## About the Author

David Swattridge has lived in South Wales all his life, has been married for forty-three years to Janet, has a daughter Emma, and two grandsons Charlie and Alfie. After working for forty-two years in the health sector, the publication in 2015 of his first novel, *Pale Battalions - The Dark Land*, fulfilled a life's ambition of becoming an author.

www.davidswattridge.com

# Dedication

For Marie Augustine Thomas, dearly loved mother of Janet and Linda.

The Alzheimer's Association.

The Commonwealth War Graves Commission.

David Swattridge

# PALE BATTALIONS
### BOOK TWO:
# THE LAZARUS POOL

Copyright © Swattridge (2017)

The right of David Swattridge to be identified as author of this work has been asserted by him in accordance with section 77 and 78 of the Copyright, Designs and Patents Act 1988.

All rights reserved. No part of this publication may be reproduced, stored in a retrieval system, or transmitted in any form or by any means, electronic, mechanical, photocopying, recording, or otherwise, without the prior permission of the publishers.

Any person who commits any unauthorised act in relation to this publication may be liable to criminal prosecution and civil claims for damages.

A CIP catalogue record for this title is available from the British Library.

ISBN 9781786294388 (Paperback)
ISBN 9781786294395 (Hardback)
ISBN 9781786294401 (eBook)

www.austinmacauley.com

First Published (2017)
Austin Macauley Publishers Ltd.
25 Canada Square
Canary Wharf
London
E14 5LQ

# Acknowledgments

The National Memorial Arboretum.
The Written Word
Ron Jones with Joe Lovejoy - 'The Auschwitz Goalkeeper'
John Coast - 'Railroad of Death'
Paul Ham - 'Sandakan'
Patricia Cornwell - 'Point of Origin'
Alexander Pope - 'An Essay on Criticism'
Ursula K. Le Guin - 'The Left Hand of Darkness'
Mahatma Gandhi - 'All Men are Brothers, Autobiographical Reflections'
John F. Kennedy - 'Farewell, Godspeed: The Greatest Eulogies of Our Time'
R. Ammons - 'Sphere: The Form of a Motion'
Charles Dickens - 'David Copperfield'
William Shakespeare - 'Romeo and Juliet': 'Hamlet': 'Measure for Measure': 'King Lear': 'As You Like It': 'Richard III': 'Henry IV Pt. 1': 'Macbeth': 'Richard II'
Virgil - 'Aeneid'
Isaac Rosenberg - 'Break of Day in the Trenches.': 'Dawn': 'Dead Man's Dump'
Siegfried Sassoon - 'Absolution'
John Keats - 'I Stood Tip-Toe Upon a Little Hill'
Robert F. Kennedy - 'Day of Affirmation Address'
Albert Einstein - 'An interview with Alfred Werner'
W. H. Auden: 'Funeral Blues'
Alexander Dumas - 'The Three Musketeers'
Thiruvalluvar
T. S. Eliot - 'A Dedication to My Wife'
John Bunyan - 'The Pilgrim's Progress'
Dante Alighieri - 'The Divine Comedy'
Lord Byron - 'And Thou art Dead, as Young and Fair'
Music and Song
Gioachino Rossini - 'The Barber of Seville'
Wolfgang Amadeus Mozart - 'The Magic Flute'
Giacomo Puccini - 'Tosca': 'La Boheme'
Eugene O' Neil - 'A Moon for the Misbegotten'
Pink Floyd - 'Comfortably Numb': 'Another Brick in the Wall (Part II)'
Ernesto De Curtis - 'Torna a Surriento'
Giambattista De Curtis - 'Torna a Surriento'
Simon and Garfunkel - 'Sounds of Silence': 'Bookends'
Mumford and Sons - 'Awake My Soul': 'Ghosts that we knew'
Art
Murray Griffin - 'Working on a Thailand Railway Cutting'

"When he shall die,
Take him and cut him out in little stars,
And he will make the face of heaven so fine
That all the world will be in love with night
And pay no worship to the garish sun."

William Shakespeare - *Romeo and Juliet*

# Chapter One

Sam Morbeck was mind-numbingly, soul-crushingly, nerve-janglingly, ass-achingly, bored. In his rapidly stagnating mind, how fishing could ever be described as relaxation, was a mystery beyond the capacity of even Sherlock Holmes.

*"What the hell's the point of this?"* he thought. *"The only things more relaxing than this, would be slug racing, or sloth surfing."*

He glared at the source of his abject misery, an innocuous red, green, and yellow waggler, knotted to a Berkley trilene XL clear monofilament line, running from a Daiwa team bait-casting reel rod. For the last half an hour, the waggler had floated defiantly motionless on the surface of the River Wye, refusing to even attempt to attract a fish.

*"Whose bloody stupid idea was this?"* Sam thought as he became increasingly down in the mouth.

*"Your dear lady-friend's,"* his other-half chipped in. Over their many years together, Sam's personal *'Jiminy Cricket'*, had become a constant, and often embarrassing feature, of his habitual 'chats' with himself.

*"You're as upbeat and charming as ever,"* Sam replied. *"Sod off, will you?"*

*"Now, now. I'm always here to put a smile on your face."*

*"And for your information, Elizabeth didn't suggest this."*

Sam recalled his consultation with Mr J G H Morrison, professor of cardiology, who'd made it abundantly clear to him, that he, and his over-stressed heart, would both come to an abrupt and premature stop, if they didn't take an immediate and extended break. The intense, endless work with Papaver Rhoeas, time travel, helping the lost souls of World War One cross over to the other side, and worrying about the strain on Elizabeth, had taken a serious mental and physical toll on him. And a week later, here he was, on the banks of the River Wye, sick and tired of relaxing.

Like a truculent child forced to do extra homework, instead of playing outside with his friends. He called to Elizabeth, who was about twenty yards further down the river bank. "Can't we just go down the pub?"

Elizabeth was concentrating on a green and black chubber trotting float. Her eyes remained fixed on it, and she shook her head. "Give it another half an hour. You're supposed to be relaxing, not getting stressed out over trying to catch a few fish."

"*Catching* a few fish?" Sam mumbled to himself. "I'd have a better chance of catching Moby Dick." He produced a sigh, which induced depression in most living creatures within a one mile radius of him.

"*Oh for Christ's sake, let's go down the pub,*" his other-half demanded.

Conversations with himself had started when he was a young boy and as an only child, they had become a normal part of his life.

"*I'm tempted.*"

"*Then let's just bloody do it. She's getting as bad as Jane. I'd hate to see you stuck in another dead-end relationship.*"

"*This one's different.*"

"*Doesn't look like that from where I'm standing.*"

"*Oh sod off back to whatever dark corner you skulk in.*"

"*Always know you're losing an argument when you revert to abuse.*"

Sam ignored him, stared at his apathetic waggler, sighed, sucked his teeth, stretched his neck, and looked upstream.

Floating serenely around the bend of the river, was what looked like a body, floating face-down.

Elizabeth glanced at Sam, saw his expression, followed his startled gaze, and saw the body, now caught in a reed bed, about thirty yards upstream.

Sam sprang up, grabbed a landing net, and ran along the bank to where his 'catch', like Moses caught in the bullrushes, was bobbing gently up and down.

Elizabeth ran to join him, and they stood gaping wide-eyed at the body, as its long blond hair, like strands of spun golden thread, gently undulated in the slow current.

"We'd better call the police," Elizabeth said with urgency, not taking her gaze from the body.

Sam nodded, and 'Mmm-ed' in agreement.

"I need your mobile."

Sam was mesmerised by the body.

"*Sam!* I need your mobile."

He jumped, and turned to Elizabeth. "Sorry. What were you saying?"

"I need your mobile to call the police!"

Without taking his gaze from the river, he pulled his iPhone from his jacket pocket, and handed it to her. "Shouldn't we get it out of the river?"

"Yes. It'll float away if we don't do something."

Sam sat on top of the riverbank, slid down to the bottom, and stood up. Elizabeth threw him a landing net. He waded a few yards out, and as he got close to the body, his confidence and enthusiasm began to rapidly seep away into the cold brown water of the river. The ravenous effect of the river, and its inhabitants on the body, hit Sam hard in the stomach. This, together with the sickly, sweet smell of putrefaction, did their best to expel his lunch from his stomach. His breathing became shallow and irregular, his pulse rate passed a hundred and sixty, adrenaline dripped and oozed from his pores, his skin glistened, and his blood pressure could have driven a steam engine.

"CAW! CAW! CAW!" screeched above his head, as the raucous cry of a crow screamed out over the river.

"SHIT!" Sam yelled.

"CAW! CAW! CAW!" The crow flew back for an encore, and flicked the 'run for your life' switch in Sam's brain.

Elizabeth panicked. "YOU OK?" Fear made her voice tremble.

Sam tentatively nodded, gingerly extended the landing net's handle, and hooked the net over a blackened, swollen foot. He tentatively pulled the handle, and the body began to swing around in the current. He looked over his shoulder at the steep bank, and realised that any attempt to get the body out of the river here would be futile. He peered downstream to a section of the river bank which was almost level with the surface of the river. "I'm going to pull it down there," he said, pointing to the low point in the bank.

Elizabeth nodded, and jogged down the bank to wait for him.

Hesitatingly, Sam towed his decomposing catch to the low bank, cautiously backed out of the shallows, and sat down next to Elizabeth.

"Can't we just leave it here until the police arrive?"

Elizabeth stared at the cadaver, and frowned. "I think we should at least try to get it out of the river. If it gets caught in any sort of current, we could lose it."

Sam swallowed deeply. "You sure?"

Elizabeth nodded uncertainly. "Sure-ish."

Apprehensively, he waded back into the river, glanced back at Elizabeth, shrugged, and loudly breathed out.

She forced a smile, and waved him on.

Sam stood over the body, guardedly bent down, rubbed his hands up and down his thighs, blew out his cheeks, grimaced, flexed his fingers, rubbed his neck, stooped down lower, and with panic coursing through his veins, diffidently took hold of a foot. The green slime coating it offered no resistance, and Sam fell onto his back.

"Try again," Elizabeth said unconvincingly.

He frowned, raised himself up onto his knees, and moved cautiously back to the body.

*"OK,"* he thought, *"get a grip Sam. Take a firmer grip."*

*"What in God's name are you doing? LEAVE IT WHERE IT IS!"* his other-half screamed at him.

*"Apart from stating the bloody obvious, have you got anything else to say?"* Sam spat back.

*"Well, at least get out of the river."*

*"Can't,"* Sam replied unconvincingly.

There was a brief mental silence.

*"Why can't?"*

*"It's a man thing."*

*"It's a moron thing. Get away from the zombie, and wait for the police."*

*"Look, piss off. I'm going to do this."*

*"It's your funeral."*

Sam took hold of the other foot and gripped it as firmly as he thought was safe, but his fingers sank into what resembled thick, chocolate mousse. His hands burst open as if they were spring-loaded man-traps, and he found himself again, sitting in the river surrounded by the half-digested contents of his stomach.

The body began to slowly turn around against the current, until its head was facing Sam. The skeletal hands flexed, sank into the river mud, and it started to push itself up into a kneeling position. What features remained of the face, made dripping socket-to-eye contact with Sam. The jaw slowly dropped, tearing the face in half, revealing glistening, white teeth, and the musculature of the jaw. River parasites erupted from the gaping throat, and the top of the skull fractured and split open, as a deluge of insects and crustaceans poured down the decomposing remnants of the face, like an unblocked sewer.

Sam's nervous system had only one response. Total shutdown.

"SAM!" Elizabeth screamed at him.

All he was capable of, was collapsing back into the river, as every muscle locked into an agonising spasm.

"SAM!"

The cadaver raised itself up, and began to shuffle through the mud towards him.

"SAM!"

It reached out, gripped his shoulders, and began to shake him.

"SAM! SAM!"

A faint, distant voice called to him. He looked up at the disintegrating face as it flew at him, bloody pieces of flesh tearing away …

The far-off voice screamed one last time "SAM!"

His eyes snapped open.

Sat close to him on the bed was Elizabeth. "You OK? What in God's name were you dreaming about?" Her fear-filled eyes welled with tears, she pulled him close, almost squeezed the breath out of him, and kissed him tenderly on the forehead. "These nightmares are happening too often. Don't you remember what the consultant said? You, that is we, have got to take a break." She released her grip on him, stood up, and walked to the window. "We're getting away from here, before this place kills us." She paused, staring at the garden. "I'm sure the Mathers said they'd got an apartment near Malaga. I could check with Mrs Mather, and see if we could rent it."

Sam shrugged, still shaken by the nightmare.

"Sam, this is wearing me down," Elizabeth said, her patience stretched to the limit. "How long have we been helping lost souls?"

He shrugged again. "Couple of months?"

"*A couple of months!* I feel like I've been here forever." She turned around, her face telling Sam, that any discussion was pointless. "*We,* are getting away for a couple of weeks' break, and I don't give a toss where it is. Jane, Adam, and Rebecca can explain where we're going to anyone who wants to know." She got up from the bed, and stabbed her finger at him. "We. Are. Going. I'll see you downstairs for breakfast."

*"Told you, didn't I. Got yourself another Jane,"* his other-half chipped in.

*"You're a real shot in the arm."*

*"I'm your own little personal ray of sunshine."*

*"God help me."* Sam groaned, as he climbed out of bed.

Rebecca had laid the table for breakfast, and the kettle had just boiled. "Coffee or tea?" she asked Elizabeth.

"Coffee would be lovely." She looked around the kitchen. "Jane and Adam not here?"

Rebecca glanced over her shoulder. "They're in the map room. What was it they said? They've been feeling some different sorts of energies? I'm sure that was it." She smiled, and made the coffee.

Elizabeth frowned, and walked closer to Rebecca. "Different energies?"

"Adam said it was as if they were from a different time?"

Elizabeth quickly turned, and walked to the kitchen door.

"Don't forget your coffee," Rebecca called after her, holding out a mug.

"Thanks." She took the mug, and headed to the map room.

Adam and Jane, were leaning over the map, staring at what looked like pulsating points of blue light, which hovered about a foot above it.

"What the hell are they?" Elizabeth asked from the doorway, as she sipped her steaming coffee.

Jane looked back over her shoulder, and shook her head. "Haven't got a clue. We've only ever seen orange points of light. But this morning …" She looked at the map, and shook her head. "These had appeared." She frowned, and glanced across at Adam. "Never seen them before, have we?"

He looked up from the map, and scratched the side of his head. "Nothing ever like these."

Sam, eating a piece of toast, followed Elizabeth into the map room, and stopped dead in his tracks. "What the hell are those?"

Elizabeth smiled. "My reaction."

Jane played with her ear lobe, leaned on the map table, and shrugged. "I haven't got a bloody Scooby."

Adam frowned. "Scooby?"

"Scooby Doo, clue? It's rhyming slang," Jane replied.

Adam shook his head, and pulled a face.

"Not important," Jane replied. "Thing is," she said and turned to Sam and Elizabeth, "what the hell are they, and what are we going to do about them?"

"Contact the experts?" Elizabeth said as she rested her elbows on the edge of the map table.

"Klaus and Guillaume?" Sam replied.

Elizabeth nodded. "Can't think of anyone better. Can you?"

Sam shook his head. "I'll call Klaus. They may have seen these in other portals." He took out his mobile, and walked to the far end of the room. A few minutes later he was back. "I couldn't get hold of Klaus, but Karsten was there. Klaus won't be back until late tomorrow, but Karsten agrees they should come over. He'll get Klaus to call us back."

"Has Karsten heard about anything similar?" Elizabeth asked.

Sam shook his head. "He sounded more surprised than we are."

# Chapter Two

Early the next day, Elizabeth arrived at the church with mixed emotions. She'd spent good years here as vicar, but her work with Papaver Rhoeas, had brought her closer to God than all her years in the clergy. She smiled at the familiar surroundings, and saw the recognisable back of Mrs Mather finishing a flower arrangement close to the Norman pulpit. "Morning, Mrs Mather."

Mrs Mather turned, and beamed at her. "My dear vicar, so good to see you. We've missed you."

"I'm afraid I've been pre-occupied with other things. How are you?" She walked up the aisle, and opened her arms to Mrs Mather, who took a few steps back."

"Hands are a bit dirty dear," she said, covering her avoidance of a hug. "I'm as fit as a fiddle." She took off her gardening gloves, and sat down in the pew just in front of Elizabeth. "What are you doing here?"

Elizabeth explained Sam's health problems, their need for a holiday, and whether Mrs Mather still owned the apartment in Malaga.

She slowly shook her head. "I am so sorry dear, we sold it … now when was it?" She rubbed her chin, pursed her lips, shook her head, tapped her temple with her index finger, and looked up for inspiration at the vaulted ceiling of the church. "Just a moment, vicar." She stood up, and walked to the open door at the back of the church.

Mr Mather, was raking dead grass and moss from the lawns close to the church, before applying an autumn feed.

"When did we sell our place in Spain?" she called out to him.

He frowned, and cocked his head to one side. "You've got a pain?"

"No dear. Our place in *Spain*."

"A sprain?" He shook his head, and tutted. "I've told you about kneeling on cold stone floors."

"SPAIN." She turned to Elizabeth. "Deaf as a post, dear. I may as well talk to that church door. He's had hearing-aids for years." She shook her head. "Never wears them." She raised an eyebrow. "He's afraid he'll lose them, so he keeps them in the bathroom cabinet." She shook her head, and turned back to her kind, but auditory-challenged husband. "WHEN DID WE SELL THE APARTMENT IN SPAIN?" She shouted at him with no signs of anger or stress.

"A DEPARTMENT STORE?"

"NO. THE APARTMENT IN SPAIN."

He shook his head. "WE SOLD IT."

"I KNOW. THAT'S WHAT I TOLD THE VICAR. SHE WANTS TO GO ON HOLIDAY."

"SHE WANTS TO WHAT?"

"TAKE A HOLIDAY."

He tutted again, and shook his head. "THERE'S NOT ANOTHER HOLY DAY UNTIL … I THINK IT'S A WEEK NEXT MONDAY." He pulled at a dandelion, and gave up as the root snapped off. "Vicars should know that sort of thing," he said to himself, as he tossed away the dandelion.

"I KNOW, BUT THE VICAR …" Mrs Mather gave up shouting, and turned back to Elizabeth. "Sorry, dear. He lives in a little world of his own."

Elizabeth had trodden this path many times before, and despite its strangely alluring charm, she could feel her will to live quietly slipping away. "It's OK. If you've sold it, I'll try something else."

"Did you want to go anywhere in particular?" she asked.

"Not really, Sam and I need a break," Elizabeth replied.

"You should go on a cruise," Mrs Mather suggested enthusiastically. "Particularly at this time of year. We love them. Wouldn't do anything else. But make sure you get an outside cabin with a balcony. Nice to have a view and fresh air. You must do the Caribbean." She stared into the far distance, remembering white sandy beaches, and warm blue seas. "Don't believe what anyone says about the islands all being the same." She turned to her husband, who was puffing away at his pipe, sitting on the grave of the late Ron Jeffris, and closely reading the instructions on a box of lawn feed.

"I WAS SAYING TO THE VICAR HOW MUCH WE LIKED CRUISING," Mrs Mather shouted.

Elizabeth grinned at the thought of these two 'cruising'.

"YOU'VE GOT BRUISING?" He shook his head, and wagged his finger at her. "THAT'LL BE FROM THAT SPRAIN." He drew hard on his pipe, and blew out a large, aromatic cloud of smoke over the headstone. "YOU SHOULD BE MORE CAREFUL AT YOUR AGE."

Mrs Mather shook her head. "Come with me, dear. Let's have a coffee." They walked together to the Mathers' house, and settled down in the lounge.

"I'll call my son. He knows the places to go," Mrs Mather said softly.

Elizabeth stared at her in amazement. "You've got a son?"

"Yes. Alfredo lives near Rome."

"Rome?" Elizabeth's couldn't hide her shock.

"He's a pilot in Civitavecchia. For ships, not planes. Civitavecchia's the port for Rome. It's where my family lives."

"You're Italian?" Elizabeth's jaw was hanging on by a thread.

"Ma naturalmente mia cara. (*But of course, my dear.)*" She got up, and walked into the kitchen, leaving Elizabeth speechless.

Ten minutes later, Mrs Mather came back, carrying a tray with two brightly patterned mugs, a plate of mixed biscuits, a cafetiere of blue Jamaican, a jug of milk, sugar, and sweeteners. She placed the tray on the coffee table, smiled, and sat down next to Elizabeth on the sofa.

"I was born in Florence, and lived there for ten years, until my family moved to Civitavecchia. I moved back to Rome when I was eighteen to find work. It was there I met Mr Mather."

Elizabeth could never remember her using his Christian name.

"It was at the end of World War Two." She chuckled. "We met at a dance, just after the liberation of Rome. Un bel soldato. He was very handsome."

Elizabeth stared at her in disbelief, enthralled by these revelations about this most English of women. "What was your name?"

"Innocenti. Caterina Innocenti. But I've gone by the name Catherine Mather, for too many years to remember."

"But I never knew." Elizabeth couldn't hide her amazement.

"You never asked me, dear."

Elizabeth blushed. "No. But you seem so … so English. Do you have a big family?"

"I had twin sisters, Carina and Valentina, three brothers, the twins, Luca and Lorenzo, who were killed in World War Two, and Angelo who died about six years ago. My mother and father died in fifty-three within a month of each other. Mia madre bella, my beautiful mother Carolina, died of a broken heart. She couldn't live after padre died." She poured coffees for them. "So, I am the only survivor. My son Alfredo, I call him Alfie, is staying with his uncle Angelo in Verona. He's gone there for the opera."

Elizabeth smiled warmly. "You're full of surprises."

"Please dear, call me Caterina."

"Shouldn't I call you, Signora Mather?"

She laughed. It was the first time Elizabeth had heard Mrs Mather laugh, and it was the joyous sound of an innocent child. "No, no vicar."

Elizabeth leaned forward in the chair. "Please call me Elizabeth. I'm not a vicar any longer."

"Well, *Elizabeth*," Mrs Mather said and leaned forward, "I think you and I shall become even closer friends."

"I'd like that, Caterina, and I'd love to hear your story."

"Come back tomorrow for coffee and cake?" She smiled. "Around two o' clock? And bring Sam?" She playfully wagged her finger at her. "I've heard so much about him. Are you hiding something from me?"

"Of course not. He'd love to meet you."

"Mrs Mather is Caterina Innocenti?" Sam shook his head in disbelief. "And Mr Mather met her in Rome at the end of the Second World War? What else does she have up her sleeve? Spying for the MI5?"

Elizabeth laughed softly. "Who knows? You could have knocked me over with a feather."

"You sure you haven't been drinking?"

She mimed knocking back some undefined booze, and slurred, "Not a drop your honour." She leaned forward, and held Sam's hand. "It's all true. We'll get the full story when we have coffee with her tomorrow."

Sam shook his head. "Italian? My God, they say nothing should ever surprise you." He scratched the side of his head, and examined his fingernails. "Have you decided where we're taking this holiday?"

She looked back at him and grinned. "Mrs … Caterina says cruising is the most relaxing thing you can do, and apparently, the Caribbean is the place to go."

"A holiday on a boat!" He shook his head. "Butlins at sea. Bloody bingo, old farts, families in matching shell suits, mixing with people you wouldn't piss on if they were on fire, scrums for lousy buffets, food poisoning, amateur-night entertainment, organised crappy games, more bloody bingo, dragged around boring bloody churches or museums by some woman with a pink umbrella, and to top it all off, throwing up with sea sickness for two weeks." He sat back, and crossed his arms. "Sounds like bloody heaven."

Elizabeth stared at him, and did her best to control her growing temper. "Not impressed by the idea then," she said through gritted teeth.

"I've seen programmes on telly. Bloody pointless way to chuck away a couple of thousand pounds."

"What programmes have you been watching? 'Carry on Cruising?'"

Sam shrugged like a spoilt child. "Maybe."

"First of all, a cruise liner is not a boat, it's a bloody enormous ship. As for the rest of your list of rubbish, you're about as far away from the truth, as thinking Hitler was a misunderstood humanitarian." She turned away, walked to the sink, and leaned against it shaking her head.

Sam shrugged, digging his heels in deeper. "Even if none of what I said is true, I still hate the sea." He shuddered. "All that bloody water."

She turned around to face him, her expression making her mood easy to read. "When have you been to sea? The nearest you've ever come to the sea, is probably on a boating lake."

Looking like a child who'd been told they couldn't stay up late, he shook his head. "I've been on a mackerel boat." He sounded hurt. "It was in Tenby, and I was ten. I was sick as a dog. They kept on saying watch the horizon, but all I could watch, was my ice-cream and candy floss, bobbing up and down on the surface of the sea."

Elizabeth sighed, and tried another tack. "OK, so the sea's out. What about a couple of weeks somewhere warm, peaceful, and quiet?"

Sam pursed his lips. "Maybe."

"OK, that's a start. Is there anywhere you'd like to go?" She was beginning to get seriously pissed off with his anti-everything attitude.

He shook his head. "Not really."

Elizabeth by now, was worn out trying to pull metaphorical teeth.

"And." Sam was struggling to find straws to clutch at. "Can we really afford to be away with these blue lights?" he said, not understanding how close Elizabeth was, to doing an impression of Mount Vesuvius.

"No blue lights, no buts. We are going. Do you want to end up somewhere hotter than the bloody Caribbean? Like the nearest crematorium? *We* are taking a sodding break! What's it going to take, to convince you that your life's at serious risk?" She was beginning to erupt. "A consultant cardiologist tells you to do it, but you still think that everything in *your* little garden's bloody rosy! FOR CHRIST'S SAKE!" The magma had found the surface, and a pyroclastic flow was heading for Sam. "PULL YOUR HEAD OUT OF YOUR ARSE, BEFORE THE REST OF YOU DISAPPEARS UP THERE AFTER IT! WHY I EVER WANTED TO STAY WITH YOU IS BLOODY WELL BEYOND ME!"

It was now crystal clear, that a major 'domestic' was kicking off. Everyone busied themselves around the kitchen, trying to look anywhere, other than at Elizabeth or Sam. Adam pretended to check the groceries in the larder, Rebecca checked the contents of the fridge, and Captain Forster made a strategic retreat to the garden.

Jane smiled broadly, poured herself a glass of wine, grabbed a bag of cheese and onion crisps from a cupboard Adam was desperately trying to hide in, grabbed two sticks of celery from the fridge Rebecca was using as a panic room, and took a ringside seat at the kitchen table as the two 'boxers' stood toe to toe, exchanging verbal blows.

"MY HEAD'S NOT UP MY ARSE!" Sam threw a left hook.

Elizabeth countered. "YOU DON'T GIVE A TOSS ABOUT ANYONE OR ANYTHING BUT YOURSELF! IT'S ALWAYS BLOODY ME, ME, ME!" She stood up, and stabbed a finger at him. "DO YOU?"

Sam threw a left jab. "WELL, IF YOU'RE THAT PISSED OFF, YOU KNOW WHAT YOU CAN DO!"

Elizabeth feinted a jab, and threw an uppercut. "YES, I BLOODY WELL DO! AND THE SOONER I DO THE BETTER!"

Sam jabbed again, looking to score points. "SHIT! I WISH I'D NEVER PISSING MET YOU!"

"LIKEWISE!" Elizabeth danced back to the ropes. "I SHOULD HAVE MARRIED THAT GOOD-LOOKING CHAP IN THE CHOIR."

Jane finished the crisps, sipped at the wine, and walked between the 'boxers'. "Excuse me," she said with a smile. She got more celery from the fridge and walked back between them. "Sorry about this." She sat back in the chair, and slowly rocked her head from side to side enjoying the contest. "Carry on."

Sam missed with a right hook. "WELL, I WAS FIGHTING THEM OFF BEFORE YOU TURNED UP."

"WHAT!" Elizabeth did an Ali shuffle. "YOU'D BE LUCKY IF A BLIND DWARF WITH HALITOSIS FANCIED YOU!"

"YOU ARE SUCH A BLOODY TART!" Sam was warned for a low blow. "WHY DON'T YOU PISS OFF BACK TO WHERE YOU CAME FROM?" He threw a weak body shot to the kidneys.

"OH, SOD OFF! WISH I'D NEVER MET YOU!" Elizabeth was deducted a point for a thumb to the eye. "WHAT THE HELL DID I EVER SEE IN YOU? I'D HAVE BEEN BETTER OFF WITH A DOG."

"DOG? YOU'RE THE PISSING DOG!" Sam was tiring, and missed with a right hook.

"WANKER!" Elizabeth breathed heavily, and glared at him.

The bell rang for the end of round one.

Jane stood up, applauding and whistling, Adam averted his eyes and slid silently out into the hall, Rebecca, having finished with the fridge, played with the washing-up in the sink, and Captain Forster was nowhere to be seen.

"For God's sake you two. We'll manage fine without you," Jane said, trying unsuccessfully to hide her sniggers.

Rebecca, keeping her eyes firmly locked on the floor, tentatively put two mugs of coffee on the kitchen table for the combatants, and quickly retreated to the sink.

Jane gestured to her that she'd like one as well. "For God's sake, give your arses a chance, and sit down." She pulled out two kitchen chairs, and stood up, until they finally sat down, avoiding looking at each other. "Listen, you pair of gobby brats, stop this stupid bloody nonsense, and take a break. You both need one. We all know what's happening here. Captain Forster will be fine about this, won't you?" She looked around the kitchen for him.

He peeked around the kitchen door, having checked the roses in the garden. "Is everything OK? Has peace broken out?"

Jane nodded. "Come in. You'll be fine if they go away for a few weeks, won't you?"

"Of course. I understand the process fully." He looked at Elizabeth. "Time to stand down for a while, mam."

"There. Straight from the horse's mouth. Now are you going to take this holiday?" Jane said pointedly to Sam.

Begrudgingly, he nodded his head. "OK. I'll go. But I'll have to check it with Guillaume first." He took his iPhone out of his pocket, marched into the garden, and five minutes later, he had his answer.

"You're sure you're OK with this?" he said to Guillaume, over a poor connection.

"Sam, I've learned much too late in life, that there is a great deal more than Papaver Rhoeas to fill our short time on this planet. Isaac and I should have done so much more together as brothers …" There was a long pause accompanied by a deep sigh. "But, well, a great deal of muddy water has passed under my personal bridge. Go away with Elizabeth, relax, enjoy some you-time, and come back refreshed. Jane can contact me if she needs help. Bring me back something ethnic, and I'll add it to Isaac's collection."

Sam smiled, remembering the dragon Isaac had bought at the Millennium Centre in Cardiff when they'd first met. "But what about the blue lights?"

"I will ask Klaus and Karsten to come to the UK. There are enough people to deal with this for two weeks. Take this chance of a break while you can."

Sam was still unsure about leaving High Wood, but Guillaume's support made him relax, and realise, as he'd said, that there were more important things in life than High Wood and Papaver Rhoeas.

"OK, we'll go. But you must contact us if we're needed."

"I will make sure Klaus does. Now go. Go and enjoy yourselves."

"Thank you, Guillaume." He slipped the iPhone into his pocket, walked back into the kitchen, and smiled at Elizabeth trying to defuse the moment.

*"So?"* Elizabeth was still fuming, and Sam's smile wasn't enough to calm her anger and frustration.

He nodded and smiled. "I'll go wherever you want." He opened his arms, but Elizabeth turned a frosty shoulder on him. He walked across the kitchen, held her tightly to him, and kissed her neck. "Come on, life's too short for us to be like this."

She resisted for a few more seconds, but then turned to face him. "I'm worried to death about you." She slapped his chest. "I don't want to lose you."

"I think I preferred it when you were at each other's throats." Jane mimed throwing up into her hands.

# Chapter Three

The following morning there was a loud knock at the front door.

"Good morning, Mr Morbeck?" A smiling Detective Sergeant Alan Morris, was outside the front door, accompanied by Constable Charlie Thompson.

Sam did his best impression of 'So pleased to see you again'. "Hello. Would you like to come in?"

*"What does this pair want?"* his other-self asked acidly.

*"Nothing for you to get concerned about."*

*"No need to turn your back on me."*

*"Not now."*

*"You'll be begging me to help when they've poked around the house."*

*"Just crawl away."*

Elizabeth popped her head into the hall, smiled, waved, and walked quickly back into the kitchen. "It's the police. Better if all of you wait in the lounge."

Jane smiled mischievously, and then waved at Rebecca, Adam, and Captain Forster to follow her.

Sam stood to one side. "Shall we go to the kitchen, and have a coffee?"

Elizabeth had the kettle boiling, and smiled, as the three men entered the kitchen. "Coffee or tea?"

"Thank you. Coffee, please," Morris replied. "Milk and two sugars for me, and black no sugar for Constable Thompson."

Sam sat across the table from them, and asked the most pertinent question he could think of. "Any news of my wife Jane?"

Morris shook his head, and gave Sam his best 'I'm sorry to say' look. "I'm afraid not." He looked across at Elizabeth, pulled a face, shrugged, and turned his attention back to Sam. "She's fallen completely off our radar, but we're maintaining a file on her. Unfortunately, due to limited manpower, we won't be able to devote as much time as we'd like to investigating it. I appreciate this is far from acceptable, but I'm afraid managing resources and budgets, is a reality of modern policing."

"I understand, and thanks for letting me know." Sam shrugged, and pulled a concerned face. "Of course, we'll keep looking, and let you know if we find anything."

Morris sipped his coffee, and frowned. "I wonder if you could help me with another matter."

Sam raised his eyebrows, and glanced at Elizabeth. "Of course, we'd be happy to."

"Sergeant Lidsay's disappeared, and more worryingly, his wife Gloria's also missing. The last time they were seen together, was when two officers were called to a domestic disturbance at their house. Gloria'd kicked Ivor, Sergeant Lidsay that is, out, and apparently his mood was… well shall we say, confrontational."

"Since his last visit with Constable Thompson," Sam said and smiled at the young constable, "we haven't seen him.

"Not a trace of them anywhere." Morris shook his head, and drank his coffee. "Damn mystery."

Elizabeth smiled at Morris, and frowned, as she remembered her last 'encounter' with Lidsay, or whatever supernatural evil he'd become.

"We found his notebook in his locker, and there were some pretty bizarre entries. Most of them related to this house," Morris said with raised eyebrows.

Sam tipped his head to one side. "Bizarre?"

Morris nodded, and finished his coffee. "We knew he'd started drinking heavily, but I don't think any of us really understood how much. The things he wrote in his notebook, can only have been written when he was drunk." He tapped the side of his head. "Had to be seeing things. You know, pink elephants?"

Jane sauntered in from the hall, chuckling to herself, as she'd been the cause of Sergeant Lidsay's pink elephants.

"What did he say he saw?" Elizabeth asked.

Morris took the notebook from his briefcase, opened it to a small post-it, and found the highlighted paragraphs. "I'm not sure how to put this, he says he saw things floating in mid-air. He lists trays, books, tool boxes, and quite a few other domestic items." He turned a few pages, and looked up. "And apparently, you've got the ghost of a mad woman in a boarded-up room upstairs. It apparently chased him 'round the house, looking for." He tapped the page, and chuckled. "'Her cat.'" He looked up, and shook his head. "Poor old sod was a bit of a dinosaur. He should have packed it in years ago." He grinned broadly. "Do you have any mad women or ghosts in the house?"

"Not the last time we looked." Sam smiled, while Jane, who was sitting on the kitchen table between Sam and Elizabeth, was in hysterics.

"It's his wife we're more concerned about. So many domestics turn violent, and what with everything which was happening to Ivor, we're worried he may have hurt her. We're very concerned for Gloria's safety."

"You don't think he's killed her, do you?" Elizabeth asked, startled at the insinuation.

Morris shrugged. "Who knows? When people are under the sort of stress he was, you wouldn't believe the things they do. If you do see or hear anything of them, we'd appreciate a call." He looked around the kitchen. "Would it be OK if we took another look around the house? I want to be sure we haven't missed anything which might give us a clue to their whereabouts. Constable Thompson will call, and arrange a day and time." He stood up, and gestured for Thompson to follow him. "Sorry to have taken up your time. Come on, Thompson, you're driving."

They shook hands with Sam and Elizabeth, and made their way down the hall to the front door.

Halfway down the path, Morris stopped, turned around, and walked back to the house.

*"What's he want?"* Sam thought in a panic.

*"Panicking?"* his other-half said, eroding Sam's already fragile self-confidence.

*"You pick the best times, don't you?"*

*"They do it to catch you off guard. He's going for your bollocks Samuel. Tighten up that sphincter. Wouldn't want any leakage."*

Morris stopped a few yards away from them. "I forgot to mention that we've had a spate of burglaries in your area. Don't know what security you have here?" He looked up at the house. "But I'd suggest you're that extra bit vigilant."

Elizabeth smiled. "Thanks. We'll make sure everything's locked."

"They don't seem to be violent, but they've made a hell of a mess of the houses they've burgled."

Sam thanked him again, waved goodbye, closed the door behind them, and turned around face-to-face with Jane. "I hope you're happy with yourself. Floating books. That was you, wasn't it?" He half-smiled, and walked straight through her.

"I wish you wouldn't do that!" Jane called after him.

# Chapter Four

Elizabeth stood outside the Mathers' front gate, with Sam close in tow.

Tack Cottage was a small, but beautifully maintained bungalow. The garden, which was the Mathers' pride and joy, had delivered summer's promise, and was now looking a little tired, as it prepared for autumn.

"Sam." Elizabeth tugged at his arm. "All you've got to do is to sit, eat cake, drink tea, and smile."

He shrugged his shoulders, and huffed.

*"Bloody hell. Tea with the Mathers? You'll be taking up knitting next,"* his other-half sniped. *"She's got you by the cajones. I warned you she was as bad as Jane."*

"She is not like Jane."

*"Hate to see you up shit creek again."*

Sam ignored him.

*"That won't work. I'll be back whenever you need me."*

Elizabeth prodded Sam hard in the chest. "At least try and look like you want to be with me."

"That bloody hurt," he said with a deep, childish frown.

"Oh grow up." Elizabeth rang the doorbell.

After a few seconds, they heard the sound of shuffling feet, three bolts being drawn back, two keys turning in their locks, and finally the door opened a few inches.

The puzzled face of Mr Mather, peered through the gap at them. "Yes?"

"Hello, Mr Mather. We're having tea with Mrs Mather. She's expecting us," Elizabeth said, as clearly as she could without shouting.

"I'm sorry, my wife's expecting visitors."

"Yes." Elizabeth nodded. "That's us." She tapped her chest, and pointed at Sam.

"You want the bus?" He shook his head. "Sorry, the council stopped our local service last year. I complained to our MP. That was a complete waste of time. Why do we bother to vote?" He shook his head again, and sighed deeply. "What's the point?"

Sam turned to leave, but Elizabeth grabbed the sleeve of his jacket, and pinched his arm.

"Ouch! Have you got it in for me today?"

The door fully opened, and Mrs Mather stood beaming at them, resplendent in a crisp, white blouse, navy cardigan, pearls, navy trousers, and tartan slippers. She gently pulled her husband to one side. "They're here for me, dear. Come in." She waved for them to follow her.

"You must be Sam," she said, as she poured tea.

He was sat in a comfortable wing-backed chair, and started to get to his feet.

"Please don't get up."

"So, Caterina." Elizabeth and Mrs Mather smiled warmly at each other. "You have a story you were going to tell us?"

Mrs Mather sat down on the sofa, and smiled. Her husband had been relocated to the next room, where he was contentedly watching cricket.

"So where shall I begin? I was born on August the tenth, nineteen twenty-six, in Rome, and my parents were Carolina and Bruno. Carolina was from Florence, where she worked as a seamstress." She paused and smiled, recalling fond memories of childhood. "When we came to Rome, she stopped working, but kept on sewing, as she made all our clothes." She sipped her tea. "Mama was also the most magnificent cook." She patted her remarkably flat stomach. "How I'm not twenty stone, I'll never understand." She sipped her tea. "Papà lived in Rome all his life, so that's where they settled. Papà fought in World War One with his brother Marco, high up in the Italian Alps, along Italy's northern border. He survived the war, but lost all the fingers on his right hand, and two on his left, to frostbite. He never worked again. We believe Marco was gassed by the Germans and his body incinerated by flamethrowers. No-one ever found what little would have remained of him. Papà never forgave the Germans for the death of his brother, or the loss of his hands." She paused, and refilled her cup with tea. "Papà died when I was twenty-seven. Cancer of the stomach." She swallowed hard. "It wasn't a peaceful end, and mamma died three months later. She couldn't live without him, and her heart just gave up." She took a handkerchief from the sleeve of her blouse, and dabbed her eyes.

Sam looked at her with his jaw metaphorically on his chest. *"Did you know about all this?"* he mouthed at Elizabeth.

She shook her head, and smiled. "Was there anyone else was in your family?"

"I had twin sisters." She smiled at their memory. "Carina was a Carmelite nun. She became Reverend Mother, at the Monastero Carmelo Sant'Anna in Rome. Valentina was a history teacher, but they both passed on a long time ago. My brother Angelo was a train driver, and he died in two thousand and eight." She smiled with the memory of journeys to the coast on the railways with her family. "My twin brothers, Luca and Lorenzo, were wonderful boys. Always looking out for their baby sister." She left this hanging in the air. "Would you like more tea and cake, Sam?"

He smiled broadly. "Thank you, yes, please. This cake is wonderful. What is it?"

"I'm glad you like it. It's Sicilian ricotta cheesecake. It was a recipe of my mama's."

"What happened to Luca and Lorenzo?" Sam asked between mouthfuls of cheesecake.

Mrs Mather picked at a scab on the back of her hand, making it bleed. She looked down at the thin crimson streak, lost in her thoughts. "They were killed in the war." She looked up at Elizabeth, an expression of hatred in her eyes which chilled Elizabeth to the bone. "That's not true. They were *murdered* by the Germans." She spat out the words.

Sam raised his eyebrows, and glanced at Elizabeth. "Murdered?"

Elizabeth shook her head at Sam. She felt uncomfortable delving into what was obviously a sensitive subject.

Mrs Mather looked up, her expression softening. "A story for another day." She cut more cheesecake, and poured more tea. "Anyway, my story is much more interesting."

Elizabeth decided, that this part of Mrs Mather's life should for now remain a secret. "When did you meet Mr Mather?"

She smiled. "Alfred." She paused for effect, as she revealed the Christian name of her husband. "He was part of the British 10th Corp who shelled the monastery at Monte Cassino in forty-four. In one afternoon they fired two hundred thousand shells into that holy place." She shook her head, and crossed herself. "It was the shelling which damaged his hearing, and over the years it's got progressively worse. I've tried to get him to wear his hearing aids, but his pride won't let him." She breathed a sigh of resignation. "After Monte Cassino, he fought up through Italy with the Allies, and followed the liberating Americans into Rome. He's got an MC, a Military Cross." She smiled wickedly at Elizabeth and Sam. "Who'd have thought it?

Elizabeth sat forward in her chair. "Never judge a book by its cover."

Mrs Mather shook her head.

"But how did you meet? Rome must have been seething with troops, and celebrating Italians."

"Another story, for another day." She looked tired.

Elizabeth looked across at Sam, and nodded her head towards the door. "We should go. You look tired, and we can always come again."

She sat upright, looked at the clock on the wall, and shook her head. "No, no, you've hardly been here any time at all. I'll tell you when I need a little nap."

Elizabeth looked questioningly at her. "Only if you're sure?"

She smiled, leaned back, adjusted her glasses, cleared her throat, and opened her hands, indicating that Sam and Elizabeth should sit back and relax.

"I was twenty when World War Two broke out, a young innocent Catholic girl with little experience of life. When my brothers died, it changed me, and I had to grow up very quickly. To me, the Germans were the spawn of the Devil, and I wanted nothing but vengeance for my brothers. Vendetta. So in late nineteen forty-three, I joined La Resistenza, the Italian Resistance, with my best friend Amelia Conti."

# Chapter Five

Morris, sat behind his desk, chewing the end of a biro like a beaver gnawing the bark off a poplar tree. He waved at Constable Thompson to join him. "Can you take a look around High Wood. It'll be good experience for you. You want to move into CID, don't you?"

"Yes, detective sergeant." Charlie was a little taken aback, as very few words had ever passed between them.

"Good." He pursed his lips, and frowned at the young constable. "You were pretty close to Sergeant Lidsay, weren't you?"

Charlie shrugged. "Not exactly close. I went out with him on quite a few visits, but I wouldn't say we were close."

Morris frowned. "Lidsay was a miserable, bad tempered, overweight, lacking in personal hygiene, pain-in-the-ass, old scrote, but do you believe he'd started seeing things?" He raised his eyebrows, leaned back in his chair, and spat a piece of splintered plastic into a waste paper bin. "It doesn't add up."

Charlie shrugged. "He'd started acting a bit weird recently."

"Had his drinking got worse?"

"I don't know much about his drinking, but I never smelt alcohol on him. He just … well, you know, he was always a bit rank." He waved his hand under his nose. "He was definitely obsessed with High Wood. I saw him a couple of times, parked up just down the road from it."

Morris picked up a note pad, and scribbled a few lines. "Did you ever see anything odd there? You know," he said and made a scary face. "Ghosts and that sort of stuff."

Charlie frowned, and shook his head. "I can't remember seeing anything weird."

"Sounds to me like there's a 'but'?"

Charlie nodded. "There were a few times when I felt I was being 'watched'. You know, those feelings you get sometimes, when someone's walked over your grave?"

Morris nodded.

"I felt it the most in the cellar." Charlie looked distant. "Although once, when I was alone upstairs, I could have sworn someone was following me around."

"So there could be something in Ivor's notes?"

Charlie chewed his lip. "Maybe? There's definitely something odd about that house. But I don't think anyone living there would have done anything … you know, killed them. They seem too nice."

"Murderers look like you and me, constable. They don't come to your front door carrying a knife dripping in blood. They're usually the husband or wife, or the next-door neighbour. Nip 'round there tomorrow, tell them you're following up on our recent visit. Take a look around, and see if you can find anything Ivor might have left."

Charlie was stood nervously outside the front door of High Wood. His first solo interview and investigation had to go well if he wanted to impress Morris, and make the move he so desperately wanted into CID.

Charlie Thompson was twenty-four, had been in the force for four years, and had enjoyed every last second of it. It was the only job he'd ever wanted to do since he was five when he'd played 'NYPD Blue' with his friends. His dad, a retired police sergeant, had Charlie late in life, and died of a major stroke when Charlie was only fourteen. He'd done everything he could to dissuade his son from his chosen career path. The years of long anti-social hours, too much alcohol, a difficult family life, mixing with the dregs of society, and avoiding death by a hairs-breadth a few times, had convinced him Charlie would be better off in any career other than the police.

However, his mother, the stronger parent, who Charlie still lived with, had done everything she could to get her 'Golden Boy' into the force. And now, he was on his own, feeling like a bull which had suddenly realised, the chap in the multi-coloured suit, funny hat, and silky towel, wasn't a German tourist looking for a sun-bed. He stared at High Wood's front door, and eventually drew up the nerve to knock. He took a step back, and stood there for what felt like ages, and nothing happened.

*"I should have called to arrange a time rather than just turning up. Not a great start,"* he thought. He took a few more steps back, and stared up at the house. It wasn't the first time he'd been to High Wood, but it was the first time he'd really paid any attention to it. The shuttered windows, like half-closed eyes, squinted down at him, daring him to enter. He walked close to the lounge window, peered in, stepped a few paces back, and studied the front of the house again. He narrowed his eyes, stared at an upstairs window, and gasped, as he thought he saw a woman's pallid white face.

*"Just a reflection,"* he thought, as his nervousness increased. *"Come on, let's go 'round the back and see if anyone's there."* With a significant degree of trepidation, he walked around the side of the house to the back garden, where the open kitchen door smirked at him, inviting him in.

In the kitchen, Jane was emptying the dishwasher and putting crockery on a high shelf in a cupboard, Rebecca was sitting at the kitchen table flicking through the pages of a magazine, Adam was lifting a bulging bin-liner out of the pedal bin, and Captain Forster was carrying a tea tray back into the kitchen from the lounge.

As Charlie walked circumspectly into the kitchen, what greeted him, fell outside any points of reference his brain possessed. Two dinner plates were levitating from the dishwasher and stacking themselves in a cupboard, the glossy pages of a magazine were turning over by themselves, a bin-liner was floating out of a pedal bin and hovering in mid-air, and a tray of tea cups was floating gracefully into the kitchen from the hall.

He managed to utter one word, "Shit," and fell into a dead faint on the kitchen floor.

"Oh, bollocks!" Jane muttered, as the crash of the now prostrate policeman hitting the fridge, span her around.

"I told you someone was at the front door," Rebecca complained.

"And who, or what, would have welcomed him?" Jane replied, with her hands on her hips.

"Well … yes, but what would have been worse? That, or this?" Rebecca said pointing at the prostrate constable.

"What the hell are we going to do?" Jane asked the three blank faces, who all simply shrugged. "Great. Just bloody great." She knelt down close to Charlie. "I think we should let him see us. We can tell him he fainted, and we were about to call an ambulance, when he started to come around. Sounds reasonable, doesn't it?"

Adam thought about it, and then said unhelpfully. "What happens when he goes back to the station, and tells them there were people in the house he'd never seen before?"

"Mmmm, fair point." Jane sat on the floor, and stared at the ceiling. "How about this then? We were visiting relatives in Australia, and got back a few days ago?" There was a lot of mmm-ing and frowning. "OK, anyone got any better suggestions?"

"Carry him back outside, and leave him by the front door. He'll think he fainted, and everything he *thought* he saw, he'll think he imagined while he was unconscious," Rebecca said quietly.

The others glanced at each other, and smiled broadly.

"Great idea. Let's do it," Jane said in a surprised tone, which changed quickly, as a frown spread across her face. "How the hell do we pick him up? He's a living thing! Our hands'll go straight through him."

Rebecca pulled a face. "Sorry, forgot about that."

Captain Forster pointed to the garden. "There's a sack truck in the garden shed. If we can get him onto that, we should be able to get him out of the house."

Jane clapped. "Always rely on the military. If we get a couple of spades, we can lift him onto it."

Twenty minutes later, after struggling, swearing, heaving, sitting, struggling, and swearing again, they got enough of Charlie onto the sack truck to wheel him to the front door which posed a new challenge as all their hands were occupied. Jane opened the front door, and started edging backwards into the porch.

At that moment, two young, well-dressed Jehovah's Witnesses stopped, and decided to deliver 'The Truth' to the residents of High Wood. To them, a secular society was morally corrupt, and under the influence of Lucifer. So, as the body of Constable Thompson came out of the front door on a sack truck pushed by no-one, and was unloaded onto the gravel drive, their beliefs were reaffirmed. Satan was alive and well, and living in Cardiff. They stared wide-eyed at each other, fell to their knees, lifted their eyes to heaven, thanked Jehovah he'd chosen them to witness this evidence of Satan's power, and closed their eyes in silent prayer, for the salvation of the damned folk of High Wood.

Jane heard the exaltations, and looked back. "Oh bugger! Quick, get him back on the sack truck, and inside the house."

"The spades!" Rebecca remembered. "They're in the kitchen."

Jane ran through the walls of the house, the front room, the 'library', and the kitchen. She grabbed the spades, ran down the hall, opened the front door, threw the spades to the others, shovelled Charlie back onto the sack truck, and wheeled him into the house, as the Jehovah's Witnesses opened their eyes.

Jane peered through the letterbox, turned around, and slid down the door onto the floor. "I don't give a toss what happens next, but we are not in."

"But we are," Adam helpfully pointed out.

"Not for those two out there we're not."

As the evangelists looked towards the house, they saw that the spawn of Satan had disappeared.

"Oh hell!" one said. "We did see that, didn't we?"

"Language Abraham!" his colleague gently rebuked.

Abraham sighed and nodded. "But we must call at this house. Those living here, must learn of the peril which envelopes them."

"Knock, and see if anyone is home," Jacob said uncertainly.

Abraham, with a considerable degree of trepidation, walked up to the front door, and knocked loudly.

In the kitchen, the spawn of Satan were in fits of laughter, until they heard the knocks at the front door. They froze, and stared blankly at each other.

"No 'odd' noises," Jane whispered. "They'll soon give up and go away."

Jacob called to Abraham to join him. "Let's go. We should seek advice on what to do next. This is beyond our understanding."

In the hall, everyone stayed silent and motionless for another few minutes, until they were sure their visitors had left, and then made their way back to the kitchen.

"As I was saying," Jane said, staring at the still unconscious body of Charlie. "What the hell do we do with him?"

"We could leave him in the cellar, and see what happens?" Adam suggested.

Rebecca looked sideways at him, and shook her head.

"And have someone else disappear from High Wood?" Jane replied sarcastically.

Adam sat down at the kitchen table, and sighed. "It was just a thought."

Charlie began to stir, shook his head, rubbed his eyes, and sat up. The dishwasher was still open, but there were no floating plates. The magazine on the kitchen table was motionless. The bin was closed, no floating bag could be seen, and there was no tray defying gravity. He pushed himself up, sat at the kitchen table, lifted the magazine, and dropped it with a satisfying slap.

*"Must have been a sugar drop,"* he thought. *"I did miss breakfast."*

Jane, Rebecca, Adam, and Captain Forster, edged closer to the kitchen door.

Charlie stood up and opened a couple of kitchen units until he found a packet of biscuits.

*"I'll get them a new packet,"* the honest policeman thought.

After demolishing half a packet of chocolate digestives, he stood up, and looked around the kitchen. He knew the layout of the house from previous visits with his erstwhile sergeant, and despite his 'sugar drop', he decided to start his 'investigation' in the cellar.

"HELLO. ANYONE HERE?" he shouted.

"Our captive policeman is up and about." Jane paused. "How about this? We'll only let him see me. I'll tell him I'm Sam's wife, I've been away in New Zealand visiting relatives, hadn't left any contact numbers, and didn't realise there'd been such concern about me."

"I'm not sure about that," Adam said warily.

A group of Tommies had gathered on the stairs.

"Yours, I think, Captain," Jane said.

Captain Forster turned to face them. "OK men, small problem, but we have things well in hand. Make yourselves comfortable in the lounge, and I'll give you a Sitrep in a few minutes."

While they'd been chatting amongst themselves, Charlie had walked out of the kitchen, and into the cellar.

"Oh shit!" Jane squealed.

"Couldn't you say something else?" Rebecca said.

"Oh crap! Any better?"

Rebecca said nothing.

Jane chuckled, and focused back on Charlie.

"Shouldn't we follow him?" Adam said.

"No. I wouldn't want him 'sensing' anything," Jane replied.

"Yes, but what if something happens down there?"

Jane shrugged, and stared at the open cellar door. "Not much we can do if it does."

Charlie found the light switch, and carefully descended the steps into the cellar. He picked up an umbrella with a charred end, and started tapping the floor, looking for anything which sounded hollow. An umbrella wasn't quite the same level of kit CSI Las Vegas had, but it would have to do. After ten minutes of fruitless tapping, and examining shelves, he decided there was nothing of any interest. He'd tell Detective Sergeant Morris he'd found nothing new. If *he* wanted to rip High Wood apart, he could get their own CSI unit involved. He walked back to the steps, and started to make his way out of the cellar when an odd smell meandered up his nose.

*"Something's burning,"* he thought.

He slowly turned on the steps, and looked back into the cellar, but there seemed to be nothing which could account for the smell. *"It must be coming from the kitchen. Someone's back in the house making toast,"* he thought as he started back up the steps. Suddenly, the overpowering pungent odour of sewage slapped him in the face.

"Shit." He grimaced at the word. "They need a good plumber."

Subtle notes of putrefaction, damp, garbage, squalor, and excrement, were added to the stench. It was as if the essence of the streets of fifteenth century London, had been distilled and bottled. The reek of decay and corruption, penetrated every pore of his skin, entered his nervous system, brought him to his knees, and dragged him into unconsciousness.

Jane was standing with her back against the wall close to the cellar door, when the senseless body of Charlie landed at her feet.

# Chapter Six

"*You* were in the Italian Resistance?" Sam said, wide-eyed and slack-jawed.

"Certo. Of course, my dear. I blew up railway tracks, disrupted supply lines, carried messages to other groups, killed a lot of Germans, and the traitorous filth of the Italian fascist party." Her face was expressionless and cold. "I hated them. Hate is a corrosive, powerful, and difficult emotion to control. The Germans were in my country, killing my fellow countrymen and good friends. What else could I do? Wouldn't you have done the same?"

Sam nodded his head. "In the blink of an eye."

"Elizabeth, would your faith have allowed you to do these desperate things?"

She stared at Mrs Mather. *"You were a member of a WW2 dark ops organisation!"* she thought incredulously.

Mrs Mather asked again. "Elizabeth? In my place, what would you have done?"

Elizabeth breathed deeply. "Alexander Pope wrote, 'to err is human, to forgive divine.' Matthew 6:14 tells us 'For if you forgive men when they sin against you, your heavenly Father will also forgive you. But, if you do not forgive men their sins, your Father will not forgive your sins.' This is what the Lord tells me, but despite these maxims, I could not have forgiven the Nazis for their sins." She took a deep breath. "And," she said and looked into Mrs Mather's eyes. "Romans 12:19 tells us 'Dearly beloved, avenge not yourselves, but rather give place unto wrath: for it is written, Vengeance is mine; I will repay, saith the Lord.' I would have exacted a vengeance on them, which would have satisfied Hamlet."

Mrs Mather smiled. "I am happy I have never got on the wrong side of you my dear. You would make a terrifying enemy." She feigned shivering with fear.

Elizabeth couldn't help but laugh. "I would have become Samael, Sariel, or Azrael. The Angel-of-Death. However, the Germans would have had a file on you marked 'Danger'."

Mrs Mather stood up. "That's enough about me and revenge. Sam, Elizabeth tells me you've been told to take a holiday. To relax more."

He nodded.

"Do you listen to music?" she asked.

"All the time."

"Does it help?"

Sam nodded. "Yes."

Mrs Mather smiled. "I listen to music all the time. It is one of my great comforts. I have my favourites I keep going back to, Sinatra, Ella Fitzgerald, Count Basie, Mozart, Puccini." She paused, and sipped her tea.

Sam smiled. She was listing, what he would have guessed were some of her favourite artists and composers.

"Although, 'Sisters of Mercy' is one of my favourite songs. I adore the music and poems of Leonard Cohen." She pulled a tissue from her pocket, and blew her nose. "I also have soft spots for Zeppelin, Floyd, Clapton, and Sonny Boy Williams."

Sam's mouth fell open.

"You should listen to a lot more music." She pointed at him. "There is no better form of relaxation. Have you ever listened to opera?"

Sam grimaced, and Elizabeth raised her eyebrows.

"I'll take that as a no." She smiled. "Opera is too readily tossed aside as an entertainment for the rich. When Luca and Lorenzo were murdered, opera embraced my deepest grief, and brought me great comfort. Can I play you two arias?"

Sam grimaced again.

Mrs Mather smiled like a dentist trying to convince a patient that drilling wouldn't hurt. "Give it a try, Sam. What's the worst that can happen?"

She walked over to an iPod connected by Blue Tooth, to a Sonos CONNECT:AMP, selected the track she wanted, tapped play, and the exquisite voice of Joan Sutherland sparkled, as 'Vissi D'Arte' floated around the room.

A few minutes later, she opened her eyes, and looked at Sam and Elizabeth. "What did you think of that?"

"Well, it's difficult to find the right words. It was pretty? But I didn't understand a word she sang. It was foreign wasn't it?" Sam struggled to put his thoughts into words.

"It was Italian, Sam. The universal language of love, and passion." She sat down, and looked at Elizabeth. "What did you think of it, my dear?"

"I've never heard anything like it before. Words are difficult to find. It made me feel gloriously uplifted. What's she singing about?"

"Tosca loves Cavaradossi, who is an artist being tortured by Baron Scarpia, the sadistic chief of police. She thinks of how the life of her lover is at the mercy of Scarpia. She sings, I lived for art, I lived for love, and at the end of the aria, she asks, 'In the hour of grief, why, why, O Lord, why do you reward me thus?' Even today, Tosca understands my loss." She dabbed a tissue to her eyes, and walked back to the iPod. "This aria is also from Tosca. It makes me think of Luca and Lorenzo, and their thoughts in their last moments. The aria is 'E lucevan le stelle'. The stars seemed to shimmer. Cavaradossi, is waiting to be executed by firing squad, and he becomes overcome with memories of love, and gives into despair. The aria ends with him singing, Everything's gone now, I'm dying hopeless, desperate! My brothers would have died hopeless and desperate."

Elizabeth shook her head, and smiled. "It's OK, you can play it for us again." She stood up, opened her arms to hug Mrs Mather, but as she closed her arms around her, they passed straight through her.

"Ah." Mrs Mather murmured. "My secret is out."

Sam jumped up, passing his chin going the other way.

Elizabeth sat back heavily on the sofa.

Mrs Mather smiled crookedly, and sat down. "You've seen through me." She chuckled at her attempt at a joke.

"You're a …" Sam said shakily. "You are, aren't you?"

"A spirit, ghost, phantom, spectre, apparition. There are so many words, but the one I like best is 'echo'." She looked up at the ceiling. "I am a suggestion, a hint, a faint semblance of what I once was."

"But you've looked after the flower arrangements in the church for years," Elizabeth said hoarsely.

"Did anyone else in the congregation ever mention me?"

Elizabeth shook her head. "Well no, but Mr Mather looked after the graveyard? I don't understand?"

"Did anyone ever mention my dearest beloved shadow?"

"A shadow? He's a ghost as well?" Elizabeth said, wide-eyed.

"I didn't mention that?" She tapped herself on the back of the hand in mock chastening. "Sorry dears."

"But how couldn't anyone have seen you, and we can?" Elizabeth muttered.

Mrs Mather cocked her head to one side, and opened her eyes wide.

"Because you didn't want them to see you, and you wanted us to see you?" Sam said.

"Like all your friends at High Wood, and those brave, sad boys from the First World War," Mrs Mather said quietly. "They want you to see them."

"You know about High Wood?" Sam barely managed to utter.

"I was a good friend of Arnold and Edith for years before we all died."

"You knew my uncle and aunt?" Sam was now almost speechless. "When did you last come to High Wood?"

"It must have been about two weeks ago. But you wouldn't have seen me. I didn't want you to. I come around fairly regularly. Busy, aren't you? I can see why you both need a holiday."

Sam and Elizabeth, sat opened-mouthed, and dumbfounded.

"Your faces will stay like that if the wind changes," Mrs Mather said cheerily.

"But why didn't you say something before?" Elizabeth asked.

"No reason to, I suppose."

"Then why now, and why are you still here? Why haven't you passed over?"

She took a deep breath. "Like your friends at High Wood, I have unfinished business, and I think you can help me."

Mr Mather wandered in from the other room. "Any tea in the pot?"

"Just about to make a fresh one. I'll bring one out to you."

He looked at Sam and Elizabeth's expressions, nodded, and smiled at Mrs Mather. "They know, do they?"

She nodded.

"Will they help?"

Mrs Mather shrugged. "I haven't asked them yet."

"I hope so. It's about time all this was brought to an end. I'll go back and watch the cricket. Let me know what they decide to do."

The conversation took place as if Sam and Elizabeth weren't in the room. They looked at each other, and couldn't help but laugh.

"He seems remarkably 'with it'," Elizabeth said with a raised eyebrow. "And his hearing seems to have recovered."

"When he's in the house, he can be as lucid as the best of them. I'll just go and make another pot of tea." She stood up, and walked into the kitchen.

Sam and Elizabeth stared at each other.

"Can you believe what we've just heard?" Sam said, shaking his head. "After all we've seen and done, what in God's name will she spring on us next?"

Elizabeth sank back into the sofa, staring into the far distance, running her fingers through her hair. "They're ghosts. All the time I was a vicar. I never had a clue."

"More tea, dears?" Mrs Mather was back, replete with tea pot, and a plate of biscuits. "You know, I think Eugene O' Neil put our situation very well in a poem 'A Moon for the Misbegotten', when he wrote, 'There is no present or future, only the past, happening over and over again now.'"

Elizabeth had just about begun to recover her composure, but poetry, on top of opera, threw her. "The past, over and over? Interesting idea." She glanced at Sam, raised her eyebrows, and then turned back to Mrs Mather. "Mr Mather said you wanted help? What is it you think we can do?"

She refilled their cups, walked through to Mr Mather with the pot and four biscuits, returned, stirred her tea, dunked a biscuit, and sat down again on the sofa next to Elizabeth.

"Two things." She sipped her tea. "Firstly, my brothers Luca and Lorenzo." She turned on the sofa to face Elizabeth. "As I told you before, they were killed in World War Two. On May nineteenth, forty-three, they were part of the seventeenth infantry of the Acqui Division, and were stationed on Kefalonia. When Italy surrendered to the Allies, Hitler issued an order, letting the Germans execute any Italian officer who resisted, for treason. On September twenty-first, nineteen forty-three, a massacre started which lasted for a week. The Germans killed Italian soldiers where they stood, with machine guns, and then marched the remaining soldiers to the San Teodoro town hall, and executed them there." She stopped, from the pain of recalling the memory of the massacre, drew a deep breath, and continued. "They threw their bodies into the dock at Argostoli." It was clear that this was becoming very difficult for her, but she carried on. "Padre Formato, who was a chaplain, said many were shouting the names of their mothers, wives, and children. The Germans offered help to the wounded, but when they crawled forward, they were machine gunned. Like the lost souls you've saved from the Great War, Luca and Lorenzo are still missing, and I will never be able to rest until they are found and we are reunited."

"I'm still not sure how we can help," Elizabeth said caringly.

"You both need a holiday?"

Elizabeth and Sam nodded.

"Kefalonia is idyllic at this time of year. Alfredo knows the owners of four beautiful villas in Sami, and they've agreed he can have the Villa Kalipso for two weeks for almost nothing. All you have to do is get there. You can take a holiday, relax in the sun, eat good food, visit Argostoli, and while you're there," she said and then paused. "See if you sense any lost souls called Luca and Lorenzo?"

Elizabeth frowned, and looked at Sam. "The problem, is the holiday is supposed to make Sam forget about these things. The last few months have worn him down." She frowned. "Worn both of us down."

Mrs Mather sank back on the sofa, and sighed deeply. "I understand. It's a lot for me to ask of you."

"Excuse us for a couple of minutes?" Sam said quietly.

Mrs Mather nodded, and smiled.

"We're not doing this, Sam." Elizabeth's face was set in stone. "I've waited all these years to find someone, and I'm not going to lose you."

"It's a cheap holiday. All we have to do is spend a day at … where was that place she mentioned?"

"Kefalonia."

"No, she mentioned a town."

"Yes." She looked up at the ceiling. "Argus? No, it was Argostoli."

"Yeah. Argostoli. We'll go to the town, and see what happens. The brothers were killed in the Second World War, and you're sensitive to the First. The chances of anything happening have got to be pretty low, and then we can spend the rest of the holiday relaxing by the pool," Sam said, as he held her hand.

"I won't take advantage of her."

"Come on. What's to lose?"

"You!"

"I'll be fine." He pulled her to him and kissed her forehead.

"That won't work," she said, desperately trying to sound serious.

He stood back, and crossed his heart. "I swear, I will relax the entire time we are in … that Greek island."

Elizabeth could see she was fighting a losing battle. "I need this holiday as well as you, Sam. But we'll have to at least try to look for Luca and Lorenzo."

He squeezed her hand, walked back into the lounge, and smiled at Mrs Mather. "We'll go."

She jumped up from her chair, and if she could have hugged them, she'd have squeezed the breath out of them. "Grazie. Grazie molte."

"Have you got any photos of Luca and Lorenzo?" Elizabeth asked.

She smiled, and called to Mr Mather. "Alfred, can you get the photo albums from the spare bedroom?"

An 'uh-huh' from the other room indicated he was on his way. Five minutes later, he appeared with three battered photo albums. "Are these the ones you wanted?"

She nodded, kissed him on the cheek, carefully leafed through the fragile pages, and nodded. "Perfect. Thank you, my dear."

"OK if I stay in here with you?" he said.

"Of course." She sat closer to Elizabeth, and Mr Mather sat on the end of the sofa. She gently lifted a few pages, made a sound which indicated she'd found what she wanted, and handed the album to Elizabeth. "There they are. Handsome boys, weren't they?"

Elizabeth looked down at the faded image of two young men in uniform. The future which lay before them, soon to be destroyed in a hail of machine gunfire on a picturesque Greek island. "They look very handsome in their uniforms. When was this taken?"

"It was, let me think, it would have been nineteen forty-one. They were so proud of serving their country, but not happy they were the allies of Germany. Our way of life was completely different to theirs, and they weren't Catholics. My brothers were strong believers, church every week, their faith central to their lives, and they saw Germany, because of their actions in Eastern Europe, as disciples of the Devil."

Elizabeth decided to change the subject. "You said there were two things you thought we might be able to help you with?"

"Yes. My Uncle Marco. The one I mentioned when you came to tea that first time." She sat back in her chair. "He was the one who died in World War One. The one who was gassed? But I'll keep his story for another time. For now let's see if you can help Luca and Lorenzo. Si?"

Sam sat forward ready to ask more, but Elizabeth gave him a sideways look which silently said, *'Not now'*.

"Caterina, can I take a copy of the photo of Luca and Lorenzo? I'll need to take it with me to Kefalonia," Elizabeth said.

"Of course, my dear." She turned to Mr Mather. "Alfred, can you scan a copy and email it to Elizabeth and Alfredo?"

Elizabeth looked at Sam, and shook her head. Could there possibly be any more surprises this couple could have for them?

# Chapter Seven

Elizabeth opened the front door, walked a little way down the hall, and stopped dead in her tracks. "What the hell's going on?"

Despite their ghostly status, Jane, Adam, Rebecca, and Captain Forster, metaphorically jumped out of their skin.

"Elizabeth," Jane said with an enormous sigh. "You frightened the life out of me." She laughed at the irony.

"Bit late to worry about that," Elizabeth said with a snigger.

"Where's Sam?" Jane asked.

"He's popped down to Tesco for some bread and milk. What's going on?" She walked closer to the group, and recognised the prostrate figure of Constable Thompson.

The ghostly quartet stared at the floor like four schoolchildren caught smoking in the toilets.

"What the hell happened?" Elizabeth asked.

"He came into the kitchen and …"

"Some Jehovah's Witnesses were …"

"Nothing to do with me …"

"I said we ought to put …"

"I told them not to."

"I was only reading a magazine …"

"He was in the cellar …"

"One at a time," Elizabeth said sharply. "Jane. What happened?"

She gave her the concise version of events which led to Constable Thompson lying unconscious at her feet.

"I suppose it's understandable what happened, but what was he doing in the cellar?"

"Don't know."

"I didn't see him."

"Wasn't me."

Elizabeth waved her arms. "OK! I'll take a look after we've sorted this out," she said, nodding at the prostate policeman. "Let's put him on the sofa. When he comes around, I'll tell him I found him in the kitchen." She began to bend down, and then stopped herself. "You can't pick him up. Can you?"

The four amigos grinned, shovelled Charlie onto the sack truck, wheeled him into the lounge, and tipped him onto the sofa.

Elizabeth rearranged Charlie into a comfortable position, pulled across a red leather pouffe, and sat down. "While I'm waiting for him to come around, why don't you put the kettle on, and make a pot of tea."

They glanced at each other, nodded, and walked out of the room.

A few minutes later, Charlie began to stir.

Elizabeth pulled the pouffe closer, and brushed loose hairs from his forehead. He slowly opened his eyes. His brain, after the 'visions' in the kitchen, was still unsure of the visual input it was receiving. However, the comforting face of Elizabeth, made it classify and file the earlier sightings, as 'must-have-been hallucinations'.

"Mrs Morbeck?" Charlie said quietly.

She decided not to correct him. "Elizabeth will do fine."

"Please call me Charlie." He peered into her eyes. "Were you here when I came to the house?"

"Yes. I'd just finished emptying the dishwasher, and was reading a magazine when you came into the kitchen." She frowned slightly. "You fainted." She held his wrist, appearing to check his pulse. "You seem OK now, but how are you feeling?"

Charlie looked sheepish. "A bit confused, I thought I saw …"

"What?"

He blushed, and looked down at the carpet. "Oh, nothing. I must have seen you, fainted, and thought I'd seen … well, seen something else. My fault really. I didn't have any breakfast, and mum would be livid if she knew."

"Imagined what?" Elizabeth gently pushed.

"Oh, nothing. Just a …" He blushed. "Some things seemed to be moving on their own in the kitchen."

"Probably just a lack of sugar. Main thing is you seem fine now, and I won't tell anyone about things floating around the kitchen if you won't." Elizabeth winked.

"Thanks." Charlie sat up. "Not sure it would help my credibility at the station."

"Like a cup of tea? Nice and sweet with a few biscuits? Get your sugar levels back up."

Charlie nodded. "Thanks." He blushed. "I've already had a few biscuits from the kitchen, but I'll get you a new packet."

Elizabeth squeezed his hand, and smiled. "I think we can manage to let you have a few biscuits." She stood up. "I'll go and make us that tea. You lie here and rest."

Jane had a pot of tea brewing. "Well?" she asked.

"No problem. Can I get him a cup of tea and a few biscuits?"

A communal sigh of relief shuffled its way around the kitchen.

After a few minutes, Elizabeth came back with a tray. "Right, let's get your sugar back to normal."

"Mrs Morbeck?"

"Elizabeth."

"Sorry. Elizabeth. Would it be OK if I came back tomorrow?" He asked. "I'd like to check if Sergeant Lidsay left anything behind. Right now, I don't have very much to tell the detective sergeant, so if I could come back, I'd be able to give him a proper report."

Elizabeth smiled, and nodded. "Of course. Two o' clock OK?"

"Thanks. You're a life saver."

Ten minutes later, he was being put into a taxi to take him home.

Elizabeth took a torch from the kitchen, and turned her attention to the cellar.

In a far corner of the cellar, a glistening pool of what looked like black mercury, was rhythmically quivering. Like a parasite seeking a host, a twitching tentacle formed from the centre of the pool, and the powerful beam of Elizabeth's torch, gave it the point of reference it was seeking.

She walked across the cellar floor, and shone the beam around. If there was anything down here, she'd either find it, or sense it.

"COFFEE?" Jane called from the open cellar doorway.

"PLEASE."

"FIND ANYTHING?"

"NOTHING YET."

"KEEP THIS BETWEEN US?"

"PLEASE."

'I'LL MAKE THE COFFEE."

Away in the corner, the quivering, stygian pool morphed into a muscular, black ribbon, and began to snake across the floor towards the cellar steps.

After a few minutes, Elizabeth, decided there was nothing to be found in the cellar, and started to make her way back up the steps to the kitchen. But something made her stop and glance over her shoulder into the darkness.

*"What was down here Constable Thompson? You felt something, didn't you?"*

She shook her head, turned, hit her hand against the wall, and dropped the torch. "Bugger!"

She made her way cautiously down the steps, knelt down, and felt around in the dark for the torch. She patted the floor with her right hand, and jumped back as it splashed into the head of the glutinous, ebony snake. She shook her hand, and wiped it on her jacket.

*"Bloody leaks,"* she thought. *"I'll have to get a plumber."*

She suddenly felt an agonising cramp in her wrist, stretched her hand, swore at the nagging pain, walked up the steps into the bright light of the hall, and sat down at the kitchen table, rubbing her wrist.

"You OK?" Jane asked with a frown.

"Yes. Probably just cramp. Cup of coffee, and a few of those biscuits will put me right."

*"Hope it's Do You Egg But,"* a familiar voice whispered at the back of her mind.

Elizabeth jumped up, and looked around the kitchen.

"Elizabeth?" Jane was concerned. "What is it?"

"Didn't you hear that?"

"What?"

*"Such a lovely cup of coffee."* The whisper strolled around her mind, finding its bearings.

"That voice." Elizabeth's eyes scanned the room.

Jane looked at the others, and everyone shook their heads. "You need that holiday more than Sam."

"You didn't hear anything?" Elizabeth stared intently into the eyes of everyone in the kitchen. Four shaking heads and deep frowns gave her the answer. "But I heard someone speak." She frowned, and shook her head. "I'm cracking up. The sooner we get to Kefalonia the better."

The whisper sniggered to itself. *"Men. They're all bastards, and there's one particularly obnoxious, overweight shit, who's going to suffer for the years of abuse I suffered."*

# Chapter Eight

"You sure you're feeling OK?" Charlie's mum asked him.

"I'm fine. It was just a sugar drop." He crossed his heart. "I promise it won't happen again."

She tousled his hair, kissed him on the cheek, and tapped the end of his nose. "Don't you let anything happen to yourself. You're all I've got." She kissed him again. "My special boy."

"Mum," Charlie complained. "I'm twenty-four."

"You're still my baby. No-one ever loves you like your mother." She paused, and adjusted the ties on her apron. "What did you think you saw? What was the house called again?"

"High Wood."

"Yes, High Wood. You said you saw things."

"Yes, but only after I'd fainted."

"OK, but what do you *think* you saw?"

Reluctantly, Charlie told her about the 'events' at High Wood.

"Floating trays, plates, rubbish bags, and a magazine turning its own pages?" Mum said.

He nodded.

She crossed her arms. "Have you seen anything else like that?"

Charlie shook his head.

"You sure? I can read you like a book, you know."

"Only my special friend Peter. We used to play together when I was little."

"Peter?"

"Yes, Mum."

"And he seemed real?"

Charlie nodded.

"Probably just an over-active imagination. You've always had a creative streak. You get it from your dad. Now call the station and tell them you won't be in today."

"But I've got to …"

Mum gave him a look which could curdle milk.

He sighed, and surrendered. "I'll call them now."

"Good boy. You can help me with the cleaning."

After vacuuming the lounge and bedrooms, steaming the hall floor, polishing Mum's knick-knacks, and taking out the rubbish, Charlie made them coffee.

"I'm going to sit in the conservatory and have a read," he said.

"OK darling. Don't spill anything on the furniture."

"No, Mum." He settled down on the cane sofa, opened 'Point of Origin' by Patricia Cornwell, and lost himself in the violent world of Dr Kay Scarpetta.

*'The story will be that this notorious psychopathic killer has contacted them while half of the law enforcement is out there looking for the bitch.'*

He finished three chapters, slipped his bookmark between the pages, got up, and walked to the kitchen.

"I'll tell him."

Silence.

"Soon. When the time's right."

Silence.

"Yes, I know he can help, but not now. Not yet."

*"Mum's on the phone,"* he thought.

As his head came around the kitchen door, he could see the phone still in its cradle, and Mum sitting with her back to him by the breakfast bar, apparently talking to the microwave.

*"Oh no,"* he thought. *Please God, not dementia."*

The conversation in the kitchen continued.

"We don't know for sure he's got it."

Silence.

"Yes, I know it looks like he does."

Silence.

"This week. I promise we'll go this week."

Silence.

"We'll find him."

Silence.

"Yes, a coffee would be lovely."

Charlie turned away and leaned against the wall of the utility room. His stomach felt like he'd been repeatedly punched by Joe Calzaghe. He edged back along the wall, and peered into the kitchen, to see the kettle float to the sink, fill itself from the tap and turn itself on. A jar of coffee floated down from a shelf, a teaspoon put coffee into a red and blue mug, and a plastic bottle of skimmed milk floated from the fridge and poured a small amount into the mug. He slid down the wall, and sat on the floor.

*"I'm going mad."* Thoughts stampeded around his head. *"High Wood, and now this?"* He pressed hard on his temples with the knuckles of his index fingers. *"How the hell can I be a policeman when I can't trust what I see with my own eyes?"* He banged the back of his head against the wall. *"Early onset Alzheimer's can start at any age. I've seen it on the news."*

# Chapter Nine

Sam and Elizabeth exited the air-conditioned cool of the Boeing 787, stood at the top of the steps, smiled, squeezed each other's hands, kissed, and descended into the pleasant late October sun of Kefalonia. They looked back from the runway at the sparkling Ionian Sea, and smiled. Cooled by a gentle sea breeze, they joined the end of a long crocodile, shuffling across the runway to the terminal building. As they entered arrivals, Sam looked around, turned to Elizabeth, grinned, and shook his head.

"This is exactly like Alicante in the sixties. Do they get many tourists here?"

"One of the most popular Greek islands." Elizabeth replied. "Read up on it on the plane. Apparently, the airport's pretty small, but very efficient. Bit like me." She laughed, and grabbed his hand. "Come on, let's get the cases."

There was only one 'well-used' carousel in the baggage claim area, and a handful of battered trolleys, which would have graced any supermarket car park. However, despite the lack of trolleys, their luggage was quickly with them. Pulling their cases behind them, they walked out of the baggage claim into a tightly packed and hectic arrivals zone.

"We should have asked for a photo of Alfredo," Sam said above the hubbub.

Elizabeth surveyed the mass of faces, and pointed to the back of the crowd. "I think that might be him."

Above head height, on what looked like the back of a piece of a large cardboard box, Sam could see their names written in large block capitals. After several excuse me's, ankles, backs and bums hit by hand luggage, and toes almost flattened by pushchairs, they reached the placard.

"Alfredo?" Sam said, struggling with a back pack and a 'light weight' suitcase.

He nodded. "Si. Benvenuti." He shook Sam's hand, kissed Elizabeth on both cheeks, pointed at his sign, smiled, and took a case from her.

Alfredo looked a few years younger than Sam, about five feet eight, slim, deeply tanned, slicked-back 'dyed' black hair, Maui Jim Stingray sunglasses, grey Hugo Boss jeans, Tommy Hilfiger polo shirt, tasteful gold crucifix around his neck, four beaded bracelets on his left wrist, a Breitling Chronomat 44 on his right, Loake tan loafers, and no socks.

"Benvenuti Kefalonia." He looked around at the madness. "Let's get outside. It's only a short walk to the car."

Elizabeth turned to Sam, nodded at Alfredo, and mouthed, *"Bit of a poser?"*

"Good trip?" His accent was richly Italian.

"Not too bad. Typical low cost airway. We'll be paying to breathe before long. Shouldn't complain, though, it was cheaper than getting a train to London," Sam said. "Is it far to … sorry, I've forgotten the name of the place."

"Sami," Elizabeth said, quietly chuckling.

"It should take us about an hour to get there. The road's pretty direct, and the island's small." Alfredo lifted the luggage into the boot. "Either of you not good with heights?"

Sam grimaced. "I'm not great with them."

Elizabeth sniggered. "Sam has panic attacks in multi-storey car parks."

"Probably best if you sit in the back behind me, Sam." Alfredo suggested. "The drive over the centre of the island, is molto mountainous. Some crash barriers have been built, but I think they ran out of money, as they don't cover the entire road."

Sam grimaced, and jumped into the back seat behind Alfredo.

After driving for a few minutes, Alfredo spoke. "Grazie molte for coming. If there is anything you can do to help, then I will be forever in your debt. Mamma has never truly recovered from my uncles' deaths."

Elizabeth looked over her shoulder at Sam, raised her eyebrows, and mouthed, *"Do you think he knows they're ghosts?"*

Sam shook his head, and shrugged.

Alfredo chuckled to himself. "You love roundabouts in the UK, don't you?"

Sam and Elizabeth smiled and nodded.

"Trouble is we have too bloody many," Sam said with a sigh. "Try driving around Swindon."

"You will love it here. Kefalonia has only three roundabouts."

They drove along the coast road which overlooked the Ionian Sea, passed through the holiday town of Lasi, and soon entered Argostoli.

"We will only pass through Argostoli today, but we will come back and visit when you are rested. We will drive around the edge of the lagoon." He paused, and smiled in the rear view mirror at Sam. "And then we start to climb." He turned to Elizabeth. "Some of the views are spectacular, but I won't stop at the viewpoints, until Sam's got his sea-legs."

The road was steep, and twisty, the crash barriers substantial and intermittent, and the viewpoints spectacular, but exposed.

Sam however, was unaware of everything, as he'd plugged in his earphones and was lost in the music of Pink Floyd.

*'When I was a child I had a fever*

*My hands felt just like two balloons.*

*Now I've got that feeling once again*

*I can't explain you would not understand*

*This is not how I am.*

*I have become comfortably numb.'*

Sam was grateful he was comfortably numb.

Elizabeth turned, and tapped Sam's knee. He looked up from Dave Gilmour's guitar solo, and raised his eyebrows.

*"What about his parents?"* she mouthed.

He took off the headphones and shrugged.

Alfredo was watching Sam in the rear view mirror, and laughed. "You British are so, riservati. In Italy we come straight to the point."

Elizabeth blushed, and Sam went back to Dave Gilmour.

"I know that mamma, and papà are spirits." He laughed out loud. "Your faces have been a picture."

Elizabeth smiled sheepishly, and nodded. "How long have you known? We only found out recently, and it was a hell of a shock."

He shook his head. "È ancora molto difficile per me capire *(It's still very hard for me to understand)*, but I will do whatever I have to, to help mamma find Luca and Lorenzo." He gripped the steering wheel. "I am sorry. When I get emotional, I slip into my natural tongue."

A motorcyclist with a death wish, revved his engine to an eardrum-shattering scream, and overtook them on a blind bend.

"BLOODY MANIAC!" Sam shouted.

"You should visit Rome, Sam. We have the best bloody maniacs in the world," he said, lightening the mood.

"The views from up here are stunning," Elizabeth said. "You should look, Sam. It's beautiful."

Sam dropped his head, and returned to safety of The Floyd.

"We've just past the highest point, and it's downhill from here." Alfredo looked in the rear view mirror and smiled. "Not too far now, Sam."

Sam was hiding behind 'The Wall'.

*'We don't need no education*

*We don't need no thought control*

*No dark sarcasm in the classroom*

*Teachers leave them kids alone*

*Hey! Teachers! Leave them kids alone!*

*All in all it's just another brick in the wall.*

*All in all you're just another brick in the wall.'*

Half an hour later, they pulled up outside the Villa Kalipso. Alfredo parked the car at the side of the villa, and with Sam's help, started unloading the luggage from the boot.

Elizabeth stood and stared. "It's beautiful, and so quiet." She couldn't help but beam. "This is where we're staying?"

Alfredo nodded and looked at the large detached villa, set in its own beautifully maintained grounds. It was part of a small development of four almost identical villas, set among olive groves surrounded by verdant hills. The only sound which could be heard was the soft bleating of sheep and goats.

"It's huge, and the setting is … it's just perfect."

Alfredo nodded again. "È un posto meraviglioso *(Is a wonderful place)*."

Elizabeth and Sam frowned.

"A wonderful place."

Elizabeth smiled. "We'll have to give you something towards the cost," she said with a degree of embarrassment.

"I believe you call these things, cavalli regalo. Gift-horses? What you are doing for mamma is payment enough."

Sam felt embarrassed about his cynical thoughts of only pretending to look for Luca and Lorenzo.

Elizabeth saw his expression, and decided to add to his discomfort. "If we can, we'll find her brothers. Now let's see what the inside of this place looks like." She wasn't disappointed.

The villa was fitted with air conditioning and Wi-Fi, downstairs was a large open plan space with marble-tiled flooring, off to the left was a modern, fully-equipped kitchen with a dining table and four wooden chairs. To the right was a bedroom with en-suite, a sitting area with a large sofa and two chairs, TV, and DVD player, and a washing machine in the adjoining garage. Just to the left were marble stairs leading upstairs to a second bedroom with en-suite, and a separate, large upstairs balcony.

"Alfredo, this is wonderful," Elizabeth said with an enormous, toothy grin. "Renting this place must cost a fortune. Are you sure we can't help?"

He shook his head, headed for the large glass doors close to the sofa in the lounge, and waved for her to follow him. "I think you'll be equally happy with the outside." He opened the heavy, wooden shutters, unlocked the patio doors, and walked out, to where directly in front was a large, well-manicured lawned area. On the patio, just outside the lounge, was a wooden swingseat, to the right was a large barbecue, and to the left was an inviting swimming pool, large lawn and garden. Sam followed them outside, put his arm around Elizabeth, and grinned like a Santa-struck-child on Christmas morning.

Alfredo smiled. "If you want to grab some sun and test the pool." He pointed to his left. "I'll email mamma to let her know we have arrived safely." He turned towards the villa. "We'll eat in Sami tonight, and get some groceries there tomorrow."

*"Sod the unpacking,"* Elizabeth thought. Five minutes later, she dropped her towel on one of the sun loungers, stared at the inviting cool blue water, dived straight in, and swam effortlessly up and down the pool. Then, relaxed and refreshed, she smiled, walked slowly out of the pool,

wrapped a soft pink towel around her head and inelegantly flopped down onto a blue sun lounger.

Sam, resplendent in a pair of long floral swimming shorts, brought out two cold beers, and sat next to Elizabeth on her lounger.

"Bloody wonderful, isn't it? I feel like a celebrity." He sipped his beer, and ran a finger through the condensation on the side of the glass. "I could learn to like this."

"Peel me a grape." She laughed. "You going to have a swim?"

Sam stared at a wasp spinning madly on the surface of the pool, as it struggled to escape a watery grave. "In a minute."

"The water's lovely. It's not cold."

Sam looked back at her, and raised his eyebrows. "I've heard that one before. Like a warm bath, is it?"

"Go on. It'll relax you. That's what we're here for, isn't it?"

Sam drained the last of his beer, and trying to retain some semblance of manhood, got up, and walked to the first step of the pool. The wasp had lost its fight, but Sam's was only just beginning. Five minutes later he'd managed to descend to the second step, and after a further five minutes, he was still stuck like a limpet to the second step. Ten minutes later, after staring aimlessly at the hills surrounding the villa, he managed to immerse his knees. After a lot of 'Oh my Gods', 'Shits', 'It's bloody freezings' and various other colourful expletives, he was stood on tip-toe, like a ballerina dancing on hot coals, desperately trying to keep his nether regions above the surface of the pool.

*"Enough's enough,"* Elizabeth thought wickedly. She stood up quietly, walked to the side of the pool, smirked, jumped into the air and 'bombed' into the pool, sending a mini tsunami crashing into Sam's chest.

"You bloody … Aagh!"

The rest of his 'thanks' were unintelligible, as he lost his footing, slipped, and with flailing arms, fell back into the pool. He resurfaced two seconds later, coughing, spluttering, and flapping his arms, like a penguin caught by a leopard seal,

# Chapter Ten

The day after Sam and Elizabeth flew to Kefalonia, Klaus and Karsten arrived at High Wood.

"Good to see you again," Jane said blowing them kisses. "Sam and Elizabeth will be sorry to have missed you."

"Our flights were cancelled because of fog, and we had to spend the night at Frankfurt Main airport." Klaus replied, sitting down at the kitchen table. "How are they? Guillaume said he thought Sam sounded very stressed when he spoke to him."

"The last few months have been tough for him and Elizabeth. If they hadn't gone away, I'm pretty sure they'd have ended up in hospital, or worse. Did you know Sam's been seeing a cardiologist?" Jane said with a frown.

Klaus shook his head, and pulled at his top lip.

"It was the consultant who told him he had to take a holiday."

Klaus glanced at Karsten, and pursed his lips. "Let's hope this break brings them back relaxed and refreshed." He looked across at Rebecca. "That coffee looks good."

She blushed. "Sorry, I wasn't thinking. Coffee for both of you?"

They smiled and nodded.

"Danke. Beide mit dwei zucker." Klaus tapped himself on the side of the head. "So sorry. Thank you, and two sugars in both." He turned back to Jane. "Do you still have the blue lights?"

Jane nodded. "Every day there seems to be more. Has anyone else seen them?"

"Biscuits?" Rebecca asked over her shoulder, as she filled the kettle.

"Bitte. Please," Klaus replied. "Those chocolate ones?"

She smiled. "I know the ones you like."

Klaus turned back to Jane. "There's hardly a Papaver Rhoeas portal which doesn't have them."

Jane leaned back in the chair, and crossed her arms. "What do you think they are?"

"Papaver Rhoeas was established to help the lost souls of World War One. The architects designed the memorials, and the portals, specifically to achieve *only* this."

Rebecca came to the table with two cups of coffee, and a plate of biscuits. "Anything else?"

Klaus and Karsten shook their heads.

"Danke Rebecca. Das is perfekt," Karsten said with a warm smile.

Klaus drank his coffee, and looked around at the attentive faces in the kitchen.

"Up and until the Second World War, the memorials and portals coped with the level of spirit-energy entering them. However, at the end of World War Two, the amount of spirit-energy which had soaked into the earth, had passed way above its saturation point." He sipped his coffee. "These spirit-energies, were not only military, but also those of millions of civilians who died. The memorials were at capacity, and these 'new' energies built up around the memorials, like a surging Spring tide. Over time, as the numbers of World War One souls has reduced, space has become available in the memorials, and as designed, they have channelled these 'new' energies to the portals."

"The blue lights are spirits from World War Two?" Jane uttered.

"Yes, my dear. That is what we believe."

"So they're the same as the World War One spirits we've been helping? Just more lost souls seeking salvation?" Jane continued.

Klaus nodded in agreement.

"But we can barely cope with the missing of World War One. If these, as they will, keep coming through to us, then we've no hope of helping them," Jane replied, running her fingers through her hair.

"I agree." Klaus sighed. "But a solution has to be found. I believe that so far, we have only been seeing a trickle of what could become a flood."

"So what do we do?" There was growing anxiety in Jane's voice. "Surely there must be memorials and portals for the missing of World War Two? Couldn't they somehow be channelled directly to them?"

"Yes, there are, but they were only ever built as memorials. So far as we know, nothing was ever incorporated into their design which would attract, store, and direct missing souls to portals." Klaus finished his coffee, smiled, and nodded his thanks to Rebecca. "These 'new' spirit-energies, have, for at least seventy years, been drifting like gossamer on the winds of time. They must be disturbed, and believe they have no hope of ever escaping from their personal Purgatory." Klaus gestured for Karsten to continue.

"We believe these spirits will be irritated and angry. They may want to take this anger out on someone." Karsten looked at his father, and raised an eyebrow.

Klaus gestured to him that he should continue.

"Perhaps on us."

There was a stunned silence around the kitchen.

"We need to contact Sam and Elizabeth," Rebecca said, tapping her fingers on the edge of the sink.

Jane shook her head. "We'll need them at their best."

"There is a meeting of Papaver Rhoeas in London in two days," Klaus said while he played with the crumbs of a chocolate digestive. "Everyone will be there, and we have to agree to a plan." He looked at Jane. "I'd like you to come."

"Are you serious?" She was taken aback. "What could I possibly say that would help?"

"You have a unique perspective, which we, the living, don't possess. The group can only benefit from your presence."

Jane thought for a few seconds, and then, with no great degree of belief, nodded her head in agreement.

Klaus stood up. "Thank you, my dear. Now, can I take a look at the map room, and I'll explain my plans further to you?"

"Of course," Jane was stood behind Karsten. "Rebecca, Adam, Captain Forster, come with us."

As they entered the map room, Klaus and Karsten were stunned into silence. Every available surface, was completely obscured by masses of pulsating cerulean, sky-blue, navy-blue, and ultramarine pin-points of light.

Klaus gathered himself. "Mein Gott! Sind das alle fehlenden Seelen? Karsten. Fotografiert." *("My God! Are these all missing souls? Karsten. Photograph.")*

Karsten ran to the hall, and came back with a Nikon P60 bridge camera.

"Die anderen müssen das sehen." *("The others must see this.")* "Wir sollten die Portale schließen." *("We should close the portals.")*

"What's he saying?" Jane said with concern.

Karsten frowned. "He is very concerned about the lights."

"And what did he actually say?"

Karsten shrugged. "Not much."

"Not much, my arse."

"Well, he said that … "

"Yes?"

"He doesn't know what to do."

"I think he does," Jane said forcefully, slapping her hands down hard on the map table.

"He wonders if we should seal up the portals."

# Chapter Eleven

Charlie was sat in the lounge, reading Mum's 'Gardener's World' magazine.

Mum, Molly, walked in with a tray, two hot chocolates, and a freshly baked lemon drizzle cake. She stopped, and looked out of the window at the strong wind bending the trees. "I'll have to get someone to look at that tree before it falls down." She shivered. "And it's gone a bit chilly, hasn't it? This'll warm you up."

Charlie sipped the hot chocolate, ate a large slice of cake, and put his mug carefully on a coaster. "Not drinking, Mum?"

"Mmmm?"

"I thought I heard you making a cup of coffee earlier on?"

"Mmmm?" Molly was sipping her hot chocolate, and trying to find something to watch on TV.

"Coffee?"

She looked up, one eye still on the TV. "With all these channels you'd think there'd be something worth watching." She glanced across at Charlie. "Don't you want the hot chocolate?"

"No, it's lovely."

"Why do you want a coffee?"

Charlie sighed, and settled back on the sofa. "Doesn't matter."

Molly shook her head, and looked back at the TV. "This weekend, I'd like to go out for the day." She sighed, gave up trying to find anything worthwhile to watch on TV, and turned back to face Charlie.

"Anywhere special you'd like to go?"

"The National Memorial Arboretum."

Charlie frowned. "The what?" He'd never heard of it, but thought he'd read that an arboretum was somewhere trees were grown.

"It's a national centre of remembrance for the fallen. Fallen soldiers, that is. I want to pay my respects to your grandad."

"Grandad Reg."

"No darling, Grandad Peter. It's a story I should have told you years ago." She settled back into the soft cushions of the sofa, and started her story.

Uncle Don, the Sheringham station-master, was forty-one years old, and still refused to accept the army wouldn't sign him up him for active service. To make things worse, his distinguished and decorated record in the First World War rubbed salt into his wounds. Admittedly, he did have moderate hearing loss in both ears, astigmatism in his right eye, a cataract in his left, severe arthritis in his left hip and right knee, and shrapnel in his right shoulder. However, what really exasperated him, was that he 'knew' he was considerably more experienced than most of the green-behind-the-ears conscripts he'd seen marching through the town. Eventually, and with extreme reluctance, he accepted the rank of captain in the local LDV. He had a parade at six o' clock, but now, at eleven, he was searching with his niece Emma, for a parcel her father had asked her to collect. After half an hour of dismantling the parcel office, they still hadn't found it, and decided to take a break.

They were sat together on a well-worn, green bench on the platform, drinking mugs of strong tea, when a young soldier accompanied by his wife and a fractious baby, asked their advice.

"Excuse me. Could you tell me when the next London train is due?" the 'green-behind-the-ears' soldier asked politely.

Uncle Don looked up and smiled. "On time as usual, sir." He glanced down at his watch. "It will be here at, eleven-twenty, or as we military types like to say, mmmm, eleven twenty hours."

The soldier, suppressing a smile, thanked Don. "Thanks. I thought I'd missed it." He turned, picked up his kit bag, and carried on to the end of the platform.

Uncle Don watched the unhappy group slowly walk down the platform, and then turned back to Emma. "What did Wally say was in it?"

"The parcel?"

Uncle Don nodded.

"Fertiliser and seeds."

"We'll finish our tea, and take a look out the back. There's a great pile of stuff out there, and it could have been put out there by mistake."

Emma looked up as the roar of hissing steam told her a train was pulling into the station. As she watched, like lost lambs appearing from an early morning mist, a line of exhausted, bedraggled, and bewildered young evacuees, emerged out of the billowing clouds of steam. She sighed deeply at the melancholy line of distressed and crumpled figures being shepherded along the platform, clutching their precious single piece of battered luggage. Emma knew that ahead of them were hours sitting in a cold village hall being inspected by locals, their new 'parents' for the duration of the war, and after meeting these strangers, they faced an uncomfortable journey on strange roads, to arrive at a strange house, with strange food, new rules, and finally, fall into a restless sleep, in a strange bed.

"Emma?"

"Mmm, sorry Uncle Don. It was the little ones." She pointed at the dishevelled crocodile shuffling past them, neither glancing right or left, staring down at their scuffed shoes.

"I know, darlin'." Uncle Don shook his head, and sighed. "Will we never learn?"

A sombre silence fell over them, as they watched the sad crocodile leave the station. It was then Emma noticed the young soldier. He was slapping backs and shaking hands with his young comrades, who, as they boarded the train, hurled mock abuse at him. He grinned, saluted, waved, turned, and marched down the platform towards her.

"Old men compared to the first war." Uncle Don shook his head. "Schoolboys, that's all we were. Hardly wet behind the ears. Should've been starting our lives, and they just marched most of us into early graves." He stood up, shook his head, and walked back to the office. "I'll have another look for that parcel." He glanced briefly at the soldiers, and sighed. "Could you get us another cup of tea, love?"

Emma nodded, as Uncle Don disappeared into his office, shaking his head and muttering something unintelligible. She looked up at the almost empty platform, except for the young soldier and his family waiting for the London train.

She got up to make the tea, as Uncle Don trotted onto the platform. "Found it! Damn thing was in the back yard. Some parcel. It's a flamin' great wooden packing case!"

They walked into the yard together, and stared at dad's 'parcel'.

Emma stared wide-eyed at the 'parcel'. "How are we going to move *that*?"

Uncle Don rubbed the stubble on his chin. "Not too sure, dear. Fred's at lunch, and he won't be back for half an hour. Bob's no use since he did his back. I told him, you're not up to helping the WI with their 'Dig for Victory campaign.'"

"Anything I can do to help?" The young soldier was leaning on the yard wall and smiling at them. "Looks like you're having a problem with that." He pointed at the packing case.

"Thank you. A little help would be much appreciated." Uncle Don said, as he walked to the wall to shake the young soldier's hand. "Good looking lad," he whispered to Emma, as he walked to open the yard gate.

Their newfound helper stood with his hands on his hips, looking the packing case up and down. "I've got a truck parked outside. Brought the lads down from the camp in it. There should be plenty of room in the back for this." He looked around the yard. "Got a sack truck, or something like that?"

Uncle Don nodded, disappeared around a corner of the yard, and came back with a battered, but functional sack truck. After twenty minutes of struggling, sweating, a little muttered-under-Uncle Don's-breath swearing, and with the help of a couple of passing local lads, they finally got the 'parcel' onto the truck.

Uncle Don held out his hand. "Thank you. Sorry, but I don't know your name."

"Peter. Peter Wallins."

"Don Thompson, and this is my niece Emma."

Peter smiled and offered his hand to her. "Pleased to meet you."

She blushed, and pointed to her battered Austin Ten. "If you follow me, it's only about three miles to the house."

Peter nodded, and climbed into the cab.

Emma kissed Uncle Don, who leaned forward and whispered, "I'd grab him with both hands, darlin'. Don't see many like him 'round these parts."

She blushed the colour of a sunset, which would have given any shepherd great delight, climbed into the Austin Ten, waved to him, and drove away down the town's main road.

Her father, Walter, was trimming hedges, when Emma pulled up outside the house. He looked up, smiled, and then turned the colour of parchment, as he saw the army truck parking just behind. The 'parcel' contained a little more than just seeds and fertiliser, and the sight of the army outside his house, brought on a feeling he'd last felt when he'd overindulged on prunes.

"What's *he* doing here?" he growled at Emma, pointing at the truck.

"Helping me with your 'parcel'. Which, I might add, weighs a bloody ton, and without Peter," she said and nodded her head towards the truck, "it would still be at the station."

"Get rid of him. Bloody army. Always poking their noses into other honest people's business."

She laughed at him. "Honest? You? Don't be so damn rude and ungrateful."

"I don't want the likes of him sniffing 'round my stuff.'

Emma screwed up her face. "Sniffing 'round what stuff?"

"Nothin'."

"You been messing 'round with that George Mellower again?" Emma was stood within inches of his face.

Dad's expression froze like a child caught with his hand in the sweet jar.

"You keeping," Emma said and looked over her shoulder at the soldier, and whispered, "that bloody black-market stuff in the shed for him again?"

Walter shrugged and kicked at the hedge trimmings.

"Right, that parcel's stayin' on the truck, and it's going straight back to the station."

His eyes shot wide open. "You can't do that! There's a lot of valuable stuff in there, and I get ten percent of the takings." He bit his tongue, as he blurted out his admission of illegal dealings. "But I only store it for him." He rubbed the top of his head, and forced a smile. *"I've never had anything to do with selling it. It's shockin' what he charges for it,"* he whispered.

Emma's expression could have curdled milk. "I'll be having a word with George when I see him."

Dad tried to answer, but her expression told him that silence was his best option.

*"I'd better speak to George, and warn him that Emma's on the warpath,"* he thought as he imagined his daughter in full flow.

Peter, with Emma and Dad's help, manhandled the packing case off the back of the truck, and Peter looked around for something to get it into the house. "Got a sack truck or something like it?" He pointed to the packing case. "This damn thing weighs a ton. What have you got in here? Feels like a tank!"

Dad panicked, and just about kept it hid. "Uh, only stuff to help uh, help turn our garden over to growing food for the country. You know, 'Dig for Victory'. Doing our bit for King and country. Got to do everything we can to support the war effort."

Peter nodded, and patted Walter on the back. "Good for you. Country needs everyone to do their bit if we're going to beat the Nazis."

*"Yes, and you won't be doing your little bit for much longer,"* she thought, flashing him a look which didn't bode well for any quiet nights he might have been considering.

"I've got just the thing in the shed." Walter had caught up with Emma. "Keep him away from the garage," he whispered.

She stood in embarrassed silence with Peter, until Dad came back with what looked like a six-wheel bogey.

"This ought to do the job," he said, dropping the handle with a flourish.

Ten minutes later, after a great deal more pushing, pulling, straining, cursing, and apologising, they got the packing case close to the garage door.

"Thanks. I'll unpack it a bit later on, and put everything inside," Dad said walking away from the garage.

"I'll give you a hand." Peter offered as he started pulling at the side of the crate.

The look of panic on Dad's face, was hard, if not impossible to disguise. "No, no, no problem at all," he said, taking Peter's hand off the crate, and shaking it vigorously. "I need something to keep me occupied this afternoon. You've been very helpful."

Peter looked a little taken aback, but shook Walter's hand.

"Like some tea and cake?" Emma said pleasantly, glaring at Dad over Peter's shoulder.

Peter smiled. "Thanks. I could do with one after shifting that," he said, wiping his face with a handkerchief.

Dad turned, cracked his head on the edge of the garage doors, and muttered some unintelligible curses.

Emma chuckled to herself and led Peter into the house.

Half an hour later, after demolishing most of the remains of an apple pie, and draining a pot of tea, Peter got up to leave. "Thanks for the tea and pie. I'd better get back to the camp." He looked sheepishly at Emma, and stared at his boots. "I'd like to thank you properly." His boots retained his attention. "There's a dance at the camp tonight. Allow us to get to know everyone in the town. You know the sort of thing."

Emma nodded. She felt her chest tightening, anticipating what she hoped Peter was going to ask.

"Would you come with me to the dance tonight?" He looked up, and blushed. "Officers will be there of course." He managed a smile. "Everything'll be above board."

"She's got too much to do, and I don't know nothing about you young man." Dad had come back into the kitchen looking for a cup of tea, and had regained his natural flair for rudeness.

Emma stood, and turned her back on him. "Thank you, I'd love to come," she answered with a beaming smile.

"Now listen to me, my girl..."

"What time should I be ready?"

"Emma, if you think you're going..."

Peter wasn't sure what to say, or who to answer.

"For the last time miss ..."

"It's OK, Peter, he's always like this. He still thinks I'm ten. What time should I be ready?"

Dad gave up, filled his tea cup from the dregs of the tea pot, grabbed the last piece of apple pie, scowled at Emma, and stabbed his finger at Peter. "You make sure she's home at a sensible time, my lad." He took a bite out of the apple pie. "Or I'll be fixing your behind to the end of my pitchfork." He shouted over his shoulder, spitting pastry and apple at Peter, before slamming the kitchen door.

"Sorry about that," Emma said. "He's been a bit protective of me since Mum died. She was at a WI meeting and the church hall got hit by a bomb. All that was left was a hole in the ground. Wasn't nothing left of her to bury, but we put up a memorial stone at the graveyard. ARP reckoned the Germans must have been trying to get rid of the bomb on their way back to Germany. Nothing much here in Sheringham worth bombing, but someone up there," she said and looked up at the sky and shook her head, "decided it was Mum's time." She frowned and sighed. "Doesn't seem fair, somehow."

"None of it's fair," Peter replied. "I've lost count of the friends I've lost in battle. Mum and Dad were killed last year in the Blitz. We live in the East End, and just like you, there was nothing left of the house. Just a rubble-filled, smoking hole in the ground." He stared into nowhere for a few seconds, and then smiled at Emma. "I'll pick you up at seven?"

"Seven will be fine." She followed him out of the house, and waved goodbye as he drove away in the truck.

"That sort is only after one thing." Dad stood behind her in the hall. "Soldiers are all the bloody same. Use the war as an excuse to get inside your … well, you know what I mean." He gave her a knowing look, and frowned.

Emma flushed with anger. "Get inside my knickers?"

"Now just a minute …"

Emma stood with feet apart, her hands on her hips, and carried on. "I suppose *you* were different to all the others, were you?"

"I managed to control my urges."

"So you could, but he can't?" Her index finger was waving like a manic conductor's baton.

Dad shrugged and pushed his hands into his trouser pockets. "They're all the bloody same. Like a herd of sex-mad rabbits."

Emma gave up and stormed upstairs to her small front bedroom, and sat quietly for a few minutes, trying to calm herself. As she stared disconsolately at her tiny wardrobe, her mood didn't improve. Clothes rationing, which had become an important part of the war effort, had hit her hard. This, and the 'Make do and Mend' campaign, meant she didn't need to waste a great deal of time thinking about what to wear. Her dresses had no pleats, elastic waist bands or fancy belts, and her black utility shoes had heels which were less than two inches high. She picked up a well-thumbed magazine from the bed, and looked intently at an advertisement for

Lorelox. A blonde, ringlet-infested moppet, and a group of permed women smiled out at her. She looked up into the small mirror on her dressing table, and her straight black listless hair stared miserably back. "Ah well." She sighed. "I'll wear a hat." By a quarter to seven, she was ready and sat in the front room. She'd done everything she could to achieve the 'Paris Look', and was nervously staring at the mantle clock.

"You make sure he doesn't try any funny business." Her father came in from the kitchen with a glass of beer, which wasn't his first. There was a small pause as he drank half of it, and wiped the froth from his moustache. "You watch what he says. I've heard them all." He drank the rest of the beer. "We've got to live for today. That's one. I may not be coming back. That's another. Lying sods are only after one thing. You know what they're after, my girl."

Emma blushed with embarrassment and anger. "I'm not that sort of girl, Dad. It's just a dance."

"Heard that one before as well." He stared at the empty glass. "Keep your hands on your drawers."

"*Dad!*" Emma was saved from any more embarrassment and fatherly advice, by a knock on the door.

*"Thank God for that,"* she thought as she jumped up from the chair and walked quickly to the door. "I won't be late," she called over her shoulder as she closed the door.

Peter had borrowed a jeep from the camp, and after a short drive, some embarrassed introductions, and a few 'lemonades', they danced the night away to an American Air Force six-piece band. Tuxedo Junction, Chattanooga Choo Choo, GI Jive, Yours, Boogie Woogie Bugle Boy, In the Mood, Ac-Cent-Tchu-Ate The Positive, When The Lights Go On Again (All Over The World), and Sentimental Journey, made the evening fly by much too quickly.

"It's ten o' clock. I should get you back," Peter said with a deep sigh.

She shrugged her shoulders. "It's been such a lovely night. Can we drive back slowly? It's so rare to have a few moments like this." She raised her eyebrows, and gave Peter her best sad puppy look.

He smiled and took her arm. "The slow way home it is, my lady." He kissed her on the cheek, and emotions flooded through her which had been waiting for the right man to wake them from their slumber. Whatever Dad had said, she wanted this young man, and was going to give herself to him.

"Can we stop here?" she asked Peter, as they came to a cornfield ready to harvest.

He nodded, and pulled the jeep close to a well-maintained hedge. They climbed out of Peter's side of the jeep, walked around the edge of a field of swaying corn, to an ancient oak tree, and lay down under its protective canopy. They lay close together staring at the starlit sky.

"Do you believe we go up there?" Peter pointed at the sky. "You know, when we die."

Emma turned her head to look at him. "Yes. Mum's up there waiting for me." She blew a kiss to the night sky. "Love you." She turned her face back to Peter. "Are you afraid of dying?"

He turned to face her. "Bloody terrified. But that's not what you say is it?" He rolled away onto his side to hide his tears.

She threw her arms around him, and pulled him close. His fear was tangible. A corrosive emotion dissolving his self-belief, and with it, any chance of him surviving the war. She felt an overpowering need to neutralise these negative feelings, and she only had one solution. Make love to this young man. Despite her total lack of experience, she offered herself up to him.

He looked down at her, not knowing how to respond to her clumsy attempts at seduction, because he, like her, was a virgin.

"I've never done this before," Peter said nervously.

Emma smiled at him. "Neither have I."

"What do we do?" he said with a face the colour of a baboon's behind.

She sat up. "Let's just kiss, and see what happens?"

A few minutes later, they lay naked in each other's arms.

"You OK?" he whispered.

"I think so," Emma replied. "Not sure how I should feel. You?"

"Sort of, tingly all over."

Emma suddenly felt exposed and embarrassed by her nakedness. She gathered up her clothes, and walked to the other side of the tree. Once dressed, she walked back around the tree to Peter, who was staring wide-eyed at the starlit sky.

"You OK?" she asked.

As he slowly turned to face her, she stumbled back, and fell against the oak tree.

Peter's eyes glowed with a brilliant, iridescent blue.

"Blue?" Charlie said.

"Yes, love. Blue. They were shining blue."

"But why?"

Molly shook her head. "No idea, but that's what she told me."

"What happened to them?" Charlie asked, as he picked up another slice of lemon drizzle cake.

"Emma, my mum, your grandma, I know about." She sat back in the chair, and stared lovingly at the chair opposite them. "But no-one knows what happened to Peter."

Charlie sighed. "Surely someone must know."

Mum shook her head. "All I know for certain, is that he fought in Burma. But what happened to him?" She left this hanging in the air.

"What happened to Grandma Emma?"

Molly glanced back at the chair opposite, and smiled.

# Chapter Twelve

After his 'unplanned' dip, Sam finally, and without a great deal of conviction, took the plunge. The water wrapped itself around him like arctic pack ice, and like a blue whale breaching, he broke the surface of the pool through the drowning local insect life.

"I told you the water was lovely." Elizabeth said as she sat up on the sun lounger, trying desperately to hide her grin.

"Piss off, it's bloody freezing," Sam said as he spat out a wasp. "Bloody penguins would be at home in here."

Elizabeth's mood suddenly darkened. "Piss off yourself! You bastard."

Sam stared at her in disbelief. "You feeling OK?"

"Who wouldn't feel good in a place like this?"

"But you just called me a bastard." He was utterly bewildered.

"I called you a bastard?" She frowned at him, and shook her head. "Me? No."

"You, yes."

"But I never use that word."

"I know, that's why I asked if you were OK."

*"She's going the same way as the other one,"* his other-half had rested long enough.

*"She's just stressed."*

*"Stressed? Are you going to stand for that? Give her a mouthful. Put her in her place now, or you'll be taking a trip down memory lane with the delightful Jane's twin sister."*

Sam ignored the jibes.

Elizabeth stood up. "Sam?"

"Mmmm? Sorry, just thinking."

"I'm sorry. I must still be stressed." She turned to Alfredo. "Where are we eating tonight?"

"There is a bella taverna, the Mellisani, at the end of the road. I've eaten there a few times, and the food and service are fantastico. Have the sea bass, it is il miglio, the best."

Elizabeth turned towards the villa. "I'm going to take a shower. What time are we leaving?"

"Seven thirty?"

She nodded, walked quickly to the villa, and trotted up the marble stairs.

"Is she OK?" Alfredo said, raising an eyebrow.

Sam frowned. "In all the time I've known her, I've never heard her swear like that." He walked out of the pool, shivering like the surface of an ultrasonic cleaner, and wrapped himself in a large orange towel. "I'm worried she's done too much. Way too much."

"Time spent here should heal the cracks. Come on, let's have a cold beer."

Sam followed him into the kitchen and sat down at the table.

Alfredo handed him a bottle of Bud Light and a bowl of olives. "What exactly is it you do, Sam? Why is mamma so convinced you can help?"

Sam swallowed half the beer, stared at the condensation running down the side of the bottle, and half-smiled at Alfredo. *"What the hell do I tell you?"* he thought. *"You know your mother's a ghost, so how much of a shock would High Wood be to you?"*

"Sam?"

He drained his beer, stood up, and walked to the fridge. "Another?"

Alfredo nodded. "Grazie."

Sam walked slowly back to the table, sat down, and took a very deep breath. "When did you find out your mother was a ghost?"

"At the funerale, or more precisely at the wake. She asked me if the buffet was good."

"At the wake? You saw her at her wake?"

Alfredo nodded. "Si."

A smile meandered across Sam's face. "Was the buffet good?"

Alfredo nodded. "Delizioso. Mamma was very happy with the catering, and especially pleased with the floral tributes." He stood up, and got a large bag of Lay crisps from a cupboard close to the sink. "High Wood, Sam? What goes on there?"

Sam gestured for Alfredo to follow him onto the patio, and they sat together on the swingseat, staring at the surrounding hills.

"Your uncles fought in World War Two, and we help soldiers who fought in World War One."

Alfredo raised his eyebrows, and nodded for him to continue.

Over the next half an hour, Sam outlined to Alfredo how he'd inherited High Wood, met Isaac Wouters, visited the memorials in France and Belgium, joined Papaver Rhoeas, how Elizabeth helped lost souls to make their final journey to the other side, how and when he'd found Rebecca and Adam, and how things were now at High Wood. He left out the problems they'd had with the 'somewhat disagreeable' Sergeant Lidsay.

Alfredo listened closely, and showed no signs of shock or disbelief. "It is no wonder you need a holiday. Elizabeth seems to have taken a lot of the emotional stress. A little outburst like that is completely understandable. Tomorrow, I'll take you to Antisamos Beach. We can sunbathe, swim, snorkel, eat good food, drink good wine, and relax. Tomorrow, sit behind Elizabeth in the car, and behind me on the way back." He smiled. "The road is a little exposed, twisty, and hilly."

The drive to Antisamos Beach was spectacularly scenic, and exactly as Alfredo had described. The views however, were well worth the short bout of acrophobia he had to suffer. They parked the car behind two tavernas, unloaded their beach essentials from the boot, walked the short distance to the pebbly beach, and planted themselves on three sun beds. The sea was the clearest blue Sam and Elizabeth had ever seen, the steep hills surrounding the bay were a verdant green, the sun beds, umbrellas, and parking were free, the waiter service from the two tavernas to the beach was efficient and friendly, and the view was to die for. It was the closest they'd been to Heaven on Earth.

They ordered three americanos with milk, and sat soaking up the view and atmosphere.

"You risking the sea?" Elizabeth said to Sam.

He grimaced, as his manhood was being brought into question again. He finished his coffee, stood up, pulled on his jelly shoes, grabbed a snorkel and mask, and strode with all the conviction of a condemned man walking to the gallows, into the sea. He was doing OK, until the waves lapped over the top of his swimming shorts, and it took all his willpower, to suppress a scream. He looked back at Elizabeth, who was hiding her face behind a magazine.

*"I'll be buggered if she's going to think I'm a wimp."*

*"Already does."* He was back. *"She's got you sussed."*

*"Look, why don't you…"*

*"I'd probably find, that whatever it was you were about to suggest, was either physically impossible, or reproductively limiting,"* his other-half chuckled. *"Go on, dive in, and give us all a bloody good laugh."*

With a considerable degree of unease, Sam 'dived' into the sea. At first he thought he'd gone into cardiac arrest, but the effect was thankfully, only temporary. After a few seconds interspersed with sharp intakes of breath, he was surprised to find that the experience was quite pleasant. He'd snorkelled a few times before, but the number of fish which were swimming close to the shore amazed him. He swam for a few metres through clear waters, and then became increasingly nervous as he swam into the darker, deeper waters of the bay. At first, it was difficult to see anything, but as his eyes became accustomed to the poor visibility, he could make out smaller fish feeding on the bottom. He lifted his head above the surface, trod water, and lusted after a black, twenty-metre catamaran, moored in the bay.

*"Let's see what else we can see,"* he thought, as he plunged his face back into the pitch-black sea. Below him to his right, he noticed a subtle movement. At first, it was just a black lump, but as it moved closer, the vague outline, began to take on the clearly discernible form of a man.

*"Great place to go scuba diving,"* Sam thought. *"I should get some lessons."*

Suddenly, the shadowy shape began to swim rapidly towards him, and as it neared the surface, intensely bright sunlight illuminated it. There was no black wet suit or aqualung, no mask, no flippers, and as it came close to him, no face. Just mottled white bone. Sam gasped, and swallowed a large sample of the Ionian Sea. He started to choke, panicked, threw his arms and legs wildly at the sea like a whirling dervish, just reached the shallows, staggered onto the pebbles, tripped, grazed his knees, apologised to a young woman whose beer he'd knocked over, and eventually got to his sun lounger, which collapsed under him as he sat down heavily on it.

Alfredo helped him up. "Are you OK?"

Sam examined his injured parts, blushed, nodded to the lady with the spilt drink, swore under his breath, and sighed. "I'm fine, thanks."

"You flew out of the sea, like a seal trying to escape from a ravenous killer whale," Elizabeth said, desperately trying not to laugh. "Was the water that cold?"

"Bloody hilarious." Sam wasn't in any mood for jokes.

"Come on, I was just pulling your leg. What happened?" She got up, from the sun lounger, and sat down close to him.

"I saw something."

"What?" Elizabeth became concerned.

"Like things we see at High Wood." He raised his eyebrows. "You know. Things. Only a hundred times worse than anything I've ever seen."

Elizabeth scowled at him. "What are you talking about?"

"I'll tell you tonight." He looked up at Alfredo and smiled.

"What did you see, Sam?" Alfredo asked, resting his elbows on his knees. "Nothing you say will frighten me."

"Something came up from the bottom of the sea."

"Spiriti, fantasmi? A ghost or spirit?"

Sam shrugged.

Alfredo pulled his sun lounger closer to them. "At their wakes, mamma and papà, didn't *let* me see them. I had already seen them at their funerals. I have always been able to see spiriti and fantasmi. This is why mamma wanted me to come with you. I can see spiriti, but I do not have the … capacità, the … abilità."

Elizabeth leaned forward. "I understand. Ability?"

"Si. Ability. The ability to find spirits and ghosts. To sense them and bring them home. A sense you and Sam have."

They nodded in understanding.

"Although sometimes it feels more like a curse," Sam replied.

"What did you see?" Alfredo asked insistently.

The three sun-worshippers leaned closer, and Sam detailed what he'd seen in the inky waters of the bay.

Alfredo looked around. "So many were thrown into the sea during the massacre. It must have been one of the Acqui division."

# Chapter Thirteen

Charlie lay back on the sofa. "What happened to grandma after she saw his eyes?"

Molly stood up, stretched her legs, got a glass of water from the tap and a small bar of chocolate from the fridge, and rejoined Charlie on the sofa. "After that night, things didn't go as well as she'd hoped."

Dad was in full flow, and nothing was going to stop him. "I bloody told you, didn't I? Only after one thing. Sly buggers will say anything to get inside your drawers. Look at you. Who the hell would marry you now? Un-unmarried woman with some other man's bastard in tow. My God. If your mother was still alive she'd turn bloody somersaults in her grave." He sat down in the armchair, finished his beer, refilled his glass, and stood up unsteadily. "And another thing." He stabbed a finger at Emma. "What's going to happen to you when *I* die?" He was getting redder and redder in the face. "Who's going to provide for you and the boy then? Haven't thought of that, have you?" He sat down and wiped beads of sweat from his forehead with his creased handkerchief. "I'll strangle the sod if I ever get my hands on him."

Emma tried to answer, but Dad, like a mill race, was in full flow.

"If you'd tell me his name," he said and glared at her, "I'd have him marching down the aisle with both barrels of my shotgun shoved up his arse." He filled his glass with more beer. "And after all this time, you haven't heard a single, bloody word from him."

"HIS NAME IS PETER. PETER WALLINS! AND MY BOY!" She waved her arms at him. "YOUR GRANDSON'S NAME IS IAN." She took a deep breath. "PETER'S DEAD! HAPPY NOW!" Emma screamed at him.

"Bloody lazy bastard. I mean how difficult is it pick up a pen and ..." Walter stared at his daughter, dropped his glass, which shattered on the floor, and tottered across the floor to her. "Darlin' I didn't know. How … when did you find out?"

She pushed him away, and he fell onto the floor. He struggled to get up, but the beer had 'relaxed' the joints in his legs, and he sat like a beached whale on the faded carpet. She slipped her arms under his armpits, and with a great deal of effort, dropped him onto the sofa.

"Someone from the camp came down and told me." She sobbed. "He knew about Peter and me and the baby, and he thought I should know." Tears streamed down her cheeks "He died in Burma." She got up, and walked to the front window. "Bloody Japanese. They forced him to work on some bloody railway 'til he dropped." She turned around, wringing her hands in despair. "How can anyone do that? For God's sake, he was only twenty-four." She fell into Walter's arms and sobbed into his shoulder until her tears dried up.

As the years passed, Ian grew fast, and Emma couldn't deny he was his father's son. Ian idolised her, which softened the gnawing pain which chewed away at her self-confidence and ability to trust anyone outside her immediate family. She built an insurmountable wall around herself, which Joshua would have had difficulty blowing down.

On September the second, nineteen forty-five, Emma, Ian, Walter, and Uncle Don, were at the church hall celebrating Ian's fifth birthday, and the surrender of Japan. Everyone in the village had pooled their rations for the celebration, and George, thanks to the blind-eye of Constable Poole, whose personal drinks cabinet had been replenished, had miraculously found oranges, chocolate, and chewing gum for the children, whiskey and tobacco for the men, and sherry, lipstick, and nylons for the women.

Emma was talking with Mrs Edwards, the baker's wife, when she noticed a face she didn't recognise. She tilted her head to Mrs Edwards, and whispered, "Don't turn around, but who's that talking to the vicar?"

Mrs Edwards' immediate reaction, was to swing around in her seat, and point at the young man. "Who, him, dear?"

Emma sank down as low as she could in her chair, and nodded.

"Oh, that's Reg. He's Mr Probert, you know, the butcher's youngest son. He got back from Germany a couple of weeks ago." After waving to the vicar, she swung back around to Emma. "Apparently," she spoke as if she was imparting some great state secret, "he saw terrible things over there. He hasn't told anyone about what happened." She leaned forward and whispered. "Mrs Murray the grocer's wife told me, that she'd heard from Mrs Robins, you know, she works at the post office, that it was something about a place called," she said and scratched her cheek, "now what was it? It sounded something like, ummm, Housewitch?" She shook her head, turned, and looked back at the butcher's son. "Apparently," she said and looked around again, as if she was working for the secret service, "he was burying bodies with a tractor." She noticed her friend Mrs Morton, and waved to her. "Lovely woman. Could do with losing a few pounds. Don't know how she does it on the rations we get." Seamlessly, she returned to Reg. "Apparently, he buried thousands of bodies, and they were all ... *Jews*." She silently mouthed the last word, and raised her pencilled eyebrows. She leaned forward, kissed Emma on the cheek, smiled, and walked over to the refreshment table for more sandwiches, and another cup of tea.

"I seem to be the topic of conversation."

Emma looked up.

Reg Probert looked down at her. "Can I sit down?"

She blushed and nodded. "Yes."

"Thanks."

"Just got back, I hear," Emma said.

Reg nodded. "About a month ago."

"Must be glad it's over."

He nodded.

"Going to work with your dad?"

Another nod. "Uh huh."

"What did you do to win all those medals?"

Reg looked down at the top pocket of his jacket, blushed, and shrugged. "Nothing really."

She called across the room to Ian. "That's enough of that chocolate. You'll be sick."

Ian smiled, trying his best to hide the remaining squares of slowly melting chocolate in the warm palms of his hands.

"Yours?" Reg asked.

Emma smiled. "Yes. It's his birthday today."

"His dad's not around?"

"He was killed in Burma."

Reg shook his head. "Bloody war. Do you know how he died?"

She slowly shook her head and her eyes locked onto her shoes.

A mutual silence fell over them like a thick, patchwork quilt on a cold winter's night.

Eventually Reg spoke. "Sorry about asking like that."

Emma looked up, wiping the tears from her cheeks. "It's fine. You sort of get used to it, and then out of the blue, the pain starts again."

"How old's your boy?" Reg asked, nodding in Ian's direction.

"Five."

"Big boy for five."

"Takes after his father. Peter was tall." Memories crashed into her mind, like autumn breakers on a pebble beach. "He …" Her eyes filled again with tears, and words became impossible.

Reg leaned forward. "I'm sorry, I didn't mean to stir up painful memories."

Emma forced a smile. "It's OK. I need, want to talk about him. Since I learned he'd been killed, I've tried to bury him at the back of my mind. But everything that's buried festers, and I won't let Peter become just a fractured memory."

Reg rubbed the stubble on his chin. "I've got a pal who was in the Chindits. He knows quite a bit about what happened over there." He paused. "I could ask him, if you like. It's a bit of a long shot, but it might help to know what happened to him."

Emma rubbed the palms of her hands together. Would knowing the details of how Peter died, make the pain of his loss any easier? The agony of understanding what he suffered would surely only make things worse. But wouldn't knowing the truth of what happened stop the nightmares? Surely the truth couldn't be worse than the imagined horrors of her dreams? She looked at Reg, and sighed. "I'm not sure, but I think I need to know."

Reg started work in his father's butcher's shop, and despite the war ending, rationing was still pinching the stomachs of the British. With meat at a premium, Reg and his father Henry, were very popular with the housewives of the town.

"Any sausages?" Mrs Baird asked Reg softly, as she leaned across the counter, exposing her substantial bosom to him.

He looked away, trying not to be drawn into the deep valley quivering under his nose, as the queue of expectant faces, tilted their heads, desperate to hear his answer.

"No sausages."

A moan of disappointment rippled up and down the queue.

Reg leaned forward and whispered, "We have got some liver, tripe, tongue, and a little bacon."

The village housewives' hearing had been so refined during the war, that the news was immediately received at the end of the queue.

"I'll make sure you all get a bit," Reg called out. "I've got enough for everyone."

"I bet he does," Mrs Petty said, none too quietly to Mrs Jonston. "Plenty of meat to go around? Eh Joany?" The two women's laughs would have graced any pub on a Saturday night.

"Careful what you say to this lot," his father said, as he came back in from the cold room. "There's a few here who'd take you at your word." He looked across and winked at Mrs Watters. "Ain't that right, Doris?"

"Oh, Mr Probert." She blushed and smiled at Reg. "I'm past that sort of thing."

"Never too old to learn a few new tricks, though. There's many a good tune played on an old fiddle." He raised his eyebrows, blew out his cheeks, and mimed playing the violin.

Giggles rippled up and down the queue.

"He could play a tune on my strings, whenever he wanted," Mrs Petty said to herself, as she gave Reg a look which screamed 'I'm yours'.

Reg looked away, terrified by the thought of being 'had' by Mrs Petty, and went back to serving Mrs Podmore.

The doorbell rang as Emma came running into the shop.

"Anything left, Mr Probert?" She called out to Reg's dad.

"Best ask Reg, dear. He's been serving all morning."

Emma, followed by the furrowed brows of the housewives of Sheringham, and particularly Mrs Petty, walked to the front of the queue. "Dad will kill me if I go home with nothing, Reg. I lost track of time. Have you got anything?"

He smiled. "You're in luck." He walked into the cold room, and came back with some liver and three rashers of very streaky bacon, wrapped in brown paper. *"Could we meet for a drink one night?"* he whispered. *"I've spoken to quite a few people, and I think I've got a decent idea what happened to Peter. How about tomorrow night? Seven o' clock at the Red Lion?"*

Emma nodded, turned, and walked quickly past a queue of scowling, sour faces.

"What would you like?" Reg was stood at the bar of the Red Lion.

"A port and lemon would be lovely," Emma replied.

He paid for the drinks, and sat next to her on a wooden bench in a corner of the bar.

"What have you found out?" she asked nervously.

Reg took a deep breath. "My pal Bernard marched into Burma with Wingate in February forty-three. Two days later, after crossing the Chindwin River, they had their first scrap with the Japanese. Two of his mates were killed, but they killed about thirty of them. They reached the north-south Burma railway in March, and demolished it in seventy places." He lifted his glass, and drank half his pint of bitter. "They were there for three months, and then drew back to India. Unfortunately, Bernard was captured by the Japanese, and made to slave on the Burma Railway." He let this hang in the air for a few seconds.

Emma sat upright. "Did he meet Peter?"

"There were thousands of soldiers working on the railway." He tried to quietly suppress her understandable excitement. "But he did say he met one young soldier who was different from the rest?"

"Different?"

"For most of the time, he kept himself to himself. Strangest thing Bernard told me, and I know this'll sound odd, was that one night he went out to take a pee, and saw this soldier standing close to the wire. Just staring at the sky."

"That's not odd."

"No. But what scared Bernard, was when this soldier turned around, his eyes were glowing."

Emma leaned forward, and knocked over Reg's drink. "What colour were they glowing? What colour, Reg?" She was shaking him by the shoulders.

Reg prised her hands from his shoulders, and stood up. "They were blue."

"What happened to him, Reg?" Emma's breathing had become shallow, her mouth dry, and she chewed her bottom lip.

He sat back and frowned. "Phil was a little sketchy, but the Japanese guards were … they were …"

"Please Reg, I need to know everything. Tell me what you know."

He looked deep into Emma's eyes, and knew he shouldn't hide anything from her. "Apparently, Peter left a diary. More of a school-exercise book really."

Her eyes flew wide open. "A diary?" She leapt to her feet, grabbed Reg's shoulders again, and shook him. "Where is it? Reg where is it?"

"It's not in great shape. Pages missing, others stained, almost illegible, and some so creased you can't read what's written on them. But from what's left, you get a fair idea of what happened."

"Anything's better than the nothing I know now." Her eyes begged him to let her see it.

"It's at my house. Locked away in a metal box." He held her hands, and squeezed them gently. "If you're sure. It isn't easy to read."

"I need to know what happened to him. Not knowing is worse than what I dream he must have suffered."

"I wouldn't be so sure your dreams are worse," Reg said. "You're sure about this?"

Emma nodded slowly.

Charlie smiled and squeezed his mother's hand. "That's quite a story. She must have been a strong lady."

"The strongest." Molly sat back and sighed. "I miss her."

"He left a diary." Charlie said wide-eyed.

# Chapter Fourteen

Matt and Mark Stroudle were twenty-eight-year-old twins, who may as well have been conjoined at birth. During their entire lives, they'd never been more than a mile away from each other. Even during their regular 'visits' at Her Majesty's pleasure.

Mark was five feet two with a body which closely resembled 'Big Hero 6', shaven-headed, to unsuccessfully hide the fact he was as bald as a snooker ball with alopecia, and as flatulent as a bulldog with a leaky anal sphincter which had devoured a particularly spicy chilli con carne. He had small feet and the body odour of a rabbit's bedding, was extremely well known to the local police as a 'bit of a joke', had an IQ well below the national average, was suited and booted by charity shops, but loved by his mum.

Matt was six feet tall, thin as a giraffe's front leg, long, lank, with black greasy hair tied back in a ponytail with an elastic band he'd found in a litter bin. He was in desperate need of the skills of an exceptionally talented dentist, school 'leaver' at fifteen with no qualifications and a lot of suggestions where the teaching staff thought he'd end up. He had an IQ marginally better than Mark's, big feet, halitosis which could strip paint at twenty yards, and was as well-known to the police as his brother. The straight man in their double-act, he had a similar taste in fashion, and was equally beloved of his mum.

After school, their career paths had been decidedly miscellaneous. They'd singularly failed as brickie's assistants, painters and decorators, warehouse assistants, shelf fillers at Aldi, Lidl, Tesco, and Asda, mini-cab drivers, pizza delivery men, park keepers, dustmen, or as the council preferred them to be known, refuse disposal operatives, and ineffective sellers of the 'Big Issue'.

Given their total washout in legal employment, they'd turned to crime, where their record was equally as bad. They'd been godawful shoplifters, twoccers, burglars, pick-pockets, purveyors of illegal cigarettes, driving under the influence, driving without tax or insurance, and general pains in the arse for a considerable proportion of the local general public.

They finally settled on burglary as a good career move, and honed their breaking-and-entry skills, on static-caravans, garden sheds, greenhouses, changing rooms, pavilions, and church halls. All with very little, i.e., no success. Despite these setbacks, they decided to move up to bigger and better things. They were sat on a park bench in Roath Park discussing their next caper, throwing stones at the ducks on the boating lake. They'd been looking for something bigger and better to tackle, and stumbled on High Wood. Sam and Elizabeth had been leaving with their luggage, and the brothers decided that this was their chance to make a name for themselves in the world of south-east-Welsh-burglary.

"It'll be a bloody doddle," Matt said, as a passing pensioner gave them a 'look'.

"Got a problem, gran?" Mark said through a scowl.

The pensioner's cheeks flushed as she walked away briskly from them, muttering to her friend about the young of today.

"Crincklies are a bleedin' pain in the arse." Mark sneered after flicking-the finger at the pensioner. He turned his attention back to Matt. "Yeah. It'll be a pissin' doddle," he said, with glistening globs of sarcasm dripping like mucus from his lips. "Just like that corner shop which was going to be a," he said and tapped his lips with his index finger, "Mmmm, 'ow did you put it? A piece of piss?"

"Bollocks. 'ow was I supposed to know about that dog?" He pulled a few loose, greasy hairs into his pony tail, and tried unsuccessfully to tuck them under the elastic band holding it together.

"Mmmm?" Mark's attention span, which was a tad above a goldfish's, was picking his nails with a broken lollipop stick he'd found under the bench.

"We'll do that big gaff 'igh Wood tonight while they're away."

Mark looked up from his 'manicure', frowned, and farted loudly. "God almighty! Smell that one." He fell back against the back of the bench, in fits of laughter. "I think I must 'ave died."

"You dirty sod." Mark waved his hands at the rising anal gases. "We doin' this tonight then?"

Mark made two ducks flap into the air, loudly quacking their indignation at being disturbed. "Break in tonight?"

Matt nodded.

"What, in the dark? You're 'avin a laugh."

"And your problem is?" Matt stood up, and shook his head.

Mark pulled his hood tight around his head, and just missed a swan with a handful of gravel. "My problem, is what I've 'eard about that place." He stood up, and walked close to Matt. "Bubs Leckie told me all about it. His mate Nicholson, 'eard that a friend of friend of 'is, saw some mad woman in one of the upstairs windows." He looked around as if he expected anyone to be actually interested in what he was saying. "And they 'eard noises." He looked around again, to check they weren't being overheard. "Woooh!" He waved his arms in the air. "You know, *them* sort of noises."

Matt shrugged, shook his head, and walked a short distance away from his brother. *"If you lived there, there'd be bloody noises comin' from it all the time,"* he thought. He stared at Mark as if he was mentally unstable, looked up at the sky, and shook his head. "Give me strength." He grabbed Mark's grey hoody, and pulled him around to face him. "What the pissin' 'ell are you talkin' about?"

"It's … well … things 'appen in that 'ouse."

"You are shittin' me. What the bloody 'ell are you talkin' about? Things 'appen? What bloody things 'appen?"

"*Things*." He raised his eyebrows, and made a face resembling a severely constipated chimp. "You know what I mean … *things*." He dragged the word out. "Like the *things* in those films we watch."

"What bloody films?" Matt was losing the will to live, and what little patience he still had.

"The one's when … you know, when nasty *things* happen." He walked around like a zombie. "*Things*!" He dragged the word out again.

"'orror films?"

"Yeah. The ones where them people who live in the 'ouse," he said and mimed using a video camera, "film all the shit things that 'appen to them."

"Paranorman's Activity."

"Yeah. That one."

"You don't 'alf talk some bollocks." He waved him away dismissively. "They're just pissin' films."

"Yeah, well anyway, I'm just sayin'."

"You wanna cut down on the stuff your snortin'? It's fryin' your brains. If you're that shit scared, I'll do it myself."

Mark shrugged. "Be my pissin' guest."

"Got the wind up 'ave we?" Matt said as if he were talking to a child. "Shit your pants scared?"

"NO!" He looked down sulkily at the grass. "No."

"So you doin' this with me or not?"

He nodded begrudgingly, stood up, and followed Matt out of the park.

As a spirit, Jane didn't need sleep but liked, as far as she could, sticking to the normal cycles and rhythms of 'living'. She was lying awake, if lying awake was possible for a spirit, and was just about to start reading David Copperfield. Since returning as a spirit, she'd consumed books. In school, they were just another boring thing she had to do to get through the day, but now, losing herself in the imaginary worlds of the classics, helped her retain her sanity.

*"Chapter 1 - I am born,"* she read to herself. *"Whether I shall turn out to be the hero of my own life, or whether that station will be held by anyone else, these pages will tell."*

An hour later she put the book down. Not through tiredness, which no longer troubled her, but because of the sound of breaking glass.

*"Careful you moron,"* Matt hissed at Mark.

"Firstly, if they're away, who's gonna 'ear us, and secondly, why are you whisperin'?" Mark said as he knocked out the remainder of the glass, and opened the kitchen door.

"Fair point well made, bruv. Don't cut yourself and leave your genies for evidence. The filth have got machines which can tell from a single fart if you've been somewhere," Matt said with a dead-pan face. "I read it in a magazine at the station."

Mark stared at him. "A fart? Piss off, you're 'avin me on."

"'onest. It's as bloody true as I'm standin' 'ere. They've got machines that's so bloody sensitive, you've only to got to leave the sniff of a fart, and they've got you. And for Christ's sake, don't take a dump or a pee."

Mark wasn't sure if he believed him, and frowned like a bulldog sucking a wasp.

"What's up now?" Matt asked with a raised eyebrow.

"I dropped one as I got inside." Mark ran to the kitchen door, and wafted it back and fore. "That ought to get rid of it."

"OK now?" Matt asked, shaking his head. "Right, you 'ave a look upstairs, and I'll see what's worth nickin' down 'ere. Back 'ere in twenty minutes."

Mark nodded, walked into the hall, switched on his torch, shone it up the stairs, and walked back to Matt. "You wanna do upstairs?"

Matt walked slowly up to him, and prodded him in the chest. "Grow up. And *no*, I am not going upstairs."

"But …"

Matt's expression, was enough for Mark to start climbing the stairs like an ibex skipping up the side of a vertical cliff with a mountain lion in close pursuit.

Jane jumped out of bed and walked onto the landing. She didn't want to disturb Rebecca and Adam, as the breaking glass could have been anything. However, the shaft of light slicing like a lighthouse-beam through the darkness, changed her mind. She ran to the end of the landing, and walked through the wall into Rebecca and Adam's bedroom.

They stirred and sat up in bed.

"Sorry. Not disturbing anything, was I?" Jane grinned wickedly.

"Jane!" Rebecca blushed.

"Well, you've a got a lot of time to catch up on."

Adam grinned. "A *lot* of time."

Rebecca elbowed him in the ribs. "Did you hear that noise?" she asked.

"That's why I came in. There's somebody in the house. Must be a burglar."

"Shall we call the captain?" Adam asked.

"No." She rubbed her hands together and grinned. "Let's make this 'visitor' wish they'd never heard of High Wood."

The three amighosts smiled at each other and walked through the bedroom wall onto the landing, just in time to see the back of Mark disappearing up the stairs into the gallery.

"Let's give him something he'll never forget," Jane said mischievously.

"MARK, YOU'VE GOTTA SEE THIS PLACE. THIS STUFF MUST BE WORTH A BLOODY FORTUNE" Matt shouted from downstairs.

"And then there were two," Jane said with a wicked smile.

Adam and Rebecca frowned and shrugged.

"It's from a poem 'Ten Little Indians'."

They kept frowning and shrugging.

"It doesn't matter." She looked at the door to the gallery. "I'll see what number one's up to in the gallery, and you two see what's going on down there." She started to walk away and stopped. "Shake him up a bit. You know. Things that go bump in the night."

Their frowns grew deeper, and the shrugs 'shruggier'.

"From ghoulies and ghosties and long-leggedy beasties, and things that go bump in the night!"

They stared at each other, and looked back at Jane like milkmen who'd just been asked in Mandarin Chinese for two pints of semi-skimmed.

"Never mind. Just scare the hell out of whoever's down there."

Mark walked into the gallery, closely followed by Jane, and walked up and down the aisles, staring at the pictures and shaking his head.

"Bloody waste of time. Not a bleedin' thing worth nickin' up 'ere. Who the 'ell wants a load of poxy old photos."

*"Me,"* Jane thought. *"And I think it's about time I got your full attention."* She walked close to Mark and whispered, *"You are not alone."*

Mark turned and assumed it was his brother. He walked down the stairs to the landing and shouted. "YOU SAY SOMETHIN'?"

Jane stared at his back. *"Something a little more physical next time."*

"THIS PLACE IS A BLOODY GOLD MINE," Matt called back.

"NOTHIN' BUT A LOAD OF SHIT UP 'ERE."

"CHECKED THE BEDROOMS YET?"

"NO."

"THEN GET A PISSIN' MOVE ON."

Mark looked up and down the landing, decided to start at the far end, and work his way back to the stairs. He picked up the sports bag he'd brought and walked to the furthest bedroom on the left.

Jane jogged down the landing, straight through Mark who shuddered, and reached her bedroom ahead of him. *"If you think you're going to turn my room into a bomb site, then you're very sadly mistaken."*

He pushed the door open and lit up the room with his torch.

*"If you need light, then let me help you,"* Jane thought with a wicked snigger.

He started opening the top drawer of the dressing table, when the ceiling light came on flooding the room with light.

"What the …?"

Matt was in the hall, walking from the lounge back to the kitchen, when he saw the light from the bedroom. "TURN THAT PISSIN' LIGHT OFF!"

Mark ran to the light switch, slapped it, and ran onto the landing. "I DIDN'T TURN IT ON!"

Matt shook his head, swore under his breath, "Bloody drugs," and walked back to the lounge.

Jane stood close to Mark and flipped the switch back on.

He turned, poked his head around the bedroom door, and slapped the switch off.

Jane, with a giggle, softly turned it back on.

This time, Mark saw the switch move, but unlike the switch, he was totally incapable of any sort of movement, except from his bowels, which left enough evidence for the police to put him away for a very long time.

Matt walked into the kitchen with a small Chinese vase, saw the light going on and off, put the vase down, and ran up the stairs two at a time. "What the 'ell are you doin'?" He hissed as he hit the light switch. "You signallin' to somebody? It's like soddin' Blackpool illuminations up 'ere. Why don't you just phone the pissin' police, and ask 'em 'round for coffee."

Mark pointed at the switch and managed to mumble. "It moved by itself. Watch."

"Watch what?"

"The switch. It'll turn itself on."

Nothing happened, and the room remained in darkness.

"Did you take anythin' before we came out tonight?" Matt prodded his brother in the chest. "I've warned you about buyin' shit from that knob Brian. 'e'll mix anything with his stuff to make a few more quid."

Mark could barely manage a shake of the head. He edged forward and apprehensively touched the light switch as if it was coated in sulphuric acid.

Matt stared at him and sighed. "I'm goin' back downstairs. *You,* go through the bedrooms, grab as much jewellery and watches as you can, and cram them in that bag." He pointed at the sports bag, turned, sniffed, and started to walk away. "You shit yourself?" He called back over his shoulder.

Mark didn't respond, grabbed his jacket, and followed Matt down the landing. "I'm comin' with you."

"Bollocks you are. Bedrooms!"

"Listen bruv, there's somethin' up 'ere." He looked over his shoulder, pleading with his brother. "There's somethin' up 'ere with me."

"Jesus! Not those bloody 'orror films again?"

Mark begged like a Labrador wanting a walk. "Let me look 'round downstairs. You're better at jewellery than me. Please, bruv!"

Matt shone his torch into Mark's face. He had the look of a puppy who'd left puddles in the kitchen. "Oh piss off downstairs. Leave this to me."

Mark grabbed him, kissed him on the cheek, and trotted off to the top of the stairs.

*"Wanker,"* Matt thought. He walked across the landing, and up the stairs to the gallery. *"OK, so what do we 'ave in 'ere?"*

Jane stood on the landing, stared at the stairs, briefly looked back at the door to the gallery, shook her head, and started down the stairs. *"Mark, you are the weakest link. Goodbye."*

In the gallery, Matt found Elizabeth's laptop, camera, and Bose sound centre. He shook his head "Nothing worth 'avin'. Jesus, if 'e wasn't my brother ... So, what else is not worth 'avin' up 'ere?"

In the far aisle, a thick, jelly-like, swirling green vapour, began to languidly emerge from between the floorboards. It slithered over the shelves like an anaconda stalking its prey, and dropped, unseen, onto the floor close to Matt.

Downstairs, Mark was a little more relaxed, but was still exuding gaseous evidence for the police. As his torchlight shakily illuminated the lounge, threatening shape-shifting shadows seemed to close in on him.

*"Sod this. I'm waitin' in the car,"* he thought. *"Matt can scream an' swear all 'e pissin' likes, but it'll be better than this."* He started to walk back to the door, when it slammed shut. There weren't enough swear words in his expansive vocabulary to capture his feelings of stark, desolate terror. He ran to the door, grabbed the handle, desperately tried to open it, but an unseen Adam's shoulder, and vice-like grip, were keeping it shut.

*"Time he heard from us,"* Jane said to Rebecca. *"Adam, keep that door shut."* She walked a few steps back and sat on the sofa.

Matt had checked enough of the aisles in the gallery to realise, that apart from the laptop, sound centre, and Nikon camera, there was nothing else worth taking. He picked them up and started to walk back down the gallery stairs. As he reached the small, halfway landing, the green mist slithered close behind him, and wrapped itself like a reticulated python around his left leg. The head reared up like a diamondback rattlesnake, and struck hard into Matt's spine, injecting the 'venom' it carried. He winced, and grabbed his lower back. "Shit! Bent down to bloody quick pickin' up that laptop." He stretched his lower back, groaned, touched his toes, and made his way down to the landing. As he reached it, he heard Mark screaming, banging, and kicking at the lounge door.

Rebecca hissed in Mark's ear. "You shouldn't have come here. You've disturbed angry spirits."

He slid down the wall, produced something rather more solid than gas, and sat paralysed on the floor.

Jane picked up two cushions from the sofa, and threw them against the wall close to Mark's head.

"YOU'RE GOING TO HELL," Adam shouted, beginning to enjoy himself. "YOU ARE CURSED."

"MATT!"

Mark's scream terrified Matt. "What the 'ell 'ave you taken? Some bastard's cut your stuff with Christ knows what." He jumped down the stairs three at a time, slammed his shoulder into the lounge door, bounced backwards, and smashed the screen of the laptop. He looked down at his shattered booty, cursed under his breath, jumped to his feet, and grabbed the door handle.

"MATT!"

"UNLOCK THIS PISSIN' DOOR!"

"THEY'VE LOCKED IT!"

It sounded like he was sobbing.

"WHO'S PISSIN' LOCKED IT?"

"THESE, BASTARD GHOSTS!"

"*'e's gone,*" Matt thought in a panic. "I'LL BE THERE NOW!"

"JESUS CHRIST, MATT! KICK IT DOWN BEFORE THEY KILL ME!"

Matt stepped back from the door and threw himself at it again.

Jane pushed her head through the wall, closely watched Matt and as his shoulder made contact with the door, she called out to Adam. *"Let go of the handle."*

Matt exploded through the door, tripped over Mark's feet, smashed into the sofa, and rolled over the top into the curtains which collapsed on top of him. He lay breathless under them for what felt like ages, eventually threw them off, and stood up. "What the fuck 'ave you been takin'?"

"I swear to God." He crossed himself. "I 'aven't taken nothin' today. Nothin'."

"So what's all the panic? Bloody door was open." He pointed at it. "Look."

"Somethin' screamed at me, and told me I was going to 'ell." He stood up and pulled his trousers away from his behind. "They pissin' threw cushions at me." He pointed at the pile at the bottom of the wall. "And that door wouldn't open."

Matt stared into his eyes, shook his head, and walked to the open door. "Come on. We'll come back tomorrow." He picked up the broken laptop and sound centre, threw them against the wall, and threw the camera strap over his shoulder. "I'm not leaving 'ere with nothin'."

A muted voice at the back of his mind whispered. *'You're not leaving with nothin'*'.

# Chapter Fifteen

Mum turned to face Charlie. "You're sure you want to read Peter's diary?"

Charlie nodded. "I need to know everything I can about what happened to him."

"OK. But you've got to understand, if he'd been caught writing, he'd have been shot." She looked around the room, rubbing her chin with her right hand. "Now where did I put it?"

On the other side of the room, a cupboard door in the Welsh dresser creaked and slowly opened a few inches.

"*Thanks, Mum,*" Molly whispered as she walked over to the Welsh dresser and pulled the door fully open. After a few seconds of lifting and moving things around, she stood up holding a rusty, blue, tin box. She walked back to the sofa and put it on the coffee table close to Charlie.

He cautiously picked it up, and tentatively lifted the rusty lid. It contained three things. A faded, badly creased, black and white photo of three men in uniform, a newspaper clipping from nineteen forty-four, and what once had been a green, school-exercise book. The corners of its cover were missing, and one rusty staple was doing its desperate best to hold the remaining pages together. He picked it up like a father holding his newborn baby for the first time.

"Have you got a tray and some tweezers I could have, Mum?"

She nodded, walked into the kitchen, and came back with a patterned, padded tray covered in pink roses, and a pair of silver tweezers.

He laid the exercise book on it and lifted some of the fragile pages with the tweezers. It was immediately obvious that a lot of them, because of age, and probable water damage, were going to be impossible to read. He looked up and frowned. "There's not a lot here, Mum. Did Grandma read this before she died?"

Molly looked into a corner of the room, stared at it intently for a few seconds, nodded, smiled, and looked back at Charlie. "When it came down to it, she couldn't face reading the truth of what happened to Peter."

Charlie stared into the corner, looked puzzlingly at his mum, frowned, and assumed she was trying to remember what Grandma Emma had told her.

"Could you get me a note pad from the drawer? And I'll write down what I can make out, before this disintegrates."

Molly walked into the kitchen, and took a reporter's note pad and a biro from a drawer, and brought them back to Charlie.

<u>Charlie Thompson - Grandad Peter's Diary</u>

*This is my record of what I can read from Grandad Peter's diary. It needs to be taken to an expert restorer, who may be able to recover the faded writings.*

*Anti aircr… guns out of amm….ion (Can't read next few lines)*

*Nip flag over Cathay Bui….g (Half the page too creased to read) Percival. surrend..ed*

*Bennet has bug..red off leaving us in the proverb…*

*(Looks like a couple of pages are missing)*

*Singapore is … dead bodies everyw…., … wire, fallen cab..s, shelled and … masonry cover stre…s. Bui..di..s burn.. (Faded words) Dead hor..s (Faded words) Peop.. wand..ing like los. sh… Bloody sha..les. (Big crease in page) Nip. bayoneting doctors wound.. and nurse in Alexandra Hos..tal*

*Group of mates shipped … on …..y hell ships God help them*

*Heard rumours of a bo.t being inter..pted by 'Nips' and the men and wo… bei.g shot.*

*(Can't read next three pages)*

*Marched to Changi A..a Goal… 3 men shot by N..s. Blood. animals. (4 faded paragraphs) 200 of us in block for 20. All filthy, infe..ed with lice, starve. Only gettin. a few o…ces of rice. (Looks like 4 or 5 pages missing)*

*Rains every day. Every..ing const..tly soaking wet. Fred's got tren.h foot. (6 faded paragraphs)*

*Men going down with dysentry, malaria and … (Next words could be Dengue Fever. Google it.)*

*(2 pages missing)*

*Marched to Bukit Timah (Bit faded - research) camp, and ... up to Bampong Camp (Badly faded paragraphs. - Research) Clothes reduced to rags.*

*Taken to Kaburi C..p (Research) marched to Ch.ngkai Camp. (Check spelling and research) ... Colonel Yanagida, and engineer officers Taram.to and Keria.a. (Confirm and research)*

*The closest camps were Tamarkan and Wun Lun. (Research)*

*(5 water damaged pages)*

*Worked on the railway, digging emba...ents, laying tracks and ...Three men beaten to dea.. in the cutting Good name Hell Fire Pa.s*

*Men dying of starvation, dysentry. (Writing's very shaky)*

*Moved to Hintok. (Confirm and Research)*

*(Next four pages are almost illegible)*

*Moved to Kinsayok Camp. (Confirm and Research)*

*Monsoon broke ... (Four water damaged pages)*

*(Next two pages are almost illegible)*

*Any attempt at escape was punished with death. (Something here about three men being made to dig their own graves, and then being shot)*

*Been a POW for about fifteen months?*

*(Pages missing)*

*Only pos..ssions old hat, boots with leaky soles, no socks, 'Jap-Happy' ... a pair of shorts, water bottle with ... cork, mess tin, sticky, sme...y, ground sheet, and two sacks.*

*Cases of ch..ra (Cholera?)... in camp.*

*(This is the last legible entry)*

Charlie put his pen and paper down, placed the tray beside him, sat back and sighed deeply. "There are more pages, but nothing's really legible. I need to get this to a professional who understands how to restore old documents."

Molly tried to smile, but was lost in tears. "That's ... the first time ... I've heard ..."

Charlie leaned across and hugged her tightly. "It's OK. There's more than enough for us to do a lot more detailed research." He kissed her on the cheek, looked deep into her eyes, and smiled. "I'll find out what happened to him. Now where's this arboretum?"

Molly brightened. "Joan went there a few months ago, and she left me a brochure." She got up and rifled through the magazine rack. "Here it is." She picked out a thick guidebook and handed it to him. "Directions must be in there somewhere. We can take it with us."

The drive from Cardiff took longer than planned, as Charlie stopped at most of the services for Molly to take advantages of their facilities. Eventually, they reached the arboretum at one o'clock, parked the car, walked the short distance to the visitor centre, bought their tickets, and decided they'd have a coffee and sandwich before looking around the extensive grounds.

Charlie took a bite out of his BLT, and opened the guidebook. "It's a big place, Mum. Is there anywhere in particular you want to visit?"

"Joan told me there's a place which commemorates those who died on the Burma Railway. I'd like to visit that."

Charlie nodded, and flicked through the pages until he found it. "It's in the Orange Zone." He tapped the map. "It looks pretty close."

After finishing lunch, they followed the map to Giffard Avenue. Molly stopped at the memorials to the British Limbless Ex-Service Association, Royal Artillery Garden, Royal Air Force Regiment, and Fire and Rescue Service, from where they could see memorial 227.

"Odd memorial," Charlie said quietly, pointing ahead of them. "It looks like the entrance to a churchyard."

Molly looked up. "What does it say in the guidebook?"

Charlie found the relevant page. "It's the Changi Lych Gate." He looked up at Mum, and then read on. "'This is the original Lych Gate from Changi Jail, Singapore, designed by Captain C. D. Pickersgill, and built in nineteen forty-two, by men from the 18th Division who were prisoners of war. They built this to mark the graves of those prisoners who'd died. After the war, their graves were moved to Kranji War Memorial Cemetery.'" Charlie raised his eyebrows and shook his head. "In his 'diary', Grandad Peter says he was here." He looked up at the lych gate. "He could have walked through this gate."

Mum sat down on the nearest bench and stroked the wooden panels.

Charlie stood back, leaving Mum alone in the moment. He stood silently for a few minutes, and then referred back to the map of the memorial site. "Mum." He touched her softly on the shoulder. "The memorials you want to visit are just up here." He pointed to his left. "The first is to the Sumatra Railway, and the other, is the one you want to the Burma Railway."

Mum took a sharp intake of breath. "That's the one." She stood up, and walked quickly away from the Changi Lych Gate.

"Mum?" Charlie jogged after her, and caught up with her, standing near a stretch of railway track. Close to it, was a bench, and a sign with a small wreath of poppies at its base. He walked close to it, knelt down, and read the sign. To the left it read, *'Thanbyuzayat 152km Burma'*, and to the right *'263km Nong Pladur Siam'*.

Mum sat down on a nearby bench and wept uncontrollably.

Charlie ran to her side and pulled her close to him.

"This is the first time I've felt really close to him." She sat up and wiped her eyes with a hanky. "What does it say in the book?"

"'The memorial was constructed from thirty metres of the original rails and sleepers used on the Burma Railway.'" Charlie stood up, uncontrollably drawn to the track. "Grandad Peter could have laid these."

Mum smiled and tipped her head to one side. "Yes, I suppose he could."

Charlie moved closer to the rails and knelt down.

"Watch you don't get your trousers dirty," she chided.

"Mmmm?"

"Your trousers. They're a good pair. You've only had them a couple of months."

Charlie leaned forward, cautiously touched the nearest rail, and a prickly, stinging heat flew up his arm. Like Scrooge clinging onto his money, his fingers clamped onto the rail. He started sweating profusely, his body trembled, and violent rigors rocked through him. Horrific images careered through his mind. Intense, coloured pictures changed to black and white, then to sepia, to black and white, and finally back to colour. It felt like an endless loop. A never-ending kaleidoscope of harrowing images of sadistic beatings, savage murders, pitiless beheadings, inhuman starvation, debilitating disease, desolate misery, and absolute exhaustion. The images changed, to intimate pen and ink, and pencil drawings, which were even more horrendous. Then an outpouring of words spewed from his mouth. "Kempeitai, Sapper Searle, Ban Pong, Teramuto, RAOC, Fufuye, Boggis, Achit, Hindato, Dunstan, Nong Pladuk."

Mum leapt up, looked around, and shouted to some visitors. "HELP ME!" She looked desperate. "PLEASE, SOMEONE HELP ME!"

Three good samaritans ran up the gravel path, and after a considerable effort, wrenched Charlie's hand off the rail. The three men carried him close to his mum, and placed him in the recovery position.

The eldest helper instructed his friends. "George, call an ambulance. Phil, run down to the visitor centre and tell them what's happened."

Suddenly, Charlie sat bolt upright, pushed himself up, and sat on the bench. "No ambulance. Thank you. I'm fine now." He smiled sheepishly at his helpers. "I'm sorry, I really do appreciate your help, but I feel OK now. Not sure what it was, but really, I feel OK." He stood up, did five star jumps, ten press ups, and held his arms out by his sides in supplication. "I really am OK."

"If you're sure?" George looked him up and down suspiciously.

Charlie nodded. "Really, I'm fighting fit. I'll just sit here for a few minutes with my mum."

"OK, but I'd get yourself checked out when you get home." The good samaritans walked slowly away, chatting to each other, and looking back over their shoulders at him.

Mum sat tight against Charlie, put her arms around him, and covered his face in kisses. "What happened to you?"

Charlie's face was scarlet, covered in sweat, and words wouldn't come.

Mum looked towards the end of the bench, shook her head, and whispered. *"You told me it wouldn't be like this."*

# Chapter Sixteen

Sam, Elizabeth, and Alfredo, sat on a wall at the seafront in Sami, watching a glorious, deep-orange sunset behind the hills hugging the bay. They were having dinner in Il Familia, and had all ordered moussaka, a carafe of local white wine, which put most good chardonnays to shame, and delicious, locally baked, crusty, white bread.

"You OK now, Sam?" Alfredo asked.

He nodded, swallowed a mouthful of bread, and washed it down with the last of the wine in his glass. "Much better."

*"Much better my arse. What the hell have you got us into?"* His other-half decided it was time to impart his opinion on today's proceedings. *"What in God's name was that in the sea?"*

"You back?"

*"Never too far away, Sam. You know me, forever picking away at things. My memory seems to be a lot longer and clearer than yours when it comes to relationships."*

*"Will you please just go away? Elizabeth is different, and in a really good way.*

*"Bloody right, she's different. She's worse than the other one."*

*"Look, just for tonight, give me a break. I need one. And for your information, compared to the old Jane, she's a saint."*

*"You'll never learn, will you? We've always been better off on our own."*

*"Just piss off."*

*"OK. But I will be back."*

"Shall we go to Argostoli tomorrow?" Alfredo asked, peering at Sam and Elizabeth over his slice of thickly buttered bread.

"Yes, and let's play it by ear when we get there." Sam refilled his glass and swilled white wine around his teeth and gums like a mouthwash. "We've only had experience with lost souls from World War One."

"Yes, Sam," Elizabeth agreed. "But we've a promise to keep." She raised her glass. "To Caterina."

They drained their glasses and Elizabeth refilled them from a new carafe.

"Alfredo, have you been to Argostoli before?" Sam asked.

"Si. I come every other year, to lay a wreath at the memorial to the Acqui Division. It is just outside Argostoli on a pine-covered hill."

"And you've never felt Luca or Lorenzo's spirits?" Elizabeth asked sensitively.

Alfredo shook his head. "No. This is why mamma asked if you could help us."

"We'll do our best," Elizabeth said softly, with the hint of a slur in her voice.

The moussaka arrived and soon disappeared with another carafe of wine.

"This food is wonderful," Sam said, wiping his lips with the corner of a serviette. He patted his stomach, looked around at the other diners, and belched quietly. "Bloody wonderful." He smiled at Elizabeth. "And *I* didn't want to come." He shook his head. "I must have needed my bumps read."

She looked across at him, smiled, and wiped her plate clean with some crusty bread. "You were a bit of a tit. But, here we are, and the food, company, and place, is just wonderful." She softly slurred her words again, loudly belched, and blushed the colour of cooked lobster. "I am so, so sorry. I do apologise."

Sam and Alfredo glanced at each other and fell about laughing. Alfredo made the sign of the cross. "Bless you my child." He ordered baklava for everyone.

"Sounds like Balaclava." Sam chuckled between hiccoughs. "What is it?"

"Layers of filo pastry, filled with chopped nuts, and bound together with honey. It's very sweet, but very delicious." He licked his lips. "I hope you like honey. This island is famous for it."

After a delicious baklava, coffee was followed by a local liqueur, and despite tasting like thick, dark, cough linctus, it was downed by everyone. They agreed that leaving the car close to the restaurant was probably a good idea, and they poured themselves out of a taxi outside the villa at around midnight. Elizabeth fell inelegantly onto her back on the grass with her feet in their air, and was lifted up by two equally unstable helpers.

"Coffee anyone?" she asked through a slur and a giggle.

Alfredo and Sam shook their heads as speech was becoming increasingly difficult.

"Me neither." She giggled, slipped on the tiled floor, and kept herself upright with the assistance of the kitchen sink. "Let's go to bed." She carried on giggling and then started hiccupping. "Sam … you'd better … undress me." The giggling and hiccupping continued as she walked unsteadily in a zig-zag to their bedroom.

Alfredo laughed. "I'll leave." He took a very deep breath, trying desperately to suppress the rapidly increasing sensation of nausea. "You two to it." He took another deep breath. "See you in the morning." And like a puppet with half its strings cut, he very slowly crawled up the stairs.

As Sam walked into the bedroom, Elizabeth was lying on top of the sheets, still fully dressed and snoring like a bull elephant seal on heat. He smiled at her, packed his ears with tissues, didn't bother undressing, and slowly sank into a local wine, moussaka, crusty bread, baklava, cough linctus, Greek brandy-induced sleep.

The drive to Argostoli lacked scintillating conversation, not due to any thoughts of the day ahead, but more the after-effects of the night before. They drove extremely slowly and carefully through the centre of Argostoli town, and followed the coast road north out of Apostolic. Not long after, they passed a marina and Alfredo pointed out a sign on the left.

'Ιταλική Acqui διαίρεση μνημείοτο'.

Close to the sign, was a plaque where an old lady was placing flowers.

"The sign is to the memorial." Alfredo sighed, stretched his neck, massaged his temples, breathed deeply, and swallowed hard as waves of nausea still washed over him. "That plaque marks the place where many soldiers were murdered. She is putting flowers there because it is close to the anniversary of the massacre."

They turned the corner onto a narrow, hilly road which meandered up through pine woods, until finally, at the end of the road in a tranquil clearing, was the memorial. It was a simple design in a clearing of trees, and enclosed by green railings. On a central, white marble wall were a large, white cross, two large, brass plaques, and three flags. In the centre, Italy, to the, left Greece, and to the right, Europe.

Alfredo climbed out of the car and took a small wreath from the boot. They walked silently to the memorial. Alfredo laid the flowers below the white cross and Elizabeth took a photo of one of the commemorative plaques.

'*AL SOLDATI DELLA DIVISIONE "ACQUI*

*MARINALE FINANZIERI DI PRESIDIO NELL ISOLA*

*OFFERTISI VOLONTARIAMENTE*

*NELLA LOTTA CONTRO GLI AGGRESSORI NAZISTI*

*CADUTI DAL 15 AL 26 SETTEMBRE 1943*

*IL COMBATTIMENTO UFF 65 SOTTUFF E SOLDATI 1250*

*FUCILATI UFF 155 SOTTUFF. E SOLDATI 5000*

*DISPERSI IN MARE: SOTTUFF E SOLDATI 3000*

*L'ITALIA RICONOSCENTE'*

"What does it say?" she asked Alfredo, pointing at the inscription.

"It says," he said and walked closer to the plaque, "the soldiers of the Acqui Division Marine Garrison, led by officers on the island, have given voluntary for the fight against the Nazi attacker. Cases from September 15th to 26th 1943. Died in combat: sixty-five officers, and twelve hundred and fifty soldiers. Executed: one hundred and fifty-five officers, and …" He paused, looked around at Elizabeth and Sam, shook his head, sighed deeply, and read the remainder of the inscription. "It says that five thousand soldiers were executed, and that a further three thousand were missing at sea." He stood back, bowed his head, said a silent prayer, made the sign of the cross, and turned back to Sam and Elizabeth. "It finishes with, 'Italy honours its victims'."

A sombre silence fell over them which Sam eventually broke. "*Five thousand* were massacred on this island? I didn't know anything about this. I've seen so much inhumanity with everything we've done with the missing of World War One, that I thought I'd become immune to the horrors of war. But this … this is …"

"*Insensato, barbaro, criminale, disumano, crudele (Senseless, barbaric, inhumane, cruel)*. The list of words is endless, but they all express exactly the same sentiment and meaning. This was nothing more than a despicable war crime." He almost spat the words out. "A crime not of passion, but of calculated cold-blooded murder."

"There are no burials here?" Elizabeth spoke softly, as she looked around the small memorial.

"No. After the war, a large number were disinterred and taken back to Italy for re-burial. There are still about two thousand who were never found, and also the three thousand who drowned at sea."

Sam frowned. "They killed them at sea?"

"No. They were being transported to labour camps and the ship was sunk. They are still lost in l'azzurro del mare *(the blue of the sea)*. It may have been one of them you saw at Antisamos. Shall we go now?" Alfredo said as he bowed to the memorial.

"They're not here," Elizabeth said, gently squeezing Alfredo's arms. "Come on let's find them."

Alfredo suddenly stood rigid and started shivering uncontrollably.

"You OK?" Elizabeth said, moving her arms to his shoulders.

The shivering became violent.

"Sam! Quick, he must be epileptic. Help me get him comfortable."

They laid him on the floor, and as Elizabeth stood up looking for help, the rigours immediately stopped. She looked at him, and he sat up as if nothing had happened.

"Something wrong?" Alfredo asked quizzically.

Sam and Elizabeth stared wide-eyed at him.

"You collapsed. We thought you were having a fit."

"Collapsed?" He shook his head and laughed. "But nothing happened. We were talking about the massacre and then we were going to look for Luca and Lorenzo." He looked puzzled. "I collapsed?"

"Yes." She stepped forward, but Sam gripped her arm.

"Whatever happened, happened when you held his arms. Have you held him before?"

Elizabeth shook her head. "I don't remember. What do you mean, when I held him?"

"When you held his arms, he collapsed. When you let go, he recovered. Elizabeth, I think he's got the same abilities as us, but they've been suppressed. When you made physical contact with him, you stimulated them. He's the same as you and me."

# Chapter Seventeen

"What happened to me at the arboretum?" Charlie asked, now fully recovered, as he sat at home drinking tea. "I think I'm losing my mind. Is there any history of mental illness in the family?"

Mum leaned forward in her chair and looked deeply into his eyes. "This, my darling, isn't going to be easy." She played with a digestive biscuit and brushed a few crumbs off her lap.

Charlie leaned forward and gently held her wrists. "What's not easy? You're worrying me. What have I got? You'd better tell me everything. It can't be that bad, can it?"

"All I ask, is that you trust your eyes. They won't lie to you, despite the fact that your mind will be frantically telling you they are. Darling, there are many types of different realities. When you look at a photo, it's a moment of the reality of a life that's been frozen in time. It's a way of looking into the past. A sort of time travel really." She tenderly touched his cheek. "This, this is our reality, and what happens tomorrow will be another. Perhaps one we'll never experience. But there are those who are capable of seeing and moving in and out of these other realities."

"Psychics?" Charlie said, amazed at where all this spiritualism had come from.

"Yes, some are called psychics by those who believe in their abilities, and for those who are too blind to see, they are charlatans, fakes, or at worst, insane. These chosen ones can see and communicate with all realities. Past, present and future." She paused and stared into the kitchen. "Ghosts and spirits occupy a reality which runs parallel to ours." She left this hanging in the air and walked into the kitchen. "Open your mind to the infinite variety of this world," she called over her shoulder.

He got up, started to walk to the kitchen, and shivered as an icy chill passed through him. He stopped and shuddered. "Brrrr, someone just walked over my grave."

"Very close. Hello, Charlie. Remember me?"

The gentle voice from behind him made him spin around.

"Grandma?"

"Yes, dear."

"Grandma Emma!?"

He staggered back against the wall, slid down it, sat on the floor, shook his head, rubbed the back of his neck, stared wide-eyed at Grandma Emma, shook his head again, leaned forward, rubbed his eyes, swore silently, and then held his head in his hands. "This isn't possible. You're dead!"

Mum walked in from the kitchen with a glass of water, knelt down, and put her arm around his shoulder. "I know this must be impossible for you to understand, but the exercise-book, and Grandma Emma, are the key to what happened to you at the arboretum. Here drink this."

Charlie sat back, and stared at her. "But Grandma's dead. I went to her funeral. I saw her in her coffin." He looked up at Emma, stood up, walked to the mantelpiece, and picked up a simple grey urn. "These are your ashes."

"Charlie, my darling," Grandma Emma said lovingly, "I should have shown myself to you long before now, but Molly, your mum felt it would be better if we didn't let you see me until the time was right."

Charlie wiped away his tears. He felt like his brain had been thrown into an industrial blender. "You're here, aren't you?"

Grandma Emma nodded slowly.

Charlie shook his head, still desperately trying to believe what his eyes were showing him. "But how? You died years ago."

Molly sat down by him. "Charlie, remember what I said, let your eyes show you the way. This is Grandma Emma's reality. She exists side-by-side with us. You have the ability to see her. You're one of the chosen."

Charlie shook his head. "I'm … I'm just so …"

Molly hugged him tightly against her.

He slowly began to compose himself and stood up. He looked back and forth, from Molly to Grandma Emma. "But how? Why are you here?"

Molly walked to a small cabinet in the lounge and came back with a large brandy for Charlie. "Drink this, love."

He sipped the harsh brandy. "Grandma, why is now so right, and before so wrong?"

Emma stood close to Charlie. "Your mum and I always thought tomorrow would be a better day. The right day. But tomorrow never came." She sighed. "Things have happened which make now the right time."

"What things?" Charlie asked.

Molly looked at him with sad eyes, paused, and took a deep breath. "I'm not well."

Charlie's breath rushed from his body, his stomach knotted, he wrung his hands, licked his lips, and felt nauseous. "Not well? How not well? What's wrong? Is it serious?"

She took another even deeper breath. "Cancer."

The word hung in the air for what felt like an eternity, and the corrosive nature of the six letters, etched themselves into Charlie's soul like sulphuric acid.

"What sort of cancer?"

"Not a good sort."

"MUM!" Charlie bit his lip. "Sorry, I shouldn't have shouted. What have you got?"

"The name's too long to remember, and my time's too short."

Charlie's breathing became laboured. "How short?"

"Six months. Maybe a few more. Maybe a few less. Who knows." Tears welled in her eyes. "Why does it take a poisonous disease like this to make you realise every day is important?"

"But … what will … when …" Charlie's world was disintegrating in front of his eyes.

"Darling, this isn't how it should have been, but there's no easy way to tell anyone you're dying. What I pray, is that you will see from Grandma being with us, that this life, this reality, isn't the end. That there's something after this, and we move on to another …" Her words were lost in a torrent of tears.

Charlie held his mum tenderly to him. "We'll find a cure. They're developing things all the time."

Molly gently pushed him a little away. "There's nothing anyone can do. It's my time. But before I go, you've got to help Grandma find someone, because until you do, she's stuck here."

Charlie started to regain a small degree of composure. "How can *I* help grandma?"

Emma turned to him. "I can't move on from here, until I know where Peter, Grandad Peter, is. Until I find him, I'm stuck here in Purgatory." She lifted her hand and stroked the air close to his cheek. "I've been here for eighteen years and I still miss him. Help me find him, see him again, so that we can move on to the other side together. Read the diary again with new eyes. With my eyes."

Charlie's attention was still with his mum. "What will happen to you, when you ...?"

"I don't have anything holding me here, so I'll move on to be with your dad, and the rest of our family who've passed over."

"Will I be able to see you when you move on?"

She shrugged. "With your abilities, I'm sure that we'll contact each other. But truthfully, I don't know. If I can, I'll come back, but I'm sure we'll meet again in another time or place."

"Stick a pin in me," Charlie said to her. "I want to wake up."

"You're awake, my darling. Will you help Grandma Emma? Please, read the diary again."

Charlie paused. How could your life change in an instant? How could one unforeseen moment in time affect so many future years? When would it be his 'instant'? What event would change his life forever? "I'll do everything I can, when I understand how I'm supposed to do it. At least with the names and places in the diary, we should be able to find out a lot more."

Molly hugged him tighter than the death grip of a boa constrictor. "You had a glimpse of what you can do at the arboretum. When you touched the rails, you saw something didn't you."

Charlie nodded.

"What did you see? You never told me." Molly asked.

Memories began to seep back into his consciousness. "They were terrible. Men dying horribly, torture, killings, executions, cruelty, starvation, misery, and such a desperate feeling of loss." He stood up and walked around the room.

Emma looked at Molly knowingly, and mouthed, *"He has it."* "Do you remember any of the words?" Emma asked.

Charlie frowned. "It's difficult, because a lot were foreign. Japanese, I think."

"Try dear," Emma said encouragingly.

He closed his eyes, trying to recall the words. "Kurrah! Buggairos! Kanayaros! Benjo no good, yasme benjo! Shoko no good! Diary kah!"

Each phrase, was clipped, and spoken with a pronounced Japanese accent.

"Mum, you've got to stop this. It isn't right. This will hurt him."

Emma shook her head. "This is only the beginning."

"同じ作業を行います。モンスーンは、作業を延期していません! *(Do the same work. The monsoon does not postpone the work!)*" Charlie screamed at the air.

Molly took him by the shoulders, and shook him. "Charlie! Stop it! Stop it now!"

"あなたは、あなたのベッドで? *(You are in bed?)*" Charlie stood arrogantly at attention, shouting, and waving his arms.

Molly slapped him across the face, and a look of rage in Charlie's eyes burnt into her.

Emma had finally seen enough. "今これを停止します! *(Stop it now!)*"

Charlie collapsed onto the floor.

"Are you happy with yourself?" Molly said angrily. "What was all that? You never told me that would happen. All you said was that he could help find Peter. If this is the help you wanted, then it stops now. How could you let this happen?"

"He'll be fine. He's stronger than you give him credit for."

## Chapter Eighteen

"I don't give a shit what you say. I'm not goin' anywhere near that soddin' place again." Mark spat at his brother. "You can call me what you like. If you wanna go back, fine, be my pissin' guest. But my arse isn't goin' within a mile of that place."

Matt sat back in the threadbare armchair they'd found in a skip, and pouted. "I told you, some moron cut somethin' into your stuff. That's all it was." He undid the buttons on the top of his jeans, easing the pressure on his stomach, and sighed. "There's a bloody fortune in that place. All we've gotta do, is pull up in a van, load it up, and piss off. We'll be set for life. I've seen stuff on 'Flog It' that was worth nowhere near what that must be." He scratched the side of his head and examined his nails. "Come on. One bloody hour? I won't leave you on your own. We'll be in and out, like a ferret on heat."

Mark's resistance weakened a little.

Matt tossed him the bottle of cheap vodka he was drinking. "You gonna help me or not?"

The vodka weakened his resistance a little more.

Matt got up and tousled Mark's hair. "Come on, you wanker. You know you want to."

Another slug of vodka did the trick.

"And you won't leave me on my own?"

"Cross my 'eart and 'ope to die."

Mark drained the last of the vodka and threw the empty bottle into a corner of the room. "One 'our?"

"Oh for God's sake. You comin' or not?"

Mark slowly nodded. "But you'd pissin' well better not leave me on my own, or I'm offsky. And one sniff of somethin' odd, and I'm gone."

"OK. We'll go back tomorrow. In the daylight. Bit riskier, but worth it."

"And we'll stay together?"

"Uh?"

"We stay together. I 'ain't goin' into any room in that soddin' place on my own."

Matt sniffed, scratched his ear, and then picked his teeth with a broken matchstick. "I promised Dad I'd always look after you, so," he said and tapped the side of his nose, "we stay together."

"Cheers, bruv."

*"Well done."* A voice murmured at the back of Matt's brain. *"We can get rid of this dopey twat later on. Just get me back inside that house."*

Matt stared blankly at Mark. "Mmmm?"

"Wha'?"

"You said somethin'"

"When?"

"Then?"

"Then?"

"Yeah just then."

Mark shook his head. "Not me."

Matt frowned, shook his head, put it down to the vodka, and picked up his mobile phone.

"Ron, you old bastard." ... "Yeah, really great. Listen, I need a favour. ... "No, not that again. I need your transit for a couple of days." ... "Brill. You're a star, mate." ... "No problem, I'll be over this afternoon to pick it up." ... "Cheers, mate."

Jane was reading David Copperfield in the garden, Adam and Captain Forster were sat in the kitchen playing backgammon, and Rebecca was watching them, trying to understand the basics of the game. Captain Forster had six pieces left, four on the five point, and one on the three point. Adam was about to offer a double back, when they heard the kitchen door open. They jumped up, and moved back against the kitchen units near the sink.

Adam glanced at Rebecca and Captain Forster and shrugged.

Jane looked up from Dickens and watched the two visitors opening the kitchen door. *"Some people will just never learn,"* she thought.

Matt walked into the kitchen and looked over his shoulder at Mark, who was stood outside. "You're not startin' already, are you?"

"I just wanna be sure it's alright."

Matt grabbed him by the arm and dragged him into the kitchen. "Make us a pissin' cup of tea and I'll have a quick look around."

"Whoa! Just a bloody minute. You said we'd stay together." Mark walked up close to Matt's face. "Didn' you?" He prodded him in the chest.

"You're in the kitchen. What the 'ell's goin' to 'appen to you in 'ere? Somebody'll toast you to death?" He pushed him away, and shook his head. "Now make us a cup of tea, and have a look in them cupboards for somethin' to eat. I could eat a scabby cat between two loafs of bread."

*"It's those two idiots again,"* Rebecca said.

*"Same as last time?"* Captain Forster said, with a wicked smile. *"Or shall I have a word with the troops and see what we can rustle up?"*

*"I think that sounds like a good idea,"* Rebecca replied.

*"Give me a few minutes and I'll work something out with the troops."* Captain Forster saluted and walked into the hall.

Jane trotted in from the garden. *"Two seconds, Captain,"* she called. *"Let's have a think about this."*

Matt walked into the lounge and saw the door at the far end of the room. "What are you 'idin' in there?" He paused, sucked his teeth, and decided to check it out later. Any jewellery, and valuables, were more likely to be upstairs.

Mark filled the kettle, grabbed a packet of bourbons from a cupboard, took a couple of mugs from a rack, and put them on the kitchen table. He walked into the hall while the kettle boiled and noticed the cellar door. He stood looking it up and down, held the handle, pulled the door open, looked at the steps, chewed his lip, and thought, *"You are 'avin' a pissin' laugh if you think I'm goin' down there."* He turned and walked back into the kitchen.

Matt stopped outside the nearest bedroom door, but something at the back of his mind, told him he should take a look in the far bedroom on the right.

Mark dropped tea bags in the mugs, and, as instructed, made the tea. "TEA!" He shouted up the stairs.

"JUST BE A MINUTE." Matt shouted back. The bedroom was a mess. *"What the 'ell's the point of comin' in 'ere?"* he thought.

A voice at the back of his mind gave him the answer. *"This is where all my shit started. I want to see if it's changed, and if she's still here."*

Matt looked behind him, and swallowed hard. "If that twat of a brother has slipped me somethin', I'll cut his bollocks off."

*"It's not that moron of a brother. It's me, inside your head."*

Matt ran for the door, which, unaided, slammed shut.

*"Not just yet, I need to make a few things clear to you."*

He tried to scream, but no sounds would come.

*"Calm down. If you just listen, then nothing's going to happen. But if you piss around with me, well let's hope we don't have that conversation. When you want to say something, just think it. It works for me."*

"What's 'appenin'? What ... who is it?"

*"I'm what's happening."*

"You possessin' me?"

*"In a manner of speaking."*

"Shit, that prick of brother of mine was right. This fuckin' 'ouse is 'aunted."

*"Yeah. But it's the living I'm more interested in."*

"You're going to tell me to kill somebody, ain't you?"

*"Spot on my friend."*

"And afterwards, I'll say the voices told me to do it. And they'll lock me up in a padded cell in some shit 'ole of a loony bin and throw away the key."

*"Not as stupid as I thought you were."*

"Why the 'ell didn't I listen to you, bruv!"

*"Because I wouldn't let you, you wanker. Now, what you're going to do, is get me into this house whenever I want, and anywhere else I might decide to go. Then I'll take over, and you can end a few shitty little lives for me. I'm going to be here for as long as it takes, so get used to it."*

"Celebrity Big Brother is on tonight, City are playing Leeds on Saturday, I'll get tickets from John."

*"Thinking about shit like that won't get rid of me. Calm down and listen. If you don't do as I say, then let's just say I could make things a little uncomfortable for you."*

Matt's brain, suddenly felt as if it had been macerated in sulphuric acid. Excruciating pain scorched every nerve ending and synapse. He tried to scream but he was still mute.

*"They said in 'Alien', that in space no-one could hear you scream, but believe me, no-one will hear you scream while I'm in here."*

As suddenly as the agony had started, it stopped.

*"What do you want, you bastard?"*

*"Tut tut, resorting to abuse will only result in another rebuke."*

The intense pain returned.

*"Now, do I have your undivided attention?"*

Matt silently nodded.

*"I don't need anything from you at the moment, other than your complete obedience. I will be paying you regular visits, and you wouldn't want that little irritation again, would you?"*

Matt shook his head, winced at the memory, and looked around the bedroom with Lidsay's eyes.

*"My God, they've tidied this up since I was last here, and the mad cow who chased me around the house seems to be gone. OK, you and that tit of a brother, get out of this house. You can come back when I'm ready."*

Matt nodded, and the bedroom door slowly swung open. He sprinted along the landing, jumped down the stairs two at a time, slipped on the wooden floor in the hall, and slid into the kitchen like an Olympic figure skater. 'Get your stuff. We're goin'."

"But your tea?"

"Fuck the tea. Pick up anythin' you brought, and let's get out of this place."

Mark sniggered. "You've seen somethin', 'aven't you? I pissin' told you this place was evil. You've had the shit scared out of you."

Matt shoved him out of the kitchen door and didn't look back.

# Chapter Nineteen

Guillaume, Klaus, and Karsten, were sat in the lounge of Guillaume's home, Bloemenwerf, drinking cold Dubbel Klok.

"The hotel is booked for three weeks from today," Guillaume said, looking up from his iPad. "Everyone has been contacted, and Ralph will be able to attend in person." He stood up and waved his glass in the air. "Another Dubbel?"

Klaus and Karsten smiled and nodded. "Ja. Danke."

Klaus poured his Dubbel. "Sacrifice, suffering, and grief are synonymous with war. Families, friends, who mourn the loss of their loved ones, need closure in order to start the grieving process. They need a place that represents their loss and celebrates the sacrifice. Are we certain there are no similar organisations and structures we know of which remember the missing of the Second World War?"

Guillaume spoke slowly, and clearly. "I have been researching this, and there are tombs to unknown soldiers of World War One all over the world. At the west end of the nave of Westminster Abbey, in the UK, is the grave of the Unknown Warrior whose body was brought from France to be buried there on 11th November 1920. In America, the tomb in Arlington National Cemetery in Virginia was established in 1921. However, it's now also the final resting place for the unknown of World War Two and the Korean War. Here in Belgium, is the Mardasson Memorial at Bastogne, which is dedicated to American soldiers who were wounded or killed at the Battle of the Bulge. There are many, but none of the size or significance of Thiepval, Vimy, Tyne Cot, or the Menin Gate. And, very importantly, as far as I can ascertain, they do not function as conduits to portals."

"What about the Arc de Triomphe?" Karsten asked. "That's an impressive structure."

Klaus smiled. "The Arc de Triomphe de l'Étoile, commemorates those who died in the French Revolutionary and Napoleonic Wars. Beneath its vaults, is the Tomb of the Unknown Soldier, but again from World War One. As far as I know, it has no direct links to World War Two."

"The Cenotaph in London?" Karsten persisted.

"It was designed and built to commemorate those who gave their lives in World War One, but subsequently, it has been the focus of services of remembrance, commemorating those who died in both World Wars. The main centres of remembrance for the second conflict are cemeteries." Guillaume continued. "But these are primarily for those whose identities are known. Our concerns are, and always have been, the unknown and the missing."

Klaus stood up and walked to the window. The view of the garden had always brought him great pleasure. "Whatever is agreed, the missing of the first conflict remain our first priority. If we get drawn into the second conflict, then we risk everything we have so far achieved. Whatever is decided, we must continue to support the activities of Papaver Rhoeas."

"I agree," Guillaume replied. "Isaac would have wanted it that way."

"But how do we start?" Karsten said, scratching his head.

"As Isaac always said, at the very beginning," Klaus answered.

"Which is exactly where we are," Karsten said with a slight hint of despondency.

"Ja Karsten. Genau, wo wir sind."

"Have you contacted Sam and Elizabeth?" Klaus asked Guillaume.

"I sent them an email last night. They have Wi-Fi in their villa, but I haven't had a response yet."

"Probably relaxing on the beach." Karsten smiled.

"I don't envy him in the least." Klaus said with a raised eyebrow and a knowing smile.

Guillaume flicked the tops off three more Dubbels, and they settled down on the sofa. "Let's talk specifics," he said as he looked for a coaster.

"We should raise all possibilities, however unpalatable they may sound," Klaus continued.

"Absolutely," Guillaume replied.

Klaus drained his glass of Dubbel. "So, why not just ignore these blue lights?"

"Because we have too much humanity, and as a nation, as Germans, we owe it to these lost spirits," Karsten said with real emotion. "Wir waren der hauptgrund für diesen krieg. *(We were the main reason for that war.)*"

"Es waren andere… *(There were other…)*" Klaus replied quickly.

"Ja, aber wir waren der hauptgrund. *(Yes, but we were the main reason.)*" Karsten wasn't finished.

"Ihre Generation wird nie … *(Their generation will never …)*"

"Please! Both of you. This will resolve nothing. Please, in English. You know I struggle with German."

"My apologies," Klaus said with a degree of embarrassment. "You are right. Arguments about the rights and wrongs of the second conflict, will provide us with no answers. Karsten and I will never agree over this, but we must put it to one side and look only for solutions."

Karsten smiled and nodded to his father. "My belief, as I stated at the last meeting of the Astrea, is that we must establish a new organisation, which would operate within, and under the control, of Papaver Rhoeas."

"I have no disagreement with what you say, Karsten," Guillaume said.

"I sense a 'but'." Karsten smiled and tilted his head to one side.

"Possibly." Guillaume couldn't help but chuckle. "But." He started to giggle, and couldn't stop.

Karsten put his hand over his mouth and spluttered as the giggles took hold of him.

Klaus got up, and walked out of the room, desperately trying not to laugh. "I'll give you a few minutes."

By the end of the morning they hadn't come up with very much, other than agreement on Karsten's suggestion of a new structure within Papaver Rhoeas. After a light lunch, they moved into the garden to see if the fresh air might help their mental gymnastics.

*"In need of my help?"*

The voice was clear and recognisable.

*"Isaac?"* Guillaume whispered. *"You are here?"*

*"Only in spirit. Only in your mind."*

"Guillaume!" Klaus said with shock. "Isaac is with you?"

Guillaume nodded.

"Have you all forgotten the meetings in thirty-eight?"

Guillaume frowned and shook his head. "In 1938 I wasn't born, and you were only nine or ten."

"Father told us about them and what had been decided."

Guillaume looked blankly at the ceiling.

"In thirty-eight, it became more and more obvious, that the lessons of the first conflict had not been learned. That is why our family escaped to England."

Guillaume nodded.

"By 1943, the Astrea could see that the number of casualties in the second conflict would be much much greater than the first. They also estimated that the energy levels of the lost souls of World War Two, would be much higher than those of World War One. So, to ensure their pledge to the missing of World War One wasn't broken, in '46 and early '47, they added structures and shields, around the memorials and portals, to keep out the spirit-energies of World War Two. All the reconstruction after the war was a perfect cover for their work."

"Was that right?"

"What is happening today would have happened decades ago, if they hadn't added the shields. And we would not have released so many lost souls from Purgatory."

"What has happened to change things?"

"I believe, as do the original architects of Papaver Rhoeas, that the pressure of so many desperate lost souls, has finally fractured the shields."

"The original architects?"

"The spirit world does have its benefits, Guillaume. They are all here, and their knowledge has been invaluable. They have some theories on what can be done, but it will take some time for them to produce actual plans. In the meantime, you must do all you can to limit the damage to our memorials and portals."

"But how? What do we do?"

"Focus everyone's attention on the UK. Too much effort spread thinly will provide no results. Make sure you have it right there, and then spread the word."

"But what do I do?"

"Speak to Sam and Elizabeth. They are already close to making contact with two lost souls of the second conflict. Speak to them when they come back from Kefalonia."

"How? But you couldn't? ... When?"

"Things not to concern yourself with. Tell Klaus everything I have told you. He and Karsten must travel to the UK."

"When will you come again?"

"In a few days."

"I miss you, brother."

"I, too. Adieu Guillaume."

"Guillaume?" Klaus said with concern.

"He is gone." Guillaume smiled sadly. "I have a great deal to tell you."

# Chapter Twenty

Sam settled Alfredo into his bed, where he slept for most of the afternoon.

"You feeling OK?" he asked Elizabeth, who was sitting on the pool's edge, dabbling her feet in the cooling water.

"Never better," she answered. "Let's go to bed."

"We can nap here." Sam pointed at the loungers.

"I don't want to nap. I want to …" She raised her eyebrows and blew him a kiss. She stood up, leaned across to him, and grabbed his arm. "Come on, or I'll have you by the pool."

Sam stared at her. The request in itself wasn't the worst he'd ever had, but coming from Elizabeth, it was disconcerting.

An hour later, an exhausted Sam 'walked' slowly out of their bedroom. They'd written six new chapters of 'Fifty Shades of Grey', reset two of Sam's displaced discs, taken a few strips of skin off his back, found creative uses for root vegetables, worn out four AA batteries, and ruined most of their bedding.

Alfredo was sat at the kitchen table, smirking. "Beer? You look like you need it."

Sam forced a smile. "Can you add paracetamol, ibuprofen, and glucose?"

Alfredo nodded and grabbed a few packets from a kitchen drawer. "She seems to be quite a woman."

"Not a woman I knew a few days ago." He shook his head, and breathed deeply. "Not too long ago she was a vicar."

"She must have had a lot of … pent-up emotions." Alfredo chuckled.

Sam sat at the table and leaned forward on his elbows. "Something's wrong with her. It started when we got to this villa. She's never behaved like this before. She wouldn't know how." He sat up and leaned back in the kitchen chair.

Alfredo sipped his beer. "Perhaps the Greek sun has brought it out in her."

"It's done more than just brought it out in her. It's created a bloody monster."

"Not the worst sort of monster, though?" Alfredo raised both his eyebrows and smirked.

Sam shrugged. "I have to admit, I learnt a few things this afternoon, which I wouldn't have believed were physically possible, but my back's better than it's been for years." He managed a grin. "But how do you feel?" he asked Alfredo.

"Ottimo. Very good. But probably not as good as you do?"

Sam breathed deeply again. "Just a little drained." He tried to cross his legs and winced.

"Yes, drained, and a little bruised?" Alfredo laughed. "Can I get you some ice?"

Sam couldn't help but join in the laughter. "Do you remember what happened at the memorial?" he asked when he eventually stopped laughing.

Alfredo shook his head. "Niente. Nothing." He frowned. "I don't remember anything. Not even how we got back here. Who drove?"

Sam smiled. "Not me. Elizabeth's the second named driver."

"What happened to me, Sam?"

"We're not sure, but I think when Elizabeth touched you, she kick-started a power in you."

Alfredo frowned. "A power?"

"Power, ability, talent, you can use different words, but it means you can sense spirits. At the memorial, it was the lost of the massacre. Elizabeth believes that it's you, not her, who can find Luca and Lorenzo. Your bloodline must be adding strength to the link to them."

"But I have no powers. I … I'm … just normal."

"Normal enough to see ghosts?" Sam stood up and stretched his back. "Mum and Dad?"

Alfredo nodded. "What you say may be true, and if it is, what do I do? What will I see? How do I help them?"

"You'll find it comes to you very naturally," Elizabeth said as she walked in from the bedroom, looking radiant. She'd slipped on one of Sam's t-shirts over a pair of shorts. "Not too long ago this was all new to me, and yet now it all seems perfectly normal."

"You OK?" Sam asked cautiously.

She beamed at him. "Never better. You?"

"Great."

"You don't sound too convinced."

"No, really, I feel great."

She leaned her head to one side, kissed him on the cheek, and smiled knowingly at him.

"What do I have to do to find them?" Alfredo asked as he filled his glass with another beer.

"We should go back to Antisamos Beach. It's the only place we've had any sort of real contact." Elizabeth replied as she popped the top off a cold beer. "You should snorkel with Sam and then play it by ear."

"Have you got that picture of Luca and Lorenzo?" Sam asked.

Alfredo nodded, jogged up to his room, and came back with his iPad. He opened the lid and tapped the 'Photo' icon. "Here they are." He turned the screen to face them. "Handsome, weren't they?"

Elizabeth stared closely at the black and white photo. "Good looking boys." She looked up at Alfredo. "Do you feel anything when you see them? Or sense anything?"

Alfredo frowned. "Something, but it's difficult to describe."

"Try," Elizabeth said encouragingly.

"It's as if they were … Come se mi stavano chiamando, come sussurra il vento… *(As if I were calling, as the wind whispers…)*"

Elizabeth smiled. "Emotions taking over again?"

"I'm sorry. As if they were calling to me, like whispers on the wind." He shrugged. "Words are difficult, but the feeling is real."

"When we get to Antisamos, hold onto that feeling."

Sam's iPhone pinged. He had an email.

"Who is it?" Elizabeth asked, looking up from the picture of the two young men.

Sam touched the mail icon and opened his account. "Guillaume."

"No problems, are there?" Elizabeth asked and then slaked her thirst with the cold beer.

"They're organising a meeting in London to agree on a way forward with the blue lights, and they want us to attend."

"We'll have to go," Elizabeth said, pouring another beer expertly down the angled side of her glass. "Alfredo should come as well. He's the only one we know who has a direct link to the second conflict."

Sam nodded. "I'll send a reply and put the dates in the calendar."

Elizabeth nodded.

"What's this?" Alfredo asked.

"A complicated story, but one you need to hear. It will help you understand what we do, and how we think you may be able to help in the future," Elizabeth replied.

Over a few more beers, they told Alfredo everything they could about Papaver Rhoeas, the events in France and Belgium, and everything which happened at High Wood.

Alfredo finished his beer and stared at them. "All of this is true?"

They nodded.

"You aren't taking anything?" He smiled.

They shook their heads.

He sucked his teeth. "I will help all I can."

They smiled and toasted him.

The following morning, they arrived early at Antisamos Beach, found sun loungers, ordered coffees, covered themselves in factor thirty, turned on their Kindles, read for an hour, and ordered more coffees.

"We're just putting it off," Elizabeth said, wiping milky froth from her upper lip.

Alfredo looked at her and shrugged. "A forse brandy. Solo per un po' di coraggio. *(Just for a bit of courage.)*"

Elizabeth raised her eyebrows. "And in English."

"Perhaps a small brandy, for, how do you say, Danish courage."

"Dutch courage, and a small brandy might help."

Sam waved to the waiter and ordered three Metaxa.

Fifteen minutes later, Sam and Alfredo were stood in the shallows, masks and snorkels perched on the top of their heads. They were staring at the intimidating interface of the shallows and the dark deeper waters of the bay.

Sam looked back at Elizabeth and smiled. Her expression told him to get a move on. "Come on Alfredo, after three."

On twenty-six, they finally 'threw' themselves 'Un-Tom-Daley-like' into the sea.

"SHIT!"

"È CONGELAMENTO! *(It's freezing!)*"

"ARGH! OH MY GOD!"

They swam close together into the deeper, darker water of the bay, but after ten minutes, nothing had happened. They lifted their faces out of the water and pulled the snorkels out of their mouths.

"We should go back," Alfredo said, treading water, and wiping dripping mucus from his nose. "Niente sta per accadere. Sorry. Nothing is going to happen."

"Give it a few more minutes?" Sam replied. "Think of Caterina and the photo. It may help."

Alfredo closed his eyes, remembering his mother and the image of his uncles. Suddenly, he looked up at Sam with startled eyes, and then, like a wildebeest being taken by a crocodile, vanished into the deep waters of the bay.

Sam fumbled for his snorkel, hurriedly put it into his mouth, and pushed his face into the sea. What he saw terrified him. Alfredo was being dragged to the bottom by what looked like five or six skeletal mermen.

Elizabeth looked up from her Kindle and immediately could see that something was very wrong. Both men had disappeared from view and the surface of the sea was an explosion of waves and bubbles. She leapt up in a panic, grabbed her snorkel and mask, started to run, but stumbled on the pebbles. She fell sideways onto two sleeping sunbathers, knocked over two cold beers, jumped up, and shouted an apology over her shoulder, as she dived headlong into the sea. When she reached the spot she judged they'd disappeared, she took a deep breath and plunged beneath the surface into the inky dark waters of the bay.

Sam was reaching the limit of holding his breath, when two mermen, now looking like Olympic swimmers, flashed past him, holding Alfredo by the arms.

Elizabeth was struggling to see anything in the murky waters, when the swimmers flashed past her.

Alfredo and his 'unearthly-lifeguards" broke the surface of the bay like 'Free Willy' making a break for freedom. They crashed back into the surface, and the two mermen, no longer skeletal, held him above the surface until Elizabeth and Sam appeared. The mermen swam to them and gently gave them Alfredo's arms. For a few brief seconds, the bizarre aquatic group stared at each other, then the mermen smiled and disappeared below the surface. Elizabeth and Sam supported Alfredo and swam to the beach, where a small crowd had gathered.

"Tout va bien? *(Everything OK?)*"

"Ist alles in Ordnung? *(Is everything all right?)*"

"Τα πάντα είναι εντάξει;? *(Everything is okay?)*"

"Wszystko jest w porządku? *(Everything is in order?)*"

Elizabeth smiled. "Thank you, yes," she said to the league of nations. "He's OK. He just got a bad cramp."

"Are you sure?" An English tourist asked.

"Quite sure. Really. He'll be fine. Thank you for your concern."

The crowd slowly dispersed, mumbling and looking back over their shoulders at them.

Elizabeth looked wide-eyed at Sam. "Did you see their faces?" she whispered.

Sam nodded.

"It was them, wasn't it?"

Sam nodded again. "It was them, or what once was them."

"My God, it was Luca and Lorenzo. We can see lost spirits from the second war."

Alfredo coughed up sea water and sat bolt upright, staring at the sea. He swung his legs over the side of the lounger and stared at Sam and Elizabeth. "What happened?"

"We think you just met your uncles," Sam said with a smile. "They saved you."

"Luca and Lorenzo?"

Sam nodded. "We're sure it was them. They must have sensed you were family and brought you to us." Sam leaned forward, offering him a cold beer. "You have a very powerful talent."

# Chapter Twenty-One

"You OK, darling?" Molly was sitting close to Charlie on the sofa, offering him a cup of sweet tea.

He sat up and looked across at Emma. "So it wasn't a dream? You're really here?"

She nodded. "Only in spirit, but yes, I'm here. Do you remember anything at all about what happened at the arboretum?"

Charlie sipped his tea, sat back, and frowned. "I can remember just about everything," he said, shaking his head and sighing deeply. "It was horrendous." He stared intently at Emma. "Why am I like this?" He tapped his chest with his index finger.

"Grandad Peter, was 'special'," Emma said. "Not special, like being really nice, but special, like having talents which most people don't have, or don't know they have. Like you. Your dad didn't have them, but things like this often jump generations. These talents you have, they've been sort of hibernating, and when you visited the arboretum with your mum, they woke up when you touched that rail." Emma peered at Charlie. "Does that make sense?"

He slowly shrugged his shoulders. "Sort of. There've been things I thought I'd imagined, but maybe they were real?"

Emma nodded. "Have you been to High Wood?"

"A few times."

"When was that?"

"I went a few times with Sergeant Lidsay. The owner's wife's, Mrs Morbeck, was missing." He breathed deeply, and sighed. "I went back recently with Detective Sergeant Morris. He wanted to check a few things about the disappearance of Sergeant Lidsay, and his wife Gloria."

Emma smiled at Molly. "And those are the only times you've been there?"

"I did go back one more time." He looked sheepish and nervous.

"And what happened?"

He began to feel this was becoming more like an interrogation. "I passed out. I think it was a sugar drop. The vicar was there, and she gave me tea and biscuits. I was right as rain then."

"Your mum said when you came home, you looked like you'd seen a ghost."

"I thought I'd seen some odd things, but I'm pretty sure I imagined them." He sat back, and rubbed his hands up and down his thighs.

"What sort of odd things? Odd things like what happened at the arboretum?"

"No! Nothing like that." Charlie was becoming annoyed. He felt like he was being badgered by his late grandma.

"Stop!" Charlie's mum had heard enough. "Leave him alone. He's been through enough. Let him rest."

Emma sat back in the chair and sighed. "I'm sorry dear. I need you to understand and embrace your talents. They're the only way I can be reunited with Peter." Tears started streaming down her cheeks.

Charlie got up and knelt on the floor in front of her. "Gran, I'll do anything I can to get him back for you. I just don't understand what it is that you want me to do."

Emma blew her nose, wiped her eyes, and smiled softly at him. "When Peter was worked to death, killed, or died of disease in Burma, the Japanese most likely buried him in a shallow grave, or just threw his body into the jungle. But his spirit-energy, his life force, like the tens of thousands of others who died in that Hell, has been drifting like spider silk on the wind. Your talents let you sense these drifting spirits. If you can find Peter's spirit, I can find a final peaceful rest. Bring him home to me. Reunite us and release me from Purgatory."

"But how am I supposed to 'sense' them?"

"I think you may have already sensed and even seen spirits."

Charlie's eyes narrowed. "Where?" He frowned. "What, at High Wood?"

Emma nodded. "That house is full of spirits. You didn't imagine those things. They were real. Your eyes can't only see the present, but also the past, and the future. You can move in and out of these realities."

Charlie stared in amazement at Emma. "Even if I believed everything you say, which, by the way, I'm having serious problems with, how the hell am I supposed to make 'contact' with someone who may have died in Burma about seventy years ago?" Charlie's brain, felt like a peach melba in a microwave. "Do I wait for him to contact me, or do I somehow contact him?"

Emma smiled lovingly. "It could be either. Go back to High Wood. Speak to Sam and Elizabeth. They'll be able to guide you."

"You know them?" Charlie couldn't hide his surprise.

"Caterina and I speak to each other all the time. We are, you might say, kindred spirits." She smiled wickedly. "She told me all about High Wood, the people, the spirits, and what everybody does there."

"Caterina?" Charlie's microwaved peach melba of a brain was now dribbling out of his ears. "Who's Caterina?"

"She's a spirit like me. She knows Elizabeth and Sam. They have talents like yours."

Charlie dropped his head into his hands. "Spirits, ghosts, people who died years ago, I'm some sort of … shit, I don't know the word …" He lifted his head, desperation and anger in his eyes. "I'm a policeman. Which is what I've always wanted to be. It's where my future lies. I can't do this as well. I don't know how." Charlie was becoming more and more exasperated.

"You'll just have to finish with the police," Emma said matter-of-factly.

"I bloody well won't! This is a load of bullshit. Bloody ghosts, spirits who miss someone, me bringing them back. I'll wake up in a minute, and have a bloody good laugh about this." He stood up, stormed out of the room, and marched down the hall. "I AM NOT GIVING UP THE POLICE FOR SOME GHOSTS. FIND SOME OTHER GULLIBLE IDIOT." He shouted over his shoulder as he slammed the door.

Molly stared at Emma. "That went well."

"He'll calm down," Emma said softly.

# Chapter Twenty-Two

The Astrea made their way into the meeting room at the Park Plaza Westminster Bridge hotel. It was the first time they'd met since Isaac's death, and the issue they faced would have benefited significantly from his knowledge and experience.

"Thank you all for coming." Guillaume opened the meeting. "There is only one agenda point. We have two days to discuss it and agree a way forward." He sipped his iced water. "If there are any other burning issues, we will deal with them, time permitting, under AORB."

There was a general nodding of agreement around the table.

"Klaus." Guillaume gestured to his right. "Will you update everyone on the situation in the UK."

"Thank you, Guillaume." He opened his laptop, tapped a few keys, and an image appeared on the projection screen.

A chorus of gasps raced around the table.

"Où est-ce? *(Where is this?)*" Patrice uttered loudly.

"Где это? *(Where is it?)*" Gilles breathed.

"Where in the name of all that's holy is that?" Ralph exclaimed.

"High Wood, Cardiff." Klaus answered. "This picture was taken a week ago."

"I have seen similar lights in France," Patrice said, as he leaned forward on his elbows. "Do you have any idea how many there are?"

Klaus shook his head. "There are too many to count. We have tried a number of computer programmes and all have failed. They are countless."

"'My name is Legion,' Ralph replied, 'for we are many,'" he said in hushed tones.

Small individual conversations broke out around the room.

"Gentlemen. Please. One meeting," Guillaume asked firmly.

The conversations continued unabated.

"JEDER RUHIG! *(EVERYBODY QUIET!)*" Klaus said loudly and sharply. "Bitte *(Please)*. One conversation at a time, or we will miss anything of value."

There were general sounds of apology and agreement.

Guillaume turned to Klaus, who nodded his thanks, and he waved for him to continue.

"Those of us who have closely studied the history of Papaver Rhoeas, will understand the detail of the design of the memorials and portals."

There were a few coughs of embarrassment around the table.

"From that, I have to assume, there may be some who would like an explanation?"

Several embarrassed heads nodded.

Klaus detailed the architect's construction of the memorials and portals, as described to Guillaume by Isaac.

A gasp of disbelief filled the room.

"Their belief? You mean the original architects?" Ralph expressed everyone's astonishment.

"Ja. Isaac, spoke to Guillaume …"

"Now you tell us that Isaac has spoken to Guillaume?" Ralph continued. "What else do you have for us? The second coming of the Messiah?"

Around the room, the murmuring started again.

Guillaume waited for it to subside, and then spoke. "Isaac's spirit spoke to me. Why should this surprise us?" Guillaume said, supporting Klaus. "Please. Listen to what Klaus has to say without interruption."

"Vielen Dank Guillaume. The situation we face is due to a number of key factors. Firstly, we should all congratulate ourselves and our hardworking teams for the success we have had giving the lost souls of World War One final rest. Secondly, the vast numbers killed in World War Two and still remaining lost or unknown, whose spirit-energies have saturated the earth of the world. Thirdly, the design of the memorials and portals incorporated shields which would only allow the lost of World War One to enter." Klaus paused, and swallowed two paracetamols. The nagging headache he'd woken with wouldn't go away. "It is these three factors which have created the problem we are confronted with today."

"How so?" Ralph asked as he leaned forward on the table.

"As the number of lost souls of World War One has reduced, the enormous number of souls from World War Two have been pressing for entry to the memorials. The architects are sure that the pressure and enormous level of spirit-energy has finally fractured the shields, and the souls have flooded into the memorials. From there, they have found their way to the portals where they wait for release from Purgatory." Klaus looked around the table at the nodding heads. "These are the blue lights we see and these are the souls we need to address." Klaus closed the lid of his laptop, and sat down.

"Thank you, Klaus." Guillaume turned to the group. "Does this make sense to everyone? Does this seem a plausible explanation for these blue lights?"

'Uh huh's, 'of course's, and 'I agree's, were heard around the table.

"Does anyone have a different theory?" Guillaume asked the group.

Ralph raised an index finger.

"Yes Ralph."

"And he asked him, what is thy name? And he answered, saying, 'My name is Legion: for we are many.'"

"Excuse me, Ralph?" Guillaume said, with a raised eyebrow.

"Mark 5:9, Luke 8:30, Matthew 8:28 to 34. 'The demons of Hell are many'. We have no idea what these blue lights are, or what they are capable of doing. Can we be sure that it isn't Satan, releasing his demons onto the Earth?"

Klaus leaned forward. "Wir nicht. I'm sorry, we don't.

"Exactly. My question is, how do we determine precisely what they are?"

Klaus shrugged. "Good or evil, they must be dealt with."

Ralph continued. "Jesus cast out the demons from the possessed man in Gadara. If these lights *are* from Hell, then I would conjecture they could possess those in the portals."

Klaus frowned. "Your work as a preacher is colouring your thoughts, Ralph."

"As Shakespeare so eloquently wrote, Klaus, 'There are more things in heaven and earth, Horatio, than are dreamt of in your philosophy'." He stopped and drank some water. "I repeat. We have no idea precisely what these lights are." He looked around the table for support and was met with nodding heads. "We must examine all possibilities."

"I agree, Ralph. But demons?" Klaus asked, with a degree of scepticism.

"If, as we all certainly do, accept the existence of spirits, souls, and ghosts, then equally, we must accept the existence of an afterlife and Heaven. So why then, should the existence of Hell be in dispute?"

There were more nodding heads.

"I accept all you say, Ralph, but my belief, based on the knowledge of Isaac and the architects, is that these lights are spirit energies of the lost of Weltkrieg Zwei, World War Two. This is further supported by their distribution."

"What have you seen in the US, Ralph?" Guillaume asked.

"I've had no reports of anything in the US. However…" He paused, and drank the remainder of his water. "My group have seen significant pockets of lights in the Pacific and the Philippines." He leaned back in his chair. "I have to concede this pattern would support your theory."

Klaus smiled. "It is also interesting to note that significant concentrations of blue lights in Japan are primarily in two locations. Hiroshima and Nagasaki." He looked deeply into Ralph's eyes. "Does this not also support the theory?"

Ralph looked across the table at Klaus and slowly nodded.

Klaus leaned forward in his chair. "This raises an interesting and possibly challenging fact. The lights being seen in Japan must be civilians, non-combatants, vaporised by the two atomic bombs." Klaus turned to Gilles. "What has been seen in Poland?"

Gilles frowned. "Significant pockets of lights around Oświęcim in southern Poland, Auschwitz II–Birkenau. They have also been seen in other similar locations."

"The Holocaust," Klaus said, almost in a whisper. "There can be nowhere on this planet, as saturated with lost souls as the sites of the Nazi concentration camps. What this must show us, is that the lights we are seeing, are of civilians and troops."

Gilles raised his hand. "This is also confirmed by what I have seen in Stalingrad and St Petersburg."

There was a general murmuring and nodding of heads around the room.

Charles Henencourt pursed his lips and raised an index finger. "Ce problème se développe plus grand par la minute. Klaus, que proposes-vous. *(This problem grows bigger by the minute. Klaus, what do you suggest.)*"

"Bon Charles. Merci," Guillaume said. "Klaus, what actions do you propose we should take?"

A group of increasingly worried faces stared back at Klaus. "I would like you to hear from Karsten, who has an idea, which I believe has merit."

"We should create a new group within Papaver Rhoeas. One completely focused on the blue lights. The situation with World War Two differs from World War One, in that there are still living relatives who have great love for their lost family members. Invite them into this new group." He looked around the room at the surprised faces and blushed. "Es tut mir leid. Es war nur eine idee. *(I am sorry. It was just an idea.)*"

Klaus smiled and thanked Karsten. "The good ideas are usually the simplest." He opened his laptop again, brought up the photo of the map room, pointed a laser pointer at the screen, and a glowing green spot danced over the blue lights. "This problem will not go away. It must be dealt quickly, before, if it hasn't already, becomes unmanageable. We cannot prevaricate over this."

"But we don't have the people, or structures, to cope with this," George Mainard said with concern.

Sounds of agreement ran around the group.

Klaus sat down and slapped the table. "We *must* do something. If not this then what else? Does anyone have any other workable suggestions?"

Silence fell on the room.

"We will have to find ways to increase our resources," Guillaume said. "Whatever these lights are, our present structure is totally inadequate to handle them."

"We don't have the finances to do it," Gilles said forcefully.

"Increase our finances then." Guillaume countered strongly.

"But how? We have never been a public organisation. Who would believe what we say? What evidence do we have?"

"We have spirits, who work with us today, and will support us," Klaus said quietly. "One of them is with us today." He paused for effect. "She can show the general public that spirits exist." He picked up a glass, refilled it with water, and drained it. "There are thousands who believe in spirits, and more importantly, there are tens of thousands who want to, but still seek proof." He paused. "We have that proof. Why would we not share that with the world? We don't need the support of banks. At first, we could draw on public contributions." He stood up, and walked to a leather couch at the side of the room. "Don't you agree, Jane?"

All heads at the table looked around the room.

Almost imperceptibly, Jane appeared on the sofa, sitting close to Klaus. "Yes."

A sharp intake of breath, like a vacuum being drawn on a sealed bag, hissed in the room.

"Gentlemen of the Astrea, let me introduce Jane Morbeck. Tell them your story, mein liebling."

Jane had been concerned about Klaus's idea, but now she saw the need for his proposal. Over the next half an hour, she retold her story of how she'd travelled back in time to World War One France, had become one with her grandmother Agnes, of Agnes's harrowing experiences as a nurse caught in the brutality and carnage of battle, how she'd helped save James from shell shock, how Agnes's spirit had left her, her return to High Wood, and finally, how she helped release the lost souls of World War One at High Wood.

Silence fell on the room as if a mute button had been pressed.

Ralph finally spoke. "This could work, but it would require very sensitive and careful planning." He chewed his lower lip. "Telling the world there are active spirits all around them, could create … well, it could create the opposite effect we want. However, this could be the answer we need." He looked at Jane. "How do you feel about becoming our spokesperson for the spirit world?"

Jane hadn't considered the possible implications of Klaus's plan, and sat quietly on the couch, studying the faces staring back at her.

Silence fell again on the group like students waiting for the results of their final exams.

"Jane?" Klaus said softly. "There is no pressure on you to do this."

She nodded. "Could I have a coffee?"

Gilles quickly filled a cup and handed it to her. "Black?"

She nodded, and slowly drank the dark bitter liquid. "Could I have a mint? I can't stand the aftertaste of coffee."

Gilles again acted as waiter.

"I believe," Jane said confidently, "that if, as you believe, what I've seen at High Wood are the lost souls of World War Two, then we have a moral duty to help them. They have suffered equally, if not more, than those of World War One." She stood up and walked to the head of the table. "However, it would be impossible for Elizabeth and Sam to cope with the number of souls at High Wood." One by one, she looked at the members of the Astrea. "They've had to take a holiday in Kefalonia, and while they're there, they're helping a friend, whose brothers died in World War Two. So unknowingly, they've already started work on your plan."

Klaus stared at her in surprise. "They are helping lost souls in Kefalonia?"

Jane nodded. "I think they're Italians who were killed in a massacre."

"Captain Corelli's Mandolin," Guillaume said as he stared at the table.

Klaus frowned. "Mmmm?"

"It's a book, but is better known as a film. I think that … now who were they … Nicolas Cage and Penelope Cruz, that was it, they starred in the film," Guillaume said.

"Very interesting," Klaus said, "but why are Sam and Elizabeth doing this?"

"To help a very nice old lady. Or more accurately, the spirit of a very nice old lady," Jane answered.

"A spirit?" Klaus said with disbelief.

"Yes, is that a problem?" She stared hard at Klaus.

"Es tut mir leid. *(I am sorry.)*" He shook his head. "Of course not. In truth, their experience will help our plans."

Ralph tapped the table with his pen. "I propose we do nothing until Sam and Elizabeth return from their vacation, and then meet again, and agree a way forward."

There was no dissension in the room.

"Excellent," Ralph said with half a smile. "A new era for Papaver Rhoeas. Guillaume, can we leave the details of the meeting to you?"

He nodded. "Of course. Is London OK for everyone?"

Heads nodded.

"Report anything that warrants attention to me on the status of the lights in your territories." He breathed deeply. "So, a new door opens for us. A very large new door." He glanced at Ralph. "Let's hope nothing unexpected, or unwanted, comes through it."

# Chapter Twenty-Three

It was three in the morning, and Mark's snoring from the next room shook the thin separating wall between himself and his brother.

Matt was lying on top of the sheet, staring at the ceiling, too terrified to go to sleep, even though the 'voice' in his head had been silent for two days.

Lidsay was recharging.

Mark's snoring reached new skull-penetrating levels, so Matt decided to get up, make a hot drink, watch a DVD, and eventually settled on 'The Shining'.

Lidsay silently watched.

Jack Torrance, Jack Nicholson, had completely broken down, and trapped Wendy and Danny in the bathroom. Matt had seen the movie loads of times, but this scene always had him on the edge of his seat. Again and again Jack smashed his axe into the bathroom door, creating a hole which grew bigger and bigger, until Jack's face leered through the hole. 'Here's Johnny!'

Lidsay was ready and spoke. *"Here's Lidsay!"*

Matt felt as if his heart had performed a triple salchow with twist in his chest.

*"I am afraid Johnny's not at home, but Lidsay is."*

*"What are you? There's gotta be tablets I can take. I'm just depressed."*

*"Not yet. But give me time."*

Matt forced himself to watch the film, to try to take his attention away from the 'voice'. Jack was chasing Danny through the frozen maze.

Lidsay considered what to do next.

The film cut back to the blue, frozen face of Jack, lost and dead in the maze. Matt had enough and needed something lighter, and 'Home Alone' fitted the bill. He slipped the DVD into the 'used' player, and pressed play. *"At least this 'ought to brighten me up."*

Lidsay decided on his next action.

Matt suddenly felt that a great weight had been lifted from him, and for the first time in days he relaxed. He walked into the kitchen, took an out of date coconut yoghurt from the small fridge, and eventually began to feel sleepy, as Macaulay Culkin set fire to the top of Joe Pesci's head.

Lidsay decided the time was right.

Matt started to push himself up out of the chair as the relative comfort and warmth of his bed finally called to him. A call which was rapidly shattered, as Lidsay began to materialise in the chair opposite him.

Matt's reactions were extreme and expansive. His blood ran cold, his hair stood on end, his flesh creeped, and he was frightened out of his wits, alarmed, and scared into a panic, as he'd had the bejesus scared out of him. And then he quickly calmed down. Because whatever it was which was sat in front of him, was actually distinctly unscary. A naked, overweight man, distinctly unattractive, with black, coarse hair covering his body, a stretch-marked stomach and thighs, sweaty, stinking of body odour, feet, and flatulence, sat picking his nose, and flicking his trophies onto the carpet, while deftly raising one cheek, and farting loudly.

Matt was struck dumb.

"Lost for words?" Lidsay said.

Matt opened his mouth, but nothing would come.

"Never mind. Take a seat."

Matt remained standing.

"I don't ask more than once," Lidsay said with menace.

Matt was hit in the chest by an invisible fist, which sent him flying back into his chair.

"Now that's much better. I only ask once, OK?"

Matt nodded blankly.

"You're probably wondering, who, sorry, what the hell I am." He sat back and crossed his hands over his not inconsiderable stomach. "Where to start." Lidsay scratched his thinning, grey pubic hair, and examined his nails. "Frankly, I can't be arsed. Just pissing listen, and do as you're told."

He stood up, ignoring Matt, and walked to the kitchen. A few minutes later, he came back with a dish filled with chocolate biscuits and sat down in the chair. "Nothing to say?"

Matt shook his head like a scarecrow flapping in a gale.

"You've been a very naughty boy, Matt. Breaking and entering." He sucked his teeth. "Very naughty." He pushed two biscuits into his cavernous mouth, chewed rapidly, swallowed them, and belched. "God I've missed these." He shovelled another two into his mouth and repeated his earlier actions. "So, what is it I want?"

Matt's head shook again, which was threatening to fall off.

"In one word. Revenge. There are a couple of arseholes I need to suffer, horrible and excruciatingly painful deaths. Not much to ask is it?"

"Wh…Who?"

"I'll let you know soon enough."

"You haven't said what … who you are." As Matt uttered the words, he regretted it.

Lidsay floated a few inches above the seat of the chair, moved slowly forward, and hovered a few inches in front of Matt's face. "There's an old adage, that silence is golden." He raised his putrid hand and touched Matt's lips.

The foulest taste Matt could imagine, began to fill his mouth. It coated his teeth, tongue, and palate with the concentrated essence of putrescence.

"If you ever open your mouth again without my permission, this delightful little shitty flavour, will not only tickle your taste buds, it will … but let's not think about that." He came even closer to Matt's face and the stench of Lidsay's breath made him want to vomit. "Am I understood?" Lidsay hissed.

Matt nodded.

"Excellent." He floated back, sat in the chair, stared at Matt for a few seconds, and smirked. "You wanted to know who I was."

Matt nodded.

"Ex-Sergeant Ivor Lidsay. South Wales police."

As Matt watched, Lidsay's form began to change back into a red vapour, which swirled and eddied, until it became a thick murky ribbon of viscous red matter. It slithered across the floor towards Matt, wrapped itself around his legs, moved sinuously up his body, reared up like a King Cobra ready to strike, and flashed into his mouth.

# Chapter Twenty-Four

Jane, Rebecca, Adam, and Captain Forster, were sat in the lounge, staring at an intense, blue glow illuminating the margins of the door to the map room.

"We'd better contact Sam and Elizabeth," Adam said.

"And Klaus," Jane added. "That," she said, pointing at the door, "is getting out of control."

"The men are getting a little jittery," Captain Forster added. "It's been quite a while since anyone's moved across to the other side and they want to know when they'll be going."

Jane opened her laptop and checked the calendar. "They're due back a week from today." She turned to Captain Forster. "Tell everyone that Elizabeth will be back in a week and then everything will be back to normal."

He nodded and walked into the hall.

"I'll email Klaus and Guillaume. There's another meeting quite soon, but," she said and looked across at the shimmering blue light, "this is getting bloody concerning." She tapped the mail icon, and found Guillaume's address. "I'll cc Klaus and Sam."

'To - *gwouters@icloud.com;*

cc - *klbauer@icloud.com; smorbeck@icloud.com*

Subject - Blue Lights - Help!

*Dear All - The blue lights have increased in number. They are so intense, that we're not sure if we should go into the lounge or map room. Don't know what to do! Don't think we can wait until the next meeting of Papaver Rhoeas. Please help!*

Regards

Jane'

Guillaume opened the email, and within a few seconds, the phone was ringing in his study.

"You've read it?" Klaus sounded concerned.

"Yes. Have you heard of the same increase being seen anywhere else?" Guillaume replied.

"I've not heard anything, but that doesn't mean they're not seeing the same thing." There was a long pause before Klaus spoke again. "I'm going back to High Wood with Karsten. I'll organise flights today and we'll stay at the house. I'll email Jane with our plans when we've finished."

"Good. I'll try to bring the meeting forward." Guillaume sounded focused. "Keep in touch daily. Phone or email, but we must keep in touch. I'll forward you any communications I get on this."

Sam heard the iPad ting in the lounge. "I'll check what that is," he said to Elizabeth and Alfredo. He read Jane's email and walked quickly outside to the pool. "We need to get back."

Elizabeth looked concerned. "What's happened?"

"The blue lights are becoming a problem. They don't know if they should go into the lounge or map room because there are so many." He turned to Alfredo. "I'm sorry, but we need to get home. Can you organise flights for us?"

Alfredo nodded. "Of course. I'll have a word with my contacts and see what can be done."

Elizabeth stood up. "Sam, another day isn't going to make a great deal of difference. Klaus will almost certainly go, so why don't we stay for another two days? We know where Luca and Lorenzo are, we just need to work out how to help them pass over." She looked pleadingly at Sam. "We can't go now after finding them."

Sam pulled a face. "It sounds pretty serious."

"It's not a problem, Elizabeth," Alfredo replied. "We can come back another time."

"Sam, come on, how much of difference is two days going to make. We're here. When will we come back?"

He sucked his teeth, examined his nails, stared at the pool, flapped at a wasp, and finally smiled at Elizabeth. "Two days, and then we fly home. I'll mail Klaus and Guillaume and let them know what we're doing."

Elizabeth jumped up and kissed him. "Thanks. I'll be extra especially nice to you tonight," she whispered.

Sam took a very, very deep breath. Extra especially nice, sounded like he'd be adding a few more new chapters to the rapidly expanding version of 'Fifty Shades of Grey'.

After a thankfully restful night's sleep, Sam was making toast, when Alfredo came downstairs. "Good morning. Sleep well?"

Alfredo mumbled something unintelligible in Italian and sat down at the kitchen table.

"Coffee?"

A nod.

"Like some toast?"

A shake of the head.

"Ground glass in your coffee?"

"Uh huh."

"Alfredo, would I be very wide of the mark if I said you were preoccupied?"

He looked up and almost managed a smile. "Doesn't this stuff scare you, Sam? What happened at Antisamos. I thought …" He shook his head and wrung his hands.

"Yes, it bothers me. But it also gives me a sense of wonder. I feel sort of 'blessed' to have been given these talents." He looked directly at Alfredo. "I've seen and done some strange things since I inherited High Wood, but what happened at the bay was unbelievable."

"Grazie a Dio. Ho pensato che stavo andando pazzo. *(Thank God. I thought I was going crazy.)*" He stood up. "Sorry, Sam. I thought I was losing my mind. Seeing mamma and papa was difficult for me to come to terms with, but … this … this is molto molto strano. *(very strange.)*"

"You OK to go back there?"

Alfredo stood up, walked to the patio doors, and stared out at the surrounding hills. "I have to. I made a solemn promise which cannot be broken." He pushed open the doors and walked out to the patio.

Elizabeth came out of their room, with a pink towel wrapped around her head. She wore red shorts, a plain blue t-shirt, and yellow flip flops.

"Everything OK?" She walked over to Sam and whispered, "Is something wrong?"

Sam nodded. "What happened at the bay disturbed Alfredo."

"Is that his coffee?" she asked.

Sam nodded.

"Let me have it. I'll take it out to him and have a chat. Make me a cup, will you?"

Sam smiled. "I'll bring it out to you."

Elizabeth walked out to Alfredo, linked arms with him, tugged him onto the swingseat, and gave him his coffee. "Drink it. You'll feel better." She waited as he drank the coffee. "I understand what you're feeling. Every time I help a spirit to the other side, it scrambles my mind. I haven't told anyone outside our circle about this. Who'd believe me? All you can do is to be led by your heart, and it will guide you."

They swung back and forth, Alfredo's eyes fixed on the mist-covered hills. "I will do it, Elizabeth. But what is the 'it' I have to do?"

She smiled caringly. "Just be there. Luca and Lorenzo will find you. You're their way to salvation and final rest."

Tears trickled down his cheeks. "It also means mamma and papa will be released from, is the word Purgatory?"

Elizabeth nodded.

"I'll lose them forever."

"Never forever," she said softly. "Come on, let's have some breakfast. Sam's omelettes are legendary."

He smiled, kissed her lightly on both cheeks, and followed her into the kitchen.

# Chapter Twenty-Five

Charlie wandered around, trying to clear his head. As days went, this one ranked very high among the 'What? Uh? No? Couldn't be. Never. You are shitting me' specials. He stopped outside Starbucks and decided a cappuccino and a blueberry muffin would put the world a small way back to rights. He sat down in a comfortable, well-worn, brown leather chair, stirred two sachets of sugar into his macchiato, unwrapped his blueberry muffin, broke it into pieces, looked around at the assembled melange of humanity, smiled to himself, sat back, and satisfyingly dunked a piece of muffin.

"OK if I sit here?"

Charlie looked up from his muffin at a young woman struggling with a blue Michael Kors handbag, primo skinny latte, raspberry and white chocolate muffin, two M&S carrier bags, and a copy of 'Hello' magazine tucked under her arm. He jumped up. "Of course. Let me help."

"Thanks. That'd be great," she replied with a warm smile.

"Busy in here." Charlie desperately tried to suppress a blush he could feel building.

"Lucky to get a seat, really." She looked around. "You're not keeping this for anyone, are you?"

Charlie smiled. "No I'm on my own." He wasn't sure if this sounded desperate, sad, or creepy.

"Macchiato?" She nodded to his cup.

Charlie nodded. "Yes. I needed it."

"Too strong for me. This," she said and nodded to her latte, "is just right." She got herself organised and started on the muffin. "Sorry, I'm Marie," she said with a voice which cascaded over Charlie like a chocolate fountain.

"Charlie," he eventually said. "Do you live around here?"

"Not far. I live with my mum and dad. Keep threatening to leave, but I suppose I've grown too used to my creature comforts and lack of bills. You?"

Charlie smiled. "I live with my mum on Alwyn Avenue, number twenty-six."

"We're in Osprey Avenue. Number six. It's called Takanun. Odd name really."

"Maybe it's an anagram?" Charlie suggested. "Aunt Kan, Tank Una, Nun Taka?"

"Don't think so." Marie laughed softly.

"So you're up in the big houses." Charlie raised his eyebrows. "Posh up there."

"It's a good size." Marie seemed a little embarrassed.

"Wish we had one." Charlie tried to recover. "It's a bit cramped in our place."

She sipped her skinny latte and attacked the remainder of the muffin.

For the first time, Charlie really looked at her. She was somewhere between pretty and plain, short, natural blonde hair, sensitive brown eyes not masked by too much make up, elfish ears, and from what he could see, a very fit body. He'd had few relationships with women, and most of them had been destroyed, as Dad had warned him, by his police work. But with Marie, he was willing to try again.

"What do you do?" Marie said as she wiped muffin crumbs off her lips with a paper serviette.

*"Do I or don't I tell her?"* he thought. *"She'll find out eventually."* He gritted his teeth. "I'm a policeman."

She smiled. "My cousin's a policeman. Alan Morris? I think he's a detective." She shrugged. "I met him when I was little, but years ago, there was a family argument, money probably, and his side of the family stopped speaking to ours." She shook her head. "How can people who were so close end up so far apart?"

Charlie shook his head slowly. "Stupid isn't it. My uncle and his brother never spoke because he married a catholic girl." He smiled. "Odd thing is, I work with your cousin. We're at the same station. He's a detective sergeant with CID." He wasn't used to making conversation and was beginning to struggle. "It's what I want to do. I was going to have another macchiato. Can I get you something?"

She smiled. "Another skinny latte would be lovely."

They sat chatting until their kidneys hinted that anymore coffee would not be a great idea until their bladders were emptied. After they'd both answered their urgent calls of nature, Charlie picked up Marie's carrier bags, and walked out with her not really knowing what to do next.

She helped him. "You ever surf?"

He frowned, confused by her question. "Surf?"

She nodded. "Yeah, you know, hang ten."

"Yeah, I know what surfing is." He laughed. "But I've only ever been on those little plywood things you had when you were a kid."

"Bodyboards."

He nodded. "Yeah, that was it."

"There's a Flo-Rider at the White-Water centre down at the bay. It's brilliant." She laughed to herself. "You should come. You'd have a great time."

"Yeah, I'd like that," Charlie replied positively, despite the fact that he possessed two left feet.

"When's good for you?" Marie pushed.

"Ummm?"

"How about Saturday?"

"Yeah."

"Two o' clock?"

"Yeah."

"I'll pick you up."

"Yeah."

"They've got everything you need at the centre, so just come in jeans, and casual clothes."

"Yeah."

Marie smiled. "Here's my number. Any problems give me a call."

"Yeah."

"Can I have yours, Charlie?" She held her hand out.

"Mmmm? Sorry. Of course." He scribbled it down on a scrap of paper and handed it to her.

"If you don't want to come, then that's fine," Marie said with a raised eyebrow.

He laughed with embarrassment. "No. No." He replied perhaps a little too enthusiastically. "No, I'd love to come. Just a bit lost for words. But really, I'd love to see you again." He'd finally said it.

"So would I, Charlie. I'll see you Saturday."

"You're back then," Mum said with a little irritation. "Where've you been? Feeling better now? Calmed down?"

He wasn't in the mood for an argument. "Just walking around clearing my head. Had a coffee at Starbucks and met a really nice girl. We're going surfing on Saturday."

"Been a busy boy." Mum frowned. "Who's this girl you picked up?"

Charlie ignored the comment. "Her name's Marie. Don't know her second name. She lives up on Osprey Avenue. House is called … what was it … Tak … Taka something."

"Takanun?" Emma said, walking in from the lounge.

"Yes, that was it." Charlie stared at her and frowned. "How do you know?"

"I knew her grandparents Alice and Henry."

Charlie stared at her in amazement. This wasn't going to be easy to get used to.

"Terrible time they had. Lost two daughters to TB. Violet was only twenty, and Edna, poor little dab, was only nine. And if that wasn't enough, they lost their two boys, Jacob and Elliot, in World War Two. How they carried on after that …" She sat down at the kitchen table and sighed. "You must have seen their house. It's the big white one next door to High Wood."

Charlie's face froze. For the second time today, he was completely lost for words.

"Cat got your tongue, dear?" Emma continued. "Both families wanted the same sort of house, so the Morbecks let the Morrises use their plans for High Wood. The Morris family always got on with the Morbecks, and neither of them saw any problem living in exactly the same design of house." She paused. "Odd how both families were hit by the wars, losing sons like that. Of course Rebecca lost her husband as well as her son, and Ethel lost her two boys. Never found Jacob, and Elliot's buried somewhere." She looked into Charlie's eyes. "Just like Peter. Missing."

# Chapter Twenty-Six

Guillaume emailed the members of the Astrea.

*From - gwouters@icloud.com*

*Subject - Blue Lights*

*The situation in the UK demands that Klaus and Karsten go there tomorrow. This means postponing our meeting. Resolution of the present crisis in the UK will help in the construction of a complete plan of action. I will update you once I have any news.*

*Best Regards*

*Guillaume.*

The replies were quick in coming and all in agreement with Guillaume's email. By eleven o' clock the following day, Klaus and Karsten were sitting at the kitchen table in High Wood.

"Any news from Sam or Elizabeth?" Klaus asked.

"I've had an email. They need to finish things off in Kefalonia and they'll be back in a few days," Jane said.

Klaus frowned. "I suppose that will have to do." He looked at Karsten, and shook his head. "Das Herz regiert den Kopf. *(The heart ruled the head.)*"

Karsten smiled. "Wie immer. *(As always.)*"

Klaus chuckled. "Ja."

"Private joke?" Jane said.

"No. We are happy that Sam and Elizabeth are having a good time." He looked at Karsten and winked. "Now, let's take a look at how bad things have got."

Everyone walked out of the kitchen and stopped in the hall.

"That bad," Jane said with a deep frown.

The door to the lounge was now locked and the door was framed by a pulsating, iridescent, cerulean aura.

For what seemed like an age, Klaus stood utterly speechless.

"Scary, isn't it?" Jane said. "It's only taken a week for it to move from the map room and engulf the lounge." She waved everyone back into the kitchen. "It'll be easier to talk in there."

Klaus and Karsten hung back, staring in amazement at the door.

"Scheiße! Was machen wir? *(Shit! What do we do?)*" Karsten said with wide, staring eyes.

"I have no idea," Klaus replied. "I have seen nothing like this before. Scheiße is a good word, although the English, shit, seems to have a little more impact."

Jane poked her face into the hall. "Joining us?"

They nodded, took one last look at the illuminations, and joined everyone in the kitchen.

"Have you any idea what to do about this?" Adam asked.

Klaus looked around the room at the attentive faces and shrugged. "Jetzt? *(Now?)*" he said to Karsten.

"Ja. Jetzt?"

Klaus took a deep breath. "Guillaume has spoken with Isaac."

"But he's dead?" Jane said with a look of shock which rapidly disappeared as she saw the hole in her argument. "But then, that's not a problem, is it?"

"They spoke in spirit." Klaus smiled warmly and detailed to everyone what Isaac had told Guillaume.

"So, we need Sam and Elizabeth," Rebecca said.

Klaus stood up. "Ja. But until then, I am at a loss what to suggest, other than sending another email with what I have told you."

Jane nodded. "I've moved everything out of the map room and my laptop's in my room." She stood up and gestured for Klaus to follow. "We can send it from there. Sam's opening everything pretty quickly."

"Guillaume called me on the way here and the situation across Europe is worsening. I may need to go to Russia, and with Sam and Elizabeth away for another few days, it provides me with an opportunity to check things over there. There are blue mists in Stalingrad, I'm sorry, Volgograd, and St Petersburg, which are seeping into the streets."

"When will you have to leave?" Jane asked.

"Tomorrow. We need to get to London to get a flight, but we will be back in a few days. I have to see what is happening with my own eyes." Klaus stepped close to Jane. "Any time of day or night, if there is a problem, call me instantly."

She nodded. *"I hope to God things don't get any worse,"* she thought.

# Chapter Twenty-Seven

It was a warm, balmy evening, and the sound of the gentle surf caressing the pebbles of Antisamos Beach played their own soft melody of the sea. Sam, Elizabeth, and Alfredo, decided that attempting to contact Luca and Lorenzo would probably be best done under the cover of darkness. Away from any prying eyes.

"You OK now?" Elizabeth asked Sam caringly. "Have you stopped shaking?"

The unlit, narrow, precipitous, twisting, goat-infested, tree-lined, pot hole-covered 'road', had made the drive torture for Sam, and his silence and expression were his answer.

"Sit quiet there for a few minutes and then we'll get started," she said.

He shook his head, stood up, and flashed the beam of his torch at the sea. "You really think this is a good idea?"

"Yes."

Sam huffed.

The sound of the waves gently bathing the stones had become almost hypnotic. The inky, black sky, apart from one cotton wool cloud, was clear, and the full moon, like a luminous pearl sitting in a black velvet case, cast dancing shadows across the bay.

"So, so beautiful," Elizabeth said to no-one in particular. She turned away from the sea and spoke to Sam. "I've been thinking."

"Yes," he answered quietly.

"The first thing which drew spirits to me was music."

"But we didn't bring anything to make music." Sam helpfully pointed out.

"We've got us," Elizabeth answered.

"Us?"

"We've got voices."

"You want us to sing?"

"Yes. Why not? Unless you've changed your mind and want to go for a midnight dip?"

The thought of swimming in the impenetrable dark waters of the bay filled him with terror and Sam responded immediately. "Sing what sort of thing?"

"I thought something Italian." She walked closer to Alfredo. "What do you think would be good?"

Alfredo had been silent since they'd arrived. "I can sing in Italian. Do you think they would respond better to that?" He suggested.

Elizabeth nodded. "That makes a lot of sense. Why don't you give it a try."

Alfredo walked close to the water's edge, stared at the gently undulating ebony sea, took a deep breath, and began to sing.

'Spira tantu sentimento, Comme tu a chi tiene mente, Ca scetato 'o faie sunnà. Guarda gua' chistu ciardino; Siente, siente sciure arance: Nu profumo accussi fino, Dinto 'o core se ne va, E tu dice: "I' parto, addio!" T'alluntane da stu core, Da sta terra de l'ammore, Tiene 'o core 'e nun turnà? Ma nun me lassà, Nun darme stu turmiento! Torna a Surriento famme campà!"

"My God, he's Pavarotti's long-lost brother." Sam turned to Elizabeth and smiled. "What an incredible voice."

Alfredo turned around to Elizabeth, shrugged, and raised his hands to the sky. "Nothing is happening."

"Keep singing," Elizabeth said encouragingly.

He turned back to the sea, and a voice like runny honey sweetened the night air.

'Vide'o mare de Surriento, che tesoro tene nfunno: chi ha girato tutto 'o munno nun l'ha visto comm'a ccà. Guarda attuorno sti Serene, ca te guardano 'ncantate, e te vonno tantu bene … Te vulessero vasà. E tu dice: "I' parto, addio!" T'alluntane da stu core Da la terra de l'ammore Tiene 'o core 'e nun turnà? Ma nun me lassà, Nun darme stu turmiento! Torna a Surriento, Famme campà!'

Sam and Elizabeth burst into spontaneous applause, their reason for being on Antisamos Beach forgotten.

Alfredo stared at the sea and then turned to face them. "Thank you, but it looks like I've had no success."

Sam and Elizabeth's eyes were fixed on something directly over his shoulder on the surface of the bay.

"*I wouldn't be so sure, Alfredo,*" Elizabeth whispered nervously. "*Take a look at the bay.*"

He turned around, instantly stumbled two steps back, and sat down heavily on the beach. "Santa Maria madre di Dio. Cos'è? *(Holy Mary mother of God. What is that?)*"

"Don't know," Sam said as he moved rapidly back. "But it wasn't there a few seconds ago."

"*What the hell is that?*" his other-half surfaced to 'reassure' Sam.

"*Why do you always manage to pick the worst possible moments?*" Sam hissed.

"*Lots of practice and an innate ability.*

"*More like, just being a twat!*"

"*That as well. But what in God's name have you got us into? I thought things had got as bad as they could when Adam turned into Count Dracula. But this?*"

"*Oh, piss off.*"

"*You'd miss me if I was gone. How's our Liz by the way? Still turning into the psycho-bitch from hell?*"

Sam tried to focus on the bay.

"*Mark my words. This one's a sandwich short of a picnic. Class A nutter. Jane will seem like a nun before this one's finished with you. That's if your prostate and the last chicken neck in the shop haven't been worn away to nothing.*"

Sam stayed focused on the surface of the bay, which as far as he could see, resembled a simmering beef casserole.

"What the hell is it?" Sam asked Elizabeth.

"Nothing natural I've ever seen or heard of," she answered, not taking her eyes off the now churning sea.

A band of small blue lights about a hundred yards across, and ten yards deep, suddenly appeared just below the surface, close to the shore.

Sam, Elizabeth, and Alfredo quickly moved back twenty yards to the grass close to the tavernas.

The pinpoints of light gradually grew to the size of tennis balls, and slowly floated to the surface.

"How far's the car?" Sam asked with increasing concern. "Who's got the keys?"

Alfredo tapped his pocket. "Ready to go as soon as anyone makes a run for it."

"Bit late for that," Elizabeth said.

"You speak for yourself," Sam said. "I'm under starter's orders."

The lights floated out of the sea, hovered about a foot above the surface, and then remained stationary.

"We should go." Sam was getting desperate.

"Oh pissing, grow up." Elizabeth tetchily spat at him. "I want to see what happens."

Sam took a few more steps back. He'd have to get her to see someone as soon as they got back. That was if they ever got back.

The blue orbs began to float towards the beach, and as they reached it, in a well-coordinated sequence, they fell to the pebbles and exploded into large clouds of glittering, sapphire dust which swirled and eddied in the gentle evening breeze.

Alfredo slowly and deliberately walked towards the orbs, and Sam jumped forward to stop him.

Elizabeth grabbed his arm. "We *really* need to see what happens."

Sam took the hint.

Alfredo stopped close to the dancing blue mists, reached out, and pushed his hand into them.

"We've got to stop this." Sam was beginning to panic.

"Not yet!"

Despite the breeze, the mists suddenly became very still, their sapphire colour changed to a greeny-blue, and they began to take on human form. The mist around Alfredo's hand sculpted itself into a hand, and steadily, by degrees, an arm appeared, then a shoulder, a neck, a torso, another arm, legs, feet, and finally a head, but no face. The body was then clothed in the grey-green uniform of the Italian Arditi.

Alfredo made no attempt to pull his hand back as a look of serene peace settled over his face.

One by one, each of the blue mists mirrored the transformation of the first, into an Italian soldier, each one with a bone-dry immaculate uniform, and each soldato with no face.

Alfredo held his hand close to the cheek, and as he did, features began to appear on the face. Slowly at first, but eventually the identity of the soldier was clear. Luca Innocenti stood proudly at attention.

"Zio Luca, bentornato, *(Uncle Luca, welcome back,)*" Alfredo said with tears streaming down his cheek. "Sai quale soldato è tuo fratello Lorenzo? *(Do you know which soldier is your brother Lorenzo?)*"

Luca stared blankly at Alfredo, bewildered and confused. "Lorenzo?"

"Sì lo zio. Lorenzo. *(Yes uncle, Lorenzo.)*"

Luca shrugged. "Dov'è questo? *(Where is this?)*"

"Cefalonia. Spiaggia di Antisamos. *(Kefalonia. Antisamos Beach.)*"

Elizabeth slowly and with a great degree of care, walked up to Alfredo. "He will be completely confused," she whispered. "Reassure him that everything is fine."

Luca was staring directly at her and smiling.

"Anastasia?"

Elizabeth's first response was to shake her head, but she resisted the urge and smiled. "Alfredo, translate for me."

He nodded.

"My name is Elizabeth."

"Il mio nome è Elizabeth."

"I am here to help you."

"Sono qui per aiutarti."

Luca tilted his head to one side and pursed his lips.

"What I have to say isn't easy."

"Che cosa devo dire non è facile."

Luca's expression changed. He looked deeply concerned. "Ciò che non è facile?"

"What is not easy?" Alfredo translated.

"You are a spirit. A ghost."

"Are you sure you want me to translate this?" Alfredo asked with a tremble in his voice.

Elizabeth nodded and maintained eye to eye contact with Luca. "Translate what I said."

"Sei uno spirito. Un fantasma."

"Un fantasma." Luca's face showed no emotion. "Io sono morto?"

"I am dead?"

Elizabeth nodded. "Si. Io sono morto."

Luca took off his feathered hat, and crossed his arms, deep in thought. The silence seemed to last for ages. "In che anno è questo? *(What year is this?)*"

Alfredo started to translate, but Elizabeth shook her head. "I think I understand." She took a few steps forward until she was face to face with Luca. "Two thousand and fourteen." She turned to Alfredo. "Please translate."

"Due mila e quattordici."

"Due mila e quattordici?" Luca's expression hardly changed. "Due mila e quattordici?"

She held her hands out to him.

He looked suspiciously down at them and shook his head. "Non."

"I am here to help you and your brother Lorenzo." She softened her expression and smiled. "Your sister is waiting for you. Alfredo translate."

"Tua sorella è in attesa per voi."

"La nostra sorella?"

"Yes, your sister, la nostra sorella?"

"E Lorenzo?"

"Yes. Si, Luca and Lorenzo." She looked around at the faceless ranks of soldati. "Help us. Which is Lorenzo? Translate."

"Ci aiutano. Che è Lorenzo?"

Luca turned away from them and studied the hundreds of faceless soldati massed on the beach. He walked up and down their motionless ranks, like a general inspecting his troops. He stopped at a few, but shook his head.

Elizabeth was beginning to get worried that Lorenzo wasn't with Luca, when he stopped, threw his arms wide, and embraced a soldato towards the back of the ranks. They linked arms and walked back to Alfredo and Elizabeth. Lorenzo's face now clear to see.

The brothers stood talking to each for a few minutes, Alfredo doing his best to translate for Elizabeth.

"What are they saying?" Sam had joined them.

Elizabeth raised her eyebrows at him, but then smiled. "Luca, he's the taller of the brothers, has been telling Lorenzo what I told him."

"And?"

"And they're finding it a bit hard to take in."

"And?" Sam repeated.

"For God's sake stop just saying 'and'."

"What are we going to do?"

"Help them across if they let us."

"And if they don't?"

Elizabeth shrugged. "I haven't met a spirit yet who's said no."

Sam was about to carry on when Luca spoke.

"Cosa vuoi che facciamo?"

"He wants to know what you want to do."

"Ask him if they really understand they're spirits."

Alfredo translated and Luca nodded.

"They understand. They're confused and frightened, but their faith tells them to trust us. They also asked about the other soldati. What will happen to them?"

Elizabeth swallowed hard. *"What can I possibly say without lying?"* she thought. *"Would I leave my comrades behind?"*

"What do I tell them?" Alfredo asked.

Elizabeth breathed deeply. "Tell your uncles who you are."

"Il mio nome è Alfredo. Io sono tuo nipote. *(My name is Alfredo. I am your nephew.)*"

Luca and Lorenzo stared at each other and then laughed out loud. "Tu sei il figlio di Caterina? *(You are the son of Caterina?)*"

Alfredo nodded. "Si."

They ran forward, opened their arms to him, and flew straight through him.

"Cosa e' questo? *(What is this?)*"

Elizabeth smiled caringly. "You are spirits. You cannot make physical contact with the living."

"Alfredo translate."

Their faces were at first puzzled, but they soon started to smile. "Cosa possiamo fare?"

"What can we do?" Alfredo translated.

"You can touch anything other than the living."

"Si può toccare qualcosa di diverso da vivente."

They smiled at each other and walked back close to Alfredo. "È è bello essere di nuovo con la famiglia. *(It is good to be back with the family.)*"

Alfredo was about to translate, but Luca and Lorenzo joined their arms, and started dancing in a circle around him.

At first he look frightened, but his expression quickly changed to a beaming smile.

The brothers danced slowly at first, but soon they were just a blur, and Alfredo's sharp outline began to become less defined.

The spinning circle around him became an azure blue.

Sam started to move forward, but Elizabeth held him back. "There's nothing we can do now."

"There must be!" Sam said with fear in his voice.

Elizabeth shook her head. "Once this starts, there's no going back."

As Sam was about to answer, the mass coalesced into a ball of blue light, and like a burning comet, rocketed into the night sky.

"They've gone to their final rest," Elizabeth said softly.

"Haven't you forgotten something," Sam said.

"Mmmm?"

"Alfredo wasn't dead."

Elizabeth looked like a rabbit caught in the headlights.

They sat down, and stared at the now empty beach, and the tranquil surface of the bay.

# Chapter Twenty-Eight

Twenty minutes before Marie was due to arrive, Charlie was waiting outside his house, making sure she wasn't exposed to an interrogation from his mum.

However, Molly was stood, partly hidden, behind the curtains at the bedroom window. She wasn't interested, just yet, in speaking to this 'other' woman, but wanted to assess the potential risk of the competition. When the VW Golf pulled up outside the house, her concerns grew, and were pushed into overdrive, when Marie got out of the car, and kissed Charlie on the cheek. *"Little tart,"* she thought.

"Is that your mum in the upstairs window?" Marie whispered.

Charlie nodded. "She thinks she's invisible."

Marie smiled. "Better not disillusion her. Shall we go?"

An hour later, Charlie was doing his best to stay on a small surfboard at the Flo-Rider. He was getting frustrated with his total lack of success, at the relatively simple task of lying face down on the board, while Marie performed like she was a native of Hawaii. To make matters worse, the three small girls in his group, all under ten, were flying down the torrent on their knees, and spinning like tops.

An hour or so later, they were sat in McDonald's, eating a McRib, and a Filet-o'-Fish.

"So, what did you think?" Marie asked between mouthfuls.

"Apart from looking a prize idiot?" He smiled. "It's probably something I'll try again when I grow a third leg."

Marie laughed. "Was it that six-year-old boy standing up?"

Charlie tried to look angry, but failed hopelessly. "No, it was his nine-year-old brother telling me I was, how did he put it? That I was a tragic?"

Marie almost choked on her Filet-o'-Fish.

"Serves you right." He laughed and almost choked on his fries.

"We'll try something a little less physical next time," Marie said as she moved onto her McFlurry.

"Next time? You'd like to see me again?" Charlie was surprised and delighted.

"Yes. Even after that dismal display, I think you're worth another go."

He leaned across the table and kissed her. "So do I."

"We could catch a film at the Dragon Centre." She looked at her watch. "It's only half past four. If there's nothing on, we could go bowling. Unless that's a little too physical?"

Charlie tilted his head and raised an eyebrow. "Coffee?"

There was nothing they wanted to see at the cinema, so Charlie had a second chance to show his prowess at physical activity. An hour later, he hadn't done anything to dissuade Marie that his skills lay with a large heavy ball and ten wooden pins.

"These hands must be good at something," she said with a wicked smile as they drained their diet Cokes. "We'll just have to find out what it is."

Charlie hadn't had many girlfriends, and this display of overt sexuality, made him speechless.

Marie patted his arm. "Come on, it's time I got you back to the home."

"Cheeky mare." Charlie laughed.

"Sorry. Back home."

"Can we drive past your house on the way?" Charlie asked. "I've been to High Wood a few times, but I've never noticed your house."

Ten minutes later, they pulled up outside Takanun.

"Like to come in for a coffee?" Marie asked.

He shook his head. "I'd better get back."

"Mum and dad won't eat you. They'll be watching some recording of a quiz show." She leaned over and kissed him softly on the lips. "Come on. You only live once." She smiled at him from under half-closed eyes. "Go on. For me."

He held onto the door handle and smiled. "OK. But not for too long."

Marie opened the front door and Charlie followed her into the hall. As they walked to the kitchen, she opened the doors to the other rooms, and he got a strong feeling of Deja vu, because apart from the decor, the house was a mirror image of High Wood. The kitchen on the left, not the right, and the main lounge on the right not the left, where Marie's mum and dad, were watching a recording of what sounded like 'Pointless'.

"Hello, darling. Good day?" Dad called out without looking away from five photos of US presidents on the TV needing identification.

"Yes. Really good. Charlie's come in for a cup of coffee."

"Lovely, sweetheart. Have fun." Dad's answer that number three was Woodrow Wilson scored only two points. "Told you it wasn't Roosevelt," he said admonishingly to the mother and daughter on the TV.

Marie made them mugs of coffee. "Come on. I'll take you on the grand tour."

Charlie smiled. "I'd like that."

Upstairs the layout was the same. Everything reversed.

"This way," Marie called as she turned left.

"What's up there?" Charlie pointed to the door immediately in front of him, the only feature he'd seen which wasn't reversed.

"Dad keeps his stuff up there. I never go in. I wouldn't want to mess anything up."

"What does he do?"

"He's a retired professor of mathematics at the university."

"No." Charlie pointed at the door. "What does he do up there?"

Marie shrugged. "I haven't got a clue. It's a bit like the elephant in the room."

Charlie looked bemused.

"If there was an elephant in your room, you couldn't miss it, could you, but anyone in the room who pretended the elephant wasn't there, must have chosen to ignore it. Something like that."

Charlie looked even more bemused.

Marie smiled. "It's a mystery what he does up there. Model trains, planes, or toy cars? The sort of thing retired men do?"

Charlie smiled.

She raised her mug of coffee. "Come on, I'll show you the bedrooms."

"It's just like you said," Charlie said a few minutes later as they walked down the stairs. "It's exactly the same as High Wood, only a mirror image."

"I've never been in High Wood," Marie said as they stopped in the hall. "What's the decor like."

"Oh, very different to this. Lots of antiques." He turned. "What's in your cellar?"

"Oh, usual things. All the crap you don't really want but couldn't possibly chuck away. Do you want a look?"

Charlie nodded.

"Give me two secs and I'll get the key." She disappeared into the kitchen and was quickly back with a large bunch of keys.

Unlike the cellar door in High Wood, Takanun's opened smoothly, and strip lighting illuminated the steps and the entire cellar.

Charlie was again amazed by the size of it. "It's just as big as next door's, and a bloody sight better lit. I nearly broke my neck on their cellar steps."

They picked their way around reasonably well-organised piles of clearly labelled plastic storage boxes, containing paperback books with pages curling at the corners, jig-saw puzzles, children's toys, DVDs, music CDs, VHS tapes, vinyl LPs, cameras, computers, luggage now too heavy for airlines, paintings, two dart boards, vacuum-packed bedding, skiing boots, rolls of unused insulation, Christmas trees, decorations, wrapping paper, old birthday cards, photo albums, odd-shaped things wrapped in tissue paper, newspapers, magazines…

"It goes on forever," Charlie said, picking up a stack of magazines he'd knocked over.

"Shall we go back up to the less congested upper levels?" she said, chuckling to herself as she walked up the steps. "You coming?" She called.

As he joined Marie on the cellar steps, unseen behind them, close to the adjoining wall between Takanun and High Wood, a vibrant, pulsing ball of cerulean light materialised between piles of old newspapers and CDs.

# Chapter Twenty-Nine

Matt and Mark were sat in Tesco's restaurant, eating fish and chips, washed down with mugs of tea.

Lidsay was biding his time and gaining strength.

Two young evangelists, sat at the next table, were discussing if they should go back to Osprey Avenue.

Jacob looked around the restaurant and leaned across the table to his colleague. "It's been a few days now. Since …"

"Shhh!" Abraham tapped his lips.

"We saw what we saw, Abraham."

"Not here, Jacob."

"If the Lord saw fit to select *us*, then we should have the courage to go back."

"We will discuss this later." Abraham sat back in his chair, picked up a finger of Kit-Kat, and frowned at Jacob.

Jacob wasn't giving up easily. "It is a test of our faith and our commitment to the church."

Abraham frowned and spoke quietly. "Malignant spirits have taken up residence at High Wood. It is a satanic temple. Our faith tells us that salvation can only be obtained by a combination of faith, good works, and obedience. Yahweh, the only true God will guide us, and the Archangel Michael will be with us. We must save the damned souls of those who are trapped in that evil house, and they will join us at the 'End of Times,' and spend eternity in paradise here on Earth."

Mark leaned across the table to Matt. "Did you hear what they just said? I bloody told you, didn't I? I said there was somethin' wrong with that place."

Matt nodded and tapped his index finger on the side of his head. *"Nutters,"* he mouthed.

Mark got up. "Nutters, my arse," he said loud enough for the entire restaurant to hear.

Abraham glanced across at them and made the sign of the cross.

Mark looked back at him as if he was something he'd just trodden in.

"Bleedin' Bible bashers. Fancy a toasted tea cake, bruv?" His volume control hadn't been turned down.

"Yeah, and plenty of pats of butter. Can't eat 'em when there's hardly any butter."

Lidsay came to the decision, that this shit-for-brains moron, wasn't the calibre of individual he needed, and it was time to take up occupancy in someone more 'useful'.

"We have to go back. I sensed many souls imprisoned in that place." Jacob continued with a religious fervour St Paul would have been proud of. "They, like us, are not one of the chosen, the 'Anointed', but they can be saved."

Abraham shrugged. "Why should we expose ourselves to this danger?"

Jacob stood up. "We are going back tomorrow, but we will need time to prepare."

Like a badly controlled marionette, Matt staggered to his feet, lurched towards Jacob, and embraced him.

A 'voice', not his own, cried out. "SAVE ME!"

Jacob looked to the heavens. "Thank you, Jehovah, for sending me this lost lamb."

For a second time the 'voice' called. "SAVE ME!"

Jacob pushed Matt away, held him at arm's length, and looked deep into his eyes. "Do you accept Jehovah as the one true God, and Jesus Christ as his first-born son?"

An invisible hand moved Matt's head, and the 'voice' cried out, "I DO!"

"Ecclesiastes 9: 5, 10 tells us 'The living are conscious that they will die; but as for the dead, they are conscious of nothing at all ... for there is no work nor devising nor knowledge nor wisdom in the grave, the place to which you are going'. Do you accept this?" Jacob continued.

The invisible hand moved Matt's head again, and the 'voice' cried out. "I DO!"

"John 5:28 - 29 tells us, 'The hour is coming in which all those in the memorial tombs will hear Jesus' voice, and come out. Those who did good things to a resurrection of life, those who practiced vile things to a resurrection of judgment'. Do you accept this?"

For a third time the invisible hand moved Matt's head, and the 'voice' cried out. "I DO!"

Jacob could contain his joy no longer. "My son, the Lord God Jehovah is with you."

By now, every face in the restaurant had turned and was staring open-mouthed at this epiphany.

Mark, tray in hand, looked across the restaurant, gaped at what he saw, stepped back, slipped on a chip, and dropped his tray on a pensioner's foot.

"YOU EVIL SOD, YOU DID THAT ON PURPOSE," the eighty-something shouted. "A COUPLE OF YEARS IN THE ARMY WOULD DO YOU GOOD. YOU THUG."

Mark turned, and came face-to-face with a 'well-fit', young man.

"Did you see that? He did that deliberately." The old lady said to anyone who'd listen, and prodded Mark in the chest with a fork. "I'M EIGHTY-TWO!"

Mark looked across in utter horror at Matt, and then back at the six-foot plus frame of the 'well-fit' young man stood behind the shit-stirring pensioner. "Look, I'm sorry, it was an accident. My bruvver," he said and pointed across the restaurant, "'e's ..." The rest of the sentence was lost in a muffled scream of agony, as the 'well-fit' young man buried his fist in Mark's face, breaking his nose.

Jacob turned and surveyed the scene of mayhem and gore, which for him was an obvious foretaste of the 'End of Times'. "JEHOVAH WILL SAVE YOU ALL!" He pointed at everyone in the restaurant. "AS HE HAS SAVED THIS LOST LAMB." He put his hand on Matt's shoulder. "Make your peace and embrace Jehovah as your salvation." He turned back to open-mouthed diners. "THE END OF TIMES WILL SOON BE UPON YOU!"

"Bloody religious nutters. Ought to find something useful to do with their time." 'Well-fit' young man said to the irascible pensioner.

"Only after your money." Irascible pensioner grumbled. "They always knock on your door when you're eating."

'Well-fit' man nodded in agreement, picked up his tray, kicked the bleeding and groaning Mark one last time in the stomach, stepped over him, and found a table in the corner of the restaurant.

Lidsay pulled Matt's strings one last time, and made him press his head close to Jacob's, and an unseen viscous red ooze slithered unnoticed from Matt's ear into Jacobs.

*"He may be saved."* The 'voice' whispered. *"But I've got other plans for you. I know two fallen souls who need to be led to salvation."*

Jacob clamped his hands together in prayer. "I hear you Lord. I am your servant. Your will is my will."

*"Fucking right it is, and you and me are going to have some fun,"* the 'voice' whispered. *"Halle - pissing – lulyah, brother."*

# Chapter Thirty

Mrs Mather was turning the pages of her family album and reminiscing with Mr Mather.

"Remember that, Alf?" She was pointing at a creased black and white photo of the Trevi fountain surrounded by crowds of ecstatic dancing Romans.

"That was the night we celebrated getting rid of the Nazis. We had such a wonderful time. The Eternal City lived up to its name. It knew we'd be together for eternity. 'Til death us do *not* part." He kissed the love of his life, and the next, tenderly on the lips, and smiled. "It was a miracle we ever met each other in that crowd. There must have been tens of thousands dancing in the streets that night." He shook his head and stroked her cheek. "Remember that spaghetti you made for me? I'd never eaten anything like that before. God bless the Americans for all those eggs and bacon, or carbonara would never have been invented." He tapped the photo. "I'd forgotten we'd been to that fountain." He frowned and rubbed the bridge of his nose. "Damn. What was it called? You know, the one you throw the coins into. We didn't because we didn't have any money."

She smiled and shook her head. "Not a single coin between us." She squeezed his cheek. "The Fontana di Trevi, the Trevi Fountain."

He nodded. "Yes, of course." He chuckled. "Remember that young urchin? The crowd was throwing coins in, he kept fishing them out, and then he ran away down the side streets." He laughed and kissed her on the cheek.

She turned the page and a family photo stared up at her. "We were all so happy then." Her eyes filled with tears. "Do you think they've found Luca and Lorenzo?"

"They'll be doing their best, my dear. You did ask a lot of them, so don't expect too much. I'll send them an email. I'm sure Sam will read it," Alfred said reassuringly.

Sam and Elizabeth got back to the villa at two am, parked the car, and walked in silence to the villa.

"What the hell are we going to do?" Sam said, as he turned on the kettle.

"What are we going to tell Caterina?" Elizabeth said with her head in her hands. "We came here to find her brothers and we've lost her son!" She shook her head. "My God, what a mess!"

Sam grabbed a bar of chocolate from a cupboard and poured boiling water over coffee granules. "Here, drink this and eat some of this."

Elizabeth lay back on the sofa and sighed. "We were doing so much good, and now, now this. Why did we ever say we'd do it?"

Sam's iPad pinged. He picked it up, and tapped the mail icon. "Oh bollocks. It's from Mr Mather."

Elizabeth shook her head, sighed deeper than the Marianas Trench, and sat up. "What's it say?"

Sam handed her the iPad, sighed, and joined her at the bottom of the pit of despair.

Her gaze drifted up and she stared at the ceiling. "What in God's name do we tell her?"

"Nothing. The mail isn't receipted, and she won't know if we've opened it. Just leave it." Sam leaned across her and closed the mail screen. "We'll fly back tomorrow as we decided, and tell her face-to-face."

"That'll be … I can't find the right words."

"Let's finish packing. We need to be at the airport by twelve."

"Any answer?" Mr Mather asked.

Mrs Mather shook her head. "I'm worried."

"Why?"

"Something's wrong. It's not like them to not answer."

"I'm sure everything's fine. Battery's probably flat or they're out celebrating."

Mrs Mather sighed as a feeling of deep foreboding grew by the minute.

The flight home was spent mostly with their noses buried in magazines. Every mile they flew closer to the UK, Sam and Elizabeth's mood, which had descended into something approaching manic depression, got progressively worse.

"Welcome home," Jane said happily. "Glad you're back."

Sam and Elizabeth followed her into the house, stopped dead in their tracks halfway down the hall, and stared incredulously at the lounge door and its pulsating luminous blue border

"What the hell's happened?" Sam asked with extreme disquiet. "How long's it been like this?"

Jane stood with her hands on her hips. "About a week."

"Has anyone been in the lounge?" Sam asked.

"No, and all the spirits have moved out. They've disappeared into the walls. Captain Forster's concerned we're going to have to rebuild some big bridges."

Elizabeth dropped her case with a bang. "Has it affected upstairs?"

"No. It moved pretty quickly from the map room, but it hasn't moved for about a week." Jane shrugged. "Who knows what's going to happen next. How was the holiday?"

Elizabeth frowned and walked into the kitchen

"Problem?" Jane asked Sam.

"It's a long story, but the upshot is, we've 'misplaced' Alfredo," Sam said, sitting down on a suitcase.

Jane's eyebrows met halfway up her forehead. "How the hell do you 'misplace' Mrs Mather's son?"

Sam shrugged. "Actually, it wasn't that difficult. Come on, let's see how Elizabeth is. She's taken it very hard. She's grown very close to Mrs Mather, and I've no idea what we're going to say to her."

Jane crossed her hands behind her neck. "What the hell happened out there, Sam?"

He shook his head. "Honestly, I haven't got a clue. Things were just bloody odd, and Elizabeth hasn't been herself."

"In what way?"

"She's been doing, and saying things, that are completely out of character. I thought she was going to having a breakdown," he said, shaking his head.

"She needs to see someone."

"Leave it, Jane. It's too complicated." He made his way to the kitchen. "Come on, let's see what she's doing."

Elizabeth was stood by the sink, looking out at the garden, lost in thought.

"*Cup of tea?*" Jane whispered to Sam.

"*Lovely. Make her one as well,*" he replied as he nodded at Elizabeth.

"*Her* is fine, thank you," Elizabeth called tetchily over her shoulder. "I am here."

Sam sighed, shook his head, and shrugged. *"Make her a cup,"* he mouthed to Jane.

"Why don't we go around to High Wood and see if anyone's heard anything from them?" Mr Mather said soothingly. "They were due back about now."

"And if they're not there, how do we explain who we are?"

"You've been to the house before. The others are spirits like us. They'll welcome us with open arms and Elizabeth must have told them about us."

"I'd rather wait. Sam and Elizabeth can call and tell us what's happened."

Mr Mather nodded. "OK, my dear." He knew that nagging her would achieve nothing.

Suddenly, she stood up, walked quickly to the back door, and into the garden.

Mr Mather followed her. "Caterina? Caterina? What is it?"

She turned to face him, her face beaming. "They've found them. And they're close."

"Sam and Elizabeth?"

"No. No." She clapped her hands together and danced a little jig. "Luca and Lorenzo. They've found them."

His brow furrowed deeply. "Are you sure Caterina?"

Mrs Mather turned and smiled. "I have a strong feeling they're close. They're at High Wood."

Mr Mather raised an eyebrow. "You're sure?"

She nodded and grinned from ear to ear.

They finished their teas and walked out of the door into the garden.

"We'll have to go around there. Putting it off's not making it any easier," Sam said as he dead-headed a few dahlias.

"You go Sam," Elizabeth said. "I can't face them."

Jane walked up to her, and put her hand close to her shoulder. "You need to go. You must have faced up to worse things when you were a vicar?"

"Grieving relatives and the terminally ill were comparatively easy to deal with compared to this." She shook her head. "We found her brothers, and within a few minutes they were gone, which was OK, I suppose. But at the same time, we lost her only son."

"They won't blame us when they understand what happened," Sam said, doing his best to make the best of a bad job.

"Do you think the same thing happened to them, that happened to Sam, Rebecca, and Adam, when we were in France?" Jane tried to suggest helpfully.

Sam frowned. "How do you mean?"

"Remember? I came back with Rebecca and Adam, but you came back on your own," Jane said. "So why shouldn't Alfredo come back to High Wood on his own?"

Elizabeth shook her head vigorously. "Antisamos Beach was completely different."

"Pretty damn close though," Sam said.

"Not close enough. It was our pissing fault," Elizabeth said angrily.

Sam looked at Jane, raised his eyebrows, pursed his lips, and nodded his head towards Elizabeth. *"See,"* he mouthed.

Jane nodded, chewed the inside of her cheek, and frowned.

"If it is the same, they'll come back in the cellar," Sam said. "Let's at least check. Has anyone looked?"

"No reason to," Jane replied.

"You can look if you like, but it'll be a bloody waste of time." Elizabeth turned and flounced back to the kitchen. "I'm going to unpack."

"Come on, Sam," Jane said without too much conviction. "It's worth a look."

Sam nodded. "OK. Let's see if anyone's down there."

After ten minutes, they'd found nothing.

"It was worth a try," Jane said disconsolately. "What the hell's wrong with Elizabeth? She never swears."

"Just the tip of an ever-growing iceberg," Sam said gloomily. "I know this may sound a bit stupid, but it's like she's possessed. Do you think any of the spirits she helped to pass over, didn't?"

Jane sat down on the cellar steps. "It's possible. None of us really understands what the hell we do, or what the risks are. Has Klaus come across anything like this before?"

Sam shrugged.

"You haven't told him have you?"

He shook his head.

"Oh for God's sake, Sam, that's the first thing you should have done. If it's happened before, he'll probably have an answer." She looked him straight in the eye. "Have you told him what happened in Kefalonia?"

He shook his head again.

She shook her head. "Jesus Sam. Before we do anything else, you're going to call him." She started up the steps.

He sucked his teeth. "I'd better go and see the Mathers. I can't put it off any longer."

"First of all, you're calling Klaus!"

He nodded. "You're right. He needs to know what's happened." He picked up his iPhone, and started to walk to the front door to get a better signal. As he got within a few feet, a soft knock stopped him dead in his tracks. He turned to Jane and shrugged. "Expecting anyone?"

She shook her head, looking as puzzled as Sam.

He opened the door and was dumbfounded to see the Mathers standing outside. "Caterina … Mrs Mather, lovely to see you, and Mr Mather. What are you doing here?"

She ran forward, arms open wide, and forgetting her 'status', ran straight through him.

"Sorry, she's a little excited," Mr Mather explained.

Sam stood to one side and gestured for him to come in.

"Excited?" Sam said questioningly.

"She's convinced you've found Luca and Lorenzo." He smiled and shrugged his shoulders. "She thinks they're here."

Sam's jaw hit the floor, along with his stomach. *"Just when you believed things couldn't get any worse,"* he thought. "Luca and Lorenzo?"

*"Up shit creek now,"* his other-half was back to lift his spirits.

*"My God, you chose the greatest of times."*

*"Always here for you in times of need. How are you planning on telling them?"*

"Not now."

*"You know, the fact that you've no idea where their son is?"*

*"Please. Not now."*

*"Or to be precise, where her brothers are either."*

Sam desperately tried to ignore him.

*"OK, ignore me if you like, but I'll be listening, and this had better be good."*

Mr Mather frowned. "She had some sort of vision. She said she knew they were close." He followed Sam down the hall. "I know she's clutching at straws Sam, but humour her for me?"

"Of course. Mr Mather."

"Please call me Alfred."

Jane appeared just behind Sam and smiled warmly.

"Of course. Alfred. Oh, and can I introduce Jane."

"Hello my dear." He smiled, and turned back to Sam. "Did you find them?"

Jane smiled and raised her eyebrows at Sam.

He looked back at Mr Mather and forced a smile. "Let's go the kitchen and we can talk there."

As they made their way down the hall, they saw Mrs Mather standing at the cellar door.

"Caterina?" Mr Mather called. "Caterina? What is it?"

She was completely unaware of them, and seemed to be whispering at the door. As they got closer to her, they began to hear what she was saying.

"Presto saremo insieme ancora una volta. Miei cari fratelli. *(Soon we will be together once again. My dear brothers.)*"

Mr Mather stopped a few feet behind her. "Caterina?"

"What's she saying?" Sam asked in a panic.

Mr Mather listened again to her repeated words. "She says. We will soon be together again. My dearest brothers."

Suddenly she stopped, her eyes fixed on the door. She reached out and her arm passed through it.

Elizabeth appeared on the landing at the top of the stairs, saw Mr Mather, and came down, just in time to see Mrs Mather disappear through the cellar door.

"My God. Where's she going? What does she think's down there?" Elizabeth squealed.

"Who, not what," Sam replied in a mild panic.

"She's convinced Luca and Lorenzo are down there," Mr Mather replied. "She was like this at home." He turned and followed his wife through the cellar door.

Sam grabbed the door handle and yanked it open. "Come on, we need to see what's happening."

Sam and Elizabeth jammed up against each other in the doorway, and Jane walked through them. Sam stepped back and Elizabeth ran down the steps.

"CATERINA!" Elizabeth shouted.

"OVER HERE! THEY'RE OVER HERE!" Jane shouted. "FAR END OF THE CELLAR. TO YOUR LEFT."

Sam and Elizabeth ran to the sound of Jane's voice.

"JANE?" Sam shouted.

"OVER HERE," she called back.

They ran around the last rack of shelving and came face to back with the Mathers who were staring intently at the cellar wall.

"What the hell can they see?" Sam asked Jane.

"Nothing I can."

"You're a ghost. Can't you see what they can?"

Jane put her hands on her hips. "Oh yes, we're all the bloody same. Just like anyone living is the same as everyone else?"

Sam nodded sheepishly. "Sorry."

Elizabeth touched his arm. "I think we've got an answer."

Along the length of the bottom six inches of the cellar wall, a blue mist was leaching out from the cracked mortar between the bricks.

The Mathers looked down, smiled at each other, and walked through the wall.

"Oh shit!" Sam shouted. "Jane, for Christ's sake follow them."

"Piss off. Do you know where they've gone?"

"Well ..."

"Exactly. And I don't intend finding out."

They all stared at the wall.

"What's on the other side of this?" Elizabeth asked, surprisingly calmly.

"No idea," Sam replied with a deep frown. "The cellar extends beyond the footprint of the house." He scratched his pate. "All that's this way," he said and pulled at his ear lobe, "is next door. Arnold told me High Wood and next door were designed by the same firm of architects," Sam explained.

"So their cellar probably extends beyond the footprint of their house." Jane suggested.

Sam thought for a second and shrugged. "If the plans are essentially the same, then there's a good chance it does."

The three turned, walked closer to the cellar wall, and softly laid their hands on it.

"So on the other side of this wall ..." Jane started to say.

"Must be another cellar." Sam finished.

"And another portal?" Elizabeth said questioningly.

The three stared at each other, the blue mist, and then ran for the steps.

"We've got to get next door." Sam called over his shoulder.

"And say exactly what?" Elizabeth said as her run slowed to a walk.

They all came to a stop.

"Ah yes. There is that," Sam said quietly.

"Why don't we just wait in the cellar and see if they come back?" Jane suggested.

Sam and Elizabeth looked blankly at each other.

Sam sighed and breathed noisily down his nose. "Can't think of anything better." He looked at Elizabeth who shook her head. "Stay here then, and if they're not back in five minutes, Jane walks through the wall, and takes a look."

Jane frowned at Sam, but nodded unconvincingly in agreement. "Why don't you get hold of Klaus like we discussed, and tell him everything that's happened? We'll wait in the cellar."

Sam shook his head. "I'm going next door."

Jane stood with her hands on her hips. "And what bright reason are you going to have for looking in their cellar?"

Sam paused and then smiled. "I'll tell them we've got a leak in ours and I want to check that it hasn't come through to theirs."

"Not bad. Almost believable." Jane conceded.

"So?" Sam looked at both women.

Jane and Elizabeth looked at each other and shrugged.

"What do you think?" Jane asked Elizabeth.

"We need to know where they've gone. OK Sam, but be discreet."

He nodded, started up the cellar steps, stopped, and turned his head. "If anything odd happens down here, get the hell out."

# Chapter Thirty-One

Molly, and Emma were sat in the kitchen discussing Charlie's reaction to their news.

"It would be a shock to anyone," Molly said as she picked at the crust of an egg sandwich.

"I know, but he's strong, and more importantly, special." Emma stood up, walked to the window, and looked out at the garden. "I loved our garden in Sheringham," she said wistfully. "It was a real picture. The war ruined it of course." She sighed. "We turned it all over to veg. Did our bit for the good of the country." She walked through the kitchen wall, up to a rose bed, bent down, and sniffed its heavy perfume.

Molly's eye's filled with tears as she walked out to her.

"Lovely, aren't they? We used to have a huge rose bed, although dahlias were the blooms I loved the most. Dana Utmost Firebird, Oreti Duke, and Lady Darlene, were my favourites." She looked up to the sky, and tilted her head to one side. "Looks like a dog. A bulldog."

"Mmmm? What does?" Molly replied, shading her eyes with her hand.

"That cloud." Emma pointed up to her right.

Molly looked up, but a breeze had already begun to destroy the image. *"Just like life,"* she thought tearfully. *"There one second, and gone the next."*

Emma was desperate to cuddle her daughter, but the afterlife had taken that away from her. "Where's he gone?"

Molly shook her head. "Not sure, but he'll be back. We can talk again then."

A loud knock rang out from the front door, and they swung their heads around.

"Talk of the devil."

"He's got a key," Molly said with a deep frown. "Why would he knock?"

"Easy way to find out."

Molly turned and walked quickly through the house. "Don't you have your key?" she said loudly as she pulled the door open.

"Afraid not." A young woman, probably in her mid-thirties, smiled back at Molly. "I'm sorry to call unannounced like this, but I've been researching our family history for my mum, and I'm pretty sure we're related." She offered her hand to Molly. "My name's Desiree Le Pley."

For once Molly was completely lost for words, but after a few stunned seconds, she stood to one side. "Come in."

Desiree followed her into the lounge where Molly eventually recovered the power of speech. "You think we're related?" She looked shocked, but slowly recovered her composure. "Please, sit down, and tell me all about it."

Desiree smiled and sat on the sofa.

Unseen, Emma walked in, sat down on one of the chairs, and pursed her lips.

"Can I get you a drink?" Molly asked.

"Thanks. Just a glass of water."

Molly soon came back, with a tumbler of sparkling spring water with ice. "Hope that's OK?"

Desiree smiled and drank half the water.

"So," Molly said, with hands raised to the ceiling, "what's all this about us being related?"

"Well," Desiree started. "What should I call you?"

"Molly."

"Thank you, Molly. My mum, her maiden name was Henriette Le Pley, was going through some old photos, and of course I asked her who they were." She drank the rest of the water. "I've always wanted to know where our name came from. I didn't know who my dad was."

Molly raised her eyebrows.

"It was one of those things. One night of passion, he was gone, and I was here."

"So where *does* your name come from?"

"Northern France. I've managed to track it back to five towns in Normandy. St Sauveur Le Vicomte, Besneville, St Nicolas de Pierrepoint, Sainteny, and Créances."

"But we haven't got any French relatives," Molly said questioningly.

Desiree leaned down, unzipped a briefcase she'd been carrying, and took out a blue A4 file. She turned the pages until she reached what she was looking for, moved closer to Molly, and turned the graphic of their family tree to face her. "The family link is through your great uncle Donald Thompson."

Emma's eyes opened wide. *"Uncle Don?"* Only Molly could hear her.

"He married Madeleine Proctor." She pointed at the graphic.

"I'd always been told he'd stayed a bachelor," Molly said, leaning forward, now showing genuine interest.

"No, he was happily married with one daughter, Susannah," Desiree continued.

Molly was now enthralled by Desiree's family story, which had a clear link to hers.

"Susannah, married Clement Le Pley in St Helier in Jersey. They had two children Aimee and Celine. Aimee had an illegitimate daughter, Henriette, my mum. Being born on the wrong side of the sheets seems to be a bit of a family trait. Henriette married my dad, Stephen Lyster, and so I think that makes me your great -great-niece? I'm not too sure if that's exactly right, but we're definitely family." She sat back with a huge smile.

Emma walked behind Molly, and looked down at the family tree. *"So Uncle Donald married her after all. Must have been after I moved away, and lost touch with him. You should tell her about me."*

*"Perhaps not just yet,"* Molly replied

*"But…"*

*"Not yet!"*

There was silence from the other side.

Molly smiled at Desiree. "It's fascinating to hear this, but I'm not sure how I can help?"

Desiree closed the file and turned to face her. "I'd love to learn as much as I can about your side of the family. Great-great Uncle Walter's side. Photos would be fantastic. I've researched a lot of the names on your side, but I've no idea what they looked like." She looked hopefully at Molly and paused. "And there is one person on your side who's a bit of a mystery."

Molly looked perplexed. "A mystery?"

"I can't find any record, of your husband Ian's father."

Emma's expression froze.

"I found his mum, Emma Thompson." She tapped the family tree. "She was married to Reg Probert. But your husband's date of birth, could only mean that Reg couldn't have been his birth-father."

Molly looked across at Emma. *"Should I tell her?"*

Emma glanced up from the family tree. *"She may be able to help us trace him."*

"Ian died in 2006," Molly said quietly.

Desiree's cheeks flushed. "I'm so sorry, I shouldn't have mentioned it."

Molly smiled. "No, no, it's good to talk about him. Ian's dad was Peter Wallins."

Desiree took a biro from her briefcase, and started making notes.

"Peter was reported as missing in action and was never found. It's always been assumed he was killed. Reg Probert and Emma married soon after the war and Reg brought up Ian as his own son."

"Where was he when he went missing?" Desiree was scribbling away.

"The far east. He was being 'used' by the Japanese, as forced labour on the Burma railway. At least that's what Emma was told by Reg."

Desiree closed her note pad. "That's absolutely brilliant, Molly. I can't thank you enough."

"Would you like something to eat?" Molly asked.

"If you're sure it's not too much trouble, then that would be lovely. Thank you, Molly." She put her briefcase back on the floor and stood up. "I'd love to bring everyone together. Would you be OK with that?"

"Yes, I'd love to meet your family, and so would Emma," she bit her lip as she said it.

"Emma?" Desiree said quizzically. "She's still alive? She must be getting on a bit now."

"No. I'm sorry, I … I still don't think of her as gone." She smiled sadly and rubbed her eyes. "She was a perfect mother-in-law, and she's always with me."

Desiree felt her eyes welling with tears. "That's such a wonderful way to deal with loss. Can I help with the food, Molly?"

"Thank you, Desiree."

They smiled at other each other as they walked into the kitchen, two strangers, now bonded together by family ties.

# Chapter Thirty-Two

Gilles Vermeulen met Klaus and Karsten at the airport and drove them into the centre of St Petersburg, a city which had always delighted, surprised, and tantalised Klaus. Gilles had booked rooms at the Stary Nevsky Hotel, which was small, only sixteen rooms, but well-located close to a lot of cafes and restaurants. They checked in, and ten minutes later, were in a taxi, headed for the Davidov restaurant. The views over St Isaac's Square were exceptional, and the cuisine contemporary European fare, alongside traditional Russian dishes. After an excellent dinner, Klaus decided, that as the vodka toasts had begun to take their toll, a walk in the cold night air of the city would benefit him. After about half an hour, they reached the Sampsonievsky Bridge, the broad river Neva flowing serenely below them.

"Is that the Aurora?" Karsten asked with wide eyes, looking down the river. It was his first visit to the city.

"Ja. Wo die erste der revolution schüsse fielen, *(Yes. Where the revolution's first shots were fired,)*" Klaus said.

"The revolution? The 1917 revolution? Lenin?"

Gilles turned to Karsten. "The Russian Revolution started there, or to be precise, the first shots were fired from the Aurora. The city was called Leningrad until 1991, when it became Saint Petersburg. It's a shame we don't have more time because the Summer Palace, and the Hermitage are magnificent." Gilles peered down into the dark surface of the Neva. "But tomorrow we must go to Victory Square. There is a monument there to the Defenders of Leningrad, and that's where the unusual activity has been seen."

Klaus frowned. "Unusual in what way?"

"Small streams of blue mist are flowing into the depression behind the column."

Karsten shrugged.

"It will make sense to you when you see it in the morning," Gilles said quietly.

The next morning, after taking a taxi to the monument, Karsten stood, gazing in awe at a tall, clean obelisk rising up from a broken ring.

"It is one of the best examples of Soviet monumental art, dedicated to the victory over Nazi Germany in World War Two," Gilles said, answering Karsten's thoughts.

They walked closer to the sobering space, where the inside of the broken ring was hung with gas torches. The engravings on the walls of the monument, Gilles told them, were dedicated to the nationwide recognition, of the courage shown by the defenders of Leningrad. As they got to the lower level of the broken ring, Karsten tugged at Klaus' sleeve, and pointed to four thin misty blue streams which were tumbling down the steps of the broken ring.

"How long has it been like this?" Karsten said with his hands in his trouser pockets.

"About a week," Gilles replied. "This is why I spoke about it at the meeting in London. We urgently need to do something, before these streams," he said, pointing to the flowing blue mists, "become raging torrents."

Klaus slowly turned around and stared at the tumbling azure cascades. He was convinced these were the spirit-energies of some of the one and half million soldiers and civilians who died in the terrible eight hundred and seventy-two day siege of 1941 - 2. "Have you heard of any other cities like this?" he said to Gilles.

"Volgograd."

Karsten tilted his head to one side.

"Stalingrad. The siege lasted from August '42 – February '43."

Karsten nodded in understanding.

"What reports has Guillaume received?" Gilles asked.

Klaus took his smart phone from his coat pocket. "I should call him. We need an update." The phone rang only twice.

"Guillaume Wouters."

"Guillaume. Bauer."

"Klaus, good to hear you. How is St Petersburg?"

"Not good. The energy streams here are growing and are concentrated on the monument to the Defenders of Leningrad. Have you had any similar reports from other cities?"

There was a brief pause. "Let me bring up the emails I've had and I'll read them to you."

Klaus switched his phone to speaker-phone and gestured to Gilles and Karsten to join him.

"This is what I've received so far. I'll tell you the city and the main elements of the mail."

"Good," Klaus replied.

"Rome. Blue streams flowing from the Vittorio Emmanuel II monument, Berlin, Paris, and Ankara, tell the same story. These spirit streams seem to be attracted to significant memorials, which have obvious links to World War Two, and also others, with no apparent association with the second conflict." There was another brief pause. "There are also reports of these streams in Poland and Eastern Europe, focused on sites of extermination camps."

"Klaus, what do we do?" Guillaume asked, doing his best to sound in control.

Klaus stared again at the spirit-energy streams. "I think there may be nothing we can do. After years lost in the viewless winds, these souls seem to have taken control of their own destinies."

Gilles frowned. "Viewless winds?"

"A quote from 'Measure for Measure' by Shakespeare. 'To bathe in fiery floods, or to reside In thrilling region of thick-ribbed ice; To be imprison'd in the viewless winds, And blown with restless violence round about The pendent world.' I studied Shakespeare while I was at München University.

There was a stunned silence.

"Any news from the UK?" Guillaume continued, amazed at this insight into what was the secret world of Klaus Bauer.

"Nothing today."

"Are they still helping the lost of World War One?" Guillaume asked.

Klaus shook his head. "Nein. Things have been, schwierig *(difficult.)*"

"Difficult?" Gilles said with a degree of controlled anger. "They must not lose sight of their primary focus."

"I agree, but things are somewhat 'unusual', and I'm sure that very soon, Elizabeth will be supporting them again. They know what they must do, Gilles. Sam and Elizabeth will continue the work." He walked a few steps away from Gilles and Karsten. "Guillaume, there isn't much else I can do here. I will make my way back to the UK." He turned back to the others. "Gilles, we must get back to the UK."

"Is there anything you need me to do?" Guillaume called out over the phone.

"Just keep me updated on the activity in the other cities. Ich werde Sie bald sprechen. Auf Wiedersehen. *(I'll talk to you soon. Goodbye.)*"

"Auf Wiedersehen, Klaus. Viel Glück *(Good luck.)*"

"We will need all the luck we can get." Klaus tapped the end-call icon.

"The flights will be organised," Gilles replied.

"Thank you, Gilles. Please inform Sam of our arrival time."

# Chapter Thirty-Three

Jacob and Abraham made their way back to the Kingdom Hall to report on their day's evangelism, and spent the next hour, typing meticulous records into a database of the visits they'd made. But no reference was made to the 'events' at High Wood.

"Surely we should include what happened at the house and the supermarket restaurant?" Abraham said with deep concern and misgivings.

"I will when Jehovah sees fit to tell me to do it. He sent me to that house of the Devil, sent that poor soul to me, and spoke to me. I am blessed."

Abraham stared at him. "You are blessed? How do you know it was Jehovah who spoke to you?"

"He said as much to me. Abraham, you are a new Witness, and time will show you Jehovah is with us at all times and points us in the right direction. Finding High Wood was no accident."

*"You must return to High Wood soon. So many souls, and so much sin."* The 'voice' spoke.

Jacob smiled angelically. "Jehovah has spoken again to me. We must go back to that damned house."

*"There are many souls in need of salvation. The house is possessed by the Fallen Angel."* The 'voice' spoke again.

Jacob's smile grew broader. "I will return and deliver them from evil."

Abraham frowned. Jacob seemed at best distracted, and at worst psychotic. "You believe Jehovah is speaking to you and has chosen you for this task?"

*"Abraham has not accepted my message."* The 'voice' spoke harshly. *"He must be made to understand."*

Jacob gripped Abraham firmly by the shoulders. "Matthew 28:19 tells us to take the gospel to all nations. This is the Great Commission. This is our purpose in life. In Luke 10:1, Jesus Christ sent the seventy-two out in pairs, and this is why we travel in pairs. The pairs are made stronger by their joint belief. I cannot be weakened by any doubts you may have."

Abraham frowned and felt real fear. "I have no doubts. My faith is solidly founded."

"But you doubt Jehovah has spoken to me." He raised his eyebrows, and tilted his head to one side.

"No ... I ... I was simply saying ..."

"You doubt my words, my vision. You doubt Jehovah." Jacob hissed.

"No. No. My faith is my life," Abraham said shakily through tears.

*"Not here and now. He must be realigned elsewhere,"* the voice whispered. *"His pernicious lies weaken your faith."*

Jacob smiled. "I am sorry, Abraham. Today has been momentous and stressful for me. It has affected my judgement and mood. I apologise."

Abraham held Jacob's arms. "I do not need to forgive you. It is you who should castigate me for my lack of faith."

*"Do not be taken in by his words. He is a threat to your mission."*

"It's late. Let's get something to eat. Your choice," Jacob said through a forced smile.

"Italian?"

"Good. How about Signor Valentino's at the Bay?"

Abraham nodded.

"A walk along the barrage will clear our heads and give us a healthy appetite."

# Chapter Thirty-Four

"I'd better make my way home," Charlie said as they walked into the hall at Takanun. "They'll be worried. I sort of walked out."

Marie looked him up and down. "You with a temper? I don't believe it."

He blushed. "Can I see you again?"

"That's very formal. If you'd like to go out with me, then I'd love to. There's a film on at the Odeon I've been waiting to see for ages. How about picking me up at four o' clock Saturday. We can go for something to eat down the Bay and catch the film at the Dragon Centre."

Charlie's cheeks flushed crimson and he rubbed the back of his neck in embarrassment. "Yeah. Great."

"Good, I'll see you Saturday." Marie opened the front door and kissed him softly on the lips.

"I'll see you Saturday, then." He thought about kissing her back but Marie had closed the door. *"It can wait,"* he thought.

Marie smiled to herself and walked down the hall towards the kitchen.

"Who was that?" Dad called, now engrossed in a recording of the 'Chase'. "ROBERT KENNEDY." He shouted at the TV. "My God, don't they educate anyone nowadays?"

She walked into the lounge. "It was Charlie. He's a friend. I was showing him the house."

"Mmmm. The house," Dad continued. "Oh for the love of Michael, everyone knows that it's gold. The house?"

"Yes, he loved the house."

"Lovely."

"Cup of tea?"

"ALBERT EINSTEIN. Doesn't anyone read anymore!"

"Cup of tea, Dad?"

He was shaking his head at a retired teacher who was struggling to remember the state capital of Alaska. "JENEAU! It's no wonder children are like they are."

Marie decided to make the decision for him and make a pot of tea.

Ten minutes later, she was sat in the lounge drinking tea, dunking biscuits, and listening to dad telling the contestants of 'Perfection', they were a bunch of idiots, because they didn't know the king who followed Victoria onto the throne.

Mum was sat in a leather, wing-backed chair, silently lost in her knitting.

The doorbell rang, getting only a response from Marie. She pulled back the front door and smiled warmly at the stranger. "Hi. Can I help?"

"Hello. Look, I'm sorry to disturb you. I live next door at High Wood." Sam pointed off to his right. "We've got a broken water pipe in our cellar and I was concerned water could be leaking through into yours. Could I take a look in the cellar? I'd feel a lot better if I knew the problem was only on our side of the wall," he said hurriedly.

"I should think so, Mr…?"

"Oh, I'm sorry. Morbeck. Sam Morbeck."

"Well, Mr Morbeck, Sam, come in. I'm sure you know where the cellar is." She smiled. "Built on the same plans, weren't they?"

Sam nodded. "Thanks." He tried his best not to run down the hall, but it was difficult to conceal his eagerness.

"Have a look around, and watch you don't fall over our stuff. There's quite a bit down there," Marie said as they reached the cellar door. "I'll wait up here in the kitchen."

"Thanks. I should only be a few minutes." Sam ran down the steps, and picked his way through the organised piles of stuff, to the wall he was certain was the adjoining wall to High Wood. As he reached it, the pulsating blue ball, hovering above a pile of bedding, confirmed his thoughts.

Subtly, it began to change size and shape and settled softly onto the bedding without a sound. It flattened into what Sam could only describe as a navy blue pancake, and then re-inflated into a sphere about five feet in diameter.

*"Come on,"* Sam whispered, urging the ball to finish whatever it was building up to, before their young neighbour came looking for him. *"Come on."*

Suddenly, as if an invisible pin had pricked it, the sphere burst into a purple dust cloud, in the centre of which, Sam could make out two figures. Slowly, like an early morning autumn mist, the cloud dispersed, leaving behind what appeared to be the outlines of two men. As the purple dust settled, and the image became sharper, it was obvious that the two men were dressed in uniform. A uniform Sam knew he'd seen on a moonlit beach in Kefalonia. The two men straightened up, stared at each other for a few seconds, turned around with a look of utter confusion, and stared at Sam as though he was the Devil incarnate.

"Chi sei? *(Who are you?)*"

Sam shrugged, trying to show them he didn't speak, what he thought was Italian.

"Chi sei? *(Who are you?)*"

Sam shrugged again, but then realised what he should say. "Luca? Lorenzo?"

The two men stared at each other in disbelief.

The soldier on the right tapped his chest. "Sì, io sono Luca. *(Yes, I'm Luca.)*"

The soldier on the left did the same. "Sì, io sono Lorenzo. *(Yes, I'm Lorenzo.)* "Chi sei?"

"Lui è Sam. *(He is Sam.)*" A voice close behind the brothers explained. "Miei fratelli. *(My brothers.)*"

Sam stepped to his right to get a clear view of what was happening and stood close behind Luca and Lorenzo, were Caterina and Alfred.

"Miei fratelli. Ci sono di nuovo insieme. Sono finalmente casa. *(We are together again. I'm finally home.)*"

"Caterina?" Sam said with mixed emotions, given that Caterina's brothers were home, but Alfredo was still missing.

"Sam, you found them. I knew you wouldn't let us down. I never thought I would see this day."

"Everything OK down there?" Marie called from the top of the steps. "Need a hand?"

"No, everything's fine, thanks. Doesn't look like there are any leaks on this side. Just need to check one more corner," Sam called back.

"OK. I'll wait for you in the kitchen."

"You need to get back into High Wood before someone comes down here," Sam said with more than a slight degree of panic. "Can you walk back through the wall with your brothers, Caterina?"

"Si. If we came this way, then going back should not be a problem." She turned to Luca and Lorenzo. "Seguimi. *(Follow me.)*"

They looked utterly bewildered, but nodded in understanding.

Caterina walked close to the wall, turned, gestured for her brothers to follow her, and together with Mr Mather, they disappeared through the wall into High Wood.

*"Thank God she didn't ask where Alfredo was,"* Sam thought desperately. *"What the hell do I tell her? And where the hell is Alfredo?"*

# Chapter Thirty-Five

Charlie stood outside his front door, thinking of the best way to apologise for his outburst and dramatic exit. Five minutes later, and finding no words which would fit the bill, he simply walked into the house, and called out, "I'm back."

"Come into the lounge, love," Molly called. "There's someone here you should meet."

Charlie frowned. *"Not another ghost,"* he thought as he opened the lounge door.

"Charlie, this is Desiree Le Pley," Molly said cheerily. "She's done some family history, and it seems we're related."

He walked to Desiree, who stood up, and shook hands.

"Hi, I'm Charlie."

"Desiree. Lovely to meet you."

"Desiree, tell him what you've discovered," Molly said enthusiastically.

Over the next twenty minutes, she showed Charlie everything she'd discovered about the Thompson family and their connection to France and Jersey. "And here I am today. I couldn't wait to meet all of you."

*"You haven't quite met everyone,"* Charlie thought as he looked across the lounge at Emma perched on the arm of the sofa. "It's fascinating," he said with as much false enthusiasm as he could muster. "Must have taken you a long time to pull all this together?"

"About a year and a half, but it's all been a real pleasure."

"Where do you live?"

"Sheringham. It's on the north coast of Norfolk."

Charlie peered up at his mum. "Isn't that where Grandma Emma lived?"

Molly nodded. "Sheringham? Yes, it's where she was born." She frowned mildly at Desiree. "You're from Sheringham?"

Desiree looked as nonplussed as Molly. "Yes, didn't I say?"

Molly shook her head.

Desiree looked a little sheepish. "Sorry. I didn't know that Emma was from Sheringham. That's amazing."

Emma stood up and walked closer to Molly. *"Ask her if our house is still there."*

Molly smiled, trying to hide her reaction to Emma's request. *"I don't know what it was called or the address, and do you honestly think she'll know?"*

*"The house was called Cambrai, and it was 26, Chaucer Road. Ask her."*

"Where do you live in Sheringham?" Molly asked.

Desiree smiled. "Well, that's a really interesting story."

*"Oh God,"* Charlie thought. *"Interesting, as in as boring as hell."*

"When Mum and Dad retired, they wanted a project to keep them occupied. So an old property they could redevelop, seemed like the perfect thing to keep them busy. You know, like on that programme on telly 'Homes under the Hammer'?"

Molly and Charlie nodded.

"Well, they looked for months, and were about to give up, when they found a lovely old place in Sheringham. It's amazing it was still there with all the development that's taken place. It was pretty run down, but they could see it had a lot of potential." She drank the remaining water in her glass. "They lived in a caravan parked next to the house."

Molly raised her eyebrows. "For very long?"

"About six months."

Charlie shook his head. "Not sure I could have done that."

"It wasn't easy. Planning permission, rising damp, complete re-wiring, new roof, the plumbing was original and had to be replaced, the windows were as draughty as hell, the garden was a jungle, and the kitchen was, let's say a bit of a mess. It took them three years to get everything finished to the standard they wanted, and now it's a lovely four-bedroomed detached house with a stunning garden."

"What's the address?" Molly interrupted.

"26 Chaucer Road."

Molly did her best to hide her surprise. "Has it got a name?"

"Yes. Mum and Dad decided to keep the original name. Odd name, really. It's something I still need to research."

"And what is the 'odd' name?" Molly asked calmly.

Desiree laughed. "Sorry. Cambray. At least that's how we say it."

"Emma and Reg lived at Cambray," Molly said, trying to hide her excitement.

Desiree slowly put her glass on the table, sat back on the sofa, squealed with delight, jumped up, and hugged Molly. "Really? That's unbelievable. I can't wait to tell Mum and Dad."

Emma glared at Mum. *"She needs to see me."*

*"She bloody well doesn't."*

*"How are you going to stop me?"*

*"Mum, for God's sake. Do you want her to die of shock?"*

Emma nodded grudgingly. *"Alright. But she needs to see me."*

*"OK, but not today. Only when she understands things a lot better,"*

Emma finally agreed. *"OK."*

*"Good."*

"How long are you down this way?" Molly asked.

"Oh, only for a few days. I'm staying at the Hilton. The one in the centre of Cardiff? I'm here until Friday."

Molly turned to Charlie. "You should show Desiree the sights."

Having to make conversation with this stranger seemed a little too much for Charlie and it showed in his expression.

"I'll be fine," Desiree said tactfully. "I love exploring new places."

"He'll show you around," Molly said with a deep and extremely meaningful glare at Charlie.

"I'd love to." He replied, forcing a non-too-convincing smile.

"Only if you're sure?" Desiree gave him another chance of a way out, but he'd had 'The Look' and he wasn't going to risk the consequences of saying no.

"No, really, it'll be a pleasure. I'll take you back to the Hilton so you can drop your things off, and then I'll show you around the city."

"OK, if you're sure, that would be great."

# Chapter Thirty-Six

Klaus and Karsten arrived back at High Wood as Sam came running up the path from Takanun.

"Sam?" Klaus called as he ran past them.

If it was possible for a person to do a handbrake turn, then Sam came very close to achieving it. "Klaus?"

"Didn't you get my email?"

"Email?"

"Yes, Sam. My email. I sent it two days ago from St Petersburg."

"Email?" Sam frowned and looked up at the sky. "Email?"

Klaus was getting exasperated with this duo-syllabic conversation. "Let's get inside and discuss it in there." He took him by the arm, and like a caring aunt, led him up the path to the house.

"I've got to get to the cellar," Sam said excitedly. "I need to know what's happened to them."

Klaus frowned at him, shrugged, and released his arm-lock. "Go on. We'll follow you."

Now free, Sam sprinted into the house, down the hall, and leapt down the cellar steps two at a time.

Klaus and Karsten followed at a slightly more reserved and leisurely pace.

"SAM?" Klaus shouted as they reached the cellar door.

"OVER HERE." A call came to their left from the far side of the cellar.

"Dies ist eine verrückte Haus geworden. Was zum Teufel geht? Karsten folgen Sie mir. *(This has become a crazy House. What the hell is going? Karsten follow me.)*" They ran to the sound of Sam's voice.

What greeted them, stretched even the imagination of Klaus. Trickles of blue mist were running from the bottom of the wall, Elizabeth was comforting an unknown man, and Sam was staring at the wall. As they stared in disbelief at the wall, almost imperceptibly, an old man, an old woman, two young soldiers, and Jane materialised in the cellar.

"Scheiße! Mein Gott! Was passiert hier? *(Shit! My God! What happens here?)*" Klaus managed to utter.

The bizarre group froze, looked around at each other, frowned, looked embarrassed, chuckled, and then burst out laughing.

Klaus and Karsten stared in disbelief.

"Scheiße!" Was all Klaus could manage to say.

Elizabeth jumped to her feet. "Klaus." She looked around at the scene. "We should probably try and explain?"

Klaus nodded. "Bitte. Bitte tun. *(Please. Please do.)*"

"Let's go upstairs, and we'll tell you everything that's happened." Elizabeth continued in a conciliatory tone. "Caterina, will you tell Luca and Lorenzo to follow you?"

She turned, smiled, and waved for her brothers to follow. "Seguimi. Tutto diventerà chiaro. *(Follow me. Everything will become clear.)*"

Luca and Lorenzo glanced at each other, looked around at the strange gathering, shrugged, nodded, and slowly followed their sister. The remainder of the disparate group shuffled after Elizabeth like lost sheep.

Klaus and Karsten shook their heads and followed like two very confused tail-gate-charlies.

Elizabeth got everyone seated in the lounge and asked Jane to help her get drinks for everyone. Ten minutes later, she stood in the middle of the room, mug of tea in hand, and brought Klaus and Karsten up to speed with recent events, interrupted by a string of questions, rhetorical and otherwise.

"You didn't know they were spirits?"

"The blue light hasn't progressed any further?"

"The young policeman collapsed?"

"Mermen pulled you under the sea?"

"These men Luca and Lorenzo came out of the bay?"

"They were killed in World War Two?

Klaus raised his eyebrows, blew out his cheeks, shook his head, pulled at his nose, looked around the room at everyone, and spoke. "Eine ziemlich normale paar Wochen dann. *(A pretty normal couple weeks then.)*"

Blank faces looked back at him.

"I am sorry. I was wondering what else could possibly happen. Mein Gott, things have moved on rapidly here in the UK."

"It all happened so quickly," Sam said. "We had no idea all this would happen. We should have told you."

"It is not a problem, Sam. In some ways, it is good, that things have happened this way. This shows you can also connect with World War Two. A connection which we are in desperate need of."

Luca and Lorenzo seemed very agitated and Caterina fell into a whispered conversation with them.

Klaus caught enough of what passed between them to allay their obvious fears. "Io sono tedesco, ma la Guerra terminò settant'anni fa. In Europa siamo tutti amici ora che lavorano insieme."

Karsten translated for the others. "I am German, but in Europe, the War ended seventy years ago. We are now friends who work together towards a common good."

"In che anno è questo? *(What year is this?)*" Luca asked.

"Due mila e quattordici. *(Two thousand fourteen)*" Klaus replied.

"Due mila e quattordici!!" Luca exclaimed.

"They want to know the year," Karsten said quietly to the others.

The two brothers and their sister moved away into a far corner of the lounge.

"This must be as a big a shock for them, as it has been for all those who've passed over through this house," Elizabeth said quietly.

Everyone turned and looked at the group in the corner.

"Anything we can do?" Rebecca asked. "We've been through the same as them. Maybe talking with us would help? Adam, what do you think?"

"Yes, that's fine. It wasn't easy at first, was it Sam?" Adam said with a smile.

Sam thought back to the first days Adam 'arrived' at High Wood, and how close it had come to Adam turning to the 'dark side'. *"Without the help of Isaac's spirit, God only knows what would have happened."*

Caterina turned and walked back to the centre of the room while the brothers stayed close to the wall. "They understand they are dead, but they can't understand how they are here, in the future. They also understand, that everyone is here to help them." She turned to the brothers. "Vieni, incontrare tutti. Sono tutti qui per aiutare. Venire. Non c'è nulla da temere. *(Come meet them all. All are here to help. Come. There is nothing to fear.)*"

Suddenly, Caterina fixed her gaze on Sam and Elizabeth. "Where is Alfredo? Where is my son?"

Sam and Elizabeth's blood froze. They looked at each other, chewed their lips, dug their nails into the palms of their hands, swallowed hard, rocked back and forth on their heels, and tried without success to hold eye to eye contact with her.

"ALFREDO, ALFIE," she wailed. "DOVE SEI? DOVE SEI? *(WHERE ARE YOU?)*"

# Chapter Thirty-Seven

Alfredo's mind was in turmoil. Sam, Elizabeth, Kefalonia, Antisamos, Argostoli, the Ionian Sea, Luca, Lorenzo … His mind was spinning out of control. He began to shiver as intense cold penetrated deep into his body, like a neuro-toxin paralysing his muscles.

*"What is this? Am I dead? Is this Hell? Sweet Jesus save me."*

Thoughts careered and ricocheted around his head. Cautiously he opened his eyes. The sight which greeted him, blew every remaining fuse in his brain. He was stood in a deep, snow-covered trench, close to the edge of a precipice, half way up the side of a mountain. He edged away from the cliff's edge until he could feel his back against the other side of the trench. He breathed a sigh of relief, but almost jumped over the edge, as he felt a firm tap on the shoulder.

"Bruno. Tutto OK? *(Bruno. Everything OK?)*"

Alfredo's mind desperately tried to make sense of the stimuli it was receiving, but for the moment, its best response was, "Oh merda!' *(Oh shit!)*" He looked right and left, up and down the icy trench, until his brain finally had a point of reference.

*"I know these uniforms,"* he thought. *"Think Alfredo, think."*

His brain threw open reference files, eventually retrieving a dossier of photographs of Luca and Lorenzo.

*"Italians. But not World War Two."*

He didn't find this revelation particularly reassuring.

*"Where the hell am I, and how the hell did I get here?"* A second important file flew open. 'Family'.

"Bruno?" The soldier offered him a mug of steaming brown liquid, smelling vaguely of coffee. "Qui, aiuterà le mani. *(Here, it will help your hands.)* Attento delle tue mani. *(Careful of your hands.)*"

Alfredo's brain nudged him, he took the mug, and thanked the soldier.

*"Of course."* His brain had made the connection. *"Bruno was mamma's papa! He lost his fingers in the Alps."*

The memory didn't improve Alfredo's mood, or reduce his now ever-increasing blood pressure.

The soldier tugged at the ice-encrusted sleeve of Alfredo's padded jacket. "Vieni, andiamo nel tunnel. Almeno c'è un incendio in là. *(Come, let us go into the tunnel. At least there is a fire in there.)*"

Alfredo followed his newly found friend into a tunnel which had been carved by hand out of the cliff face.

"Vieni più vicino al fuoco. *(Come closer to the fire.)*" A voice from somewhere in the shadows called to him.

He didn't need a second request and sat as close as possible to the warm glow of the smoky wood fire. He pulled off his gloves and was sickened by the sight of his swollen and blackened fingers.

"Sergente. Sue mani! *(Sergeant. His hands.)*" A soldier, wrapped in ragged woollen blankets, leaned forward and frowned deeply

A second ice-warrior shuffled across the tunnel floor and tenderly held Alfredo's hands. He looked up into his eyes and shook his head. "Bruno. Si dovrà tornare a valle. *(Bruno. You will have to return to the valley)*.

*"How am I Bruno? Is this because of my 'abilities?' Is this nothing more than a dream?"*

His mind was doing its almighty best to drag him back to a reality he understood.

"Qualcosa da mangiare? *(Something to eat?)*" A soldier, wrapped in what looked like filthy sacking, offered him black, mould-covered, stale bread, with a slice, of what once had been salami. Alfredo looked around and tapped his chest. "Per me? *(For me?)*" He'd found his voice.

"Sì. Per te. *(Yes, for you.)*"

"Grazie. *(Thanks.)*"

He struggled to hold the bread, so the soldier sat down beside him, broke off small pieces and fed him. He worked against a massive gag reflex which was doing it's best to reject everything headed for his stomach.

Suddenly, from outside the tunnel was the not-too-distant sound of an explosion, followed by an ominous rumbling.

The sergeant crawled as quickly as he could to the tunnel entrance. "Valanga! All'interno del tunnel. *(Avalanche! Inside the tunnel)*."

The already cramped space in the tunnel soon resembled a cage of battery chickens, and as the last soldier began to crawl into the tunnel, a tsunami of snow and ice, swept him away down the side of the mountain. As the last of his screams were lost in the thunder of the avalanche, the tunnel was plunged into a stygian blackness.

"Gli austriaci hanno fatto questo. Bastarde! *(The Austrians have done this. Bastards!)*"

Alfredo shook his head. "Austriaci? *(Austrians?)*"

A voice in the dark replied. "Attaccano dalla vetta. *(Attack from the summit)*. Questo è non come combattere. *(This is not how to fight.)*"

As soldiers blindly jostled for position in the blackness of the tunnel, they thumped into Alfredo, sending him sprawling onto the unforgiving tunnel floor. The excruciating pain from his hands was like none he'd ever known, or would ever want to know again. It flashed along nerve fibres, charring synapses and searing the pain centres in his brain. He was close to breaking point. He called out to his faith in prayer.

"Oh Mother of Perpetual Help, grant that I may ever invoke your powerful name, the protection of the living and the salvation of the dying. Purest Mary, let your name henceforth be ever on my lips. Delay not, Blessed Lady, to rescue me whenever I call on you. In my temptations, in my needs, I will never cease to call on you, ever repeating your sacred name, Mary, Mary." He was becoming weaker by the second and close to being subsumed by Bruno. Lost forever in his reality, his time, his space.

"Alfredo!"

The voice was disconnected and remote. The merest suggestion of a presence, briefly there, and then gone like dew on a morning glade. He staggered to his feet and tripped over a boulder. The agony returned.

"Alfredo! Torna da me! *(Come back to me!)*"

His mind resisted the call. The strength of Bruno's spirit growing by the second.

"ALFREDO!!" The call became clearer, and more insistent.

*"Ignore it."* Bruno's mind said.

*"I know the voice."* Something whispered.

*"It is the voice of Satan. He speaks to you in tongues."* Bruno replied.

*"I know this voice."*

*"It is the voice of the Fallen Angel."*

*"It is ..."*

"It is LUCIFER! He speaks to you in tongues, to hide his true self." Bruno insisted.

Alfredo prayed for the rapture to leave him and his body began to shake.

*"You have returned to the tunnel. Satan has taken you back to that God forsaken place to freeze to death."*

His body shuddered. He could hear other sounds. His personal reality was calling to him. Dim light began to filter through his eyelids. He forced them open and immediately shut them as the intense light seemed to scorch his retinas. He cautiously opened them again to small slits, and he began to discern shapes. Human shapes. Shapes which were helping him to stand. Hugging him. Shapes which were speaking to him. Shapes he began to recognise.

"Alfredo?" It was a comforting woman's voice.

His throat managed only one hoarse word. "Mamma?"

# Chapter Thirty-Eight

"Shouldn't we book somewhere?" Abraham suggested.

Jacob leaned on the railings, watching families disembark from the water taxi, children talking animatedly about their visit to the 'Dr Who Experience', old couples walking arm in arm past the Corn Exchange, seagulls dive-bombing anyone eating ice cream or chips, a group of women on their way to the Millennium Centre, and a police helicopter circling Penarth Heights.

"Mmmm?"

"Shouldn't we book somewhere to eat?"

"No. Not on a weekday. They should have plenty of tables."

"What do you fancy?"

*"Getting rid of your dozy arse,"* the 'voice' said.

Jacob didn't look away from the activities in the Bay and leered. *"We will resolve this tonight."* The 'voice' continued. *"You must to go back to High Wood. The possessed souls need salvation."* The 'voice' said with false sincerity.

Jacob closed his eyes in silent prayer. *"I hear Jehovah. They will be saved from the End of Times."*

*"There are two special spirits we must save. They need all your powers to save their demonised souls."*

"Jacob?" Abraham was becoming increasingly concerned by his behaviour.

*"Ignore him."*

"Jacob." Abraham grabbed him by the arm.

"LET GO OF ME!" Jacob screamed, attracting the attention of the crowds.

Abraham dropped his arm as if it was electrified.

"DO NOT DO THAT AGAIN!"

Abraham was about to speak, but the look of hatred in Jacob's eyes, terrified him.

"Do you like Italian?" Charlie asked Desiree.

"Does pizza count?" She said with a wicked smile.

Charlie tried desperately not to laugh.

"Or spag-bol?"

"You cordon bleu chefs are all the same."

She linked arms with him. "Come on then, Antonio Carlucci, let's find Pizza Express."

They heard shouting and looked behind them.

"They seem to have a problem," Desiree said. "Is it always like this in Cardiff, Mr Policeman?"

"I'll have a word."

Desiree blushed and panicked a little. "You're off duty. Please don't. I've had a lovely time. Let's not spoil it." She raised her eyebrows and half smiled.

"Never off duty."

"Just for today?" She gave him a lost-puppy look. "For me."

Charlie smiled at her. He'd had little or no contact with the opposite sex, and now in two days, he'd fallen for two.

*"It should be pretty easy,"* he thought. *"One lives in Cardiff, and the other in Sheringham."*

"Let's get that pizza," Desiree said, pulling Charlie away from the disturbance.

He smiled. "Pizza Express is just over here." She slipped her arm to his arm and held his hand.

Abraham stood back, stared at Jacob, shook his head, and walked away along the boardwalk.

"COME BACK! WE HAVEN'T FINISHED!"

Abraham stared in front of him, avoiding the looks of the astonished faces, and headed for the Norwegian Church. He needed somewhere which would provide an atmosphere of calm and tranquillity.

*"Follow him,"* the 'voice' said. *"He can't speak to anyone about this."*

"Jehovah, what would you have me do?"

*"Sacrifice. I demand sacrifice."*

"What should I sacrifice to you, Lord?"

*"A human."*

"Human, Lord?"

*"Do you question me?"*

"No Lord. But ..."

*"Listen to me, you little shit. Silence that twat who just walked out on us, and then there are a few more in need of 'help'."*

Jacob's mind questioned this demand, and its use of profane language, but then remembered his scriptures. *"Am I being tested like Abraham with Isaac?"*

*"Yes, like Abraham. Now get on with it,"* the 'voice' said impatiently. Lidsay was beginning to tire of this second host. *"Pissing Holy Joes."*

Jacob looked up at the sky, crossed himself, and jogged after Abraham.

Charlie looked over his shoulder and watched Jacob following Abraham. He lightly tapped Desiree on the arm. "Do you think we ought to follow them? That one looks pretty pissed off. Sorry." He blushed and looked away.

"I've never heard such language," she said with a chuckle. "Oh, come on then. But don't get involved unless you have to. Agreed?"

Charlie nodded his head. "Agreed. Come on, or we're going to lose them."

They walked quickly after them and caught sight of Jacob disappearing into the Norwegian Church. They slowed to a walk and soon entered the church.

"What's this place?" Desiree asked, looking around.

"Cardiff at one time, was one of the greatest sea ports in the world. Norwegian ships brought Scandinavian timber to South Wales to use as pit props in the coal mines, and then took the coal back to Norway. There was a large Norwegian community here, and they built this church to worship in. Roald Dahl's family worshipped here."

Desiree raised her eyebrows. "Really?"

"His father Harald was from Oslo, and he co-founded the ship broking company, Aadnesen & Dahl, in Cardiff in 1880."

"You learn something new every day," she said with a smile. "Is it still used as a church?"

"As far as I know, it's mainly an Arts Centre. Fancy a coffee?" He pointed across the large room to a coffee bar."

Desiree nodded. "Skinny cappuccino please."

Abraham was ordering a decaffeinated latte when he felt a hand on his shoulder. He turned and looked into the now smiling eyes of Jacob.

"How can I apologise? I have been stressed recently. My father is very ill and Seattle is so far away."

Abraham held his arm. "My brother, I didn't know. You should share your troubles. Keeping things like that to yourself can have a devastating effect on your health. Let me get you a coffee."

Jacob smiled and nodded. "I'll have whatever you're having."

"Looks like they've kissed and made up," Desiree whispered. "Still have that coffee, though?"

Charlie nodded. "Skinny cappuccino, wasn't it?"

"And a chocolate muffin, please. I've gone off the idea of a pizza. My sweet tooth has taken over."

Charlie laughed to himself. How could he have found two such perfect women in such a short time? *"Mind you, I could have worse problems than this,"* he thought. "You grab a table, and I'll get the coffee and cakes."

Lidsay was looking around through Jacob's eyes, when he noticed Charlie. *"Well, I'll be buggered. If it isn't that snotty-nosed Constable Thompson. You little shit, what are you up to?"*

He watched Charlie carry the tray of coffees and muffins back to the table and took a long lecherous look at Desiree.

*"You sly, little bastard. Where have you kept her hidden? Now I wouldn't mind spending my time exploring her assets."*

He looked across at Abraham, back at Charlie and Desiree, and decided he'd had enough of this Bible-bashing pair.

*"Walk over to that table with the young man in the blue sweater, and the woman in the jeans and red top."*

Jacob jumped up, like a clown on the end of a spring in a Jack in the Box.

"Jacob?" Abraham asked in surprise.

There was no answer.

Desiree looked up from her skinny cappuccino. "He's coming over," she said with a degree of panic in her voice. "Do you think he's recognised us?"

"Who?" Charlie asked as he spilled his coffee over the table. "Shit."

"Him." She gestured at Jacob with her head. "One of those two who were shouting at each other."

"Oh bugger. Don't worry, I'll deal with it." Charlie stood up, and met Jacob half way. "Can I help?"

"Mmmm?" Jacob mumbled.

*"Leave this to me,"* Lidsay said. *"Just shake his hand, and apologise for the shouting and arguing."*

Jacob took Charlie's hand, and pressed it just a little too firmly for his liking.

"I would like to apologise for the shouting earlier on. We were having a heated debate about Heaven and Hell which got a little out of hand." He carried on gripping Charlie's hand. "We're Jehovah's Witnesses."

A deep, painful heat rapidly moved up Charlie's arm, across his shoulder, up his neck, and into his head.

*"Gotcha! You're my ticket into High Wood, Charlie. They know you, and they won't be worried about you walking around the house. Welcome back, Constable Thompson. Good to have the old team back together."*

# Chapter Thirty-Nine

Sam and Elizabeth stared at the cellar door. A few minutes after being reunited with her brothers, Caterina had run from the kitchen and back through the cellar door.

"Come on, you two. We need to see what's got her so excited," Jane called out, as she raced after Caterina, through Sam, and the cellar door.

As Sam and Elizabeth reached the cellar floor, they saw Jane's back disappearing in the direction of the far cellar wall, and as they got closer, they could hear body-quivering sobbing. Elizabeth was a few strides ahead of Sam, and as she reached the wall, she screamed. Sam was quickly by her side and a soft pillow of downy-feathers could have knocked him over. Kneeling on the ground was Caterina, and close by, was the prone, motionless body of her son Alfredo.

"You … brought them … all … home." Mrs Mather said between sobs. "I knew … you … you would."

The sound of footfalls behind them told them they had company.

Everyone's reaction was the same. Shock, joy disbelief, tears, and a lot of fist-punching, and high-fives.

Alfredo began to regain consciousness, but his mind was fearful of what it would see, so kept his eyed tightly shut.

"Alfredo. È tua madre. *(It is your mother.)*" She whispered something in his ear and the result was immediate.

He opened his eyes, looked up at her, around at the others, and beamed at Luca and Lorenzo. "Ciao. Luca, Lorenzo. Benvenuti a casa. *(Hello. Luca, Lorenzo. Welcome home.)*"

Caterina jumped up, and danced a little jig. "Grazie mille, grazie mille"

"This must be a wonderful moment for you, Caterina. It is so good to meet you at last," Jane said with a caring smile.

Caterina hugged Jane, both being spirits, and kissed her on both cheeks. "Grazie." She looked around the room at everyone. "Everyone, please call me Caterina. This is my husband Alfred, my son Alfredo, and my dearest brothers Luca and Lorenzo." She laughed. "It is only Alfredo who is living."

Klaus walked close to Caterina. "It is now my turn, Caterina. Elizabeth and Sam you know, this is my son Karsten, Rebecca and her husband Adam, Captain Forster, and this is Jane. She is, was, Sam's wife." His cheeks flushed. "Myself, Karsten, Sam, and Elizabeth are also living."

Caterina laughed. "Thank you, Klaus."

He nodded, and came to attention.

"After 1943, I swore I would never speak to another German," Caterina said with a slight frown.

Klaus's expression slightly darkened, but soon lightened, as Caterina smiled.

"You have shown me, Klaus, that times and peoples change. Hate will only destroy. Life may be too short, but eternity, well, it lasts forever." She laughed again. "Too long a time to bear a grudge." She walked forward, blew kisses to Klaus and Karsten, and looked again at Luca and Lorenzo. "This is a time of great joy for me, but tinged with great sadness, for now we are reunited, it is time for us to move on."

Klaus opened his arms to Caterina. "Before moving on, would you stay a little longer and help us? Will you and your family join us? I know from Sam and Elizabeth, that you already know about us, and what we do."

She nodded.

"We have only ever helped the lost of World War One, but now the lost of World War Two have made their presence felt to us and we must help them. But we do not have the resources to support them. We are trying to establish a new structure, one which can help these drifting souls cross over to salvation." He paused and stepped back. "I think you could help us to save these lost souls." He paused again, trying to assess her response. "What do you think?"

"I, as you say, know what you do here. It is admirable and everyone should know about what you do."

Klaus smiled. "We have plans to do that."

"Excellent." Caterina's face relaxed. "I understand the panic which could be caused if the general population knew ghosts were flying around everywhere. However, I am delighted and humbled you've suggested this. Please give us a little time to discuss it. So much has happened in such a short time, that we all need to catch our breath and gather our thoughts. We will go home and talk about it there. We will come back tomorrow afternoon and give you our answer."

"I could not ask for any more. I look forward to seeing you tomorrow, Caterina. Grazie molte. È meraviglioso vedere la tua famiglia insieme dopo tanti anni. *(It is wonderful to see your family together after so many years.)*" Klaus bowed deeply from the waist.

Caterina smiled broadly. "L'italiano è eccellente, Klaus. Si discuterà questo correttamente e ci vediamo domani. *(The Italian is excellent, Klaus. We will discuss this properly and see you tomorrow.)*"

Half an hour later, Klaus was sat at the kitchen table with everyone discussing the day's events.

"You have been busy, my friends," Klaus said with a raised eyebrow. "Sehr beschäftigt. *(Very busy.)*"

Captain Forster walked into the kitchen.

"Yes, Captain," Sam said and then frowned. "You know, after all this time, we still don't know your first name."

Captain Forster smiled. "Edward. Edward Albert Forster."

Sam stood up and saluted. "Well, Captain Edward Albert Forster, how can we help?"

"I need to tell the men what's happening, Sam." He nervously rubbed his hands down the sides of his legs. "It's been quite a while since anyone has passed across."

Elizabeth shuffled uncomfortably in her chair. "Klaus, you need to make your plans without me. I can't ignore these spirits any longer. I'll be happy to be involved at some point in the future, but now, I need to help Captain Forster and his men."

Klaus nodded slowly. "You are completely correct, my dear. These souls are our main reason for being here. Elizabeth, you go with the captain and help them. We will decide what to do with the blue lights and keep you informed of our plans. I will wait for you to tell us, if and when you are able to help. There will be no pressure put on you." He paused. "Is there anyone else who should come with you?"

She looked around the table. "Rebecca and Adam, but I may need some extra help in the future."

"Let us know and you can have whoever you need," Klaus replied. "Whatever plans are made, everyone else will still be here, so never feel alone or isolated."

She nodded, waved to Rebecca and Adam, and they followed Captain Forster into the hall.

"Keep a close eye on her, Sam. We sometimes expect too much of her," Klaus said with genuine concern.

"She's not been acting like herself, and I'm worried if we ask too much of her, she could have a breakdown," Sam said with obvious worry.

Klaus frowned deeply. "We should stop her then."

Sam shook his head. "No. I'll keep a very close eye on her, and if she seems to be getting worse, then I'll stop everything."

Klaus nodded, but looked unsure of his decision.

"Tun mein Freund, was wir? *(So my friend, what do we do?)*" Sam slowly, but surely, said.

Klaus and Karsten's eyebrows almost met at the back of their heads.

"Mein Gott ist Sam, Ihr Deutsch ausgezeichnet, *(My God Sam, your German is excellent,)*" Karsten said with a huge smile.

"I've been learning," Sam replied with some embarrassment. "My German isn't great, but it's getting there."

"Sehr gute, Sam. Sehr gut," Klaus said as he leaned across the table and shook his hand. "Sehr gut."

"So Klaus, what are we facing and what do we do?"

# Chapter Forty

Guillaume couldn't sleep. He tossed and turned, listened to music on his iPod, counted herds of Belgian sheep, planned out the next three days, read a few chapters of 'Eagles at War', finally gave up, and got up at three o' clock. Even in the early hours of the morning, Bloemenwerf felt like an old friend, as it put a comforting arm around his shoulders, but even this didn't ease his heartache. Without his brother Isaac, Bloemenwerf would never be the home it had been. He walked slowly from room to room, stroking the furniture Isaac had loved, and by and by came to the dining room. It had always been his favourite room in the house, and the memories forged here, shone like beacons through the fog of his mourning.

"So many good times here, brother," he said softly to Isaac's photo, sat on an 1880 ornate French, Black Forest, oak desk. It sat at the front of a group of photos of members of the Wouters/Rosenberg family. Rosenberg had been the family name, prior to Hitler coming to power in Germany. Guillaume tenderly touched each image and ran his fingers over the exquisite carvings of the desk, lingering on the stag's head which he'd loved since he was a boy.

"Do you remember what we called it, Isaac?" Guillaume prayed for an answer, but none came. "Ah well. You will come when you can."

He pulled a 1900, Spanish, walnut and leather chair away from the dining table and sat at the desk.

*"What did we keep in here?"* he thought, as he looked closely at the three drawers. *"You first."* He pulled open the small drawer on his right, but there was nothing of any real interest. *"Now you."* He opened the large centre drawer, where there was the usual collection of old pens, pads of writing paper, decks of playing cards, rubber bands, erasers, paper clips, envelopes … *"Remember the games we played with these?"* He tenderly picked up a deck of playing cards with images of French chateaus on their backs, and unsuccessfully attempted a riffle shuffle which sprayed the

cards all over the floor. He picked them up, put them back in their box, and back in the drawer. *"Last chance. What are you hiding?"* The small drawer on his left didn't disappoint. Under a programme for La Boheme from 1998, he noticed the corner of a red notebook. He lifted the programme, gently held the corner of the note book, and pulled it slowly out of the drawer. The name inside the cover made his heart jump.

*Isaac Rosenberg*

"Uncle Isaac!" he said loudly, disturbing the stillness of the house. He stood up, pushed the chair back to the table, sat down, and put the note book on the polished surface. The cover was faded and worn, and as he carefully turned the pages, their fragility became apparent. The first few pages, were notes on holidays spent in Normandy and Brittany, before the start of the second conflict. What followed was what Guillaume had been hoping to find. Isaac's poetry. He painstakingly turned the fragile pages until he came to the poem which had always moved him. *'Break of Day in the Trenches.'* It had always been one of Guillaume's favourites, written during the First World War. He leaned forward and silently read the poem in his mind, but as he came to second half of the poem, the words demanded to be read aloud.

"Sprawled in the bowels of the earth,

The torn fields of France.

What do you see in your eyes

At the shrieking iron and flame

Hurled through still heavens?

What quaver - what heart aghast?

Poppies whose roots are in man's veins

Drop, and are ever dropping;

But mine in my ear is safe,

Just a little white with the dust."

He sighed, ran his finger over the faded written words, and turned more pages. He was about to close the note book, when he saw several lines of another poem heavily underlined. He tapped the title with his index finger.

'Dawn.'

The words echoed in his mind.

*'And then, as sleep lies down to sleep*

*And all her dreams lie somewhere dead,*
*The iron shepherd leads his sheep*
*To pastures parched whose green is shed.*
*Still, O frail dawn, still in your hair*
*And your cold eyes and sad sweet lips,*
*The ghosts of all the dreams are them,*
*To fade like passing ships.'*

He leaned back in the chair, tears tracing glossy lines down his cheeks. "To fade like passing ships. Come to me, brother." He looked up to the ceiling, offering a silent prayer. "Please come to me." The silence around him, was profound and smothering. "You will come when you are ready. I know this."

He picked up the note book, and held it close to his heart until giddiness and nausea overcame him.

*"Sleep is calling,"* he thought. *"I'll sit here for a little longer until this nausea passes."*

He started to feel himself drifting away and soon slipped into the arms of Morpheus. He woke with a start, feeling stiff and aching from head to toe.

*"Teach me to go to bed when I want to sleep."* He gently chided himself. He stretched and cracked his knee on something rough, wooden, and hard. *"It must be the table. I need to get a French polisher to take a look at it."*

He sat up quickly, and cracked his head on a rough wooden surface. *"What is this?"* His brain had no answer. It sent unheard signals to his eyes to snap open, but they resisted.

*"What is this?"* His brain had no answer to his demands. It sent more and more signals to his eyes to snap open, and finally they obeyed, but only for an instant. The input the brain received was incomprehensible. Nonetheless, it fed its analysis and instructions to Guillaume's eyes, which, by tiny degrees, opened. Directly above his head were stained, dirt ingrained, rough wooden planks, with what appeared to be filthy straw and rags hanging in the gaps between them.

"אלוהים! אני איפה? *(My God? Where am I?)*"

Before he could look away, his other senses were assaulted by a cacophony of noises and smells. The air was heavy, a miasma of unwashed bodies, festering sores, rotten meat, faeces, urine, and the discordant chorus of wretchedness, despair, suffering, separation, and grieving.

*"Breathe deeply and slowly."*

He turned his head to one side, and the intense white beam of a searchlight cruised across a cracked, icy window, making it sparkle like crystals caught in the rays of the sun. He raised his hand, touched the window guardedly, and pulled it away rapidly from the freezing temperature of the cracked pane.

*"This is a nightmare."*

Guillaume's desperate belief he was in some bizarre dream was being badly shaken. He lifted his hand once again to the cracked window, pressed the palm of his hand against the bitterly cold glass, and held it there, hoping the intense pain would wake him up. All he achieved, was to leave a layer of skin adhered to the glass. Like a Jenga puzzle, Guillaume's mind only needed one wrong move to send it crashing to the floor.

*"Not a dream? Another reality?"*

He lay back on the filthy straw of the bunk, and pulled the thin ragged covers up to his shoulders. He tried to push away a cold pair of feet on his side of the bunk, but the legs were unbendable, rigid. Guillaume reached down, touched them, and his hand flew away from the freezing cadaverous cold.

*"I'm lying with a corpse?"*

The shrill call of reveille, brought him to full consciousness with a jolt. He jumped down from the bunk, and his bare feet slipped on oiled wooden planks. He edged passed a Häftling, snuggly wrapped in a blanket on night watch, asleep in a chair. A stinking pail of urine near the bunk, was close to overflowing, but so was Guillaume's bladder, and he was soon paddling in warm urine. Suddenly he heard music.

*"A brass band?"*

The music got louder and louder, and unseen to Guillaume, a Kommandos band marched past to the 'Beer Barrel Polka'. He heard baskets scraping along the floor as orderlies began to distribute 'rations'.

*"This is another reality. Another time and place!* איפה אני! אלוהים*? (Dear God! Where am I?)"*

"ZIJ ZULLEN HIER SPOEDIG! JE MOET OPSTAAN! *(They will be here soon! You must get up!).*

Guillaume recognised the language as Dutch, and he turned his head to look at the source of the bellowing. A shaven-headed, emaciated face with hollow eyes, stared back at him. The rags he wore barely covered his skeletal body, but it was the design of the rags which froze Guillaume's blood. They were blue and white stripes.

"ZIJ ZULLEN HIER SPOEDIG! JE MOET OPSTAAN!

The poor wretch turned and called to an older man. "Isaac. Over here."

*"Isaac?"* Guillaume thought. The Jenga pieces of his mind now were lying in a jumbled heap.

The older man, in a similar condition to the poor wretch who'd spoken to Guillaume, shuffled across the barrack. "Thank you, Levi." He stared through red-rimmed eyes at Guillaume. "I don't know your face. You're new to this barrack?"

Guillaume stared blankly at him. *"Barrack? Blue and white striped uniforms? Jewish names? Filthy, stinking conditions?"* An unnerving thought scorched through his mind.

"Who are you?" The dishevelled figure asked.

"Guillaume Wouters." His response was automatic. "I am from Brussels."

The dishevelled figure looked at him suspiciously. "I know Guillaume Wouters." His eyes burrowed deep into Guillaume's face. "He is a small boy." His eyes scanned every nook and cranny of Guillaume's face. "He escaped to England with his family in '38" He lifted a filthy hand and touched Guillaume's cheek. "Are you related? Do you know them?"

Guillaume's brain was desperately trying to make some sense of everything that was being hurled at it. It threw open every dust-covered cupboard, drawer, and file it could find until under a grubby pile it found 'Childhood'.

A filth encrusted finger, suspiciously prodded Guillaume in the chest. "Who are you?"

"You are Uncle Isaac!" Guillaume uttered in disbelief. "Isaac Rosenberg. You wrote poetry in World War One."

Isaac nodded. "Yes, I am Isaac Rosenberg." His frown deepened. "You say you are my nephew?" He frowned deeply and shook his head. "That is impossible. I told you. He is a child."

Guillaume frowned and then spoke. "'Moses, from whose loins I sprung, Lit by a lamp in his blood Ten immutable rules, a moon For mutable lampless men.'"

Isaac was clearly shocked. "Where did you learn that?"

"You wrote that, didn't you? You wrote it for our family. Father used to read it to me."

"You could have read this anywhere." His voice was dismissive.

"Could a small child remember this? 'The blonde, the bronze, the ruddy, With the same heaving blood, Keep tide to the moon of Moses. Then why do they sneer at me?'"

Isaac stood open-mouthed and speechless.

Before they could continue the conversation, the door to the barrack flew open.

"AUFSTEHEN! SCHNELL! RAUS HIER! *(Get up! Quickly! Get out!)*"

Two muscular SS guards pushed through the barracks, randomly smashing the butts of their rifles into anyone they felt deserved it, which was pretty much anyone.

A whip whistled through the air and lashed anyone who didn't emerge fast enough from under their blankets, and lash in hand, the stubhova *(barracks leader)*, flew up to the third tier in the centre of the bunks, whipping faces and legs still numb with sleep and cold.

"Follow me!" Isaac hissed. It was an urgent instruction which didn't need repeating.

Guillaume took a firm hold of Isaac's arm and became part of the congested river of desperate humanity flowing out into the bowels of IIcll.

"Where is this?" Guillaume whispered to Isaac.

Isaac put his finger to his lips. "Speak only when you are spoken to. They will shoot you for a great deal less."

Guillaume pressed Isaac. "Where are we?"

Isaac stared deep into his eyes and shook his head. "You don't know, do you?"

Guillaume shook his head.

Isaac's answer numbed every cell in Guillaume's body. "Auschwitz-Birkenau."

# Chapter Forty-One

Charlie turned and walked back to the table. As Desiree saw his expression, she jumped up, walked quickly to him, linked arms with him, and led him back to his chair.

"You look terrible. What happened? What did he say to you?"

Charlie stared straight through her.

*"Don't screw things up. Just make normal conversation,"* Lidsay instructed.

"Sorry." Charlie shook his head and rubbed his eyes. "I think it must have been another sugar drop. I seem to be getting them fairly regularly."

Desiree frowned. "I'll get some chocolate."

Charlie nodded. "Thanks. Anything will do." He leaned back in the chair and closed his eyes.

Lidsay chuckled. *"Well done. We don't want to upset anybody do we? Well, not just yet."*

Charlie nodded. *"Not just yet."*

Desiree came back with a bag of Revels. "Get these down you."

Charlie opened his eyes and smiled. "Thanks." Five minutes later, he seemed to be himself again. "Sorry about that. I really need to see my GP."

"Still want that pizza?"

He nodded. "Hawaiian." He covered his eyes in mock shame. "Not the best choice in the world, but I love them."

Desiree dropped her head into her hands and shook her head. "I'm glad you've come clean." She paused for a few seconds. "Because so do I." She laughed, stood up, grabbed his arm, and pulled him to his feet. "Come on, I'm starving."

*"So am I."* Lidsay snarled. *"Starving for a chew on that devious son of a bitch Sam, and his sanctimonious whore of a vicar."*

After pizza, they strolled along the bay to the Millennium Centre, and unbelievably managed to get a couple of returns for the Lion King. Four hours later, Charlie pulled up outside Desiree's hotel.

"Thanks so much. I've had a fantastic time. The show was amazing. I've wanted to see it for years." She leaned across and kissed him on the cheek. "Do you want to come in for a nightcap?"

*"Go on my son. Older women are gagging for it,"* Lidsay said lecherously.

"I'll need to park the car."

"I'll meet you in the bar in ten minutes," Desiree said with a cheeky smile.

After a few glasses of Pinot Grigio, and a few shots, Desiree turned to Charlie and kissed him on the lips.

"Do you want to come up?"

"To your room?"

She nodded, looking him straight in the eye.

"I'd love to," he said shyly.

She leaned forward and whispered in his ear. "I hope you don't think I've done this before."

*"You don't seriously believe that, do you? I'd bet she's responsible for more merry men than Robin Hood."* Lidsay roared with laughter.

Charlie ignored him. "Me neither."

They finished their drinks, stood up from the booth, held hands, and walked to the lift.

"This is us," Desiree said, as they reached room 222. "Still want to come in?"

Charlie nodded. His chest was so tight that he was finding it difficult to breathe.

The light cast from the bathroom illuminated the room just enough for them to undress with only slight embarrassment.

*"Now then, my boy, let's have some fun."* Lidsay hissed in his ear. *"You may not have much experience, but, whatever she says, I'd bet my last pound she's worked as a test pilot for Ann Summers. And you're*

*talking to an expert."* He laughed malignantly. *"Leave this to me, Charlie. She's not going to forget you."*

As Charlie rode home in a taxi, he didn't know if he should feel satisfied, energised, worried, disturbed, or deeply ashamed. He'd no idea where the words he'd said, or things he'd done had come from. Even in the few 'adult' web sites he'd visited, he couldn't remember seeing anyone do anything close to what they had. She'd not thrown him out of her room, but her face was enough to tell him that he shouldn't contact her again.

*"Proud of you, Charlie. That's all they're good for. Pieces of meat for our pleasure,"* Lidsay crowed.

Charlie's mind had had enough of this and began to fight back. *"What are you?"*

*"More like who was I? Don't remember your sergeant?"*

*"You're only missing."*

*"Bit more than missing. Stone-cold dead."*

*"How did you die?"*

*"Ah, that's where you'll be helping me."*

*"To do what?"*

*"To bring two people a lot closer to me."*

*"Closer to you?"*

*"Close enough for them to sample the 'afterlife' they buried me in."*

There was a long mental silence.

*"You want them dead?"*

*"Hit it right on the nail."*

*"You want me to kill them?"*

*"Can't think of another way."*

*"I'm not doing that."*

*"I should warn you, that if you chose not to assist me in my personal quest for revenge, then I'm afraid I have ways to help you change your mind."*

*"Like what?"*

*"How about this."*

An excruciating pain, moved from Charlie's neck, down his spine, and concentrated its toxic energy in his pelvis. He squealed in agony and collapsed across the back seat of the taxi.

"DON'T YOU BE SICK IN MY BLOODY CAB!" The taxi driver shouted into his rear view mirror. "Bloody piss-artists."

Lidsay flicked the off switch. *"On the same page now?"*

Charlie struggled to sit up.

*"Want a reminder?"*

He shook his head. He'd deal with Lidsay later.

The taxi pulled up outside Charlie's house, the driver grabbed his ten pound note, and accelerated down the road.

It was one in the morning and there was still a light glowing in the front room. He ran his fingers through his hair, did his best to tidy himself, blew into his hand to check his breath, nearly passed out with the alcohol, clenched his fists, stared at the front door, and finally got up the courage to face mum and her 'music'.

"Morning, dear. Have a nice time with Desiree?" There wasn't the merest hint of annoyance in her voice.

"Lovely. We went to see the Lion King at the Millennium Centre, and had a bite to eat and a few glasses of wine. I thought I'd be sensible and got a cab home."

"Did she enjoy herself?"

"I think so."

"Only think so?"

"We had a really good time together."

"Are you going to see her again?"

"Probably not."

"Why's that?"

"She lives so far away." He sat down on the sofa, exhausted. "Hard to be friends with someone who lives on the other side of the country."

"I suppose so. But we need to keep in touch with her about the family tree."

"Uh huh."

"When's she going back to Sheringham?"

"Tomorrow, I think."

"Didn't she say?"

This was becoming an interrogation and Mum was an expert. Charlie decided retreat was his best option.

"I'm off to bed, Mum. I'm shattered. I'll call her in the morning."

"OK, dear. She called about an hour ago."

Charlie froze. "What did she say?" His mouth was bone dry.

"She wanted to thank you for such a lovely time. She said she'd call around in the morning before she gets the afternoon train." She stared at her exhausted son. "You don't look too pleased?"

"No, that's great. I thought her train was in the morning. It'll be lovely to see her again."

"She said she'd be around about ten, so you'd better get to bed." She walked past him to the stairs. "Night, love."

He kissed her on the cheek. "Night, Mum."

*"What does she want?"* Lidsay muttered. *"Probably more of the same if I'm any judge of character."*

*"Piss off."*

*"Now now, don't want a repeat of that earlier 'irritation' do you?"*

# Chapter Forty-Two

Elizabeth walked briskly upstairs to the gallery where Captain Forster, Rebecca, and Adam were waiting for her. They walked methodically up and down the panels of photographs, where before, faceless sepia images had been, smiling eager young men now happily looked back at them.

Elizabeth glowed at the memories of the souls she'd helped passed over and then turned to Captain Forster. "How many do you think are still left?"

"A lot more have come through since we stopped, and with those already waiting," he said and scratched his chin, "I'd say there were still about a hundred?"

"A hundred?" Elizabeth gasped. "We've a lot to do Captain. Who's going to be first?"

"I've been talking to the men and they agree it should be those who've been waiting the longest. I can have a list in about ten to fifteen minutes?"

Elizabeth smiled with relief. Things seemed to be well in hand and back on track. "I'll meet you back here."

Captain Forster sharply saluted, snapped his heels together, and walked down the gallery stairs.

Elizabeth looked around the gallery and frowned. "My laptop, sound centre, and camera are gone."

Rebecca looked at Adam, and he gestured at her to tell Elizabeth what had happened. "We had burglars while you were away. They probably took them," she said with some embarrassment.

"Burglars?" The question immediately seemed pointless. "Apart from my stuff, did they take anything else?"

"We don't think so. We sort of, caught them at it." Rebecca looked sheepishly at Adam. "I don't think they'll be back. We … well we gave them a bit of a shock."

"What have you two been up to?" she said with a chuckle in her voice.

Rebecca avoided eye contact with Elizabeth and told her about Matt and Mark's visit, the voices, the flying cushions, and the other 'effects' the brothers had experienced.

Elizabeth couldn't help but laugh. "I must tell Sam. He'll wet his pants."

"He's incontinent?" Adam asked with surprise.

"No, no, it's just something we say when someone's laughed a lot."

Adam looked at Rebecca and shrugged.

"I don't think we'll be seeing them again any time soon," Elizabeth said as she returned her attention to the photos.

Rebecca and Adam decided not to say anything about the brothers' second visit.

"Rebecca," Elizabeth said. "Can you tell Captain Forster I need to pop down to Curry's, to get a new laptop, sound centre, and camera? I'll meet him up here in about an hour."

She nodded. "OK."

*"Thank God everything's backed up on my external hard drive, cloud, and a memory stick,"* Elizabeth thought. "While I'm away, could you start taking down all the photos with faces? It'll make things a lot easier to help those who are left." She started to leave, but turned at the top of the stairs. "Put them in alphabetical piles." She stopped again and frowned. "See you in about an hour." She turned away and walked quickly down the stairs.

Captain Forster was glad of the extra time, as it allowed him to reassure all the Tommies that things were back to normal.

Elizabeth's new Bose sat in pride of place on a camping table, paired through Blue Tooth to her new laptop.

*"OK, what are we going to start with?"* she thought. *"Something gentle and melodic I think."* She opened iTunes and selected 'Simon and Garfunkel's Greatest Hits'. *"Should be perfect."*

The flawless harmonies of Paul and Art filled the empty space of the gallery with the 'Sounds of Silence', the lyrics having a deep resonance with Elizabeth. Next, she selected her favourite song, 'Bookends', and the lyrics this time, moved her to tears.

She looked at the remaining faceless photographs. *"I promise to preserve your memories,"* she thought as she dabbed her eyes with a tissue.

*"What a bloody waste of time."* Her inner-voice said petulantly.

*"Leave me alone,"* Elizabeth said angrily.

*"Not just yet, vicar."* It replied softly. *"When Gloria's satisfied, I'll pass over."*

"GLORIA!" Elizabeth exclaimed.

*"Yes. I did so enjoy our cups of coffee together."*

"I thought you were just missing? What do you want?"

*"An ex-husband of mine made my life a misery, and I want to make sure his afterlife is a real pain in the arse for him."*

"Sergeant Lidsay?"

*"That's the bastard I'm talking about."*

Elizabeth felt faint and swallowed hard. *"I'm not going within a country mile of him. He's evil. You'd better find somebody else to do your dirty work."*

*"Ivor never liked unfinished business. He'll come back for you, and when he does, I'll be there."*

"LEAVE ME ALONE!" Elizabeth screamed at the air.

"ELIZABETH!?" Captain Forster called in a terrified voice from the top of the gallery stairs.

She wiped her eyes. "IT'S FINE. I'M OK."

"Shall I tell the men we'll start tomorrow?" he said with concern as he walked into the gallery.

"No, they've waited long enough. Helping them across to the other-side will calm me down." She wiped her eyes again. "Ready when you are, captain. Who's first?"

He walked to the nearest aisle and tapped a photo. "Private Maurice Carpenter."

Elizabeth stared at the faceless Tommy surrounded by his family and shook her head. "Such a happy group. This," she said and tapped the photo, "well-dressed couple must be his parents, and these two cheery young things his brother and sister?" She sucked in her cheeks and sighed. "Their lives destroyed in one catastrophic instant." She tried to smooth a few creases out of the photo. "And we still haven't learnt any lessons. Let's get him home to his family." She turned, smiled, and gestured with a tilt of her head for Captain Forster to bring Private Carpenter up to the gallery.

Elizabeth replaced Simon and Garfunkel with Elgar's Enigma Variations, selected Nimrod, turned the volume low, and stood waiting for Private Carpenter. It wasn't long until a tall, young man slow marched into the gallery, closely followed by Captain Forster.

"Attention private," Captain Forster ordered quietly.

Private Carpenter came to a sharp stop a few paces in front of Elizabeth.

"Stand at ease," Captain Forster said in a kind tone. "At ease, private." There was a final short pause, followed by. "Stand easy."

"Sir."

"Private, this is Elizabeth. She's going to get you home."

Elizabeth looked deep into his eyes. "Maurice?"

"Maurice Alan Peter Carpenter, marm."

"Are you ready to go home, Maurice?"

"Yes, marm."

"Is there anything you want to ask me?"

He looked nervous.

"Ask me anything."

"Will I meet everyone again, marm? You know, my family."

"I don't know, Maurice."

He looked confused. "Marm?"

"I still have to make this journey, but my belief and my faith tell me you'll meet them again." She lifted her hand close to his face. "Do you have faith, Maurice?"

"Yes, marm. Although it hasn't helped me much, has it? Stuck here for God knows how long. Pardon the language, marm."

"What you've suffered would strain the faith of a saint." She pressed her hands together as if in prayer. "Will you place your trust in me?"

He frowned, sighed, looked deeply into her eyes. "I trust you, marm." He took one pace back and looked up at the ceiling. "Am I going up there?" he said, pointing up, his voice tremulous. "You know, marm. Heaven?"

"I don't know, Maurice. We discover the truth when we take this final journey."

"Will it hurt?"

She shrugged and shook her head. "I don't think so."

He took a few steps back and stared at his boots. "If it's alright, marm, I think I'll stay."

Captain Forster walked up beside him. "Is there a problem, private?"

"Yes sir."

"What is it?"

"Lady doesn't know what's going to happen to me, sir." He glanced across at Elizabeth. "Beg pardon, marm."

Captain Forster looked across at Elizabeth and raised his eyebrows.

She smiled softly. "Maurice, there are many mysteries interwoven into the lives we lead. Unexplainable events shape this life and others we still have to live. Until we make this final journey, none of us know what lies next. But what must be true, is if you're still here after a hundred years, there is life after death."

He frowned and nodded.

"You've had no-one to guide you to journey's end. Let me be your guide."

He carried on frowning, then slowly nodded.

"Shall we finish the journey you started so many years ago, Maurice?"

He swallowed hard, looked at Captain Forster, saluted, and despite his fears, nodded to Elizabeth. "Thank you, marm. It's time to go home. I miss Edna and the baby. Wherever I go next, can't be worse than drifting in this endless nothing. What have I got to do, marm?"

"Just stand a little closer to me and hold out your hands."

He shuffled a little closer to Elizabeth and held out his hands. "Like this, marm?"

"Perfect. Bless you and God speed, Maurice."

Elizabeth positioned her hands directly over his and a spark of energy connected them. He gasped and looked up wide-eyed at the ceiling. Elizabeth's hands began to tremble and then shake as a red aura began to form around Private Carpenter. She struggled to keep her hands above his, as powerful forces did their best to force them apart. Little by little, Maurice's form became fuzzy, and less distinct. Elizabeth struggled to keep her hands close to his, but eventually had to stand back, exhausted by the effort. The hazy outline of Maurice was finally lost, as it metamorphosed into a turbulent red cloud which shrank to the size and shape of a football spinning rapidly on its axis. She backed away from Maurice and moved closer to Captain Forster. The ball of spirit-energy began to vibrate and hum like a child's spinning top, its shape stretched and elongated into a tube as it rose slowly into the air. It hovered, suddenly rocketed to the ceiling, and disintegrated into a thousand glittering red shards.

"Is it always like this?" Captain Forster asked, his eyes fixed on the ceiling.

Elizabeth frowned, wiped away a tear, and then smiled. "You haven't seen this before, have you?"

He shook his head. "No. This was the first time. It's … well it was…"

"Difficult to find the words, isn't it?"

He nodded again.

Elizabeth smiled. "You go down and tell the next Tommy I'll be ready," she said and looked at her watch, "in about half an hour."

He snapped to attention and saluted her. "Marm, you are a saint." He turned sharply and made his way downstairs.

Elizabeth pulled her camping chair close to the window, sat down, turned on the sound centre, and successively opened iTunes, artists - Mumford and Sons, albums - Babel, and selected track five - 'Ghosts that We Knew.' She pressed play, and as the song washed over her, she could no longer contain her emotions. She buried her head in her hands, and her body racked with sobs as she thought of Private Maurice Carpenter.

"That was so beautiful."

"Rather wonderful, wasn't it Gloria? Wouldn't you like to take that journey? Things would be so much better for you on the other side."

"Too late for me now. I'm already damned for eternity."

"Damned for what? For hating a vicious, wife-beating pig of a man? That's not a sin. What is a sin, is letting this hate fester and carrying it beyond the grave. God only seeks forgiveness. Forgive him and you can move on."

# Chapter Forty-Three

Klaus came into the kitchen and stood close to the sink while the others sat around the table drinking tea.

"Also meine freunde, lassen sie uns loslegen. *(So my friends, let us get started.)*"

Sam raised his eyebrows and smiled. "I don't think we're quite up to that level of German."

"Sorry, Sam." He gently slapped his wrist and smiled. "I was saying we should make a start."

Jane sat playfully at attention. "You have our undivided attention."

"Let's start. I have been a member of Papaver Rhoeas for longer than I care to remember, and in all that time, I have never seen anything like this." He glanced towards the gently oscillating blue glow around the edges of the lounge door.

Sam sat forward and leaned on the table. "I'd like to discuss next door."

Klaus raised one eyebrow. "Is that where you were running from when we arrived?"

Sam nodded. "Takanun was built with copies of the plans for High Wood."

Karsten and Klaus glanced questioningly at each other.

"Takanun is identical to High Wood?" Klaus's expression gave away his shock.

He nodded.

"In every detail?"

Sam nodded. "From what I've seen, it is a mirror image of High Wood."

"But Arnold and Edith said nothing of this to us," Klaus said with a mild degree of annoyance in his voice.

"I don't believe they knew," Sam replied. "Marie told me the families were close friends and agreed to use the Morbeck's plans for both houses."

Klaus shook his head. "This is unheard of. Plans for portals were only drawn up to build portals." He walked to the sink, filled a glass with tap water, and drained it. "They should not have done this." He raised his hands to his face. "My God, how many other places has this happened in?"

Sam shrugged. "I can only tell you what I've been told."

"The question is," Klaus said, his anger slowly beginning to subside. "does Taka … What was it called, Sam?"

"Takanun."

"Yes Takanun. Does Takanun possess the same powers as High Wood?" He walked around the kitchen, his fingers intertwined around the back of his neck. "Structurally, it is entirely possible it could function as a portal."

Sam nodded in agreement. "Luca and Lorenzo materialised in their cellar."

"You saw this?" Klaus's interest was tinged with annoyance. "A materialisation in Takanun?"

Sam nodded. "From a blue orb.

"Blue? You are sure of this, Sam?"

Sam edged back, turned his head towards the lounge door, and pointed. "Exactly the same colour as that."

Silence fell over the room.

"I need to go next door," Klaus said as he stood up.

"Now?" Sam said wide-eyed.

"Ja. Jetzt. Now!"

"At least let me go around first. They know me and I can explain to them what it is we want to discuss."

Klaus blew noisily through his nose. "Ja. Call me immediately you have spoken to them."

Sam felt like a schoolboy being chided for forgetting his homework. "Yes, Klaus."

Marie was making herself a ham omelette when the front door bell rang. She turned the heat down as low as it would go and walked to the front door.

"Sorry, it's me again," Sam said, blushing with embarrassment.

"Still got a problem, Noah?" She giggled and stood to one side. "Come in. Still got a problem with your flood?"

Sam stepped into the hall and laughed. "Ah, my flood. I was wondering if I could speak to your parents? I wanted to ask them about our houses."

"Come into the kitchen. I was just cooking an omelette." She turned and trotted down the hall.

Sam followed her, and sat at the kitchen table as she turned out her omelette onto a plate, and began to eat.

"What exactly was it you wanted…?"

"Sam. Please call me Sam."

Marie smiled. "How can I help you, Sam?"

He breathed deeply. "I wanted to have a chat with your parents about our houses." He shifted uncomfortably in his chair. "It's to do with how they were built."

Marie frowned as she picked at her omelette. She pushed her plate to one side and wiped her mouth with a serviette. "How they were built? Odd sort of question."

Sam sucked in his cheeks. "Can I talk with your parents?"

Marie pursed her lips and shook her head. "You'll have to talk to me. Mum and Dad are getting on, and their memories aren't as sharp as they used to be." She pulled her chair closer to the table, rested on her elbows, and looked closely at him. "Tell me what's so obviously bothering you."

He leaned back in his chair. "Before I start, please understand that what I'm about to tell you is true. You'll need to suspend your beliefs in what you think is … well, normal."

She smiled and raised her eyebrows. "Now you've got my undivided attention. So the flood was just a little fib to get into the house?"

"Something was leaking into your cellar, but it wasn't water."

Marie leaned forward and felt Sam's forehead. "You're not running a temperature? Taken any illegal substances?"

Sam smiled. "Not for quite a few years."

"Then you've firmly pressed my curiosity button."

Sam spoke calmly and slowly. "Do you believe that after death, we go on to another place?"

Marie leaned back in her chair, narrowed her eyes, and stared at him. "Is this a wind up?"

Sam shook his head. "I wish it was."

She stared silently at him for a few seconds, chewed her lip, sat back in her chair, and crossed her arms. "Carry on."

"As I said, do you believe in a life after death?"

"Possibly."

"At least that's better than a straight no." He sat back and relaxed a little. "Do you believe in ghosts?"

"Yes."

*"Odd she doesn't seem particularly surprised by the word ghost?"* His other-half decided it was time to have a say.

*"Do you deliberately wait for the most inappropriate moments?"*

*"I'm only saying, that it seems bloody odd to me that you walk into someone's kitchen, ask them if they believe in ghosts, and they just smile, and say yes. That's all I'm saying."*

*"Well, piss off, and say it to someone else."*

His other-half huffed and disappeared.

"You do?" Sam couldn't hide his obvious surprise.

"I've believed in them for years."

Sam was nonplussed. "What … but how did you …?"

Marie took out a gold stud earring and pulled at her ear lobe. "A few days after my Auntie Audrey died, I went to pay my respects at Pidgeons, they're a funeral home on Cowbridge Road. I was stood by her open coffin." She shook her head and swallowed hard. "I hate the way they make-up the dead. Looks so wrong. Auntie Audrey looked more like a doll than how I'd known her. In a lot of ways, I wish I hadn't seen her like that." She pulled at her top lip. "I bent down to kiss her goodbye, and as I did, it felt as if something passed through me. You know, when you say someone's walked over your grave?" She looked questioningly at Sam.

"Yes."

"I turned around, and standing close behind me was Auntie Audrey. We had a chat. She said she was fine and she knew she'd soon move on. It was so comforting to know there was something more after this," Marie said in a perfectly matter-of-fact tone.

Sam was speechless.

"Cat got your tongue, Sam?"

He stared open-mouthed at this singular young woman.

"Catching flies now?" She was finding it difficult not to laugh out loud.

Sam took a deep breath and gathered his thoughts. "Ever wonder what goes on next door?"

She shook her head. "I often spoke with Arnold and Edith, but I didn't think about what they did. I've always 'felt' there was something odd about High Wood. It seems to give off a sort of warm glow?" She suddenly shook her head and pointed at Sam. "I *knew* I'd seen you before. You used to visit Arnold and Edith, didn't you?"

He nodded. "They were my uncle and aunt. I used to take them to lunch, and on trips, but sadly, they recently passed away. I inherited the house and everything which came with it."

"Are you going to tell me what the 'everything' was?"

He leaned forward. *"In for a penny in for a pound,"* he thought. "High Wood is a 'special' place." He paused and clasped his hands together. "In the First World War, tens of thousands of soldiers were slaughtered. They were cut to pieces by machine guns, blown into atoms by shells, and dismembered by shrapnel. But their bodies were unidentifiable, or just impossible to find. So they were never buried and their families could never mourn. Their spirits are marooned and unable to pass onto the next life."

Marie said nothing, but gestured for him to continue.

"An organisation was established called Papaver Rhoeas, to find these missing souls and help them find their way home."

"Papava Reeza?"

"It's the Latin name for the Flanders poppy."

Marie smiled, remembering the deep bed of red poppies in their garden. "Carry on, Sam. You haven't lost me yet."

"High Wood's a portal, a sort of gateway, where the souls of these soldiers are helped to escape Purgatory." He paused and blew his nose in a crumpled tissue." I'm probably not explaining this very well."

"You're doing remarkably well, given what you're trying to tell me."

"Once they've passed over, we believe they're reunited with their families and loved ones." He sighed about as deeply as was possible, without sucking all the air out of the room.

Marie stared deep into Sam's eyes. "And you want to discuss this with my parents?"

"I was hoping to," Sam said. His hopes now significantly deflated by her response.

She carried on staring at him and then smiled. "Even if they wanted to, they couldn't help you, Sam. They've both got dementia." She breathed deeply and chewed the inside of her cheek. "The bloody thing started about three years ago, and it's just got progressively worse. Dad just watches recordings of TV quiz shows, and Mum knits the same scarf over and over again." She wiped a tear away from her eye and swallowed hard.

"I am so sorry. It's a horrendous disease."

"It's OK. Well, to be honest, it isn't, but you get on with life don't you." She stood up. "But before the 'long goodbye' took hold of him, Dad told me about the history of this house." She stood up. "Cup of tea? This could take a while."

Sam nodded. "Thanks. I'll call next door and tell them what we're doing."

Marie nodded, got up, and walked to the stove.

Sam tapped Klaus's contact icon on his iPhone.

"Bauer." It was Klaus's usual abrupt response.

"Klaus. It's Sam."

"Ah, Sam. I'll come around now."

"Not yet."

"Bitte?" There was no attempt to hide the aggravation in his voice.

"I'm speaking with Marie. I need more time. Her parents have dementia."

"Sugar?" Marie called over her shoulder to Sam.

"Just milk, please. Please, Klaus, leave this with me for a few more minutes?"

There was the sound of a frustrated sigh. "Ja." The line went abruptly dead.

Marie brought tea and biscuits back to the table.

"URANUS!" An excited shout came from the lounge. "NOT JUPITER!"

"Sorry about that." Marie swallowed hard. "Quiz programmes. Like I said, they're all he's got."

"Don't apologise." Sam smiled and sipped his tea. "You were going to tell me the story of Takanun."

"My great-great-grandfather, I think that's right, Joseph Stridham, was a grocer and lived above the shop with his family. Adam Morbeck, a lifelong friend, was a successful local butcher, and they were both Freemasons."

Sam choked on a custard cream. "Adam Morbeck was my great grandfather."

Marie chuckled. "Small world, isn't it? In 1912, Joseph and Adam bought a plot of land together to build two houses. Unfortunately, it wasn't until after the First World War that any building work started. From what I've managed to discover, Adam already had plans drawn up, and let Joseph copy them."

"And they built High Wood and Takanun."

"Not quite. Originally, the houses were called Outlook House, and Prospect House."

"I can make an educated guess why Rebecca changed Outlook House to High Wood, but what happened to change the name of Prospect House?" Sam said, finishing his tea.

"I'll come to that. In 1919, Joseph's business went bust and he didn't have any money to finish building Prospect House. When Outlook House was completed, Adam Morbeck suggested to Joseph that he and his family lived with them until they had the funds to complete Prospect House."

"Their friendship must have been unbelievably strong," Sam said. "Two families in one house?"

"They were bound together by a shared grief and High Wood's a big house."

Sam looked questioningly at Marie.

She continued. "As you know, Adam and Jack Morbeck were both lost in the First World War."

Sam nodded.

"Joseph's twin boys George and Henry, were killed within two days of each other at the Battle of the Somme. His wife Edna was devastated by their deaths and couldn't cope with the loss. She died in 1918 of a broken heart. She's buried at a local church with Joseph."

Sam's mind was torn by the thought of the concentrated anguish of the two families seeping into the bricks and mortar of High Wood.

"By 1922," Marie continued. "Joseph, with Fred and Bert's support, established a successful new hardware store, and work finally started to complete Prospect House. It was then Fred Morbeck changed the name of Outlook House to High Wood. But you know that, don't you?"

Sam nodded.

Marie drained her tea, stood up, and walked to the fridge. "Something a little stronger? I've got a lovely Verdicchio Castelli at just the right temperature."

He didn't need much persuading.

"Good, isn't it?" she said with a satisfied smile.

"Mmmm. Very good." He took the bottle and read the label. "Must get some of this." He looked up at Marie. "So Joseph finally finished building the house?"

"Yes. It took longer than they thought, but by 1924, the family had moved into Prospect House."

"So who changed the name?"

"My great-grandfather Maurice. Prospect House became Takanun in 1959."

"Any particular reason?"

"The birth of his son Edward." She paused. "He was named after his grandfather, who was killed in the Second World War."

"But why Takanun?"

"Edward died in Burma. He was a POW and was worked to death by the Japanese. The house should really be called Tarkkanun, with an 'r' and a double 'k'. Edward died in Tarkkanun Camp, and the name must have been misspelt as Takanun."

Sam sat back in his chair and finished the glass of Verdicchio.

"Another?" Marie asked. "You look like you need it."

Sam nodded. *"Why didn't I know about this?"* he thought.

*"Why the hell should you? None of your business, was it?"*

*"Back are you?"*

*"Just trying to bring some balance to the discussion."*

*"Balance my arse."*

"Sam?"

"Mmmm?"

"You seem a bit distracted?"

"No. Just trying to take it all in."

"Do you want me to go on?"

He nodded. "Was Edward found and buried?"

"No. From what I've researched, the Japanese weren't too fussy about how they disposed of the bodies of POWs. It was something which always upset great-grandad Maurice, and finding Edward's body became an obsession with him. He tried for years to find him, but it was never going to be possible." She shook her head. "But at least Edward's remembered on a memorial in the National Arboretum."

Sam's phone rang in his pocket. "Sorry, I should have had it on silent."

She gestured for him to take the call.

"Sam."

"You've been there for almost an hour. Am I coming around?"

"Klaus?"

"Ja. Of course." The reply was curt.

"Leave it with me, and I'll tell you everything when I get back."

There was silence on the other end of the line.

"Klaus?"

Silence.

"Problem, Sam?" Marie said.

Sam put his hand over the phone. "I've a visitor from Germany who wants to come around." He raised his eyebrows and shrugged.

"That's fine. The more the merrier. Ask him to come over."

"Klaus? Marie says to come over."

"Gute. Ich werde es in ein paar sekunden sein. *(Good. I'll be there in a few seconds.)*"

"What did he say?"

"Not sure, but I think he'll be here shortly."

# Chapter Forty-Four

Desiree rang the doorbell at one minute to ten.

"Come in my dear. Lovely to see you again." Molly shepherded her into the front room. "Charlie's in the kitchen. I'll give him a call."

A few seconds later, he walked slowly into the room. "Hi. Didn't expect to see you again so soon."

She patted the sofa for him to sit down next to her. "I had such a lovely time last night." The word lovely was drawn out slowly. "Never had such a lovely time." She squeezed his hand. "You're quite a dark horse."

Charlie was paralysed with fear. Completely incapable of speech or movement.

Lidsay took over. "Great time, wasn't it?" He leaned across and whispered in her ear. "I didn't know anyone could be so flexible."

Molly came in from the kitchen with a tray of tea. "Lovely to see you two getting on."

"I was just saying to Desiree that I'd like to see a lot more of her." Lidsay continued. "Get to know her really well." Charlie struggled to regain control. "I've learnt so much in the short time she's been here."

"Me, too, Mrs Thompson. Charlie's got a real appetite for family history." She chuckled and prodded his arm.

Emma came in through the wall from the garden and stared distrustfully at Desiree. *"I don't like her."* She crossed the room, walked through Desiree and the sofa, and sat down next to Molly. *"She's hiding something. Can't quite get it, but she's not telling us everything."*

Molly ignored Emma's comments. "Charlie, you'll have to go up to, where was it again, dear?"

"Sheringham." She clapped her hands together. "I think that's a great idea. There are things I couldn't bring, which I could show Charlie." She looked at her watch and stood up. "Any chance you could run me to the station, Charlie?" She smiled at him. "We could agree some dates for you to visit Sheringham."

Charlie jumped up, Lidsay still pulling his strings. "No problem. I'll get the keys from the kitchen."

Emma walked through Desiree and across to the kitchen door. *"She's up to something."*

Molly continued to ignore her. "They're by the bread bin, dear." She got up and stood next to Desiree. "Thanks so much for coming. I think Charlie visiting you will bring him out of himself. You seem to have had a good effect on him."

"Yes, I probably pressed a few buttons no-one else has." She smirked to herself. "Family history can be addictive."

"Good. It'll take his mind off the police. I know it's always been his dream, but it's all he ever talks about."

"Yes, he did say he'd show me his handcuffs."

"There you are. Perfect example. You take him in hand, my dear, with my blessing."

"Thank you, Mrs Thompson, but I think I'll need both hands."

Molly laughed, despite not understanding the double-entendre. "Yes, he needs a lot of help." She chuckled. "Both hands."

Charlie came back with the keys, kissed Mum, and linked arms with Desiree. "Shouldn't be too long."

"Nice girl," Molly said with a pleasant smile as she turned on the TV.

*"Nice my left foot. He'll come to no good with her."* Emma hadn't given up.

"How soon can you come up?" Desiree asked.

Charlie agreed a date to visit Sheringham and dropped her at the Central Station.

"See you soon," she called over her shoulder as she pulled her case into the station.

Lidsay was tired after the efforts of last night and gave Charlie back control.

*"I need some fresh air,"* Charlie thought and decided to take a walk along the front at Penarth. He parked the car close to the pier, walked up

the hill to 'The Top', bought himself a pretty average coffee in the cafe, and sat down on a bench on the cliff top, overlooking the Bristol Channel, and the north coast of Devon.

"Constable Thompson?" The voice was unmistakably Detective Sergeant Morris's. "How are you? Refreshed, and ready to come back for the fight against crime?"

*"If I wasn't so knackered I'd sodding have you Morris. Still, softly softly, catchy arse head,"* Lidsay thought.

"Yes, thanks detective sergeant. I'm feeling a lot better." He looked out at the view. "I always come up here when I need to restore my belief in life and recharge the batteries." He turned slightly. "Any news on Sergeant Lidsay and his wife?"

*"You devious little shit,"* Lidsay spat at Charlie.

"What, Lord Scrote?" Morris chuckled. "No, nothing. Not too bothered about that miserable old bastard of a sergeant, but I'm still concerned about his missus. I've got a sneaking suspicion he's killed her." He blew on his steaming tea. "What do you think, Thompson?"

*"Watch what you pissing say."*

"He was always a little abrupt, ignorant, drunk, flatulent, smelly, unwashed, poorly dressed, overweight, pissed off with life, with pretty disgusting eating habits, but he never seemed like a murderer. The only person he ever seemed to really hate was … well, it was you detective sergeant. No offence."

*"You know me pretty bloody well,"* Lidsay said.

"Me. Can't understand that." Morris laughed out loud.

*"Laugh while you can, you twat. You're close to the top of my list."*

Charlie got up. "I'll see you at the station tomorrow detective sergeant?"

"Look forward to it, Charlie." It was the first time he'd ever used Charlie's name. "We can decide what to do about our 'late' colleague." He looked at the view and sipped his tea. "Take another look around that house before we meet. It might bring something extra to the discussion."

Charlie nodded and smiled.

# CHAPTER FORTY-FIVE

Guillaume stood close to Isaac in the rear rank of ten. He looked around him at row upon row of bedraggled, grimy, foul-smelling, emaciated men in ragged blue and white striped uniforms.

"What is this?" Guillaume whispered to Isaac.

Isaac's expression screamed, *"BE QUIET."* He looked around slowly, and seeing no-one was paying them any attention, he whispered out of the corner of his mouth. *"Roll call. Every morning and night, whatever the weather or time of year, they count the living and the dead. Some days they make us stand here for hours."* He shook his head and nodded to the man stood arrogantly at the front. *"He is the Kapo (Work foreman). He is selecting men for either work detail or punishment."* Isaac suddenly stood rigidly to attention and stared blindly to his front as the Kapo swaggered close to them.

"YOU TWO!" The Kapo was pointing a well-used leather whip at Isaac and Guillaume.

"SIR!" Isaac shouted out.

"And you?" The Kapo moved directly in front of Guillaume. "You have a problem?"

"Sir?" Guillaume's response wasn't what the Kapo wanted to hear, and the handle of the whip crashed into the side of his head.

"CONCRETE ROLLER!" He turned to Isaac. "AND YOU" The whip's handle flashed again as Isaac's shoulder felt its full force. "He screws up, you get the beating. NOW MOVE!"

Isaac grabbed Guillaume's arm and started to drag him away.

"STOP!" The Kapo screamed at them. "After the roller, report to the latrines. They need cleaning." The guards around the Kapo laughed and patted him on the back.

"Guillaume. Follow me." Isaac started to run. "*Now!*"

They ran around three barracks, until they came to an abrupt stop, close to 'The Roller'. It was a huge concrete roller which needed three men to pull and another three to push.

Guillaume glanced at Isaac and grimaced.

Isaac's eyes remained fixed on the roller. "Just do what I do."

For the next three energy-sapping hours, together with two French, and two Belgian prisoners, Isaac and Guillaume pulled 'The Roller', which compacted the earth of the 'street' which ran through the camp. Two men collapsed, and after being severely beaten, they were dragged away behind a barrack. The crackle of gunshots announced their fate. Guillaume, Isaac, and the other men collapsed onto the floor and leaned their backs against 'The Roller'.

The fat, sweaty Kapo in charge of their detail, a convicted murderer released from a Munich jail, knelt down in front of Isaac and Guillaume. "Not you two. GET UP." The words were spat in the faces.

They got to their feet, exhaustion doing its best to drag them back to the relative comfort of 'The Roller'.

"You have other duties." He prodded them hard in the chest with the handle of his whip. "LATRINES! NOW!" He helped them on their way with a kick to their backsides.

"We have to clean out the toilets?" Guillaume asked wide-eyed.

Isaac looked at him quizzically. "How long have you been here? You seem very naive about what happens in the camp."

"As you say, I know very little." Guillaume replied.

Isaac leaned forward and spoke quietly but firmly to him. "We will talk about this later. For now, do what I do, or they will shoot you."

As they got closer to the latrines, the stench became stronger and increasingly unbearable which made Guillaume spontaneously vomit as he ran. They gasped as they entered the long, wooden building containing the latrines. Guillaume almost passed out under the violent assault on his senses. Two wooden benches only separated by a few inches interspersed at regular intervals with holes about nine inches in diameter, stretched the entire length of the building. It was from these open sewers, that the miasma was spewing.

"My God, I've died and I am fallen into Hell," Guillaume said between short gasps for breath. "'Lo! Death has reared himself a throne, In a strange city lying alone, Far down within the dim West, Where the good and the bad and the worst and the best, Have gone to their eternal rest.'"

"'No rays from the holy heaven come down, On the long night-time of that town.' Poe has always been one of my favourite poets," Isaac said as he began to regain his breath.

Guillaume nodded. "How does anyone survive in this Hell?"

"Mostly they don't," Isaac said softly. "But for now, be grateful for an arrogant stupid Kapo."

Guillaume turned to look at Isaac. "Be *grateful*?"

"This place may not be the most 'fragrant', but it is considered by us, as one of the best job details."

Guillaume was beginning to think Isaac had gone completely insane. An understandable survival mechanism in this Gehenna, this nether world. "One of the *best* job details?"

"Most certainly the best and there are two reasons."

"Shouldn't we be working?" Guillaume interrupted.

Isaac shrugged. "The smell is so bad, that the guards never come in here. This is where news is exchanged, trades are made, and guerrilla activity is planned. This is the first reason." Isaac smiled. A rare thing in this abyss from which death was the only one means of escape. "The second, is we will reek of shit and piss. We will stink so badly that the guards won't come near us. Giving up our pride and vanity is a fair exchange for the promise of living another day. They try to dehumanise us, but all they do is give us opportunities to communicate and strengthen our resistance to their evil."

Guillaume looked closely at him and grimaced. "Isaac."

"Yes?"

"Exactly where are we?"

Isaac looked astonished at this question. "You don't know?"

*"Make this lie a good one,"* Guillaume thought rapidly. "I'm suffering from amnesia. I was caught in a shell blast."

Isaac raised an eyebrow but then smiled. "I have seen this before." He took his arm. "Come with me."

They walked to the back of the latrines and stepped outside.

Guillaume's expression of panic was quickly eased by Isaac. "They won't come anywhere near us." He smiled. "Our personal odour doesn't attract many companions. We'll have a few minutes before they'll expect us to go back inside." Isaac stretched out his arms. "This is Monowitz, a camp for Jewish slave labour. Over there is the Zigeunerlager, the Gypsy Camp. There are probably around fifteen thousand men, women, and children crammed into those barracks." He nodded to his right. "Over there, is E715. It's a POW camp. British, American, and Australians who all work as slave labour."

"But the Geneva Convention states…"

Isaac shook his head. "There are no conventions here. We have only one maxim. Survive this day." A black cloud suddenly enveloped the sun. Isaac looked up and nodded at a churning pall of smoke, hanging malevolently over an entrance to the bowels of Hell. A gateway that no particle of good or pulse of humanity could escape from. He struggled to maintain control of his emotions. "Three miles over there is Birkenau." That's the 'Death Camp'.

The word on its own was enough to tighten every muscle in Guillaume's chest. Slowly, his mind added a second name, which congealed his blood. "Auschwitz-Birkenau?" He barely managed to utter.

Isaac nodded and turned back to the latrines.

As Guillaume started to turn around, the direction of the wind changed and he was struck by a sickly, sweet smell. It was the nauseating odour of burning flesh from the crematoria. He dropped to his knees and buried his head in his hands, tears flowing down his face, sobs racking through his chest.

Isaac walked back to him, lifted him up, helped him into the latrines, and sat him down on the benches. "Now you remember?"

Guillaume nodded, looked up, and wiped his eyes and face with his filthy sleeve. "I remember."

A young man, once handsome, but now a wasted desolate shell, approached Isaac. His eyes were flashing everywhere, checking they were alone.

"I have what you wanted." His words were hushed and laboured.

Isaac stood close to him, and Guillaume watched as two small packages were exchanged.

Isaac walked up to Guillaume, shook his hand, and handed him the packages he'd been given by the young man.

Guillaume's eyes flew open in shock, but as he opened his mouth to speak, Isaac shook his head.

"Shhh. Hide them away. I need to get more." Isaac whispered, as he turned to join a group of three men sitting over the holes in the wooden benches.

A few minutes later, Isaac rejoined him. "I have everything I need." He looked around, and then pointed to a far corner. "There are buckets and mops there. Bring them over and we can do our 'cleaning'.

As Guillaume dropped the buckets between himself and Isaac, he noticed a group of four men, stood either side of the latrine-bench. Between them, he could see a small child with his ragged trousers still up. He was about to look away, when the child jumped up onto the bench, forced himself through the hole, and dropped down into the excrement filled trench beneath. Guillaume tugged his sleeve, started to point, but Isaac stopped his arm in mid-air.

"We never point."

"But that child, he'll … he'll drown in that … that filth."

Isaac shook his head. "He won't drown. He is hiding. We will bring him what food and water we can. There are others down there with him."

"But how can anyone … my God … how can he?"

"Down there, he won't be whipped, beaten, gassed, or shot." He shrugged. "It's a terrible price, but it is worth paying."

Guillaume was about to speak again, but Isaac shook his head.

"Mop the floor."

As they pushed their mops around the latrines, Guillaume watched as men, women, and children came into the building, and sat by side emptying their bladders and bowels into the already overflowing open cess pit below, and over its 'inhabitants'.

As darkness fell, Isaac gestured to Guillaume to put the buckets and mops back, and follow him out of the latrines. As they shuffled back on the compacted earth to their barracks, he realised how right Isaac had been about the value of their personal malodour, as everyone scowled at them, and gave them a very wide berth. It had been a price worth paying.

# Chapter Forty-Six

A beaming Elizabeth left the gallery and made her way down to the kitchen. "I'd forgotten how wonderful that made me feel."

Captain Forster walked slowly past her. "Tea?"

"Please."

Klaus strode purposefully past her.

"Klaus? Where are you going?" she asked civilly.

"Next door." He replied abruptly and carried on towards the front door.

"Just asking," Elizabeth said to his back, with obvious irritation in her voice.

He turned, slightly red faced, and apologised. "Es tut mir leid. *(I am sorry.)*" I am going next door to see Sam and our neighbour."

"I'm coming with you," Elizabeth said as if it wasn't up for discussion.

Klaus raised an eyebrow. "Shouldn't you carry on with what you have started?"

She grimaced. He was right. How could she start, and then after saving one soul, stop? "You're right. I'll stay and carry on."

"The right decision, my dear. Was there something you wanted to ask him?"

"Not really. I just wanted to know more about that house."

"I will tell you everything when I get back. Karsten, contact Guillaume, and let him know what has happened."

"Ja, Vater."

Klaus turned, and walked to the front door.

"Cup of tea?"

Elizabeth turned around and saw that Captain Forster was holding out a cup of tea to her. "Thanks."

As they sat down at the table, a loud knock from the front door echoed down the hall.

"Father has forgotten something," Karsten said with a smile. "I'll go. You finish your tea." He pulled open the front door. "Vater."

"I could have walked through the door, but I didn't think it would have been very good manners." Caterina replied. "Hello, Karsten."

"Guten Morgen, Frau Mather. Please come in."

Caterina walked into the hall, followed by Mr Mather, Alfredo, Luca, and Lorenzo. They peered at the blue glow around the lounge door, glanced briefly at each other, shrugged, and walked into the kitchen.

"Caterina. So lovely to see you again," Elizabeth said with genuine affection. "And all the family."

Caterina smiled at everyone in the kitchen. "I promised you I would come back."

"Sam and Klaus are next door." Elizabeth got up from the table. "They're meeting our neighbours." She patted her chair. "Sit down."

She shook her head. "That's OK. I didn't say a time when I might come. How long do you think they'll be?"

"Let me call Sam and find out for you."

Klaus joined Sam and Marie in the kitchen. "Hallo. Ich bin Klaus Bauer."

"Willkommen bei Takanun. Ich bin Marie Stridham."

"Sie sprechen ausgezeichnet Deutsch. *(You speak excellent German.)*"

"Danke, Klaus."

Sam scratched the side of his head and raised his hands. "And for those of us who aren't fluent in German?"

"I'm sorry, Sam. We were just introducing ourselves to each other," Marie replied. "I lived in Germany for three years, and I don't often get a chance to speak German."

"You speak like a native, my dear." Klaus silently clapped. "Now, please, tell me everything you know about the house."

Sam's mobile vibrated in his pocket. "I'll take this while you tell Klaus the story."

Marie nodded and started to outline to Klaus what she'd told Sam earlier.

"Hi Elizabeth."

"Sam, Mrs Mather and her family are here. Remember she said she'd come back?"

"Yes. They were considering whether they'd help us or not."

"I don't know what she's decided, but she wants you and Klaus to be here before she tells us."

"Can't leave here for a while yet."

"OK, but how long do you think 'a while' will be?"

"Difficult to say, to be honest. Half an hour? Could be longer?" There was a pause. "Why don't we go around to her house later today when we've finished here?"

"Let me see what she says."

There was a pause.

"That's fine, Sam. She'll bake some cakes and have high tea ready for us at three o' clock."

"Thank her for me, and ask her if she could make one of those cheesecakes. We'll be as quick as we can." Sam walked back into the kitchen.

"THE LITTLE RED BOOK."

Klaus looked around him and frowned. "Was zum Teufel war das? *(What the Hell was that?)*"

"Es tut mir Leid Klaus. Mum and Dad have dementia."

Klaus's expression saddened. "Demenz." He shook his head. "I am so sorry. It is a terrible condition."

"Why are you here?" Marie's question was direct.

"To the point, my dear," Klaus replied. "I like that. We have a problem, and I believe that you, or rather your house, may be able to play a part in a possible solution."

Marie sat back and crossed her arms. "You intrigue me sehr geehrter Herr."

"I should explain who and what we are, what we do, and why I believe this house, may play a part in solving a big problem we are facing."

"Please carry on."

Over the next twenty minutes, Klaus explained the history of Papaver Rhoeas, the function of the memorials and portals, how High Wood operated, and the dilemma of the blue lights.

"That would make a brilliant film," Marie said with a mischievous smile. "But how does this house play any part in helping you with these blue lights?"

Sam leaned forward. "Can we go down to the cellar?"

"Still got a fixation on my cellar, Sam?" Her mischievous smile was back. "I'm sure Klaus wants to take a look." She looked at him, and raised an eyebrow.

"Ja natürlich." He liked this singular young woman.

"I'd say follow me, but you know the way."

"Come with us?" Klaus said.

"I planned to. I wouldn't miss this for the world."

"OH FOR GOODNESS SAKE."

"Sorry again about …"

"HE WAS THE KING OF SWEDEN."

"His mind seems to be pretty sharp," Sam said with a frown.

"The answers he gives, have unfortunately got nothing do with the questions."

"Sorry, I didn't…"

"How could you, Sam? Come on, show me the secrets of the cellar." She chuckled to herself, opened the cellar door, made a dramatic gesture of looking around, and then trotted down the steps to the cellar. When she reached the bottom, she stopped abruptly, and again looked all around her.

"What colour did you say those lights were?" She called out.

"Blue."

There was silence from the cellar floor.

"Marie?"

"You'd better come down," she said softly.

Sam reached the cellar floor, stopped abruptly, and Klaus walked into the back of him.

"Sein Sie vorsichtig. *(Be careful.)*"

As far as the eye could see, the cellar was a mass of twinkling blue stars.

Marie turned to face them. "Now you have my full attention."

"Scheiße!"

"Shit indeed, but what the hell are they, and how come I can suddenly see them?" she said, with an expression like parents who have just seen their teenage daughter's mobile phone bill.

"We should go back upstairs. There is nothing we can do down here," Klaus said quickly and headed back up the steps.

"Do you have the original plans of the house?" Klaus asked Marie, as they sat down at the kitchen table.

She screwed up her face in thought. "Never mind the plans. What the hell was that in the cellar? Why are they in our house? And how come I can see them?"

Klaus leaned across the table, and gently held her hand. "My dear. You must have abilities which you were not aware of."

Sam smiled at Marie. "I think you'll find Klaus, that she does know about at least one of her abilities."

Klaus shrugged. "Was meinst du? *(What do you mean?)*"

"As the boy in the Sixth Sense said, 'I see dead people,'" Marie said with a wicked smile. "'De profundis clamo ad te, domino.'" Her voice was suddenly a rich baritone.

Sam was struck dumb. His expression frozen in fear.

"It's Latin Sam. 'Out of the depths I cry unto thee, O Lord.'" Klaus translated. He peered deep into Marie's eyes. "Bist du OK, meine Liebe? *(Are you OK, my dear?)*"

"Ich bin mir nicht sicher. (I'm not sure.)" Marie was clearly badly affected by the 'voice'.

"You have strong untapped abilities which make these other realities visible to you. To most, these other realities are sensed, but never seen. They are only aware of a trace of their presence. It can be a sudden unexplained chill in a room, a single pure white feather, a whispered voice, a familiar smell, an old toy which suddenly plays a tune, a stair or floorboard which creaks. But only a few, a special few, can see beyond these whispers and echoes to the true causes. Ghosts, spirits, phantoms, they have many names, but there are only a few who can enter their reality and communicate with them."

"And you believe I can do this?" Marie had recovered her composure and was now remarkably calm.

"I know that. Sie sind etwas Besonderes. *(You are something special, my dear.)* I believe, that the enormous concentration of spirit-energy in this house has finally overcome your mind's natural resistance to accepting the existence of these things."

Marie raised an eyebrow. "Bin ich was besonderes? *(I'm something special?)*"

Klaus nodded and smiled. "In many ways. You and I should speak further on this. I am certain you can help us."

Marie squeezed Klaus's hand. "Ich würde gerne. *(I would like to.)*"

Klaus glanced at Marie and pursed his lips. "If I could see the plans to Takanun, I may be able to provide an answer to the blue lights."

"They could be up in Dad's room in the loft. That's where he keeps all his 'stuff'. It's probably the best place to make a start."

"High Wood's are with my solicitor." Sam chipped in.

"Can you get them, Sam? I believe that together with the plans of Takanun, they could hold the answer." Klaus stood up, steepled his fingers, pressed them to his nose, and walked around the kitchen table. "So, to summarise, Takanun was built with the copied plans of High Wood."

Marie and Sam nodded.

"At first Takanun was partly built and completed at a later date."

Sam and Marie kept silent and still, as Klaus was clearly constructing a possible hypothesis.

He stood up and walked to the sink, looked up, and stared out at the garden.

Minutes passed.

Finally he turned, and walked back to the kitchen table. "I need to see the plans."

"Give me a few minutes," Marie said. "Dad has the keys."

"You know, don't you?" Sam said as he sucked in his lips.

Klaus's expression gave nothing away. "I believe I may have an insight into what is happening." He looked after Marie. "But first, I must see the plans." He turned back to Sam. "Call your solicitor, and get him to bring the plans to High Wood. I need to compare them with this house."

# Chapter Forty-Seven

Desiree arrived back in Sheringham early in the afternoon and got a taxi home. As she walked through the front gate, her father was eagerly waiting for her.

"How did it go?" He asked as he took her case from her.

"Really well. You'll never believe what I've discovered."

"I'm afraid I left my psychic hat in the cupboard," Dad said, as he held the front door open for her.

Desiree ignored the soft sarcasm. "I know who Ian Thompson's father was." She left it hanging in the air for a few seconds. "He was a man called Peter Wallins. The most unbelievable thing, is Ian's mum and dad lived here!"

Dad frowned.

"Emma and Reg lived in Cambrai for about fifty years."

Dad's eyebrows raced each other to the top of his head. "Fifty years?" He dropped Desiree's case and walked quickly into the lounge. "Henry, Desiree's found that Ian Thompson's mum and dad lived here for fifty years." His eyebrows began to subside from the summit.

"There you are. I said she wasn't wasting her time," Mum said with a small degree of self-satisfaction.

A beaming Desiree followed Dad into the lounge. "Isn't it brilliant?"

"Amazing, darling. Can I get you something?" Mum asked as she carried two empty mugs to the kitchen.

Desiree looked a little crestfallen.

Mum stopped and put down the mugs on a coffee table. "I'm sorry, Des'. It's amazing what you've done. Dad and I really want to hear all about it, so you have a shower, and I'll get some food together."

"Good idea. I feel grubby, hungry, and tired."

After a relaxing hot shower, glass of wine, lasagne, a few more glasses of wine, cherry pie and cream, and coffee and Amaretto, Desiree cuddled up on the sofa, and told mum and dad almost everything that had happened in Cardiff.

"Remind me again who was there?" Dad asked.

"Charlie and his mother Molly."

"Will they come?" Dad asked as he bit into an apple.

"Only Charlie. I think his mum's very ill. She didn't say anything, but she was the colour of parchment. Like someone with cancer."

"Oh no," Mum said with compassion. "Poor woman."

"You didn't say anything about us?" Mum asked as she chased a grape off her lap and onto the floor.

"Of course not." She sat down, breathed deeply, stared at the ceiling, and loudly sucked her teeth. "But, you know, there was something other-worldly about Charlie."

Mum smiled as the grape disappeared under a chair. "Other-worldly?"

"As if he could see things like we do."

"Did you see anything dear?" Dad asked.

Marie nodded. "Emma was there."

"You're sure it was her?

She nodded. "I'm certain. Charlie could see her, and I heard his mum whispering to her. She used her name."

# Chapter Forty-Eight

Klaus's phone vibrated in his pocket. He took it out, glanced at the caller, and stood up. "Entschuldigen Sie mich, Marie. Ich muss den Anruf annehmen. *(Excuse me, Marie. I must take this call.)*"

Sam frowned.

"Gilles?" Klaus said as walked into the hall.

"Good afternoon Klaus."

"What is it? The lights in St Petersburg?"

"No. I can't get hold of Guillaume. He's so reliable and always at the end of the phone. I have called a number of times and he hasn't answered. I am very concerned."

Klaus frowned. Gilles was right, reliability was Guillaume's watchword. "When was this?"

"Yesterday, and again today. I have left messages on the land line, and his mobile, but I've had no replies. This is not like him, Klaus."

Klaus walked slowly up and down the hall.

"Klaus?"

"Yes. I was thinking." There was another prolonged pause. "I can think of no reason why he wouldn't answer. How soon can you get to Bloemenwerf?"

"No earlier than tomorrow. Shouldn't we call the police? He may have been taken ill."

"I'd like to avoid that if I could, but it may be that it is our only option." A belt was tightening around Klaus's chest, when a light came on in his head. "Call Renaat. He lives only a few kilometres from Bloemenwerf. I'll text you his number. Tell him to call me as soon as he gets there."

"I'll do it as soon as you put the phone down. How are things in the UK?"

"Elizabeth has restarted her work with the lost souls and Sam is working with me. Their holiday has helped a little, but it has also added a lot more scheiße for them to deal with. Now, please call Renaat. Auf Wiedersehen." The call ended and Klaus slipped his phone into his jacket pocket.

*"Klaus."*

"Isaac?" Klaus was startled but happy to hear his old friend, even if it was only in his head.

*"I cannot contact Guillaume. Do you know where he is?"*

"Gilles called me, and Renaat will check Bloemenwerf in the next hour," he answered, trying to hide his concern.

*"Good. I will come back to you then."*

"Why did you come, Isaac?"

*"I have spoken again with the architects and they believe they have a possible solution to the blue lights."*

"Klaus," Sam called from the kitchen.

*"I have to go."*

*"I'll speak to you in an hour. I'll tell you then what their proposal is."*

*"Auf Wiedersehen."*

*"Auf Wiedersehen."*

Klaus walked back into the kitchen. "Yes, Sam."

"We really should go. The Mathers will be expecting us."

Klaus nodded slowly. "Yes. Sorry, I'd forgotten. Marie, while we're gone would you look for the plans for me?"

She smiled. "Of course."

"If it's alright, we'll call back later today?"

"Yes, that'll be no problem." She picked up a pad and pen. "Give me your number in case something comes up."

Elizabeth was stood outside the front door reading emails on her phone as Sam and Klaus came out of the house *"Bloody spam,"* she thought. *"As soon as you unsubscribe from one, another ton of crap takes its place."*

"You coming?" Sam asked.

"Of course I'm coming. Don't get pissing arsey with me." She stormed past them with the car keys in her hand. "Are you coming?"

Klaus stopped dead in his tracks and turned to Sam. "Is this what you meant about her acting strangely?"

Sam nodded. "I've got to get her to a doctor."

Klaus stared at the back of her rapidly disappearing head. "She is too valuable for us to risk losing. You must take her tomorrow."

Sam nodded. "I'll do my best."

The sound of the car horn indicated Elizabeth was getting impatient.

After a thankfully brief car journey of smothering, uncomfortable silence, they arrived at the Mathers's.

# Chapter Forty-Nine

Charlie felt 'normal' again. He was back in uniform, back at the station, back on coffee duty for Detective Sergeant Morris, and thankfully back in mental silence, as his 'visitor', had been struck dumb for a few days.

However, the sight of Detective Sergeant Morris sitting behind his desk drinking coffee, joking with his mates, and sucking up to the detective inspector, brought Lidsay out of his stupor.

*"Let him make his own pissin' coffee. Lazy, devious, greasy-pole-climbing bastard."*

Charlie ignored him, his inner strength and untapped abilities, had begun to act as powerful psychic buffers.

*"I can still hurt you."*

*"Do your worst."* Charlie rasped back at him. *"You need me more than I need you."*

*"I can hurt those wankers you love."*

*"You'll need to go through me first!"*

*"Getting angry, constable? Looks like I've got your attention. And what have you got that would stop me."*

*"You'd be surprised what..."* Charlie bit his tongue.

*"I'd be surprised by what?"*

*"That's for you to find out. Now sod off and leave me alone."*

Lidsay decided to pull his neck in and keep his powder dry, uncertain about Charlie's threat.

Detective Sergeant Morris looked up from his desk at the steaming mug of coffee. "Cheers, Charlie, you must be telepathic. Handy thing for a policeman. Especially one who wants to be a detective." He tapped the side of his nose and gave him a knowing wink.

Charlie gave an embarrassed shrug. "More about remembering things, really."

"Still, bloody handy skill to have." He took the mug of coffee. "Sit down." He patted the stool close to him. "Let's catch up on Lord Scrote."

*"You cocky twat, Morris. Who the hell does he think he is calling me that?"*

Morris sipped his coffee and opened the file in front of him. "What information have you been able to pick up on our dearly departed sergeant?"

Charlie detailed as precisely as his memory and notes would allow, all the 'events' at High Wood, omitting the fact that Lidsay had taken up residence in the back of his mind.

"I've had an odd feeling about that place. Nothing I could put my finger on, but something just didn't feel right." Morris scribbled a few notes in the file and chewed the broken end of a cheap biro. "Perhaps our ex-sergeant was actually onto something." He pursed his lips. "I haven't got a bloody clue what, but I hate itches I can't scratch." He drained the last of the cold coffee in his mug and shuddered. "I do that every time. Bloody disgusting, cold coffee." He ran the biro over his notes and looked up at Charlie. "I'll get you wired and fixed up with a hidden camera. Go back to High Wood, and tell them you need to take one last look around the house. Examine every room and record everything you see and hear."

Charlie's smile stretched from ear to ear. He felt like Tom Cruise in 'Mission Impossible.'

# Chapter Fifty

Caterina had prepared a spread which Sam was overjoyed to see included his favourite cheesecake. She saw his expression. "Especially for you, Sam. Can I cut you a piece before my family devours it?"

He almost displaced a disc in his neck as he nodded a tad too vigorously.

Caterina got everyone food and drink, and then stood in the centre of the room. "Thank you all for coming."

Sam, Elizabeth, and Klaus smiled despite mouthfuls of Caterina's exquisite culinary and baking skills.

She smiled. "I'm happy you approve of the food."

"Sank you so mutt." Sam managed to mumble through a mouthful of half-chewed cheesecake.

Caterina mimed brushing crumbs from her dress and smiled. "Thank you, Sam. And so to business."

Alfred placed a dining table chair behind her. "There you are, my dear."

She smiled and sat down. "As I was saying, to business. The last few days have been the most interesting, intense, and illuminating of this life, and any others I may have lived. It's given me," she said, turned, and smiled at Luca and Lorenzo, who were stood close behind her, "my two sweet brothers back, shown me things, which even in this reality I didn't know existed, and posed problems which you have asked for our help. We have discussed this at great length." She looked over her shoulder at her husband. "Alfred, will you tell Sam and Elizabeth your thoughts?"

He spoke from where he sat. "My beloved Caterina has waited a long time to be reunited with her brothers, so why should she risk separation again on a journey to who knows where. However strong our beliefs are, I am not willing to take a chance of my dearest love losing everything so soon after she has found it." He paused, emotions taking hold of him. "I believe we should stay."

Caterina turned to Alfredo and gestured for him to speak.

"If everyone moves on, I'll be left on my own. This may seem selfish, but I have had mamma and papa with me since they died." He looked at his mother and father. "Most people suffer bereavement only once, and the thought of suffering this trauma twice, is too much to ask of me. We should stay and help you."

Caterina finally turned to Luca and Lorenzo. "Miei fratelli *(My brothers)*, Che ne pensi? *(What do you think about this?)*"

"I will speak … as good as is for me … in English." Luca replied uncertainly. "We … have for ever been … gone, lost. Now we are … trovato *(found)*, I think finded, we will not wish to go … go where we not know." He looked to his brother and smiled. "We think … both we stay."

Caterina smiled. "I understand. Sono d'accordo *(I agree with you)*. Having found you again," she said, and her eyes twinkled as she spoke, "I will not risk losing you again. When the Lord wants it of us, we will move on to a new life. But I want more time with all of you before we do this. We all say we should help you. Eventually we will think of a new life. But not just yet."

# Chapter Fifty-One

Klaus and Karsten decided it was best to stay at High Wood, and after a convivial supper of fish and chips eaten straight from the tray, they decided an early night was in order.

Klaus was sitting on the edge of his bed, looking out of the window over the back garden. Having spoken to Renaat, he was dreading Isaac making contact again. He didn't have to wait long.

*"What have you heard? Tell me exactly what Renaat saw at Bloemenwerf."*

*"I spoke to him a few minutes ago and he was very agitated. In the lounge at Bloemenwerf, there were some empty beer bottles, a half-eaten sandwich, the radio was playing, his shoes were next to the sofa ..."*

*"What else?"* Isaac's tone was fraught and impatient.

*"He found him on the floor, close to a chest of drawers."*

*"And?"* The level of concern in Isaac's voice increased.

*"At first, Renaat couldn't find any signs of life."*

*"WHAT!"*

*"He thought he was dead."*

There was a long painful silence.

*"Isaac?"*

*"Continue."*

*"The strangest thing, is that he was still warm, and when Renaat tried to move him, he sighed. Renaat ran for blankets to keep him warm, called an ambulance, and then called me."*

*"Call him now, and tell him to cancel any medical support. Do it now, Klaus!"*

A few seconds later, Klaus tapped the end call icon on his iPhone. *"It's done, but Renaat is very concerned and afraid of harming Guillaume."*

*"Guillaume is fine. Now tell me what else Renaat told you."*

He thought back on Renaat's account. *"Nothing really out of the ordinary."* There was a brief silence. *"It appeared he had been reading, but that's not unusual, is it?"*

*"What?"*

*"Mmmm?"*

*"What was he reading? It's important, Klaus."*

*"Poetry. He was reading World War One poetry."*

*"What poetry?"*

*"How should I know that?"*

*"Think, Klaus. What did Renaat say?"*

There was a long silence.

*"He said a book was open at a poem called, what was it, a month, yes, it was August 1914."*

There was silence from Isaac.

*"Isaac?"*

*"The poem is by Isaac Rosenberg. He was our uncle. We left Germany before the war started in '39, but Uncle Isaac stayed on. We know he was taken by the Nazis and I know where he died. His body was never found."*

Klaus was getting increasingly concerned. *"Isaac what is it? You know, don't you?"*

*"I believe I know where he is."*

*"Mein Gott, Isaac! Where?"*

*"Guillaume has additional abilities which you and I don't possess. He is able to move back and forth in time, to locate the missing, and to direct them home."*

*"Like Sam?"*

*"Almost like Sam. Although, Sam has abilities even I don't fully understand."*

Klaus was confused, worried, and he needed answers. *"Was tun wir? (What do we do?)"*

*"Isaac Rosenberg, our uncle, has cried out from the past, and Guillaume has answered. He has travelled to another reality, another time and place. Uncle Isaac's time and place. Guillaume's spirit has found him. However, Guillaume is unpractised in this. He will need help to return."*

Klaus was getting increasingly nervous. *"What help?"*

*"A Spirit Walker."*

Klaus blew out a long breath, and sniffed. *"I remember the last Spirit Walker who 'travelled', He is still in a psychiatric hospital. Not too long after that, the Astrea unanimously agreed Spirit Walkers would never again 'travel'."*

*"Klaus, Guillaume has 'walked' back and I will not leave my brother trapped in another reality."*

Like a calm before the storm, a stillness settled on the conversation.

*"Isaac?"* Klaus broke the silence.

*"With Adam's rescue, Sam has proved his ability as a Spirit Walker."*

*"You cannot expect him to do this. He has too much to lose."*

*"No risk is too high for my brother."* Isaac's tone was cold. *"If not Sam, then your son Karsten has the necessary abilities."*

Klaus was dumbstruck.

*"Think over what we have said and we will finish this conversation tomorrow. For now, I will tell you what the architects have told me."* Isaac was again in control of himself.

Klaus remained shocked and silent.

*"In late '46 and early '47, the memorials and portals were fitted with shields to prevent the lost souls of World War Two overwhelming their storage capacity. Concrete trenches, six feet deep, were poured around the existing foundations. The solution is simple. Replace the concrete."*

*"But why are they not working?"* Klaus asked.

*"They have been buried for almost seventy five years, and the concrete has corroded. Any work at High Wood, can be easily explained as necessary repairs to the existing foundations."*

*"And what of Takanun?"*

*"You will need to see the plans. If they match the plans for High Wood, then the solution is the same. However, as Takanun was never intended to be a portal, shields probably weren't added. It is our conclusion that the*

*house is overwhelmed with spirit-energies, and they are bleeding through into High Wood."*

"That makes sense." Klaus was still concerned. *"Do we have time to complete these repairs?"*

Isaac was silent for a few seconds. *"I don't know."*

*"How long do the architects say one repair will take?"*

"Two weeks?"

*"Isaac! Wait. I need detailed plans. What do I do about Guillaume? What do I tell Sam and Karsten?"*

*"Start typing and the words will come to you. I will speak with you again tomorrow and agree who is best placed to become the Spirit Walker."*

*"Isaac, one last thing. You said you knew where your uncle was."*

There was an unsettlingly long pause, but eventually the silence was broken by two devastating words.

*"Auschwitz-Birkenau."*

Klaus lay back on the bed and buried his head in a pillow.

# Chapter Fifty-Two

Charlie was outside Asda, with a list of mostly high-calorie, high-fat, high-sugar, high-salt, low-health, low-fibre snacks for the boys at the station. *"And they wonder why we've got an obesity problem,"* he thought to himself. *"Better call High Wood before I buy all this crap, and make an appointment for a visit. Don't want a repeat of last time."* He took out his mobile from his back trouser pocket and called High Wood.

Elizabeth took the call in the kitchen. "Constable Thompson, good to hear from you." There was a short silence as she listened to him. "This afternoon would be fine. Can you make that?"

"Yes. What time's best for you?"

"Two o' clock?"

"Two o' clock it is then. Goodbye, Mrs Morbeck."

Elizabeth chose not to correct him. "See you then, constable."

Sam walked in from the garden. "Who was that?" he said as he filled the kettle to make pot of tea.

"That young policeman wants to take another look around the house, to see if that obnoxious sergeant left any clues to his whereabouts."

Sam nodded and sat on the edge of the kitchen table, waiting for the kettle to boil.

After giving everyone their snacks, Charlie went to see Detective Sergeant Morris.

"I've got an appointment at High Wood this afternoon. Is there enough time to wire me up?" Charlie was like a child on Christmas morning with a new toy that needed batteries.

"No problem, constable. Good to see you acting so quickly. Sign of a good detective." He raised his eyebrows and waved at Charlie to follow him.

Two o' clock on the button, Charlie was stood nervously outside High Wood's front door with a concealed microphone taped to his chest and a hidden camera in the bag he was carrying.

"Come in, constable." Elizabeth stood back, inviting him in. "Cup of tea before you start your … not sure what to call it. Investigation?"

Charlie smiled. "Investigation's fine, and a cup of tea would be lovely. Thank you …"

"Please call me Elizabeth," she said warmly. "And can I call you something other than constable?"

"Charlie. Please call me Charlie."

He followed her into the kitchen, where the rest of the 'family' were gathered. Jane stopped changing the batteries in the wall clock, Adam backed out into the garden, Rebecca walked backwards through the wall into the hall, and Captain Forster and two Tommies marched through the oven into the sitting room.

"So Charlie," Elizabeth said as she handed him a mug of tea, "what is it you want to do?"

"Just take a final look around and see if there's anything which might give a clue to what's happened to the sergeant and his wife."

*"Don't worry about me, Charlie. I'm doing just fine and I really don't give a shit about what's happened to my darling wife."* Lidsay was back in High Wood. Exactly where he wanted to be.

After tea and a chat, Charlie started his 'tour' of the house. He walked through the downstairs rooms and then made his way upstairs. An hour later, he came back to the kitchen and thanked Elizabeth for her hospitality.

"Did you find anything?" she asked.

"No, nothing of any real interest. We'll keep this on file and see what happens." He shook Elizabeth's hand and made his way to the front door. "Thanks again for your help. I don't think we'll need to bother you again."

Later that afternoon, Charlie reviewed the video he'd recorded on a computer back at the station. The image from the small hole in the bag wasn't brilliant, but despite its high boredom quotient, Charlie payed close attention to the computer screen. He watched, as the various rooms passed across the screen until finally they came to the gallery.

Something indistinct, and almost oily in appearance, passed across the screen. It was like looking at a picture through frosted glass. He frowned, chewed his bottom lip, scratched the side of his head, steepled his fingers, rested them against his teeth, and alternately pressed rewind, pause, and play, slowly edging the image forward and back, frame by frame. Then an indiscernible shape haltingly made its way across the screen. He pressed pause, leaned forward, and peered intently at the shape. He moved the image forward, and sat bolt upright in the chair. There, in the centre of the screen, was the undeniable outline of a man in uniform. He moved the recording on, and two other hazy figures crossed the screen. For half an hour, over and over he re-ran the recording, but the gauzy figures were always there.

Detective Sergeant Morris walked to Charlie's desk. "Find anything?"

Charlie looked up from the screen. He wasn't ready to show his 'ghost' film to his superior yet. "Nothing yet. I didn't see or hear anything when I was there, and there doesn't seem to be anything on the video."

Morris sighed and shrugged. "Ah well, at least we tried. Thanks, Charlie. Good work." He turned and walked back to his desk.

*"My God, one visit on your own, and you think you're Inspector Morse."* Charlie had Lidsay under 'semi-control', but he was still vocal.

Charlie smiled to himself. He'd found that ignoring Lidsay was proving to be an effective way of controlling him. It was only when Lidsay was seething with emotions that his malevolent spirit-energy came close to overcoming Charlie's strong abilities.

*"I know you're there, and that's where you're staying. Now piss off and leave me alone,"* Charlie snapped.

Lidsay was tempted to respond, but decided restoring his energy levels, was the best plan. *"I'll be back, you cocky little shit,"* he thought to himself.

Charlie looked back at the screen, and rewound the video to the beginning. He tapped fast forward, and the images moved from the kitchen, into the hall, up the stairs, and into the bedrooms. He checked, and re-checked everywhere, but there were no more frosted images. No more 'ghosts'. He restarted the video in the gallery. It moved onto the landing, the stairs and finally into the cellar. As the camera scanned along the walls, he almost slapped the pause key. Moving, in and out of the walls, like a gentle Atlantic swell, were what looked like, hundreds of 'ghosts'. He took a screen shot and printed the image. That night, back at home, he opened Google Images, and searched them for 'Silhouettes- soldiers'. At the third row of the images, he stopped, and compared what he could see on the screen, to the screen shot he'd printed. It was an almost exact match.

"*Does Elizabeth know about these?*" he thought. "*Should I tell her about this? Those things I saw at High Wood must have been real. Was it ghosts moving things around?*" He walked to the kitchen and took a can of diet Coke from the fridge. "*What else could those things be?*" He sat down at the desk and accompanied the diet drink with a half a bar of chocolate.

"*You haven't listened to the sound recording.*" He reminded himself.

He plugged the memory stick into a USB port, loaded the file, and put on his headphones. There was a lot of conversation with Elizabeth, puffing and panting as Charlie climbed the stairs, a lot of silence, and in what had to be the kitchen, barely audible, was the sound of voices.

"*When I got back, only Elizabeth was in the kitchen.*" His mind was doing somersaults. He opened settings, and cranked up the background volume to maximum.

"*You sure he doesn't susp... anyth...*" A woman's voice.

"*I think he s... everyth....*" An older man's voice.

"*I thought ... first time ... came here, he nearly saw ...*" A different man's voice.

"*But he's ... said a word.*" Another woman's voice.

"*Elizabeth can ... he'll soon...*" First woman's voice.

The rest was so indistinct, he couldn't understand anything. He put the photo in a plastic file, picked up his laptop and memory stick, walked to the car park, jumped in the car, and drove to High Wood.

The loud insistent knock at the front door made Elizabeth jump. She ran from the lounge and pulled open the door. "Charlie? Is something wrong?"

He nodded his head, and blank faced, followed her into the kitchen. He sat down in the kitchen chair, leaned forward on the table, and stared intently at Elizabeth.

'What on earth is it, Charlie?" Elizabeth was concerned. She'd never seen this young policeman in this mood before. "Charlie, what's wrong?"

He put the laptop on the table, turned the screen to face Elizabeth, and played the video and audio.

She looked up, her face expressionless.

"I saw things here, and you lied to me. I thought I was going mad." He looked into her eyes. "Then I saw this and heard the voices." He tapped the screen of the laptop and tipped the photos onto the table. "Elizabeth, what is all this? What's going on in this house?"

She picked up one of the photos, ran her finger sensitively around the silhouette, looked up at Charlie, and smiled wistfully. "I think it's time you met some friends of mine, learned what we do here, and found out what I think you are." She stood up. "Come with me?"

They walked in silence upstairs to the gallery.

"Let me explain things to you as simply as I can." She walked up and down the aisles of photos, explaining the faceless images, and what happened at High Wood.

"So you help them go to heaven?" Charlie said with less amazement than Elizabeth was expecting. "Somehow they find their way here, and then you do your thing?"

Elizabeth smiled. "That's the best summary I've heard since I came to this house."

"Are there lost souls in the house now?" Charlie asked with genuine interest.

"Souls and ghosts." She looked at Charlie for a reaction, but none came. "Do you believe in ghosts?"

He nodded, thinking of Grandma Emma. "Not until recently." He smiled. "Then I met my grandma."

"A ghost?"

"Yes."

"You seem remarkably calm about all this."

He had one of the photos in his hand. "Until I saw this," he said and held up the photo of the 'frosted' silhouette. "I thought I was going insane. But with this, and meeting grandma, I'm happy I'm not stark raving mad." He smiled at Elizabeth.

"Good. Well, let me test your sanity a little further."

They walked downstairs to the kitchen.

Elizabeth spoke to an apparently empty room. "I've explained everything to Charlie and I'd like him to meet everyone." She paused. "And one at a time please." She turned to Charlie. "You might want to sit down."

He looked around the empty kitchen, when a frosted silhouette began to appear close to the sink. Gradually it took on more density, and within seconds, Jane appeared, leaning against the sink.

Charlie simply said, "Hi."

"Hi, I'm Jane, and I'm a ghost," she said with a chuckle. "We've met before, although all you saw was the dishwasher unloading itself."

Charlie rubbed the back of his neck and pulled a face. "There was a magazine turning its own pages, a tray floating into the room, and a bin emptying itself."

Jane put her hand over her face in mock embarrassment. "Sorry about that. Not all my doing, though."

Rebecca, Adam, and Captain Forster appeared, all extending their apologies.

Charlie stood up. "It's lovely to finally meet you all. You have no idea how pleased I am."

"Would you like a coffee, Charlie?" Rebecca asked.

"Milk and two sugars, please."

"Charlie." Elizabeth spoke quietly. "You've seem to have similar abilities to me. You're not fully tuned into them yet, but you're definitely 'special'. People like you are rare, and we need as much help as we can at the moment. It would be brilliant if you joined us."

He took the mug from Rebecca, put it down slowly and deliberately, pursed his lips, drummed his fingers on the table, looked closely at everyone in the kitchen, turned to Elizabeth, and looked back at Rebecca. "Could I have a biscuit, please?"

"What do you think?" Elizabeth gently prodded him.

"How would I earn any money?"

"We're well funded, and we could pay you a lot more than you currently get in the police. You're a rare commodity." Elizabeth gently held his arm. "Have a think about what I've said, and come back to meet the others? The living others that is."

Charlie smiled. "I'll call you in a few days." He drank his coffee, ate his biscuits, shook his head, and chuckled quietly to himself.

# Chapter Fifty-Three

Guillaume stood close to Isaac's 'hutch' among the mass of stacked, wooden bunks. It reminded him of a terrible morning spent at a battery farm for chickens, who, like this tortured assembly of humanity, sat silently waiting for slaughter. Although in this case, slaughter in a far from humane manner.

Guillaume frowned deeply at Isaac. "How do you survive this?"

"The belief I have in His name, and to survive one day at a time. My horizons are short. If, when I close my eyes, it is only to sleep, I have won a small victory. There is a light in me, which no matter what torment they put me through, will never be extinguished. It shines and illuminates my darkness. The smallest act of kindness appears to me like a giant spark, and I chose to remember only the sparks. I still believe in kindness, and I will not let their evil and my anger drive me out of this world."

Guillaume was in awe of this man's inner strength to get up each day and not accept the inevitable. To not hate the sadistic dregs of humanity who made his daily life as horrendous as they could, and to somehow see good in this deepest, blackest, malignant pit of Hell.

"Do you still write poetry?" Guillaume asked with genuine interest.

Isaac shook his head. "I haven't written anything since the last war."

"Do you remember them?"

"Of course. They are imprinted on my mind. It was the images of consummate horror seared into my memory which composed the verses for me. The horrors were a hundred times worse than anything I have seen here. You become deadened and anaesthetised to death in all its many and varied forms." Isaac took a long deep breath. "'Horror of wounds and anger at the foe, and loss of things desired; all these must pass. We are the happy legion, for we know Time's but a golden wind that shakes the grass.'"

"Sassoon?"

Isaac nodded. "'Absolution.'"

"Could you recite some of yours for me?" Guillaume asked softly. "It would bring me comfort."

Isaac shrugged. "It has been too long since I spoke my words."

"I was brought up on your poems." Guillaume tried again.

Isaac shrugged. "I am too tired, Guillaume. These are not easy days, but I will recite a little of a poem I love." He closed his eyes, recalling the words. "'After a hundred years Nobody knows the place, Agony, that enacted there, Motionless as peace. Weeds triumphant ranged, Strangers strolled and spelled At the lone orthography Of the elder dead. Winds of summer fields Recollect the way, Instinct picking up the key Dropped by memory.'"

Guillaume gently squeezed Isaac's arm. "That was so wonderful. Who wrote it?"

"Emily Dickinson."

Isaac sat up, leaned forward, and stared deep into Guillaume's eyes. "Who are you? You say you are Guillaume Wouters, but that cannot be possible. Guillaume Wouters is a young boy." He looked him up and down. "You are a young man. Thirty at most? Your accent is possibly French?"

Guillaume frowned deeply. *"I am occupying a body."*

"I ask again. Who are you? The SS place spies amongst us. Are you in their pay? I know the Wouters well, and I do not remember you. The name, yes. But this face?" He reached down, touched Guillaume's cheek, and his hand flew back, as if it had been electrocuted. "The question I should ask," he said and ran his index finger across his lower lip, "is not who you are, but rather, what you are?" He cautiously reached forward closer to Guillaume's face and small sparks crackled between them.

"If I told you, you would not believe me." Despite all his years in Papaver Rhoeas, saving souls, time travel, and talking with ghosts, Guillaume's confidence in explaining to Isaac who he was, wasn't particularly high. However, his inner strength, belief in his abilities, faith, and knowledge of an afterlife, were safeguarding his sanity.

"Please try me." Isaac dropped down from his bunk. "Come, we can talk at the end of the barrack."

They huddled together in a far corner. "I am Guillaume Wouters, the small boy you know, but now grown up. I have taken possession of this body." He paused and took a deep breath. "I am from the future."

Isaac's expression remained remarkably calm and gestured that he should continue.

Guillaume did his best to explain Papaver Rhoeas and their mission. He tried to explain why he'd been drawn back to Auschwitz-Birkenau by Isaac's extraordinary high level of spirit-energy and his powerful family links.

Isaac stood in silence listening to everything Guillaume had to say, and then stretched his arms, nodded slowly, cracked his knuckles, looked deep into Guillaume's eyes, nodded again, and linked arms with him. "Come. We need to rest. Tomorrow will be hard. Many die at I.G."

Guillaume was baffled by Isaac's reaction, but given that he hadn't screamed for the guards, or called him insane, he felt he may have believed some of what he'd said. "What happens tomorrow?"

Isaac chuckled. "A man from the future, comes to save me. 'God moves in a mysterious way, His wonders to perform; He plants His footsteps in the sea And rides upon the storm. His purposes will ripen fast, Unfolding every hour; The bud may have a bitter taste, But sweet will be the flow'r.' William Cowper, if you didn't know. Very appropriate, don't you think?"

Guillaume's confidence that Isaac may have believed some of what he'd said, began to strengthen.

Isaac chuckled again. "The order of the day for tomorrow, is breakfast, in the loosest and smallest sense of the word, roll-call, line up for delousing, latrines or washing, ten hours work in the hardest sense of the word, and physical exhaustion. For lunch, scraps of cabbage or turnip in hot water, roll-call. For dinner, the same soup as lunch, plus some rotten potato or swede, lie down, close your eyes, and pray that you wake up." He paused, looking a little more serious. "Or not, as the case maybe."

"Sounds like a very full day," Guillaume said with a hint of irony.

"Tomorrow we have the pleasure of 'working' at I.G. Farben."

Guillaume frowned. "I.G. Farben?"

"I have it from a very good source that I.G. financed the building of Auschwitz-Birkenau for the Nazis, and so consequently they own it. Thus, it provides them with the singular opportunity of exploiting the dramatic cost reduction of using slave labour. If I survive this Hell, I will ensure those responsible are brought to book for their sins."

"What do they make there?"

"Mainly synthetic rubber, heating oil, and tar. They've been trying to make synthetic petrol from coal, but so far they've had very poor results. And they also make pesticides. Mainly Zyklon B."

Guillaume's face froze. "The chemical … the one they …"

"Gas our people with?" He nodded and scowled.

Guillaume's expression was frozen in disbelief. "We are forced to help them make Zyklon B?"

Isaac nodded. "I think we should go to sleep."

# Chapter Fifty-Four

Klaus sat back, his mind still in turmoil over the thought of his son becoming a Spirit Walker. He needed to focus on solving the main issue of the blue lights, so he scrolled through the few pages of text, calculations, and images, and started to read the brief summary.

Trench and concrete specification

1) 6' outside the existing foundations.
2) 3' wide, 6' deep.
3) Concrete specified to BS EN 13670, and ICE - Specification for piling and embedded retaining walls.

The mobile in his pocket vibrated, and the ubiquitous 'old phone' ring tone, told him he had a call. He looked at the small photo of Patrick in the top corner of the screen and smiled.

"Bauer."

"Klaus, what's going on? I've not heard from you for weeks, and Guillaume seems to have disappeared off the face of the earth."

"There have been a few developments."

There was a silence which demanded that Klaus continued.

"Guillaume has …" He took a deep breath. "We believe he may have been drawn back to 1944, by his family bond to his uncle Isaac Rosenberg."

The silence could have been cut with a chain saw.

"I am thinking of sending a Spirit Walker to bring him back."

"We still use them? After the last 'problems', we voted to stop their use? Who authorised this?"

"Isaac."

"Wouters!?"

"Yes. His spirit speaks to me."

This seemed to be readily accepted and Patrick continued. "Who will you send? I'm not aware of any 'active' Spirit Walkers?"

"I have limited choices, but I'm sure that whoever I select, will return Guillaume to us."

"Has there been any progress on the blue lights?"

"Yes, but I need a little more time before I can make recommendations to the Astrea. Patrick, can you please communicate this to the other members? Without Guillaume, it has become very difficult to manage everything."

"Of course. Is there anything else I can help with?"

"Communicate with the others for me. If I can use you as a single point of contact, it will remove a lot of my concerns."

"You have my full support in this, Klaus."

"I need to go, Patrick. I have much to do."

"Take care, Klaus. Call me if you need anything. Au revoir."

"Auf Wiedersehen."

As Klaus ended the call, the phone rang immediately. His first thought was to ignore it, but he saw it was from Marie.

"Bauer. You have news?" As always with Klaus, pleasantries were ignored.

"Yes. I found the plans in an old tin box."

"Das ist wunderbar! *(This is wonderful!)*"

"You need to come around."

"Of course."

"I need you to see what's in the loft."

"The loft?"

"Come around. It's hard to explain."

"I'll be around now!"

The line went dead. Marie stared at it for a few seconds, and then shook her head. *"Must be in their genes,"* she thought. A loud knock at the front door told her that her German 'advisor' was good to his word.

"Klaus, please come in."

He bowed from the waist and indicated he would follow Marie into the house.

"We should go upstairs," she said urgently.

Klaus almost imperceptibly nodded. "Ja. Sicher. *(Sure.)*"

Marie walked briskly up the stairs, pulling a small bunch of keys out of her jean's pocket. The door opened easily. "I gave it a good soaking with WD40. I could barely open it the first time I tried."

Klaus followed her to a second metal door, which was significantly more substantial than the first.

Marie spoke over her shoulder to Klaus. "It looks like it belongs in a bank." She inserted a brass key, turned the handle, and pulled it open. The sound of a loud hiss, and a cool breeze, indicated the room was under positive air pressure. "The whole loft is temperature and climate controlled," she said. "I found gauges, dials, and units in the loft, which maintain a constant cool dry environment." She smiled. "I only know this because there's a maintenance manual up there."

Klaus examined the cold metal of the door, frowned, and followed Marie up the two short sets of carpeted stairs leading to the loft. The first time he'd seen the gallery he was taken aback, but what confronted him now left him speechless. He took a few steps into the room, slowly trying to take it all in. It was enormous, and matched the size of the gallery. To his right, at the far end of the loft, was a projection screen, supported by a black tripod and stand. Klaus smiled, recalling the one his father had at their home, where they'd watched shaky holiday films. A few yards in front of the screen, were four comfortable-looking padded camping chairs. The remainder of the loft was crammed from floor to ceiling, with row upon row, of what looked like post office pigeon-hole racks for organising mail, all of which contained shining metal cans of film. He gingerly picked up the nearest can, and read the faded printed label taped to its rim. *'Kasserine Pass, February 1943'*. Klaus's hands trembled and he almost dropped the can. Fearing what might happen to the film if the can spilt its contents onto the floor, he carefully placed it back in the rack, and turned around to Marie.

"Not what you'd expect to find, is it?" Marie said with genuine disbelief. "It had the same effect on me."

"You saw this for the first time today?" Klaus finally managed to utter. "You haven't been in here before?"

"Never. It's always been locked. This must be the first time it's been opened, since mum and dad got ill." She walked closer to Klaus "What do you think they are?" She waved her hands at the racks of film. "I mean, I know they're cans of film, but what of?"

Klaus nodded at the can he'd replaced. "The label on that one I know. The Kasserine Pass, is in the Atlas Mountains in west central Tunisia. My father fought there with Rommel in '43."

Marie frowned, walked along the racks, mentally trying to calculate how many cans there were.

"What are you thinking?" Klaus called out.

"There must be at least," she said and paused, thinking through the numbers, "somewhere around a couple of thousand cans stored in here."

"Question is," Klaus said, as he walked closer to her, "how many of these films have survived? Because over time, they are prone to degradation."

"Let's find out," Marie said cheerfully, reaching for a can labelled *'Crucifix Hill 1944'*.

Klaus jumped forward, and grabbed her arm. "Nein! You may destroy anything which still survives in the can." He quickly let go of Marie's arm and blushed. "I am so sorry. Forgive me."

"Glad you stopped me."

He quickly regained his composure. "I have had experience of this before," he said, gesturing at the racks. "Ralph, our chief of operations in America, has contacts at the Packard Humanities Institute in Los Altos, California. They have experts in film preservation. Before we open any of these, I will contact him, and seek his advice."

Marie walked to the end of the loft, sat on one of the camping chairs, and stared at the blank screen. "What do you think he did up here?"

Klaus sat next to her and swung around to look at the racks. "He couldn't have managed all this on his own." He replied. "Did you ever see anyone else come up here with your father?"

She leaned back in the chair, and closed her eyes. "I do remember two men who came at the end of every month. Although at the time, I thought they were probably from the Electricity Board checking something in the loft."

Klaus frowned. "No-one else?"

Marie shook her head. "Not that I remember."

"Would it be possible to speak to your father?"

Marie shook her head. "Not really. He has moments of lucidity, but they're very infrequent now. Mum isn't quite as bad, but her moments of clarity can't be arranged. They just happen. I did explain this to Sam."

"I'm sorry. We haven't seen much of each other recently."

Marie leaned back in her chair. "In that case, I should tell you everything I told him."

"Bitte." Klaus was intrigued.

Ten minutes later, Marie had brought Klaus up to speed with everything she knew.

He was rarely at a loss for words, but his lips were locked together, unlike his eyes, which were wide open.

"You're surprised," she said with a twinkle in her eyes.

Even the dour German had to smile. "Ein bisschen. *(A little)*."

"Tut mir Leid. *(I'm sorry.)*"

"That explains a great deal, but it also poses many other questions." Klaus had recovered himself. "Have you seen anything unusual in the house recently?"

"Do blue fairy lights without wires count as unusual?"

"You have seen them?" He leaned forward almost tipping the chair over.

She nodded her head, as if seeing them was the most natural thing in the world.

"Where?"

She waved her hands in the air. "All over the house." She stood up and looked around. "Haven't you seen them? They were here when we came up." She turned to Klaus.

Klaus nodded, and followed Marie's gaze to the other end of the loft, where it was gradually filling with pinpoints of Prussian blue light.

Klaus stood up and took Marie by the arm. "We should go."

Marie pulled away. "Why? What harm can they do to us?"

"Please, let's go."

"I've seen these before in the cellar, and they didn't hurt me then." She crossed her arms across her chest. "You go if you want to, but I'm staying. I want to see … I'm not sure what I want to see, but somehow I know that I need to stay."

Klaus had met his match and cursed under his breath.

She looked at him from under her eyebrows and grinned. "Denken Sie daran, dass ich fließend Deutsch sprechen. *(Remember, I speak German fluently.)*"

Klaus blushed. "Tut mir Leid. I will stay."

The lights inexorably filled the loft and finally 'washed over' Marie and Klaus.

"Do you feel anything?" he asked.

"Nothing physical. No pain. I just feel desperate sadness." Tears were streaming down her cheeks. "They have a consciousness." She waved her hands through the circling lights. "There's only grief, isolation, and abandonment." She wiped away some of her tears. "But they're no threat to us." She blew her nose in a tissue. "Klaus, I have a sense of whispering, and murmuring." She closed her eyes, deep in concentration. "I can't make any sense of it. It's just gibberish."

He touched her elbow. "Until we understand this better, we should go."

She nodded in agreement and they cautiously made their way downstairs.

"Would you help me," Klaus said as they sat in the kitchen, "find an answer to these lights, and help them find their way home?"

"I'd love to. Mum and Dad never explained to me what they did here at Takanun, and then the dementia started. Whatever they did, hasn't been done for at least three years." She looked at Klaus and tilted her head to one side. "Does anyone in High Wood know what they did?"

"No-one mentioned them, and Takanun seems to have come as a surprise to everyone. However, my guess is they did the same here as we do in High Wood, only for the lost souls of World War Two. If, as you say, nothing has happened for three years, then these blue lights must be the lost souls who haven't been helped across." He glanced at Marie. "Their numbers have grown and grown. I need to speak to your father. He may be able to recall something. Even the smallest memory could be a great help to us. Do you think I could try?" Klaus said caringly.

"OK. But I doubt you'll get anything from him."

They stood up and made their way to the lounge.

"When do you want to look at the plans?" Marie asked as she poured two glasses of cold water.

"Scheiße. Ich hatte sie vergessen. *(Shit. I forgot it.)*" He slapped his hands on the kitchen worktop close to the sink. "Can I take them with me?"

"Of course. I'll pop them into an envelope for you."

He picked up his glass and drained half of the water. "Shall we go?"

Marie nodded, sighed deeply, and walked to the lounge.

"BEETHOVEN, NOT MOZART." Dad shouted at a forty-something bus driver trying to win ten thousand pounds.

# Chapter Fifty-Five

"When you get to Sheringham, take plenty of photos." Molly was finishing packing Charlie's case. "Ask them if they'd like to come down to us."

He nodded. "I'll take as many as I can, but I'm not going to be there all that long." Charlie was a shy person, and his pet hate was making conversation with strangers. The thought of spending days with Desiree's parents filled him with apprehension.

Emma walked through the wall from bathroom. "Find out everything you can about what they know about Peter. Take lots of pictures of the house. Inside and out." She handed him a hand-written list. "If you get a chance, try to find these places, and take some pictures. I'd like to know if they're still there."

Charlie took the list, scanned the names, looked up, and frowned. "They're mostly shops and pubs."

Emma nodded. "Those are the shops and pubs where I worked, rested, and played."

He smiled. "I'll do everything I can, Gran." He looked across at Molly. "Mum, does everyone in our family have special abilities?" he asked.

Emma glanced at Molly who nodded.

"Not really, dear. It started when your dad Ian was born. That's why he was such a good policeman. He could see things the others couldn't. Until recently, we thought it had missed a generation, but now it's clear you've inherited Peter's genes."

"Do you know anything about a house called High Wood, Gran?"

Another glance passed between Emma and Molly.

"No, dear. I'm only here, because your mum is my only living relative. If I didn't 'stay' here, I'd be who knows where."

"Why's that, love?" Molly asked.

Charlie told them what he'd learned from Elizabeth and what she'd asked him to do.

Molly had been praying for a way to get Charlie out of the police force, and despite her obvious concerns about High Wood, she thought her prayers had been answered.

"You should do it. If it didn't work out, you could always go back to the force."

Charlie scratched the back of his head. "But it took me so long to get where I am, and my detective sergeant says I could get into CID."

"Decide after you've been to Sheringham. I'm sure it can wait 'til then."

Charlie nodded and pulled at his ear lobe. "It'll give me more time to think about everything."

"Yes, darling." Molly zipped up his case and pushed it towards him. "Now you'd better get a move on."

He'd considered taking the train, but decided he wanted to be in control of his travel and chose to drive. As he crawled around Peterborough in a five-mile tail back, he regretted the decision, and very late on a windswept, rainy Friday night, he finally parked outside the Sunrays Guest House. He checked in and the owner showed him to his room, which for the money, was well above his expectations.

The following morning at eight thirty, Desiree walked into reception dressed in jeans, trainers, and a cream, argyle sweater. "Morning. Sleep well?"

Before he had time to answer, she'd wrapped her arms around his neck and was doing her best to swallow his face.

"Room OK?" She leaned close to his ear, licked it, and whispered lasciviously. "How's the bed? Hope the springs are industrial grade."

"They took them off a Chieftain tank," Lidsay whispered. He was woken by his thought of Desiree's energetic performance in Cardiff.

"Who'll be at the house?" Charlie asked as he adjusted his seat in Desiree's VW Golf.

"Just mum and dad." She slipped the car into first, and with a right foot contained in a lead boot, accelerated flat-out, out of the guest house car park.

Charlie metaphorically tossed his policeman's helmet onto the back seat, and buckled up for the ride.

"Thinking of booking me, Charlie?"

"Only if I can find my handcuffs," Lidsay said with a leer.

"Why constable, what kind of girl do you think I am?" she said through fluttering eyelashes.

Lidsay just leered and Charlie licked his lips.

They raced past fields covered in amber stubble, harvested weeks before of their grain.

"Can we stop?" Charlie squeezed his knees together and pulled a face. "Too many coffees and orange juices at breakfast."

"You sure?" The eyelashes fluttered again. "Not trying to get me into a field for a quickie?"

Charlie leapt, as best he could with a bursting bladder pressing on his abdominal wall, out of the car, over a five bar gate, and looked for cover. He saw a large oak tree, and ran behind it. The feeling of relief was indescribable as his bladder emptied. How a simple bodily function like taking a pee could give so much pleasure, was beyond him. He opened his eyes to tidy himself, and after zipping himself up, he looked up at the tree and frowned. He could just make out the faint outline of a heart carved into the bark. He stood closer, and rubbed away some of the moss and lichen which obscured the letters, written either side of the heart. After a short time, the letters became clearly visible.

P W E T.  ♡

# Chapter Fifty-Six

However hard he tried, Matt couldn't get High Wood out of his head. "There's a bloody fortune just lyin' there waitin' for us," he said to the ceiling as he drained his fifth can of cheap, strong lager.

"Like I've 'eard it all before." There was a long pause as Mark crushed his sixth empty can of even cheaper cider and threw it onto a pile in the corner of the room. "And if you think I'm goin' back to that band of soddin' mad ghosts, then you are pissed." He picked up his last can of cider. "I pissin'," he said. A loud belch, followed by the stench of rancid apples, slapped Matt full in the face. "Told you. I ain't goin' back," Another thundering belch took a strip of flaking paint off the skirting board. "Into that mad shit hole of a place. Not now, not never!"

Matt grimaced. "Listen, I'm sick of livin' like this." He looked around at the grimy, damp, malodorous pit that was their two-bedroom flat on the third floor of a decrepit Victorian house, above a chip shop.

Mark farted, sniffed his handy work, grimaced, wafted his hand around, smiled, and looked around at the 'decor'. "S' not that bad. Lick of paint." He studied the small, cramped space. "I can think of worse pissin' places to live."

"Name one." Matt stood up, cursed, lifted his foot, and scraped off a piece of mouldy pizza. "BOLLOCKS!" He shouted at no-one in particular. "We're getting out of this fuckin' pit, and if some bastard ghost wants to get in my way, then bloody good luck to it. 'Cause I 'ave 'ad enough."

"I am not goin' back in there, and I don' give a shit what you think." He looked around again at the 'accommodation'. "S' cheap, and better than sleepin' on the bloody streets."

"Only just." Matt spat at him. "If you're 'appy with this shit 'ole, then you're pissin' welcome to it. Be my fuckin' guest. I'm going back to that 'ouse. I know where the good stuff is, so it'll be a quick in and out."

"Good pissin' luck." Mark belched and was nearly sick. "Like you're goin' to need it."

Matt walked into the kitchen and stared in despair at the congealed grease on the surface of the water in the sink, which concealed unwashed dishes, plates, cups, mugs, knives, forks, and pans. The rest of the kitchen didn't improve his mood. There were saucepans on the stove with baked-on tinned spaghetti, a frying pan with what looked like the remains of a fried egg, and oven trays with burnt on pizza. Close to the sink was an overflowing, stinking bin with most of its contents on the floor, tea stains on the table, a pile of used tea bags next to the rusty kettle, crumbs just about everywhere, and stains on the floor which he didn't want to know the source of. Brother or no brother, he was getting out of this. If he crapped out at High Wood, then there were plenty of other places in Cardiff he'd try burgling. Even getting caught, and banged up, had to better than this cess pit. He turned to face what did it's best to be the lounge, and grimaced at Mark who'd fallen into a deep, drunken stupor, drool and vomit coating his chin, and was snoring like a walrus with a severe head cold and sinusitis.

Matt shook his head. *"Well, bruv,"* he thought, *"I've done my bit for enough years. Time you stood on your own two feet. You can come with me or rot in this ..."* He couldn't find any more words which would describe the level of squalor they were living in. He shook his head, waved, and headed for the nearest pub.

# Chapter Fifty-Seven

Sam and Elizabeth walked in through the kitchen door at High Wood.

"Evening everyone." Captain Forster wandered into the kitchen with a plate and mug. "The men were asking who'd be next."

Elizabeth glanced at Sam, breathed deeply, and then smiled. "Tell them we'll start again at nine sharp, o nine hundred, and I'll leave it with you to decide the order."

Captain Forster beamed. "They'll be very happy. Thank you, Elizabeth." He turned away whistling 'It's a Long Way to Tipperary'.

The following morning over an early breakfast, Sam and Elizabeth were discussing 'events', and particularly, the possibility that Constable Thompson might join them.

"More coffee?" Rebecca said with her usual early morning smile. Something, which everyone apart from Adam, found unbelievably annoying at such an early hour.

"Please," Sam replied, hiding his irritation. "I need a strong injection of caffeine."

Captain Forster came in with a sheet of paper, snapped to attention, saluted, and then grinned broadly. "Running order for today, marm."

"Coffee captain?" Jane was making herself a cup.

"Please, marm … sorry, Jane. I'm afraid old habits die hard."

Elizabeth patted the chair beside her. "Sit down and have some breakfast."

"Why not? I haven't had a piece of toast since … You know, I can't remember when."

"When do you plan to go home?" Elizabeth asked.

"Mmmm?" Captain Forster replied, as he tasted toast and marmalade for the first time in a very long time. "Me, marm … Elizabeth? Only when all the men are accounted for. Not until then. I have a duty to them. Can't fall down on that."

Elizabeth smiled, there was a lot to be said for this almost forgotten level of responsibility and care for his fellow man. "When you're ready, just let me know." She smiled. "Toast good?"

His expression said everything.

By eleven o' clock, Privates Morrison, Handley, and Juttery had been helped across to the other side with blissful smiles.

*"Wonderful. Just wonderful."* The 'voice' was quiet and wistful.

Elizabeth stood up and looked around the gallery. *"Is that you Gloria?"*

*"I can't keep this up. I've tried my best, but I haven't got it in me. I can't break up your relationship. Mine was terrible, but what you and Sam are doing is just wonderful. Ivor's not worth it."*

*"Gloria?"* Elizabeth softly said.

*"Mmmm. Uh huh."*

Elizabeth shuddered as a coldness ran down her spine and into her feet. She bent forward holding her knees, as her breath shortened and her pulse raced.

*"Sorry about that, but there's no other way of leaving you."*

Elizabeth straightened up, and looked straight into the eyes of Gloria Lidsay. A Gloria who at first she didn't recognise. The matted hair, unkempt appearance, extra weight, greasy skin, body odour, and bushy eyebrows were all gone. Standing close to her was a young attractive woman with long, shiny auburn hair, sparkling brown eyes, a body with curves where curves should be, gleaming white teeth, and who was dressed immaculately. "Gloria? Is that you?"

She looked herself up and down. "Yeah. Great, isn't it?" She sat down inelegantly on the floor. "Where does it all go? You've plans, you don't think anything's going to get in the way, then life sits up, slaps you in the face, and says that's not for you." She slowly shook her head, and looked deep into Elizabeth's eyes. "Don't waste a minute while life's good, because things have got a habit of very quickly going sour." She stood up. "Look at me. I was happy once. Actually, I was happy for quite a few years. Then Ivor didn't get the promotion he thought was his and he got cynical. Cynicism turned to depression, which he'd never admit to, depression turned him to alcohol, alcohol turned him into an aggressive bully, and that was the straw which finally broke my personal camel's back."

"Why didn't you tell me this before?"

"I was hurt, and someone was going to suffer. But seeing that, has thankfully brought me to my senses." She chuckled. "I'm glad it's over."

"So am I, and so is Sam."

"Bit naughty, wasn't I?" She blushed and looked up from under her eyebrows at Elizabeth.

"I don't think Sam was complaining. Although any more of it, and he'd have been in traction for months." She looked at Gloria, smiled, and they both burst into laughter. "Where did you learn to do all those things?"

Gloria blushed. "It's probably why Ivor stayed with me for so long."

"I don't think he was depressed. Just bloody worn out." Elizabeth sniggered and the two women collapsed into fits of laughter. Eventually they regained a little self-control. "Do you still want to find him?"

"Ivor?" She shook her head and scowled. "Not now. That bastard isn't worth the effort."

"What are you going to do?" Elizabeth said, scratching the side of her head. "Not too many options, I suppose."

Gloria tilted her head to one side. "Could I help you and the others?"

Elizabeth was speechless.

"Sorry, I shouldn't have asked." Gloria flushed scarlet with embarrassment.

"No. No." Elizabeth quickly recovered herself. "I was just, well, just a bit shocked."

"So can I?"

"I'd need to speak to the others, but if you and I are OK, then I can't see any reason why not. Things have got pretty mad around here, and another pair of hands would be very welcome."

Gloria ran forward to hug Elizabeth and went straight through her.

Elizabeth turned and smiled. "Something you'll get used to. Come on, let's go down stairs and meet the others."

# Chapter Fifty-Eight

After a drive around the surrounding points of interest, Charlie and Desiree arrived at Cambrai at twelve thirty, where Desiree's mother and father were waiting at the gate to meet them.

Stephen, Desiree's father, opened the gate and walked out to meet them. He was a short man, slightly overweight, with surprisingly large feet, small hands, intensely green eyes hidden behind black heavy rimmed glasses, and short curly hair which looked as if it would work well as a scouring pad. What struck Charlie most about him, was how young he looked to have a daughter of thirty-five.

Stephen smiled broadly. "Welcome to Cambrai, lovely to meet you. Heard a lot about you, Charlie. She," he said and nodded at Desiree, "hasn't stopped talking about you since she came back from Cardiff. You made quite an impression on her."

Lidsay woke up and chuckled. *"Spent enough time on top of her to make a permanent dent."*

Charlie ignored him. "Nice to meet you." He felt uncomfortable, but was hiding it well. "Nice to meet family I didn't know I had."

"Yes, indeed. Family." Stephen smiled at Desiree. "All down to this little beauty. She's spent months tracking down family members." He looked to his right. "This is the trouble and strife, Henriette, or Henry as she's better known to her friends."

She smiled shyly and waved a limp hand at Charlie. "Nice to meet you, and please call me Henry." She turned towards the house. "Come in. Lunch is ready. Hope you like cottage pie."

"It's one of my favourites," Charlie said, winning early brownie points with Henry. *"She looks younger than he does,"* he thought. *"Must be the sea air."*

"Well, come on then, there's plenty to be eaten." Desiree linked arms with Charlie, and they headed into the house.

"You've a lovely home," Charlie said, as he sat down at the dining room table. "How old is the house?"

He'd hit on Stephen's favourite subject. "It was originally built in 1896 as a cottage for a farm manager, it was virtually rebuilt in 1919, for a Major Coussmaker who came home from the war as a decorated hero, and he lived here until he died in 1932. It would have been then that your grandma moved in. Your dad Ian was born in the house in …" He turned to Desiree for help.

"He was born in 1942."

"Thanks, darling. Your dad and grandma lived here until 1966, when the house was bought by the local station manager, who died in 1969. We saw the house on the internet," he said and smiled at Henry, "and were looking for a project to keep us busy in our retirement. It had been left unattended for a year, but when we saw Cambrai, we fell in love with it and bought it in 1970. Over the last forty-odd years, we've added a bit here, and improved a bit there. All the work's been carried out to a particularly high standard, with great respect to the original architecture, but without compromising on the essential modern additions we required." He beamed satisfyingly. "I'd say that overall, we're very happy with the results of our labours."

Charlie opened his eyes wide and raised his eyebrows. "You should be very proud of what you've achieved." More brownie points were clocked up.

"Thank you, Charlie. Would you like some wine or beer?" He walked towards a drinks cabinet like a cockerel who'd just been let loose in a hen house full of sexually active chickens.

After a very good lunch, and some exceptionally good wine, they all moved into an orangery at the back of the house for coffee.

"Why don't you show Charlie around the grounds?" Stephen suggested. "I say grounds, Charlie. We've got a couple of acres out the back." He pointed out of the orangery windows to a large field which ended at a deciduous wood. "To be honest, I like it, because I can cut the grass with my McCulloch MC12597SD 38" 2 in 1 Lawntractor," he said like Jeremy Clarkson describing a new Aston Martin. "If you like, you can take her for a spin. Grass could do with a cut." He mimed driving. "Great fun."

"Loves his toys," Henry said with a grin. "Doesn't matter how old they are, men have got to have their toys."

"It makes cutting the grass a lot easier and quicker," Stephen replied, trying to justify the significant financial investment he'd made in grass-cutting technology.

Henry looked at Charlie and raised an eyebrow. "And it makes him feel like Lewis Hamilton."

Charlie did his best, without too much success, not to laugh.

"Come on," Desiree said as she held Charlie's arm and pulled him to his feet. "Let's show you the 'estate'."

As they walked up the slight incline to the woods, Charlie stopped, and looked back at the house. "You've got a really nice place."

"I've got an even nicer place for you to take a look around, when we make it into the woods," Desiree said, kissing him on the cheek.

*"We've struck the mother lode, Charlie. She's got more moves than Strictly Come, Dancing."*

Charlie continued to ignore him, but was struggling to argue with his thoughts.

"DESIREE!" Her father shouted from the back garden, waving a mobile phone. "PHONE FOR YOU."

"Looks like we'll have to forget our fun in the forest," she said as they turned and walked quickly back to the house.

*"Shit!"* Lidsay was a 'little' disappointed.

Desiree took the phone, laughed, and walked into the house.

"Can I use the bathroom?" Charlie asked as the wine and coffee did their best to burst his bladder.

"Upstairs, and first on the right." Stephen smiled.

Desiree came back into the garden and looked around for Charlie.

Her father pointed upstairs and mimed pulling a chain.

They leaned on the garden fence together, watching rabbits happily feeding at the edge of the wood.

"He has the 'skill'," Dad said softly. "I sensed it when we first met."

"Can he help you?" Desiree asked hopefully.

"To move on?" He shook his head and shrugged. "Who knows, he seems a very pleasant young man." He looked back at the house. "Ask him to sleep over, and I'll ask him in the morning. Perhaps the house will help him make his decision."

Charlie came back from the toilet looking a lot more relaxed.

"Dad suggested you should stay here tonight. We could take a good look at all the family research, have a few more glasses of wine, and have a nice relaxing evening." She tilted her head to one side and raised an eyebrow. "What do you think?"

The meal and wine had already made Charlie feel 'relaxed', and the offer of a bed, and no ride back to the hotel, didn't need much thought. "Thanks, I'd love to."

Dad offered Charlie a fresh glass of Cabernet Sauvignon.

Charlie tapped one of the A4 sheets spread out on the dinner table. "This is your branch of the family?"

Desiree nodded. "Only as far back as Donald Thompson." She tapped the dates 1898 – 1969. "I've managed to go back further, but I thought this would be enough for us to look at for now."

Charlie nodded. "Eugene Thompson died very young. Twenty three's no age at all." He looked up. "From the date 1944, he must have died in World War Two?"

"Yes," Stephen replied. "The records we," He corrected himself. "Desiree found, show he was a POW in Burma. He must have died of disease, starvation, or being worked to death by the Japanese. His body was never found."

"One of my relatives died building the Burma railway." Charlie turned to Desiree. "The one you couldn't find."

"Peter Wallins," she recalled.

Charlie nodded. "My grandad. How spooky is that?"

After a convivial evening, at eleven o' clock everyone decided that bed was calling.

"I'll show you the way," Desiree said and then whispered, "but we won't be able to have any fun tonight. I'm a bit too vocal for that." She stopped on the landing. "Bathroom's over there, and this is your room."

She opened the door, and he followed her into a small, but very cosy bedroom. He stood at the head of the bed and gazed at the wall where a pale silhouette remained of what must have been a large painting.

"It's in the attic." Desiree answered his silent question. "It's called, 'Working on a Thailand Railway Cutting', July 1943, by Murray Griffin. Dad told me it's one of the most famous images of the terrible conditions experienced by POWs, when they constructed the Thai–Burma railway. It used to dominate the room, but it isn't the most pleasant thing to have in a bedroom. So now it lives in the attic." She walked to a bedside cabinet and took out a battered book. "There's a picture of it in here somewhere." She flicked through a few pages, and handed it to Charlie. "That one," she said, tapping a photo at the bottom of the page.

"That's appalling!" It was all Charlie could say. He peered closer at the picture to get a closer look, and rediscovered the power of speech. "It's like a vision of Hell. My God, Hieronymus Bosch would have struggled to paint something more monstrous."

"Her, Ronny, who?"

"An art teacher introduced me to his paintings when I was in the sixth form. They're a bit odd, but they struck a note with me."

"You'll have to show me," Desiree said, as she studied the painting in detail for the first time.

"Good night," Dad called from the landing.

"Night, Dad. See you in the morning." She turned and kissed Charlie on the lips. "Sorry, but that'll have to do for now." She squeezed his hand and smiled. "Sleep well."

Charlie quickly slipped into a wine-induced sleep, but was woken by the same fluid, demanding release from his bladder. Feeling relieved, he walked back from the bathroom onto the landing, where the silence of the house was almost palpable. His mouth was as dry as a mummy's scalp, so he made his way downstairs to the kitchen.

In his room, the silhouette of the painting on the wall began to glow an iridescent blue.

*"Hot or cold?"* he thought, as he looked at the fridge and the kettle. The kettle won. As it started whistling loudly, he leapt up from the kitchen table, and turned off the gas before he woke the rest of the house. He made a large mug of tea and sat down on a kitchen chair. Charlie sipped the steaming tea, when the silence of the kitchen was suddenly broken by a

high-pitched buzzing. "What the hell's that?" He walked to fridge, checked the phone, put his ear close to the radio, shook his head, and sat down again at the kitchen table. The buzzing continued, and his brain trawled through its memory banks looking for an answer. It found it under 'Natural History'. *"Cicadas? In Norfolk?"* he thought. He shook his head, found a biscuit tin, ate five digestives, made his way back to his room, and climbed under the duvet. The heavy silence of the room was broken again by the same high-pitched buzzing. He sat up in bed and peered into the dark of the bedroom. The light switch was too far away for him to be bothered to look for the source of the sound, and silence once again settled on the room. A thunderous whooping call and the sound of something large, and probably very angry, crashing above him, through what sounded like branches, made Charlie jump out of bed. He felt along the edge of the mattress, and across the floor, until he reached the window, and threw the curtains open. His blood chilled as he saw the shadowy facsimile of the painting of the Burma railway reflected back at him. He sat back on the window ledge, gripped his thighs, but his pyjama shorts felt frayed and tattered. His hand shot up to his chest, and came away with a piece of grubby, torn, pale brown material. In the bright moonlight from the window, he looked at his hand, his chest, his legs, and finally his feet. Panic set in. He looked like an extra from a 'Bridge over the River Kwai'. He looked up and around for the bedroom, but it had disappeared, and been replaced by dense jungle.

# Chapter Fifty-Nine

Klaus followed Marie into the lounge, where the decor was significantly different to High Wood. Particularly the fifty-inch Panasonic Viera TX-50CX802B, fixed very securely, Klaus hoped, to the wall above the fireplace.

Mum's hair and make-up were done, she was dressed smartly, and sat on a leather recliner with her feet resting on a foot stool. From behind silver framed glasses, her eyes were fixed in a determined stare at her knitting.

Dad was centre stage on the sofa, grey hair brushed, and smartly dressed in blue slacks, red striped shirt, and navy blue sweater. He was holding worry beads made from yellow amber, which he coiled and twisted, smoothly and expertly through his fingers. He was completely focused on the TV, and particularly the contestants of 'The Chase', who were struggling with the questions posed by the host.

"They're all recordings," Marie said softly. "He can miss all the ads then. Otherwise they make him a little upset." She bit her bottom lip and her eyes filled with tears.

"How long have they been unwell?"

"Mum's been like this for about three years, although I'm pretty sure it started about five years ago. Dad's had it," she said, paused, and swallowed hard, "probably about a year longer? It's impossible to know when it starts. The signs at first are so subtle, that you can easily miss them." She walked across to her father, moved his glass of water from the coffee table in front of him, brushed away a loose hair from his face, kissed him on the cheek, and indicated that Klaus should join them on the sofa. "Talk to him quite normally. His responses will vary, but in amongst the silences and vague answers, will be little nuggets of gold. If we both make mental notes, then we shouldn't miss anything."

Klaus nodded and unrolled the plans of Takanun on the coffee table.

Dad took little notice, as a retired taxi driver was having trouble remembering the capital of Bolivia. "No, not *Lima*." There were a series of tut-tuts, followed by a very deep sigh. "LA. PAZ!"

"He knows his stuff." Klaus said to Marie, across Dad's shoulders.

"He was a professor of mathematics at UWIST before this parasite started eating away his brain."

"It's a dreadful condition," Klaus said with compassion. "The loss of someone who's still with you is unbearable. I have a brother who has been in a coma for many years."

Marie smiled wanly. "No. It's not easy. It's a terrible thing to say, but I wish they could just …" she said and choked away a tear, "simply pass away quietly in the night."

Klaus squeezed her hand and nodded at the coffee table. "Shall we see if these stimulate any memories?"

Marie nodded and gestured for him to start.

"What is your father's name?" Klaus asked quietly.

"Robert, but everyone calls him Bob, and mum's name is Patricia, Pat." She whispered.

Klaus leaned forward and ran his hand over the plans. "Do you remember these, Bob?"

Bob stayed completely focused on the TV. "It's a HYENA."

Klaus gently tapped the plans with his index finger. "These are the plans of this house. Your great-grandfather, Joseph Stridham, copied them from plans of his good friend Adam Morbeck."

"Do you like these?" Robert nodded towards the TV, without taking his eyes from the programme.

Marie tilted her head for Klaus to answer.

"Ja. I very much enjoy them."

"You're German, aren't you?" His tone wasn't aggressive.

"Yes Bob. I am German."

"Damn fine engineers the Germans." His eyes didn't leave the moving images on the TV. "Need good maths to be a good engineer." His eyes didn't blink or move from the TV. "Are you an engineer?"

"No."

"Shame. World needs engineers."

Klaus looked across at Marie.

Her eyes were streaming with tears. *"Keep going,"* she mouthed.

"I was never very good at maths, Bob. Marie told me you were a professor of mathematics."

He nodded, staring intently at the TV. He shook his head, sighed as if all the ills of the world were on his shoulders, and shouted, "SHIKOKU!" at a seriously overweight, older woman, in a skirt which was too short, shoes with heels too high, make-up too thick, and teeth in need of a good vet.

"Shikoku, Bob?"

"Largest island in Japan. She should have known that. Is everyone as stupid as this in Germany?" For the first time, he turned and looked at Klaus. "What was your name again?"

"Klaus. Klaus Bauer. I think every country in the world has people like that." He nodded at the TV.

"Same the world over. Education …" The word was left hanging in the air.

"Have you been to Japan, Bob?"

"Do you think they deliberately put stupid people like her in these shows, just to make the rest of us feel clever?"

"The questions are sometimes harder," Klaus said softly.

"No, that's not it. They're all just plain stupid, and damn pig-ignorant." He leaned forward, stared at the coffee table, and tapped the plans. "What are these?"

Marie and Klaus sat up, frowned at each other, and shook their heads.

"You don't remember these, Dad?" Marie had to speak.

Silence was the only answer she got.

"I've seen them before."

Marie's eyes met Klaus's.

It was her mum's voice.

"Does she speak very often?" Klaus asked almost in a whisper.

"That's the first time in, in weeks." Marie's was startled.

Klaus got up, folded the plans in half, and opened them in front of Patricia.

"You've seen these plans before, Pat?"

Her eyes moved slowly from her knitting to the plans and nodded. "Yes."

Klaus gasped. "You have seen them before?"

"Yes." She looked at him questioningly.

"Be sensitive, Klaus. I don't want her pushed too hard," she said softly as she wiped her nose.

Pat put her knitting on the arm of the chair, leaned forward, picked up the plans, and looked closely at the detail. "I remember Bob's dad showed me these." She looked up at the ceiling, trying to glue together microscopic shards of fractured memories, of happier times spent with family. "He told me … Now what was it … That was it … It was the money. They couldn't … hard times." She leaned forward dropped the plans, as if to pick up her knitting, but then sat back and smiled. "And his father … his father …" She seemed to be drifting away. "He couldn't … not the same."

Marie looked amazed at her mother's recall, and struggled to maintain self-control, as a momentary glimpse of what she'd lost, fluttered by like a butterfly on a summer breeze. She swallowed hard and spoke softly. "What wasn't the same, mum?"

"They're nearly the same." She slowly rubbed her hands together, and stared into the far distance, memories beginning to disappear like a snowman on an unseasonably mild winter's day. "They should … something in the ground." She shook her head, but her eyes had begun to lose their focus. "Concrete …" She picked up her knitting, and started again on the never-ending scarf, as the memory shattered into a million fragile shards.

Klaus was speechless. "Concrete, Pat? What did they do with the concrete?"

"Arch duke FRANZ FERDINAND." Bob was engrossed in another contestant's lack of knowledge.

Klaus stared intently at Pat, and then back at Marie. "I would like to carry on, or do you want me to stop?"

Marie nodded, tears flowing freely down her cheeks. "I think … we should … stop," she said through loud sniffs. "Mum … hasn't been that lucid … for months."

Klaus was shaking his head, and staring at the floor. "Dieses haus sollte nie gebaut worden sein. *(This house should have never been built.)*"

"Why not?"

"The architects only drew up plans for one portal. High Wood. There were never plans to build a second portal." Klaus picked up the plans and gestured for Marie to follow him into the kitchen. "High Wood was built as a portal to rescue the lost souls of the Great War. The plans were drawn up to only allow the lost souls of World War One into High Wood."

Marie sat back in the kitchen chair. "So the only reason Takanun was built to the same specifications as High Wood, was because Adam and Joseph were such close friends?"

Klaus nodded. "Ja. Beste Freunde. *(Best friends.)*"

"And unless Adam told him, Joseph probably wouldn't have known the reason High Wood had been built."

"Ja. Any house which was used as a portal, was always kept secret. For Joseph, Takanun was only ever going to be a house and home." He pursed his lips, and then chewed his bottom lip. "But because of their friendship, this house unintentionally became a portal, which Joseph would not have been aware of. It became an open door for any lost soul seeking salvation and final rest." He frowned deeply. "My fear is that other spirits who are, shall we say, less than friendly than the lost souls we save, find their way into this time and reality."

Marie looked shocked. "Demons and poltergeists?"

Klaus nodded. "I think this may have already happened. 'Something,' which was once a policeman, came through in High Wood, and tried to kill Elizabeth." He frowned deeply. "It must have found its way in through here. But thankfully, we have seen nothing like that since." He sighed. "At least not that I am aware of."

"Could they stay in this house?"

"Ja."

"I've seen the blue lights. But how do I know if they're searching for salvation, or intending to create mayhem?"

"You have an ability to see everything which moves in and out of our reality." He stared at the walls. "Spirits have been finding their way into Takanun, through its unprotected foundations, until the house reached saturation point. Then they found a way out through the cellar wall into High Wood, and since then they have been pouring through."

"How many?"

Klaus shook his head. "This room glows with a blue light, and there are many spirits creating it. But how many?" He shrugged. "However, these spirits do not appear to want to harm us."

Marie's eyes flashed to her mother and father. "Do you think they could possess them, because of their damaged minds?"

"If they were going to be affected, then I'm sure it would have happened by now."

Marie chewed her top lip. "What do I have to do?"

"Sam and Elizabeth will be able to guide you. Have they met Bob and Pat?"

"No." She chuckled softly. "Sam 'heard' dad, but he hasn't spoken to him."

"Then we need to arrange this quickly," Klaus said as he stood up.

"You're leaving?"

"I have to speak with a friend in Belgium. He needs to know everything I have discovered. It will help him construct the plans we need."

"When will Sam and Elizabeth be able to come?" She glanced across at her parents.

"Soon, but there are important things which must be dealt with first." Klaus kissed her on both cheeks. "Do not fear what lives in the house with you. I am sure there is no evil here. Only great sorrow, loneliness, and isolation." He briskly walked the short distance to High Wood, and as he pushed open the front door he almost walked through Jane.

She stood back and sniffed loudly as he walked around her to the kitchen.

"Wer ist zum Teufel das? I am sorry. Who is this?" Klaus said, pointing at Gloria.

Elizabeth decided she'd be best placed to do the introductions, as she knew who, or rather what, Gloria was. "Klaus, this Gloria Lidsay. She was the unfortunate wife of Sergeant Ivor Lidsay, who I 'met' in the gallery. Gloria and I have grown very close over the last few weeks." She turned and smiled at her.

Klaus bowed slightly. "You have my deepest sympathy, my dear. Your husband was an extremely unpleasant man and you are better rid of him. Welcome to High Wood." With his usual abrupt manner he turned to the others. "I have been in Takanun and believe I know the cause of the major part of our problem."

Rebecca smiled and nodded. "A few biscuits?" She knew Klaus's fondness for chocolate digestives, and his warm smile told her she'd hit the right button.

"So the architects of Papaver Rhoeas never meant for it to be built? It was only because Adam and Joseph were such good friends?" Elizabeth asked rhetorically.

"Ja."

"And they didn't know about the shields?"

"Nein."

"And their shields would have protected High Wood from these blue lights?"

"Ja."

"From these other spirit-energies?"

"Ja."

"And they've been coming through the cellar wall?"

"Ja." He smiled at Rebecca as she placed his coffee and biscuits on the kitchen table. "The entire wall connecting High Wood with Takanun must be reinforced with concrete. This will at least stop these spirits finding their way into High Wood." He sipped his coffee. "But unfortunately, that does not help us with the problem we already face." Klaus turned in his chair and stared at the intense blue glow around the lounge door. "What we do about that and the spirits in Takanun."

# Chapter Sixty

After breakfast and roll-call, Guillaume found himself with Isaac and one other Polish prisoner being marched to the I.G. Farben factory.

"Just follow me," Isaac whispered. "The Kapos are mindless thugs. The Nazis pay them to make our lives as miserable as they can."

Guillaume looked across at three large iron cylinders, about sixty to seventy feet tall.

Isaac saw his gaze. "That's why we're here. They're filled with clay filters and one will need cleaning. They run two and clean one. We'll have to go up there." He raised his eyes and looked to the top of the iron towers.

The Kapo, a tall, thick-set German with a shaven head, had been released from a Berlin prison for beating to death two students in a bar. His defence had been that they were either communists or Jews and deserved to die. He strutted across to them, cracking a long leather whip, pointed to the Polish prisoner, and then to the top of the nearest tower. "Da oben Sie, und reinigen Sie den Filter. *(Up there and clean the filter.)*"

The Pole, who had a badly sprained wrist, shrugged, and despite some pointing, and broken German, he couldn't make the Kapo understand his problem.

The Kapo snarled at him again, and punched him in the face. "Da oben Sie, und reinigen Sie den Filter."

With blood streaming from his broken nose, the Pole tried again in his pigeon German to explain. "Mein Handgelenk, nicht gut. *(My wrist, not good.)*"

This time, the Kapo punched him to the ground, kicked him in the stomach, and called over a guard.

Isaac sighed. "Unteroffizier *(NCO)* Bruno Franks."

The unteroffizier marched up to the collapsed Pole, pulled out his Luger pistol, and ordered him to get up immediately. The Pole struggled to his knees, but then collapsed.

"Mein Handgelenk, nicht gut. *(My wrist, not good.)*"

Franks laughed, grinned at the Kapo, and shot the Pole in the head. He looked down at the blood splatter on his boots, wiped them clean on the Pole's back, and turned his attention to Isaac and Guillaume.

"DU!" He pointed his Luger at Guillaume's head, and then waved it at the tower. "AUF DEM TURM! *(UP THE TOWER!)*" The words were screamed at them.

Isaac pushed Guillaume gently in the back, but he needed no persuasion.

The guard stared at Isaac as if he was something he'd trodden in, waved his Luger, and shouted. "DU! AUF DEM TURM."

Telling this vicious sadist he suffered from vertigo would be close to a death sentence, so Isaac slowly and deliberately started up the tower. Guillaume, having set off first, looked down, and seeing Isaac struggling up the tower, slowed to wait for him.

The guard fired his Luger into the air, the bullet ricocheting off the tower. "SCHNELLE JUDEN!"

Three hours later, Guillaume and Isaac, exhausted and caked in thick, red clay dust, made their way shakily down the precarious side of the iron tower. When they finally reached the ground, Isaac's legs collapsed under him. Guillaume ran forward to help him, but was tripped by the returning Kapo, and kicked in the head.

"Helfen Sie ihm nicht, Jude. *(You will not help him, Jew.)*"

The Kapo kicked Guillaume four or five times in the ribs, before becoming bored, and leaving Guillaume battered and bruised, sitting propped up against the tower.

"LATRINNEN!" he screamed at them. "SCHNELLE!"

The injured friends helped each other up and unsteadily hobbled to the latrines.

"At least we will be able to sit down," Isaac said with a cut lip, broken tooth, and blood soaked shirt.

Arm in arm, they supported each other as they stumbled to the latrines.

"We need to walk quicker," Isaac said with fear in his voice. "If they believe we are of no use as slave labour, they will gas us."

Guillaume straightened up in panic, pulled Isaac up with him, and did his best to appear 'fit and healthy'.

The stench from the latrines told them they didn't have far to go to keep up the pretence. As they entered the latrines, they fell onto the floor, utterly worn out. A group of prisoners ran over and lifted them up onto the latrine benches. Even the fetid stink of excreta wasn't enough to make them move.

"I can't keep this up," Isaac said weakly. "The gas chamber or a bullet, would be a kind release." He painfully turned his head to look at Guillaume. "Leave me to them. Remember. Survive one day at a time. That's what you have to do my friend. I can't do that anymore. I'm broken and my days are numbered." He looked away and bent forward to lean on his knees. "I will pray when I sleep tonight that I don't wake tomorrow." He sighed deeply. "'I lift my eyes to the mountains -- from where will my help come? My help will come from the Lord, Maker of heaven and earth. He will not let your foot falter; your guardian does not slumber. Indeed, the Guardian of Israel neither slumbers nor sleeps. The Lord is your guardian; the Lord is your protective shade at your right hand. The sun will not harm you by day, nor the moon by night. The Lord will guard you from all evil; He will guard your soul. The Lord will guard your going and your coming from now and for all time.'"

Guillaume couldn't say anything to lift this crushed man, and if he couldn't escape from these barbarous conditions, he had no doubt, he'd also be praying for release from this torment.

# Chapter Sixty-One

Charlie's mind had been shattered, like an antique Chinese vase given to a hyperactive toddler with a hammer.

At the back of his mind, Lidsay lay stewing, stunned and silent.

Charlie's breathing was laboured, his pulse raced, and his mouth felt like the bottom of a hamster's cage. "Bugger my special abilities. What the hell is real, and what isn't?"

A voice screamed to his left. *"KURRAH! (HERE YOU!)"* It chipped away a little more of his sanity and attachment to his own reality. Through the trees, Charlie could see a column of soldiers. The tattered condition of their uniforms made it almost impossible to tell their nationality, but from the odd word he could make out, it was clear they were British. Stumbling over tree roots and rocks, he cautiously approached the dishevelled column, and without thinking, stumbled out of the undergrowth, and joined them.

*"Shit! What the hell's going on?"* he thought. His mind desperately struggled to assimilate, evaluate, and establish some points of reference. Any degree of understanding, anything it could gather from his surroundings which would restore some level of sanity. His brain cross-referenced everything, and soon calculated there was a high degree of probability he was a POW in Japanese-occupied territory during World War Two.

"You OK?" A weak voice to Charlie's right whispered.

He glanced over his shoulder at a severely malnourished, unshaven soldier, 'dressed' in the tattered remnants of his uniform.

*"KURRAH!" (HERE YOU!)* The yell bellowed out from just behind them. This was quickly followed by a crashing blow across Charlie's back from a long, thin bamboo cane, which drew blood. He turned his head to be faced with an ugly, short, bespectacled, Japanese soldier, unbelievably wearing immaculate white gloves.

"FACE THE FRONT!" He screamed, then stepped closer to Charlie, and hit him across the face as hard as he could. The glove took the worst of the sting out of the smack, and the soldier's toupee fell off. He bent down, picked it up, and hit Charlie again with the bamboo cane. Again his hat fell off, and grunting savagely, he took a vicious swing at Charlie's chin which didn't connect. His pride and status damaged, the guard screamed "BUGGAIROS!" *(fool)* at Charlie, which was followed, by a final, agonising blow with the bamboo cane across his upper arm.

Charlie grimaced and managed to maintain a blank expression.

"Do as they say and just keep walking. Don't look back and keep quiet."

Charlie winced at the stinging wounds on his back, face, and arm, but kept pace with the column.

Twenty minutes later, they stopped for a rest.

"OK Cha? *(OK Tea?)*" a British officer asked the Japanese officer in charge.

"More ten minutes," the officer mumbled back through a sneer.

"Ten minutes, boys. Get some tea going," the British officer called to the column.

Charlie followed his newly found comrade in arms and sat under a tree.

"Not seen you before," his friend said with a questioning stare. "You're new. Not a Nip spy are you? The slit-eyed bastards have been planting them everywhere. If we ever catch them …" He left the words hanging in the air and drew his thumb across his throat.

Charlie shook his head. "I came up from another camp."

"Which camp?"

"206." Charlie answered. *"Where the hell did that come from?"* he thought in somewhat of less a panic than he'd expected.

"Christ, you've had it tough. I've heard terrible things about 206." He shook his head and offered Charlie some water. "What's your name?"

"Eugene. Eugene Thompson. But most people call me Swot. Started when I was in school" The answer was quick and effortless. *"Wasn't Eugene Thompson Desiree's great-uncle or something?"*

"Fred." His newly found friend offered his bruised, grazed, and callused hand. "Fred Larcombe. What regiment you with?"

"137th Field Artillery Regiment. You?" More information easily spilled from Charlie's merging mind.

"4th Battalion Royal Norfolk Regiment." Fred glanced at a soldier who was hobbling slowly to the trees. "Don't be too long, George."

George looked back, grimaced as a spasm ripped through his bowels, and rushed for the jungle.

"Dysentery." Fred nodded to George's back as he disappeared into the trees. "Poor sod's already shit himself twice today." He looked to his left and jumped up. "I'll grab us some cha before these bastards get us moving again."

Charlie nodded, his thoughts struggling back to his conversation with Elizabeth.

*"Your abilities are some of the strongest I've ever seen. ... We help lost souls find their way home. ... Some can travel in and out of different realities. ... In and out of different times. ..."*

Lidsay was seriously unhappy with this change to his well-laid plans. *"Who the fuck is Eugene Thompson?"* he murmured to himself. *"You little shit, Charlie, you were my ticket into that pox-ridden hole High Wood, and not here in some pissing Nip POW camp. I can bide my time."*

Suddenly a flood of snarls filled the air. "SHOKO! *(Officers.)* KURRAH! KURRAH! *(Here you!)*"

The British officer in charge of the column ran across to the Japanese officer screaming at the troops, and pointed at the jungle. "Yes, Nippon, but one man benjo *(latrine)* jungle."

The Japanese officer shouted back. "OK NIPPON? HE BACK SOON!" He flexed his bamboo cane. "NO OK!"

Two minutes later, the soldier stumbled out of the jungle fastening his jap-happy.

The officer screamed, "KURRAH!"

The soldier cowered and turned to face the officer. "I benjo Nippon."

"Benjo no good. Yasme benjo. Shoko no good."

The British officer stood between them. "This man dysentery, Nippon. Stomach no good Nippon."

The Japanese officer's hand flashed through the air, crashing into the officer's face. He pushed him onto the floor, kicked him, and lashed the cowering officer's arms with his bamboo cane.

No-one moved to help the officer up, understanding the brutal consequences if they did. After more screams and lashes, the column started marching again.

Charlie fell into step with the soldiers in front of him, and deep in his brain, Lidsay's spirit-energy, smouldered like the embers of a camp fire.

# Chapter Sixty-Two

Sam got back to High Wood at ten o' clock and made his way to the kitchen. His throat was as dry as a popcorn fart, and only the largest mug of tea would slake his thirst.

"Evening, Sam. Long day?" Jane was sat at the table reading Wolf Hall. "Bloody good this. I was never into history, but this, this is a really good read." She looked across the kitchen at him as he filled the kettle. "You should read it," she said to his back. "Bloody good read."

"I take it you like it?" Sam said over his shoulder.

"Never your strongest point that," she said as she dipped back into the life and times of Thomas Cromwell.

"Mmmm?" He was trying to disprove the maxim that a watched kettle never boiled.

"Sarcasm."

Sam ignored her. "Elizabeth about, Rebecca?"

"You didn't tell him?" Rebecca said softly to the top of Jane's head.

"Tell him what?" Sam said a little too loudly, as he carried on watching the kettle.

"Tell you Elizabeth was possessed by Lidsay's wife Gloria, that Gloria was so moved by Elizabeth helping a Tommy over to the other side," Jane said and breathed in noisily, "that she, not really sure what the word is, dispossessed, left her, and now she's going to join the team." She looked up at Rebecca. "Did I miss anything?"

Rebecca shook her head and looked sheepishly at Sam. "Tell you that."

Sam looked at Jane and tilted his head to one side. "You are pulling my leg?"

"Cross my heart and hope to … Ah, can't really use that one can I?" She smiled. "I am not pulling anything. Did enough of that when we were married."

"Seriously?"

"Seriously. Christ, what does it take for you to believe me?"

"Oh piss off. Come on, what really happened?"

She sucked her teeth, tapped the side of her head, blew out a long breath, pointed at Rebecca, and lost herself in Tudor England.

Rebecca stared at Sam sheepishly. "What she said."

Sam looked like a man who'd discovered too late on his first date that his new girlfriend was a well-endowed transvestite rugby player from Hull. He opened his mouth, but no sound would come out. He coughed, clearing his throat. "She was …"

"Possessed." Jane closed the book and sighed.

"Possessed?"

"Jesus Christ! How many ways do you need me to say it? The spirit of Gloria Lidsay, ex-wife of Sergeant Ivor Lidsay, took possession of the soul of Elizabeth."

Sam was about to dismiss this as Jane's perverted sense of humour, but he thought back to his exertions in Kefalonia, and changed his mind. "So where are they?"

"Behind you Sam." The sound of Elizabeth's voice span him around.

This time, he was fully struck dumb.

"Sam, this Gloria. Gloria, this is Sam." Elizabeth smiled wickedly at Gloria and back at Sam. "You may remember him from a night in Kefalonia."

Gloria, rapidly followed by Sam, turned the colour of tomato ketchup.

"Nice to meet …" The words were lost as Gloria's cheeks reached an even deeper shade of red.

"And you." Sam stayed seated, his eyes remaining fixed on the top of the table.

Elizabeth tried to hide her smile, but couldn't stop herself giggling. "I think we all learnt a few new things in Kefalonia." She looked at Gloria. "We should thank her for introducing us, to … some different ways of 'doing' things."

Sam's face had passed all available shades of red and had progressed to purple.

His other-half couldn't contain himself. *"So it wasn't her who was bonking your brains out. Who'd have believed it? Shame about that, Sammy boy. What is it they say? A cook in the kitchen, an angel in the living room, and a whore in the bedroom? Well, something like that anyway."*

Sam wasn't going to respond to the jibes.

*"Gone a bit puce, haven't we. Come on, you know you enjoyed it. Jesus she just about wore the skin off your…"*

*"Sod off!"*

*"That's more like the Sam I know and love. Shame you didn't meet Gloria when she was still Adhuc vivo…"*

*"Look, enough's enough. I get the point. Now piss off."*

*"Like Arnie said, 'I'll be back.'"*

Jane looked sideways at Elizabeth. "Care to share the joke?"

"Just some advice Gloria gave us," Elizabeth said, looking away from Sam and collapsing in laughter.

Sam stormed out of the kitchen into the garden.

# Chapter Sixty-Three

On the other side of the street from High Wood, Matt and Mark, who'd settled their differences, were sat in their Fiesta, 'casing the joint.'

"Let's go 'ome." Mark wasn't a happy camper.

"Just a bit longer."

"Oh come on." It was a drawn-out whine. "Please." The word sounded like it was squealed by a spoilt brat who'd been refused sweets.

Matt turned his head to Mark. "I want to see what's goin' on."

"Don't know how. You can't see sod all from 'ere."

"I can see enough."

"Bollocks you can."

"Anymore coffee in that thermos?"

Mark shook it theatrically. "What, after an hour and a half of freezin' my balls off. Not a pissin' drop."

Matt looked up and down the avenue. "Nip over to next door, an' ask 'em if we can 'ave some 'ot water." He pointed at the thermos. "There's some sachets of coffee in the glove box."

Mark looked at him as if he'd asked him to run stark naked through John Lewis. "Piss. Off."

Matt curled his upper lip, frowned at him, snatched the thermos, got out of the car, and walked across to Takanun.

"Prick," Mark said when he was sure Matt was far enough away not to hear him.

Klaus had his hand on the door handle, when Matt knocked loudly on the other side.

"I'll get it," Marie said.

"I was wondering," Matt said as he started mentally undressing Marie, as she opened the door, "if you could let us *have* some *hot* water?" He lifted the thermos. "My brother and me was walkin', and it's pretty cold tonight."

Marie held out her hand and took the thermos. "Wait here. I'll fill it with hot chocolate for you. If that's OK?"

"Brill'," Matt said. "Thanks."

Klaus eyed Matt up and down and shook his head. He leaned forward and whispered in Marie's ear. "Seien Sie vorsichtig mit fremden. *(Be careful with strangers)*."

Marie smiled. "I will."

"Gute. Rufen Sie mich an, wenn er weg ist. *(Good. Call me when he's gone.)*"

She smiled again and gently touched his arm. "I'll call. I promise."

Klaus smiled and gave Matt a look which said, don't even think about it, or I'll track you down, rip off your head, and feed it, and the rest of you to the pigs.

"German?" Matt said.

*"Bright, one this,"* Marie thought.

Five minutes later, Matt was stood in the hall with a thermos full of steaming hot chocolate.

"THEY LIVED IN AUSTRALIA." Bellowed out from behind the lounge door.

Matt jumped back and stared wide-eyed at it.

"Sorry about that. Just my dad. He's got dementia."

Matt tried to look as sorry as he could. "Sorry."

"Thanks." She looked towards the front door and Matt took the hint.

"Thanks again for this," he said, waving the thermos.

"No problem. Bye." She closed the front door, made sure it was locked, walked to the lounge, and as requested, called Klaus to tell him all was well.

"Where 'ave you bin?" Mark squawked as Matt climbed back into the car. "I was brickin' it."

Matt waved the thermos under his nose, screwed off the lid and cap, and poured hot chocolate into the plastic cup.

"You're shittin' me. You got this?"

Matt nodded. "Got somethin' else as well."

"Wha'?" Mark said between sips of hot chocolate.

"*That* house, is exactly the same, as *that* one," he said, pointing towards High Wood and Takanun. "And the only people in *there*," he said as he pointed at Takanun, "is some young, fit tart, and her dippy old parents." He rubbed his hands together. "Piece of piss compared to that." He tilted his head back towards High Wood. "An' not a pissin' sniff of a ghost."

# Chapter Sixty-Four

Charlie shuffled along in the centre of the column. At first, they were forced to struggle through eight feet tall, unforgiving clumps of elephant grass, whose razor sharp blades sliced into hands, arms, and legs. Thankfully, it was soon left behind and they skirted fields of peanuts grown by small-holding Chinese. Soon, the terrain got a lot wilder as it became scrubby jungle, and the column had to duck under and around bushes and the low boughs of trees. After an hour of energy sapping 'marching' through gaps in the bushes, Charlie began to make out the outlines of the atap huts in the camp. As they 'marched' into Tarkkanun, soldiers wearing patched shorts and clompers, shambled out onto verandahs to watch them enter camp. The path through the camp was inches deep in black mud and carried on a short way until it ended in a square. At the top of this was a beautifully constructed Japanese hut, which was the camp office and H.Q. This, under the shade of six colossal trees, formed the heart of Tarkkanun camp.

"Keep quiet, Swot. Any excuse, and they'll beat you up," Charlie's newly found comrade whispered. "But then, you know all about that."

Charlie nodded, his eyes fixed forward, and his body locked at attention.

After roll-call, the camp commandant, Colonel Kaito Yanagida, a short, bull-necked man, wearing lavender gloves, cavalry jodhpurs, brown leather riding boots, stiff-peaked cap, and a jacket covered in medals, strutted from the office, stood arrogantly at attention on the verandah, and surveyed the assembled bedraggled mass of suffering humanity.

A junior Japanese officer, Haruki Adachi, stood to one side of Yanagida, translating his brief 'welcoming' speech.

"イギリスの兵士、戦争は終わったです"

"British soldiers, the war is over."

"ここにビルマから鉄道を構築します."

"You are here to build a railway through Burma."

"ハードと元気を操作します。あなたは健康的な自分自身を維持しています."

"You will work hard and cheerfully. You will keep yourselves healthy."

"不従順は容認されません。これが迅速かつ容赦なくで配られます."

"Disobedience will not be tolerated. This will be dealt with swiftly and mercilessly."

"残りの部分、食べ、眠る。明日、堅く、よく働きます."

"Rest, eat, and sleep. Tomorrow, work hard and well."

Yanagida slowly looked over the assembled mass of malnourished, exhausted, beaten, infected, dying soldiers, sneered to himself, turned on his heels, and marched briskly back into the office.

"Go to your huts," Adachi snarled.

"Follow me." Fred was gesturing for him to follow.

Charlie nodded his understanding, and struggled through the black treacle to one of the atap huts. It had an inverted V-shaped roof, thatched with atap and nipah palm, which leaked badly, and was supported on a crude bamboo framework. Down the middle of the hut was a central gangway, flanked on each side by a split bamboo shelf about six feet long, and raised a couple of feet above the ground. It was divided into fourteen foot bays, where anything from four to ten men lived and slept, on bed-bug-infested, bamboo slats.

"Not much room, I'm afraid. But better than it was in 206?"

Charlie nodded. "Spent most of the time sleeping on the floor."

"How come you ended up here?" Fred asked.

"I bribed one of the guards for easy work details, and had to threaten to blow the whistle on him when he got nervous. He made up some story about me stealing food, and after a few weeks in solitary, they sent me up here." Charlie looked around the hut and frowned. "Any chance you could show me where the latrines are?"

Fred grimaced. "This way."

As they walked across the camp, their feet stuck in the mud, and as they dragged them from its glutinous grip, it made a sound like a plumber's plunger clearing a blocked drain. To his right, Charlie saw the cookhouses, simple atap shacks with giant frying pans made of crude iron boiling and steaming food. The approach to the latrines was through a morass. The latrine 'pit' was a deep trench floored over with bamboos with open slits about nine inches wide. The whole area was alive with grey-white maggots, which crawled out of the trench looking for ground where they could burrow and chrysalise into gross, fat bluebottles.

"That's where you squat, Swot." Fred pointed at the bamboos and laughed at his 'rhyming'. "Not much privacy, sitting cheek-to-cheek."

Charlie tried unsuccessfully to hold his breath, and the noxious 'aroma' of the cocktail of human excreta, vomit, and urine in the trench reached down his throat and dragged out what little there was in his stomach.

"Never get used to it, do you?" Fred said as he pulled up his rags.

Charlie wiped his mouth on his sleeve, and followed Fred back into the quagmire.

On the way back to their hut, they came to the 'hospital'.

"You should get the MO to take a look at your back. Better get it cleaned up before it gets infected," Fred said firmly.

The 'hospital' was another atap hut and was in a low point of the camp which meant it was permanently flooded. There was over a foot of water right through the hut, and in several places, it was only a few inches below the bamboo slats on which the sick lay.

Charlie and Fred paddled into the hospital, where the MO was doing his rounds in gum boots. He looked back over his shoulder and mouthed, *"Lift up your shirt."*

Charlie slowly and painfully did as asked.

The MO noisily sucked his teeth. "Bamboo cane?"

Fred nodded. "It was that bastard Takeo."

"Bit too handy with his stick that one." The MO shook his head and sprinkled Sulpha powder on Charlie's wounds.

He winced, but made no sound.

"Take a couple of these as well," the MO added, as he dropped six Sulpha pills in Charlie's hand, "and hopefully I won't see you again. Good luck." He turned away and splashed his way back up the hut.

"Hell of a man," Fred said with genuine feeling. "With everything he's got to deal with, it's amazing he survives this place."

They paddled back into the black, stinking mud and made their way to their hut.

Charlie stared around him, shook his head, felt like crying, swallowed hard, ran his fingers through his lank, greasy hair, rubbed the stubble on his chin, shook his head again, and followed Fred through the morass.

"Do you think he's OK?" Molly asked Emma, as they sat playing Scrabble. "We haven't heard from him since yesterday." She frowned. "It's not like him."

"He's fine. Probably having a good time with that tart Deirdre."

"*Desiree,* and she seemed to be a nice quiet girl."

"Yes, and you know what they say about the *quiet* ones."

"Which is?" Molly said with a degree of annoyance in her voice.

Emma simply smiled, tapped the side of her nose, and shrugged. "He's fine. He'll call tonight. Why don't you give *Deirdre* a ring?"

"*Desiree*. It's *Desiree*." Molly thought for a few seconds and then found the note Desiree had left with her contact numbers. "I'll wait 'til tomorrow. I don't want to seem like a fussy old mother hen."

# Chapter Sixty-Five

Klaus was sitting in the garden, typing up notes on his laptop, when Isaac came back to him.

*"Any news on Guillaume?"* Isaac asked.

*"Nothing,"* Klaus said with a note of significant frustration in his voice.

Isaac chose to ignore Klaus's mood. *"Have you decided what to do about the Spirit Walker?"*

*"Nein."* His frustration became even more obvious.

Ignoring his mood was now no longer an option. *"What is the problem, Klaus?"*

There was a prolonged silence, which was finally broken by a very deep breath. *"I have always been in control of events, but all of this seems beyond me."*

*"We have faced worse situations, but together, we always found a way. Nothing is insurmountable, Klaus. We will solve this. We have a workable solution for the blue spirit-energies, and if you and I can agree who should be the Spirit Walker, we have a way forward."*

Another silence filled the gap. *"What you say is true, but I feel ... I feel ... Ich kann Dinge nicht kontrollieren. (I cannot control things.)"*

Isaac thought very carefully about what he should say next. *"You are my general. You have always had the confidence of everyone in Papaver Rhoeas. You need Guillaume's support and knowledge. Decide who is the Spirit Walker, and get him back from Auschwitz-Birkenau."*

*"How do I chose one?"* Klaus was regaining his composure.

*"Sit by your computer and start typing."*

Twenty minutes later, Klaus was sat opposite Sam at the kitchen table, reading Isaac's notes.

"Tell me again what this is about?" Sam said with a raised eyebrow.

"Guillaume is missing and Isaac is certain he has been transported back to World War Two. It is vital we bring him back, because his input into the problems we are facing, is critical."

"Because of what I did with Adam, you think I could bring him back?"

"Ja. It is my ... our belief, Isaac's and mine, that you have the abilities to become a Spirit Walker." Klaus finally used the words he'd been avoiding for days.

"Spirit Walker? Sounds like a new game for the X-Box."

"Ja." Klaus gathered his thoughts. "A Spirit Walker is a person who is able to move from place to place, time to time, and reality to reality, and importantly, return home."

"And you think I'm one of these ... these Spirit Walkers?"

"Yes, but I need to confirm it."

Sam sat forward and leaned on the table. "Because even if I am a Spirit Walker, Elizabeth won't let me wander through time. Check away my friend."

Klaus referred to his notes. "I need you to think about Guillaume. Only him and *nothing* else. Clear your mind of all other things and focus only on him."

Sam closed his eyes and rested his head on the table.

Klaus leaned forward, not sure what to expect, and gave Sam a few minutes to focus on Guillaume. "Do you see only Guillaume?"

Sam nodded. His eyes moved as if he was in REM sleep.

"Imagine his heart beat, and see it as you would on a heart monitor. A moving trace of peaks and troughs, each one a point of life, an indication of his being."

In his mind, Sam could clearly see the moving trace.

"Do you have it, Sam?"

He nodded.

"Good. Now view the Earth as if using Google Earth, but don't focus down on anything yet."

A minute passed, and then Sam nodded.

"Overlay the trace on the Earth."

Two minutes dragged by, until eventually, to Klaus's great relief, Sam nodded.

"Now let the trace take control of the map."

In Sam's mind, the globe of the Earth stopped spinning, the trace shrank to a single peak, which rapidly focused down onto Europe, Poland, Małopolska, a province of southern Poland, and the town of Oświęcim. Sam's mind fought to regain control, but the Spirit Walker had taken over, and the process wouldn't stop until Guillaume had been precisely located. The peak zoomed again and hovered over a wooden building, a barrack, where the single peak returned to a complete moving trace of Guillaume's heartbeat. The Spirit Walker in Sam had achieved its objective, shut down. Sam jumped up, and violently pushed his chair away from the table into the cabinets under the sink.

"You want me to travel back to *Auschwitz*! Are you mad! They murdered millions there." He shook his head vigorously. "No. No way, Klaus. I'd never survive."

"So do you think Guillaume will survive? He needs our help."

"He might need help, but it's not going to be mine." He shook his head again. "Elizabeth wouldn't allow it. And anyway, why wouldn't the SS guards see me? Last time, I started changing into … How will Guillaume know me? How do I get back? My God, Klaus, when I got involved in all this I didn't expect I'd be asked to turn into Dr Who."

"Who?"

"Dr Who. He's a character on TV who travels through time and space."

Klaus nodded, despite not understanding Sam's explanation. Isaac had been right. Sam had the powers to be a Spirit Walker, but could he risk Sam's life to bring Guillaume back? What if neither of them came back? He would need to speak with Isaac again.

"What is important, is we know you have the abilities of a Spirit Walker. There are others in the group the same as you, and they may be able to do this."

*"Aber nicht mein Sohn! (But not my son!)"* Klaus thought.

# Chapter Sixty-Six

Guillaume and Isaac 'rested' for half an hour in the latrines, while others completed their duties. They'd been given water, and some 'edible' scraps, and felt just about strong enough to make the hazardous walk back to the barracks.

Guillaume stood first and helped Isaac to his feet.

"I will walk on my own," Isaac said, looking as if he was well past his breaking point. "If they see any hint of distress, they'll gas me, or just shoot me where I stand."

"None of that!" Guillaume said firmly. "We will get through this together."

Isaac managed a half-smile, but his face gave away that he'd lost all his fight.

"We will walk arm in arm," Guillaume said firmly. "It will look as if we are simply friends."

Isaac did his best to smile, swallowed hard, and nodded. "Simply friends."

They thanked those who'd helped them and walked outside into the 'fresh' air where no-one paid them any attention. Within yards of the barrack, a bored, fat, Polish Kapo, strutted across to them.

"Draniu Żydów! *(Bastard Jews!)* Co robisz? *(What are you doing?)*"

Isaac shrugged.

"We don't understand," Guillaume said, panic growing in his voice.

"CO ROBISZ!" He screamed at them and smashed the handle of his whip into the side of Isaac's head.

Isaac dropped to his knees, and Guillaume bent down, desperate to help him up, but this was only met with three lashes of the Kapo's whip. Guillaume cried out with pain, and rolled into a foetal ball.

The Kapo laughed, kicked him in the side, and then turned his attention back to Isaac. "WSTAWAJ!! *(Get up!!)*" he bawled at him. "WSTAWAJ!!"

*"I cannot and will not,"* Isaac thought peacefully. *"Yahweh, take me into your arms. I am already dead. Shema Yisrael Adonai Eloheinu Adonai Echod. (Listen oh Israel, the Lord, Our God is One. God is acknowledged as the source of all, the Source before whom we are all equal.)"*

The Kapo looked around him and called over an SS guard.

Guillaume, like a relaxing hedgehog, began to unroll. He staggered to his feet and looked up to see the SS guard puling his Luger from his holster. It was the same SS guard he'd seen in the factory. Bruno Franks.

Franks walked calmly up to Isaac, smiled at the Kapo, and shot Isaac in the back of the head. He turned, wiping the blood off his boots on Isaac's arm, and stared at Guillaume. "Haben Sie ein Problem Jude? *(Jew, have a problem?)*"

Guillaume's stare bored scorching holes through Franks.

Franks knelt down within inches of his face. His rank breath was as bad as anything Guillaume had suffered in the latrines. Franks raised his Luger and pressed the still hot barrel into Guillaume's temple. Smoke rose as it burnt into his flesh, but Guillaume refused to show any pain or emotion. Franks moved the barrel of the gun away and pointed at the blistering burn to the Kapo. He changed hands with the gun, and pressed it into Guillaume's other temple. Smoke rose again, but Guillaume's expression remained frozen in hate.

Franks roared with laughter. "Diesein ist besondere Aufmerksamkeit gekennzeichnet. *(This one is marked for special attention.)*" He spat on Isaac's twitching body. "Dieses loszuwerden. *(Get rid of this.)*" He instructed the Kapo. "Der Jude kann in Birkenau arbeiten. *(The Jew can work at Birkenau.)*" He nodded his head at Guillaume. "Es gibt eine Menge zu begraben. *(There is much to bury.)*" He started to march away, laughing to himself, but then stopped, and looked back at Guillaume. "Oder Block 11? *(Or Block 11?)*" He thought about the idea for a few seconds, sucked his teeth, tilted his head to one side, shook his head, and marched away.

Guillaume stared at the disappearing back of Franks, and back to the grinning Kapo. *"You are abominations, and you will pay for this barbarism. You will descend to Gehinnom, where every sin you have committed has created an angel of destruction, and you will be tormented and punished by the demons you have created in life."*

As he was dragged to his feet by the Kapo, he took one last heart-rending look at the now still body of Isaac. *"Be at peace, uncle. However long it takes, you will be avenged."*

# Chapter Sixty-Seven

Matt and Mark waited for the lights in the house to go out before breaking into Takanun.

"You sure 'bout this?" Mark whispered as they forced the kitchen door.

"Still shittin' it?"

"*No*. Just wanna be, like sure we don't get caught," he said unconvincingly.

"My arse," Matt muttered to himself.

"Wha'?"

"Nothin'," Matt said as he gave him a sports bag. "'ave a look around the downstairs rooms, and bag anythin' we can sell."

Matt lifted his torch and pointed the beam directly in Matt's face.

"Fuck off will you, you're blindin' me."

He moved the beam to his right, and choked back a scream, as it reflected back from the face of a wall clock. "Jesus!" He looked up at Matt. "What 'appened to stayin' togeva?"

"Look, we want much as we can get, so goin' on our own's gotta be better."

Mark shook his head. "Not sure about that."

"Look, if you don't get a pissin' move on, they'll be comin' down for breakfast." He pushed him towards the kitchen door. "Now jus' piss off, and grab what you can. I'll do upstairs. Only 'dopey old man', 'dippy old woman', and well-fit bint up there." He pushed Mark out of the door, started up the stairs, and called back over his shoulder. "Back 'ere in ten."

Mark shuffled down the hall, muttering to himself.

The layout upstairs was pretty much as Matt remembered High Wood, with the exception of it being reversed. He tried the door to the loft, but it was locked.

*"Shit!"* he thought. *"Hopin' there'd be another laptop up there."*

He turned right, stopped at the first bedroom, and the door opened easily. Snoring loudly in the bed, Matt could just make out Pat. *"Jewellery!"*

Downstairs, Mark was like a pig in shit. He'd collected an iPad, laptop, DVD player, some cash, three expensive-looking picture frames, a box-set of Game of Thrones, a BT hub, and three phones. "Piece of piss," he said satisfyingly to himself. "I think I'll 'ave a drink to celebrate." He found the drinks cabinet, and poured himself a very large twenty-year-old malt whisky. "I could get used to this." After another even larger malt, he decided to impress his brother and see what he could find in the cellar. "Nothin' to worry about in this soddin' place." He belched loudly and started giggling. "Oops. Don' wanna wake the locals." He fell back and spilled the remainder of his whisky over the sofa. "Oops."

Matt was also having a good time. A jewellery box contained enough rings, watches, bracelets, and necklaces for him to leave Takanun, but greed soon blew away any common sense, and he made his way to the next bedroom.

Matt pushed Marie's bedroom door open. Marie was sleeping soundly, exhausted after an intense day with mum and dad.

He walked to a low shelf covered with make-up, pulled open a small drawer, illuminated it with his torch, and smiled. An open box was filled with rings and ear rings. As he tried to quietly lift the box out, he knocked over a bottle of perfume.

Marie stirred in the bed and began to sit up.

Matt let go of the box and edged to the door.

"Mum?" Marie peered into the dark of the room, but sleep called to her, and she soon returned to the warm embrace of her duvet.

*"Shit,"* Mark thought as he moved slowly along the landing.

Mark, plus the remains of the bottle of malt, having missed the light switch, was unsteadily groping his way down the cellar steps. He got within two steps of the bottom, stumbled and fell into a pile of blankets.

"Oops," he said, still giggling. "Soddin' lucky, that." He got up unsteadily and beamed as, illuminated by his torch, he saw the piles of 'stuff'. "I'm gonna need a bigga bag." He threw his arms wide and fell unconscious onto the blankets.

Matt decided not to push his luck and made his way to the kitchen. "You 'ere?" He hissed into the darkness. He did the same in all the downstairs rooms, his mood growing increasingly worse. As he came back down the hall, he noticed the cellar door was open. "'e'd never go down there on his own, would 'e?" He flicked on the lights and walked about halfway down the cellar steps, chewing his bottom lip, when he saw Mark lying prostrate on a pile of blankets, arms spread like a crucifix, legs wide apart, and snoring like a bull elephant mounting his mate. He walked quickly down, but his concern was soon extinguished as he smelt his brother's breath. "You bastard. Fuckin' booze." He kicked Mark's leg and pushed him with his foot.

"Wha'! Uh! Who the fu' …" The rest was lost as Mark started snoring again, but the slaps to the face did the trick.

Matt picked him up by the neck of his jacket. "You twat. One pissin' night. One sober pissin' night was all I needed from you, and you couldn't even bastard well manage that." He dropped him onto his back. "You and me are finished. Pissed or not, you can find your own bleedin' way back."

Mark looked up at him through half-open eyes. "Matteeee. Matteeee. I wa' … jus' like one … one fu' …don' be a twat …" His eyes closed and he slipped back into his alcohol-fuelled stupor.

Matt looked down at him, shook his head, picked up Mark's bag, walked back to the kitchen, and left the house.

In the cellar, blue lights gathered around Mark's unconscious body.

# Chapter Sixty-Eight

"Has anyone tried to go into the lounge?" Sam asked. He was feeling peckish and was making toast.

"Haven't you?" Jane replied.

Everyone turned, looked at everyone else, and everyone shook their heads.

"So who decided we couldn't go into the rooms where the lights are?" Sam turned away from the toaster and frowned. "Anyone?"

A chorus of shaking heads gave the answer.

"No-one?" Klaus said with disbelief in his voice.

"I suppose we all just assumed it was dangerous," Elizabeth said defensively.

"Then we need to see what's in there," Klaus said, as he walked out of the kitchen into the hall.

"I'll take a look." Karsten was stood close to Klaus. "We need to know if it's dangerous."

"Bist du sicher? *(Are you sure?)*"

"I am sure."

Klaus frowned, but then nodded in agreement. "Pass auf dich auf. *(Take care.)*"

"Ich werde. *(I will.)*"

Everyone came out of the kitchen and stood around Klaus.

Karsten stepped forward, stretched his fingers, took a deep breath, stared at the door handle, looked back at Klaus, half smiled, reached out, and gripped the handle. Nothing happened. He turned, smiled at everyone, opened the door, walked into the lounge, and closed the door. The scene which met him, wasn't what Karsten had imagined. With the exception of the door to the hall, the walls, floor and ceiling, were covered in a thick carpet of pulsating blue lights. He took a few steps into the room and the lights on the floor moved aside like the wake from a power boat. Karsten stopped and stood stock still.

"You can come in," he called. "It's OK."

"Why have they stopped there?" Elizabeth asked, staring at the lights packed against the edges of the door. "The door seems to be acting like some kind of barrier?"

Klaus walked up to the wall, reached out, and gently moved his hand through the lights. "It feels like a warm bath." As his hand disturbed them, they rippled back, and clung to the wall, like limpets to the hull of a ship.

"I have never seen anything like this." Klaus stood back, his eyes fixed on the wall.

"We should take a look in the map room," Sam suggested, walking briskly down the connecting corridor.

Jane, Gloria, Adam, and Elizabeth, followed Sam. Karsten and Rebecca stayed with Klaus, whose gaze hadn't left the wall.

"There can only be one thing holding them back," Klaus said softly. "The structure of the house is still saturated with the lost souls of World War One." He started chuckling to himself. "They won't give up their place for these 'new' lost souls, so the 'intruders' have to gather on the surface, and wait their turn." He stood up, walked towards the wall, brushed his hand through the deep coating of blue lights, and watched as they flowed through his fingers. A loud knock from the front door made him jump and stumble back against the wall. The lights erupted in an explosion of spirit-energy, but soon settled back into a gently undulating swell.

"Scheiße! Das machte mir Angst. *(Shit! That scared me.)*"

Elizabeth ran back from the map room. "I'll get it."

She opened the lounge door and walked quickly to the front door. Outside, the Mathers were assembled.

"Caterina. Come in. Come in. Follow me," Elizabeth said with genuine pleasure at seeing her again.

Caterina kissed the air close to her cheeks. "Grazie, Elizabeth. So good to see you again."

"Ciao," Elizabeth replied.

"Molto bene. Molto bene, Elizabeth. You have been practicing."

"Si. But I'm afraid that's the limit of my linguistic skills."

Caterina shook her head. "You have tried for me, and that is meraviglioso, wonderful."

Elizabeth turned and walked to the lounge. "We have visitors," she said as she waved the Mathers in.

Klaus smiled. "Così bello vederti. *(So good to see you.)*"

"Your Italian is excellent, Klaus," Alfredo said, as he shook Klaus firmly by the hand. "I'm the only member of the family who can do this," he said with a huge smile.

"And to what do we owe this pleasure?" Klaus asked as he gestured for Caterina to sit on the sofa.

"Grazie, Klaus." She looked around the room and smiled. "I see you have visitors?"

"Ja." Klaus shrugged. "This is why I asked for your help."

"Ah. Yes." Her gaze dropped to the floor.

"Caterina, is there a problem?" Elizabeth felt Caterina's embarrassment.

"You are perceptive, my dear. Since we met, we have spoken a great deal about the situation we find ourselves in." She clasped her hands in front of her. "And after much soul searching, we, all of us that is, think it better if we move on. Our time passed long ago, and this is Alfredo's time. We will be sad to leave, but our faith gives us the courage and belief that this is the right thing to do." She glanced at Alfredo who was clearly upset. "Alfredo will stay and work with you."

"It makes me, tanto triste *(so sad)*, to be losing my family so soon after finding them, but mamma wants it this way. I have been fortunate to have mamma e papà for so many extra years, but still, parting is not easy." His eyes were glistening with tears. "For me, a page turns, and a new chapter starts. I am here to learn and to help." He paused briefly. "If you will have me?"

Klaus shook Alfredo warmly by the hand. "You are already one of the team. It is good to 'officially' have you with us. As you can see," Klaus said and pointed at the blue lights coating the wall, "we need all the help we can."

Elizabeth took a few steps forward. "Caterina, I thought you'd all decided to stay. What's changed your mind?"

She smiled wistfully. "I have lived and loved a full life. I miss those who have gone before me. I miss them more than I believed it was possible. It's time to be reunited." She shrugged slightly. "È il mio momento. *(It's my time.)*"

Elizabeth hid her sadness. "When will you leave?"

Caterina smiled and tenderly held her hand close to Elizabeth's cheek. "I was hoping you would help us with that, mio caro."

"Me?"

"Of course. You have helped so many others. Will you do it for me?" She moved her face close to Elizabeth's ear. "Essere il mio Salvatore. Be my saviour."

Elizabeth clasped her hands together as if in prayer. "I will do everything I can for you. When do you want to be reunited?"

"Now?" Caterina said, tilting her head to one side. "Strike while the iron is hot?"

Elizabeth was taken aback. She looked at Klaus who shrugged, and mouthed encouragingly, *"You should help her."*

Elizabeth swallowed hard and nodded. "OK."

Caterina blew her a kiss. "Mio uno speciale. Dio vi benedica per questo. *(My special one. God bless you for this.)*"

"I help lost souls pass over in the gallery, but it's only ever been one at a time."

"Why change?" Caterina said happily, a look of serene contentment on her face. "Shall we go to the gallery, Elizabeth?"

"Of course, but can we do this one person at a time?"

Caterina shook her head. "Alfred and I haven't been parted from each other for too many years to remember. At this time, more than any other, we have to be together. Luca and Lorenzo want the same. Draw on your faith, Elizabeth. It will give you the strength you need. Dio non si lascerà ora. God will not desert you now."

Elizabeth chewed her top lip, blew out a long breath, folded her hands at the back of her neck, pinched the top of her nose, smiled, and finally said, "I'll meet you in the gallery. Sam will show you the way." She looked around the room at the others. "I think we should all leave. There are some goodbyes which … which …" Everyone understood, and walked out of the lounge saying their goodbyes.

Klaus was the last to leave. "Viaggio sicuro. Dio sia con voi, Caterina. *(Safe journey. God be with you, Caterina.)"*

Alfredo was shattering into emotional fragments and words were impossible.

Luca and Lorenzo stood silently close to Alfredo, saluted, and joined Sam in the hall.

"Nostro figlio diletto. Ci incontreremo nuovamente. *(Our beloved son. We will meet again.)"* Caterina and Alfred blessed Alfredo, and then joined Sam in the hall.

Caterina closed her eyes and made the sign of the cross. "It will take time, but he is strong. Alfredo knows it is the right time." She took a very deep breath. "Now Sam, where is this gallery?"

Sam stopped at the top of the stairs and pointed at the door opposite them. "She's up there." He was fighting to keep hold of his emotions. "I will miss you, Caterina. Especially your cheesecake."

"The recipe is in the kitchen cupboard above the toaster. It is my gift to you, Sam. Cook it, eat it, and with every mouthful, remember us."

"I will." Tears like mill streams were flowing freely down his face. "Addio."

"Addio, Sam." She blew him a kiss, and closely followed by Luca and Lorenzo, started up the stairs to the gallery.

Elizabeth stood alone in the gallery, recalling the Tommies who'd passed over. She'd cherished each one, for the pure joy of seeing a lost soul, now found, returning to their loved ones.

"Elizabeth?" Caterina and her family stood close to her.

"Mmmm?"

"Are you alright?"

Elizabeth dragged her vicar's hat out of 'cold storage' at the back of her mind. She would need all her faith to get through the next few minutes. "I'm fine, Caterina. I'm sure you should make this final journey together."

"As it should be," Caterina said calmly. "What do we have to do?"

"Stand close together and hold hands." *"Dear Lord guide me now."* She moved closer to the group and stood directly behind Caterina, an invisible hand guiding her. Controlled by a spiritual puppet-master, her arms rose into a cruciform, and she uttered words from another time, language, and place.

"Caritas Christi. *(The love of Christ.)* Concordia cum veritate. Nunc ite in pace. *(In harmony with truth. Go now in peace.)* Christus nos liberavit. *(Christ has freed us.)* Ave Maria, gratia plena, Dominus tecum. *(Hail Mary, full of Grace, the Lord is with thee.)* Benedicta tu in mulieribus, et benedictus fructus ventris tui, Iesus. (*Blessed art thou amongst women, and blessed is the Fruit of thy womb, Jesus.)"*

Caterina, Alfred, Luca, and Lorenzo, moved closer to each other, their faces lifted to the ceiling and the heavens beyond.

Sancta Maria, Mater Dei, ora pro nobis peccatoribus, nunc, et in hora mortis nostrae. (*Holy Mary, mother of God, pray for us sinners, now and in the hour of our death.)*" Elizabeth continued.

Caterina pulled her family tight around her, and uttered her final words on earth. "Signore ci porterà tra le tue braccia. *(Lord take us in your arms.)*"

Pale yellow mists began to gently drift from the family, their outlines became less distinct, until it was impossible to distinguish one family member from another. The four spirit-bodies, imperceptibly became one pulsating orb of radiant, rainbow light. Like the Orion nebula, it began steadily spinning, and by degrees, began to hover above the floor. The orb's pulsations became stronger and more rhythmic. It emitted a deep throb like a human heart which reverberated around the room. The rainbow orb trembled, stretched, and formed an arch over Elizabeth's head. It remained motionless for a few seconds, coalesced again into an orb, soared to the ceiling, and in an instant, it was gone.

Elizabeth collapsed into a senseless heap on the floor, physically and emotionally, utterly drained.

Sam heard the crash and raced up the stairs with Alfredo.

"Elizabeth?" Sam was thrown into a panic as he saw her lifeless body.

Alfredo calmly felt for her pulse, and smiled, as he felt it was strong and regular. "She is fine, Sam. Four souls at once must have exhausted her."

They sat with her quietly, and soon, her eyes began to flutter open. Supported by Sam, Elizabeth sat up. Her expression told Alfredo all he wanted to know.

"They've gone?" Alfredo said remarkably calmly, controlling the storm of emotions coursing through him.

Elizabeth nodded, her face a picture of pure bliss. "It was wonderful. They went together, united by love."

"Grazie, Elizabeth. Molte, molte grazie." Alfredo looked to the ceiling, crossed himself, dropped to his knees, and finally gave in to the flood of emotion.

# Chapter Sixty-Nine

Molly was frantic. She hadn't heard from Charlie for three days, couldn't raise him on his mobile, and to make matters worse, despite leaving messages, she couldn't get hold of Desiree.

"This is your faults," she called to Emma, as she tried again, unsuccessfully to contact Desiree. "What in God's name's happened to him? He always calls and tells me where he is. I'm going to call that policeman Morrison he works for."

"Morris," Emma corrected as she walked through the kitchen wall into the lounge. "Detective Sergeant Morris. Still can't get hold of Charlie? We should go up there and see them. Take the mountain to Mohammed?"

"That's the first sensible thing you've said for weeks." Steam was coming out of Molly's ears. "I'll pack a bag, and we can leave in the morning."

"Why don't you call that policeman first? There's probably a simple explanation for this."

"OK," Molly said grudgingly. "Probably should have done that earlier."

"Hello. Detective Sergeant Morris. How can I help?"

"Hello, detective sergeant, this is Mrs Thompson. I'm Charlie's mum."

"Hello, Mrs Thompson. I've heard a lot about you from Charlie. Good policeman, your son."

"Do you know where he is?"

"*You* don't know where he is?"

"I haven't heard from him since Friday. He was visiting some people in Norfolk."

"No, I'm afraid I haven't heard a thing from him. But he isn't due back on duty until tomorrow. I have your number Mrs Thompson, and if hear from him, I'll call you immediately. Bye now."

Whether Molly wanted to end the call or not, it was clearly over. "Bloody charming! Ignorant sod! Right. I'm booking a rail ticket. I want to be at their house tomorrow, and they'd better have some bloody good explanations." She turned on her laptop and checked the availability of Great Western. "There's a train leaving Cardiff at 09:11 which gets into Sheringham at 15:42. Bit later than I'd like, but it'll have to do." She checked for an inexpensive hotel, and decided on the Sandcliff Hotel close to Cromer pier. "Thirty-five pounds a night. Perfect." She printed the details of the hotel, put them in her handbag, and turned to Emma. "You stay here. You'll cause too much trouble up there."

Emma's eyes flashed. "I'm coming. I want to see what they've done to our house, and I know a damn sight more about Sheringham than you ever will. You'll need me there. And you need someone with you if you're ill."

Molly thought about arguing, but wasn't in the mood. "If you come, you stay quiet, and you stay invisible." She gave Emma a stare which could have curdled milk. "Right!"

"OK," Emma said, her fingers crossed behind her back.

The discussion was cut short by a knock at the front door.

"Why do people always call when you least want them to?" Molly said with irritation. She was ready to give anyone selling anything, her 'honest and frank' opinion of their trade or product, but held this back when she saw the young woman outside the front door. She frowned and peered at the young woman. "I know you. You picked up Charlie."

The young woman nodded and smiled. "We haven't been introduced properly. My name's Marie. Charlie and I have seen each other a few times and we've become good friends."

Molly's mood relaxed a little, she stood to one side, and waved her into the house. "Come in."

Marie followed her into the lounge. "Hello."

Molly looked back at her. "Hello?"

"Sorry, I was just saying hello to the lady on the sofa."

Molly sat down flabbergasted, utterly lost for words.

Emma leaned forward and patted the sofa. "Hello, my dear. Come and sit down next to me."

Molly finally regained the power of speech. "You ... you can see her?"

Marie looked at Emma, and then back at Molly. "Of course." She reached out to pat Emma's hand, and discovered the reason behind Molly's question. "Ah. I see."

Molly raised an eyebrow, pulled at her ear, shook her head, and stared at Marie. "You can see Emma?"

Marie nodded and smiled, not understanding Molly's reaction.

"She died in 1996." She paused for this to sink in. "You don't seem very surprised?"

Marie shrugged. "A couple of weeks ago, I'd have run screaming down the road, as if the Devil himself was chasing me." A smile flickered across her lips. "But I met some new friends recently, and let's say they changed my understanding of 'people' like Emma."

"But haven't ghosts got to let you see them?" Molly asked, astonished by Marie's calm acceptance of her deceased mother-in-law sitting next to her on the sofa.

"They showed me I have abilities which let me see them without their permission."

Molly frowned, looked across at Emma who was laughing, and finally sat down. "Why did you come here?"

"I can't get hold of Charlie, and I wondered if you knew where he was," Marie said with concern in her voice.

Molly sighed. "I wish I knew. He hasn't been in touch for days, and it's not like him." She leaned forward, her elbows on her knees. "He went up to Sheringham, to look into some family history." She decided to leave Desiree out of the conversation. "He should have been back today, but I can't get hold of him, or anyone he was going to see." Her eyes welled up with tears. "I'm worried to death, Marie. This isn't like him. I'm sure something's happened to him. Policemen make a lot enemies."

"The first time I saw her, I knew there was something wrong with her," Emma mumbled to herself.

"Wrong with who?" Marie asked.

"Oh, nothing dear." Molly tapped the side of her head, and mouthed, *"Bit loopy."*

Emma crossed her arms and sat back on the sofa. "Bloody loopy, am I? Mark my words, that girl was up to something."

"What girl?" Marie persisted.

"A young woman came to the house. She'd done a lot of research on our family history, and found we were related. Charlie went up to Sheringham to meet her family." Molly explained.

"Pure poison she was." Emma wouldn't give this up without a fight. "Right little tart."

Molly's face suddenly grimaced in pain. She doubled over, and moaned in agony, as wave after wave of excruciating spasms ran through her colon. The cancer was spreading, and delivering its signature of torment, agony, desolation, suffering, and hopelessness.

Marie jumped up from the sofa and did her best to comfort her. "Is there anything I can get you?"

Molly grimaced, and shook her head. "It … will … pass." She whispered between gritted teeth.

It took five minutes, but eventually the spasms passed. Molly blew out her cheeks and laid her head back on the chair. "I'll have to cancel that rail ticket. Could you call them for me, Marie?"

"Of course. Who do I need to ring?"

"Cardiff central station. I was planning to go to Sheringham tomorrow." She grimaced as the cancer gave her one last painful reminder.

Marie sat back on her haunches. "I could go for you. I've nothing on at the moment. I could use your ticket and you could give me details of who he went to see."

Molly frowned. "I'm not sure. They wouldn't know you." Her face was grey.

"But Charlie would. And that's all that matters."

"Let her go," Emma said softly. "You need to get back to the hospital."

"OK. But call, and let me know what's happened."

"And you, if he comes back," Marie said with a gentle, reassuring smile.

Molly gave Marie all the details she needed for the hotel, the rail ticket, and the contacts she had for the family in Sheringham.

"Now come on. Let's get you to bed." Marie said, taking Molly's arm. "Do you have a number for your GP?"

Molly nodded. "In that drawer. There's an address book."

"I'll call him and get him to come around as soon as possible."

Ten minutes later, Molly was settled into bed with her medications and a cold glass of water.

"I'll call you as soon as I get there," Marie said reassuringly. "Now rest. Sleep's the best thing."

Molly took little convincing and was soon asleep.

Marie quietly closed the door and made her way downstairs.

"Thank you dear," Emma said with genuine warmth. "You take care up there. Let's say I've got a feeling about them."

"She's sleeping now. I've spoken to the clinic and a GP should be here in a couple of hours. I've told them the back door will be open. I'd better go. I need to pack."

Emma smiled. "Bring him back to us."

"I'll do everything I can." Marie blew her a kiss. "Keep an eye on her."

# Chapter Seventy

Klaus opened his laptop to check his emails. He was waiting for a reply from Ralph on what to do with the cans of film. After trawling through enough spam to make a dozen meat loaves, he found what he'd been waiting for.

*From - Ralph*

*To - Klaus*

*Subject - Preservation of film*

*Been in contact with my friends at the Packard Humanities Institute in Los Altos. Their advice is on the attachment, but to summarise their recommendations, if the film has been kept in its can in a temperature and humidity-controlled environment, it should be OK to review. I can put you in touch, if you want to speak directly to them.*

*Any news on a date for the next meeting? My diary's filling up.*

*Best regards*

*Ralph*

Klaus closed the lid of the laptop and walked into the lounge. "I am going next door. It's time to take a look at these reels of film. Is Sam still with Elizabeth?"

Jane looked up from her magazine. "Yes. She's sleeping. The Mathers took it out of her."

Klaus nodded. "I won't disturb her. Karsten, come with me."

"Of course. I want to know what is in those tins of film," he replied.

"Cans, not tins," Klaus added helpfully. "If Sam and Elizabeth come down, and want to come around, their input would be very helpful," he said to Jane.

"Of course. I might pop around myself. I'd like to see what all the fuss is about," Jane answered.

Klaus knocked on the front door, and after waiting for some time, decided to call Marie on her mobile. The phone rang four times before she picked up.

"He … o, Klau..., I'm on a trai … Sign … is bad."

To overcome the poor reception, Klaus took the standard approach of speaking louder. *"I'm at your house. I want to look at the films."*

"Da… won't hear y… The bac… door is op… They won… disturb you. Call m… wh… you… watch … some."

"Thanks. I'll call you later." Klaus's reply was unheard as the signal on Marie's phone completely gave out.

They opened the side gate, and walked around to the kitchen door, which as Marie had said, was open.

"ACKER BILK!"

Klaus turned to Karsten. "It's her father. He is demenz."

Karsten smiled and slowly shook his head. "Der lange Abschied. *(The long goodbye.)*"

Klaus nodded. "Ja. Es ist eine grausame Krankheit. *(It is a cruel disease.)*"

They quickly made their way upstairs to the loft, moved the 35mm projector from the wall in front of the four chairs, lowered the screen, and walked to the cans of film.

"Is there anything in particular we should be looking for?" Karsten asked.

"No. I want to check if a sample we select is OK. If it is, we will need a plan to review everything." He waved his arms at the racks. "See if anything sparks our interest. You go right, and I'll go left."

*"OK,"* Karsten thought. *"Where to start?"* He walked to the first rack, and picked up a can of film. The label on the rim read, *'Battle: Location - Metz, NE France: Date - 27 September – 13 December 1944, Territorial changes - German-held territory captured by US forces.'* He shrugged. *"As good as any."*

Klaus had also made his choice, *'Siege: Location - Leningrad, Russian SFSR, Soviet Union: Date - 8 September 1941 – 27 January 1944: Result - Soviet victory, Red Army counter-offensive'*.

"Yours first," Klaus said to Karsten, as he unlocked the side of the projector. "I haven't seen this done for … it must be, anyway, it was a long time ago when I worked in the cinema." Ten minutes later, after a great deal, of winding and unwinding film, cursing, kicking chairs, and blaming Karsten for just about everything, Klaus was ready to view the first film. He turned the projector on, Karsten turned off the lights, and a shaft of flickering light, lit up thousands of sparkling, dancing particles of dust trapped in its beam.

The black and white film showed skirmishes in and around the town of Metz, and seemed to be nothing more than a historical documentary of interest only to chroniclers of World War Two. That was until it neared the end. It showed troops of the US 5th Infantry Division entering Metz on 18 November 1944. The column marched past the camera, each soldier waving and smiling at the camera.

"There! There!" Karsten called out, pointing at the screen. "Can you run it back?"

Klaus rewound a short amount of film and started it playing again.

Karsten jumped to his feet. "There! Stop it now!"

Klaus stopped the film.

"There! Do you see it?" Karsten said, excitedly tapping the screen.

Klaus gasped. "Ja. Herrgott! Er hat kein Gesicht! *(Yes. For God's sake! He has no face!)*"

# Chapter Seventy-One

Charlie was stood on the verandah of his hut and watched as three guards dragged a badly emaciated soldier out of a punishment cage at the top of the camp square. He turned and called to Fred. "Who's that poor bugger?"

Fred walked out of the hut, stood beside him, and peered to where Charlie was pointing. "Not sure. Could be quite a few of the lads. The Nips throw them in there for stealing food or anything which annoys them. You can see for yourself what it does to them."

"Is there more than one cage?"

"Yeah. They had to build a so-called 'bigger' one, because there were so many stealing food."

"Bigger?"

"Yeah. Ten foot by twenty foot and they managed to cram in seventeen."

"Anyone you know in there?"

Fred scowled and spat over the railings. "Yeah. Bill Moffitt. He was put in there without food, and they let him out twice a day to go to the latrine and get water. He had no hat or shirt, and was made to sit up to attention all day. Every morning and afternoon, the bastards would take him out of the cage, and for about five minutes, they'd beat him with sticks, fists, and kick him. He was a completely broken man. He died about two months later."

Charlie left it at that.

A few minutes later, the guards dragged the soldier up to Charlie's hut, and threw him onto the ground close to the verandah. Charlie and Fred jumped down with another two men, carefully picked up the unconscious form, and carried him into the hut.

"George, give the MO a shout will you?" Fred asked urgently. "Although if you ask me, he looks like another one for the graveyard."

"Who is he?" Charlie asked as he tried to make the lifeless soldier comfortable.

"Not sure. Difficult to tell who he is under all that shit. Best to leave him 'til the MO gets here."

Charlie looked down at the emaciated, blackened body, covered in scabies, his hair and beard, caked in dirt. Then there was the overpowering smell of sweat, filth, and excreta. *"Fred's probably right,"* he thought. *"This guy's past the point of no return."*

The MO came running into the hut, and took a deep breath when he saw the condition of the soldier. "Sweet Jesus. Is it possible for these bastards to sink any lower?"

Charlie turned, and walked outside to the wire, which despite the impenetrable jungle, the camp commandant felt was a necessary deterrent to escape.

*"How the Hell do I get back home? I got here, so there's got be a way back. Every way in has a way out. Come on, Charlie, think."* Like a caged lion, he paced up and down the length of the fence. *"I was in the bedroom at her house, walked out of the jungle, joined the column, and arrived here."* He stared at the wall of trees and dense undergrowth. *"How did I end up here? Was peeing on that tree the way in?"* He stopped, utterly confused, and sat down on a tree stump, his stomach growling like a rampant grizzly bear.

"CHARLIE," Fred called from the hut. "Dinner's served."

*"Thanks,"* Charlie thought with a chuckle. *"Bursting my roast beef, carrots, cabbage, roast potato, Yorkshire pudding, and steaming gravy dream. At least I'm losing some weight."* He patted what used to be his stomach. *"Losing a bit too much and a bit too quickly."*

He looked back at the jungle. "See you later." He started to make his way to the mess tent, when something made him stop at the hut to check on the 'man in the cage'. The MO had cleaned him up, and he looked almost human. Charlie stood close to the bed and pulled the sheet up a little higher. He leaned over, and closely studied the face, but there was nothing familiar about it. Slowly, the soldier's eyes partially opened. The small slits between his eyelids were glowing an iridescent blue.

Charlie stumbled back and fell over a bamboo stool. *"What was it mum said in that story she told me about grandma?"* His mind frantically searched for the memory. Bells jangled, memory files crashed open and spilled their contents on the floor. *"His eyes were a bright, iridescent blue."*

He stepped back and frowned so deeply his forehead looked like a freshly ploughed field. "Peter?" The word struggled to pass Charlie's lips. "Are you Peter?" He sat down on the opposite bunk, the air around the bed suffused with a blue radiance. "But you don't look anything like the photo." Charlie looked around for anyone to confirm what he was seeing, and saw the MO coming back to the hut with what looked like a bottle of water.

"Sir?"

"Yes, private …?"

"Thompson, sir. Eugene Thompson."

"Yes, Thompson, what is it?"

"His eyes sir. Are they OK sir?"

"His eyes?" He looked at Charlie as if he was the patient. "Well despite being out in the blazing sun for hours with no protection, I'd say they were in reasonably good shape."

"You can't see anything wrong with them. Their colour?"

The MO stared quizzically at Charlie. "Not entirely sure what you're getting at, Thompson. Stridham's eyes are as good as yours or mine. Now if you'll excuse me, the delights of dinner are calling." He placed three white tablets and a bottle of water close to the bunk. "Get him to take these when he wakes up."

Charlie was about to speak again, but bit his tongue. *"Stridham?"* He dropped his head into his hands. He looked down again at Stridham's eyes when they suddenly flew open and flooded the hut with a radiant, azure incandescence.

# Chapter Seventy-Two

Alfredo was sat in the map room, watching the blue lights hovering above the table and the maps on the walls.

Elizabeth, closely followed by Sam, walked in with a blanket around her shoulders.

"How are you feeling now?" Alfredo asked caringly. "I was very concerned for you. You took on too much at one time."

"I'm fine. Just a little drained, but that'll soon go with rest." She walked closer to him. "More's the point. How are you?"

"Non male. *(Not bad.)* Well, not as bad as I thought I would be." His expression belied his comments. "I suppose I lost mamma and papa a long time ago, and yesterday was just …"

"Final closure?"

"Sì. Un addio finale. *(Yes. A final farewell.)* But enough of sadness and things past. We must think of the future."

"Let's have a glass of wine and talk about how you become part of Papaver Rhoeas," Elizabeth suggested as she linked arms with him. "Sam, can you get a bottle of Merlot from the kitchen and meet us in the lounge?"

Sam made his way to the kitchen, and was almost knocked over by Klaus and Karsten as they ran down the hall.

"Tut mir Leid, Sam, *(Sorry, Sam,)*" Klaus said, resting his hands on his knees as he struggled to get his breath. "We … need to … speak." He followed Sam and Karsten into the kitchen and sat down heavily on a chair. "Where is everyone?"

Sam looked concerned. He'd never seen Klaus like this before. "Here. In the house. Elizabeth's in the lounge with Alfredo. We were going to have a glass of wine and you look like you need one."

Klaus's laboured breathing was slowly easing and he smiled. "A glass of wine is an excellent idea."

"Merlot?" Sam asked, looking at Karsten, who nodded.

"I'll bring it into the lounge. You go and sit down. I'll just be a few seconds."

Elizabeth jumped up as Klaus and Karsten entered the lounge. "What on earth's happened? You look like you've seen a ghost and run a mile."

"You are correct on both counts." Klaus said as he eased himself onto the sofa.

Elizabeth frowned, shrugged, and raised her hands to the ceiling. "You have my undivided attention."

"First a glass of wine," Klaus answered as Sam came in with a tray, glasses, and two bottles of Merlot.

"You looked like you needed a couple of glasses," Sam said as he put the tray on the coffee table.

Klaus quickly drained his first glass and held it out for a second. He took a deep breath and relaxed. "We have been next door in the loft." He described what they found.

"Cans of 35mm film?" Sam said as he pulled the cork from the second bottle. "Hundreds you say."

"Possibly thousands," Karsten replied.

"The loft is packed with cans of 35mm film. Reels and reels of film containing moving pictures of war."

Elizabeth sat forward on her chair. "You've looked at them?"

Klaus nodded. "Ja. A few."

"You've discovered something, haven't you?" She continued.

Klaus nodded again. "Ja."

"Are you going to tell us?" she said, with the slightest hint of impatience.

He smiled. "We only looked at two reels. One was the battle of Metz, and the other was the siege of Leningrad." He finished his second glass of Merlot, smiled at Sam, who understood, and topped up his glass. "Danke."

"Shall I continue?" Karsten asked Klaus, who nodded. "Towards the end of the Metz film, it showed a column of American troops marching past the camera into Metz. The film showed close ups of the smiling victorious GIs." He looked sideways at his father, who nodded. "Six of the GIs who marched past," he said then paused, and looked around at the intense expressions on everyone's face, "had no faces."

A butterfly launching itself into flight, would have sounded like a 747 taking off.

"No faces?" Elizabeth said incredulously. "Like the photos in the gallery?"

"Exactly the same, other than these were moving images," Karsten replied.

Silence fell again on the group, as they took in the implications of what Klaus and Karsten had seen.

"You're certain about this?" Sam asked.

"Absolut. Ich habe keine Zweifel. *(I have no doubt.)*" Klaus replied confidently and slightly slurred.

"We should all see this," Alfredo said softly.

Klaus smiled warmly at Alfredo. "An excellent idea." He stood up, reasonably steadily, and drained his glass. "Come. As you say, hit the steel while it is hot."

Elizabeth stood up and patted Klaus on the shoulder. "Close enough."

Ten minutes later, Elizabeth, Sam, and Alfredo, were sat in front of the screen, as Klaus and Karsten rewound the Metz film. It ran for some time with general shots of the fighting, but nothing, which showed close-ups of the faces of the US troops.

"Now! Watch closely!" Klaus said with excitement in his voice.

Everyone leaned forward on their chairs as the camera panned and focused on the column marching into the town of Metz."

"Very soon," Klaus said with growing excitement. "THERE! Karsten, hold it." He ran close to the screen and pointed at two soldiers. "There. Can you see? They have no faces."

Elizabeth, Sam, and Alfredo stared at each other, slowly stood up, walked close to the screen, and stared at the faceless GIs.

Alfredo softly touched the screen. "Captured moments of another reality, time, and place. Fleeting points of lifetimes, there and gone in an instant, but frozen here for us to see."

Klaus moved away from the screen and sat down. "This is the solution we have been seeking. These, as do the photos in the gallery, provide us with the way to help these blue lights, these lost souls to their salvation."

Everyone slowly turned, and looked at the racks of films and the enormity of the task they faced.

"But this would take forever," Sam said. "How do we start? Where do we start?"

*"Wouldn't pissing bother, if you ask me. Total waste of time."*

*"No-one was asking for your opinion,"* Sam said with frustration to his other-half.

*"Well, if you were asking me, I'd be saying you'd be a first-class tit to take this on. You'll bloody kill yourself and your friend."*

*"She does have a name. Now piss off."*

*"Look ..."*

Sam switched off the connection.

"Looking at that," Klaus said and nodded towards the racks of film, "I would agree. But I am sure it can be managed. I will speak to Ralph. He has contacts at an institute, who are experts in everything relating to film." He tapped his temple with his index finger. "I am sure on a TV programme I watched, they were using, I think in English it is called, face recognition software. If this does exist, then why couldn't it be programmed to recognise and filter out faceless images?"

Sam was uneasy. "You'd still be faced with what Elizabeth does? Assisting them to the other side. Who's going to do that? Not Elizabeth. There are still hundreds at High Wood."

Klaus smiled and turned to face Alfredo. "I think someone did something similar in Kefalonia?"

# Chapter Seventy-Three

The train to Sheringham, despite four connections, was on time. Marie hailed a taxi, made her way to the hotel, and asked the driver to wait. After checking in and leaving her case with the concierge, she returned to the taxi which took her to Cambrai.

*"So what do I do?"* Marie thought nervously. *"It's a long way to come to not say or do anything."*

Her agitation was eased as Desiree appeared from the back of the house. "Can I help?"

"Yes. Do the Le Pley family live here?" Marie quickly assessed Desiree and decided she wouldn't trust her.

Desiree nodded. "Sort of. Le Pley is mum's maiden name, but our name is Lyster. Why were you looking for them?"

"Sorry about the getting the name wrong." Marie blushed. "A *friend*," She placed a special emphasis on the word. "Charlie Thompson?" She let the name hang in the air for a few seconds. "He came to see you recently?" She noticed a subtle change in Desiree's expression. "The problem is that he hasn't arrived home, and his mum's very ill. I offered to travel for her and see if I could find out what's happened."

"Charlie? Yes, he was here last weekend. I dropped him off at the station on Sunday, to get the train to Cardiff." She frowned, but Marie could see there was no real emotion behind her eyes. "And he didn't make it home?" The false concern continued.

"No." Marie was getting increasingly worried about Charlie. "Do you think I could have a drink?" she asked as she licked her lips.

Desiree's act continued. "I'm so sorry. Come in, and I'll put the kettle on."

Marie followed Desiree into Cambrai, and looked around for signs of anyone else, but couldn't see or hear anything. "Do you live on your own?"

Desiree paused before answering. "Yes. I was left the house when Mum died. Been on my own now for about a year. They died so recently that I still think of them as here with me." She smiled. "If you'd like to take a seat in the lounge," she said and pointed to her right, "I'll make some tea."

Marie walked into the lounge, another room which looked like it needed dusting, and sat near a bay window at the front of the house. The view at one time must have been wonderful. But now, the housing development close by, had consumed just about everything green.

Desiree was soon back with two cups of tea. "I made it white without sugar. Is that OK for you?"

Marie nodded, took the cup and saucer, and put it down on a glass coaster with pink dahlias. "I understand your family links with Charlie's family go back a long way?"

"Yes. All the way back to my great-grandad Donald and beyond. That's where the family link is. Great-grandad Donald. He was Charlie's great-grandad Walter's brother." Desiree carried on to explain where the families' roots were and their links to Normandy.

Marie sat back in the chair. "Couldn't have another cup of tea, could I? I've got a terribly dry throat." She sniffed. "Must be going down with something."

Desiree's smile assumed new heights of insincerity. "Of course. No problem at all." She turned, hardly trying to hide a loud sigh.

Marie could sense something wasn't right. She heard the back door open, and there was the muted sound of voices. She got up and walked closer to the kitchen door. The voices were faint, but she could just about understand what was being said.

"She's who?"

"Charlie's mum … didn't … she's looking … him."

"Get rid … her."

"Another cup of … and … be gone."

"OK … don't … her …"

Marie heard the noise of a cup and saucer rattling, and she trotted back to the bay window.

Desiree came back into the lounge, with only one cup of tea, and very obviously glancing at her watch.

"Do you have to be somewhere?" Marie asked with her own brand of insincerity. "Only I thought I heard voices in the kitchen."

Desiree was almost lost for words. "No. No, it was just the milkman asking for his money."

Marie smiled. "I'll drink it as fast as I can." She stood up. "OK if I finish my tea in the garden?"

"No, not all. Lovely day, isn't it?"

The garden was clearly someone's pride and joy, and the view from the back of the house hadn't as yet been destroyed by developers where a gentle, grassy slope, about fifty yards long, ran up to a deciduous wood.

"Beautiful view," Marie said with genuine feeling. "Did Charlie go anywhere when he was here?"

Desiree looked over her shoulder and nodded. "He wandered up there, into Lateau Wood."

"Unusual name."

"The local council changed it in 1919, same time as my grandad changed the name of the house to Cambrai. Apparently, Lateau Wood, was part of the Cambrai battle. The first time tanks were used. You should take a look before you go. It's beautiful up there at this time of year."

Marie was suspicious of Desiree's motives, but her interest was stimulated. "Good idea. A quick stroll in the woods will put some colour back in my cheeks. Are you coming?"

"No. I've been up there too many times to remember. I'll wait down here for you."

Half way up the slope, Marie stopped and turned around. Desiree was standing with her back to her, talking to an older man and woman. *"Voices in the kitchen,"* she thought. But what shook her was when the unknown couple walked back into the house, through the kitchen wall. *"My God! More ghosts? What have they done with Charlie?"*

# Chapter Seventy-Four

Klaus asked Sam and Karsten to join him in the kitchen and they settled down at the table, feeling distinctly uneasy.

Klaus took a deep breath. "We have to name a Spirit walker."

Sam shook his head. "Not me! I told you, Elizabeth would never consider it."

Klaus sighed. "I know, Sam. You have much to lose." He sighed, slowly turned to Karsten, and swallowed hard. "There is no-one else."

Karsten frowned and stayed silent.

"Guillaume must be brought home, or he will be lost forever."

"And you believe I can do these things?" Karsten's calm demeanour was beginning to crack. "How many Spirit Walkers have there been?"

"Probably around a hundred."

"In all the years of Papaver Rhoeas, only a hundred individuals have become Spirit Walkers?" It wasn't a question, but an expression of disbelief. Karsten frowned, the cracks deepening. "Because Spirit Walkers were rare individuals, or only a few were prepared to be one?"

Klaus stared at his son across the kitchen table. "Wahrheitsgemäß. Ich weiß es nicht. *(Truthfully. I don't know.)*"

Karsten stared deep into his father's eyes. "So, there were very few men, who were either brave, honourable, gullible, or just stupid enough to become Spirit Walkers?"

Klaus nodded. "Probably."

"There are no Spirit Walkers now who could do this?" Karsten continued.

"None."

"All dead?"

"No."

Karsten tipped his head to one side. "If they're not dead, then where are they?"

Klaus wrung his hands. "The only two I know of, are living … but they are unwell."

Karsten sat silently, waiting for Klaus to expand.

"They are in mental institutions."

Karsten remained calm. "And the others?" He slapped the table. "The truth, father."

Klaus shook his head "Wahrheitsgemäß? Ich weiß es nicht. *(Truthfully? I don't know.)*"

Karsten remained unnaturally calm. "You don't know?"

Klaus pursed his lips, stared at the table, avoiding Karsten's eyes, breathed softly down his nose, and bit the skin on the side of his thumb. "What I have heard, is that most returned, a few lost their minds, and some … some never came back. To be exact, their sprits didn't come back. As Spirit Walkers, only the spirit travels. The physical body remains behind."

Sam leaned his elbows on the table. "Is there no other way to save Guillaume?"

Klaus shook his head.

"Isaac can't help us?" Sam asked sceptically.

"Isaac told me to find a Spirit Walker." Klaus looked across at Sam and Karsten.

Karsten shook his head. "But I have never travelled through time."

"No, my son. But I know you can."

Elizabeth wandered into the kitchen. "I've been listening." She looked at Sam. "Why didn't you discuss this with me?" She turned to Klaus. "How long has Guillaume been missing?"

"About a week."

"And how long can he survive there before it becomes impossible for him to come back?"

Klaus shook his head. "Every situation is unique. However, I don't believe he can survive very much longer before he becomes a permanent part of the past reality he is in."

"Which is where and when?" Elizabeth persisted.

Klaus's expression froze in fear. "Isaac is sure he is in 1943. The place … the place is … Auschwitz-Birkenau."

Elizabeth put her hand across her forehead, a look of utter panic on her face. "A man of his faith in a place like that? Surely he can't survive very long? If he hasn't already been …" She couldn't say the word, and turned to Sam. "You have to be the Spirit Walker. Karsten has never done anything like this." She sat down on the edge of the table. "I don't want to risk losing you Sam, but we owe it to Guillaume. This group owes it to him."

Sam stood up, looked at everyone, and walked silently out of the kitchen into the garden.

"Elizabeth." Klaus stood up. "This is too much to ask of you and Sam." She started to speak, but Klaus shook his head. "It pains me to say it, but Karsten is best suited to rescue Guillaume. He speaks German and could best fit in as a member of the SS." He turned to look at his son. "My love for you is so deep, that part of me will be ripped out if you go. It has to be you mein geliebter Sohn. *(my beloved son)*."

"In truth, my mind was already made up to go," Karsten said with a sigh. "It is not the risks which frighten me. It is seeing what we Germans did in that Gottverlassene *(God-forsaken)* place." He held his father gently at arm's length. "What do I have to do?"

Klaus looked around the kitchen. "We need to be on our own."

Everyone nodded, left the kitchen to Klaus and Karsten, and closed the door behind them.

Klaus stared deeply into Karsten's eyes. "Dazu bist du sicher? *(You're sure?)*"

"Nein, aber es muss getan werden. *(No, but it must be done.)*"

The voice was clear and identifiable. *"Do you need my help?"*

"Isaac?" Klaus uttered.

*"Yes, my friend. You send your son for my brother."*

"I wish there was another way, but …"

*"They will return."*

"I wish I had your confidence."

*"My faith and experience tells me this."*

"You offered help."

*"Yes. Go to a bedroom."*

Karsten's expression brightened. "Isaac?"

*"You will need to rest."*

Klaus and Karsten walked into the hall, past the others, and made their way to a bedroom.

Isaac spoke directly to Karsten. *"The task you face is fraught with danger. Keep your concentration high, your attention focused on the task, and you will bring Guillaume home. But if your attention is drawn away, you will become part of their reality, and never return. Whatever you do, will not change the Holocaust. But you can save Guillaume."*

"I understand."

*"You say you understand, but you have only read books, and watched films and seen pictures. Your senses and emotions have not been assaulted, as they will be, when you enter the hell of Auschwitz-Birkenau. If you remember only one thing, remember this. Do not lose your self-control, or you will be lost forever."*

"I understand."

*"Lastly. Guillaume will not recognise you. A Spirit Walker must inhabit a body to merge into their surroundings. However, Guillaume will recall important things about his life which only we know. When you find him, quickly remind him of Bloemenwerf, Papaver Rhoeas, Chef Charon, High Wood, and his brother Isaac. Once he knows it is you, kiss him on the forehead, and your spirit will move into Guillaume. He will find his way home, and you will be released to return here. Now, lay back, clear your mind, and think only of Guillaume. His spirit will draw you to him."*

Klaus sat on the edge of the bed, his eyes fixed on his son's face. For a few minutes, nothing seemed to happen. Then Karsten's breathing became shallower, and Klaus edged closer to him.

*"Do not disturb him, or he could become lost between realities,"* Isaac said sharply.

Karsten's breathing became shallower, until suddenly, it stopped.

"KARSTEN!" Klaus screamed. "Isaac, he's dead."

*"KLAUS! Be calm. His spirit has left him. His body is in stasis, and will remain like this until his spirit returns."*

Klaus dropped to his knees, his tears soaking into the duvet. "Im Namen Gottes was habe ich getan? *(In the name of God what have I done?)*"

# Chapter Seventy-Five

Matt finished his third can of lager, belched, leaned over to his right, picked up the sports bag, unzipped it, and smiled broadly at the night's spoils from High Wood.

*"Mansten will get rid of this lot for me. Few more 'trips' like this, and I'll be out of this shit 'ole, like a rat on steroids up a drainpipe,"* he thought.

Despite this rare moment of success, something niggled away at the back of his mind, and wouldn't let him enjoy this rare moment of pleasure. He sighed, threw the empty can against the wall, and opened another. "Why did you 'ave to get pissed? And where the 'ell are you?" He spat at the empty chair opposite him. "Still in that pissin' cellar? Shit, you're nothin' but pissin' trouble. Aw, sod this for a game of soldiers." He lowered his hand to pick up another can, and the lack of any weight in every one he picked up didn't lighten his mood. He shambled over to the sink, plunged his hand through the solid layer of grease sitting on top of the now cold water, pulled them out, shook off the excess grease, splashed water over his face, and under his arms, tucked his stained t-shirt inside his boxer shorts, pulled an oversized, cheap, sweater over his head, dabbed his fingers into the sink water, ran them through his hair, didn't bother with socks, as they seemed to be growing some rare undiscovered fungus, pulled on a pair of trainers whose laces had long since departed, and left to find his brother.

Mark woke up. Every bone, muscle, tendon, ligament, hair, nail, orifice, and exposed piece of skin, were doing their best to overload the pain centres in his brain. Added to this, was the team of miners trying to tunnel their way out of his skull with jack hammers. He gingerly sat up and slowly looked around. The cellar was in complete darkness. He staggered to his feet and walked into an ancient vacuum cleaner.

"Bollocks! My pissing knee."

He limped to his right and stumbled into a plastic container of CDs. He hopped about, tripped over a pile of newspapers, and fell into a black bin bag full of plastic toys.

"YOU BASTARDS!" he screamed at the darkness. "WHAT THE FUCK HAVE I EVER DONE TO YOU?"

Upstairs in the kitchen, Sam and Elizabeth were making a pot of tea for themselves and Marie's mum and dad. They looked around them at the 'constellation' of blue lights covering the kitchen ceiling.

"At least we've got a better idea why they're here, and they don't seem to pose any threat," Elizabeth said.

"Not much more we can do now," Sam replied, as he filled the tea pot with boiling water. "Pointless looking at any more reels of film until Ralph comes back with an answer on digitisation. Once they're on computer, we should be able to make a lot more sense of them."

Elizabeth was getting mugs from a cupboard. "Are we asking too much of Alfredo?"

"He should be fine." Sam was about to continue, when they heard a muffled shouting, coming from what sounded like the cellar. "Did you hear that?"

Elizabeth frowned and nodded. "Cellar?"

Sam pulled a face. "Take a look?" Odd sounds from cellars were so commonplace that rarely did they merit any attention.

"Probably should."

"Tea first?"

"Yeah. It can wait."

Mark picked himself up from the floor and tentatively felt his way through the obstacle course laid out on the cellar floor. After cracking various parts of his lower extremities, he eventually found his way to the bottom of the cellar steps. He dropped onto his hands and knees, crawled quickly to the top, and smashed his face into the door.

Sam jumped at the sound of Mark's head making contact with the cellar door. "I think we should check that."

They ran to the cellar door, just in time to hear some extreme cursing and loud banging on the door.

"SHIT!!" Mark stood up and leaned against the door. "BOLLOCKS!! MY FUCKIN' FACE!!"

"WHO'S THERE!?" Sam shouted.

Even in Mark's under-used brain, it struck him that explaining why he was in their cellar might prove a little difficult.

"PLEASE HELP!"

Sam glanced at Elizabeth and shrugged. "WHO ARE YOU?"

"I WAS LOOKING FOR STUFF FOR A CHARITY SHOP, AND I FELL OVER THE PILES OF STUFF."

Sam looked at Elizabeth and scowled. "Do you believe that garbage?"

She shrugged. "Could be. You told me there's piles and piles of stuff down there."

Sam sucked his teeth. "It's possible, but who let him in? I sure as hell didn't. Marie?"

Elizabeth shook her head. "Definitely wasn't me."

"HELLO, ANYBODY THERE?" Mark shouted, banging on the door.

Sam stared at the door. "Shall I open the door or call the police?"

Elizabeth nodded and took a step back. "Let's see what we've got, shall we?"

Sam yanked the door open and Mark fell out into Elizabeth's arms. "Jesus. Thanks. I thought I was piss..." He bit his lip. "I thought I'd be stuck in there forever."

Elizabeth pushed Mark away and mouthed to Sam, *"He stinks of drink."*

Sam nodded in agreement. The alcohol oozing from every pore and orifice of Mark's body would have easily put Sam over the limit.

"How'd you get locked in there?" Sam asked forcefully, his arms crossed over his chest.

"I was looking at all the stuff down there to see if it was alright to sell in our charity shop and the lights went out. I fell over something and must 'ave knocked myself out." *"Bloody work of genius,"* Mark thought proudly.

"Who let you in?" Sam was beginning to lose his patience.

Mark vaguely remembered his brother telling him who lived in the house. "Uh, ... an old man."

Sam turned to Elizabeth and shook his head. "Possible, but not probable?"

She shrugged. "Benefit of the doubt?"

Sam pulled a face and turned back to Mark. "*You* smell like a brewery," he said through gritted teeth. "Drink much in charity shops, do they?"

Mark's brain was approaching overload. "I … I was thirsty and found some bottles down there. They … they must have been some sort of booze."

"Which charity do you work for?" Sam couldn't hide his irritation.

Mark's brain was now melting, and had only one response. Flight, with an enormous 'F'. He jumped forward, pushed Sam and Elizabeth onto their backs, and ran as if his life depended on it through the front door. He tripped and fell onto the sharp gravel of the drive. Ignoring the pain of the cuts and grazes, which were numbed by the alcohol, he scrabbled back to his feet and legged it down the road.

Sam leaned back against the wall. "What the hell was all that about?"

# Chapter Seventy-Six

Klaus was sat close to Karsten's bed. It had been two days, and his son still showed no signs of life.

"I've made you a sandwich," Jane said softly as she entered the room. "You need to eat something."

"Thank you, but I am not hungry."

"When Karsten gets back, he will need all your strength and support." She walked closer and placed the tray on Klaus's lap. "Eat." She tapped the top of the thermos. "There's coffee in there, and sugar and milk on the tray."

Klaus shrugged and started to give the tray back to her.

"I don't want to have to feed you. But if that's what it takes." She left the words hanging in the air, and stood staring down at him. "I'm not going anywhere."

Klaus sighed, took a bite out of the sandwich, looked up at Jane, and smiled. "Very nice." He took another bite. "Smoked salmon, horseradish mayonnaise, and dill pickles?"

Jane nodded.

"My favourite sandwich." He leaned his head to one side. "How did you know?"

"I have my ways." She smiled. "Now, a cup of coffee, and the Klaus we know and love will be back with us." She leaned forward and kissed the air just above his cheek. "We need you back." She stood back and opened her arms. "Rebecca will sit with Karsten. We need you downstairs."

Klaus slowly stood, looked lovingly at his son, bent down, kissed him on the forehead, whispered a short prayer, and chewing his sandwich, followed Jane downstairs.

"Relax in the lounge," Jane suggested, handing him his laptop. "Catch up on emails." She started to walk away, and then turned. "Have a sleep. None of us will disturb you." She raised her eyebrows and pointed at him with a wagging finger. "*Rest!*"

He managed half a smile, opened the laptop, and tapped the mail icon. A stream of emails filled the screen. He quickly filtered through them, deleting everything he didn't recognise. The mail he was waiting for, was last but one of the hundred he'd received.

*From - Ralph*

*To - Klaus*

*Subject - 35mm Film*

*I've spoken with the institute, and they're sending a tech-guy over to you. He'll bring the equipment he needs. They are very excited by your discovery. Not for the same reasons as you, but nonetheless, their enthusiasm provides the expert support you need. His name is Bill Burrough. He will be with you on the 24th. He will email you separately with his travel details.*

*Good luck with this.*

*Regards*

*Ralph*

Klaus wrote a quick reply.

*To - Ralph*

*From - Klaus*

*Subject - 35mm Film*

*Thanks for all your help. Tremendous news. He will stay with us in Takanun. Will mail you with results.*

*Regards*

*Klaus*

Sam was passing the lounge door and saw Klaus was awake. "OK if I come in?" It was the first time he'd seen him since Karsten 'walked' to Auschwitz-Birkenau.

Klaus tapped the sofa. "Sit with me."

"It should have been me." Sam's voice was trembling with emotion.

"It was never going to be you, Sam. You are too valuable here."

He shrugged. The deep feelings of guilt would be hard to ease.

Klaus closed the lid of his laptop and set it to one side. He turned on the sofa to face Sam. "Guilt is a corrosive emotion, and I need you to be focused. We all need you focused. We still have a big job to do. Thousands still wander lost and confused, and we are their doorway to salvation."

Sam breathed deeply. "I know you're right, but I still …"

"No buts, stills, maybes, or perhaps. Just focus?"

Sam nodded, stood up, walked to the door, stopped, and turned. "We are all here for you."

Klaus smiled. "I know. I am blessed to have such friends."

# Chapter Seventy-Seven

Guillaume was crammed into the back of a truck with fifty other spent echoes of human beings. Barely clinging to life, they moved like a herd of sheep who could smell the blood of the abattoir, and without a struggle, simply accepted their fate. Free will and resistance, had been beaten, kicked, whipped, and 'worked' out of them. There was no fear of death's cold embrace which offered a blessed release from their torment. The truck pulled away and Guillaume glimpsed the menacing red glow above the crematoria.

Some lines from Isaac's poetry came to him. *'These dead strode time with vigorous life, The air is loud with death, The dark air spurts with fire,'*

The short journey from Monowitz to Birkenau took ten minutes. On arrival, the majority of 'passengers' were dragged off the truck and marched away towards a low, grey concrete blockhouse which Guillaume knew was a killing room. He watched as they shuffled silently to their deaths, and as the pathetic group reached the entrance, Max Grabner, head of the Political Department, a branch office of the Gestapo, stood on the flat roof of the building and addressed the victims.

*"When this war is finally over,"* Guillaume thought, *"there will be days of reckoning. I will be there to be judge, jury and executioner."* His grip on his own time and reality was slipping fast.

Karsten felt he was floating on a waveless sea, until he became aware of a sickly, sweet smell which reminded him of failed barbecues.

"Bruno?" A voice from somewhere close called to him. "Bruno? Stimmt etwas nicht? *(Is something wrong?)*"

"Nein." Karsten's response was immediate and without thought.

"Haben Sie eine Zigarette. *(Have a cigarette.)*"

"Vielen Dank." Karsten lit the cigarette with a match from a Kapo. *"But I don't smoke,"* he thought. He sucked a deep lungful of acrid tobacco smoke and didn't cough. He remembered Isaac's words, 'maintain your self-control'. *"This is the reality of this German soldier. I occupy only his spirit, and not his physical self."*

"Ja potrzebować twój współpracownik. *(I need your help.)*" The Polish Kapo spoke nervously to Karsten's host.

Karsten took a step forward and slapped him across the face. "Sprechen Sie in Deutscher, Pole." *(Speak in German, Pole.)*"

The Kapo fixed his eyes on the floor, terrified of whoever it was Karsten had possessed. "Es tut mir leid Unteroffizier Franks. *(I am sorry NCO Franks.)*"

"DEMO! *(Show me!)*" Franks screamed at him. "SCHNELL!"

The Kapo, followed by Franks, walked briskly, until they came to two cowering figures stood close to a barracks doorway. A wretched man looking considerably older than his years, due to malnutrition, disease, beatings, and the daily spectre of death, was hugging a young boy close to him. The expression of horror in his lifeless hollow eyes, screamed that he knew the reputation and brutality of the SS officer marching towards him.

The Kapo dragged the man and boy out of the doorway and quickly told Franks they'd been caught stealing 'food', which was nothing more than a bowl of stinking, rancid cabbage stew.

Franks called them over and Karsten's spirit began to quake.

"AUF DIE KNIE. *(On your knees.)*" He ordered the young boy's father. He roughly grabbed the boy's hand, forced his Luger into it, and pointed it at the kneeling man. "Erschieß ihn, *(Shoot him,)*" he said, as if simply requesting a cup of coffee.

The young boy, probably no older than eleven or twelve, was terrified and confused.

"Französisch? Français? French?" Franks asked with venom.

"Oui. Je suis Français. *(I am French.)*" Terror and tears overflowed from the young boy's eyes.

Franks, calmly and coldly, gave his instruction. "Tirer sur lui. *(Shoot him.)*"

The young boy fell to his knees, his hands clasped in prayer. "S'il vous plaît. Je vous en prie. Je ne peux pas tuer mon père. *(Please. I beg you. I can't kill my father.)*"

"JUDE!" Franks spat at the boy, ripped the pistol from his hand, and kicked him to the floor. He grabbed the father's hair, and forced him to look at his son's face

The father, who knew only too well what was to follow, stared deep into his son's eyes, and silently mouthed to him, *"Dieu vous bénisse, mon fils. Avoir le courage. Nous nous retrouverons dans le ciel. (God bless you, my son. Have courage. We will meet again in heaven.)"*

Without the slightest hesitation, Franks shot the boy in the head, and forced the father to keep looking at what remained of his son's face. "Juden minus eins. *(Jews minus one.)*"

Karsten's spirit wept invisible tears. It required a superhuman effort to maintain his focus and control and not get lost in this reality. He needed time to understand how he could control Franks, find Guillaume, and get back to High Wood. He looked around at the scattered corpses, on the packed earth, in varying stages of decay. *"Why has God has forsaken this place? Has the Fallen Angel gained dominion over this Earth?"*

For the first time he saw the pall of black, acrid smoke, and the tongues of scarlet flame lasciviously licking the dark sky over the crematoria.

*"'They will throw them into the fiery furnace, where there will be weeping and gnashing of teeth.'"* Having studied for three years in a Catholic seminary, Karsten was well versed in the Bible. *"'But the fearful, and unbelieving, and the abominable, and murderers, and whoremongers, and sorcerers, and idolaters, and all liars, shall have their part in the lake which burneth with fire and brimstone: which is the second death.' You will burn in Hell, Franks."*

# Chapter Seventy-Eight

Charlie woke to the shrill blast of a whistle. *"Six am again. Don't slip too deep into this place and time. Keep a grip on who you are, or you can say goodbye to getting home to the ones you love."*

Lidsay stirred. *"And just how do you suggest we get back home?"*

*"Stick with me, leave me alone, and we'll get back. You start pissing around with me, and you're going to be stuck in this cess pit. OK?"*

Lidsay hated not being in control, but if he ever wanted a chance of getting back, then Charlie was his only real hope. *"I'll just sit back here and leave you to it,"* Lidsay said, temporarily admitting defeat.

*"Good. Because I'm going for what they call 'breakfast'."*

He walked through the cloying black mud to the mess tent, where 'breakfast' was the usual mushed-up rice, which everyone called pap-porridge.

"How's the soldier they dragged out of the cage?" Fred asked between mouthfuls of tasteless grey slop.

"MO left some tablets for him. He was sleeping when I left."

"Best thing probably." He looked secretively around the mess tent. "Want to get out of here?"

*"Who doesn't, but you couldn't get me to where I want to go,"* Charlie thought.

"If I don't get out of here soon, I swear I'll go mad or die."

"And if you do get out of here, you *will* almost certainly die. The chances of surviving in that jungle are pretty slim. That's what they rely on." He nodded to one of the guards. "Our fear of what's out there."

"Do you want them," he said and nodded at the guards, "to either kill us, work us to death, shoot us, cut our bleedin' heads off, or take a chance on making it through to allied lines? If we're lucky, we could bump into a Chindit patrol."

"I'll think about it," Charlie whispered.

"Don't think about it too long." He looked around secretively. "I'm planning to go in a couple of days."

Charlie finished the 'wallpaper paste', got up, and leaned over the table to Fred. "I'll think about it." He turned and ploughed back through the mud to his hut.

The caged soldier was sitting up, looking rested. "MO tells me I've got you to thank."

"Thank?"

"For being alive."

"It was nothing. We've got to stick together."

The soldier offered his hand, and as they touched, an electric shock, raced up Charlie's arm. It wasn't destructive, or painful, just warm and relaxing like a hot stone massage. The invalid smiled and raised an eyebrow. "You're one of us? Am I right?"

Charlie kept his powder dry.

"You're not sure what you are, are you?"

Charlie still didn't respond.

"And you're not sure what the hell's going on."

"I understand a fair bit." Charlie did his best to sound in control.

"If you know or understand any of this, then you must be something special." The soldier examined Charlie's face. "Have you looked in a mirror since you got here?"

"Why?"

"Have you?"

"No. Waste of time. I only wash the bits I can see." Charlie rubbed the growth on his face. "I haven't shaved for days. Just haven't needed a mirror."

The soldier gingerly got out of bed, picked up a battered cardboard box, peered inside, and came back with a small, cracked mirror. "Take a look at yourself."

Charlie took the mirror, stared at his face, and dropped the mirror onto the bed. "Who the hell's that?" He picked up the mirror, and peered at his fractured reflection. Staring back at him, was the face of a complete stranger. He looked up, wide-eyed, desperately struggling to think clearly. *"I said I was Eugene Thompson, but ... Didn't I just remember the name from Desiree? I can't be him, can I?"*

The soldier patted the bed. "Sit down. There are a few things you need to know."

Twenty minutes later, Charlie had been given a refresher course on Papaver Rhoeas. What was new, and of real interest to him, was what the soldier told him about Spirit Walkers. "Only your spirit travels? And you can control the body of the person you're looking for? And all this happens in their time and place?"

The soldier nodded. "That's a decent summary."

Charlie stared deep into the soldier's eyes. "If I hadn't watched them drag you out of that cage, smelt the stench of the latrines, felt the agony of the lash of a bamboo cane, and tasted the pap we have for meals, I'd say you and I were bloody deranged. Basket cases. But how the hell else, is all this explicable, and how in God's name, do you know all this?"

"My name's Peter Wallins. I'm a member of Papaver Rhoeas, and a Spirit Walker." He looked closely at Charlie. "And yours?"

The remainder of Charlie's face joined his chin on the floor. "Charlie Thompson." He stared intently at Peter's face. "You're Peter Wallins? *The Peter Wallins who spent time in Sheringham?*" He walked up and down the hut shaking his head, and then came back to Peter. "You're the one Grandma Emma's been searching for."

Peter's expression made it clear that Charlie had shocked him. "You've got a grandma called Emma? And she's looking for me?" He rubbed the tip of his nose and breathed deeply. "What year are you from?"

Charlie frowned. "2015."

"You've travelled back seventy years to ..." He stopped and chewed his bottom lip. "Why have you come back? And who sent you?"

"I've no idea why I came back, and as far as I know, no-one sent me back. I know about Papaver Rhoeas. They told me I've got 'talents', but they didn't send me. What I remember, is staying in a house called Cambrai, in Sheringham."

"CAMBRAI!" Peter looked around checking no-one had heard his exclamation. "A house in Sheringham called Cambrai, and your gran's called Emma." He gathered himself. "Emma Thompson?"

Charlie couldn't believe how calm he was, having this bizarre conversation. "She's been trying to find you since World War Two."

"But she can't possibly still be alive. Can she?"

"No. But I can see her ghost." He sat down on the bed next to Peter. "Mum told me how Reg Probert told gran you'd been killed in Burma, and your body was never found. Now grandma can't move on until she knows you're at rest."

Peter frowned. "So I die out here do I? Bit of a shocker, that." He lay back on the bed for a few seconds, then sat up as he seemed to recover from the shock of Charlie's news of his imminent death. "Thing is, I don't think I do die out here. Reg Probert was a lying, devious sod. Was always after Emma, and by the sound of it, he did his best to make her believe I was dead." He took a deep breath, trying to control his anger. "I'm here to recover lost souls. This is my present, and your past. What's *extra* special about me, is the blue light you sometimes see in my eyes."

Charlie nodded. "It scared the shit out of me."

"Sorry about that. It shows that I'm one of a very few who can sense the lost *before* they die. Be there when it happens and bring them home."

Charlie touched his face. "Who's this? Whose soul are you saving?"

"Edward Stridham, presently of 129 Field Regiment, RA of the 17th Indian Division of the 14th Army."

Charlie stood up and walked around the hut. "Marie told me about her great-uncle Edward Stridham. It's not a common name. You've got to be him."

Peter shrugged. "I need to tell you what's going to happen, because we may be able to help each other. Eugene and Edward will both die in a few days."

"How do you know that?"

"Papaver Rhoeas maintains comprehensive records of all lost souls, past, present and future. That's why I'm here now."

"So when do we die?"

Peter shook his head and sat down on the bed. "Dates and times can't ever be exact, but it will be in the next two or three days." Peter patted the bed for Charlie to sit down. "The only difference between you and me, seems to be that your eyes don't produce the same glow as mine. But like me, you can sense the souls of the dead who are about to die. You've been drawn back here to save Eugene's soul. This is what Spirit Walkers do." He put his hand gently on Charlie's shoulder. "This is what *we* do, Charlie."

Charlie's blank expression hadn't changed.

Peter continued quietly. "I don't know exactly when or how, but Eugene and Edward will die soon, and probably at the hands of those brutal bastards out there. Otherwise you wouldn't be here. I was sent here to bring Edward's spirit back, to rest in peace, and not rot, lost and alone in some jungle graveyard. You," he said and tapped him on the chest. "You've been dragged back here, to bring back the soul of Eugene Thompson."

Charlie slowly nodded, as an understanding, like the first rays of dawn, began to shed an ever-growing light over his ignorance. "I remember I was in a bedroom, and that a painting moved. They knew, didn't they? All along, they bloody well knew. That little bitch used me. Does Eugene know he's possessed by me?" Charlie had left surprise behind long ago, had accelerated past shock, was looking at astonishment in his rear-view mirror, and would soon overtake stupefaction.

"No. Once a Spirit Walker has taken possession of a body, the host's spirit will 'sleep', and we can control the corporal self, the body."

Charlie frowned, trying to make some sense of this baffling state of affairs. "Let me see if I understand any of this." He closed his eyes and crossed his arms. "You came here as a soldier, in your body, as a member of Papaver Rhoeas?"

"I got as far as Singapore and managed to get out before the Japanese invaded."

"So your body's... Where is your body?" Charlie asked, his frown almost reaching his hair line.

"In a village on the Burmese border. They think I'm a Nat."

Charlie couldn't help chuckling.

"Not a bug." Peter laughed. "They believe that Nats are spirits which resemble a human in shape. When Edward's home, I'll 'travel' back to the village, get back with my Nat, rejoin my regiment, and carry on finding lost souls."

Charlie's face froze in fear. "Jesus Christ! Where's my body?"

"Where's the last place you remember?" Peter asked.

"That bedroom in Cambrai."

"Your Grandma Emma, Reg Probert, and me, have only two things in common. Sheringham and Cambrai."

An expression of understanding slowly crossed Charlie's face. "My body's still in that bedroom in Cambrai."

"Unless anyone's moved it, it's still in that bedroom." Peter frowned. "Cambrai must still be a portal. Quite a few smaller portals were decommissioned, but Cambrai must have kept its power."

Charlie decided to give up trying to make sense of anything, and to just go with the flow. He waved his hand towards the camp. "You've left me in no doubt that I'm either completely psychotic, or I must have some 'unusual' skills." He pulled a face like a bulldog sucking a lemon. "If this is your present, then when were you born?"

Peter grinned like a donkey eating nettles. "1920."

There was a long pause. Charlie shook his head, closed his eyes, scratched his ear, swallowed hard, sighed, and began to chuckle. "So if you were in my reality, you'd be about ninety-five." The chuckling became stomach-aching laughter. "Well, given everything else that's happened, why shouldn't I believe you?"

"I'm twenty-two." He smirked. "Remember, this is my present, and my reality."

"And in my present, and my reality, I'm strapped to some bed in an asylum, heavily medicated, and doubly incontinent."

"You're here Charlie, and you're a Spirit Walker."

"Fine. So I'm this Spirit Walker who travels through time and can save lost souls. But how do we get back?"

"How do you think we get back?" Peter asked with a knowing smile.

Charlie pursed his lips and shook his head. "Not a bloody clue." He looked around the hut. "Haven't got any water, have you? God, I'm thirsty."

Peter shook his head. "The Nips don't give a toss if it's starvation or thirst which kills us. It's one less for them not to have to murder." He pressed Charlie's arm and stood up. "The way back home is simple. Our physical bodies yearn for our souls, because without reuniting with them, they die and we join the lost souls drifting around the earth. The physical self is constantly trying to pull us back and we have to resist this. When we have the lost soul we came for, we simply give in to the power of the attraction of your corporal self, and it will take us home."

Charlie was standing close to Peter. "Strangely, what you've said, makes perfect sense. But how do I get Eugene's soul back? Surely, if I took it when he's alive, wouldn't it kill him?"

"As you're Eugene, you'll be there at the point of death. It's at that moment, you give in to your body's pull, and Eugene's spirit will be drawn to a portal." He looked around and put his index finger to his lips. "There is one other thing. Portals only allow two pairs of united spirits to return at any one time."

Charlie frowned. "But that's not a problem. Is it? Eugene and me, and Edward and you."

Peter softly touched the side of Charlie's head. "You brought something with you. I sensed it when we shook hands. You're already united with another spirit."

"Shit, yes." Charlie nodded. "I'd forgotten."

"We have to get rid of it, or it will take the place of Eugene."

"And come back with me?"

Peter nodded. "From your expression, that's not something you'd want?"

Charlie shook his head. "Christ no. To leave it here, would be perfect."

Peter smirked. "There is a way, but we don't want it to know, do we?" He put his hand on Charlie's shoulder. "Trust me Charlie, I know a way."

Lidsay was awake and taking a real interest. *"Fucking try anything, and you pair of bastards will regret it."*

# Chapter Seventy-Nine

Bill arrived by train at Cardiff Central and was met by Sam.

"Glad I brought the van," Sam said with a smile as he looked at Bill's luggage. "Brought enough kit with you?" he said as he lifted the fourth and last aluminium case into the back of the van.

"Is it far?" Bill asked. He was a clean shaven, thirty-something Californian with closed-cropped black hair, brown eyes the colour of mahogany. He was about six feet tall and wore a quilted jacket, a red Polo shirt, faded Boss jeans, and tan Timberland boots. A confirmed travel virgin, Bill had to apply for his passport before travelling. He thought Wales was either any of the larger marine mammals of the order Cetacea, something big, great, or fine of its kind, the constellation Cetus, possibly a streak, stripe, or ridge produced on the skin by the stroke of a rod or whip, or the texture or weave of a fabric. But not a division of the United Kingdom.

"Only about fifteen minutes. High Wood's pretty close. Been doing this sort of thing for long?" Sam was not a great conversationalist.

"Since I was ten."

"Must be pretty good at it by now then."

"Passable."

Bill's tone and manner told Charlie he didn't want to chat, and after twenty minutes of uncomfortable silence, they pulled up outside High Wood.

"You understand everything that happens here?" Sam said to Bill, leaning his head towards the house.

"Yes."

*"I'm sure somebody loves you,"* Sam thought.

"I'll help you with the cases," Bill said as he hopped out of the van.

Sam quickly followed him, opened the back doors, grabbed two of the aluminium cases, and gestured for Bill to take the other two and follow him.

Klaus was stood at the open front door. "Willkommen, Bill. Welcome to High Wood. I am glad you are here."

Bill put a case down and offered his hand. "Thanks …?"

Klaus's cheeks flushed. "I'm so sorry. I am Klaus Bauer." He turned around. "This is Elizabeth and Alfredo, and if these fine folk will do the honours," he said as Jane, Rebecca, Gloria, Jane, and Adam, materialised in the hall, close behind him, "they are our …"

"We're ghosts," Jane said helpfully with a twinkle in her eye.

"I was told there were entities here." Bill answered without the slightest hint of surprise. "Can I see the films?"

"Of course." Klaus waved him into the hall. "Follow me." He turned to the others. "Could everyone grab a case, and bring them across to Takanun?"

Bill nodded. "Is that where the films are?"

Klaus nodded. "Follow me."

"Chatty," Jane said as she struggled to lift a case. "Never been called an entity before. Cheeky sod. Sounds like we're poltergeists."

"Shhh." Sam put his finger to his lips.

"Shhh yourself."

As they walked into the loft at Takanun, even the unflappable Bill's expression showed the merest hint of surprise. He walked into the racks, studied them for a few minutes, and then turned to Klaus. "Have you made a count?"

"No."

"Mmmm. OK." He sounded like a disappointed parent and walked in and out of the aisles, mentally calculating the number of reels. "Around nine hundred. I'll ship some back to the institute." He walked to the front of the loft and moved the chairs against the wall. "I'll need two decent-sized tables and plenty of power points. Can you get Hershey Kisses over here?"

Klaus looked confused, but Elizabeth nodded.

"Excellent. I'll need a lot. How about Dr Pepper?"

Elizabeth nodded again. "Anything else on your shopping list?"

A sheet of reporter's note pad later, he was finished, and he handed it to Elizabeth.

"This shouldn't be a problem. Not sure about the Tootsie Rolls, Jolly Rancher Hard Candy, and Twinkies, but I'll check on the internet."

Bill sucked his teeth. "OK. If I can get the tables and power, I'll get started." It wasn't a request.

An hour and a half later, Bill had digitally remastered the first reel. "I decided to use this one." He held out the empty can.

Klaus read the label. 'Battle of Tarawa *(US code name Operation Galvanic)* fought from November 20 to November 23, 1943.' "Any particular reason for picking this?"

"US theatre of war." Bill looked back at his computer screen. "I've digitised it and run a face-recognition programme over it which will eliminate everything other than soldiers with no faces." He waved Klaus and Sam over. "These are the faceless soldiers who've been identified. I've created a new file specifically for this battle, and I'll do the same for the others."

"Bloody impressive, Bill. How many are there?" Sam asked.

"Faceless soldiers?" Bill looked at the bottom right of the screen. "Total's three hundred and fifty-six."

Sam, Klaus, and Alfredo pulled up chairs and sat next to Bill.

Klaus tapped the computer screen. "We need to prioritise these. Bill, is there a programme you can run over World War Two battles, and rank them in order of Allied casualties by country? If there is time afterwards, could you do the same for Axis casualties by country? When we have this, we can send the individual files to the various countries for action."

"No problem," he said with absolute confidence.

"How long should it take?" Alfredo asked.

"Timing is down to how long it takes you to get the films to me. I can run you the first list of casualties in the next hour."

"Excellent. Let's reconvene here in an hour." Klaus was pleased with their initial progress. "Do you want to join us for a snack and a drink before you get started?"

Bill nodded. "Uh huh."

"You OK?" Sam asked Klaus quietly.

Klaus shrugged, "If he can do what he says, I will tolerate any type of behaviour. His work will go a long way to helping our spirits on their final journey."

Alfredo stopped at the bottom of the stairs and clicked his fingers. "I think I get it."

Looking somewhat confused, Klaus stopped next to him. "I am very pleased to hear it Alfredo. But what is *it*?"

"*It* is I think I now understand why images are so important. The films and the photos next door."

Klaus shrugged.

"I was thinking about an old western I saw, maybe twenty years ago? Cowboys were stealing Indian territory. I think the film was called 'The Black Hills.'"

Klaus interrupted him. "There is a point to this?"

"Mi dispiace. *(I'm sorry.)* There was a cowboy, no he was a 'city slicker'. I can't remember who the actor was, but he was trying to take pictures of the Indians, Apaches I think they were." Alfredo frowned, waved his arms like a crazed conductor, and then smiled." And this is the important part, they wouldn't have a picture taken because they believed the camera stole their soul."

"And?" Klaus was edging away.

"EVEREST IS NOT THE HIGHEST IN MOUNTAIN CANADA!"

Alfredo's head span around.

"You'll get used to it," Sam said with a shrug. "It's Marie's father. She lives here with her parents. They suffer from dementia."

Alfredo crossed himself and said a prayer. "All praise and glory are yours, Lord our God. For you have called us to serve you and one another in love. Bless our sick today so that they may bear their illness in union with Jesus' sufferings and restore them quickly to health."

Klaus started to walk down the hall. "You were telling us about Indians and cameras."

"The Indians, yes. I think they were almost right. The camera captured only a piece of their soul. Lost souls are attracted to faceless images, because they possess the final piece of the jig saw of their spirit. Without this final piece, they're incomplete and can't pass across."

Klaus's expression couldn't hide his amazement. "Alfredo … It is an excellent, and highly feasible theorem." He took his arm. "Let's go to High Wood. I need a drink."

Everyone was sat in the lounge at High Wood, demolishing packets of BBQ-flavour crisps, salted popcorn, and cans of Diet Coke.

Alfredo sat back on the sofa, deep in thought. "Klaus, the situation with the lost souls of World War One is now almost manageable."

"Ja."

"And they were helped across, using the photos without faces?"

"Ja. This is we already know." He sounded a little impatient.

"Bear with me. At present, the way we plan to deal with these blue spirits, is to stop them entering the portals by adding new concrete ditches?"

"Ja."

Alfredo turned to face Bill. "You're an expert on old film?"

Bill swallowed his mouthful of popcorn, his ego stroked, and sat up. "Over the years I have gained some knowledge of them."

"How many other films, like those next door still exist, and importantly, are intact?"

Bill sat back on the sofa, stared into the distance for a minute, and then looked back at Alfredo. "That's a very good and pertinent question, to which I don't have an accurate answer. However, I know someone who does." He stood up and walked to the lounge door. "I won't be long. I need to send an email to the Institute."

"What are you thinking Alfredo?" Klaus asked, believing he had a possible answer to their problem.

"I believe that if more of these films exist, they could be analysed like those next door." He coughed as he swallowed a sharp piece of crisp. "Sorry." He coughed again, clearing his throat. "35mm films are the way out for these blue spirits, as are the photos in High Wood, for World War One spirits. We need to capture screen shots of faceless troops from all available films, save them by battle or country, circulate them to the specific Papaver Rhoeas teams, and let them, with some initial assistance, deal with them as they have dealt with the lost souls of World War One." He drank some water, washing away the last unyielding fragment of crisp, which was doing its best to lacerate his throat. "Then we would not need to build the concrete shields." He looked at Klaus's expression, which didn't give a hint of what he was thinking. "There have been conflicts and lost souls before and after the 1914 - 18 war. Vietnam, Korea, Iraq, the Killing Fields of Cambodia, the Massacre of Nanking. Lost souls will go on being created as new wars inevitably happen. It is a problem which building ditches will not solve. It will only create a greater problem, as these spirits seek salvation."

Everyone in the room was staring open-mouthed at Alfredo, who blushed.

"I'm sorry. I have said too much. It wasn't my place to suggest such things."

Klaus opened his arms wide in incredulity. "Sie sind voller Überraschungen. I am sorry, Alfredo. I said you are full of surprises. Let me communicate this to the other members of the Astrea, which, I believe, will meet with their approval. For now, we will do what you have suggested and I will delay building the shields."

Sam walked to the fridge in the kitchen. "I've got something in here which I've been waiting for an excuse to open." He took out a crumpled brown paper bag.

"Been splashing out?" Jane asked.

Sam smiled, opened the bag, put his hand in like a Las Vegas magician, and pulled out a bottle of Veuve Clicquot Yellow Label Brut NV. "Thirty-five quid from Sainsbury's."

"Just bloody pour it." Jane just about managed to say, with her tongue hanging out like an over-exercised bull mastiff.

# Chapter Eighty

Matt was taking the last few twenties from Pete Mansten, when Mark, panting like a fox on Boxing Day, fell in through the front door.

"Thanks, Pete. Sorry about my moron brother."

Pete shook his head and picked up some of the jewellery. "Listen, if you get any more stuff like this, I'd be very interested."

Matt smiled and shook his hand. "Give me about a week, and I'll give you a bell. It'll be the same quality."

"Look forward to it. Cheers, Matt. Shame about dopey." He looked down at the prone, panting figure of Mark. "You could do great things without him dragging you back all the time. If you ever fancy dumping that," he said pointing at Mark, "call me."

Matt dragged Mark up the lapels and threw him, onto what did it's best to be a sofa. There was no point talking to him, as he was barely able to breathe, so he opened another can of lager, and started watching some grainy black and white film.

Half an hour later, as Matt was slipping into the cosy land of nod, Mark finally recovered most of his senses, "Chuck us a can, bruv."

No answer.

"BRUV!"

"Shit, what the …!" Matt narrowly escaped whip lash, as he jumped off the sofa. "You dopey twat!" He massaged the back of his neck. "I nearly broke my pissin' neck."

"Didn't wake you, did I?" Mark said with a stupid grin which he immediately regretted.

Matt's expression, could have shot blast a finely polished finish on a pumice stone. "You … words pissin' fail me." He ground his teeth, grimaced, and finally recovered a little control of his anger. "I've sold everythin' I took from that 'ouse." He paused for effect. "For three 'undred quid."

Mark almost fell off the sofa. "'ow much?"

"Three, 'undred, quid, and Pete'll take as much of the same as I can get. So we're goin' back, and this time, you'll stay pissin' sober." He stabbed his index finger into Mark's chest. "'cause if you don't, then you and me, bruv, is over. You can look after yourself. 'Cause right now, you're about as much soddin' use to me, as an ashtray on a motor bike."

Mark felt hurt, so he pouted, scratched his head, thought of asking for a can of lager, but thought better of it, stood up, sat down, crossed and uncrossed his legs, picked his nose, closely examined it, flicked it across the room, and finally folded his arms. "'ow can you say things like that to me? We're like blood, we are. Mum would turn in her grave, if she 'adn't been cremated."

Matt pointed at Mark. "You've pissin' 'eld me back for years. I'm only 'ere 'cause I promised Dad I'd look after you."

"Can't break a promise then."

"Just bloody watch me. *You* 'ave got one more chance. Tomorrow night we're goin' back to that 'ouse."

"I know where they keep most of their stuff." Mark was desperately trying to win some badly needed brownie points with his brother.

Matt looked up and threw him a can of lager. "Wha'd you say?"

"When you left me there, an' I was like stuck in the cellar, I saw tons of stuff down there."

"Like wha'?"

"Well … it was dark."

"Like I said, you're pissin' useless."

"No, listen. There was loads of like, stuff down there. Even if I can't remember wha' it was, some of it's gotta be like decent stuff." He scratched his chin. "Come on bruv, it's gotta be worf a'avin a look? There is one fing though I should 'ave mentioned."

"Which is what?" Matt was losing patience.

"Well," Mark said. He looked down at his hands and steepled his fingers. "There was some 'uvver punters in the 'ouse."

Matt stared at Mark in disbelief. "And you thought you'd tell me now." He shook his head, and threw an empty can, which caught him a glancing blow on the side of the head.

"Piss off. You could 'ave 'ad my eye out."

"You piss off. How many others were there?" He shook his head, picked up another empty can, but decided not to throw it.

Mark was getting increasingly nervous with his brother's reactions. "Just two ov 'em, I think. But I'm pretty sure they didn't live there."

Matt's sigh almost sucked all the air out of their 'flat'. "So they probably *don't* live there."

Mark shook his head and walked behind a chair for cover. "No."

"OK. So it's probably just the tart who'll be there."

"Yeah."

"I wasn't askin' for your pissin' opinion."

Mark ran his fingers across his lips, zipping them up.

"We'll park up on Friday night and see what 'appens."

# Chapter Eighty-One

Guillaume was herded together with ten others from Monowitz, and they marched towards the low concrete blockhouses.

*"They're going to gas us,"* he thought, and the memory of his real identity, now only a drifting shadow, passed fleetingly across his mind.

The young man beside him, a French communist, saw his expression of terror. "Nous allons y travailler. Ils ne seront pas gaz nous. Pas encore. *(We will work there. They will not gas us. Not yet.)*"

"Merci."

The young Frenchman shook his head and sighed. "Il serait mieux si ils nous gazés. *(It would be better if they gassed us.)*"

Guillaume looked sideways and frowned.

"Vous le verrez. *(You will see.)*"

The conversation was ended by a club across the young Frenchman's back.

"MILCZ! *(Be silent!)*" A tall, heavily tattooed Kapo yelled.

They 'marched' past the gas chambers and into an open area at the back. The sight which met them convinced Guillaume he'd been condemned to eternal damnation. Directly in front of him, were three pits, approximately fifty to sixty yards long, thirty feet wide, and nine feet deep. They were filled with corpses which were licked by the tongues of a thousand tiny blue flames.

Guillaume fell to his knees and recited a prayer. "O God, full of compassion, Who dwells on high, grant true rest upon the wings of the Shechinah *(Divine Presence)*, in the exalted spheres of the holy and pure, who shine as the resplendence of the firmament, to these souls who have gone to their world, for charity has been donated in remembrance of their souls; may their place of rest be in Gan Eden. Therefore, may the All-

Merciful One shelter them with the cover of His wings forever, and bind their souls in the bond of life. The Lord is their heritage; may they rest in his resting-place in peace; and let us say: Amen."

The young Frenchman dragged him to his feet as a Kapo moved towards them.

Guillaume smiled at the young Frenchman and looked back at the pit where the fire had grown fiercer. In the furnace-like heat, a few of the dead began to stir, writhing as though in unbearable pain, as their arms, and legs strained in slow motion. Their bodies hesitantly straightened a little, as if, with their last strength, they were trying to rebel against their doom. But eventually, the fire became so fierce that the bodies were enveloped by the towering flames. One by one, the blisters which had formed on the corpses' skin, began to burst. They glistened as if they'd been greased. Bodies burst open. The sound of the hissing and sputtering of frying corpses in the terrible heat violated Guillaume's senses. The flames, fanned by the wind, now took on a fiery, white hue, and Guillaume finally had to look away from the pit. Lines from Milton's 'Paradise Lost' came to him.

*'As one great furnace flamed; yet from those flames, No light; but rather darkness visible, Regions of sorrow, doleful shades, where peace, And rest can never dwell, hope never comes, Still urges, and a fiery deluge, fed, With ever-burning sulphur unconsumed.'*

One particular line encapsulated his feelings of utter hopelessness.

*'As far removed from God and light of Heaven.'*

The young Frenchman, despite the clubbing, whispered to Guillaume. "Ils ont tué dix mille Juifs en un jour. Maintenant ils doivent utiliser des fosses. *(They killed ten thousand Jews in one day. Now they must use pits.)*" He stared at his feet. "Et maintenant, nous creusons eux. *(And now we are digging them.)*"

Two long columns of sonderkommandos, whose primary responsibility was the disposal of corpses, stopped alongside Guillaume's group, making their number around a hundred and fifty. Picks, shovels, and spades were quickly distributed amongst them. Over the next two days, for what the guards regarded as an acceptable loss, eight sonderkommandos were shot, four beaten to death, nine buried alive under a collapsed wall of earth, six thrown alive into a burning pit, and twelve died due to complete exhaustion, the fourth cremation pit was completed.

Guillaume stood outside the brick barrack and carried on the breeze with the sickly, sweet stench of the crematoria, he could faintly hear his favourite aria from Tosca, being sung by a wonderful tenor.

'E lucevan le stelle, Ed olezzava la terra, Stridea l'uscio dell'orto, E un passo sfiorava la rena, Entrava ella fragrante, Mi cadea fra le braccia.' *(And the stars were shining, And the earth was scented. The gate of the garden creaked, And a footstep grazed the sand, Fragrant, she entered And fell into my arms.)*

'O! dolci baci, o languide carezze, Mentr'io fremente le belle forme disciogliea dai veli!, Svanì per sempre il sogno mio d'amore. L'ora è fuggita, e muoio disperato! E muoio disperato! E non ho amato mai tanto la vita, Tanto la vita! *(Oh, sweet kisses and languorous caresses, While feverishly I stripped the beautiful form of its veils! Forever, my dream of love has vanished..."*

The sound of a gunshot ended the aria prematurely, and the reality of 'life' in Auschwitz-Birkenau had been restored.

*'And I never before loved life so much, Loved life so much!'* Guillaume recalled the last words of the aria, and the firing squad which ended Cavaradossi's life. The aria's tragic, heart-rending words, and the cold-hearted murder of Cavaradossi, finally shattered Guillaume's carapace and he disintegrated into uncontrollable tears.

Out of the dark, a tall figure walked slowly towards him, and stood over his bent, quaking body.

"Jude Steh auf! *(Jew Get up!)*"

Guillaume, like Isaac, couldn't and didn't want to move. Death was the only release from this diabolical place.

"JUDE STEH AUF!"

Guillaume gave himself up to his maker as he felt the cold end of the barrel of a Luger pressed against his temple. He felt hot fetid breath on his neck, as the barrel of the Luger moved to his chest. But it was one word whispered into his ear, which found in the deepest recesses of his mind, the remnants of Guillaume, and breathed life into him.

"Bloemenwerf."

Guillaume struggled to his feet and came face to face with Unteroffizier Bruno Franks.

"How do you know of Bloemenwerf?" The words were spat into Frank's face.

Karsten wiped his sleeve across Franks's cheek, leaned forward, and whispered two more words in Guillaume's ear. "Papaver Rhoeas."

Guillaume ignored what was said, stepped forward, grabbed Franks by the throat, and started to choke him.

"Guillaume," Karsten wheezed, "Isaac sent me."

Guillaume was incensed. "ISAAC IS DEAD.YOU SHOT HIM. I WAS THERE." One quote ran over and over through his mind. *"'Hell is empty and all the devils are here.'"*

Karsten began to feel dizzy, unsteady on his feet, and his vision began to blur. "Isaac Wouters. Your broth.. … Klau …" The words were left hanging in the air as Karsten went limp in Guillaume's hands, his weight freeing him of Guillaume's death-grip.

"MÖRDER! *(Killer!)*" Screamed out to Guillaume's left. A Luger smashed into his temple and he collapsed unconscious onto the floor. "Du wirst langsam dafür sterben. *(You will die slowly for this.)*"

Two Kapos roughly grabbed Guillaume's arms and dragged him to his feet. The SS guard said few words. "Stammlager, Block elf. *(Auschwitz I main camp Block 11.)*" Words, which in Auschwitz-Birkenau, held the greatest terror among its inmates.

# Chapter Eighty-Two

Marie sat on a tree stump at the edge of the wood, deciding what she should do next. She didn't have complete confidence in her newly found abilities, and was hoping they would show her what to do next. She sat for a few more minutes and gradually her thoughts became calm and calculated.

*"If Charlie was here, where's his car? Not here, so call the hotel."* She tried to remember what Charlie had been driving when he picked her up to go surfing at the Florider. *"It was black, small, and a BMW, or was it a VW?"* She thought back to the car park at the White Water Centre. *"Definitely a black BMW 1 series. No idea of the number plate. It did have a sticker in the front window. It was green."* She struggled to open more memory files, and eventually got what she wanted. *"National Trust. Member for 2014."* She took her mobile out of her pocket, searched through her recent calls, and found the guest house.

"Hello, Sunrays Guest House. How can I help?"

"Hi, it's Marie Stridham, I'm staying with you."

"Ah yes. Here until tomorrow. What can I do for you?"

"I'm trying to find a friend who recently stayed with you. Charlie Thompson? Could you confirm that he did?"

There was a short silence. "Yes, he did stay, but he didn't sleep in his room, his things are still here, *and* he didn't pay his bill." There was a note of annoyance in the voice.

"I'll settle his bill when I come back."

"That's very generous of you, but guests always have to leave a credit card impression, and we've charged it to that."

"He drove to you, so his car should still be with you? I don't have the registration, but it's a black BMW 1 series. Can you check if it's still there for me?"

"Oh, it's definitely still here. Guests always have to leave details of their vehicles in the register when they check in."

"Thank you. You've been very helpful."

"I hope you find him. Is there anything else I can help you with?"

"Yes. Could you book me a table for dinner at eight tonight? Thanks again. Bye."

She sat silently for a few seconds, realising how deep her feelings for Charlie had grown. *"Where are you? I miss you."* She looked down the hill at the house. *"OK. Time I asked a few awkward questions."* She stood up, girded her loins, and purposefully strode down the slope.

Desiree was stood outside the kitchen door, smiling.

*"My God,"* Marie thought, *"she's used that a few times. That smile's about as false as Cressida's."* She was amazed by her knowledge of Shakespeare. *"Thanks, Dad. I did learn something from all those quizzes."*

"Everything OK?" Desiree continued her impression of a faithless lover. "Like a cup of tea before you go?"

*"Can't wait to get rid of me, can you?"* Marie managed to contain her growing anger. "Tea would be lovely." She followed Desiree into the kitchen. "Charlie didn't get back to the hotel," she said to Desiree's back, as she was filling the kettle at the sink.

"No, he stayed the night here. We spent the evening looking at the family trees and drinking wine. It got rather late and staying seemed the most sensible thing to do."

"He never collected his things from the hotel and his car's still there."

Desiree turned on the kettle and slowly turned around. "What? But the next morning, he got a taxi from here."

*"Didn't you say you dropped him off at the station? Don't ever take up acting, dear,"* Marie thought. "So you've no idea where he could be?" Marie was struggling to keep her cool.

"Absolutely none. I'm as surprised and worried as you."

"Does anyone else live here?" Marie decided to start pushing.

"Why do you ask?" Desiree's mask slipped a little.

"I saw you talking to two people in the garden." She omitted the part about walking through the wall.

"You must have imagined it. I live here on my own." Her acting started again. "Ah, you must have seen our …" She quickly corrected herself. "*My* neighbours. They wanted to borrow some coffee. Nice couple."

"That must have been what it was." Marie leaned forward on the table. *"OK. Gloves off,"* she thought. "Are they magicians?"

"*Pardon!*" Desiree's reaction for once was very real. "Magicians?" What the hell do you mean?"

*"That's better. Let's see the real you,"* Marie thought with satisfaction. "Only when I was sat up there in the wood, I could have sworn they walked straight through your kitchen wall."

Desiree slowly wrung her hands, sniffed loudly, sat down, stood up, adjusted some dying flowers in a vase, stared at Marie, poured two cups of tea, sat down again, and sipped her tea. "Through the wall?" She just about managed a seriously forced laugh. "You shouldn't drink and drive. How much have you had?"

"Not a drop. Now where is he? He's still here, isn't he? He's a policeman, he would have contacted someone if there was a problem, and he'd never have left his pride and joy. His BMW. What have you done with him?"

Desiree attempted anger, but her eyes gave away her fear. "I think you should leave now. You're bloody demented. I go to see someone about family history, and you … you accuse me of … well, you should leave right now."

"Not until I've taken a good look around this house and satisfied myself he's not here."

"You can't do that!"

"Watch me. What are you hiding? Why don't you want me to look around?"

"This is my house. Now piss off."

*"Ah, anger. Cut through all the layers of bullshit, have we?"* Marie was enjoying herself. She stood up and started to make her way out of the kitchen.

Desiree stood in her way. "You can't fucking do this! GET OUT!"

Marie pushed her to one side and started looking through the downstairs rooms.

"I'm going to call the police." Desiree blustered.

"Use my phone." Marie offered her mobile.

"I'd rather use my own."

"Bullshit. You wouldn't call them if your arse was on fire. So what's upstairs?"

Desiree's manner became frantic. "NO! You will not go up there. It's where my parents' things are. You're not going through them." She was close to tears.

"Out. Of. My. Way." Marie prodded her between her breasts. "Or *I'm going to call the police.*"

Desiree moved to one side, sat down on the stairs, and burst into floods of tears.

Despite her bravado, Marie was now terrified at the thought of what she might find. She'd watched enough TV programmes about murders to fill the Albert Hall, and in her fevered mind, Charlie had suffered a fate similar to any of the worst kinds of horror she could remember. She made her way through to what must have been Desiree's parent's bedroom, Desiree's pink boudoir, the bathroom, until she came to what had to be the guest room. She pushed the door open. The room was in darkness, so she felt along the wall for a light switch and illuminated the 'crime scene'. She walked around the door and staggered back against the wall, knocking a mirror off a dressing table. Lying on the bed, covered up to his neck with white sheets was Charlie, looking like a corpse in an open coffin for viewing at a funeral home.

"She's killed him and kept his body. She must be related to Dennis Nilsen." She slipped down the wall and buried her head in her hands.

"It's not what it seems, my dear." A soft voice to her right made her look up. Through her tears, she could see a middle-aged couple, kneeling on the floor close to her. "Charlie is fine."

Marie's abilities, which up and until then were in suspended animation, were now fully awake and honed to a razor's edge. "You're her parents, aren't you? Her dead parents."

"Don't blame her for this." The man nodded his head to the bed. "We were desperate, and it was more by luck than judgement that Desiree found Charlie. If she'd contacted other family members, we'd have never found him." Stephen looked down at the floor. "We should have asked, or told someone what we were looking for, but you get carried along by things."

"What have you done?" Marie had never felt more alive than she did at this moment. She was buzzing. "What have you done to him?"

"He's gone to find someone who can help them."

Marie looked across to the door where Desiree was stood.

"Let *me* explain, dear," Stephen said lovingly to Desiree. "We, as you've guessed, are ghosts, and we are stuck here because we've unfinished business to deal with."

Marie held up her hand. "And that unfinished business I would guess, given what she," she pointed at Desiree, "said, is that you need someone or something to help you move on, and Charlie's trying to find them for you." She got up, moved to the bed, and felt Charlie's forehead. "He's still warm." She then felt for a pulse and couldn't find one in his wrist or neck. She stepped back from the bed, turned, and stared at the bewildered trio. "He hasn't got a pulse! He's dead! How's he still warm?" She ripped back the blankets. "You've got an electric blanket under him, haven't you?"

"He's not dead. He's just, 'sleeping'. His spirit has gone to find Eugene."

"*Willingly?*" Marie was now barely able to suppress her anger.

The trio looked sheepishly at each other and shook their heads.

"So you forced him!" She could contain it no longer. "WHAT THE HELL HAVE YOU DONE TO HIM!"

"It wasn't us," Desiree's mother said through tears. "It was that." She pointed at the wall behind Marie's head. "That damn thing." She turned to her husband and started beating her fists on his arm. "We should have burnt it years ago. Years ago …"

Marie sat on the bed close to Charlie's feet and stared at the wall behind the headboard where there was the clear outline of where a large painting had been hanging. "What was there?"

"A painting," Desiree said with a scowl. "It's in the attic."

"What, a painting in your attic did this? Pull the other one, it plays Westminster bloody chimes."

"Honestly." Henry looked at her husband. "Tell her."

He shook his head.

"Tell her now."

Marie screwed up her face, and lifted her arms above her head. "For God's sake, someone just bloody tell me."

"We," Stephen said and nodded to his wife, "were members of a group called Papaver …"

"Rhoeas." Marie finished his sentence.

"You know about the organisation?"

Marie nodded, but said nothing.

"We were the keepers of this portal. Two years ago, we were killed in a head-on car crash with a petrol tanker on the A148. Our bodies were burnt to ash and never recovered. Cremated before we could be cremated. Since then, we've been here, locked in Purgatory. Desiree has no powers and she only sees us because we let her. But then you know about that, don't you?" He sat on the bed close to Marie. "We have helped so many lost souls move on, but now, we don't know how to do it for ourselves. When Desiree met Charlie, she felt he could help, but before we could ask him, the evening had flown by. We asked him to stay, and planned to ask for his help the following morning. When he didn't get up, we came to wake him, and found him like this." He turned, and did his best to smile at Marie. "Please believe me, we never meant for this to happen. The painting acts as a gateway to Burma. This, plus the pull of Eugene, was greater than we ever imagined. We'll do all we can to help you bring him back."

# Chapter Eighty-Three

Klaus put his arm around Alfredo's shoulder. "Bill should have enough faceless images by now to test your theory."

Alfredo nodded. "I have been thinking how we could do this."

Klaus called to Sam, Elizabeth, and Jane to join them in the lounge. "Alfredo tell us your thoughts."

"Create a gallery of the faceless images from the 35mm reels, and like our gallery, we could see if they attract any lost spirits?" He shrugged, blushed, and sat down.

The others exchanged glances, nodded, and Sam gestured to Klaus to speak for them. "We should do it as soon as possible. What do you need?"

"Very little to start. Six panels which we could fix to the wall, something to fix them to the wall, and some sticky tape to fix the photos to the panels."

Klaus turned to Sam. "Can you organise that?"

"Yes. Any DIY warehouse will have them." He stood up. "I should be about an hour." He turned to Alfredo. "If you can get the pictures organised, we can start when I get back."

Jane's expression, showed something was niggling her.

"Problem?" Klaus asked her.

"Where do we try this? Here or next door?"

"Excellent question."

"You don't need to sound so surprised, Klaus."

"Es tut mir leid. You raise a very good question." He turned to face Elizabeth. "What do you think?"

She breathed in deeply, scratched her neck, and leaned forward in her chair. "I'd do it next door. It's probably 'cleaner'. The only spirits in

Takanun, as far as we know, are associated with the blue lights, but in High Wood, there are both."

"Gute. I agree that this would be the best option." He stood up and walked to the hall. "I'll speak to Bill to get the pictures printed." He started to walk away, but stopped. "How many do you think we should have?"

Jane and Elizabeth, glanced at each other, shrugged, and mouthed twenty or thirty at each other.

"Twenty or thirty?" Elizabeth suggested.

"Gute. Zwanzig oder dreißig."

"Anyone fancy a cup of coffee and some toast?" Elizabeth asked. "I'm parched and starving."

Twenty minutes later, thirsts slaked, and hunger sated, the trio settled back into the comfort of the lounge.

"Klaus?"

"Yes, Jane."

"Something's been niggling me. It's probably nothing, and I'm sure someone's asked this before." She paused. "What used to be in those empty shelving racks in the cellar?"

"Here in High Wood?"

She nodded.

Klaus looked bemused. "Well, they … surely they … I have no idea."

They both looked at Elizabeth. "Don't look at me. I've never thought about it until you mentioned it. They've always just been there. I never gave a thought to what they were used for."

"Don't you think the shelving in the cellar, looks a lot like the racking in the loft next door? Admittedly, ours are more modern," Jane said quietly.

Klaus jumped up from his chair. "Natürlich. *(Of course.)* Wie haben wir das verpasst? *(How did we miss that?)* Ich bin so dumm. *(I'm so stupid.)*" He walked around the room, muttering to himself, stopped, and spiritually hugged Jane. "They were for film storage. Many films were made of the first conflict, so why wouldn't they have used film, as well as still photos?" He paused, his mind trying to pull together the last few pieces of the jig saw. "The cellar isn't a controlled environment. Wouldn't they perish?"

Bill walked briskly into the room, carrying a clear plastic sleeve containing photos. "As requested, thirty young men with no faces."

Silence and serious expressions greeted him.

"Something I said?"

"Bill!" Klaus jumped up. "Sit down. Sit down. We need to pick your brains."

"Pick away."

Klaus outlined their thoughts about the shelving. "Could film survive in the conditions in cellar?"

"Give me a moment, let me check it out." He walked into the hall, and after a short time, came back to the lounge. "The shelving could and probably has been used to store film. There are obvious marks on the shelves which are about the right dimensions for cans. It's pretty dry and cool down there, and provided the cans were sealed, then film could have easily been stored down there. The question is," he said and scratched the back of his head, "if cans of film were stored there, where are they?"

Klaus pressed his hands into his cheeks. "You are right. We must find them."

Bill sat on the sofa and took a sheet of A4 paper out of his pocket. "I've had an answer from the Institute about the films."

Klaus hid his irritation. "What did they say?"

"There are thousands of archived films, mostly in public and private collections going all the way back to Gettysburg. But none have been analysed in the way we are proposing. The magnitude of the task would be colossal."

"But possible with the right number of people trained in using the software?" Elizabeth asked.

Bill nodded and sucked his teeth. "Possible, but time consuming, and damn expensive."

Klaus stood up and paced around the room. "How many people, and what would the costs be?"

"You'll have to give me time to work that one out. I should have an answer for you by tomorrow."

Klaus nodded. "Das ist gut. Let's regroup in Takanun's cellar in the morning at nine thirty. We can put up the panels, test Alfredo's theory, and discuss Bill's conclusions."

# Chapter Eighty-Four

Accompanied by Franks, Guillaume was dragged to Block 11 which was part of the Stammlager *(Auschwitz I main camp)*.

*"For the moment, let him have some control,"* Karsten thought. *"Guillaume needs to be somewhere a lot more private before I speak to him."*

"Stehbunker. *(Standing cell.)*" Was all Franks said.

The guards sharply nodded their understanding, roughly took Guillaume's by the arms, and disappeared down a dimly lit, stark concrete corridor.

As they walked through the maze of dank soulless corridors, the screams, wails, dull thuds of metal on flesh, and pleas for mercy made Karsten feel like Aeneas travelling to the Underworld.

*"This is Tartarus,"* he thought, remembering Virgil's Aeneid. *'From hence are heard the groans of ghosts, the pains of sounding lashes and of dragging chains.'*

This was Dante's tenth circle of Hell. Its true names, Diyu, Naraka, Tartaros, Gehenna, Xibalba Hölle.

Hell's given name was now Auschwitz-Birkenau.

Karsten recalled from his studies descriptions of the levels of Diyu, a version of hell in traditional Chinese culture, which captured the horrors of Auschwitz-Birkenau and particularly Block 11. The Chamber of Tongue Ripping, Chamber of Scissors, Chamber of Pounding, Pool of Blood, Chamber of Dismemberment, Mountain of Knives, Mountain of Flames, and Chamber of Saw. As they passed a riveted wooden door, it burst open, and the scene inside dragged Karsten deeper into this accursed, malevolent abyss. Inside the cell, suspended by chains hung from the ceiling, was a meter-long iron bar, and bent over it was a naked prisoner, with his wrists manacled to his ankles. A guard was pushing him across the room in a slow arc, while another guard was smashing a crowbar into his buttocks.

"Was ist das?" Karsten spat at the guard.

"Boger-Schaukel. *(Boger-Swing)*. Gut ja?"

Karsten didn't answer and kicked the door shut to mute the screams of the victim being broken on the diabolical apparatus. A few yards further down the corridor, they stopped, and the guards dragged open the door of a cell. The stench of human excreta and death which flew out of the cell, made Karsten instantly vomit. The guards grinned at each other, making sure Franks hadn't see them. They reached into the cell, dragged out two corpses, grabbed Guillaume, and pushed him into the cell. Forced by the lack of space, his only option was to stand.

Karsten tapped into Franks's mind, immediately regretting his decision to allow Franks to bring Guillaume here.

*"It will have to be done now,"* Karsten thought. *"One night in there will kill him."* He lifted the elegant bamboo walking stick he was carrying, and prodded one of the guards in the back. "Hol ihn da raus! *(Get him out!)*"

"Herr Unteroffizier?"

"HOL IHN DA RAUS!"

The guards shrugged at each other, but knew from Franks' reputation that he wasn't one to question. They unceremoniously dragged Guillaume out of the standing cell, stood at attention, and waited for instructions.

"Geben Sie mir eine leere Zelle. *(Get me an empty room.)*"

The guards looked puzzled, but obeyed without question and took Karsten to a room close to the main office. They opened the door and stood back.

Karsten looked at them and barked an order. "JETZT VERPISS DICH AUS MEINEN AUGEN! *(Now get the fuck out of my sight!)*"

They saluted, and marched down the corridor, glad to be away from Franks.

Karsten slammed the door, turned the key in the lock, sensitively helped Guillaume to a chair, and sat him down. "My dear friend. What in God's name have they done to you?" Like the melting ice of a summer glacier, tears flooded down his cheeks. "I will … soon have … you …

safely home." As he stepped closer to Guillaume, he tried to place a kiss-of-return on Guillaume's forehead.

From deep in the fathomless depths of his weakened state, Guillaume tapped into an elemental strength. He leapt up from the chair, grappled Franks to the floor, pinned his arms with his legs, and began to violently throttle him. "BASTARD!" His grip grew tighter on Franks's throat. "Death is too good for you. Dear God, let this evil sinner fall as far as Lucifer fell." He lifted Franks's head and smashed it into the concrete floor, showering him in Franks's blood.

Karsten desperately tried to speak, but no words would form. Life was leeching out of Franks. If Karsten couldn't bond with Guillaume's spirit, they would be lost forever in another reality, in another time.

The crash of the chair hitting the concrete floor, brought the guards running back. They hammered on the door. "HERR UNTEROFFIZIER!? ÖFFNEN SIE DIE TüR!? *(Open the door.)*"

*"Your help he doesn't need!"* Karsten thought in a daze, as Franks's oxygen saturation levels dropped to critical levels.

Guillaume's eyes were reflections of pure undiluted hatred, but in his severely malnourished condition, his grip began to loosen on Franks's throat.

Karsten felt the small reduction in pressure on his arms and throat, struggled, pulled one arm free, prised three of Guillaume's fingers from his throat, and hoarsely croaked. "Bloemenwerf. Klaus. Papaver ..." His remaining words were lost, as Guillaume regained the pressure on his throat.

Somewhere deep in 'the undiscovered country' of Guillaume's brain, Karsten's mental flint struck steel, and a spark glimmered briefly in the stygian darkness. The spark fell onto Guillaume's mental 'tinder', and breathed life into his memories. A small wisp of smoke billowed, and the 'tinder' burst into flame.

Franks was close to death.

Guillaume whispered. "*Bloemenwerf. Klaus. Papaver.*" His hands were choking what little life was left out of Franks. He looked down at his hands, stared incredulously at Franks, and threw his hands in the air.

"ÖFFNE DIE TÜR! ÖFFNE DIE TÜR! *(Open the door!)*" The guards screamed as they hammered at it.

"Karsten?" Guillaume released his grip, lifted Franks' limp head onto his lap, and rocked back and forth. "אלוהים, אלוהים, לא אותו. *(God not him.)*"

The wood of the door began to crack as rifle butts were 'applied' to the problem.

"Karsten? Is it you?"

A panel of the door exploded into the room, sending splinters over Guillaume and Karsten.

An SS officer peered through the hole, and quickly understood what he saw.

"Er hat ihn umgebracht! *(He's killed him!)*"

The barrel of a Luger appeared through the hole in the door. A deafening crack echoed around the room and a bullet ricocheted off the walls.

Guillaume sat Franks up, and slapped his face, which resulted in nothing more than a hoarse groan.

"KARSTEN WAKE UP!"

There seemed little sign of him regaining consciousness before the SS guards kicked down the door. A second bullet ricocheted off the walls, and grazed Guillaume's cheek. He laid Franks back on the concrete floor, as another two panels exploded into the room. He knelt down by Franks, and fearing the worst, began to softly recite, 'A Song of Ascents'.

"'I lift my eyes to the mountains - from where will my help come? My help will come from the Lord, Maker of heaven and earth. He will not let your foot falter; your guardian does not slumber. Indeed, the Guardian of Israel neither slumbers nor sleeps. The Lord is your guardian; the Lord is your protective shade at your right hand. The sun will not harm you by day, nor the moon …'"

The last of the door finally gave up the ghost, the SS guards crashed into the room, a Luger fired, Guillaume bent down, ready to meet his end, and kissed Franks on the forehead.

Klaus had been sitting with Karsten for hours, and although he didn't attend any church, he felt a desperate need to ask any greater power which existed, to bring his son back to him. He dropped to his knees and prayed.

"If I'm heard by anything or anyone who may or may not care what I say or ask, look on my son with kindness and help him find his way home to me. Amen." He pushed himself up from his arthritic knees and groaned.

It was the second and third groans which tightened his chest and shortened his breath. He turned, almost not wanting to look at the bed.

Karsten was lifting himself up on his elbows.

At the same moment in Bloemenwerf, Renaat was dancing around the room as Guillaume sat up in bed.

# Chapter Eighty-Five

Charlie limped back into camp after a day digging out massive boulders in a cut. His limp was due to the 'attention' of a particularly vicious Korean guard who'd lashed his thighs and buttocks with a bamboo cane.

"You OK?" the MO asked as Charlie hobbled back to his atap hut.

"Just a bit sore, sir."

The MO raised an eyebrow. "Let me take a look."

Charlie reluctantly limped into the hospital.

"Show me."

Charlie lowered his tattered shorts and the MO whistled. "I'd say you were a bit more than just sore, private. Lie down there." He pointed to the only empty bamboo 'bed'. "I'll get something for that."

Charlie looked around the ward at the remnants of what until recently, had been human beings, now reduced by disease, inhumanity, and the cruelty of the Japanese, to mere vestiges of men. *"How many of you will I have to search for?"* Charlie thought, accepting his abilities and place as a Spirit Walker.

"Afraid there's not much I can do … Thompson, isn't it?" The MO dabbed some sulpha powder on Charlie's angry, bleeding gashes. "Can't do anything for the pain, but hopefully I can stop any infection setting in. I'll put you on sick detail. You can't work with these cuts."

"If you're sure, doc."

"Report to me in the morning and I'll give you a chitty. They'll probably get you on graveyard duties."

Charlie hadn't noticed, that in four of the beds, the single sheet was pulled up over the faces of the soldiers. "Bad night, sir?" He nodded in the direction of the dead soldiers.

"Bloody dysentery. Haven't got a cat's chance in hell of replacing the volume of fluids they lose through vomiting and diarrhoea." He walked away, shaking his head and muttering to himself. "Eight bloody years of training, and all I can do is watch men die. What the hell's the point of the Hippocratic Oath at times like this? These bastards won't have heard of Hippocrates. My God, I stood and swore, 'I will apply, for the benefit of the sick, all measures which are required'. So where, in the name of all that's holy, are these measures which are required which I'm going to apply?" He tossed his head back and walked outside.

Charlie lay on the 'bed' for half an hour, waiting for the pain to reduce from unrelenting agony, to just about bearable severe pain. After an hour, and with the support of another soldier, he limped back to his atap hut.

"Bad day?" Peter asked with his tongue deeply in his cheek. "Jesus, your legs. What the hell happened?"

"Keriama …"

"Ah?" Peter said knowingly. "Him again."

"We were working on the embankment, and one of our officers, Captain Dale I think, was made to stand on the top of the embankment with his shovel above his head. We dropped our tools, sat down, and refused to work. Then others, up and down the line did the same and I got these." He looked down at his legs. "Three Korean privates laid into us with canes." He gingerly sat on his bunk. "Colonel's in with them now. MO's put me on sick parade."

"Well, they say every cloud has one, and this gives us time to decide how and when we get out of here."

"The sooner the better. Not sure I can take much more of this. If these get infected, I'm finished. And if they don't, I'm not sure how long my mind and body will hold up. What do you have in mind?"

"Tomorrow, we'll get on a work detail."

"I'm not sure if I can manage it, and what about the MO?" Charlie grimaced.

"It has to be tomorrow. That's when I'm pretty sure it will happen, so that's when we've got to leave."

"When Edward dies?"

Peter nodded.

"But what about Eugene? When does he die?"

"The thing is, he's going to die here, and if it's a few days early, then it really doesn't matter. This way, his soul is saved, and you get home."

Charlie looked unsure, but had no other plan. "Tell me what I have to do."

Peter leaned forward, and whispered. "Once we're in thick jungle, we'll make a break for it. I'll go left, and you go right. This won't be easy for you Charlie. Getting killed for the first time is … well, it's not good. But Eugene's death is the only way of you getting back from this." Peter moved closer to him, and held his shoulders. "You'll be fine. Treat it like a trip to the dentist. Usually shit when you're there, but soon forgotten."

Charlie looked a little more relaxed. "So we let them catch us."

"Yes, but don't make it too easy. If they catch you quickly, then it'll be the cage." Peter shook his head. "And believe me, you don't want that."

The following morning after breakfast, they joined the working party for the embankment. Twenty minutes into the march in deep jungle, Peter turned to Charlie and nodded. It was the signal they'd agreed the previous day.

Peter mouthed to Charlie, *"On three. One, two, three."*

Charlie ran to the right, crashing through small saplings and into thick jungle. He heard unintelligible screaming behind him and then the unmistakable crackle of gunshots.

*"Not too fast,"* he thought, his mind in panic mode, terrified of what was about to happen.

The screaming became louder and closer. Charlie's breathing became laboured, his legs screaming in pain from the gashes in his legs, and the effort of running through the undergrowth and jumping over roots. His foot landed in a deep muddy rut, and he fell headfirst into a clump of elephant grass which ripped deep gashes into his face. He couldn't contain the scream of agony. The voices were closing in. "Should I pray?"

"彼はここ *(Here he is.)*" Was loud, clear, totally unintelligible, and very close.

He rolled onto his back and looked up at two smirking Japanese guards pointing their Type 38 Cavalry Carbines with forty cm. bayonets at him. His breathing became rapid and shallow, as he stared fixedly into their dead eyes which offered him no hope of mercy. The shorter of the two guards smirked at the other, pressed his bayonet against Charlie's chest, and leant on the butt of his rifle with just enough pressure to puncture his lung, and despite the agony and terror, he remembered Peter's instructions. *"When the time comes, grab hold of the guard. Hold on tight, empty your mind, and your passenger will be gone."*

With an evil grin, the guard twisted the bayonet and slowly pulled it out.

Charlie grimaced, coughed up blood, threw himself at him, grabbed his wrist, and emptied his mind.

The guard screamed abuse at him, but his grip couldn't be broken. He yelled to his crony, who smashed the butt of his rifle into Charlie's head, rendering him unconscious, and ensuring his mind was now utterly clear.

Both guards repeatedly bayoneted Charlie, tearing his aorta, and puncturing the heart eleven times. Death was instantaneous. The guards kicked him a few times, and fired eight bullets into his head. Satisfied he was dead, they left the body for the jungle predators.

Lidsay felt like scummy bathwater cascading down a rusty drain pipe. *"What have you done you bastard? Why would you commit suicide like this?"* A distant light began to flicker. If Charlie was dead and gone, then where the hell was Lidsay? *"You devious shit."*

"彼は死んでいます. *(He is dead.)*"

Lidsay felt as if he'd been sucked through a narrow bore pipe by an industrial vacuum pump. *"Thompson, what the fuck have you done?"* His question was met by silence. *"Try and ignore me if you want, but you'll soon have to talk. I can still hurt you. You, your mates, and your loved ones."*

"英語? *(English?)*" The guard span around, staring all around him.

Lidsay panicked when he looked through his new 'friend's' eyes, and saw Charlie's butchered, blood soaked-corpse.

"英語? *(English?)*"

*"You bastard! You won't stop me from getting Mr Shit for brains and Mrs Whore. And now, Constable Thompson, you're on my shit list. You, and anyone you know."*

"英語。どこに隠れている？ *(English? Where are you hiding?)*" The guard walked into the elephant grass, prodding it with his bayonet.

*"Spin on it, you slant-eyed twat! Watch your back, Thompson. I'll find you."*

Charlie felt utterly at peace, floating in deep space, in a sensory attenuation tank, an isolation chamber. His thoughts began to meander and float around him.

In the stygian blackness of the spirit-cosmos, Charlie, saw a myriad of pinpricks of light. A micro-galaxy, rotated around him, and accelerated like a centrifugal fairground ride with no brakes. Shooting stars broke away from the galaxy and fixed themselves to him. More and more broke away until they resembled a crystal waterfall. Charlie became encased in a scintillating diamante suit which would have graced Liberace.

Marie was looking out of the bedroom window when Desiree came in with a tray of sandwiches, tea, and cakes.

"You should eat something." She turned her head and looked at the still figure of Charlie in the bed. "Don't worry, he'll come back. I'm sure of it."

Marie shook her head. "I'm really not hungry."

Desiree gently pulled her away from the window. "Please. Eat something. Even if it's just a cake." She smiled. "They're homemade."

Marie sighed deeply, took a ham and tomato sandwich, then another, a tuna mayonnaise roll, a slice of lemon drizzle cake, and washed them down with three cups of tea.

"Feeling better?"

"Yes. You were ..." Marie's eyes were fixed on the bed. "He moved."

Desiree ran to the side of the bed. "You're sure?"

Marie leapt close to the other side of the bed. "Watch."

A minute passed, nothing happened, and Marie started to cry.

"You like him, don't you?" Desiree said softly. "Love him?"

Marie wiped her eyes. "Since we met." She blew her nose on a serviette. "There was something, ..." Tears overcame her.

*"The sex was great. Shame really. It'll be bloody difficult to find another one like him,"* Desiree thought pragmatically. *"And that was all it ever would have been. As long she doesn't know, why rock the apple cart?"*

The two women walked back to the window, staring at Lateau Wood.

"Did you say something?" Marie asked Desiree.

"Mmmm? Say something?" She shook her head. "No."

A faint whisper from behind them span them around. Their faces dissolved into a cocktail of disbelief, wonder, joy, and tears.

"Hi," Charlie whispered hoarsely, sitting up in the bed. "Miss me?"

Marie ran to the bed and threw her arms around him. "I thought I'd lost you." She softly punched him in the chest. "Where the hell have you been?"

Desiree stayed close to the window. There was no love between her and Charlie, only a longing for another night. This was Marie's moment.

He looked across the room at Desiree. She touched her lips, shook her head, waved goodbye, and mimed locking her lips with a key and throwing it away. Charlie understood and mouthed, *"Thank you."*

"So what happened?" Marie pressed him for an answer.

Charlie pushed himself up in the bed and rested back on the pillows. "Where to start?" A yellow mental post-it note, fluttered down with two words carefully written on it - Eugene Thompson. He looked to Desiree, still stood by the window. "I found him. I'm pretty sure I brought him back."

Desiree looked confused. "Found who Charlie?"

"The one you sent me to find." His face was deeply creased by a frown. "Or to be more precise, you, and your mother and father's ghosts, sent me to find."

Desiree blushed and whispered. "Eugene?"

Charlie nodded. "Yeah, Eugene." He looked around the room. "He should be here. This had to be where the strongest pull was from." He looked up at Marie and stared deep into her eyes. "You know something, don't you?"

Marie sat on the bed. "I talked with Klaus."

Charlie sucked his teeth. "And what did he tell you?"

"Everything. Everything about the houses, the organisation, the people, and the lost souls." She picked at the sheets with her fingers.

"I talked with Elizabeth." Charlie answered softly, taking her hand, and stroking her fingers. "She told me the same as you, but she also told me I had powers like them."

"Klaus told me the same. Not about you that is, about me."

Charlie's eyes almost popped out of their sockets. "We're the same?"

Marie slowly nodded. "Sounds like it."

Desiree moved closer to the bed. She didn't want to miss a word of this conversation.

"Have you sensed any new spirits?" Charlie asked Marie, as if this was a perfectly normal thing to ask.

She nodded. "Not in the house, but outside."

Charlie pushed the sheets back and climbed out of bed. "Where?"

Marie looked him up and down and chuckled. "You might want to put some clothes on first."

He looked down at his naked body and then at Desiree. "You …?"

She nodded. "Mum helped." She walked across to an old mahogany wardrobe and took out three hangers with his clothes. "Shoes are on the other side of the bed."

Five minutes later, Charlie, Marie, Desiree, and the spirit family, were stood outside in the garden.

Charlie closed his eyes, trying to re-establish contact with his spirit-hitchhiker.

Marie's face slowly turned, peering up at the wood. "There's a spirit up there, in amongst the trees. Is there a tree up there linked to someone in the family?"

Mum glanced up at the wood and quickly back at Marie. "The only person who would have a link to the woods, would be Peter."

"Peter?" Charlie opened his eyes and held Marie's hand. "Peter Wallins."

# Chapter Eighty-Six

It was one o' clock in the morning, and Matt and Mark had been freezing their important male parts off for the last hour, watching Takanun from their car.

"OK now?" Matt asked with ever increasing frustration.

"Just a bit longer." Mark said, squinting at the house.

"Oh for fuck's sake you …" Anger was beginning to take over from frustration. "I'm goin'. You comin'? If not, then bollocks to you." Matt got out of the car and resisted the urge to slam the door.

Sat in the car on his own in the dark was all the stimulation Mark needed to follow his brother. "'Old up, bruv.'" He called out rather too loudly.

Matt hit himself on the side of the head, bit his lip, turned around, put his hand over his mouth, and raised his eyebrows about as high as they would go. *"Twat."*

"What's the problem?" Mark said again too loud for the circumstances.

"Will you pissin' shut up, or at least just soddin' talk quiet?"

Mark looked hurt and pouted. "For Christ's sake, I was only tryin' to catch up."

Matt gave up. "Now listen, and I mean really listen, not your usual brassed-off teenager 'avin' a bollockin' listen."

Mark pouted like a Grouper after lip pumping with dermal fillers.

"When we get into that 'ouse, we only do the cellar. We'll just take a sample of what they've got, and see if Pete Mansten thinks it's worth anythin'." He tossed a piece of strawberry gum in his mouth. "Only take things that's worth somethin'. No crap." He threw two sports bags at him. "Fill these up, and we should be in and out in twenty minutes." He chewed the gum, squeezing out the last drop of flavour, before spitting it into the hedge. "Capiche?" He'd waited years to say it since he'd heard it on the Sopranos.

"Wha'?" Mark wasn't at his most communicative. "Wha' d'you say?"

"I will punch you in the face if you don't start listenin'." He prodded him in the chest.

Mark reacted as if he'd been hit by a taser. "Piss off. That soddin' hurt."

"Fol ... low ...me. Do ... what ...I ...do."

"I'm not a moron."

"So you say," Matt said to himself as he turned away and walked towards the house. "Where's the car?"

"Wha'?"

"Where's the car?"

"Wha' car?"

"The fit piece. The daughter. If she's away, there's only the two old duffers in the 'ouse."

Breaking in was simple, as the kitchen door had been left unlocked.

"She must be away. She'd never leave this open," Matt said to himself. "Still, makes life a lot easier, and quieter." He flicked on his torch and shone it into the kitchen. Shadows pirouetted around the room.

"Don't do tha'," Mark muttered.

Matt grabbed hold of Mark's arm. "Right, come on. The cellar. We grab stuff and piss off."

Half way down the cellar steps, Mark stepped on an untied lace from his trainers, 'skied' down three steps, free fell three, span down two, tripped over his own feet, and finally crashed into a pile of clear plastic storage containers.

"You clumsy bastard! Can't you even walk down steps without causin' pissin' chaos?" Matt walked down the last few steps and shone his torch on the crumpled heap. "Get up and get some stuff." He turned to walk away, and had one last shot. "And only stuff worth selling."

Upstairs, the two nurses who Marie had arranged to care for her mum and dad, were on the landing, staring at each other, mobile phones in hand.

"Shouldn't we check what that was?" Audrey asked Pam, the answer already reflected in her eyes.

Pam shook her head and looked down over the bannister rail. "Call the police. They can deal with this. I'm going back with mum and locking the door. If I were you, I'd do exactly the same."

"What service do you require?' The calm voice asked.

"Police. I think we've got burglars."

The conversation continued as Audrey gave all her details and a brief account of what had happened.

"We'll have a car with you in a few minutes. Is this the best number to get you on?"

Audrey nodded. "Yes. Thank you. Please be as quick as you can!"

"Lock yourself in the bedroom until someone gets there."

Audrey needed no encouragement and tiptoed as quickly as she could back to Dad's room.

The brothers met at the bottom of the cellar steps. Matt looked into Mark's bulging bag, looked up, smiled, pinched his cheek, play-punched him in the stomach, and ruffled his hair. "You clever sod."

"Told you I wasn' no moron."

"No, bruv. No moron," Matt said with a smile. *"Just agree with 'im. Doesn' 'appen very often,"* he thought.

"We could get some more, couldn't we?"

"Don't overstretch the little bit of grey matter you've got. Plenty of time for more visits. Seen any scary monsters?"

Mark shook his head.

"Good. So let's get out of 'ere."

Mark was growing unjustifiably confident. "I think like, we should leave wha' we go' in the 'all, and come back down for more." He waved the beam of his torch, at a pile of 'shop for life' bags near the steps. "We could use these."

"We go together. I'm not leavin' you on your own again in this place. You're a car crash waitin' to 'appen. Let's get out of this pissin' place!"

"Fine. Keep your shirt on. Mr pissin' perfect."

Matt ignored him, picked up his bag, and walked quickly up the steps.

As they stepped out of the back door, the blue light flashing against the side of the house, tested their sphincters. The powerful, white beam of light, which flashed down the side of the house, followed by a call of, "I'll check around the back, Dave," made them spin on their heels, and run back into the kitchen.

Matt stopped, sniffed the air, and grimaced. "You dirty bastard. Wanna leave any more DNA evidence?"

Mark grabbed a towel from the sink and waved it like a myopic matador, trying to drive the aroma of rotten eggs out of the kitchen.

Matt ripped the towel from his hand. "With me. Quick. Back into the cellar." Once on the cellar floor, Matt grabbed Mark's arm, and dragged him to the adjoining wall with High Wood. "Get behind that pile of magazines, and I don't wanna 'ear your 'air growin'."

Mark crawled behind the pile of magazines and settled down for the duration.

"Looks like you've had burglars. The back door was open, and there are muddy footprints on the kitchen floor. What sort of mindless toe rags, steal from old people who can't take care of themselves?" The constable was saying to Audrey. "Do you know if there's anything of value worth stealing in the house?"

Audrey shook her head and looked at Pam who shrugged. "I'm afraid I wouldn't know, constable. Probably best to come back when their daughter gets back from Norfolk. She can tell you if anything's missing."

"Well," the older policeman said reassuringly, "apart from that locked room upstairs, we've had a good look around, and they're not here."

"Have you checked the cellar?" Pam asked nervously, pointing to the hall.

"There's nothing down there, Pam," Audrey said. "I remember Marie saying it was just full of rubbish."

The older policeman smiled. "I think you're safe. I haven't met many burglars who specialise in nicking crap. Excuse me, ladies. We'll leave now, so lock the front door behind us and make sure the back door's secured."

Both nurses nodded their heads vigorously.

As they walked into the hall, the younger policeman turned, and looked at the cellar door. "Make sure that's locked. Best to cover all bases."

Matt heard muffled voices in the hall, and a door slam. What concerned him, and seriously pissed him off, was the sound of a key being turned in the cellar door. This was the final straw which fractured his personal camel's back, until he heard the sound of snoring from the pile Mark was hiding behind. *"What did I ever do to deserve this? Flash my arse at a nun? Shag a sheep? Nick a boy scout's soddin' woggle?"* He swung his foot at Mark's arse, and made a satisfying solid contact.

"Wha'! Who the …? I'll bleedin' do you!"

"How can you sleep?"

"It's warm down 'ere. Bloody site warmer than our place. Feel the wall. It's lush."

"Brick walls in cellars aren't warm, you tit."

"Stick your hand on this," Mark said, as he gently stroked the bricks with his hand. "Warm as the spark Prometheus stole."

Matt stood dumbfounded. "Wha' did you just say?"

"Warm as the spark Prometheus stole."

"And what the fuck does that mean?"

Mark stared at Matt, as if his lack of knowledge of Greek mythology was an embarrassment to him. "Prometheus snuck quietly into Zeus's domain, and stole a spark from Zeus's lightning bolt. He touched the end of a long reed to the spark, it caught fire, and burned slowly. He hurried back to his own land, taking with him the precious spark, and when he reached home, he called the shivering people from their caves, built a fire for them, showed them how to warm themselves by it, and how to use it to cook their food. Of course Zeus made him suffer." Mark said, as if it was perfectly natural for him to know such things.

"You been taking stuff 'aven't you?"

Mark was indignant. "Absolutely not. Nothing could be further from my mind. Poisoning my intellect with that sort of thing."

Matt stared deep into his eyes. "What's 'appened to your voice? You sound like a ponce."

Mark's indignance grew deeper. "I am speaking perfectly naturally, and it would do you no harm to improve *your* grammar and diction."

Matt pushed him out of the way, and slapped his hands against the bricks. "I told you the wall was…" It was warm, approaching hot. He edged along the cellar wall for about five yards, feeling his way with his hands, and then edged back the other way. "There's a stretch in the middle about six or seven yards wide that's 'ot, then it's warm on either side for another two, and then it's cold." He scratched his head and shivered.

"Somebody walk over your grave?" Mark said, trying to lighten the moment.

Never had a truer word been spoken. The 'Hot Spot' on the cellar wall, was where concentrated spirit energies were passing back and forth between High Wood and Takanun. Powerful surges of spirit-energy, were also passing through Matt and Mark, each one leaving a tiny amount of residual spirit-energy behind. The effect was significantly magnified by the numbers passing through them, which were having profound restorative effects on their cells.

Mark shone his torch in Matt's face. "Are you running a temperature, brother? Your face is as red as a ripe Martina's Roma tomato."

"Are you sure you're alright?" Matt stared at Mark, reached up, and held his wrist. "Shit, your scorchin'. No wonder you're talking bollocks." He stared at the bricks in the wall, illuminated by their torches, which shimmered like a heat haze on hot desert sand. He walked closer to the wall and glanced back at Mark. "Stay there. Don't bloody move."

"No need for that sort of language," Mark said with real disdain in his voice.

*"His brain's finally gone,"* Matt thought. *"After all the abuse it's 'ad, it can't be much of a surprise. I'll 'ave to get him sectioned."* He walked cautiously to where he judged the centre of the 'Hot Spot' was, and touched it as if he was petting a kitten. The more he 'petted' the wall, the more he wanted to. It generated a feeling of well-being in him and a sensation of total contentment.

"Good, isn't it?" Mark called to him. "

"Mmmm?"

"Makes you feel … feel somehow new and enlivened."

Matt turned his back to the wall and slid down to the floor. Absolute euphoria washing over him.

Mark joined him, and the brothers slipped into a deep and restful sleep.

The brothers woke the next morning feeling more alive than they ever had.

Matt yawned and stretched. "We should return tout suite to our abode."

Mark took a deep breath, patted the wall, pushed himself up, and helped Matt to his feet. "I am in agreement, as I am somewhat peckish."

"We should seek assistance in extricating ourselves from our present difficulty."

"I concur."

They walked together across the cellar, up the steps, and tapped politely on the door.

"There appears to be no-one at home, brother."

"Perhaps knock a little harder?"

Matt nodded. "Excellent suggestion." He swallowed hard, stretched back his shoulders, and knocked firmly on the door.

Alfredo came back to Takanun, to take another look around the loft, and as he reached the bottom of the stairs, he heard knocking from the cellar door. He walked close to it as Matt chose to give it one last heavy knock. "Santa Maria madre di Dio. *(Holy Mary mother of God.)*"

"Hello? Is someone there?" Matt called, from behind the door. "Could you please help us?"

Alfredo turned the key, opened the door, and stood back to let the brothers out.

"Thank you. Thank you so much for helping us out of our predicament."

"Chi sei? Who are you?"

"We are Matt and Mark. We were locked in your cellar."

"Why were you locked in?" Alfredo took a few steps back, wary of these rather bemused men.

The brothers smiled at each other, shrugged, and raised their hands to the ceiling. "It is a complete mystery to us."

Jane had followed Alfredo to Takanun. *"Not these two clowns again,"* she thought to herself, as unseen by the brothers, she walked down the hall. *"Bollocks. I'm going to let them see me."*

"And how can we help you two?" Jane asked with extreme politeness.

Alfredo span on his heels. "They see you," he whispered.

She nodded. "I let them." She turned to the brothers. "We've met before."

Matt smiled inanely at her. "But, soft! What light through yonder window breaks? It is the east, and Juliet is the sun."

Jane was dumbstruck.

"Wisely and slow; they stumble that run fast."

Jane stared, dumbfounded at Matt. Where was this coming from? Her previous 'meetings' with this pair of boneheads didn't suggest they'd seen, heard, or read, a great deal of anything, and particularly not Shakespeare.

"What are you doing here?" she asked, her annoyance growing by the second.

"I must be gone and live, or stay and die."

Jane chewed her top lip, her temper reaching just below boiling point. "I can't be arsed to find out why you're here, so why don't the pair of you piss-heads just bugger off?"

Matt bowed low to Jane. "And where two raging fires meet together, they do consume the thing that feeds their fury."

"Oh, just sod off, will you! NOW!"

Alfredo stepped in, took a firm hold of Matt's arm, marched him down the hall, closely followed by Mark, who 'helped' them out of the front door.

Matt swept low again. "Good night, good night! Parting is such sweet sorrow, That I shall say good night till it be morrow."

Jane slammed the door in their faces.

# Chapter Eighty-Seven

Sam and Alfredo had been up since six, fixing white melamine panels to a wall in Takanun's cellar. They were sticking the last of the photos on the panels, when Elizabeth and Klaus came down the cellar steps.

"Perfect timing. That's the last one." Sam stood back and high-fived Alfredo. "Good job."

"They look very good," Klaus agreed. "How many do we have?"

"Exactly fifty," Alfredo answered.

"Excellent." Klaus fell silent and looked around at everyone. "Any suggestions what we do next?"

"Well," Elizabeth said and took a step towards the panels. "I'm the one who sees the souls across, so why don't I stand close to a picture, and see what happens?"

Everyone nodded their heads in agreement.

She walked close to the prints and stopped. "We should have everything as close as we can to things in the gallery. Sam, can you get my chair, the Bose, and my iPod from next door?"

He nodded and tapped Alfredo on the shoulder to follow him.

"Klaus," Elizabeth said as she walked up and down the prints. "We didn't answer Jane's question. Did we?"

Klaus walked closer to her. "Which question?"

"Where are all the reels of film from High Wood? I was thinking about it in bed last night. Wouldn't Sam's uncle and aunt have found somewhere secure to make sure the films were safe and protected?"

Klaus frowned and then smiled. "Yes, they'd have moved them to a professional storage facility. And one that can't be too far away?"

Elizabeth took her mobile out of her pocket, and searched in yell.com for storage warehouses in Cardiff. She looked up a little disappointed. "Thirty."

"That's good," Klaus reassured her. "Can you narrow them down to only those close to High Wood?"

Elizabeth's finger scrolled up and down the available storage sites. She looked up, her expression much brighter. "I'd say there are probably only two, both on Newport Road. Storage Giant and Safestore Self Storage."

"Ausgezeichnet. (*Excellent.*) Something Sam can do while we start things here."

Twenty minutes later, Sam and Alfredo came back with Elizabeth's 'extras'.

"Where have you been?" Elizabeth asked tetchily.

Like a Las Vegas magician, Alfredo pulled out a flask of coffee from under his coat. "We thought this might help."

Elizabeth's displeasure was almost assuaged. "Phone next time."

Sam and Alfredo quickly set things up for her while she poured coffee into four Styrofoam cups.

"Sam," Klaus said as he crushed his empty cup. "We need you to go to these storage units and find out if your aunt and uncle left anything there."

"Now?"

Klaus nodded. "Ja. Jetzt."

"What am I looking for?"

"The missing 35mm cans of film."

"Where are these units?"

Elizabeth handed him a post-it note with two addresses. "They're close together on Newport Road. If the reels of film are there, they'll need quite a bit of storage space."

Sam took the post-it and made his way out of the cellar.

Elizabeth walked up and down the prints, until she was drawn to a photo. "This one." By his insignia and regimental badges, the soldier had been a sergeant in the 12th Battalion, the Devonshire Regiment.

Klaus had very mixed emotions as he watched Elizabeth touch the selected print. The power of the stream of spirit-energy passing through the connecting wall to High Wood, was causing the 'stars' in the cellar to rebound off the walls, ceiling, and floor, as if they were balls in a game of celestial pin ball. A loud knock at the front door snapped Klaus back into the moment.

Elizabeth span around, the picture temporarily forgotten. "We'd better go," she said, looking directly at Klaus. "Alfredo, will you keep an eye on things down here? We'll be back in a tick."

"Si." Alfredo nodded, although he had no idea how long a tick was.

Elizabeth opened the front door, and smiled at Detective Sergeant Morris. "Detective sergeant, any news for us?"

Morris's expression said 'what the hell are you doing in this house.'

Elizabeth could see what he was thinking, glanced at Klaus, and answered very convincingly. "You're wondering why we're here, and not in High Wood?"

Morris nodded, still frowning deeply.

"We pop in regularly to keep an eye on Marie's parents." She paused. "They both have dementia, and we try to give her a regular break."

Morris nodded in understanding. "I have an aunt with the same problem. Put's a terrible strain on a family. It's very good of you to do this." He gestured with his head, if it was OK for him to come in.

Elizabeth stood to one side and waved him in. "I'll get us some tea."

Once in the kitchen, the kettle boiling, biscuits on a plate, with everyone sat at the table, Morris took out his note book, and flicked to the pages he needed. "No news I'm afraid on Mrs Morbeck." Jane was leaning against the fridge. "I'm afraid that after this length of time, it's unlikely we'll find her."

"Sam will be upset," Elizabeth said with apparent and genuine sadness, desperately trying not to look at Jane, who was in hysterics. "He's just had to pop out. Probably be about an hour?"

Morris nodded and referred back to his notes. "Same report on the sergeant and his wife. They've all completely disappeared off the radar. Whatever's happened to them, I think it's highly unlikely we'll ever discover what it was." He sipped his tea. "The main reason I called, is that Constable Thompson seems to have gone missing. Apparently, he went to," he said and referred to his notes, "Norfolk, but never came back. Very unlike him, his mother said." He glanced at his notebook again. "We also received a report from a passer-by, of a break-in here a couple of days ago. I was wondering if you knew anything about either?"

Elizabeth swallowed hard. *"Those two idiots are doing their best to drop us in it,"* she thought. "The last time I saw Constable Thompson was about a week ago, and he said he was going, as you said, to somewhere in Norfolk. As far as any break-in goes, we," she said and looked at Klaus who shook his head, "would probably have been in High Wood, and wouldn't have seen or heard anything. I'm sorry I can't be of any more help than that."

Morris finished his tea and picked up a custard cream. "Thanks. It was a bit of a long shot, but worth a try." He stood up and shook Klaus and Elizabeth's hands. "I'll see myself out. Thanks again for the tea and biscuits." He turned, and a few seconds later, they heard the front door open and close.

Klaus sat down, frowned, and stared at Jane. "Was he talking about the two in the cellar you told us about?"

Jane nodded. "They're just a pair of idiots."

"Idiots, you told me, who quote Shakespeare?" Klaus wasn't amused. "They could cause trouble for us, Elizabeth?"

She turned in her chair to face Jane. "Tell us everything you know about these two."

Jane sat at the kitchen table, and told Klaus and Elizabeth about the two failed break-ins at High Wood, and the recent events at Takanun.

Elizabeth drummed her fingers on the table. "So, two incompetent, barely literate, thick as two short planks, frightened of their own shadows, burglars, after being stuck in Takanun's cellar, are transformed into well-mannered, polite, Shakespeare-quoting, young men?"

Jane stood with her hands on her hips and nodded slowly. "That's about it."

Elizabeth rocked back in her chair. "But in God's name how could that happen?" She rocked the chair back too far, and it tipped back onto the floor. She stood up, trying not to look embarrassed, walked around the kitchen, pursed her lips, ran her fingers through her hair, picked up the chair, sat back down, leaned on her elbows, and finally sucked her teeth. "How long were they locked in?"

"Most of the night I should think," Jane replied, trying to hide her smirk, and feeling more relaxed.

"Did they say where they'd been in the cellar?" Elizabeth continued, massaging her temples.

"I heard one of them say he was glad to feel cooler, after sleeping against the wall," Alfredo said calmly.

"Cooler?" Klaus asked with a scowl Scrooge would have been proud of.

Alfredo nodded. "I'm certain he said cooler. He was panting, and his face was bright red."

Klaus put the tip of his index finger between his teeth, and gently chewed it. "Then he must have been warmed by the wall?" he said softly to no-one in particular. "We need to go back down into the cellar."

"What about the pictures?" Alfredo asked cautiously.

"They can wait. There is something in that cellar we have missed." He stopped and tapped the side of his head. "But first I must call Renaat. I have to know how Guillaume is recovering."

# Chapter Eighty-Eight

Charlie was sat in the kitchen at Cambrai, eating a hearty full English breakfast, feeling almost recovered from his 'travels'.

"I spoke to your gran to say you were OK," Marie said as she finished her coffee.

"How's mum? What did gran say?" Charlie put down his knife and fork and became very agitated.

"She's so pleased you're OK, and is really looking forward to seeing you when you get home. I said we'd probably be back early afternoon tomorrow."

"She was OK with that? I thought we could travel today?"

"She sounded fine with tomorrow." Marie's tone was a little too reassuring.

"What aren't you telling me? It's the cancer, isn't it?"

Marie was hoping to avoid getting Charlie emotionally stressed, but there was clearly no avoiding it. "She's going to the hospital today for chemotherapy, is staying overnight, and will be coming home tomorrow. They don't want her to be on her own after such aggressive drugs."

"I should be with her. Mum shouldn't be on her own." Charlie stood up and ran into the back garden.

"Shouldn't someone go with him?" Desiree asked quietly.

Marie shook her head. "No. Leave him. He needs some time on his own."

Molly was resting in bed on the ward after her third dose of Folfox, Folfiri, and Capox. By now she knew what to expect, but it didn't make it any easier to bear. Fatigue, nerve pain, nausea which rose and fell like the tides, temperature which spiked and fell, ulcers in her mouth, throat, and bowel, constipation, diarrhoea, tingling in her fingers, problems with balance, and worst of all for her, 'chemo-brain'. Fuzzy thinking and problems with memory. She stared at the PICC line in the crook of her arm, which would stay in for the whole course of her treatment. A long, thin, flexible tube, possibly delivering, a few extra months of life.

Emma came with her, but remained unseen by everyone except Molly. "How are you feeling?"

"Honestly?"

Emma forced half a smile and nodded.

"Like a giant pile of steaming shit." She lay back on the bed, grimaced in pain, moved around to try to get comfortable, and finally closed her eyes, trying to lose herself in a 'better place'. "If I've got to go through this, just to get a few more months…" She opened her eyes and sighed. "I'm not coming back for any more treatment. I can't take any more of this. What's the point? I'd rather die."

"You don't mean that. No-one *wants* to die."

"That's easy for you to say." Molly looked up at Emma, and couldn't help but smile at the irony. "You've already done it."

"Well, sort of, I suppose." She stood up, walked through the bed, and looked out of the window, at the world outside. "Enjoy it while you can." She was addressing the tangle of humanity walking in and out of the hospital. "One minute the world's your oyster, and the next, it's … it's a bloody stinking, rotten fish."

"Emma? I've never heard you … well, almost swear."

Emma carried on watching the sick, the dying, and their visitors enter the hospital, some whose prayers would be answered, and some whose world, like a child's kaleidoscope, would be twisted and shaken, and the image of their world transformed forever. "What sort of God thinks up cancer? I mean, what's the point. Mind you, He's got a good track record on thinking up shit for us. Alzheimer's, AIDs, Ebola. I could keep going all day." She turned away from the window, shaking her head.

"Emma! This isn't a good time to be bad mouthing someone or something, which may be sitting up there waiting to judge us."

"He can do whatever he wants." Emma sat down close to the bed. "Oh, I forgot to say that I spoke with Marie. Charlie's fine and they'll be back tomorrow."

"Where's he been?" Molly was overjoyed.

"I didn't ask. I was just pleased he was OK. We can ask him when we see him."

"He's not going to deal with this very well." Molly sighed. "Not well at all."

"Charlie'll be fine. He's a strong lad." Emma paused. "And we haven't talked about his skills."

"Not now. I'm too tired." Molly lay back, closed her eyes, and prayed to whatever deity would listen, to let her sleep and never wake up.

Charlie was up at first light hammering on Marie's bedroom door. "We need to be on the road before the rush hour traffic kicks off."

A pair of bleary eyes appeared in the doorway. "What the hell's the time?"

"Don't know. It's early. Grab your things. We can grab something to eat on the way." He turned with a bag in his hand. "I'll wait for you in the kitchen."

Desiree had heard Charlie moving around, and was already in the kitchen with a teapot of freshly brewed tea. "Thought this would help." She pointed to the table, at four piles wrapped in aluminium foil. "Ham sandwiches, chocolate cake, some tomatoes and celery, two apples and some grapes, a couple of Swiss rolls. And I've just filled a flask with coffee. That should keep you going."

Charlie smiled. "Thanks, and thanks for not saying anything about Cardiff? You know. In the hotel?"

"Don't know what you're talking about Charlie." She winked at him, and made a face. "You go very well together."

"Mmmm?"

"You and Marie." She squeezed his arm. "You know she's in love with you, don't you?"

Charlie looked surprised. "In love with *me*?"

"My God. You call yourself a policeman, and you can't even see what's happening under your nose. She adores you." She wagged a finger at him. "Don't you make her unhappy, or I'll track you down."

Charlie smiled. "I'll do my best."

"Morning," Marie said cheerily as she walked into the kitchen. She looked at the packed feast on the table, smiled, walked across to Desiree, hugged her tightly, and kissed her on the cheek. "You didn't need to do this. But thanks so much for thinking of us."

Desiree gathered up the packages and the flask and dropped them into two carrier bags.

Charlie picked them up, kissed her on the cheek, and whispered in her ear. "Thanks again. I'll do my best to make her happy."

As they reached the front door, Marie turned around. "You must come and visit us in Cardiff. I want to hear all about the family tree."

Desiree waved as they walked to the car. "I'd love to," she called out. "Keep in touch."

They were on the road by six, and by eleven thirty, they were pulling up outside Takanun.

"I really want to come with you, but I need to check on mum and dad." Marie leaned across and kissed him tenderly on the cheek. "Let me know how she is, and give her a kiss from me." She started to get out of the car, and then stopped, and leaned back inside. "I think I might have fallen in love with you, Charlie." She kissed him passionately on the lips and walked quickly to Takanun.

"I love you, Marie," he whispered as she opened the front door and disappeared into the house.

He drove home as quickly as his police training would allow him, and ran into the house. "MUM!"

"In here, Charlie. I'm in the lounge."

He ran to the weak voice and burst into tears. For the first time, he saw the full effect of the cancer and the chemotherapy on his mother. He sat down carefully on the sofa, close to her. "How … you're … I was …" The rest was lost in chest-heaving sobs.

Molly took his head, laid it softly in her lap, and stroked his hair. "You're home now. That's all that matters. I'll be fine now. Grandma's been with me."

Emma walked slowly in from the kitchen. *"Is he OK?"* she mouthed to Molly.

She shook her head and carried on stroking his hair. "Put the kettle on, would you?"

Charlie sat up. "Straight away mum."

"No darling. I was asking grandma."

Charlie looked across at Emma and smiled. "Thank you for being with mum."

"That's OK, my dear. I'll make us all a cup of tea." She turned, and ignoring the door this time, walked through the wall.

"She's been a rock. I don't think I could have got through it without her."

Charlie's chest heaved again, as an overwhelming sadness rocked him. "I sh … I should have been …"

Molly held his hands tightly and looked deep into his tear-stained, red eyes. "I'm fine. Now tell me what happened in Sheringham? I want to know everything."

"Shouldn't we wait for grandma?"

Molly looked towards the kitchen door and smiled. "Yes. She needs to hear this as well."

Over cups of tea, slices of madeira cake, and chocolate biscuits, Charlie told them, within reason, everything that happened in Sheringham and Burma.

Emma sat, staring wide-eyed and open-mouthed at him. "You were with Peter?"

Charlie nodded.

"My Peter?"

He nodded again. "We were together most of the time I was in the camp."

"Did he talk about me?" Her lips were quivering, and her voice tremulous.

Charlie's smile was full of love. "He spoke a great deal about you gran, and how he'd try to come to the future to see you." He frowned slightly.

Molly shook her head. "Are you sure he got away?"

Charlie shook his head. "I don't know. We ran in different directions." He shuddered as he remembered the bayonets. "But it wasn't the first time he'd done it. Saving spirits that is. Spirit Walking. His body was downriver in a native camp, and once he got back to it," Charlie said, then shrugged. "Who knows what happened next." He frowned. "The war still had years to run."

"But if I'm still here, he must have been killed and is still lost. Why else would I still be here?"

He looked caringly at his grandma. "The little I've been told about the reasons a spirit remains, are either unfinished business, a strong resistance to moving across to the other side, or a really strong attraction to a place, event, or person. I suppose it could it be any of them."

Emma sat back in the chair, deep in thought, and after a few minutes of silence, she sat forward. "I've always believed that after he saw his baby and went back to war, he was killed. Reg constantly reminded me Peter was dead, and so for me, it became the truth."

Molly looked across at her from the sofa. "You have to let go of what you thought was true and let the real truth in."

Emma nodded. "But what is the real truth? What do I let in? How do I know what's true and what isn't?"

Charlie desperately wanted to throw his arms around Emma and hug her. "From the brief time I've been involved in this, gran, I've understood, that sometimes, things just happen. If Peter is, as I know he is, a Spirit Walker, then he can time travel and he should be able to come to you."

"I told you Peter was special," Emma said with exaggerated satisfaction. "Always knew. Just like you, Charlie." Emma stared into his eyes. "You're special, aren't you?"

"Yes," Charlie said with some embarrassment.

Molly looked across at Emma. "Looks like you were right all along."

"Where's Mary?" Emma asked Charlie.

"*Marie's* at home. She's checking her parents are OK."

"You like her, don't you?" Molly said, through her laboured breathing.

Charlie blushed and nodded.

"Nothing to be embarrassed about son. Bit more than *like* is it?"

Charlie's cheeks could have toasted bread.

"There's nothing you can do here, so why don't you go and see her? You can come back later today. I'll still be here."

"I'm staying."

"You're going, unless you want to stress me out."

Charlie realised that arguing was pointless. "Do you want me to get you anything when I'm out?"

Molly thought for a few seconds. "A couple of magazines. You choose."

Charlie kissed her tenderly on the cheek, squeezed her chin, smiled at Emma, and walked slowly backwards out of the lounge. It would be good to see Marie and get some comfort.

# Chapter Eighty-Nine

Matt and Mark decided to stop on their way home for a drink at the Fox and Hounds. The bar was heaving with their friends and others who were less than warm towards them.

"EVENING LADS," Phil the landlord shouted above the noise. "Usual? Two pints?"

"Good evening, landlord." Matt smiled inanely. "Could I possibly have a glass of your finest sauvignon blanc for my brother? Preferably Kim Crawford if you have it?"

Phil leaned forward on the bar and stared in utter disbelief at Matt. "Kim pissing who?"

"Kim Crawford, Phillip. The producer of the wine is from New Zealand."

Phil stopped blinking, and just stared, his chin scraping along the floor.

"I would like," Matt said, holding his chin, and scanning the shelves and cabinets behind the bar, "a bottle of ginger ale if you would be so kind." He requested politely.

Phil stared at him as if he'd grown a second head. "What ginger ale? You mean Crabbies?"

"No, no, just a plain ginger ale with ice, and perhaps a slice of lime?"

Phil leaned across the bar and firmly held onto the collar of Matt's sweater. "Have you lads been taking anything? 'Cause you know I don't have that sort of thing in my pub," he said, stabbing a finger into Matt's chest. "Or are you just taking the piss?" He focused on their eyes, but their pupils were normal. "You going down with something?"

Others close to the bar had started to take an interest in this conversation.

"Never felt better. In fact, I feel ten years younger."

Phil wasn't giving up and looked around the ceiling. "Where's the cameras? You're in some bloody TV programme, aren't you? It's something like that, ain't it?"

Matt shook his head and looked at Mark who did the same.

Phil was now losing his cool. "OK! So you're just taking the piss. You've been coming in 'ere for ten years, and you've always ordered two pints of Brains SA. Now you want some fucking poncey wine and a ginger beer?" He slammed his hands on the bar and nodded his head towards the door. "Now sod off. And don't come back until you've … shit, I don't know what, but if you do come back, then it better not be like this."

Matt and Mark looked at each other in utter amazement. "If our custom is not welcome at this establishment, landlord, then I'm afraid we will have to seek another hostelry with a rather more welcoming ambience." They turned, and to a cacophony of cat calls, whistles, raucous laughter, and 'Goodbye petals', they walked out of the pub.

"What an ill-mannered oaf," Mark said softly to his brother. "We are better rid of that sort."

"We shall find 'A goodly portly man, i' faith, and a corpulent; of a cheerful look, a pleasing eye' and give him our business," Matt said with an enormous smile. "Come brother, let's find our own Boar's Head."

After being thrown out of another four pubs, the brothers decided to call it a day and go back to their 'flat'. Twenty minutes later, they were stood in their 'apartment', taking in the disarray. They gaped in disbelief at each other, burst into tears, wouldn't sit down for fear of catching something, held hands, and walked out.

"We can't possibly live in that?" Matt said between sobs. "Can we?"

"It must have been ransacked by young ruffians." Mark put his arm around Matt's shoulder and squeezed gently. "We most probably lived here some time ago. Those oafs in the hostelries, have so upset us that we must have returned to where we began."

They stopped and looked up at their only window.

"Problem lads?" a reassuring voice said from behind them.

Matt turned around, wiped his eyes, and did his best to smile at the police constable. "We have almost certainly been burgled, and the rascals have ransacked our abode. It's terrible up there. How can people do such things?"

"Don't worry, sir. Let me take a look." The constable tried to look reassuring and not smile. After a brief time, he came back shaking his head. "My God, I've never seen anything like it. They've completely wrecked the place. It looks like a tornado's gone through it. I'll contact the station. What's the name, sir?"

"Matthew Stroudle."

As he spoke to the station, the constable walked away a few paces, and then looked over his shoulder and stared at Matt and Mark a few times.

"Are you better known as Matt Stroudle, sir? And is this your brother Mark?"

"That is correct," Matt answered very politely. "We are brothers."

The constable walked a few paces away again, spoke into his radio, and came back. "Would you wait here with me, sir? I've asked for some extra support to look into this crime."

"Of course, officer. If it helps apprehend the scoundrels who committed this crime, we will do everything which is required of us."

Half an hour later as they sat in an interview room at the station, Matt wasn't too sure about his earlier offer of support, and the way they were being treated. "Why are we in here?" he asked the constable stood in a corner of the room.

"Someone will be along very soon, sir."

"Thank you. I'm sure we can resolve everything very quickly."

Detective Sergeant Morris walked into the interview room with Detective Constable Jean Andrews. "Hello lads. Excuse me for a few seconds. I need to make all this official." He turned on the recorder, explained who was present, and sat back to listen to the Stroudle's tale of woe.

"Tut, tut. What is the world coming to, Detective Constable Andrews, when two young gentlemen like this, can't go out for a pleasant evening together, and expect their property to be in the same condition when they get home?" He leaned his elbows on the table, breathed deeply, sucked his teeth, and scratched the side of his nose. "OK, what are you pair of wankers are trying to pull? Is this some insurance scam?"

Matt and Mark looked at each other, aghast at the suggestion.

"We have absolutely no idea what you are talking about or suggesting. We came here in good faith to report a crime, and now we find ourselves slandered in this manner."

"Oh, piss off, Matt. How many times have you and dopey," he said and nodded at Mark, "been with me in this room?"

"I have a vague recollection of meeting you before. However, be assured that this will be the last time you will see myself or my brother."

Morris sat back in his chair, pursed his lips, and stared intently at both brothers. "You're bloody serious, aren't you?"

Matt nodded. "Most certainly. Why else would we be here? Away, and mock the time with fairest show; False face must hide what the false heart doth know."

Morris almost fell off his chair. "I need to talk with someone. Preferably a psychiatrist." He glanced over his shoulder at the brothers. "Tea?"

"Thank you. Do you have any Earl Grey?"

"Only Baron Builder's I'm afraid."

"In that case, white with two sugars, and Mark is white with one sugar. I'm glad to see that common-sense has at last prevailed. An apology will not be necessary."

Morris almost responded, but chose, at least for the present, to ignore Matt. He slammed the door behind him and stood outside the cell with Detective Constable Andrews. "I've known those two arseholes for ten years, and admittedly they're a prime-rib pair of nobs, but I've never seen them act like this before." He shook his head and walked up and down the corridor talking to himself. "There's something wrong. I'm wondering if all the shit they've snorted, dropped, ate, drank, and shoved up their arses, has finally fried their brains." He leaned back against the wall. "I'm nipping upstairs to call the MO. I want him to take a look at this pair. They're either up to something, or on something. You stay here and keep them topped up with tea and biscuits."

After discussing the brothers over the phone with the MO, Morris returned to the interview room. "Tea OK?"

"Not too bad. Not up to Lapsang Souchon. Do you know how they achieve its evocative, smoky, rich flavour?" Mark directed his question at Morris.

"No … no I don't, Mark," he said, trying to disguise any shock or disbelief in his voice. *"And how the fuck does a numpty like you?"*

"Well, to give this tea its unmistakable flavour, the plucked leaves are withered over pine fires, pan-dried, rolled, placed in bamboo baskets, and smoked over smouldering pinewood fires. Extraordinary, isn't it?"

Morris metaphorically pinched himself. *"Any second now, I'm going to wake up."*

"Are you OK Detective Sergeant?" Matt asked with genuine concern.

"Yes, thanks. But I'm not so sure about you two."

"I'm sorry?" Mark exclaimed.

"Have you been anywhere you shouldn't have? Somewhere you normally don't go? Or taken something you don't normally take?"

"I'm not entirely sure I understand what you're asking," Matt said with a deep frown.

Morris repeated his questions.

The brothers put their heads close together and spoke secretively to each other. After a few minutes, they looked up, and Matt took the lead. "We have a recollection of recently being trapped in a house."

Morris looked up from his notes. "Trapped?"

The brothers nodded. "Well, I suppose we were locked in, really." Matt answered.

"Where was this?"

The brothers put their heads together again. "Not exactly sure about the name, but it began with a 't', and sounded a bit like," he said and stared at the ceiling seeking inspiration, "a bit like … tax-something. Or was it … tacky? Oh, what was it?"

"Takanun?" Morris suggested.

The brothers, looked at each other as if Morris had discovered the cure for the common cold, high-fived each other and turned beaming at him. "Exactly," Matt said with a smile from ear to ear.

Morris stood up and gestured for the detective constable to follow him. "Let them go, Jean. I'm going back to that house to check on that reported burglary and I'd bet my pension it was those two who were involved."

"But why would they say they were locked in? They're as good as admitting guilt," Jean asked.

"Don't know, but there's something bloody odd and smelly about all this. My antennae are twitching and I need to know why." He turned and headed off down the corridor.

# Chapter Ninety

Guillaume half woke, from what his mind was desperately trying to convince him, had been the most harrowing nightmare of his life. As he opened his eyes, he found himself looking up into the concerned eyes of Renaat. But all Guillaume saw, were the eyes of Unteroffizier Bruno Franks.

"BASTARD!" He threw the sheets back and flew at Renaat, like a hungry crocodile at a wildebeest.

"BASTARD! EVIL BASTARD! THIS TIME YOU WILL DIE!"

Despite the ferocity of the attack, Renaat easily pushed the weakened body of Guillaume back onto the bed. "It is me, my friend. It is Renaat. Guillaume, it is Renaat." He maintained gentle pressure on his shoulders because the fire in Guillaume's eye hadn't dimmed.

"BASTARD! SS BASTARD!"

"I know my friend. Shhh. Relax. I'll stay with you."

"FRANKS! DEVIL! FRANKS!"

"Shhh, my dearest friend. Shhh."

"I will kill …" Guillaume drifted back into a restless state of semi-consciousness.

Renaat pulled the sheets back and tucked them in tightly around him. He walked to the window, took out his mobile, and called Guillaume's family doctor.

"I'll be there in about fifteen minutes. Keep him in bed. I'll administer another sedative when I get there." Doctor Van Moot answered. His voice didn't hide his concern for one of his closest friends.

Renaat sat down in the chair he'd brought up from the lounge, and his mobile rang. He looked at the screen. 'Bauer'. "Hallo Klaus, how is Karsten?"

"He is back with me, but I am unsure about his mental state. How is Guillaume?" Klaus's voice was uncharacteristically flat.

Renaat thought for a few seconds before replying. "He's mostly been sleeping." He thought that mentioning his outburst, wouldn't help Klaus's obvious concerns about his son.

"Karsten is the same." There was a short pause. "Guillaume has said nothing?"

"Only some garbled words which meant nothing to me." Renaat regretted saying the words as soon as he'd uttered them.

"Garbled words? Has he lost his mind?"

"No, nothing like that, just some things in his sleep."

"Oh." Klaus sounded even flatter. "Is anyone there to help you?"

"His doctor will be here in a few minutes, and I have some friends locally who'll help me take a few days off. But I'm fine. I sit, drink coffee and beer, watch TV, listen to music, do crosswords, and read mostly." There was a pregnant pause, and Renaat spoke again. "We should call a meeting of the Astrea Klaus. So much has happened and we need to update each other."

"I agree. Who would be best to arrange this?"

"Probably Ralph. I know he's in the US, but he has very strong persuasive powers."

"Could you email him on behalf of both of us, Renaat?"

"Of course. Any particular dates?"

"Any time, anywhere. I will make myself available."

"Leave it with me. Keep me updated on Karsten's progress."

"And you also on Guillaume. Auf Wiedersehen."

"Auf Wiedersehen Klaus. Viel Glück *(Good luck)*."

Klaus turned to the others. "OK meine Freunde. Let's take a look at that wall." He walked quickly down the cellar steps and trotted across to the adjoining wall.

Elizabeth was close behind him, and almost ran into his back as Klaus came to an abrupt stop.

"Careful," she said rather louder than she planned.

"Tut mir leid mein Schatz, *(Sorry my dear,)*" He turned to face her and his expression scared Elizabeth. He turned and pointed at the wall.

Elizabeth and the others followed the line of his finger, and their expressions soon matched his.

Swirling into the wall on their left, and out of the wall on their right, was what looked like half of a vortex of blue 'stars'. A spinning azure whirlpool, with what looked like a half of a black hole at its centre.

Bill sauntered down the cellar steps, across the cellar floor, and in his own inimitable way, stood calmly next to Elizabeth, studying the phenomenon. "The theory of general relativity predicts, that a sufficiently compact mass can deform space-time to form a black hole. That darker ring at the boundary of the region, from which no escape is possible, is called the event horizon. Moreover, quantum field theory in curved space-time, predicts that event horizons emit Hawking radiation."

"Are you seriously suggesting this is a black hole? And is possibly emitting some form of radiation?" Klaus said with remarkable control. "Something which normally exists far out in our universe, also exists here in this cellar." He swallowed hard and stared at Bill. "That is your theory?"

He looked hurt. "It's a workable hypothesis. The energy levels which have built up in here and next door are vast. Who knows what could happen."

"But a black hole?" Jane said without hiding her disbelief. "No way. Why haven't we all been sucked into it?" She stood with her feet planted wide apart, daring Bill to argue with her.

"Well," Bill gently started to back-track, "maybe not a black hole, but something very like one."

"And if it was," Klaus asked, not taking his eyes off the vortex, "it would emit some form of radiation?"

Bill nodded. "With black holes, it's 'Hawking radiation'. In 1975 Hawking published a shocking result, that black holes should glow slightly with 'Hawking radiation', consisting of photons, neutrinos, and to a lesser extent, all sorts of massive particles. But what's emitted from this?" He shrugged and scratched his head. "Who knows? But I would bet that it's emitting some form of radiation. All these particles of spirit-energy, spinning and colliding with each other, must be generating some form of radiation."

Elizabeth and Alfredo slowly began to back away.

"Are we in any danger?" Gloria asked nervously.

"Who knows? I sure as hell don't." Bill chuckled to himself. "But it's brilliant, isn't it?" He took out his iPhone and started taking video and photos.

Klaus was now wholly focused on determining what it was. "Is there any way of measuring or checking if there is any radiation?"

Bill walked close to the vortex and ran his fingers through the outer currents, like a child running his fingers through the surface of a fast-moving brook. "It's warm. It somehow seems to penetrate into your muscles and bones." He pulled his hand out of the spinning stars and staggered back two or three steps, onto Klaus's foot.

Klaus hopped around, muttering unintelligible German expletives under his breath. When he finally stopped, he turned his attention back to Bill, who was sat on the floor, staring wide-eyed at his right hand. Klaus knelt down beside him. "Was ist es? What is it?"

Bill said nothing and simply held up his hand.

Klaus examined it closely, turning it over several times. "It appears to be perfectly normal."

Bill looked up at Klaus. "Yes. But a few minutes ago, that palm had a deep cut with four stitches."

Klaus looked up and walked slowly around the cellar, examining the piles of collected 'stuff'. Eventually he found what he wanted. An empty, clear plastic CD case. He walked back, cracked the case under his heel, picked up a large shard, and cut himself in the palm of his right hand. He grimaced, walked close to the vortex, and pushed his bleeding hand into the azure whirlpool. He stood calmly for a few minutes, lifted his hand out of the maelstrom, closely examined it, walked back to the Elizabeth, and showed her his hand.

She took a step back and gasped. "It's a trick! You didn't cut yourself, did you? That sort of thing can't happen."

"WHAT THE HELL?" Jane shouted, as they all grouped around Klaus's hand.

"SHIT!"

"My God, it's gone."

"How in the name of …"

"But it was …"

Klaus rubbed the palm of his hand with his thumb. "No cut, no scar, no pain." He looked over his shoulder at the vortex. "Whatever else this may be, it seems to have the power to heal. Es ist ein Wunder. *(It is a miracle.)*"

"I'm not sure if Jesus managed this sort of thing." Elizabeth stared deep into the spinning blueness. "It's a twenty-four carat miracle."

Klaus's mind had slipped into overdrive. "Will you help me carry Karsten here?" He looked at Alfredo and Elizabeth. "He hasn't really recovered since his return. Gott hilf mir. *(God help me.)* Gott hilf mir."

Elizabeth held Klaus gently by the wrist. "None of us have any idea what this is, or least of all, what it could do to anyone." She pointed at the vortex. "Until we know what the hell that is, we shouldn't be experimenting with it. God knows what it's done to your hand, and more importantly, what it might do to Karsten." She looked tenderly into his eyes. "The risks are too high."

Klaus tried to pull away, but Elizabeth held him back. "Now is not the time, Klaus."

"When will be the right time?" He was close to tears. "Do any of you know?" He looked imploringly at the others. "Who can help my son? Your earlier employer, Elizabeth?"

Elizabeth frowned at Klaus and pointed to the sky. "God?" she said with growing concern. "And should I also check with Jesus, Mary, and the band of angels?"

Klaus prised her hand away with his other, and sighed so deeply that Alfredo expected the walls to collapse in on themselves. "You are right. This could just be some trick vom Teufel *(trick of the Devil)*. We should go back to High Wood and discuss what we do next."

Everyone was in agreement, when a loud knock at the front door changed their plans.

"You carry on," Elizabeth said. "I'll see who this is and meet you at the house."

Klaus heard the ping from his mobile and stayed behind, while the others made their way to High Wood. It was a text from Ralph, with two dates for a meeting of the Astrea, and a text from Renaat. He responded to the second text first.

# Chapter Ninety-One

Sam parked close to the entrance of Safestore, a large, red-brick warehouse with blue cladding on the upper third of the walls.

The young woman behind the desk stopped tapping away at her computer and gave Sam her full attention. "Good morning, sir. How can I help?"

"Hi, I'm Sam Morbeck, and I'm not exactly sure what I need to ask for." He stumbled over his words.

"Just tell me what the problem is, and let's see how I can help." She exuded customer service training. "Would you like a coffee?"

"Please. White with two sugars."

They sat together in reception, drinking their coffees on a green leather sofa, which was badly worn and in need of some TLC.

"So Sam. What is it I can help you with?"

"I've inherited a house in Cardiff which belonged to my aunt and uncle. I've been going through their papers, and there was an old receipt for this place, for storing reels of film, and I need to find them."

Nicola smiled. "Shouldn't be a problem. I'll need some proof of identity before I can check anything for you."

Sam searched through his pockets, found his driving licence in his wallet, and handed it to Nicola.

She took it and smiled. "Perfect. Give me a couple of minutes, and I'll check our records." She walked back to the reception desk, and started tapping away at the computer. A few minutes later she was back. "I've found something."

Sam put his cup on the floor.

"A Mr A Morbeck did rent a unit from us."

"That's my Uncle Arnold."

She looked down at her print and nodded. "I'm afraid there's some money owing."

"That's the sort of thing I'm tidying up," Sam said in a very conciliatory tone. "How much do I owe?"

She glanced back at the form. "It comes to six hundred and forty-three pounds and eighty-six pence."

He hid his shock well, took out his wallet again, and gave her his Master Card, praying his balance was still deep enough in the black to pay for this.

She nodded and took the payment. "I'll get the key for you and show you where the storage unit is."

Sam took the key from her, and followed her to the unit which looked like a steel double garage door.

"I'll leave you to it. If you need anything, I'll be in reception." She turned and walked away.

He put the key in the lock and slowly raised the hinged door. Inside, both sides were packed from ceiling to floor with white cardboard boxes sealed with brown packing tape. A small aisle, about a yard wide, ran down the middle of the unit, providing access to the boxes. Close to the door was an aluminium step ladder, which Sam pulled into the unit. He climbed to the top of the first row of boxes, and pulled out a dusty white box, which, being a lot heavier than he'd anticipated, fell straight through his hands to the floor. It split open on impact, and silver film cans spilled everywhere.

*"At least I know I'm in the right place,"* he thought.

# Chapter Ninety-Two

Lidsay had lain low, as far back as he could, in the mind of the Japanese guard. He'd tried a few times to move closer to the front of the guard's mind, trying to regain some control, but he couldn't take the terrible spectacle of constant violence, abuse, killing, summary executions, disease, and above all, the bloody Japanese language.

*"Why can't you understand me, you slant-eyed tit!"*

He decided to give up on the abuse and find a new host.

*"Question is?"* He mused. *"I should be able to just split away from this Nip whenever I want to. So why wouldn't I?"*

He pondered on this for a few minutes.

*"OK. Let's give it a ..."* He metaphorically stopped dead in his tracks. *"Not yet. I know I can get back, but I still haven't got a bloody clue how to. Last time I was a lot closer in France. This pissing place is a bit further away."* Lidsay's thoughts of escape were brought to an abrupt end as his host suddenly felt as if he was free falling.

The guard's scream stopped instantly, as Gurney snapped his head back, exposing his throat, and Jonson simultaneously slashed his windpipe with a stolen knife.

"One less slit-eyed bastard to torment us. Back to the camp." Jonson hissed as they pushed the guard's body over the edge of the ravine.

The two men briefly waited, heard the splash in the river below, smiled at each other, turned, and ran back to the camp.

The guard's body bobbed back to the surface of the river like a rubber ring in a child's swimming pool and was rapidly carried downstream by the raging current in the rapids.

The chief of the village poked his head through the entrance to Peter's hut. "There is a body in the river."

Peter sat up on the bamboo bunk. "British?"

The chief shook his head. "Nippon."

Peter sat back on the bunk. "Let it float by."

"The body has weapons. The death grip has a firm hold on a rifle with bayonet."

Peter stood up again, walked out of the hut, and followed the chief to the edge of the river.

The body had been brutally battered by the current and rocks, but as the chief had said, a rifle, with a bayonet still attached, was held in a death grip by what remained of the guard's hand. Two villagers walked out into the river, took a firm hold of the boots, and pulled the body onto the shore. The shattered end of the tibia, was protruding through the torn trousers, the left arm was only attached by a few tendons, and what remained of the head and face, was unrecognisable as human. But despite the mutilated condition of the guard, the rifle appeared to be in reasonably good condition, and the pistol at the waist also appeared to be OK. The villagers stepped back, unhappy to take anything from a spirit which they believed could still harm them.

Peter smiled, understanding their reticence, stepped forward, and tried unsuccessfully to wrench the rifle away from its owner. He turned to the chief and gestured for his knife. After removing three fingers from the hand, the rifle fell to the riverbank.

Lidsay, had been quietly observing events, and saw a way out of this rapidly disintegrating Japanese soldier.

Peter tossed the rifle back to the chief, kept the bayonet, and turned his attention to the pistol. *"Unfasten the belt?"* he thought. *"No point. Just cut it with the bayonet."*

Lidsay, like a lioness stalking an antelope, was waiting for his moment, which soon came, as Peter reached down, and gripped the belt to cut it. Lidsay struck with the speed of a Death Adder and the venom of a Papuan Taipan.

Peter dropped the pistol as if it was red hot, fell onto his back, stared blindly at the sky, vomited, sat up, wiped his mouth with the back of his hand, shook his head, massaged his temples and neck, breathed deeply, and finally, with the help of the chief, stood up.

The chief looked concerned. "Are you OK, Peetah?"

"I don't know." He was unsteady on his feet. "I think I'll go back to the hut and lie down." Two hours later, he woke from a very disturbed sleep. *"I knew this would eventually come,"* he thought. *"You can't see and do and what I have, and not be affected by it."* He got up from his bunk, walked to the edge of the clearing, found the tree he wanted, dug at the roots, and lifted out a thick canvas bag. Back in the hut, he opened the bag, and took out the radio. "Know when it's the right time to stop." He checked his watch and dialled in the frequency of his contact in the Chindits.

"AQZ1. AQZ1 over." Peter tweaked the dial, but there was no answer.

"AQZ1. AQZ1 over."

Nothing.

"AQZ1. AQZ1 over."

"Maluku. トーク *(Talk)*."

"私は私の歯を取り出す必要があります *(I need my teeth taking out.)*"

"とき *(When)*?"

"できるだけ早くすることができます *(As soon as you can.)*"

There was a brief silence.

"明日 3 時 *(Tomorrow at three.)*"

"ありがとう。あるでしょう *(Thanks. I will be there.)*"

Peter closed the radio, replaced it in the canvas bag, pushed it under his bunk, and walked out to find the chief. "I'll be leaving tomorrow, but another soldier will come to replace me.

"We will miss you, Peetah. You have been a good friend."

Lidsay chuckled to himself. *"Good lad. Don't know where we're going, but it's got to be a fucking side better than this."*

Three weeks later, after thorough physical and mental assessments, Peter was back in the UK, for a month's leave before returning to the Philippines. He decided to find the young woman he'd met in Sheringham, and if she wasn't there, then at least the sea air would help his recovery.

With so many young men away at the war, Uncle Donald was finding running the station too much. Every Monday, Thursday, and Saturday, Emma and her father helped him out in the ticket office and as station guards.

It was an unseasonably cold day, and Walter, Emma's father, and Uncle Donald, were sat on a bench outside the station office, cuddling steaming mugs of tea.

Emma was making sandwiches for them when the London train arrived at the platform. She wandered out of the office, into a dense cloud of steam and smoke which obscured the disembarking passengers. Soldiers, sailors, and airmen home on leave, sad, confused young evacuees from London, mail, provisions for the town, parcels, two or three dogs, a few cats, too many young men in wheelchairs, four bicycles for the local Home Guard, and Peter Wallins.

Peter stood on the platform, waiting for the cloud to dissipate to get his bearings.

"I'll get you those sandwiches," Emma said to her father and uncle. But as she turned to go back to the office, an invisible hand tugged at her shoulder, and an invisible whisk stirred the contents of her stomach into a churning soup. Not knowing what to expect, she slowly turned, held her breath, and stared into the rapidly dispersing cloud. A figure moved toward her, and she screwed up her eyes to make out the features. As Peter appeared from the cloud into the crisp, fresh, clear air, Emma collapsed in a dead faint.

Walter leapt to his feet and pointed at him. "You're dead!"

Peter smiled, patted himself, saw Emma's body lying on the platform, dropped his bags, ran to her, picked her up in his arms, and carried her into the station office.

"But you're dead." Walter remained pointing at Peter.

Emma's eyes flickered open, and what she saw, made her almost faint again, until Peter spoke.

"It's me. Peter. I told you I'd come back."

"But you're …"

"Dead? Your father seems to think so." He smiled at her. "You as well?" He kissed her on the forehead. "I'm here. I kept my promise."

"But Reg asked … and they … they told him …" Her words were lost in uncontrollable sobs and tears.

Peter pulled her close to him and waited for her to calm down. Five minutes later, she was almost in control of her emotions.

"OK now?" he asked tenderly.

She stood back a little from him. "You've been away so long, you didn't write, and when Reg told me you were dead, what else was I supposed to think? You can't just walk back into my life like this.' She turned away, her emotions again taking over.

"I think you'd better go." Walter was stood in the doorway of the office. "She's right. You take her out for one night and expect her to wait for you like a bloody nun?" He was angry. "You're not wanted here."

Peter looked longingly at Emma's back, wanting desperately to tell her why he hadn't written. Tell her about the secret missions, the selfless work he'd done saving POWs, his 'abilities', and his deep love for her, which he was sure was reciprocated.

"You still here?" Walter had taken a few steps into the office.

"DAD!" Emma screamed at him. "GO AWAY!" She gathered herself. "I'll be fine."

"Don't you listen to his bloody lies again, my girl."

Emma's expression melted his heart. "Please, dad. Let me speak to him."

"OK, but just … well just be … Oh bugger me, I don't know." He pointed at Peter, wagged his finger, and walked onto the platform.

She held out her hand to Peter. "Let's take a walk. You can leave your bags in here."

Lidsay, was enjoying the show. *"See, bloody women. Never trust them. Lying cows. You'd be pissing better off without her."* He didn't share his thoughts as he didn't want to rock this particular personal boat too much until he had a decent idea how to get back to Cardiff and 2015.

# Chapter Ninety-Three

Elizabeth slowly opened the front door and a beaming smile spread across her face. "Marie! So good to see you." She stood back and waved her into the house. "Welcome back."

"How's mum and dad?"

"Fine. The nurses have been brilliant with them. You couldn't have had anyone better."

Marie smiled. "I'll get some flowers for them to say thank you. Where are mum and dad now?"

"In the lounge. I think they've been improving their general knowledge." Elizabeth chuckled, as Marie's dad's voice bellowed from the lounge, that John Adams was the second president of the US, not Lincoln.

Marie smiled. "He sounds in good spirits."

Elizabeth linked arms with her. "Let's have a coffee. I need to bring you up to date with everything that's happened while you were away."

Marie frowned slightly and walked with Elizabeth into the kitchen.

After several coffees, Marie stood up and walked to the kitchen window. "And you say his cut had completely disappeared?"

"There wasn't a sign it had ever been there."

"And it did the same for Klaus?"

Elizabeth was beginning to understand where Marie was going with her questions. "Yes, but we haven't got a clue how it does it, or what the short or long term effects could be. It still needs to be investigated."

"But it works?" Marie turned around to face Elizabeth. "And have Alfredo or Klaus had any problems?"

Elizabeth shook her head.

Marie chewed the inside of her cheek, steepled her fingers, stared into the far distance, turned around again to face the window, talked quietly to herself, folded her arms, sighed, scratched the back of her head, turned around again, and pushed her fingers through her hair.

"I want to try this with dad."

Elizabeth had seen this coming and was struggling to find an argument against it. "But it's still untested. Who knows what it might do to him."

"What could it do? If nothing new is done, dad's going to die pretty soon. Who gives a toss about any side effects? Whatever the hell this is, it's been put here for a reason, and I'm going to use it." She stared intently at Elizabeth. "And no-one's going to stop me."

Elizabeth shrugged. "OK, but I'm coming with you."

They walked into the lounge, helped Marie's dad from his chair, and together helped him walk down the cellar steps.

Marie stood frozen to the spot, gaping at the spinning blue stars. "My God, it's so beautiful."

Elizabeth and the others had used many adjectives to describe it, but not beautiful, and she couldn't believe they hadn't. It was beyond beautiful. Almost ethereal. Spiritual.

Marie took her father's right arm and led him into the vortex.

"What's this darling?" Dad asked without any sense of fear.

"A way back to the way things used to be, dad. A key to unlock all your forgotten memories."

"That'll be nice, darling."

Marie started to cry softly. "Yes, dad. It will be nice to have you back with me."

Elizabeth stood in awe and watched as the father and daughter bathed in the spinning cerulean spa.

Marie's father smiled at his daughter, but it was a smile she hadn't seen for years. It was an understanding smile, a smile which said 'I remember'. Marie flew into his arms and hugged the breath out of him.

"Careful, darling. You'll break a rib if you're not careful," he said with a chuckle she'd almost forgotten. "Let's get your mother, shall we?"

Marie took his hand and together they ran across the cellar floor, up the steps, and into the lounge. Two minutes later they were back with Marie's mum. The 'bathing' was repeated, and soon, a re-united family, stood smiling in front of Elizabeth.

"Mum, dad, this is Elizabeth."

They stepped forward and shook her warmly by the hand.

"It's a real pleasure to meet you, my dear. Weren't you the vicar at St Barnabus?" Marie's father asked with a slight frown. "I remember a particular sermon you gave. It was based on … now what was it? Love, yes that was it, love. Luke 6:35 'But love your enemies, do good to them, and lend to them without expecting to get anything back. Then your reward will be great, and you will be sons of the Most High, because he is kind to the ungrateful and wicked.'"

Elizabeth sat down on one of the piles of old cushions and stared at him wide-eyed, in complete shock and bewilderment. "That was five Easters ago…" She was unsure what to call him.

"Robert. Please call me Robert, my dear. You obviously don't wear the cloth anymore, and of course that's none of my business." He turned to his wife, as if the last five years of affliction hadn't happened. "You remember the vicar, dear."

She smiled and nodded. "Please call me Patricia, but we can't call you vicar, can we?"

"Elizabeth. Call me Elizabeth."

Robert turned to Marie. "Excellent. Now that we've completed the formal introductions, shall we go upstairs where it's a lot more comfortable?"

They settled down around the kitchen table, for the first time in what felt to Marie like a lifetime. Despite her cheeks aching, she couldn't stop smiling, and for the next hour, they talked and talked about everything and about nothing.

*"Lazarus's family couldn't have felt any better than this,"* Elizabeth thought. "I'd better go back next door. They'll be wondering where I am," she said softly.

"Will we see you again?" Robert asked as he buttered a piece of toast.

"Of course. I live next door."

"At High Wood?"

"Yes." She looked deep into the penetrating eyes. "Do you remember the people who lived there?"

"Of course. We were very close friends with Edith and Arnold."

"Do you know what they did at High Wood?"

"Of course. But I couldn't possibly discuss that with you, my dear. Very hush-hush. Very secret." He tapped the side of his nose.

"They helped the souls of missing soldiers from World War One pass over to the other side," Elizabeth said as if it was a simple matter of fact.

At first, Robert and Patricia showed no response to Elizabeth's words, but then they slowly turned to face her. "And how do you know this?"

"I've been helping souls to move over for quite a while. I have an ability to do it."

"You?'

"Should that be a surprise?"

Robert's cheeks flushed. "I'm very sorry, Elizabeth. Forgive my rudeness. Please tell me what's happened at High Wood."

"Shall we go into the lounge?" She suggested.

An hour later, after much shaking of heads, glasses of wine, smiles, intense conversation, tears and explanations, an understanding of what had recently happened in High wood was achieved.

"That's High Wood," Elizabeth continued, "but what can you tell me about Takanun?"

Robert looked at Patricia, and she nodded that he should be their spokesperson. "You know the story of how Takanun was built?"

Elizabeth nodded. "I know the history of Prospect House and Outlook House.

"What High Wood is capable of, so is Takanun. They were built to the same plans, and sit on the same conjunction of ley lines. Arnold and Edith were our closest, and best friends, and we," he said and looked across at Patricia, "let's say, are 'associate' members of Papaver Rhoeas."

Elizabeth retained a calm exterior, but inside, her stomach was churning. "So you've been doing the same as we have?"

"Sort of. We, and the previous owners of Takanun, have played a small part in supporting High Wood. That is, until the outbreak of World War Two, when we became overrun with lost souls. It seemed that Takanun was the only point on these ley lines, where they could find an exit point. All other portals were already overloaded by the lost souls of World War One, and protected by shields. Takanun, I now understand, had most of the structure of a portal, but no shields. So my father, we took over after his death, started to help World War Two souls pass over. But for the last five years or so, since our illness, they've had to remain here, confused and frustrated." He paused and sipped whiskey from a cut glass tumbler. "From what you have described, they have created a weak point between the houses and have found a way out. What on earth the vortex, is I have no idea, but thank God for it."

"Or thank the Devil?" Elizabeth said softly.

Robert, Patricia, and Marie's eyes flashed at Elizabeth in a complete lack of understanding.

"The Devil?" Patricia finally spoke.

"We have no understanding of how it works, what after effects it may have, how long the effects may last. Will it make you live forever?"

"It heals and cures. Surely that must be a blessing," Robert said with exasperation.

"Let's imagine this is the only vortex in the world. Would it still be a blessing?"

There was silence.

"Who decides who stands or falls? The sane or insane, benign or malignant, blind or seeing, deaf or hearing, alive or dead, wife or widow?" Elizabeth continued.

The silence grew deeper, and for two or three minutes, they all sat deep in thought.

Robert finally broke the calm. "I'll see my GP and get tested. I won't tell him how I recovered my faculties, and let's see what science can tell us about this miracle." He looked around at the others. "'Jesus said to her, 'I am the resurrection and the life. The one who believes in me will live, even though they die; and whoever lives by believing in me will never die.' Do you believe this?"

Elizabeth nodded her head. "I believe in Christ and his miracles." She stared deeply into Robert's eyes. "You believe that you are similar to Lazarus?"

Robert smiled and nodded.

Elizabeth shook her head and then continued. "We should keep this between ourselves and those who know next door. If this got out, then God only knows what would happen. For the next few weeks, let's keep this our secret." She looked at Robert and Patricia, and raised her eyebrows, seeking their agreement.

Begrudgingly, Robert nodded his head. "OK."

# Chapter Ninety-Four

"Bauer. How is Guillaume?"

"Thanks for getting back to me," Renaat replied, accustomed to his friend's abruptness. "He's up and about, but still very weak." There was a long pause. "He won't discuss what happened."

"Is he able to travel?"

"Possibly. But only with support."

"Can you bring him to Cardiff?"

"Why?"

"I have my reasons."

"Which are?"

"I'd rather not say?"

"Why?"

"Renaat, we can go around in circles like this, or you can simply bring Guillaume to High Wood."

Renaat was annoyed with Klaus's attitude, and didn't feel like continuing this irritating conversation. "I'll book flights, and email you. Goodbye."

Klaus saw nothing wrong in this and smiled to himself. His friend would soon be with him, and they would get things moving. If Guillaume, like Karsten, had suffered from his Spirit Walking, then he had a remedy in the cellar. He walked back towards the kitchen and remembered the other text from Ralph. *"He'll still be asleep,"* he thought. *"I'll call him later."* He made his way back into the kitchen, where the 'discussion', like a bobsleigh, was running headlong down the mountain.

"We don't know how it works."

"But look at my hand."

"How long's it been there?"

"Why hasn't anyone seen it before?"

"Will someone just look at my hand!"

"And don't forget Klaus's hand. You can't ignore that."

"But how do we know the blue thing did it?"

"We need a doctor to look at your hands."

"Cuts don't just disappear."

"And Klaus."

"What about Karsten? We all know what Klaus wants to do."

"I want my son back. Nothing more, nothing less." Klaus was filling the kettle at the sink. "You would want the same? What if this thing can cure cancer? Would we keep it to ourselves? Would we deprive humanity of this miracle?"

"We could make a lot of money from it." Jane regretted the words as they left her mouth.

The silence was a powerful reply.

"Sorry. I wasn't thinking."

Alfredo stood up and walked to the kitchen door. "Jane makes a difficult but good point. Someone, not one of us, but someone could take advantage of this, and they would make a lot of money. We have to protect this until we are certain what to do."

There was a lot of head nodding, mmming, uh huhing, and 'he's right'.

The discussion briefly halted as the front door opened. A few seconds later, Elizabeth appeared at the kitchen door with Marie, Robert, and Patricia.

"Hello everyone. My name is Robert Stridham." He turned and smiled at his wife. "This is my wife Patricia, and I think you already know our daughter Marie."

Klaus's face was a picture of utter confusion and incredulity. "But weren't you … you were … demenz?"

"Yes, I was suffering from dementia, but I have bathed in the blue light. 'What a piece of work is a man! How noble in Reason! how infinite in faculties! in form and moving how express and admirable! In action how like an Angel! in apprehension how like a god! the beauty of the world! the paragon of animals! and yet to me, what is this quintessence of dust? Man delights not me; no, nor Woman neither; though by your smiling you seem to say so.'" He smiled at Klaus. "Hamlet. Do you think I could have a cup of tea? I'm absolutely parched. Oh, and one for these lovely ladies."

Klaus, and everyone else in the kitchen, was either speechless, dumbfounded, thunderstruck, or tongue-tied.

"Cup of tea? Milk and two sugars?" Robert smiled at their frozen expressions. They looked like waxwork figures on phenazepam.

Eventually, Elizabeth stepped forward, walked to the sink, and took the kettle from Klaus. She turned and smiled at everyone. "Your faces. The things you see when you don't have a camera."

Ice, thicker than the polar shelf, finally cracked.

Charlie arrived, walked halfway down the hall, and called out. "Marie!"

She panicked. "He can't see mum and dad like this. He doesn't know about the blue thing."

Klaus nodded. "Go and meet him in the hall, and take him back to Takanun."

"OK, but what about mum and dad?"

Klaus paused and rubbed the tips of his fingers together. "We'll do something. You …"

The rest of his words were lost as Charlie, popped his head around the kitchen door. "Ah, you're in here. Looks like everybody's …" He walked closer to Marie and whispered to her. "Is it alright for your mum and dad to be out of the house?"

"My hearing is acute, and my vision twenty-twenty, young man."

Marie buried her face in her hands. "Oh shit!"

Charlie's jaw missed the floor and carried on few feet into the foundations before he regained control of it. "You spoke?"

Robert looked at Marie. "Picked a bright one this time, darling."

"You spoke."

Robert moved close to Charlie, and prodded him gently in the chest. "I am real, and yes, I can speak."

Charlie was stuck in a seemingly endless loop. "You. Spoke?" He prodded Robert in the chest.

Marie linked arms with Charlie and led him into the garden. "There are a few things I need to tell you."

# Chapter Ninety-Five

Matt and Mark were strolling back from the police station.

"They were a little officious." Mark complained. "Especially that officer in the interview room."

"'The prince of darkness is a gentleman!'" Matt replied.

"Just so, brother. King Lear?"

Matt nodded and smiled.

"Shall we go back to our 'room', and do what we can do to restore it to some semblance of order?"

"Good suggestion. 'Nothing can come of nothing.' But let's stop first for something to eat. I think … I think … I think." Matt's words dissolved into silence.

"Brother? What is it?"

Matt stared vacantly into the distance.

Mark gripped him by the shoulders and shook him. "BROTHER! What is it?"

Matt sniffed loudly, shook his head, sat down on the step of a chip shop, buried his head in his hands, muttered something unintelligible to himself, looked up at Mark, massaged his temples, and started to rock back and forth.

"Matt, what is wrong with you?" Mark put his hand across his mouth and blushed.

Matt looked up at him. "Don't you pissin' swear at me. I'll bleedin' chin you."

"Fuck off, you wanker. You 'aint got the bottle."

The ensuing scuffle drew the attention of a passing police van.

Detective Sergeant Morris was preparing to leave when he heard the noise from the custody desk. As he pushed open the connecting doors, he stopped dead in his tracks. "Oh for the love of… What the hell are you two doing back here?"

"Just when you thought things couldn't get any worse, this twat turns up," Matt said through a sneer to his brother.

"Yeah. Captain Wanker." Mark spat on the floor, which won him a 'prod' in the kidneys. "Soddin' police brutality."

"Why are these two dick-heads back here?" Morris asked the arresting constable.

"Disturbing the peace outside a chip shop. Assaulting a police officer, and until we know better, drunk and disorderly, or under the influence of substance or substances unknown."

"Piss off! We 'aven't touched a soddin' drop, or taken anythin'. Lyin' bunch of bastards." Matt cursed at anyone in a uniform within earshot, and got a similar 'prod' to his brother.

Morris stared at them, and sucked his teeth. *"What the hell's going on?"* he thought. *"How come Derek Jacobi's fan club's have sunk back to their normal selves so quickly?"* He waved the constable over who'd arrested them. "Chuck them in the interview room. I want to have a word with this pair."

The constable nodded, and with the help of three other officers, frog-marched Matt and Mark, kicking and swearing, to the interview room.

Morris sat opposite the brothers, his arms stretched out behind his back. He cracked a few knuckles, stared at Matt, pursed his lips, sipped the coffee he'd brought with him, belched, and started the recorder.

"Any chance of a cup?" Matt asked as politely as it was possible for him to do with a split lip.

Morris just laughed and dunked a chocolate digestive biscuit.

Matt jumped up, leapt across the desk, and didn't reach Morris, because his testicles crashed into the corner of the table. He uttered a stifled, agonised moan and collapsed into a crumpled, writhing, heap on the floor.

Morris turned his attention to the dimmer of the brothers. "So Mark, my favourite numpty, like a cup of coffee or tea?"

Mark had prepared himself for a rather more 'robust' questioning from Morris and was lost for words.

Morris spoke to him as if he was talking to a toddler. "Cup. Of. Tea?" He mimed drinking from a cup. "Or would you like a coffee?"

"Uh, tea."

"And what's the magic word?" Morris slightly raised his eyebrows.

"Uh, please." It wasn't difficult to confuse Mark, but he'd now reached a level of bewilderment never before achieved.

"Good boy." He turned to the constable guarding the door, "Tea please." He turned his attention back to Mark. "Now then. Tell me everything you've done over the last couple of days."

"Don't say a fuckin' word to that bas…"

Morris kicked him in the stomach, which produced a stream of unintelligible expletives.

"So, as we were saying Mark, tell me about the last couple of days."

As he drank his tea and ate as many biscuits as Morris provided, Mark gave him a surprisingly detailed, and colourful description of events.

Morris rocked back in his chair and chewed the end of another rapidly disintegrating biro. After a few minutes, he stood up, walked to the door, and spoke to the constable. "Let them go. They're just a pair of useless boneheads, and I can't be arsed to waste my time on them." He looked down at Matt. "Give him a couple of minutes, and an ice-pack for his bollocks." He walked up to his office, grabbed a few things, and told the sergeant on the front desk he was going out. Half an hour later, he was parked across the road from Takanun. For the first time, he noticed its remarkable similarity to High Wood. *"Call yourself a detective,"* he thought.

# Chapter Ninety-Six

Emma and Peter walked up the hill towards Lateau wood and sat close to each other under an elm.

"So you thought I was dead," Peter said as he stared deep into Emma's eyes.

She nodded and blushed. The feelings she held for him had only been given a shallow burial, and they were doing their best to reach the light. "It's what he told me."

"Reg?"

"Yes."

"I suppose he could only repeat what he'd been told." Peter conceded.

She reached out and held his hand. "It's so wonderful to see you." She glanced back at the house. "Ignore what Dad said. He's always been a little over-protective." A smile played around her mouth. "Peter. You have a son."

A hummingbird's feather could have knocked him over. "A … You said … I've … I've got a …" Peter said with tears torrenting down his cheeks.

Emma swallowed hard, and chewed her bottom lip. "A son." She smiled. "His name's Ian." She held Peter's hand and squeezed it. "He's well." She kissed him tenderly. "He looks just like you." She stroked his cheek. "He seems to get bigger every day."

"Really?" Peter smiled as if world peace had been declared. "Can I see him?" He asked tentatively.

Emma jumped up. "Come on. He's due a feed."

Walter had left for the pub and wouldn't be back for hours, so they sat together in the kitchen feeding Ian.

"Do you want to hold him?" Emma asked.

Peter nodded, and nervously held out his arms. Emotions coursed through his veins as he held his son in his arms.

"Feels good, doesn't it?" Emma said through a smile which almost stretched from ear to ear.

"Better than good. I wish I'd had the education to find the right words."

"Your face says enough."

They sat together, basking in the love and warmth which flowed between them. A haven of peace in a world corrupted by war.

Peter held out his arms and Emma took Ian from him. His expression changed, and Emma feared what she knew he was about to say.

"You're going back, aren't you?" she said in hushed tones.

"Uh, huh. In a few days."

"And you can't tell me where, can you?"

He shook his head. "Will you wait for me?"

"Of course."

"No matter what anyone says, and however long it takes, I will come back for you."

"I know." She looked deep into his eyes. "When have you got to go?"

"I've got to be back in London tomorrow."

*"I am going to be pissing sick."* Lidsay's warmer side had begun to show. *"Shit. I need to get out of you. At least I'll be back in Britain."* As Peter leaned forward to kiss Emma, Lidsay decided that this was his moment. But as Peter neared Emma, she held up the baby for him to kiss, and at that moment, Lidsay chose to move.

The baby screamed.

Peter jumped back. "I'm sorry. I only kissed him."

Emma kissed Peter on the cheek. "Probably your stubble." She soothed the baby. "He's fine." She took the deepest breath of her life. "You'd better go or you'll miss your train."

He pulled her tight against him. "I will never love another. Always remember that." He kissed her forehead, stroked her cheek with his fingers, kissed the end of her nose, swallowed hard, held back his tears, stood back, gently caressed the baby's face, mouthed, *"I love you"*, blew her a kiss, turned, and left the house. "I'll come back for you." He called from the gate.

Emma ran back into the house, buried her face in a cushion, and disintegrated into stomach-wrenching sobs.

Lidsay was confused. He'd invaded quite a few bodies, but never a baby. *"Bit of a poser this. Suppose I could just get out quick into mum."* He suddenly had an epiphany. *"You're Ian Thompson. You couldn't possibly be related to my erstwhile Constable Charlie Thompson, could you? I'm bloody sure he said his dad's name was Ian. If you are, then you're my ticket back to Cardiff, where I'll reacquaint myself with Constable Thompson, when I get back to 2015."*

# Chapter Ninety-Seven

Unteroffizier Bruno Franks screamed obscenities at three Jewish labourers, raised his Luger, and shot the old man supported by two young women, in the right knee. Franks sniggered and shot the old man in the left knee. The two young women tried to pick him up, but Franks kicked them both to the ground. "Jude Hündinnen! *(Jew bitches!)*"

He walked closer to the old man, and fired three bullets into his emaciated, sunken chest. The younger of the two women, leapt at him, and scratched his cheek. He punched her in the face, breaking her nose. The other sister started to get up, but was kicked onto her back. He spat on them and bellowed. "Dieses Stück Scheiße zu begraben! *(Bury this piece of shit!)* Schnell! Schnell!"

Karsten tried to scream, but no sound would come.

The young women struggled to pick up the body of the old man, his blood soaking the rags they wore. One word, was barely audible between their sobs. "Vader. *(Father!)*"

Karsten tried to cry, but no tears would come.

Franks followed the women to the second of the 'pits'. "Schnell Jude!!" As they rolled their father's body down the slope onto the piles of corpses, he walked close behind them. "Auf die Knie. *(On your knees.)*", He kicked them, and watched as they knelt together and held hands with each other. He hit their hands with his whip and shot them both in the back of the head. Like rag dolls, they rolled down the slope, and came to rest against their father's corpse. The family reunited in a grotesque final embrace.

Karsten tried to wake, but no deliverance would come.

Franks laughed. "Ein paar weniger Schweine zu füttern. *(A few less pigs to feed.)*" He grinned at two guards and urinated over the corpses.

Karsten screamed. "FRANKS! NICHT MENSCHLICHE! DÄMON! *(NOT HUMAN! DEMON!)* He sat bolt upright in bed, punched the air, cried, sobbed, thrashed about in the bed, and finally woke feeling nauseous. Even in his own time and reality, Franks still haunted him.

Jane was on the landing and heard his screams. "KARSTEN!" She forgot her 'status' in 'life', ran to hug him, ran straight through the bedroom wall, and after a brief delay floating over the back garden, she came back through the bedroom wall. "Oops. You OK?"

Karsten smiled weakly. "I wish I could do that."

"There is a rather 'unique' qualification." She laughed. "I think perhaps you should wait a little longer?"

He pushed back the sheets and slipped out of bed.

"I'll wait downstairs for you," Jane said as Karsten's naked bum disappeared into the bathroom.

He shaved, showered, dressed, and walked slowly downstairs to the kitchen at an interesting point in the discussions. "I seem to have missed quite a lot," he said to the backs of heads, all of which instantly flew around.

Klaus was like a mother hen. "Should you be up?" He felt Karsten's pulse and forehead until he gently pushed his hand away.

"Mir geht es gut. Was ist passiert? *(I am well. What happened?)*" Karsten asked.

"Es ist eine lange Geschichte. *(It's a long story.)* Let me introduce those you haven't met." Klaus 'did the honours', and gave Karsten an outline of what had happened.

"You want me to bathe in this blue whirlpool?" Karsten asked his father.

Untypically, Klaus was slightly embarrassed. "I was concerned about you. Ich hatte Angst um Ihren Verstand. *(I was afraid for your mind.)* Ich dachte, ich hätte dich verloren. *(I thought I'd lost you.)*"

Karsten pulled his father to him and hugged him tightly. "Ich bin OK."

Klaus turned away and wiped away his tears. "And so to business."

Charlie's words were coming at the speed of a bullet. "And this whirlpool heals people? It repaired Alfredo's hand, Klaus's cut, and your mum and dad's dementia." His mind had only one thought. *"Get mum here and cure her cancer."*

"Charlie." Marie took hold of his arm and squeezed it gently. "Calm down."

"I know, but if it's done this for them, then it could cure mum's cancer. She doesn't need to die. My God this is wonderful." He kissed her. "It's a bloody twenty-four carat miracle." He jumped up and down like a child on a pogo stick. "Thank you Jesus, Mary, Archangel Michael, and any other heavenly being I've missed." He kissed Marie again. "This is going to change the world. My God no more deaths from cancer or any other terminal illness."

Marie's grip grew a lot firmer and she led him into the garden. "You need to calm down. The reason everyone's here, is to decide what we do about this 'miracle'. Please, my darling, calm down. No-one should go anywhere near it until we properly understand everything about it."

Charlie pulled away from her. "That could take years. Mum will be dead by then."

"How would you explain your mum's miraculous cure to her doctors?"

"Couldn't give a shit. I just wouldn't take her to the hospital."

"And no-one would follow-up on your mum? Try to discover what had happened to her?" She raised her eyebrows at him. "Really?"

"Sod 'em."

"Charlie, let's see what's decided before we start making any other plans. Will you at least do that for me?"

There was a long pause before he nodded.

"Thank you. Now let's go back and join the others."

He took her hand like a toddler with his mum and walked back to the kitchen.

Klaus looked around the kitchen at the 'crowd'. "To paraphrase Roy Scheider in *Jaws*, I think we're going to need to bigger room."

Everyone laughed and the emotional tension was eased.

"Let's go next door." Robert suggested. "We've knocked through the front room and lounge. It's a big space with plenty of chairs."

Morris watched, as everyone trooped out of High Wood into Takanun. "Constable Thompson? Well, well? I thought you were on the sick. What the hell's going on in these houses?" He leaned forward on the steering wheel. "Looks like there'll never be a better time to find out." He reached behind him, picked up a file on the 'Brothers Stroudle' from the back seat, and made his way to the 'empty' High Wood.

# Chapter Ninety-Eight

"I'm gonna do that bastard." Matt wasn't in any mood for forgiveness. "Pig kicked me in the bollocks. Twat. I'll 'ave 'im."

"Ah, forget it. We'll only lose. Pissin' pigs 'ave the cards stacked against us." Mark wasn't feeling forgiving, just not in the mood for picking a fight with the local police. "What are we gonna do? I 'aven't got any brass."

Matt pulled out his jean pockets, halfway to doing his famous elephant impression. "Not a pissin' bean. Anythin' in the flat?"

Mark shook his head, sat on a low wall, picked his nose, examined his trophy, flicked it over the wall, pulled a face like a badly constipated baboon, pulled at an ear lobe, sighed, stood up, sat down, and finally swore at no-one and nothing particular. "Aw, fuck it. Why don't we go back to that 'ouse? There's plenty of stuff there. Last time was just a bit of a cock up, and we know more this time, so…" The pressure of thinking up something had seized up his brain.

"So what?" Matt was beginning to recover some composure. "We could always mug some OAP?"

"They'd probably kick the shit out of us. Let's just go over there and take a look. Sod all else to do."

Matt finally gave in. "Yeah. Alright. But only a look. Whatever shit you believed about those houses, is catching."

To add to their joys, it started chucking it down with rain.

An hour later, a pair of what appeared to be bedraggled, shipwrecked sailors, stood huddled together under a chestnut tree opposite High Wood.

Matt suddenly bristled like a ginger tom seeing a black lab. "It's that twat Morris!" He pointed across the road at the front door of High Wood. "Cheeky bastard's goin' in." He looked at Mark. "Did you see anyone let 'im in? Coz I didn't. 'e's pissin' breakin' an' enterin'. Well, well, Officer

Morris, what *are* you up to?" He grabbed Mark by the arm. "Come on, we're gonna make a citizen's arrest."

Morris walked cautiously into High Wood. "Hello. Anyone here?" His words echoed back off the silence. He walked slowly up the hall, taking a look in all the rooms. *"Shit, they must have had some money at one time. All this must have cost a bloody fortune,"* he thought as he made his way up the stairs.

Captain Forster, Rebecca, Gloria, and Adam, watched Morris as he walked down the hall, decided to follow him, ran straight through him and waited on the landing.

*"Grab hold of the handle to the gallery,"* Captain Forster said to Adam. *"We don't want him going up there."* He turned to Rebecca. *"You and I can follow him around."*

*"Shouldn't I get someone?"* Rebecca suggested. *"I mean, this is burglary, isn't it?"*

*"She's right. He's breaking the law,"* Adam said, supporting Rebecca.

*"Rebecca, you go next door, bring back someone, preferably living, and we'll keep an eye on what he does."*

She nodded, turned to go down the stairs, and walked through Morris as he reached the top. As she reached the bottom, two bedraggled excuses for humanity, walked in through the front door. *"Oh, for goodness sake. Not you two again. How many times does it take for you to understand that coming in here isn't a good idea?"* She turned and trotted back up the stairs. *"They're back."*

Adam looked across at his wife. *"Who?"*

*"That pair of idiots who broke in recently. The ones we messed around with."*

Adam couldn't help but smile. *"Better bring Jane as well."*

Rebecca turned, ran down the stairs, stopped near Matt, couldn't resist blowing in his ear, and ran out of the front door in hysterics.

Matt threw himself flat against the wall, with his finger in his right ear. "It's soddin' started already!" He started shuffling along the wall towards the front door. "I'm pissin' off."

Mark's skin began to tingle like a mild sunburn. Images of green pastures, idyllic lakes, snow-topped mountains, calm, blue seas, heather-covered moors, rolling downs, and babbling trout streams filled his mind.

Snatches of poems and lines by Shakespeare whispered in his inner ear. 'Closer of lovely eyes to lovely dreams,' 'As stars that shoot along the sky Shine brightest as they fall from high.' They carried on running through his mind until he started reciting them. "'A knave; a rascal; an eater of broken meats; abase, proud, shallow, beggarly, three-suited, hundred-pound, filthy, worsted-stocking knave; a lily-livered, action-taking knave, a whoreson.'"

Matt stopped shuffling along the wall, stared at his brother, and grabbed him by the collar of his jacket. "I'm a fuckin' wha'? Are you taking the piss?"

"'The prince of darkness is a gentleman!'"

"I'm the pissin' devil!?" Matt pulled back his fist to punch Mark in the face, but his mind was suddenly overwhelmed by a tsunami of operatic arias. He didn't have the greatest voice in the world. In fact hyenas in the Serengeti with strangulated hernias would have sounded more tuneful. In the original Italian, he started to sing at the top of his voice. "'Largo al factotum della città. Presto a bottega che l'alba è già. Ah, che bel vivere, che bel piacere, per un barbiere di qualità! di qualità!'"

Mark smiled broadly. "Magnifico fratello. *(Magnificent brother.)*"

Upstairs, Morris was struggling to believe what he was hearing. He shook his head in disbelief. "Jesus. No way. It can't be those two wankers again. I know they're bloody stupid, but my God, they make gravel look intelligent." He walked slowly back to the stairs, cautiously made his way down, and sat down on the last stair. The brothers Stroudle were serenading each other in what sounded like Italian and German.

"'Der Hölle Rache kocht in meinem Herzen, Tod und Verzweiflung flammet um mich her! Fühlt nicht durch dich Sarastro Todesschmerzen'." Mark was in full flow, duetted by Matt in French. "La boheme, la boheme. Ça voulait dire on a vingt ans La boheme, la boheme et nous vivions de l'air du temps'."

Adam and Captain Forster had followed Morris, and were stood in utter dumbfounded silence.

Rebecca returned with Jane and Elizabeth, and like the others, stood in total amazement at the spectacle which greeted them.

The serenading continued, until Elizabeth walked into the hall. "Hello. Can I help you?"

"My apologies, sweet lady," Matt replied. "Sometimes the muse simply takes us. We visited here not long ago, and as we were passing, we thought we'd drop in and reacquaint ourselves with you. 'I like this place, and could willingly waste my time in it.' Which, as I'm sure you know, is from 'As You Like It'." He bowed very slightly from the hips. "I hope I wasn't being too presumptuous?"

Elizabeth wasn't often lost for words, but her mind was screaming, *"NO POINTS OF REFERENCE!"*

"What are you two arse-heads up to?" Morris joined the conversation in his usual cultured manner, despite his 'illegal' entry into the house. "Where is all this educated, upper-class, bullshit coming from? Since I've had the misfortune of knowing you wankers, you've struggled to string two bloody words together. Have you swallowed a pissing thesaurus?"

"A thesaurus, dear inspector, is a book that lists words in groups of synonyms and related concepts. It does not contain quotations."

"Detective Sergeant Morris?" Elizabeth said with surprise. "I didn't see you there. I didn't know you were coming?"

Morris, if nothing else, could think as quickly on his feet as Usain Bolt could sprint. "We had a report of a possible break in and I was in the area." He stood back and pointed at the brothers. "I found these two in your house. I can only believe from their behaviour, that they've taken something illegal, and pretty damn potent. I'll get them back to the station and charge them with breaking and entering."

"'Out of my sight! Thou dost infect mine eyes.'" Matt waved at Morris, and then turned to Elizabeth. "We have committed no such crime madam. As I said, we were simply passing. The front door was open, and after calling out, we came in to wait." He glanced at Morris. "We have had previous experience with this person and would not believe a word he uttered."

"You cheeky bast ..."

"If I were you madam, I would contact the local constabulary and confirm what he says is true."

Even Morris's quick-thinking mind, wasn't prepared for this little gem.

Matt stared intently at him. "Well, officer, shall we call your superiors? I fear 'Something is rotten in the state of Denmark.'"

Elizabeth had never had a good feeling about this policeman, and she was fascinated by this exchange.

Morris started to back down. "However, as no damage seems to have been done, and you don't want to press any charges?" He turned to Elizabeth.

She shook her head.

"Then perhaps we should forget this unfortunate misunderstanding." He was addressing his comments through gritted teeth at Matt and Mark.

"'The weak can never forgive. Forgiveness is the attribute of the strong'," Matt said with a small nod of the head. "Mahatma Gandhi, 'All Men are Brothers, Autobiographical Reflections.'"

Morris shook Elizabeth's hand and left with his tail between his legs.

Matt and Mark smiled at Elizabeth. "Will you introduce your friends to us?"

Elizabeth looked at Matt with a puzzled expression.

Matt looked towards the door, and then back at the top of the hall. "The two extremely pretty women, the army officer, and the young soldier."

Elizabeth was as speechless as a mute swan with severe laryngitis.

# Chapter Ninety-Nine

Klaus realised, late in the day, that he hadn't responded to Ralph's text. He flipped open the lid of his MacBook Air, tapped the Face Time icon, and waited for the call to connect.

"Thought you'd forgotten me." Ralph's tanned, smiling face appeared on the screen with a view of the Pacific behind him.

"On holiday again?" Klaus knew what answer was coming.

"Every day's a holiday when you're retired, my friend." The pleasantries over, Ralph's expression changed. "What's happening over there Klaus? I can't keep putting off this meeting."

"Gute oder schlechte Nachrichten?"

"And for those of us who don't speak German."

"Good news, or bad news?"

"Let's start with the bad."

"No final answer to the blue lights."

"And the good?"

"We are making good progress towards an answer."

"And could you share that with me?" Ralph hid his frustration with his old friend.

Over the next twenty minutes, Klaus outlined the discovery of the cans of 35mm film, the faceless troops, Takanun, and although he wasn't sure if he should, the effect of the vortex.

"Let me get this straight. This ... this, whatever the hell it is, repairs damaged cells and bodies? And you say it healed two long standing cases of dementia?" Ralph's face couldn't disguise his amazement. "This is astonishing, Klaus. My God." He reached to his right, picked up a tumbler of bourbon, and drained it. "This could change the world."

"Ralph." Klaus's tone was purposeful and direct. "This must remain a secret until we understand how it works, its effects, and potential side effects. This may be the only one of its kind in the world. I know of no other location where two portals are linked together like conjoined twins. The risks are far too great to make this public just yet. This *must* remain between us. Don't share this with any other members of the Astrea."

"They're pressing for a meeting. I need a date, Klaus."

"Give me another week. Whatever the status then, we will hold a meeting."

"I'm coming over. I need to see this with my own eyes." Ralph didn't sound as if he could be dissuaded from his decision.

"If you think that will help?"

"It will, and I do."

"Let me know your travel plans and I'll arrange transport from the airport."

"Thank you. I'll be with you as soon as I can arrange a flight."

"I look forward to seeing you. Abschied. *(Farewell.)*"

*"Not Auf Wiedersehen."* Ralph thought to himself. "Have a good day, Klaus."

"Are you joining us?" Alfredo popped his head around the kitchen door.

"Ja, Ja. I was speaking with Ralph in the US." Klaus quickly closed his laptop, jumped to his feet, brushed past Alfredo, marched into the converted front room, pulled up a chair, sat down like a sack of coal, and leaned back in his chair. "I am ready. Who will... Where is Elizabeth? And Sam is not back yet?"

"Just arrived." Sam strolled into the room, looked around, threw a cushion on the floor, and sat down.

"Excellent. What did you find?"

"They were all there. The storage room was about the size of a double garage, and there were hundreds of them sealed up in white cardboard boxes." He got himself comfortable on the cushion. "Bloody expensive, storing stuff. I had to pay them nearly six hundred and fifty quid, and it's about a hundred quid a week as long as we leave it there! We'll have to rent a van to get them back here."

"Can I leave you to arrange that Sam?" Klaus asked.

He nodded his head.

"I'll also reimburse the monies for you."

"Thanks." Sam replied. "My bank balance needs it."

"Now we only need Elizabeth." Klaus continued.

"She's next door," Marie answered. "There is a bit of a problem which she's dealing with."

Klaus tipped his head to one side. "Was für ein Problem? *(What kind of a problem?)*"

"Zwei Einbrecher, und ein Polizist. *(Two burglars, and a cop.)*"

"Your German remains excellent my dear. Is it something we need to attend to?"

Marie shook her head. "I'm sure Elizabeth will come back if she needs any support.

Sam started to get up, but Klaus waved him to sit down. "She will be fine, Sam. She is a strong woman."

Charlie's mobile buzzed in his pocket, he read the message, whispered something to Marie, and stood up. "You'll have to excuse me. Mum's very ill, and I need to check on her."

With a look of unexpected compassion, Klaus slowly nodded.

As Charlie engaged first gear, a strange tingle ran across his shoulders and down both arms. He shook them and steepled his fingers, stretching the joints. *"I need to drink more,"* he thought.

A snigger meandered its way around Charlie's head, which was followed closely by the feeling of claws being dragged down the inside of his skull. He grimaced, massaged his temples, screwed up his eyes, sucked in an enormous deep breath, slowly rotated his neck, cracked his cervical vertebrae, and unbuttoned his collar.

*"It's been a long, boring fucking wait, but I'm back."* Lidsay hissed.

Charlie was shocked, but covered it well. *"I left you in Burma."*

*"You certainly did, but fate took a hand, and here I am."*

*"And how the hell did you get here?"*

*"Pretty simple really. Surprised you haven't worked it out."* He paused for a few seconds. *"Want to have a go?"*

Charlie stayed silent. He was more interested in finding an antidote for this poison, rather than knowing how it had infected him again.

"Not a clue? Always thought you were not quite up to the scratch on intelligence."

Charlie didn't respond.

"Well, the short version, is as follows. From you to Nip, from Nip to Peter, from Peter to Ian, your dad, from Ian to Molly, your mum, and from Molly to you when you last saw her. Mind you, I made sure it was painless this time. Shit, do you realise it's taken me seventy-one fucking years to get back to you? Slept most of the time. Fortunately, when you're, whatever the hell I am, time seems to adopt its own rules."

Charlie didn't want to encourage him.

"Giving me the cold shoulder? I may have made the move painlessly, but I can still make your life a misery."

The intensity of the pain in Charlie's head went up by a factor of ten.

"Tongue a little looser?"

"If you piss around with me anymore, you'll regret it. I'm a lot stronger than I was in Burma, and I can do things to you you wouldn't want me to."

"I am shitting my pants."

"You will be, you toxic bastard. As soon as I find some shit place to dump you, you'll be gone. So crawl away to whatever cess pit you skulk in and leave me alone."

"Just remember I can move when I want to, and I may choose to 'jump' over to something a little 'softer' than you. Pretty little thing that friend of yours."

Charlie decided to ignore him, although the threat to Marie terrified him. He unlocked his car, climbed in, and drove home.

Molly was lying on the sofa, wrapped in a comfy, drinking sparkling water. Emma was sitting opposite her, still trying to take in everything Charlie had told her.

"You OK, mum?" Charlie asked as he walked briskly into the lounge from the kitchen. "Gran, you OK?"

They both looked at him, smiled wanly, and nodded.

"Can I get either of you anything?"

The smiles continued accompanied by shakes of the head.

"Just going to make myself a cup of tea." He turned and walked into the kitchen.

As he sat on a pouffe close to his mum, Charlie stroked her hair, puffed up her pillows, kissed her on the forehead, took her glass of water, and moistened her lips. "How you feeling?"

"Not great. Completely washed out. But they told me I should expect this. Worst things are these ulcers in my mouth. Everything's like swallowing razor blades."

Charlie winced. "Nothing they can give you?"

She shook her head, trying not to swallow any spittle.

"What have they told you?"

"About what?"

Charlie didn't want to ask the question. His next actions would be led by her answer. "How long … well … when will …"

"They can't be sure, but months at the most." Molly was remarkably in control.

Charlie stood up. "I'm just going out for some fresh air."

She nodded understandingly.

*"How the hell do I get her to Takanun?"* Charlie thought desperately. *"And if I do get her there, how do I her get past the others?"* He bent down, and tugged at some dandelion leaves which snapped off just above the root. "Shit! Bloody thing'll grow again." He dug into the soil with his fingers, trying, without a great deal of success, to get as much of the root as he could. He gave up, walked to the top of the garden, scraping the dirt from under his nails, and watched the sun beginning to set over the rooftops. *"Middle of the night."* A light flicked on in his mind. *"Everyone's asleep and I can use the key Marie gave me."*

*"Shouldn't be doing this,"* his other-half chipped in. *"You were told."*

*"Piss off! Sod all to do with you."*

## Chapter Hundred

"You can see them?" Elizabeth asked in amazement.

"Of course. Why wouldn't we?" Matt answered as if seeing ghosts was the most natural thing in the world.

"But you haven't seen them before?"

"No, we haven't seen them before. But in our misspent days, I believe they may have made 'contact' with us." With sparkling eyes, Matt looked at Jane. "Isn't that correct, my dear?"

Jane smirked and nodded. "We did have a little 'fun' with you. But what's happened to you? When you were here before, you were … well, you weren't as eloquent as you are now." She pursed her lips, and sucked her teeth. "To be honest, you seemed as thick as two short planks. No offence, of course."

"None taken. Our memories of what we call, our 'earlier days', are somewhat thin, and we seem to have gained a certain clarity of perception since we were locked in the cellar. The one next door, that is." Matt tipped his head in the direction of Takanun. "I've a memory of a blue light. Very bright it was. Very bright, and very warm. Odd sensation, really."

"What made it odd?" Elizabeth was now interested in hearing what these two had experienced in the vortex.

"When you touched it, you felt … it made you feel sort of, in the pink, fit as a fiddle, right as rain. I'd never felt better in my life. Odd thing was," Matt said and left this hanging in the air.

"What?" Elizabeth said encouragingly.

"When we returned to that despicable policeman's station, we seemed to have lost it all. I felt as if I'd been drained of everything. Well-being, knowledge, just everything. But now, thank the Lord, we're back." He smiled broadly. "We feel," he said, then glanced at Mark who nodded, "tickety boo, and fighting fit. My brain feels like it needs an external hard drive. Ask me anything. Go on, anything."

Elizabeth stared at him, and frowned. If she hadn't known about the vortex, she'd have had him committed. "Capital of Taiwan?"

"Oh, really, Taipei. Come on, something a bit more juicy."

"What did Jesus say of the Pharisees?"

"Matthew 23: verses 1-39 says 'Then Jesus said to the crowds and to his disciples, "The scribes and the Pharisees sit on Moses' seat, so practice and observe whatever they tell you—but not what they do. For they preach, but do not practice. They tie up heavy burdens, hard to bear, and lay them on people's shoulders, but they themselves are not willing to move them with their finger.'"

"That's impressive." Even Elizabeth's theological training wouldn't have made her capable of such a precise answer. "How do you do that?"

"Truly, I don't know. The answers just come to us. Try Mark."

"What are the three directions of Buddhism?"

Mark smiled at Elizabeth, like a child being asked what two plus two was. "The three great directions are Tantric, Mahāyāna, and Hīnayāna."

"How long were you 'touched' by the 'warmth'?" Jane was now spellbound.

The brothers looked at each other, and Matt spoke. "We estimate all night."

Jane looked at Elizabeth. "Shit. That must be at least eight or nine hours. Klaus and Alfredo were only in it for one or two minutes at the most." She shook her head, ran her fingers through her hair, walked up and down the hall mumbling to herself, sat down on the stairs, looked up at Matt and Mark, shook her head again, closed her eyes, steepled her fingers, breathed down her nose, opened her eyes, and looked up at the ceiling. "It doesn't only heal, somehow the knowledge that's contained in that spirit stream, is absorbed by the brain." She closed her eyes again, spoke quietly to herself, drummed her fingers on her knees, tipped her head to the right and left, chewed her upper lip, and smiled. "This miracle has a drawback."

Elizabeth shrugged. "Which is?"

"If what they say is true, then as you move away from it, the effects weaken or disappear. That's why these two keep ending up back in the police station. One minute they're cultured, high-IQ, raconteurs, and the next, they turn into a couple of low-IQ numpties."

Elizabeth put her hand over her mouth and massaged her cheeks. "We need to test this."

"How?" Jane replied quizzically.

"Easy. Walk away from Takanun with either Klaus or Alfredo, and if your theory is right, then at some point their hands should lose the healing effect."

"We should do it now," Jane said as she made for the door.

"Wait," Elizabeth said. "What about these two?"

Jane shrugged. "Bring them with us. They're the evidence."

Elizabeth tipped her head to one side, and pursed her lips. "Follow us please," she said politely to Matt and Mark.

Their entrance at Takanun was met with shock.

"Wer sind sie? Sie sollten nicht hier sein."

Elizabeth frowned at him and shrugged. "I don't sprechen Deutsch."

"Sorry, Elizabeth." He gestured for her to follow him into the hall. "What are they doing here?"

Elizabeth explained to Klaus what had happened to the brothers.

"Come with me. I must know if this is true." Klaus popped his head around the door. "Elizabeth and I are going out. We will be a few minutes. Have some refreshments while we are gone."

Alfredo frowned and raised his eyebrows at Jane. "What was that about?"

"Wait 'til they get back and then everything will be clear."

"How far do we have to go?" Klaus asked, looking down at his hand.

Elizabeth shrugged. "We'll just have to play it by ear. But if the brothers had lost everything by the time they reached the central police station, then the maximum range, after a maximum exposure, must be around four or five miles?" She looked back to the house. "Give me two seconds. There's something we need in my room."

She was quickly back, and as she got closer to Klaus, he could see her adjusting something on her belt.

"What is that?"

"Pedometer. It won't be very precise, but it will give us a good idea on dose and exposure, versus distance and effect."

"Excellent." Klaus nodded towards the gate. "Let's start walking."

Twenty minutes later, Klaus cried out, lifted his hand to his face, frowned, stopped, and lifted his hand up to Elizabeth. An angry red line had appeared where the gash on his hand had been. "How far?"

Elizabeth checked the pedometer. "About three quarters of a mile."

"Let's keep walking," Klaus said in an uncharacteristically friendly manner.

As they walked, Elizabeth took Klaus's arm, his eyes remaining locked on his hand.

"That's far enough," he said. "Look."

Elizabeth examined his hand. The gash had opened and blood was dripping from his hand onto the pavement. She looked up at him. "We need to get back."

"How far?"

Elizabeth looked up at him. "Just under a mile."

# Chapter Hundred-One

Charlie drove around for a few hours, stopped and bought a double espresso at Starbucks, drove around some more, and got a takeaway at McDonalds. At around eleven in the evening, he got back home, and parked a couple of hundred yards away from the house. At one o' clock in the morning, he decided it was late enough. Gran could be anywhere, but Mum should be sleeping and relatively easy to get into his car. Whether she'd be compliant was an entirely different question.

"Mmmm?" For the first time in weeks, Molly had been in a deep sleep. She rolled onto her back and rubbed her eyes. "Charlie?"

"Yes, Mum."

"What time is it?"

"About one."

"One! What are you doing up at this time? Is something wrong?"

"Nothing's wrong. Are you able to come with me? It's not far, and I think it could help you."

Molly gently rubbed her eyes, and slowly, with Charlie's help, pushed herself up onto her pillows, stared at him in the dim light of the room, and took his hand. "What is it, son?"

"Just come with me."

"Not if you don't tell me what's going on." She was shivering, so he grabbed her dressing gown and wrapped it around her shoulders.

"What are you two whispering about?" Emma was stood a few feet behind Charlie, with her hands on her hips. "*Well?*"

He stood up and turned to face her. "I just need Mum to come with me."

"That's all, is it?" Emma said with her head on one side, with an expression of 'you are pulling my leg'.

"Yes."

"You expect *her*," she said and nodded to Molly, "who has just had chemotherapy, and is at best weak, to get up in the middle of the night, and follow you to some unknown place for some unknown reason?"

Charlie nodded. He was beginning to regret this idea.

"She's not going. End of." Emma sat down opposite them, with her arms folded and an expression which screamed 'this is not open for discussion'.

Molly looked up at Charlie with exhausted eyes. "Darling, I couldn't make it. Let me rest and we can talk in the morning. I need to sleep."

"But it needs to be now, when they're asleep."

Molly and Emma's expressions changed dramatically.

"When who are asleep?" Emma asked deliberately.

Charlie sucked in his lips, stared at his feet, shook his head, wrung his hands, glanced up at Molly and Emma, and walked out of the room. "Anyone want a drink?" he asked, pointlessly trying to change the subject.

"Get back in here!" Emma said firmly.

"Tea or coffee. I'm having tea."

"NOW!"

He appeared at the door with the kettle in his right hand. "Hot chocolate?"

Molly was more conciliatory. She patted the bed, and gestured for him to join her, sans kettle. "Now. What's going on? Something important's bothering you. What is it?"

Like a child who'd been caught feeding the goldfish to the cat, Charlie shuffled across the room, and still staring at his feet, sat down close to Molly.

"Charlie?" She lifted his chin and stared lovingly into his eyes. "Whatever it is can't be that bad, can it?"

"I wish I could say, but I can't." He began to cry uncontrollably.

"Darling." Molly reached out to him and hugged him as close to her as she could. "I know this is difficult, but you've got to be strong for me." She sat back a little. "When I go, grandma will be waiting for me. I'm not going to be alone."

"I ... will. You won't ... have ... any reason to ... stay."

"I'll stay for as long as I can, but we'll be together again. Hopefully not for some time, but we will be back together. You've got your life still ahead of you. I've had a wonderful life and I'm not afraid of dying. It's just a door to another life."

Charlie's words were lost amongst sobs.

"Make us all a cup of tea, will you?" Molly asked Emma, who nodded and walked to the kitchen.

After several mugs of tea, and the remains of an apple tart, Charlie was almost in control of himself.

"Are you going to tell me what this is all about?" Molly asked her son.

Half an hour later, he'd told them what he knew about the people at High Wood, Takanun, what they did, Papaver Rhoeas, Burma, Sheringham, everything. Everything apart from the vortex.

"But you've already told us most of this." Molly said with a slight frown. "What haven't you told me?"

"This must stay a secret."

Molly nodded.

"A real secret. A pinky secret. Like we used to keep when I was little. We never broke pinky secrets, did we?"

Molly shook her head, and held up her little finger. "Pinky promise."

Charlie was happy that an unbreakable promise had been made. "There's something in the cellar at Takanun. Something like nothing else on Earth. Probably not even in the universe. Something like nothing in heaven or Earth. Something which …" He stood up, and walked slowly around the room.

Molly gave him a few seconds, and then spoke softly. "What something?"

He turned to face her, the light from the window casting a soft orange glow on his face. "Something which can heal the sick, the injured, the lame …" he said and sat down next to Molly and held her hands, "and the dying."

Molly looked at him with staring eyes. "You were taking me to this … what did you call it?"

"I call it the Lazarus Pool."

"What have you got to gain from this?"

"You?" Charlie eyes were fixed on his shoes.

"*Me!* Don't you think I should be involved in decisions about me, and particularly ones about whether I live or die? Who do you think you are deciding this for me?"

"Your son." Charlie had never seen or heard his mother like this. "I was only thinking of you."

"Of yourself more like. What about what I ..." Her anger couldn't be sustained any longer and she dissolved into tears.

Charlie looked up and hugged her. "Mum, I'm so so sorry. I can't lose you. I'd do anything to keep you here. Anything. I thought this was a miracle sent to me to save you."

Molly wiped her eyes in a tissue and gently pushed him away. "Darling." Her tone was more composed and caring. "We all die and nothing can stop that. Not even your 'pool'. Life can get to a point when you've just had enough. When everything aches, creaks, and groans, when getting up in the morning is a massive effort, when even cooking for yourself becomes an unnecessary task. I'm so tired, son, and death offers me relief. I know that for you, it only offers fear, loss, and the pain of bereavement. But you must think of me. When our dogs were in pain and suffering, we did the right thing by them. It was painful, but we knew that for them it was for the best. I'm suffering, darling. Simply being is an agony. Do the same for me. Allow me to go. Don't keep me a like a drooling mannequin in a corner of the room, simply to ease the pangs of separation. Be a strong understanding son for me. Do this for me."

Charlie heard what he didn't want to hear, but came to the realisation that nothing he could say or do, would dissuade his mum from this course of action. "I'll do whatever you want."

# Chapter Hundred-Two

Back at the station, Morris was drumming his fingers on his desk, deciding whether or not to file a report on 'goings-on' at High Wood and Takanun. He'd been staring at a blank computer screen for five minutes, chewing things over in his mind.

"Problem?" Morris's boss was stood behind him looking over his shoulder. "It'll never boil."

"Mmmm?"

"That will never boil?"

"Oh … yeah. Sorry, deep in thought."

"About?"

"Oh, just things in general. Nothing specific. Lot going on at the moment and I need to prioritise stuff."

"How's that little helper of yours? Thompson?"

"Should be back this week." He said with a forced smile.

"Good. That lad's got a lot of potential. In line for a detective constable's job. You have my full support."

"Thanks boss. He's pretty much ready to move on. Bit wasted doing what he does. I'll get the paperwork in next week."

"Excellent." The 'boss' was turning to leave, but stopped and glanced back over his shoulder. "Any news on our dearly departed sergeant, and his lovely wife?"

"Not a whisper. I see it as one we keep on the back burner?"

"Good idea. There's plenty to keep us occupied without worrying about that piss-head. Let me know when Thompson's paperwork is heading my way."

*"Be happy if I knew what the hell Constable Thompson was up to?"* Morris thought. He picked up his mobile off the desk, found Charlie in his contacts, tapped the green call icon, and waited for an answer.

"Detective sergeant." Charlie was unsure what sort of 'pep-talk' he was about to get.

"Charlie, how are you? Ready to come back to the front line?"

*"Thank God. He seems in a good mood,"* Charlie thought. "Yes. Feeling really good. I'll be back tomorrow first thing."

"Excellent. The super and I were discussing you, and we believe it's time for you to join CID. What do you think of that?"

There was silence at the end of the line.

"Never heard you speechless before."

"Sorry. It's just that this is all I've ever wanted. I'm … that's brilliant. Thanks so much." Charlie's smile, if it could, would have met at the back of his head.

"Tell you what," Morris replied. "I've got to be in Cardiff this afternoon. Can you meet me at Pret a Manger in St David's Centre around one o' clock? We can discuss the move to CID."

"I'll be there."

Morris picked up a chef's chipotle chicken salad and flat white coffee, and Charlie bought a teriyaki salmon salad and white americano. As they ate their food and chatted about 'stuff', Morris explained how the transfer from uniform to the CID would happen.

"OK with all that?"

"Sounds brilliant. I can't wait."

*"Lovely to see you two so chatty."* Being so close to his Nemesis, Lidsay couldn't stay quiet any longer. *"He hasn't changed. Supercilious, self-opinionated, arrogant, shit-for-brains, wanker."*

"Still got a high opinion of him then." Charlie was happy that he was in control of this parasite.

*"You're getting pretty close to him. Detective sergeant's pretty boy, are we?"*

"Abuse? Always a good sign you're losing the argument." Charlie answered calmly.

*"Oh, fuck right off."*

*"Abuse and cursing. You really are pissed off and exactly where I want you."*

"Oh am I?" Lidsay had had enough of Charlie's resistance, and decided that screwing up Morris's life would be a more satisfying option. He summoned up all his spirit-energy and forced Charlie to offer his hand to Morris, and in that instant, he took up residence in the man he most detested in this world, and if he had any chance, the next.

Charlie felt as if a great weight had been lifted from his shoulders. "You're in there, aren't you?"

Lidsay smiled to himself. *"You bet your sweet life I am. And I'm going to screw around with this poisonous little shit."*

Morris looked about as confused as a chameleon in a bag of Skittles.

Charlie's mind was in a panic, trying to find a plausible reason for his outburst. "Sorry, I'd lost some keys, and I suddenly remembered where they were. Just shouted out. Sorry."

Morris's expression gradually relaxed. "I do that all the time. Bloody odd, isn't it? Your brain and mouth just decide to connect without telling you." He smiled and shook his head.

"Yeah," Charlie replied. *"Think I got away with it."*

Morris got up to leave. "I need to get back to the station." He saw that Charlie hadn't finished his salad. "You stay and finish that, and I'll see you tomorrow at the station."

"See you tomorrow, sir."

*"Yeah. See you tomorrow, Charlie."* Lidsay chuckled to himself.

# Chapter Hundred-Three

As they got back to High Wood, the gash on Klaus's hand had healed.

They walked into the kitchen, Klaus filled a glass from the tap, and sipped the cold water. "The effects are either temporary or limited. At a specific distance, the effect is lost." He drained the rest of the water. "The latter would seem to be supported by the brothers. The detective sergeant said that when they were at the station, I can't remember his exact words, but he didn't have a very high opinion of them. And yet when they are here, they are highly educated intellectuals." He leaned back in the chair. "We should take them for a walk and see what happens."

Elizabeth nodded and stood up. "I'll find them."

Klaus stood up. "I'm coming with you. You don't know how they'll react when the effects of the vortex wear off."

"A walk in the fresh air would be delightful. 'This blessed plot, this earth, this realm, this England,'" Matt said with genuine pleasure.

Elizabeth turned to Klaus and whispered. "Effects seem to working at a hundred per cent."

He nodded and smiled. "Magst du Shakespeare? *(Do you like Shakespeare?)*"

Matt looked a little bemused at him, smiled at Mark, and replied. "Ja. Er ist ein wunderbare. *(Yes. He is wonderful.)*"

"Sprechen sie deutsch?"

"Ja. Ein bisschen, *(Yes. A little bit,)*" he said modestly.

Elizabeth was fascinated by the effect of the vortex on the brothers.

"Do you speak any other languages?"

"Un petit français. Qualche italiano, y suficiente español para sobrevivir. *(A little French. A little Italian, and enough Spanish to survive.)*" He moved towards the front door. "Shall we go?"

Elizabeth reset the pedometer. "Let's go. It's such a lovely day."

After a mile, Klaus stopped outside a Shell garage, and turned to Mark. "Do you have a preference for a brand of petrol?"

Mark looked up at the Shell sign. "I've never been too fond of this particular brand. We typically purchase our gasoline according to the keenest pricing accessible on the fore-courts within a convenient radius of our dwelling."

"No change yet," Klaus said quietly to Elizabeth.

"Not with them," she replied. "But it looks like you need a tissue," she said softly, as she looked down at the spots of blood on the pavement.

Klaus quickly covered the blood spots with his foot, took three tissues from Elizabeth, and pressed them into the oozing gash in his palm. "Danke."

After further stops at a newsagent, library, and a post office, there was still no obvious deterioration in their mental abilities.

Elizabeth checked her pedometer. They'd walked four and a half miles from the house.

A mile later, Klaus asked Matt for his thoughts on Europe.

"Continent… we're part of it … we joined it … the Euro?"

"It's starting to slip," Klaus whispered to Elizabeth.

After another half a mile, Elizabeth stopped outside a pub. "Shall we have a drink?"

"My mouth's as dry as a parrot's chuff," Mark said with a wicked smile. "What's your tipple, Liz?"

"Pint of lager for me, bruv," Matt said as he patted Elizabeth's bum.

She smiled, taking no offence, turned to Klaus who was desperately trying not to laugh, and said quietly, "I think we should go back?"

Klaus nodded, suppressing a giggle. "I agree. But let's take a taxi."

Back at High Wood, Klaus called everyone together. "Elizabeth and I have some things we need to tell you about the vortex." He explained how far they'd walked, and that the effects of the vortex had worn off. "My cut opened up at just over a mile, but my exposure to the vortex, was very short." He massaged his temples, his headache not getting any better. "These miraculous cures, can only be sustained, if the person involved remains close to the source of the energy, or has a massive, prolonged exposure to it."

"So it is probably of very limited value?" Alfredo said with obvious disappointment.

"Nein," Klaus said firmly. "The value of the vortex still remains, but its benefit to mankind can only be made more broadly available if we understand how it works. It may be that it can be altered and its effects made permanent. The value to us may not be only therapeutic, but also financial. Think of the revenue we could generate if we were able to licence the use of the vortex to a global community."

"You talk like a businessman, Klaus," Jane said with a small degree of satisfaction in her voice.

"But isn't that what I am? Papaver Rhoeas can only be sustained with strong finances." He waved his arms around him. "Everything we do has a cost we must bear. If we can increase our income stream by a significant factor, then we will be able to do so much more."

"So if I want to remain like this," Robert said quietly. "I have to stay within a relatively close radius of the house, or I will once again succumb to the dementia?"

"That is our," he said and gestured to Elizabeth, "belief. The experiments we made are very simple and small in number. However, it is my belief that this is the reality of the situation."

"So in an odd way, I'm damned if I do, and damned if I don't."

"You're certain about this?" Charlie had only just arrived, but had caught the gist of what had been said. "The Lazarus Pool works, but only if you stay close to it?"

Klaus frowned at Charlie. "What did you call it?" His tone wasn't aggressive, but it was at best irritated.

"The Lazarus Pool," Charlie said uncertainly. "It's just a name. I thought it sort of said what it did?"

"Ist Jesus Christus im Zimmer? *(Is Jesus Christ in the room?)*" He replied angrily.

Marie came to Charlie's defence. "Danke Klaus. Solche Überlegungen. *(Thanks, Klaus. Such consideration.)*"

Klaus pursed his lips, took a deep breath, swallowed hard, and nodded a few times towards Marie. "You are quite correct. What does it matter what we call this thing?"

"Sounds like a very good name to me." Rebecca chipped in, supporting Charlie.

"She's right, you know," Jane replied. "If we do ever come to sell this thing, it will need a name. That's what marketing people do isn't it?" She waved her arms theatrically. "The Lazarus Pool. We should … Oh what do you do when you want to own something?"

"Buy it?" Rebecca suggested naively.

"No, my dearest Rebecca. But a good suggestion," Klaus said kindly. "If it is a name, then we should copyright it, trade mark it, or register the name as trademark." He paused, thinking things through. He walked towards Charlie who slightly flinched. Klaus smiled. "I only eat human flesh after midnight."

The room was reduced to laughter which slowly settled.

Klaus put his arm around Charlie's shoulder. "You have made an excellent suggestion. I will raise this at the next meeting of the Astrea." He took another deep breath, and like a gust of chill damp wind out of a long-closed vault, sighed. "We will have a great deal to discuss."

# Chapter Hundred-Four

Morris got back home late from the station, and his wife was already in bed fast asleep. He walked into the bedroom, undressed, dropped his washing on the landing, something which irritated the hell out of his wife Frankie, decided to have a bowl of cornflakes before going to bed, added a mug of hot chocolate, and caught up on the news on Sky. At one am, he cleaned his teeth, climbed into bed, and set the alarm for six. He looked across at Frankie, and couldn't remember the last time they'd made love. In fact, he couldn't remember the last time they'd done anything together. For the last five years, police work and a burning ambition had taken priority over everything else. He knew things were rapidly coming to a head, but they never seemed to have had the time to resolve anything. He turned his back on her, pulled the duvet up to his neck, and eventually fell into a disturbed sleep.

*"Jesus Christ,"* Lidsay chirped to himself. *"I thought my marriage was crap, but yours is a shit-fest compared to mine. Still, I think I'll piss around with your head. My God, I owe you a shitload of pain, so why not start now."*

Somewhere in the endless corridors of some unknown foreign airport, Morris was lost. He was late, very late. He'd lost his ticket and passport, his breathing was laboured like a hay fever sufferer in a freshly mown field, he was sweating like an overweight jogger running a half marathon, and panicking like an over-the-limit driver at Christmas. Everyone was shunning him like a tramp with the plague, and to top it all, the battery in his mobile was flat.

*"Fuck me,"* Lidsay hissed. *"If you already dream like this, then carry on your own sweet way,"* he thought about this for a few seconds, and then changed his mind. *"Then again, you should go where I've gone. See what I've seen. Smell what I've smelt."* Lidsay grimaced at the memory. *"Let's take a trip through Flanders Fields."*

In the distance, Morris saw a flashing, bright green exit sign. He crashed through the doors, deep into No Man's Land. He dragged his feet through the glutinous mire and stopped on the edge of a shell crater. He grasped at fresh air, as the edge gave way, sending him headlong down the side of the crater into a rancid pool at the bottom. He surfaced, spitting out most of the filth he'd swallowed, but something caught in his throat. He wretched, coughed two or three times, and the offending object, flew out of his throat, onto the menacing dark brown surface of the pool. He gaped at it. In disbelief, his brain desperately refused to accept the signals it was receiving. Like a loaded pellet waggler float doing its best to attract a giant carp, the top joint of a severed human finger was gently bobbing up and down on the surface. Morris's response was immediate and violent. He threw himself at the side of the crater, desperately trying to claw his way up the gelatinous side, but the brown goo simply squeezed between his fingers like overripe banana. He kept clawing madly at the slope, until his hands found purchase on something firm. He breathed a small sigh of relief, as his fingers closed on it, gripping whatever it was like a vice. He started to pull against it, and for a few seconds it resisted and supported his weight. Slowly he began to make some progress up the slope, but held his breath as he felt the resistance beginning to weaken. Suddenly, he was tumbling back down the side of the slope and disappearing under the surface of the fetid 'pond'. His fingers remained locked, onto what for a short time, had seemed to be his saviour, but as he surfaced, his fingers snapped open from the dismembered head, and partial spinal column of a British soldier. He sat bolt upright in bed, and let out a scream which would have tested the nerves of Professor Abraham van Helsing.

Frankie woke with a start, rolled away from him, and fell out of bed with a thud onto the floor. "Jesus Christ! What the hell's wrong with you! You bloody idiot. I could have had a heart attack!" Her tone quickly changed as she turned on the bedside lamp, saw his rigid, paralysed face, sweat-soaked pyjamas, and the look of absolute terror in his eyes.

*"Good night's work that,"* Lidsay said, very pleased with himself. *"And there's plenty more where that came from."*

The next morning, Morris was sat with his head slumped forward on his desk, with a headache which felt like a JCB excavating a drainage trench inside his skull. Four paracetamols and two ibuprofens hadn't touched it, and the thought of the day ahead wasn't helping his mood.

"Coffee, sir?" Charlie asked cheerily, on time, on routine, and happily aware that Lidsay had 'left' him. What he wasn't expecting was Morris's response.

"Fuck off, will you! And leave me alone!"

"Sir?" Charlie was unprepared for this sort of response.

Morris cautiously lifted his head. "Sorry. I thought it was that prick from the front desk." He pressed his index fingers into his temples. "Got a cure for the mother and father of headaches on you? Shit, my head feels like someone's trying to chisel their way out through my eyes with a blunt screwdriver."

"Bad night?"

"Bloody terrible. Worst nightmares I've ever had. It was one of those when you just won't wake up. It felt like something was stopping me. Part of the pissing nightmare I suppose. But it was the oddest sensation…" He stared into the distance, lost in the memory of the night before. "Any way, enough of that." He gingerly sat up and picked up his notepad. "I've spoken to the boss, and after some paperwork's been signed, by the beginning of next week you should be officially Detective Constable Thompson. So between now and then, you can start learning the ropes."

Charlie beamed. It was rare his dreams actually came true.

"I'd like you to sit in on a couple of interviews I've got today. It'll be good experience for you." He stretched his neck and groaned. "I've got some court appearances this afternoon, so while I'm there, I'd like you to take another look at those houses."

Charlie frowned.

"High Wood and Takanun. Something just won't stop niggling at me about them. Give them a final once over, and re-interview everyone. It's probably nothing, but I need to scratch this itch. We can discuss what you find tomorrow morning. Oh, and thanks, I'd love a coffee."

As he waited for the kettle to boil, Charlie's thoughts and emotions were like a pair of boxer shorts in a tumble dryer.

Marie - Love, frustration.

Burma - Fear, consternation.

Mum - Abject-grief, frustration.

Morris - Delight, anxiety, concern.

Papaver Rhoeas, Klaus - Confusion, indecision.

He returned with the coffees.

Morris was sat on the edge of a desk he'd had cleared. He stood up and patted the top. "All yours, detective constable."

Charlie's face was a picture of absolute undiluted joy. He sat down in what wasn't the most comfortable of chairs, but to him it felt like an Italian leather recliner. "Thanks, detective sergeant. I'll repay your confidence in me."

Morris waved for him to follow him to the interview rooms. "OK. It starts here. Sit behind me and observe, and make as many notes as you want. Say nothing. Just observe."

Charlie nodded nervously and followed Morris into the room.

*"Well, well, how can I screw up this interview?"* Lidsay was enjoying himself.

Fifteen minutes later, a bemused Charlie was sat in the interview room not quite believing what he'd just witnessed.

The suspected drug dealer, of eastern European origins, and his solicitor, were as bemused as Charlie, but also ecstatic, as they were now walking away from what they were sure was going to be a lengthy prison term.

Charlie, as instructed, made notes, but they made strange reading. *"Called the suspect a shit for brains, arse-poking fuck wit, and a drain on society. Leaned across the desk and placed a bag of heroin in the suspect's pocket. Threatened the suspect's family with threats of violence, false imprisonment, or deportation. Suggested his wife could be sexually molested by people he knew from the sex offenders register. And finally demanded a substantial bribe from his solicitor to get his client off the charges."* He looked up, attempted a smile, apologised for Morris's behaviour, and accompanied the solicitor and his shaven-headed, unemployed, six feet two, body-building, smirking Latvian immigrant to the desk sergeant.

Detective Inspector Robinson, who'd been observing the interview, grabbed Charlie by the arm and pulled him into the toilets. "What the hell was going on in there? I've never seen anything like that before! Pissing open and shut case, and he gives them a get out of jail free card?"

Charlie stared blankly at him.

"Well?"

"I've no idea sir. I was told to sit and observe."

Robinson punched the towel dispenser, leaving a deep dent and three bleeding knuckles. "We've been trying to get that bastard for three years." He contemplated punching the dispenser again, but the pain in his hand made him think twice. "Finally, when we get him banged to rites, what does that bloody, dozy, fucking moron do!" He turned his attention to the waste paper bin, and kicked it across the toilet into a cubicle. "JESUS! What in God's name was he thinking?"

Charlie was in shock. Working with Klaus was beginning to look a much more promising career path for him to take. "I really don't know sir."

"Well, you fucking well should." He turned, looking embarrassed. "Sorry, Thompson. It's so bloody frustrating. I don't know who the hell that was in there, but it wasn't Morris." He patted Charlie on the shoulder, smiled, and walked out of the toilets, muttering to himself. "Not like him, not like him at all."

*"No,"* Charlie thought, *"but it was a lot like that bastard Lidsay."*

# Chapter Hundred-Five

"Elizabeth?" Captain Forster called out as she walked into High Wood. "Everyone's getting jittery. We made a good start, but everything's slowed up again. They want to know when you'll be back in the saddle?"

*"Bugger. Bloody short memory you've got,"* Elizabeth scolded herself and smiled sheepishly at Captain Forster. "First thing in the morning." She crossed her heart. "Organise five men for the morning, and five for the afternoon. Tell everyone we'll stick rigidly to that schedule for the rest of the week."

Captain Forster looked up from under his eyebrows at her. "Everything OK? Only you look stressed, and you seem to be spending a lot of time next door lately."

"Trying to find an answer to the blue lights."

"Any luck?"

"Possibly. But nowhere near a real solution."

"Anything I can do?"

"For now, keep reminding me about my responsibilities here. Whatever's happening with these blue lights, these lost souls must be my first priority." She frowned and shook her head. "I've been very remiss recently, but I intend to correct that. The others can focus on everything else. We have unhappy souls to help." If she could have put an arm around the captain and squeezed him, she would have.

Captain Forster snapped his heels sharply together, and saluted extravagantly. "At your command, marm."

Klaus was very concerned about Karsten. He seemed lost in himself and had contributed little to the meeting at Takanun. "You don't look as if you've fully recovered? How are you feeling?"

Karsten smiled weakly at his father, but his eyes were focused on some unseen thing on the other side of the room. "I'm OK. Probably need a few more days' rest and I'll be fine."

Klaus followed his eyes, but couldn't see anything.

Karsten glanced at his father, saw the direction of his eyes, and looked down at the floor.

"You've hardly said a word since you 'came back'. Do you want to talk with me?" Klaus was hiding his concern well. Perhaps too well.

"Vielleicht in ein oder zwei Tage. *(Maybe in a day or two.)*"

Klaus bit his lower lip. Now wasn't the right time to push this. He looked into Karsten's eyes, and again they were focused on a far corner of the room. Klaus glanced over his shoulder and gasped. Standing close to the doorway, was the fuzzy shape of what Klaus was sure was a German officer of the Second World War. He looked back at Karsten, whose expression was one of pure hatred. When Klaus looked back into the corner, the figure was gone. He held Karsten firmly by the shoulders. "What was that? What did you see?"

Karsten's expression didn't change.

"KARSTEN!" Klaus shouted with fear in his voice. "Tell me, what is going on. Was ist es? *(What is it?)*"

Karsten's face turned back to his father, but his eyes remained fixed on the corner of the room.

Klaus slapped him across the face. "KARSTEN! LOOK AT ME!"

The look in Karsten's eyes made Klaus release his grip on his son's shoulders, and take a couple of steps back. "Karsten. Karsten. Ich bins. Es ist dein Vater. *(It's me. It's your father.)*"

Karsten closed the space between himself and Klaus. "Du bist ein Teufel. *(You are a devil.)* Ein Mörder von Frauen und Kindern. *(A killer of women and children.)*' He threw himself at Klaus and knocked him to the floor. "TEUFEL!" As he locked his hands around Klaus's throat, Sam walked into the lounge.

"KARSTEN!" Sam used what little knowledge of rugby he knew, and like an All Black entering a ruck, smashed Karsten into the wall, knocking the wind out of him. Sam crawled back to Klaus and helped him onto the sofa while Karsten sat, painfully gasping for breath. "What the hell happened? He was trying to kill you."

Klaus gently rubbed his throat and looked up at Sam. "It wasn't me he was trying to kill, it was …" He pointed at an empty corner of the room.

Sam's gaze followed Klaus's finger. *"He must be dazed. There's nothing there,"* he thought. "I should call a doctor to check you out."

Klaus shook his head. "And how would I explain my condition?" He slowly shook his head. "No. Whatever caused this bizarre behaviour, was something in this room."

Sam looked nervously over his shoulder at the corner and shook his head. He helped Klaus to his feet and they dropped onto the sofa.

"Sam, please believe me when I say there was something in that corner. Something which stirred up memories I have struggled to suppress." He clasped his hands together. "Memories of my time in the Wehrmacht on the eastern front."

Sam looked again into the corner, and his stomach did a triple somersault with pike. A rippling cloud of grey smoke, vaguely in the form of a man, drifted across the window like a cloud across the sun.

"You saw it?" Klaus whispered.

Sam silently nodded, his eyes never leaving the corner, and the door to the map room.

"What did you see?"

"A tall military man. But not a Tommy. His…" Sam frowned, trying to remember every detail." It was the cap. It was high peaked."

"Deutsch?" Klaus suggested.

"Yes. German."

"It was Franks." Karsten, still panting, had recovered, and was stood close to them. "Somehow he has followed me back here." He stroked his father's face as tears ran down his cheeks. "Tut mir so leid. *(I'm so sorry.)*"

Sam patted the sofa and Karsten sat alongside them.

"Who's Franks?" Sam asked.

"That is a little difficult to explain," Karsten answered.

"Try me," Sam said with a warm smile.

"When I was seeking Guillaume, I occupied the body of an SS officer. He was the most evil of men. His actions were those of someone psychopathic or possessed."

"But all I saw was a shape, just the impression of a man. How do you know it's this man Franks?" Sam said with increasing fear in his voice.

"I would know Unteroffizier Bruno Franks if he was within a ten kilometre radius of me. The rank stench of his evil and crimes polluted the air, corrupted the earth, and perverted everything he touched."

Klaus had been silent, taking in everything his son had been saying. "I knew of this man Franks."

Sam and Karsten turned their heads.

Klaus's expression was distant, lost in faded memories. "He was a member of the SS - Totenkopfverbände."

Sam frowned, not understanding.

"Death's-Head Units. They were the SS organisation responsible for administering the Nazi concentration camps for the Third Reich," Klaus explained. "Franks was infamous for his actions at Auschwitz-Birkenau. After the war, he was never found. I would have killed him myself if I had come across him. In peace time, he would have been diagnosed as a psychopath killer and locked away in an asylum. But the war gave him opportunities to satisfy his sick lust for causing pain and misery."

"And you think he's followed you here?" Sam said with alarm.

"It's his … I'm not sure if spirit is the correct word," Karsten replied.

"I saw the vapour in the shape of a man." The voice was Alfredo's.

All three heads turned to the hall door, where Alfredo was stood listening to their conversation.

"It was uno dei propri del diavolo." Alfredo dropped this bombshell, as if it was something normal he did every day. "One of the Devil's own."

Klaus's face was the embodiment of incredulity. "A demon?!"

"Why not? We know that spirits exist, and that there is an afterlife. So why not the existence of demons and Hell?" He walked a few steps into the room. "I can smell it."

Klaus had no answer.

Sam's expression was a mixture of curiosity and terror. "So what is this thing? Does it have a name?"

Alfredo sat in an armchair and steepled his fingers under his chin. "I believe it is an Afrit. I took a deep interest in religion and demonology at university."

Sam, Karsten, and Klaus stared wide-eyed at Alfredo.

"An Afrit is the ghost of the victim of a murder." He stared intently at Karsten. "Who killed this man?"

Karsten shrugged.

"Not you?"

Karsten shook his head.

Alfredo continued. "The Afrit returns from the dead to take revenge on his killer." He frowned and sat down in a chair. "Whoever, and whatever Franks was, after he was killed, was condemned to hell. He has been changed into this demon Afrit." He leaned forward, and glanced at all three men. "And now he is seeking revenge."

Karsten swallowed hard, his breathing becoming shallow.

"Karsten?" Klaus uttered with growing fear. "What is it?"

Karsten peered up through his fingers at his father and shook his head.

"Tell me!"

"Guillaume strangled him."

Klaus, Alfredo, and Sam stared at each other in disbelief.

"How?" Sam asked, now utterly confused.

"In Block 11."

"Go on," Sam encouraged. "What happened?"

"I was in Franks body, trying to bond with Guillaume." He fought to bring back the memory. "Guillaume was on top of us, strangling me … Franks, that is. We were writhing on the floor. The door was being smashed in by guards. Bullets were ricocheting around the room, and I felt myself losing consciousness. The next thing I remember, I was back here."

A loud knock at the front door abruptly stopped their conversation.

"I'll go," Sam said, walking quickly to the front door. A few seconds later, he was back. "We've got visitors." He walked into the lounge followed by Elizabeth.

"They came to High Wood." She stood to one side, and Renaat and Guillaume walked into the lounge.

"Guillaume?" Klaus was overwhelmed by a cocktail of emotions. "Mein Gott. Mein Freund, wie geht es dir? *(My God. My friend, how are you?)*"

"I think we agreed that all meetings should be conducted in English." Guillaume had a glint in his eye. "But I am well, and Renaat insisted that you needed me here." He replied with a beaming smile. "Sam. Elizabeth. It is so good to see you again. And who are all these fine folk?"

Sam did the necessary introductions.

"You are building quite a team in the UK?" Guillaume said, as they moved into the kitchen. "Yes, quite a team. Do you have any cold beers, Sam?"

He nodded, and fetched a bottle of Kriek.

Guillaume smiled. "You remembered. That is very thoughtful of you, Sam. Thank you."

Klaus had barely improved to a state of semi-shock. "How did you get here?"

Guillaume put his arm around Klaus's shoulder, and like a father and younger son, led him into the lounge and onto the sofa. "Now, are you feeling more relaxed?"

Klaus smiled and nodded. "Ja. As they say, I have control. It is so good to have you here. There is so much to catch up on."

"Excellent. Tell me everything."

Over several cups of coffee, Klaus brought Guillaume up to speed with happenings at High Wood and Takanun.

Guillaume leaned towards Klaus. "Let me see your hand." He took it as if it was made of priceless porcelain, turned it over several times, examined it closely, shook his head, and sat back. "Quite extraordinary. And this happened when you held your hand in this blue vortex?"

Klaus nodded slowly.

"And the cut came back as you got further away from the house?"

Klaus nodded again.

Guillaume lay back on the sofa and closed his eyes.

Klaus knew this was a time to leave Guillaume deep in his thoughts.

*'What do you think brother?"* Guillaume spoke to the other side.

There was a short delay before Isaac answered. *"This is all completely new to myself and everyone here."*

"What on earth do we do with it? Or rather, what is it going to do with us?"

*"Have you seen it?"*

*"No. I wanted to speak with you first."*

*"View it, establish your own thoughts, and then let's speak again."*

*"Of course."*

*"How are you after your 'trip'?"*

*"Mentally battered and bruised, but physically, I'm ... I'm fine. I'll take a look at this phenomenon and speak to you again. Vous parler bientôt. (Talk to you soon.)"*

*"Au revoir."* And like an early morning mist, Isaac was gone.

Guillaume stood up, adjusted his belt, removed his tie, unbuttoned his collar, and offered Klaus his hand. "Come on, old friend, we have a lot to do. Show me this wonder."

Alfredo and Sam joined Klaus and Guillaume, while Elizabeth returned to the gallery with Captain Forster to continue returning lost souls to their loved ones.

Guillaume stopped about six feet from the vortex, and whistled. "Doux Jésus! *(Sweet Jesus!)*" He turned his face to Klaus and shook his head. "Doux Jésus!" He took a step closer. "You can feel warmth from it." He stepped back. "How long do you know it has been here?" He addressed his question to Sam.

"We saw it for the first time only a few days ago. How long it's actually been here is unknown." Sam scratched the side of his head. "It definitely wasn't here the first time I came into the cellar, which was about eight or nine days ago."

The sound of footsteps behind them made them turn around.

"Thought I might be of some use," Bill said.

Klaus smiled and nodded. "Guillaume, this is Bill. He's our resident computer, photographic, and black hole expert. Ralph and Bill know each other."

Bill stepped forward, and shook Guillaume firmly by the hand. "Pleasure to meet you. I've heard a great deal about you."

"All of it good I hope?"

"Actually it was." Bill smiled. "So what can I tell you about this anomaly?"

"Anything and everything. Help me understand what it is."

Ten minutes later, Guillaume was more knowledgeable, puzzled, amazed, and utterly at a loss what to do. "I understand why this has become the problem it has. What do we do?" He focused his eyes back on the vortex and walked close to it.

"Guillaume?" Klaus's voice had an edge of concern. "Not too close."

Guillaume looked back, smiled wickedly, winked, and walked into the vortex.

Klaus jumped forward, but Alfredo and Sam grabbed his arms.

Guillaume pulled a digital recorder out of his pocket and started to speak. "It's hot, but not uncomfortable. Like a jacuzzi."

*Pause.*

"I feel refreshed? It is as if my entire body was repairing itself at a cellular level."

*Pause.*

"The constant throbbing sciatic pain I've had for months, has gone." He looked down at the skin of his hands. "The skin on my hands appears smoother."

*Pause.*

"My brain feels like a sponge. I can almost feel the synapses firing. Knowledge is pouring into me."

*Pause.*

"Questions to be answered. One. Are there any others like this? Two. Precisely establish the range of its effect. Three. Video is required for Astrea. Four. Video conference needed as soon as possible. Five. What in God's name do we do with it?"

*Stop.*

He stepped out of the vortex.

There was silence for a few seconds.

"How do you feel?" Klaus asked nervously.

"Like a man in his twenties, with the experience and knowledge of a man in his seventies. The perfect combination every man has always prayed for." Guillaume chuckled to himself. "I have never felt so energised. We need to arrange a video conference as soon as possible with the members of the Astrea. This can't be left until we can coordinate everyone's travel plans."

Bill raised his hand. "I think that falls within my remit. If you can provide me with all their contact details, I should be able to get it organised within twenty-four hours?"

"I'll need my iPad. You can have them as soon as we get back upstairs," Guillaume answered. "I don't think there's any more we can learn here. Let's go upstairs. I need one of your famous English breakfasts."

As they climbed the stairs, wisps of amber and green smoke, undulated up the stairs after them, like a reticulated python in pursuit of its prey.

# Chapter Hundred-Six

Matt and Mark, left to their own devices in High Wood, and despite the risks, decided that a trip to the National Museum of Wales, would be beneficial, to their physical and mental well-being.

"'If art is to nourish the roots of our culture, society must set the artist free to follow his vision wherever it takes him'," Matt said, waving his right arm toward the front door. "'Things go away to return, brightened for the passage.'"

Mark smiled. "John F. Kennedy and A.R. Ammons?"

"Absolutely. Spot on, brother. Shall we go?"

Mark nodded, linked arms with Matt, walked briskly together out of the front door, and caught a bus from a nearby bus stop. By the time they'd reached the central bus station, Mark had made several immoral, and probably illegal suggestions to two schoolgirls, harangued three pensioners about the need for compulsory euthanasia, and questioned the bus driver's parentage as he threw them off the bus.

"Up yours, you old bastard!" Matt spat at him as they were 'assisted' off the bus.

"Yeah!" Mark chipped in. "Old git. You should be in a pissin' cemetery with the other stiffs."

"Drink?" Matt suggested, as he raised the middle finger of his right hand to the bus driver and most of the passengers.

Later that day, they were back in the central police station, cooling their alcohol-fuelled heels in separate cells, mopping up vomit, hurling abuse at anyone and no-one in particular, and trying to pee into, and mostly missing, the metal toilet pan.

"Shall we call him?" the desk sergeant asked the constable on duty with him.

"Nah. Let 'em stew 'til the morning. Morris Minor can have a chat with them then if he wants."

The following morning, a very compliant Detective Sergeant Morris, 'driven' by Lidsay, was stood outside High Wood, while the brothers continued to stew in the cells.

*"Now my friend, nice and easy. Get me inside, and as close to those two bastards who got me into this pissing mess."* Lidsay instructed.

"Detective Sergeant Morris." Sam did his best to disguise the 'what the bloody hell do you want this time' in his voice, "Come through to the kitchen. Most of us are in there." He led the way and sat Morris close to Klaus at the kitchen table.

"Guten Morgen. Einen Kaffee? I apologise. Good morning. A coffee?" Klaus asked pleasantly.

"Thank you. That would be very nice. I think I know everyone, apart from this gentleman?" Morris asked.

"Guillaume Wouters. I am a close friend of Sam and Elizabeth's. And you are?"

"Pardon me. Detective Sergeant Morris. I've been investigating the disappearance of a sergeant we used to have at the station and his wife." He glanced at Sam. "And the disappearance of Mr Morbeck's wife."

"Sounds like a classic Swedish crime series," Guillaume said innocently.

Morris paused as Lidsay gave instructions.

*"Tell them you want to see the room where the photos are. I'm pretty sure they call it the gallery."* Lidsay directed.

Marie brought Morris his coffee.

Morris made small talk before raising the gallery. "I understand you've got a room full of photographs?"

Klaus glanced at Sam, frowned, shook his head, smiled as Morris turned around to look at him, and said questioningly, "Photographs?"

"Yes. I have information which would indicate that the room at the top of the house contains hundreds of old photos?" He paused and made it clear from his expression that he expected to be taken upstairs. "I'd like to take a look."

"Why?" Sam asked quite reasonably.

"It's the only room we haven't checked to see if sergeant Lidsay, his wife, or Mrs Morbeck, may have left clues to their disappearance. I know it's a bit of a long shot, but it's worth a try. Is there a problem?"

"No, no, of course not," Sam replied as innocently as he could. "Elizabeth is already up there. I'll show you the way."

After a fruitless twenty minutes of searching the gallery, and asking Elizabeth questions about the photographs, Morris seemed satisfied that there was nothing to cast any light on the disappearances. "Thank you both. It may have seemed a bit pointless, but I want to be sure I've covered every possible avenue of inquiry before I close the cases."

"You don't expect to find them then?" Elizabeth asked.

Morris shook his head. "No, not really, and there are much more serious cases to be …" The sentence stopped short as Morris, like a scarecrow without a pole and string, sank into a shapeless heap on the floor.

"Oh shit, that's all we need. The sudden death of a police officer in the house." Sam whined as he slapped his forehead with the palm of his hand. "Bloody perfect."

"Sam," Elizabeth whispered. "Step back. Quickly, step away from him and make your way to the door."

He looked at her, and shrugged. "Not suggesting we just leave him here, are you?" Elizabeth's expression sent a shiver down his spine, and his eyes followed the direction in which she was pointing. A dark brown, viscous fluid, resembling liquid shellac, was dribbling from Morris's ears and nose, and was pooling on the floor.

"Shit he's had a … Oh bollocks, what do they call it?" He shook his head and sighed. "It was in a documentary the other night. This old chap came into A&E with stuff coming out of his ears and nose. It was a stroke, but they called it …"

"Sam, much as this is fascinating, I don't like the look of that stuff, so let's get the hell out of here." Elizabeth grabbed his arm and ran for the door which refused to open.

"I wouldn't bother," a familiar voice behind them said. "Lucifer himself couldn't open that."

Sam and Elizabeth glanced at each other and simultaneously mouthed a single word, *"Lidsay?!"*

"Come on now, don't be shy. After all, we've grown to know each other so well. I even got to know that dip-shit Constable Thompson. Do you know it's taken me nearly seventy years to get back here? Miss me?"

Sam and Elizabeth remained frozen to the door.

"TURN THE FUCK AROUND NOW!"

It was a howl that reverberated through the house.

"Scheiße! Was zum Teufel war das? *(Shit! What the hell was that?)*" Klaus exclaimed.

"Es klang wie der Teufel persönlich, *(It sounded like the Devil himself,)*" Karsten replied.

"Ich habe gehört, dass vor, *(I have heard that before,)*" Klaus said, regaining control of himself.

Karsten raised his eyebrows. "Wann? (*When?)*"

Klaus looked up at the ceiling. "The gallery! It is Lidsay!"

"Der böse Geist? Der Dämon? (*The evil spirit? The demon?)*" Karsten said in hushed tones.

Klaus slowly nodded. "Ja. Der Dämon."

"Even though I speak excellent German," Marie said, "I'm not sure that everyone else really got the gist of that."

Klaus apologised and gave them the short version.

Guillaume stared wide-eyed at Klaus. "This is the same spirit which you 'exorcised'?"

Klaus nodded. "Ja. It would seem he is proving more resilient than we thought." He looked caringly at Guillaume. "Stay here. I do not want you exposed to this after what you have recently suffered."

Guillaume started to move towards him, but Klaus held him firmly by the arms. "For me. Bitte. Stay here with the others."

Reluctantly Guillaume nodded. "Sei vorsichtig. *(Be careful.)*"

Alfredo and Gloria stared at them, not understanding the fear which was apparent in everyone's eyes.

Alfredo clasped his hands together, and shook them like a mafia don caught by the FBI with a smoking tommy gun at his feet, and a bleeding corpse resembling a Swiss cheese close by. "What is this demon? Why is it here?"

Klaus explained about Lidsay, and as he was doing so, he caught a glimpse of Gloria's expression. "My dear, I am sorry. It was very insensitive of me."

Gloria shook her head. "No. This is something I need to deal with. He's ruined too many lives, and it stops here and now." She walked towards the hall. "Everyone stay here. I'll deal with this."

# Chapter Hundred-Seven

Matt and Mark were released early the next morning with a slap on the wrist, a kick up the arse, and a 'don't you pair of useless bastards ever darken our door again' from the desk sergeant.

"My mouth's like a Sumo wrestler's jock strap. I could drop a rhino at twenty feet with my breath," Matt said as he poked his tongue in and out of his mouth like a cat licking sour milk. "That shit at the station they called breakfast, only made it worse. Wha' the 'ell was it?"

"Was alright. Filled a bloody 'ole," Mark said as he tied the tattered laces on his trainers.

Matt looked down at the top of his head. "Let me have men about me that are fat, Sleek-headed men and such as sleep a-nights. Yond Cassius has a lean and hungry look, He thinks too much; such men are dangerous."

Mark fell onto his back, rolled onto his side, shook his head, and stared up at Matt like a Pope who'd been told St Peter was a woman.

"What you pissin' starin' at?"

"You, you wanker."

"Why?"

"Cause you are a number one, class A wanker."

"Why. Am. I. A. Wanker?" Matt kicked him rhythmically in the arse to each of the words.

"Piss off will yu, that bastard well 'urts." Mark got to his feet, not bothering to brush off the leaves and dirt stuck to his jeans. "You are a wanker, 'cause of all the shit you were spoutin' jus' then?"

"Shit?" Matt thought about kicking him again, but held back as his feet were hurting. "What shit was I spoutin'?"

"That bollocks about some fat men, Cassius Clay, oh shit, I don' remember."

"Yond Cassius has a lean and hungry look, He thinks too much; such men are dangerous."

Mark jumped forward, and prodded him in the chest. *"That bollocks!"*

"Mmmm?" Matt was staring at a poster for Aida.

Mark stood close to his brother and looked deep into his eyes. "'Ave you taken some shit?"

Matt pushed him away. ""Shall I compare thee to a summer's day? Thou art more lovely and more temperate."

Mark clenched his fists, and struck a pose like Sugar Ray Leonard. "You turnin' queer? Brother or no brother, you ain't takin' me up the arse. My shit goes one way. Down'ill!"

"What are you talkin' about? Let's see if we can wangle a cup of coffee at Tesco." Matt trotted off down the road. "You comin'?" He called over his shoulder.

An hour later, after being 'helped on their way' from Tesco, for claiming they were in costume, and raising charity for Comic Relief, Matt suggested they went back to High Wood. "They know us there. See if we can scrounge a meal?"

"Why the 'ell do you wanna go back there?" Mark had about as much desire to revisit High Wood, as he did to have a Prince Albert without anaesthetic.

"Can't explain it, but I've got a feelin' in my water, that we ought to go back there."

"I'd need a feelin' from Charlize Theron to make me wanna go back there." Mark smirked at his brother. "Her or that other one who was in … oh bollocks, wha' was 'er pissin' name. She was in that film with that, that poncey British twat."

"What bloody film?"

"That one where, no, it was Captain America! That was it. She was, oh I don't know. But she could 'ave me." He sat down on the pavement, trying to remember his fantasy lover's name, when he suddenly jumped to his feet. "Scarlet O' 'ara! That was 'er name. Bloody gorgeous."

"Scarlett Johansson, you tit. Not bloody O' 'ara. She was in Gone with the Wind with Clint Eastwood." He started walking away. "You comin'?"

"S'pose so. Sod all else to do. May as well 'ave the shit scared out of me again."

As they got nearer to High Wood, the conversation slowly began to 'improve'.

"Did you read that review of Jonas Kaufmann in Wagner's Parsifal. He has everything, handsome, charismatic, a great actor and a wonderful singer," Mark said.

"Opera is lucky to have such a star as Kaufmann," Matt replied.

"I understand this will be followed in spring by his appearance in Verdi's Don Carlos at Covent Garden. We should try to get tickets."

"Marvellous idea. We'll do it."

As they walked into the avenue, a young couple absorbed by their smart phones, allowed their toddler to run ahead of them, and almost into the path of a car. The conversation then elevated itself to another level.

"'Two things are infinite: the universe and human stupidity; and I'm not sure about the universe,'" Matt said calmly, as he watched the parents sprint down the avenue shouting at the tops of their voices.

"'There may be times when we are powerless to prevent injustice, but there must never be a time when we fail to protest,'" Mark replied eloquently.

"'Those who know do not speak. Those who speak do not know.'"

"Ah yes," Mark said, pointing very deliberately at High Wood as they arrived. "'The eye sees only what the mind is prepared to comprehend.'"

# Chapter Hundred-Eight

Gloria took a deep breath and started up the main stairs.

In the gallery, Sam and Elizabeth slowly turned around.

Sam wasn't nearly as terrified as he'd been the first time he crossed swords with Lidsay's demonic alter ego. He stared impassively, at the obscene, naked figure, floating a foot above the floor, a few yards in front of him. Lidsay reminded him of Count Vladimir Harkonnen in Dune.

"Question is," Lidsay slavered, brown mucus dripping down his chin, "who's first?" He raised a decomposing arm and wiped it across his face, leaving pieces of green flesh hanging from his cheeks, like rancid banana peel. "Mmmm. Such a choice. Who shall it be?" He floated down to the floor and shuffled across the gallery, leaving smears like a slug on a paving slab.

Gloria heard the howl, stood paralysed for a few seconds, and then quickened her pace.

Elizabeth dug deep into the furthest recesses of her mind, and dragged out anything she could remember, on exorcising evil spirits. "'From all evil, deliver us, O Lord.'" She rifled through her memory banks. "'From all sin, From your wrath, From sudden and unprovided death, From the snares of the devil, From anger, hatred, and all ill will …'"

"IS THAT ALL YOU GOT!?" Lidsay screamed with laughter which tore into Sam and Elizabeth's brains like a jackhammer in overdrive.

"'By your death and burial, By your holy resurrection, By your wondrous ascension, By the coming of the Holy, Spirit, the Advocate, On the day of judgment …'"

"BLAH DE PISSING BLAH. Fucking holy joe bullshit." He shuffled to within a few inches of her face. His breath was fetid. A distillation of excrement and putrefaction. His blistered, peeling skin exuded a pus-like fluid which dripped onto the floor, leaving smouldering yellow stains.

What little hair remained on his scab-covered head, hung like oily rat's tails, over holes on the either side of his head out of which crawled a menagerie of insect life. "When will you lot realise that it's Abaddon, Beelzebub, Leviathan, or whatever the hell you want to call him, who runs this poxy planet. Jesus was just some hippy who got nailed to a cross."

Gloria reached the door to the gallery and pressed her ear against it.

Elizabeth didn't blink and stared Lidsay straight in the eye. "'That you spare us, That you pardon us, That you bring us to true penance …'"

"SHUT THE FUCK UP YOU SANCTIMONIOUS, SELF-RIGHTEOUS, HOLIER-THAN-THOU, SMUG …"

"'That you confirm and preserve us in your holy service, That you lift up our minds to heavenly desires, That you grant everlasting blessings to all our benefactors …'"

Lidsay shuffled a few feet back. His eyes giving away a hint of uncertainty. "SHUT YOUR MOUTH!"

"'That you deliver our souls and the souls of our brethren, relatives, and benefactors from everlasting damnation, That you give and preserve the fruits of the earth, That you grant eternal rest to all the faithful departed, That you graciously hear us, Son of God!'"

For the first time, Lidsay didn't feel totally in control. There was something different about this. He didn't know what, but something was definitely not right. The banging and shouting from the door, gave him the answer.

"IVOR! OPEN THIS BLOODY DOOR AND LEAVE THOSE PEOPLE ALONE!"

*"Gloria?"* he hissed like a deflating balloon. *"Gloria?"*

Seeing Lidsay was distracted, Sam tried the door again, and after wrenching at it with every ounce of strength he could muster, it crashed open, and Gloria fell into the room at the 'feet' of Lidsay.

She stood up slowly, taking everything thing in. Her erstwhile husband's appearance not fazing her, she brushed herself off and met his now slowly reducing crazed gaze. "You caused me too many years of grief, untold sleepless nights, covering up my bruises with long sleeves, blaming black eyes on door frames, running out of tears, not having kids, wasting a life, and not being there for my mum and dad when they died." She slapped him across the face and wiped off the putrefied goo on her jeans. "And if you think you're going to bloody ruin my afterlife as well, then you are so far off the mark, that you may as well be on the other side of this world."

Lidsay's maw opened, but Gloria hadn't finished.

Sam and Elizabeth stood in the doorway and stared in disbelief at each other as the drama unfolded in front of them.

"What the hell are you? Have you looked in a mirror recently?"

Sam put his hand over his mouth and chuckled.

Elizabeth turned away and bit her lip.

Lidsay had no points of reference to fall back on. How the hell did he respond to the ghost of a woman whose life he'd made a misery, and now, in something which was maybe an afterlife, wanted who the hell knew what. Sounds started to emit from him, but Gloria was in full flow. Like Niagara Falls, nothing was going to stop this long-restrained torrent.

"You don't belong here. This world is for the living. I don't know what comes next, but," she said and walked up close to Lidsay, and tenderly touched his cheek. "it has to be better than this." She looked him up and down and sighed deeply. "There were times at the beginning when we were happy. Good times. Let's see if we can find them again," she said and looked up at the ceiling, "out there somewhere in another place and time."

Sam and Elizabeth felt as if they were gate-crashers on something very private, but they couldn't look away.

Where Gloria touched Lidsay's cheek, the green putrid flesh started to fall away, revealing pink unblemished skin beneath. She reached again, and put the palms of both hands on either side of his head. Large flakes of yellow skin sloughed off the underlying corrupt flesh. She resisted the almost uncontrollable urge to pull away, and pressed her hands tighter against his head. Like an anaconda shedding its skin, Lidsay's features slowly began to appear from beneath the rank sludge, which had formed the anatomy of his face and head. Gloria maintained eye-to-eye contact as the process of metamorphosis began to accelerate through his body, like a dragonfly nymph, transforming into a fragile glassy-winged dragonfly. The 'goo' slipped from all over Lidsay's body, and lay in a glistening steaming mound on the gallery floor. A few feet in front of Gloria, lay the naked, prostate figure of a much younger, fitter Ivor Lidsay. He slowly stood up and the sheen of his body refracted rays of sunlight into a kaleidoscope of rainbows.

Lidsay's mind, like his body, became softer, warmer, unbrutalised after years of policing. Slowly, the memory of his 'other' self began to fade. He looked for something to cover his nakedness and embarrassment, and picked up a blanket Elizabeth used when the gallery became cold and wrapped it around himself. "Gloria?" He looked around the gallery, utterly confused. "Where am I? What's happened?"

She smiled affectionately at him. "That's a very long story." She linked her arm with his. "Come on, let's get you some clothes." She looked over at Sam. "Can we try some of yours?"

Sam nodded, still in a state of absolute shock at seeing his nemesis transformed into this pleasant young man. "Of course. Take what you want."

After raiding Sam's wardrobe, Lidsay appeared in the kitchen with Gloria, dressed in jeans, trainers, a white shirt, and a red sweater.

"Sorry for the problems I seem to have caused," Ivor said softly, his eyes fixed on his trainers. "I can't remember any of it, but from what Gloria's told me, I'm surprised that you'd want to be in the same room as me."

Klaus patted the seat next to him. "Please. Sit next to me, and we will tell you who we are, and what has happened.

An hour later, a bemused Ivor was sat in the lounge with everyone. "I did all those things?" He managed to utter to Sam. "And we've travelled through time?"

Sam shrugged and nodded. "I'll admit it sounds a little 'odd', but it's all true." He smiled at Ivor. "Shit, you were an evil bastard."

"Sam!" Elizabeth elbowed him in the ribs.

"But he was."

Another elbow swiftly followed.

"Sorry."

"It's me who should be sorry, Elizabeth." A subdued Ivor replied. "Evil bastard sounds like a bit of an understatement." He looked intently at Gloria. "And now we're ghosts?"

"Yes. Ghosts, spirits, whatever you want to call us. They all add up to the same thing," Gloria replied. "But it's fortunate we came to this house, because here, we've found each other again." She leaned over and kissed him softly on the lips.

A soft hiss was unheard by everyone in the room, as a ribbon of smoke wrapped itself around the base of a standard lamp.

# Chapter One Hundred-Nine

A loud knock at the front door drew an immediate reaction from Klaus. "Wer ist zum Teufel das? *(Who the hell is that?)* Alfredo will you go? Tell them we are too busy to see anyone."

He nodded, and made his way to the front door. "Ciao. Chi sei? *(Hello. Who are you?)*" He was hoping a stranger wouldn't waste their time on a foreigner who couldn't speak English.

"I am Ralph Jefferson," he said firmly and slowly. "I have just flown in from the US."

"Mi dispiace. Mi scusi. Io non parlo Inglese. *(I'm sorry. Excuse me. I don't speak English.)*"

Ralph looked in the gaps either side of Alfredo into the hall, and deciding he had nothing to lose, shouted. "KLAUS! IT'S RALPH!"

Klaus leapt to his feet and ran to the front door. He gently pushed Alfredo out of the way and shook Ralph by the hand. "I am so sorry, Ralph. I told Alfredo to get rid of whoever was calling."

Alfredo blushed and offered his hand to Ralph. "Mi dispiace tanto. *(I am so sorry.)*"

Ralph shook his hand warmly. "No problem." He stopped in the hall and looked around. "So this is High Wood." He walked in and out of the ground floor rooms. "Very impressive, Klaus. I've been waiting a long time to see this."

"Let me show you to your room." He turned to Sam and Alfredo. "We do have a room, don't we?"

"First on the left is still free," Sam replied. "Although space is beginning to disappear at a rate of knots."

They dropped Ralph's bag in his room and Klaus took him up to the gallery. "Impressive isn't it?"

"Very. How many are still left without faces?" Ralph asked as he surveyed the panels.

"Elizabeth will know precisely. We can ask her when we go down."

"And she's the one who helps them pass over?"

"Yes. She has an innate ability to bring them comfort in their passing. She is the most empathetic person I have ever met."

"I look forward to meeting her," Ralph said with a smile. "Shall we go down?"

Klaus nodded and led the way.

Guillaume jumped to his feet as they entered the kitchen, which had become the hub of the house. "My dear friend." He shook Ralph by the hand so firmly that he eventually had to pull his hand away. "When did you arrive?"

"A few minutes ago. I'm glad you're here. I want to arrange a video conference in the next few days?"

"Our thoughts precisely." Klaus answered as if his idea had been stolen. "Bill is working on it, and we should be, I think you say, 'good to go' by tomorrow."

"Take a look if you want," Bill said as he walked in from the garden. "I've pulled in a few favours, and it's all set up next door."

Klaus stepped forward. "Ralph, this is Bill, he's our on-site tech-guy."

"Yeah, we know each other well. How are you Bill?"

"Good. Shall we go?"

There was a general nodding of heads and everyone made their way to Takanun.

"Jesus!" Ralph exclaimed as they walked into the 'lounge'. "This looks more like mission control at Kennedy Space Centre. Where the hell did you get all of this stuff?"

Five office chairs with microphones, set up in front of them, had been placed facing a semi-circle of four Sony Bravia KDL60W605 Smart 60" LED TVs.

Bill tapped the side of his nose. "I didn't know how many we'd be connecting to, but I can split screens to accommodate two per TV, which gives you a potential of eight."

"That'll be plenty," Ralph answered. "I'm impressed, Bill. Great job." He turned and high-fived him. "Should be an interesting show. Guillaume, let's agree a time and get on the phones. Klaus, you'll help?"

"Ja. Of course."

An hour later, the video conference was set for the next day at three pm.

Klaus turned to Bill. "Can we connect any of the 35mm films into the conference call?"

Bill grinned. "I'm ahead of you on that one. Just let me know when you want it. I've cut together five different scenes, all of which show faceless troops in different locations."

Ralph smiled broadly and high-fived Bill again. "Can you get some video of this vortex for the call? It's essential everyone sees it." He glanced over at Klaus. "Probably make sense for me to see it before they do."

"Of course. Come with me. Bill, can you bring a camera?"

Bill opened a black plastic case designed to carry ammunition for the US marines, and took out a Cubicam Waterproof 1080p HD Micro Sports Camera.

Klaus looked concerned at his choice. "Will that do the job?"

"This camera may be small, but it shoots in stunning 1080p HD quality." Bill replied with a satisfied smile. "It'll do the job."

Another high-five followed, which was beginning to irritate Klaus.

Ralph's first view of the vortex brought a loud, "Well kiss my hairy arse!!"

Klaus as always, was never sure how to respond to Ralph's diverse use of language, and simply smiled. He looked away from him towards the vortex, and his jaw metaphorically hit the floor. "Küss meinen Arsch. *(Kiss my arse.)*"

Ralph couldn't help but laugh. "I'll make you an American yet." He followed Klaus's stare. "What is it?"

"It's changed its shape, and it's bigger. A lot bigger."

The diameter of the vortex had increased by about twenty-five per cent, but the most significant change, was the spinning disc now resembled a whirlpool. The spiralling bottom seemed to be drilling itself into the cellar floor, sending shards of what looked like blue forked lightning, ricocheting off the cellar walls.

"Can I touch it?" Ralph asked.

Klaus shook his head. "With these changes, I wouldn't, until we fully understand it."

Ralph's expression showed a small level of disappointment, but heavily overlaid with understanding.

Klaus turned to Bill. "Can you capture this?"

He nodded, and circled the spinning, cerulean maelstrom.

Ralph watched closely as Bill captured the phenomenon. "We should call this Charybdis."

Klaus looked perplexed.

"Greek mythology. I studied it at university. In some variations of the story, Charybdis was simply a large whirlpool. A later myth makes Charybdis the daughter of Poseidon and Gaia, and living as a loyal servant to Poseidon. She aided him in his feud with Zeus, and as such, helped him engulf lands and islands in water."

Klaus nodded, looking bemused, not interested in the least in the story.

"Greek mythology not to your taste, Klaus?" Ralph asked with a knowing smile.

"Δεν. *(No.)*"

"Excellent, Klaus. Μιλούν την ελληνική γλώσσα? *(Speak Greek?)*"

Klaus's expression clearly indicated that he didn't. "Do you have enough, Bill?"

He nodded.

"Good." Klaus turned to Ralph. "Hungry?"

"I could eat a dead cow between two loaves of bread."

"Is that a new McDonald's happy meal?" Bill asked as he put the camera back in its case.

"Yeah. The Triple Mooc-Donald." The two Americans fell about laughing and high-fived each other.

The three men walked upstairs, said their goodbyes to Marie, Rob and Pat, and walked back to High wood.

"Who the hell are those two?" Ralph asked Klaus, as he saw Matt and Mark standing forlornly at the gate.

Klaus looked skyward. "Nicht wieder diese zwei Idioten. *(Not these two idiots again.)*"

Ralph looked at him and frowned. "What the hell did you just say?"

Klaus looked down and sighed. "Sorry, Ralph. These two are, how do you say, lost pennies? They keep turning up."

"Bad pennies," Ralph said with an unconvincing smile.

Matt turned and saw Klaus.

"Hereof one cannot speak, thereof one must be silent."

Ralph frowned. "What the hell did he just say?"

Klaus glanced at Matt. "He was quoting Wittgenstein. I studied philosophy at Ruprecht-Karls-Universität Heidelberg."

Ralph frowned again.

"Heidelberg University."

"Touché," Ralph said. "Come on, let's get inside. I'm starving." He walked past Matt and Mark and smiled.

"'The only thing that makes life possible is permanent, intolerable uncertainty: not knowing what comes next,'" Mark said to Matt as Bill walked past them.

"'To be alone is to be different, to be different is to be alone,'" Matt said as Klaus approached them.

"How are you?" Klaus asked pleasantly. "You look as if you have been sleeping outside."

The brothers looked at themselves and quickly recovered. "We have been doing some work for charity. These are our work clothes."

Klaus knew they were lying, as their 'work' clothes were the same they'd worn on every visit to High Wood. "What do you want?"

Matt looked confused. "The house it, it called to me."

Klaus stared deep into his eyes, and knew he was telling, what he believed to be the truth. "You'd better come in."

The brothers smiled, and like two puppies, followed Klaus into the house.

# Chapter Hundred-Ten

After several weeks of intense counselling, re-education with the male elders and ministerial servants of the Kingdom Hall, Jacob was deemed fit to return to his evangelism. Joshua, his accompanying Witness, had been taken ill after a dodgy chicken sandwich, and now, a street away from High Wood, Jacob was delivering the 'message' and handing out copies of 'The Watchtower - Announcing Jehovah's Kingdom' to the apathetic residents. He was 'preaching' to an elderly couple about an article in the Watchtower he was holding. "Have you asked yourself these questions? What is the purpose of life? Why do people suffer and die? What does the future hold? Does God care about me?"

The husband, a seventy-year-old retired professor of history and philosophy at Oxford University, pursed his lips, tapped his temple with his index finger, looked intently at Jacob, frowned, breathed deeply, and answered. "To address your first question. According to the Bible, our purpose, the reason we are here, is for God's glory. In other words, our purpose is to praise God, worship Him, to proclaim His greatness, and to accomplish His will. In respect of your second, we suffer and die because of sin."

Jacob was at a loss what to say, so nodded and mmm'd in agreement.

"As to the third point you raise, I think Eleanor Roosevelt put it best. 'The future belongs to those who believe in the beauty of their dreams.'"

"You have some exceptional answers. Can I ..."

"Four is much more difficult to answer."

*"Thank the Lord for that,"* Jacob thought.

"However, one of the most touching verses in Scripture that perfectly captures this truth of God's heart toward us, is found in Zephaniah, which states: "The Lord your God is with you. He's mighty to deliver. He takes great delight in you. He will quiet you with His love. He rejoices over you with singing."

"I'm afraid I have to go," Jacob said over his shoulder as he walked quickly down their path.

"Do call again." The elderly gentleman called after him as they closed the front door.

Jacob's self-will and patience had been stretched to their limits. He was ready to call it a day, when an invisible hand pulled him down a road which rang a peel of church bells which would have given the Hunchback of Notre Dame tinnitus. As the rooftop of High Wood came into view, he gasped.

"'Satan was the first angel to fall from heaven after he rebelled against God, and he resides in you.'" He pointed at High Wood and spoke in a loud clear voice. "'Be sober-minded; be watchful. Your adversary the devil prowls around like a roaring lion, seeking someone to devour.'" He walked in through the gate. "'And the great dragon was thrown down, that ancient serpent, who is called the devil and Satan, the deceiver of the whole world - he was thrown down to the earth, and his angels were thrown down with him.'" He called out to the house. "'SUBMIT YOURSELVES THEREFORE TO GOD. RESIST THE DEVIL, AND HE WILL FLEE FROM YOU!'"

Klaus was stood in the hall and heard the shouting. He turned, told the brothers to go upstairs, and wait there. He watched them climb the stairs, and then walked to the front door. "Mein Gott! Mehr verrückte Leute *(My God! More crazy people!)*"

"PUT ON THE WHOLE ARMOUR OF GOD, THAT YOU MAY BE ABLE TO STAND AGAINST THE SCHEMES OF THE DEVIL!" he shouted at Klaus, jabbing his index finger at him.

Passers-by had begun to gather at the gate, drawn by the shouting.

Klaus looked past Jacob, and noticed the small crowd at the gate. "Come with me, and let's talk in the house." He grabbed hold of Jacob's arm and tried to pull him towards the house.

Jacob resisted, glanced back at the people at the gate, turned and screamed at Klaus. "'AND ANOTHER SIGN APPEARED IN HEAVEN: BEHOLD, A GREAT RED DRAGON, WITH SEVEN HEADS AND TEN HORNS, AND ON HIS HEADS SEVEN DIADEMS!'"

Alfredo joined Klaus in the drive, and gripped Jacob's other arm. Together, they pulled him into the house. As they pulled him in through the front door, Jacob turned and screamed, his last words as the door was slammed. "'AND THE ENEMY WHO SOWED THEM IS THE DEVIL. THE HARVE …'"

Inside the hall Jacob shook himself free. "What do you demons want of me?" He clasped his hands in prayer and looked up to the ceiling. "'Behold, I have given you authority to tread on serpents and scorpions, and over all the power of the enemy, and nothing shall hurt you.'"

"We don't mean you harm," Klaus said as calmly as he could. "We were concerned you were having some kind of convulsion." He shouted to the kitchen. "Could I have a glass of water?"

Rebecca brought the glass to Klaus, and Jacob's expression was enough to tell him he'd seen something he shouldn't have. Klaus turned and took from Rebecca what Jacob had seen as a floating glass. "Thank you. Tell the others to stay in the kitchen, until I say it's OK to come out," he whispered.

Jacob's beliefs that High Wood was the dwelling place of demons, was reaffirmed in block capitals a foot high. "'You believe that God is one; you do well. Even the demons believe - and shudder!'"

Klaus stepped forward. "Please come into the lounge and let's discuss this." He glanced at Alfredo and mouthed, *"Fetch Ralph and Guillaume."*

Jacob looked down at the hand as if it was coated in pus, stepped back, pointed at Klaus, and screamed at him again. "'FOR THE LORD HIMSELF WILL DESEND FROM HEAVEN WITH A CRY OF COMMAND, WITH THE VOICE OF AN ARCHANGEL, AND WITH THE SOUND OF THE TRUMPET OF GOD.'"

Sam, Elizabeth, Gloria, and Ivor, hearing the commotion in the hall, came in from the lounge to see what was happening, and stood for a few moments, staring in disbelief at the ranting evangelist.

"We need to do something about him, before he attracts attention to us," Sam said in ignorance of the small crowd already assembled outside, one or two who'd already called the police.

Ivor smiled. "Leave it to me. I've a lot of experience of this sort of thing."

Gloria turned to him. "Don't do anything stupid. I'm not losing this opportunity for a second chance, even if it's in the next life."

Ivor kissed her tenderly. He'd forgotten how something so simple could give so much pleasure. "I'll only be gone a short while."

Jacob was in full flow, waving his arms at Klaus. "GET BEHIND ME, SATAN! YOU ARE A HINDRANCE TO ME. FOR YOU ARE NOT SETTING YOUR MIND ON THE THINGS OF GOD, BUT ON THE THINGS OF MAN."

Ivor strolled past Klaus, and softly took up 'spiritual' residence in Jacob. The transformation was immediate, and within two minutes, Jacob was gratefully accepting the offer of tea, and walking with Klaus into the kitchen.

The desk sergeant knew Morris, was in, or close to High Wood, so called him on his mobile.

The ringing and vibrations in his pocket, brought Morris back from wherever he was, into semi-consciousness. "Mmmm? Wha'. This is …"

"You OK, detective sergeant?"

"Mmmm? Yeah. What is it?"

"Are you still at High Wood?"

Morris stood up unsteadily and looked around at where he was. "Think so. Why?"

"We've had reports of a disturbance. Lot of shouting and a man being dragged into the house. Can you look into it?"

Morris leaned against the gallery door, desperately trying to clear his head. "Yeah. I'll see what's going on. Give me a few minutes. If I need back up, I'll call it in."

In the kitchen, Jacob was like an obedient Labrador.

Morris made his way unsteadily downstairs and into the kitchen.

Sam stared wide-eyed at Elizabeth. *"Shit! I'd forgotten about him,"* he mouthed.

She shrugged, and put a comforting arm around Morris's shoulders. "Feeling better?"

"Mmmm? Thanks. Yes. I feel OK." He looked around the table and assumed Jacob was the captive. "Everything OK, sir? Only we've had a report of a disturbance here."

Jacob smiled, looked up, and Ivor replied. "Very good, officer. We were just discussing the merits of different religions. Bit of a misunderstanding earlier, but I'm perfectly OK now." He glanced around at the faces around the table. "Very nice people. Would you like a cup of something? If you don't mind me saying, you look like you need something."

Morris shook his head. "Thank you, no. I should be getting back to the station." He turned and looked over his shoulder at Jacob. "Can I give you a lift anywhere?"

Ivor shook Jacob's head. "Very kind of you, but I've quite a lot of visits still to make."

Morris uh - uh'd. "I'll see myself out." When he got to the gate, he told the small crowd that everything was in order and to disperse.

In the kitchen, the discussion was focused on what to do with Jacob. After a few minutes, Ivor lifted Jacob's hand for silence. "I'll walk him a reasonable distance away, and leave him there. When I leave him, he won't remember a thing about his visit."

Two hours later, Jacob was sat in the Kingdom Hall, bemused, battered, and bewildered, and asking for a transfer back to the US.

# Chapter Hundred-Eleven

The brothers had lifted down a couple of large tomes from the bookshelves in the lounge, and were deep in a philosophical debate about the existence of God.

Ralph walked into the lounge. "You guys OK?"

"Ah our colonial cousin," Matt said with a smirk. "Come in, come in. Your thoughts would be much appreciated."

"Well, firstly, I think you'll find that the Declaration of Independence, was signed by the Continental Congress on July 4, 1776, announcing that the thirteen American colonies, then at war with Great Britain, regarded themselves as thirteen newly independent sovereign states, and no longer a part of the British Empire."

"Indeed," Matt conceded. "And you've never looked back since." He continued with a small degree of sarcasm in his voice.

Ralph ignored this. "So what were you discussing?"

"Mark insists that the complexity of our planet, points to a deliberate Designer, who not only created our universe, but sustains it today. While I on the other hand, believe that, life on Earth began more than three billion years ago, evolving from the most basic of microbes into a dazzling array of complexity over time," Matt said without batting an eyelid.

Ralph sat down heavily on the sofa.

"Secondly, he believes that God exists because he pursues us, and is constantly initiating and seeking for us to come to him."

Mark frowned. "Anyone understands that unlike any other revelation of God, Jesus Christ is the clearest, most specific picture of God revealing himself to us."

Klaus followed Ralph into the room. "You have met the brothers?

Ralph smiled.

Klaus shrugged. "What do we do with them?"

Ralph held out his hands, palms up, and raised an eyebrow. "Not a clue. But there must be something we can do with their level of knowledge?"

Klaus breathed deeply and nodded. "Let's discuss this later." He sat on the sofa close to Ralph. "How are things in the other locations? We have been very engrossed in things here, and I need to catch up before our video conference."

Ralph leaned back, stroked his chin, and looked deep into Klaus's eyes. "The situation in St Petersburg, and the other localised concentrations, have improved"

Klaus looked less than convinced. "Wie? How?"

"I followed your suggestion at the last meeting of the Astrea."

"Which was?"

"The talk which Jane gave, made enormous sense to me. That was the reason you brought her?"

Klaus shrugged, rocked his head from side to side, pursed his lips, and finally nodded.

"This was why I decided Papaver Rhoeas should go public. I found other spirits who would help us, organised interviews on TV and Radio, and the response was astonishing. Financial contributions came flooding in, and our accounts have never been so healthy. Within a month I'd taken on spiritualists, psychics, mediums, clairvoyants, mystics, pretty much anyone who could, or believed they could, communicate with the other side. By throwing all these people at the problem, the situation has become much more manageable."

Klaus was incandescent. "*You* decided to do this?"

Ralph nodded.

"Without discussion with myself?"

Ralph nodded.

"Why wasn't I consulted?"

Ralph sensitively took him by the arm, led him through the kitchen, and into the garden. "As you said, you've been preoccupied with resolving the situation here. I felt that disturbing you with this would be counter-productive. The others supported that view." He paused, judging Klaus's mood. "You have to understand, Klaus, that as far as I was concerned, I was only implementing your proposal."

Klaus stood up, walked to the garden shed, and turned to face Ralph. "But this is unprecedented. Who gave you this authority?"

Ralph ignored his comments, and continued. "The situation here is unique. Two portals, side by side, one shielded, one not, and operating independently of each other? Add to that the existence of this vortex, and you have a completely separate, and singular set of problems which needed your complete undivided attention. This was meant as no personal affront to you. If you feel that, then I can only apologise unreservedly. You are the closest to Guillaume. Closest to the Chef Charon. We needed your experience and expertise focused on this problem."

Klaus's mood was *very* slowly settling, and despite his immeasurable anger at the decisions which had been taken without his knowledge, he had to admit they'd been correct and in line with his own thoughts. The results Ralph had told him were impressive, but he wasn't going to admit that just yet. "Why then do we still need this video conference?" he said, still with obvious, but reduced irritation.

"To discuss the vortex?" He frowned slightly. "What did you say Charlie had called it?"

"The Lazarus Pool."

"The Lazarus Pool." Ralph drew out the words with almost religious fervour. "It would make a great brand name. Marketing this would be a dream come true for any consultancy. My God, if only half of what you've told me is true, then Papaver Rhoeas could have discovered a cash generator of stratospheric proportions."

"Cash generator?" Klaus said, almost himself again.

Ralph nodded vigorously. "My God, Klaus, this could be as big as … shit, I can't think of anything big enough to compare it to." He narrowed his eyes and peered questioningly at him. "You don't agree?"

"Ich bin mir nicht sicher. Sorry. I am still undecided."

"My friend, we've been trying to address a global problem with local resources. This additional funding would allow us to manage this issue properly, and send all our lost souls home. Military or civilian. We've kept ourselves secret for too long." He stood close to him and put his arm around his shoulder. "You and I are dinosaurs, and we need to leave it to the young bucks. People who understand this social media stuff. Shit, I've probably only got a few years left." He stood back, and playfully looked Klaus up and down. "And you … I'd give you a few months." He softly punched him in the stomach. "Come on, you miserable kraut. It's the future and we won't be a part of it for much longer." He held Klaus's cheeks and pulled them up in a mock smile. "'Put a smile on your face, and don't bring everybody down. Ooh, ooh ooh ooh. Don't worry. Ooh oo - ooh ooh ooh. Don't worry, be happy. I'm not worried, I'm happy.'" He sang in a very poor impression of Bobby McFerrin.

Klaus couldn't keep the anger going and burst out laughing. "Narr. *(Fool.)* Don't you Americans have a saying about a good tune being blown on an old flute?"

"A fiddle not a flute."

Matt and Mark sauntered into the garden to join Klaus and Ralph.

"Was it something we said?" Matt asked politely.

"No, no. We just needed some fresh air," Ralph replied. "Jet lag catches up on you."

The brothers nodded in understanding.

"Yes. It can be extremely debilitating." Mark stroked his chin, deep in thought. "I have read that nonbenzodiazepines, such as zolpidem, eszopiclone, zaleplon, and benzodiazepines, such as triazolam, are very effective in treating the symptoms."

Ralph gaped back at him. "Thanks for the advice."

Mark wasn't finished. "Light therapy has also been shown to help. It involves exposing your eyes to an artificial bright light or lamp that simulates sunlight for a specific and regular amount of time during the time when you're meant to be awake."

"Thanks. I'll give it a try. Could you give us a minute?" Ralph asked politely. "Couple of personal things we need to discuss."

""And thus the heart will break, yet brokenly live on.'" Matt smiled at Ralph and Klaus.

"George Gordon Byron," Matt said as he walked back to the house with Mark.

"Why don't we let them stay, and help with the work at Takanun? They're 'geniuses' and we could give them things to do. We can be completely open with them, now we've gone public. Give me two seconds." He stood up and walked quickly into the house. A few minutes later he was stood at the kitchen door with his laptop. He waved to Klaus to join him. "Left it in there this morning." He lifted up the lid, waited a few seconds, tapped a few keys, and turned the screen to face Klaus. "Doesn't anyone here look at the internet?"

"We have been somewhat preoccupied," Klaus replied from under raised eyebrows.

"Fair point." Ralph tapped the screen. "We've, I believe the phrase is, gone viral." He clicked on the play arrow on the small screen, and an interview appeared with Ralph. It ran for five minutes, during which Klaus didn't blink, "There." Ralph said proudly. "What do you think?"

Klaus continued to stare at the screen. "This is viral?"

"Three million hits, in the last two weeks. We're more popular than Marvel's Ant-Man."

"And people have sent money?"

"A fair sum."

"But what do they get for their money?"

"The pleasure of knowing they're donating to an extremely worthwhile cause. And the definitive proof that an afterlife does exist."

"This is so different to what we have done before."

Ralph smiled. "One word, my dearest friend. Change." He turned the laptop to face Klaus, clicked a few more buttons, and smiled." Here it is. I bookmarked it." He ran his finger across the screen following the words. "Change management is an approach to transitioning individual teams, organisations, to a desired future state."

Klaus looked like a rabbit caught in the headlights.

"Change is everywhere, and if we're going to survive, we have to embrace it." He held Klaus's shoulders and squeezed them. "You and I need others to follow behind us and carry the torch. I'm due a bypass when I get back, and this knee," he said and massaged his right leg, "needs replacing with metal and plastic." He squeezed Klaus's shoulders again. "We deal with events that happened a hundred years ago, but we live in the twenty-first century. We have to adopt these new technologies. If only for the sake of the everlasting lives of the lost souls we save."

The message was slowly beginning to penetrate Klaus's shuttered mind. "I can't believe I wasn't aware of this?"

"You, and everyone else in this house, and the others, have been drowning in problems and stress. What's happened outside has become secondary. But now we're all, as they say, on the same page. Well, we will be, once we get everyone together in the morning, and explain what's going on." He looked deep into Klaus's eyes. "Good to go?"

Klaus nodded. "Ja. Gut zu gehen. Ja. It is good to go."

"Why don't you, me, and Guillaume go into the city, and have a quiet dinner in a good restaurant?"

# Chapter Hundred-Twelve

Elizabeth was taking a well-earned break, relaxing in the garden, watching the sunset, after helping more Tommies pass over.

Sam joined her with two glasses of cold beer. "Fancy one?" He smirked. "Beer that is."

"Perfect." She ran her finger around the rim of the glass and doodled in the condensation on the sides. "Couldn't manage much else."

"I'll have a word with Gloria," Sam said with a wicked smile.

Elizabeth choked on her beer and spat it out on Sam's shoes. "Dozy sod."

"Many souls left?" he asked, as he mopped his shoes with a tissue.

"Enough to keep me occupied for a good few months. The issue is what will be needed with these 'new' souls?"

"Apparently, there's news on the way forward. I spoke very briefly with Ralph, but he was off out with Klaus and Guillaume. He wants to update everyone on the latest news in the morning."

Elizabeth stretched her neck and opened her eyes wide. "Wonder what that's all about?"

"Getting a bit chilly out here," Sam said with a badly mimed shiver.

"Thank you, Brad. We'll call you." Elizabeth playfully slapped him on the cheek. "Go on in if you're feeling cold. I'm fine."

"Sure you wouldn't like to come in?" Sam asked as he walked behind her and massaged her neck and shoulders.

"Tell you what," she said with a chuckle in her voice. "Get me another beer, and I might consider an early night."

Usain Bolt couldn't have been any faster, and he was soon back with a bottle of San Miguel.

"Careful, Sam, you'll have a coronary, and that would cramp your style. Now go away and leave me alone with my beer."

He gave her his best hang-dog expression, smirked, and walked back to the house. "I'd better have that chat with Gloria." He called back over his shoulder.

Elizabeth was tempted to respond, but resisted the urge.

He meandered back into the kitchen and met Karsten walking in from the hall.

"Beer?" Sam asked with his head in the fridge.

"Bitte, Sam."

"I though you liked lager." Sam laughed at his pun, and emerged from the fridge smirking, until he realised his attempt at humour was completely lost on Karsten.

"Ja. Lager, bitte, Sam."

Sam was now confused. "You want lager or bitter?"

"Yes, Sam. Lager bitte."

Sam held out a bottle of Kriek. "This OK?"

"Ja. Vielen Dank."

Sam was tempted to continue this endless loop of a conversation, but decided his brain had had enough stress for one day. "How are you feeling now?"

"Much better. The nightmares still come, but they aren't as bad as they were."

"What happened when you were Spirit Walking?"

Karsten drained half the bottle. "Another time, Sam. It is still very roh. Raw."

Sam lifted his bottle to Karsten's and they clinked them together. "Cheers. Good health."

"Prost. Gute Gesundheit."

Sam smiled gently. "We sometimes say that when we sneeze."

Karsten shrugged.

"Guzundite? Well, that, or mostly bless you."

Karsten chuckled. "Gesundheit. But yours is close enough Sam, and bless you is also gesundheit."

"Let's sit in the lounge. More comfortable than this." He patted the seat of the wooden kitchen chairs.

"Can we listen to some music?" Karsten said to Sam as he massaged his temples.

"Of course. Headache?"

He nodded. "Someone is clearing a mine field inside my head."

Sam made a gesture of zipping his mouth, picked up the iPod, selected an album he knew Karsten liked, pressed play, reduced the volume, and sat opposite him in an easy chair.

As the music washed over them, Karsten smiled at the familiar words and music.

*'How fickle my heart and how woozy my eyes*

*I struggle to find any truth in your lies*

*And now my heart stumbles on things I don't know*

*My weakness I feel I must finally show'*

"Do you like Mumford and Son, Sam?"

"I only started listening to them after you told me about them. I think they're brilliant."

The song played on until it came to the last verse.

*'Awake my soul*

*Awake my soul*

*Awake my soul*

*For you were made to meet your maker*

*You were made to meet your maker'*

"I have all their albums, Sam. I will save them to a memory stick for you." He looked up at him.

Sam's eyes were wide open and fixed on something behind Karsten. He started to turn his head to look, but Sam shook his head without taking his gaze from whatever it was his eyes were fixed on.

"*Don't move,*" Sam whispered.

Karsten's frown grew deeper and deeper. He shrugged, and raised the palms of his hands to the ceiling, seeking an answer.

Like Dracula rising from the tomb, Sam slowly and deliberately stood up, and gestured for Karsten to get up and walk across to him. As Karsten reached him, he spoke softly in his ear. "Turn around slowly, but for God's sake don't shout or make any sounds."

Karsten glanced at Sam, his eyes screaming 'why', but as told, he slowly turned, and immediately understood the reason for Sam's instructions.

Standing a few feet behind the sofa was what looked like a semi-inflated balloon in the shape of a Second World War German officer. Karsten and Sam's need for flight was being overwhelmed by their need to see what would happen in front of them. More 'gas' was pumped into the balloon, until it stood solid, erect, with its head bowed. What froze Karsten's blood, and was pressing hard on his flight button, was the gleaming silver Death's Head emblem on the peaked cap.

"Schutz-Staffel," Karsten said loudly. "SS-Totenkopfverbände."

Sam frowned.

"Nazi SS Death's Head unit. The worst of the worst. They ran the death camps. They made certain the requirements of the 'Final Solution' were fulfilled. They were the embodiment of evil."

Sam froze.

The SS officer gradually lifted his head until the face was completely visible to Karsten and Sam.

"FRANKS!!" Karsten stared with hatred at the face. "Even death hasn't changed you."

Franks leered at Karsten and undiluted hatred radiated from his eyes. "Der Teufel hat mich zurück geschickt. *(The devil has sent me back.)*" He raised a crooked index finger, and pointed it directly at Karsten. "WO IST DER ANDERE? *(Where is the other?)*" He screamed. "DER JUDE, DER MICH TöTEN! *(The Jew who kill me!)*" The fetid stench of his breath filled the air.

"Nicht hier. *(Not here.)*" Karsten spat back at Franks.

Franks bent his head back through ninety degrees, until his neck cracked like dry winter twigs underfoot. He sniffed the air, like a wolf hunting its prey. "Der Gestank der Juden ist unverkennbar. *(The stench of the Jews is unmistakable.)*" Franks snarled at Karsten.

Karsten maintained his granite expression. "Nicht hier. *(Not here.)*"

Franks smirked, licked his lips, spat a glob of green mucus on the floor, and gestured at Sam with his finger, to come closer. "Ich werde dich bringen. *(I'm going to take you.)* Sie kommen zurück mit mir, und *ich* wird aus der Hölle entkommen. *(You come back with me, and I will escape from Hell.)*" "Eine Seele für eine Seele. *(A soul for a soul.)*"

"NEIN!" Karsten screamed at him. "NEIN! Nehmen Sie niemand. *(Take nobody.)*"

# Chapter Hundred-Thirteen

Gloria, Ivor, Rebecca, Jane, and Adam, were in the kitchen when they heard the shouting coming from the lounge.

Guillaume, Ralph, and Klaus arrived back at around nine, to see their spirit-helpers racing into the lounge.

"They are in a hurry," Klaus said, his mood mellowed by some very good food, conversation, wine, and brandy.

The three friends smiled inanely at each other, until an unearthly scream echoed around the hall. "DER JUDE! JETZT! *(THE JEW! NOW!)*"

"Scheiße! Was war das? *(Shit! What was that?)*"

Guillaume's mood was instantly transformed. "I will never forget that voice," he said calmly, but with an underlying deep hatred. "It is the SS guard from the camp. Franks."

Ralph looked confused. "The camp?"

"Auschwitz-Birkenau."

Ralph had to sit down on a hall chair, or fall down. "Auschwitz? But how?"

"A story I will tell you at another time. I believe we are required in the lounge." Guillaume ran down the hall and into the lounge. As he ran into the room, he saw the apparition and his worst fears were confirmed. "Franks. It is no wonder you are a demon. You will fit in well with the others of your kind in Hell."

"I am called Afrit, and I wear the shell of the one you call Franks." It sucked in air, sounding like Darth Vader with emphysema. "I seek retribution, Jew." Vader breathed again. "And I am here to take you back to Hell."

Ralph and Klaus ran into the back of Guillaume, and fell into a tangled heap on the floor. Sam ran forward and helped them up. For the first time, Ralph and Klaus saw the demon Afrit.

"You are shitting me! What in the name of Uncle Sam is that?" Ralph exclaimed. "Shit, it looks like…"

"It is a demon." Guillaume finished his sentence. "And to be precise, it is a demon called Afrit. It is inside the shell of Unteroffizier Bruno Franks. The sadistic animal who made my life a hell, and cold-bloodily tortured and killed thousands of other Jews at Auschwitz. I killed him when Karsten brought me back, and now it wants revenge."

Klaus was speechless.

Guillaume calmly continued. "'You have heard that it was said, 'Eye for eye, and tooth for tooth. But I tell you, do not resist an evil person. If anyone slaps you on the right cheek, turn to them the other cheek also. Matthew 5:38-48.'"

"You are going to turn the other cheek?" Ralph said with incredulity.

Guillaume glanced across at him and smiled. "I believe you say, hell no."

Ralph patted him on the shoulder, but had no idea how to stop this evil in their midst.

Ivor had been calmly taking everything in and assessing the options.

Gloria looked at him and knew what he was thinking. *"No,"* she whispered.

Ivor turned his face towards her and smiled. "I will never leave you again." He kissed her on the cheek. "Believe me, and hold onto that thought. I *will* be back."

Gloria paled. "Back? But back from where?"

Ivor kissed her again. "I *will* be back. Keep thinking that. I'll need your love to help me back."

Gloria tried to speak, but Ivor pressed his finger to her lips, and mouthed three words, *"I love you."*

"Now then, you twisted bastard," Ivor said loudly and confidently as he walked through Sam and Guillaume. "We seem to have a problem." He walked to within three feet of the Afrit.

Elizabeth ran into the kitchen and Googled Afrit on her iPad. A few minutes later, she rushed into the lounge and spoke softly to Klaus,

Guillaume, Sam, and Ralph. "This Afrit, is the ghost of the victim of a murder. It returns from the dead to take revenge on the murderer. In early folklore, the Afrit was said to be formed from the blood of the murder victim. These creatures were reported to be able to take the form of the murder victim."

"Franks," Guillaume said quietly. "Is there anything we can do?"

"This is, well it's just stories and legend. But," she said and referred back to her iPad, "it says here that driving an unused, new nail into the blood of the murder victim was supposed to stop their formation." She shrugged. "It's got to be worth trying. But where are we going to find any of Franks's blood?

Guillaume glowered. "When I killed him, his concentrated corruption percolated into my spirit. When I returned, the canker seeped onto my pyjamas and bedding."

"Where are they?" Elizabeth asked.

"JUDEN!" The Afrit roared. "JUDEN! ICH BIN IMMER NOCH HIER! *(JEW! JEW! I AM STILL HERE!)*"

Guillaume looked directly at the Afrit, but spoke over his shoulder to Elizabeth. "In my room, under the bed. They're in a red sports bag."

Ralph, Klaus, Sam, and Elizabeth quietly backed out of the room.

*"You two get the sports bag, and bring it to the kitchen. Sam, you go to the garden shed, and get an old ..."* Elizabeth whispered.

"New." Ralph quickly corrected her. *"Remember. You said they had to be new."*

*"New nails and a new hammer."* Sam repeated and ran into the garden.

Ivor was still trying to distract the Afrit's attention away from Guillaume, but no matter what he did, its eyes remained locked on Guillaume.

# Chapter Hundred-Fourteen

Still not understanding what had happened to Morris in the interview-room, Charlie made his way home from the station. He intended to spend as much time as he could with his mum, and hadn't as yet given up on using the Lazarus Pool to help her. He walked across the poorly lit car park, fumbled for his keys, and was about to climb into his car, when Morris pulled up and parked nearby. Charlie decided that showing a degree of concern for his new boss should win some 'brownie points,' and he walked over.

"OK boss?" Charlie called across the car park.

Morris, still bewildered by recent events at High Wood, looked up and forced a smile. "Charlie. See you in the morning." The reply was offhand and Morris disappeared into the station.

*"Mind on other things,"* Charlie thought. *"Like a serious bollocking from the DI."*

As he got closer to home, his skin began to tingle like a nettle rash. He parked his car alongside the house at around eight, and by then the tingling had increased to something like a severe sunburn. As he walked in through the back door, the reason for his discomfort became clear. Sitting with Grandma Emma at the kitchen table was Peter Wallins.

"Hello Charlie. Good to see you again, and in much better circumstances," Peter said with an enormous smile. "Your gran and I have been catching up." His expression softened. "So sorry to hear about your mum."

"Yeah, thanks." He switched his gaze to his grandma. The fact that he was talking with two spirits who'd been lovers during the Second World War, one of whom had time travelled with him, didn't faze him. "Where's mum?"

"In bed, dear." She smiled. "Thanks for helping to get us back together."

"That's alright, Gran. Does this mean you can move on?" Charlie asked.

Emma smiled at Peter and nodded. "I've got nothing keeping me here anymore, and I need to be waiting on the other side for your mum."

Charlie swallowed hard, pressed his nails into the palms of his hand, sighed deeply, held back his tears, and chewed his bottom lip. Even he was softened by Emma's expression.

"Nice to see you so happy, gran." He turned and made his way to his mum's bedroom where she was in a deep, drug-induced sleep. *"Whatever she says,"* he thought, *"I've got to try it. I'm not losing her without putting up a fight."* He couldn't accept that at any given point in someone's life, death could appear more attractive than living. That it was a price worth paying to end suffering, to end loneliness, and a chance of reunion with lost loved ones. He could only see a desperate future. The loss of his dearest friend and companion, emotional and physical pain, unforgiving emptiness, unyielding never-ending sorrow, and an unquenchable desire to bring them back, or join them. His mind couldn't accept this, and the draw of the Lazarus Pool was too much for him. As quietly as he could, without disturbing the reunited couple, he pushed Molly's wheelchair close to the bed, gently pulled back the sheets, and lifted her from the bed. He gasped and almost dropped her as he felt her child-like lightness. She couldn't have weighed more than five stones. Tears streamed down his cheeks, but he held his soft grip on his still sleeping mum, put her in the wheelchair, wrapped a couple of blankets around her, and wheeled her out of the house to his car. Twenty minutes later, he was parked outside Takanun, with Molly strapped in the front passenger seat, still sound asleep. He got out of the car, took the wheelchair out of the boot, lifted the feather-light sleeping Molly out of the front passenger seat, placed her gently in the chair, and wheeled her up to the front door. Charlie knocked, time passed, and eventually Marie opened the door.

Her expression said everything. *"What the hell are you doing here?"* She looked at Molly. "You haven't drugged her, have you? My God Charlie, what did I say to you? You can't do this. I won't let you."

"I have to." He frowned and narrowed his eyes. "It was OK for your mum and dad. So what's the difference?"

Marie ignored his comment. "What did your mother say about it?"

His eyes gave him away. "She said that …"

"You weren't to take her anywhere near it. That's what she said, wasn't it?"

He looked down at the floor and mumbled something.

"What?"

"She said I wasn't to do it."

"But you're still here. Despite everything we told you."

He nodded, still staring at the floor like a golfer found replacing a lost ball with new.

Marie stood back, holding the door open. "Come in. It's freezing out there."

Charlie tipped the chair back and pushed it into the hall. "Thanks."

"Right, let's get your mum onto the sofa."

Ten minutes later, after several cups of strong tea, two rounds of toast and honey, and a cuddle from Marie, Charlie was seeing things in sharper focus.

"So the effect only works if you stay in the house?" he said to Marie as he sat in a chair close to Molly.

Marie nodded. "It weakens when you move away from the house, and eventually the effect's lost altogether." She sat on his lap and kissed him on the cheek. "It would never have worked. Sometimes there are things which are, just bloody well not meant to be."

Charlie looked at Molly through his tears and buried his head in Marie's shoulder. "I just don't want her to go."

"But she probably does?"

He nodded. "She said so. She's worn out and in constant pain. She just wants peace."

"Death's not the final chapter Charlie. You and I know this, and that must give you some degree of comfort. It's just a door to the next life, the next reality. A reality which we will share with those who've gone before us."

Molly's eyes flickered open. "I don't want to leave you. But I want to leave peacefully, not suffering like this. I don't want you remembering me like this. This echo of who I was. This body's not what I remember in my head, and not what I want to be your last memory of me."

"But Mum ..." Charlie was finding words almost impossible through chest-heaving sobs.

"Let me go, son."

He sat up and dropped onto his knees close to Molly. Words simply wouldn't form in his throat, and his vision was blurred by his tears and swollen eyes.

"Let her go, Charlie." Marie was sat next to him, stroking his hair. "Let her go with your blessing."

Molly coughed weakly.

"While there's still time, Charlie." Marie gently urged him.

Charlie knelt up, leaned forward, kissed Molly tenderly on the forehead, pushed a piece of hair from across her eyes, held her close, and closed his eyes.

Marie's inner strength finally collapsed, and she sat back on the floor in an inconsolable, sobbing heap.

Charlie held Molly's hand, and felt her spirit leaving her, as a soothing feeling of euphoria, flowed through him. As suddenly as it had come, it was gone, replaced by dysphoria, misery, fear, and anxiety.

"Come and sit over here, Charlie. She's at peace now." Robert and Patricia had been silently watching the grief-stricken events from the doorway.

"I'm not leav ... her. I'm ... sta ...ing with ... her."

"Of course. You must stay. But sit here." They gently lifted him up and sat him on the sofa. "Pat, will you get a drink from the cabinet?"

She nodded, and Robert helped Marie up and onto a chair close to Charlie. Pat poured out four large ten-year-old malts and silently handed them out.

Charlie wasn't a whiskey drinker, but the smooth warmth of the amber liquid in his throat and gullet was comforting. He sat back on the sofa and drained the last few drops.

"Another?" Pat asked softly.

Charlie nodded and managed to force a weak smile, which broadened as he looked from the still body of Molly, to the fireplace where she was standing with grandma Emma, smiling angelically at him.

*"Everything's fine, darling. I've never felt so at peace."* Molly's mind spoke only to Charlie. *"Don't mourn me, remember only the best of times. There is so much joy in remembrance."*

*"How do I fill this hole?"* He held his hand against his heart. *"It feels bottomless."*

*"It will never fill, but it isn't bottomless."*

*"Stay."*

*"I can't, and this will sound cruel, but I don't want to. There are so many friends and family waiting for me."*

Charlie finally began to accept this was only an interlude, a break in transmission, and normal service would be resumed, at some, as yet undetermined time in the future.

Mother and son smiled at each other, and like Chinese lanterns, Molly and Emma glided slowly up to the ceiling, joined together in a scintillating eye of heaven, and slowly melted away like snow crystals under a warm winter sun.

# Chapter Hundred-Fifteen

Klaus and Ralph quickly found the red sports bag under Guillaume's bed, glanced inside it, nodded to each other, zipped up the bag, ran down the stairs, peered cautiously into the lounge, where the stand-off between Ivor and the Afrit hadn't changed, and tip-toed to the kitchen.

Elizabeth was stood with Sam, leaning on the kitchen table, a hammer and a clear-plastic packet of new nails on it. "Did you get it?" she asked in a panic.

Ralph held up the bag. "Have you got any rubber gloves?"

"Yes, of course." She turned and started fishing around in a cupboard under the sink, looking for an old pair of Marigolds. After a minute or so, she stood up, waving a pink pair in the air.

Ralph sniffed, but smiled. "They'll have to do." He unzipped the bag and put everything on the table.

"Looks like the sheet's our best bet?" Klaus suggested uncertainly.

"I'd cover all bases and drive nails into everything," Ralph suggested.

Sam nodded in agreement, laid out the sheet, picked up a hammer and four nails, and drove them through it into the kitchen table.

"Always claim for a new one," Ralph said helpfully.

The Afrit winced, and moved forward through Ivor, its snake-eyes fixed on Guillaume. It raised a crooked finger, which was now oozing blood from its nails, and croaked at Guillaume. "Jude Schmutz. *(Jew dirt.)* Scheiß auf eure Familien. *(Fuck your families.)* Der Teufel schreit für Sie. *(The Devil screams for you.)*"

*"Pray God it works,"* Guillaume thought in ever increasing fear.

Sam hammered four nails into a pillowcase.

The Afrit grimaced and glared towards the kitchen.

Guillaume saw the change, and spoke to the Afrit. "Deutscher Abschaum. *(German scum.)* Deutschland züchtet Bastarde. *(Germany breeds bastards.)*"

From its mouth, the Afrit flashed a stream of energy at Guillaume, which knocked him onto his back, and it continued on its unrelenting way to find the source of its torment.

Sam hammered more nails into the pillowcase and sheet.

The Afrit arched its back, and an agonised roar like a tiger caught in a poacher's trap, shrieked through the house.

Elizabeth glanced into the hall. "It's coming, but it's wounded. Have you got anything left?"

The three men in the kitchen glanced briefly at each other, and stared worryingly at the two remaining items on the kitchen table.

Elizabeth ran her fingers through her hair. "Ah."

A stench like an execrable synthesis of gangrenous flesh, rotten fish, raw sewage, vomit, and a dog fart, slithered into the kitchen, closely followed by the Afrit, which was badly hurt. And like any wounded beast, it was now at its most dangerous.

"SAM! HAMMER!" Klaus screamed.

Sam looked down at the pyjamas on the table, and frowned. *"Dear God, please be enough."*

The Afrit fixed its malignant gaze on Sam, the hammer, and the nails.

Sam picked up a nail, and a stream of energy smashed into the table, sending the nails spinning across the kitchen floor. "SHIT!" Sam shouted. "FOR CHRIST'S SAKE SOMEONE GET ME SOME NAILS!" He glanced at the Afrit, picked up the pyjamas, and with the last nail gripped tightly between his teeth, he sprinted into the garden.

"KOMM ZURüCK! *(Come back!)* JUDE LIEBHABER! *(Jew lovers!)*" It moved like a slug on steroids across the kitchen floor, knocking aside Klaus and Ralph, leaving a trail of slime across the tiles.

Sam sprinted into the garden, and in the dark, he didn't see the rake. It flew up, hitting him hard in the face, and breaking two teeth. By the time he reached the garden shed, his dictionary of cursing was exhausted.

In the kitchen, Elizabeth flicked the switch for the outside lights, and the garden was flooded with stark white light.

As Sam reached the garden shed, he glanced over his shoulder, and shielded his eyes against the glare of the two eighty watt LED floodlit security lights. As his eyes became accustomed to the glare, he couldn't look away from the horror which confronted him.

The Afrit's shell was covered in cracks like the mud at the bottom of a dried-out Serengeti water hole. Through the growing cracks, flickering flames the colour of lava, licked at the Afrit's rapidly disintegrating shell.

Sam was paralysed by fear.

"SAM!" Elizabeth screamed from the relative safety of the kitchen door. "HAMMER AND NAILS!"

He nodded his head, forced his eyes away from the horror which was now close behind him, and took a firm hold of the door handle of the shed.

The Afrit's 'shell' completely fragmented and fell into a smoking heap around the hooved feet of what Sam could only imagine was a powerful, winged demon.

He turned the door handle of the shed and pushed against the warped wooden frame which resisted his attempts to open it. The unseen energy stream which smashed into Sam's back, easily overcame the resistance and sent him and the door hurtling to the back of the shed.

Elizabeth screamed and covered her eyes.

Klaus tried to dash out of the kitchen, but Ralph grabbed his arm. "There's nothing we can do now. It's up to Sam."

Inside the shed, Sam tried to push away the splintered door, tools, paint tins, broken shelves, and old newspapers which covered him. He caught his breath as he felt the pyjamas in his left hand. The garden floodlights created a narrow shaft of light across the shed floor. Sam panicked. There was no sign of the hammer, or nails. After a few seconds he got to his knees and scrabbled through the debris. There were tools everywhere, but no hammer. A splinter dug deep under the nail on his right thumb, and he let out a scream which the Afrit would have been proud of. He stood up, grimaced, peered out of the small shed window, and for the first time saw the true appearance of the Afrit. *"Oh bollocks!"* he thought, crouched down, searched desperately amongst the shattered remains of the shed, cut the palm of his hand on a piece of broken plastic pot, and squealed as a tin tack dug deep into his knee. As his levels of panic reached the stratosphere, under a used paint tin he found a crowbar. *"That'll do as a hammer."* Another stream of energy hit the side of the shed, showering him in jagged wood splinters and shards of window glass. He winced as two shards pierced the skin on his back. *"Nails, Sam. Come on."* He looked around him, saw that a large splinter had upset a rusty sweet tin, and poking out from under it, was a pack of new nails. He ripped it open, and tipped four into the palm of his hand.

*"Sure they're not used?"*

*"Jesus Christ! Not now. Piss off. They're bloody new!"*

*"Important question, Sam. Can't get this one wrong."*

Sam did his best to ignore him, laid a pyjama top on what remained of the shed floor, and drove three new nails into it.

The Afrit fell to its knees and uttered a wail more terrifying than the last.

Elizabeth's hands were clasped in front of her face. "Come on, Sam. One more. It's hurt."

Inexorably, the Afrit moved the few remaining yards to the shed.

Sam knew the end was close as the shed was illuminated by a blood-red glow.

*"DON'T LOOK BACK, JUST HIT THAT BLOODY NAIL!"* his other-half screamed.

Sam had no other thought in his mind. He laid the pyjama trousers on the shed floor, placed a new nail on it, raised the crowbar, and froze.

Behind him, the Afrit started reciting what sounded like a curse. "'Thou who hath shunned me, thou who hath pained me, may your soul burn to fiery flames and ash. I hereby banish you to the flames of Hell forever.'"

*"SAM!"* his other-half screamed.

He glanced over his shoulder into the burning eyes of the Afrit, and screamed, "GO TO HELL!" He drove his last nail into the pyjama trousers, and waited for either eternal damnation or salvation.

Ralph pointed at the Afrit. "Look. It's hurt."

Klaus moved closer to him, ground his teeth, rhythmically tapped his thighs with his fists, rocked back and forth on his heels, blew out loudly, sucked his teeth, and swallowed hard.

The Afrit imperceptibly staggered, its burning, black, leathery wings twitched, the flames engulfing it flickered, and slowly it dropped to its knees. What looked like black treacle, started to bubble up from the soil under its clawed feet. Steam billowed into the air as the 'treacle' met the furnace-like heat of the Afrit. It looked down at the growing pool as it began to sink, and let loose a howl of fear and agony. It sank deeper and deeper into the 'treacle' until its flaming body was extinguished. It reared up into the air, revealing a blackened, charred scaly body, and fell back into the pool. As its head began to disappear beneath the boiling surface of the pool, it screamed out a final curse. "'THOU WHO HATH SHUNNED ME, THOU WHO HATH PAINED ME MAY YOU BURN ...'" The final words of the curse were lost in a seething cloud of steam.

An uneasy silence fell over everyone, their minds trying to convince them that the beast would suddenly reappear from the pool, reinvigorated and ready for revenge. But after a couple of minutes of silent tension, there was a great deal of deep breathing and sighs, until the remainder of the shed collapsed in on itself.

"SHIT!" Jane shouted.

"SCOPARE! *(FUCK!)*" Alfredo bawled.

"Good heavens," Matt said as he joined everyone in the garden. "Bit of a shock that." He turned to Mark. "You alright, brother?"

"Absolutely ticket-y-boo."

"SAM!" Elizabeth screamed, bursting into a flood of tears, and burying her face in her hands.

Alfredo gripped her arm. "Look."

From behind a pile of smoking, splintered wood, Sam emerged limping badly, but smiling like a possum eating peach seeds.

# Chapter Hundred-Sixteen

Charlie and Marie were stood outside the front door of Takanun getting some fresh air.

"You OK?" she asked tenderly.

He managed a half smile. "Not as bad as I thought I'd be." He scratched his nose. "But I'm sure reality will soon kick in."

Marie kissed him on the cheek. "It was a beautiful goodbye."

"Yes. But still a goodbye," Charlie said wistfully.

"I've been saying goodbye for the last five years," Marie said soulfully. "The dementia dissects them, and takes them away from you piece by little piece." She turned and looked back at the house. "And then one day there's nothing left but an empty shell of someone you loved. I think I'd prefer your goodbye Charlie. You still knew each other at the end."

He put his arm around her, pulled her close, and kissed her softly on the forehead. "We'll never leave each other."

The unearthly wail from the direction of High Wood, brought an end to their tête-à-tête.

"What in the name of everything that's holy was that?" Robert exclaimed as he trotted out of the front door. "It sounded like it came from High Wood?" He glanced at Marie and Charlie. "You two alright?"

Charlie did his best to smile and took a deep breath, but words wouldn't come.

Robert put his arm around his shoulders. "Pointless me using all the usual platitudes, my boy. It hurts and no amount of words will help. But believe me when I say that you can count on our support for anything you need."

A second wail of even greater volume and malevolence cut through the air like a machete.

The three glanced at each other, nodded, and ran for High Wood. The scene which greeted them was one of total mayhem. Sam was lying on his front wincing, as Elizabeth appeared to be pulling shards of glass out of his back, the garden shed looked like the smouldering remains of a giant game of Jenga, like a gently simmering casserole, a previously non-existent garden pool now sat in the middle of the lawn, the whole garden seemed to have been scorched by an industrial flamethrower and further ruined by a series of what looked like deep hoof prints. Everyone else was either helping Elizabeth, staring at the pool and shed, or looking shell-shocked.

Marie found Klaus and tapped him on the shoulder. "Was ist passiert? *(What happened?)*"

He shrugged, shook his head, pulled at his ear lobe, looked back at what remained of the garden, shook his head again, and gestured for her to follow him into the relative calm of the house. "In all the years I have been involved with Papaver Rhoeas, I have never experienced anything like that."

"Was?"

"Ein Dämon."

"Demon!" Marie was temporarily lost for words.

Klaus nodded. "It could have been nothing else." Before Klaus was able to say anything further, the calm of the kitchen was shattered by the unmistakable sound of fire engine sirens.

"Someone's called the emergency services!" Marie said with alarm. "How the hell do we explain that?" She pointed out of the kitchen window at the bomb site which had once been the garden.

The hammering on the front door indicated the fire service had arrived and were eager to help.

"I'll let them in before they decide to batter down the front door," Marie called over her shoulder as she ran down the hall. "Hi." She blushed and tried to look as if she'd made a terribly embarrassing mistake. "Someone saw the flames? We had a bit of a problem with the barbecue. Couldn't get the charcoal to light, so I thought some paint brush cleaner might help. Made quite a show and didn't leave very much of the barbecue or the garden shed. I was just getting ready to cook the burgers in the kitchen. Bit embarrassing, really."

The fire officer remained perfectly calm, and smiled understandingly. "Get these quite frequently, madam. Dangerous things barbecues. I'd like to take a look if I could. Just to make sure everything's under control and there are no remaining risks of fire. I will have to put a report in, so I need to take a look."

Marie understood, that saying no was not an option and gestured for him to come in.

The fire officer turned to the rest of his crew and told them to stand down.

Marie tried to gain a little time. "Would they like some coffee or tea?"

"No thanks, madam. They live on the stuff back at the station. If I could take a look?"

She turned and walked down the hall, and the fire officer followed.

Klaus and the others were desperately trying to make the garden look a little less like a bomb site when Marie emerged from the kitchen with the fire officer in close in tow.

"Quite a mess." He scanned the garden, shed, and people. "Miracle no-one was seriously hurt."

*"You have no idea,"* Sam thought, sitting gingerly forward on the garden bench, doing his best not to grimace in pain.

*"You jammy bastard. I think you might have got away with it?"* His personal life advisor said supportively.

*"Not yet I haven't."*

*"Yeah, 'cause he looks like someone who takes a really, really, close look at things."*

*"Always ready to light up the dark times with a little ray of sunshine."*

*"That's me. Little Johnny Sunbeam."*

"I'll just take a look around," the fire officer said with disbelief in his eyes. He walked around the garden, speaking to everyone, shaking his head, taking photos, picking things up, shaking his head again, looking back at Marie, pursing his lips, and after about twenty minutes, he came back to the kitchen. "And all of that…" He nodded back to the garden. "You say all of that," he said and nodded again at the garden, "is because of a barbecue?"

Marie nodded.

"Odd that. Only you see, I can't seem to find the remains of a barbecue?"

Marie stared wide-eyed at Klaus, Guillaume, and Ralph for help.

"Wasn't very much left to see." Ralph lied effectively. "So I threw all the charred bits away."

*"Please don't ask to take a look."* Marie silently prayed.

The fire officer looked back at the garden and smiled at Ralph. "Well, you all seem to be OK. No-one hurt?"

A group head shake answered his question.

He sucked his teeth, looked at his note book, glanced again at the garden, shook his head, and finally offered his hand to Ralph and Marie. "As long as everyone's OK, and there doesn't appear to be any on-going risk of fire, I'll leave you in peace. I'll have to file a report in the event you put in an insurance claim for the damage. You'll need it."

"Thank you for coming, and I'm so sorry it was a waste of time," Marie said, still showing as much contrition as she could.

"Never a waste of time, madam. Our first concern is always to ensure everyone is OK."

Marie accompanied the fire officer to the front door and waved him off.

"Think we got away with it?" Alfredo said unconvincingly.

The silence gave him his answer.

# Chapter Hundred-Seventeen

Everyone assembled in the lounge at Takanun and spread themselves out in front of the four large flat screen TVs.

Bill sat behind a table covered in laptops and what looked to Sam like a mixing desk. "OK Klaus."

He nodded. "Ja."

"OK. I'm going to patch everyone in, and to avoid people talking over each other, I'd suggest Guillaume chairs the session."

There were no dissenting voices.

An image with HD clarity appeared on TV #1. "Hi." Patrice Beaudet smiled down at them. "Good to see everyone."

"I'll introduce everyone in a few minutes, Patrice."

"OK."

Gilles Vermeulen, appeared next, followed by George Mainard and Charles Henencourt.

After introductions, a general catch-up, and debate over what needed to be discussed in the allotted time. The Astrea settled on five subjects; Blue Lights, Lazarus Pool, Takanun, Spirit Walkers, and WW1 lost souls.

After an hour of exhaustive discussion, Guillaume referred to his notes and summarised the agreed actions to the group. "The overall situation isn't worsening, and the support we have been receiving is improving things. Bill has agreed to stay in the UK for a further month to manage the smooth introduction of the 35mm film analysis, and Sam and Alfredo will support him. After this, he will spend another month with yourselves to introduce the programme to all other countries." Guillaume looked at the screens and confirmed their agreement. "Excellent. Now with regard to the rather more difficult subject of the Lazarus Pool." He turned to Charlie and smiled. "Is everyone happy with the name? It seems to have become our name of choice."

There were no dissenting voices.

"Thank you. The Lazarus Pool it is then." Guillaume breathed deeply. "However, it is clear that a great deal of further work is required before we can make any solid decisions about what we do with this phenomenon. Consequently, we will reconvene in two weeks to review what has been discovered. Remember, it is *vital* that this remains confidential."

There were no dissenting voices.

Guillaume referred to his extensive notes. "Next. Takanun will become our centre for assisting Blue Lights. This will be supported by Marie, Robert, Patricia, and Bill's face recognition algorithm."

There were no dissenting voices.

"Penultimately, Spirit Walkers. We need to create a list of all known and potential Spirit Walkers. This programme will be headed up by Klaus, and supported by Charlie and Karsten.

There were no dissenting voices.

Finally, and the easiest subject to deal with, is the support of the lost souls of WW1. Elizabeth will control the on-going programme in the UK, with the support of all our spirit friends, and all other programmes will continue." He paused and drank the remains of his water. "We need to determine how our new friends the Stroudle brothers will assist us."

"We must understand how they became so changed, and how they lost their abilities," Gilles said with a deep frown. "This could be a blessing or a curse."

"Your point is well made, and will be an important part of the analysis of the Lazarus Pool." Guillaume scanned the faces on the screens. "Does anyone have any further points to make before I close the meeting?"

Patrice raised a hand. "I'd like to say that I'm glad to see Guillaume and Charlie looking so well after their 'adventures'. Au revoir tout le monde et bonne chance à nous tous. *(Goodbye everyone and good luck to us all.)*"

"Remain focused on supporting the lost souls of World War One, maintain the on-going work with our new volunteers, and keep in touch. I will circulate notes from today, and I look forward to speaking to you all again in two weeks." Guillaume drew the meeting to a close.

# Chapter Hundred-Eighteen

Not much was said over breakfast at High Wood, as the after effects of the Afrit were still being felt by everyone. Everyone apart from the brothers.

"And you'd like us to live here, sorry next door, become part of a team, *and* be paid?" Matt said with a degree of disbelief.

"That's it in a nutshell," Ralph replied.

"But what do *we* bring to the party?" Mark asked.

"Two enormous intellects." Ralph felt that a little ego massage wouldn't do any harm.

The brothers looked at each other and smiled.

"That is true. I'm sure we'll be able to contribute once we understand what we're contributing to," Matt said positively.

"Start today. All the teams will be meeting this morning at ten to decide how to move forward." He looked at his watch. "You've still got half an hour."

"Well it was well said that 'Only those who dare to fail greatly can ever achieve greatly.'"

Ralph smiled. "Robert F. Kennedy."

"Bravo, Ralph," Matt said as he clapped. "Bravo indeed. How about, 'Only those who attempt the absurd can achieve the impossible.'"

Ralph frowned, sighed, and smirked. "Albert Einstein, I believe."

Mark joined the applause, and everyone else at the kitchen table turned and looked at this early morning edition of 'Quote Unquote'.

"OK," Ralph said feeling invigorated by these two unique individuals. "How about this. 'If you want to make God laugh, tell him about your plans.'"

"Oh, you will have to try a lot harder than that, Ralph. It is of course Woody Allen."

"OK, let's call it a draw. I've got to get some things before we start the meetings." Ralph turned and walked to the hall. "Good to have you both on-board," he called over his shoulder.

"nuqneH," Matt called after him.

Ralph reappeared in the doorway with an enormous frown and a wide smile. "And that is?"

"Klingon. We thank you."

Ralph shook his head, pulled a hanky from his trouser pocket, and waved it. "I surrender." He grinned at the brothers, shook his head, and left.

Bill, Sam, and Alfredo strolled next door and made their way to the loft which they'd christened 'The Roxy'.

"I've arranged for fifty cans from storage to be delivered this morning," Sam said. "We can find out what they contain and prioritise them? Or do you want to digitally remaster everything first, Bill?"

Bill mmm'd. "Until they arrive, I think we should make a start on working with what we have." Bill picked up his iPad and gave it to Alfredo. "If you don't have any other suggestions, can you start taking photos of all the cans, and I'll start on this programme ranking World War Two battles, by allied casualties, and country. Once I've entered the images into the system, we can prioritise them. At least that'll give us a starting position. I'll run the face recognition programme over the digitised films, identify faceless soldiers, sort them by country, and mail the files to them for action." He checked with Alfredo and Sam. "OK with that?"

They looked at each other, nodded, and made their way to the racks.

Elizabeth stayed in the kitchen with Gloria, Ivor, Rebecca, Adam, Jane, and Captain Forster.

"Bit mob-handed?" Jane said as she tilted her head to one side.

Elizabeth looked around at the assembled spirits. "Mmmm? Probably right. What do you think?"

"Captain Forster has to stay."

Elizabeth nodded.

"Adam's known by the Tommies."

"Yes."

"We'll need someone to provide refreshments." Jane looked at Rebecca and smiled. "OK?"

Rebecca smiled. "Of course."

"That leaves, Gloria, Ivor, and myself. What do you think?" Jane asked Elizabeth.

"Gloria and Ivor could work with Marie on the Lazarus Pool?"

"And me?" Jane said with a raised eyebrow.

"Sam, Bill and Alfredo?"

Jane chuckled. "Putting the old team back together?"

Elizabeth nodded.

"Sounds like you've got a plan," Klaus said from the kitchen door. "Makes sense to spread our resources a little more evenly." He walked in and sat next to Elizabeth. "I'd like to spend some time with you. It would comfort me to see that our main objective is still achieving success."

"Delighted to have you," Elizabeth said as she kissed him on the cheek.

In the cellar at Takanun, Marie was staring at the Lazarus Pool, when Charlie jumped up and grabbed her from behind.

"You stupid sod!" She span around and punched him in the chest. "You scared the living daylights out of me."

Charlie stepped back and blushed. "Sorry. Stupid thing to do."

"Stupid? You …" Marie's face softened. "What are you doing here? I thought you were part of the Spirit Walkers?"

"I am. Klaus has a few things to do and Karsten's having a rest. He still hasn't recovered fully from his 'trip'." He pulled her to him and kissed her softly on the lips. "So I thought I'd come over, and see if I could help."

"See if you could scare the pants off me."

"Well, if it had that effect …"

She pushed him away and wagged her finger at him. "It'll take more than that to get mine off."

Charlie smiled and looked back at the Lazarus Pool. "Seems bigger?"

Marie followed his eyes and frowned.

"Bloody odd, isn't it?" He took a few steps closer to the Lazarus Pool and Marie grabbed his arm.

"Near enough."

Charlie held out his hands towards it. "I'm sure it's hotter than it was."

Marie linked arms with him, and looked around the cellar at the light show. Stars of every shade of blue were rebounding off the walls, colliding with each other, and ricocheting off at crazy angles, forming mini constellations. Constantly, they left and rejoined the Lazarus Pool, occasionally hovering close to the ceiling, and then like star shells, bursting into myriads of tiny azure shards.

"How the hell do we find out what makes this thing so damn special?" Sam asked Marie.

"I've contacts in the fields of maths and astro-physics who I'm sure would love to help."

Marie and Sam span around. Robert was stood with his hands on his hips with a broad smile on his face. "Don't forget, I was a professor of mathematics at the university."

"Could you make some calls, Dad?" Marie said with a smile which would have taken pride of place in an exhibition of 'The Greatest Smiles of the World'.

"Of course, darling. Give me a couple of hours. Explaining this," he said and nodded at the Lazarus Pool, "could take a little time."

"Well, give it your best shot," Matt said as he and Mark arrived. "A little reading and research, and I'm sure we'll have a rough hypothesis pulled together in no time at all."

"Stay close to the houses." Marie reminded them. "Don't go visiting any libraries or museums. Why don't you go with Dad? He's got a room full of stuff which you'd love."

"I think we now understand the importance of these properties to our mental well-being," Mark replied.

"Follow me," Robert said with enthusiasm, and deep in conversation, the three men started up the cellar steps.

"While Bill's working on identifying the faceless, it's probably better if we concentrate on how to get their spirit-energies across to the other side," Charlie suggested.

Marie had a moment of inspiration. "Are the photos still on that whiteboard?"

Charlie glanced over his shoulder and pointed. "They're over here."

"Come on, let's have a go with them."

Charlie took the lead and found the white-board, the photos of the faceless soldiers, staring blankly back at him.

# Chapter Hundred-Nineteen

After a severe bollocking from his DI, Detective Sergeant, hanging on by his fingernails, Morris, decided it was time to close the file on the Lidsays, and Mrs Morbeck. However, he was going to put those two little shits the Stroudle brothers away for a very long time, even if it took him the rest of his life. His DI, had told him to 'take a few days off', so he decided to spend a quiet afternoon in the multiplex cinema at the bay, watching 'Avengers: Age of Ultron'. He read the blurb close to the ticket desk, *'Earth's Mightiest Heroes return in 'Avengers: Age of Ultron', to combat the threat of a genocidal artificial intelligence which Tony Stark has accidentally brought to life.'* He got his ticket, and then spent a small fortune on a bag of Pick n' Mix.

"*How much?*" he said to the young, if you want it you pay for it, I could make more on benefits, do I look like I give a shit, quick look at his watch, could do with a damn good wash, manners of an ill-bred neo-Nazi assistant.

"Six pounds ninety-six." The assistant scratched his head and examined his nails. "Sir."

Morris looked into the bag. "You've seen what I've got in here, have you? Only I didn't notice the Beluga caviar."

"Like, only priced on weight, sir. Don't serve car veer." He pulled up his jeans, whose crutch had sank down to his knees. "Sir. Like, I can take them back if you don't want 'em."

"You can shove …" Morris bit his lip and handed over a ten pound note.

"Three pounds and four 'p' change." His jeans had sunk again and were only being kept up by him spreading his knees. "Sir."

Morris unceremoniously took the change and threw the assistant a 'look'.

"Twat," the assistant said quietly as Morris walked away.

Morris heard the 'compliment', but decided he'd had enough aggravation for one day. The film was just what the doctor ordered. Pure escapism for two hours. As he drove home, he was caught up in the rush hour traffic, and as he bent down to pick up a mint he'd dropped, he glanced out of the passenger side window, and saw a face he knew only too well. *"Afternoon, Mr Morbeck,"* he thought.

Sam had been to the storage unit to collect as many cans of film as his car would carry, as the delivery man had missed their drop.

*"This is a bloody pain in the arse,"* his other-half complained. *"Cocked up delivery, and now this shit traffic."*

*"There is sod all we can do about it. So shut up."*

*"Keep up with the traffic, you wanker,"* his other-half complained to an eighty-something driver in a pale blue Fiat Cinquecento, who was at least ten yards behind the car in front of him. *"Jesus, don't they know how to drive? Probably never took a driving test. I'd introduce compulsory testing for anyone over sixty-five, take their licence off them when they reach eighty, attach speed limiters on all cars driven by anyone under thirty-five, restrict lorries to fifty miles an hour, and only allow them on the roads between midnight and six am."*

*"And the point of that rant was?"*

*"Nothing really, but it made me feel a lot better."*

*"I am so glad to hear it. Now piss off. I want to listen to the news."* Sam ended the 'conversation'.

Morris couldn't take his eyes off Sam and assumed he was talking to someone on his mobile. *"Forget it? One bollocking off the DI is more than enough for this year,"* he thought, desperately trying to suppress the urge to follow Sam. *"But what if I just happened to be in the same jam? Nothing wrong in that."* He wasn't being very successful at convincing himself.

Sam turned on the radio, and tuned it to radio four for the news. As a discussion got underway on the need, or otherwise, for an independent nuclear deterrent, he glanced out of his side window, saw Detective Sergeant Morris, waved, and shook his head. *"Bloody traffic,"* he mouthed.

Morris frowned and shrugged. *"What the hell do you want?"* He thought.

Sam opened the side window and gestured for Morris to do the same. "I was saying that the traffic is bloody terrible at this time of day. I'll be glad when the schools are off again. Most of this is mothers picking up their kids. Didn't happen in my day. It was the bus or you walked."

Morris smiled.

"Going anywhere?"

*"I'm sat in my car, and you want to know if I'm going anywhere?"*

"I've been down to that storage place on …"

The conversation was abruptly ended as the traffic finally began to move forward.

*"What the hell are you keeping in a storage unit?"* Morris's antennae twitched. *"Interesting place to store a lot of things."* He tapped on Charlie's mobile number. *"Including a body."*

"Yes, detective sergeant?" Charlie put his hand over the phone and mouthed, *"Morris"* to Marie.

"Charlie. I've got a little job for you. Chance for you to hone your detective skills."

"Great." He tried to sound as interested and enthusiastic as he could, given what had happened at Takanun and High Wood.

"I want you to contact all storage units in Cardiff, and see if they're keeping anything for Sam Morbeck."

Charlie's mouth suddenly went dry.

"You still there?"

"Yes. Sorry, I was just making some notes. Making sure I didn't forget anything."

"Well done, detective constable. Good practice that. As soon as you've got any news, give me a call on the mobile. Don't leave any messages at the station. Only speak to me." Morris ended the call and made his way home.

*"Why are you still interested in Sam?"* Charlie thought suspiciously. *"I thought you'd given up on finding Jane."* He put the phone back in his pocket and turned to Marie. "Where's Sam?" His expression gave away his thoughts.

Marie could see he'd been disturbed by the call. "What's up? What did Morris want?"

"He," Charlie said scratching the side of his head, "wants me to check storage units in Cardiff, to see if Sam's got anything in them."

Marie wandered a few feet away across the cellar floor, and after a minute or so, came back to him. "Just get a list of units off the internet, leave it for a day or so, and then call him. Tell him you've checked them all thoroughly, and Sam hasn't got anything stored anywhere. He's hardly likely to check what you've done, otherwise he'd have done it himself." She squeezed his arm. "Remember, I told you he's my cousin, although admittedly we haven't spoken to each other for, God I can't remember when. Why don't I invite him round to the house, and I can try and find out what he's really up to?" She kissed him softly on the cheek. "Go on. What have we got to lose?"

Despite the support Morris had given Charlie in his career, there had always been something, an itch he couldn't quite scratch, something about him he couldn't quite take to.

# Chapter Hundred-Twenty

Klaus and Guillaume were stood together in the gallery.

"Are you fully recovered now?" Klaus was concerned about the mental and physical effects of the 'trip' on his friend.

"I will never recover from that man and that place." Guillaume's frown was deep and his eyes gave away the intense emotions churning inside him. "You read about it, listen to eye witness accounts, watch films, but nothing can prepare you for such inhumanity. What they did …" His words dissolved in tears.

An ethereal sobbing made them gently start.

"Isaac?" Guillaume whispered.

The sobbing continued unabated.

"Brother? Is it you?"

*"I was wrong ... sent you ... too much ... I knew but hadn't seen. I ... I..."* The rest was lost in heart-rending sobs.

"I am back, and I am stronger now than I have ever been. Being a part of their suffering has given me wisdom which would never have been achieved in any other way."

*"But the evil you were exposed to, and the devils that inflicted such terrible torment on you, must have created deep wounds in your psyche."*

"At times like this, I am comforted by the words of W H Auden. 'Don't get rid of my devils, because my angels will go to.'" Guillaume softly smiled. "Over the years, Auden has stirred every possible emotion in me. With the lost souls we save, he perfectly encapsulates my feelings." He took a soft, deep breath. "'Stop all the clocks, cut off the telephone, Prevent the dog from barking with a juicy bone, Silence the pianos and with muffled drum Bring out the coffin, let the mourners come." Guillaume closed his eyes and raised his face to the sky. "'The stars are not wanted now; put out every one, Pack up the moon and dismantle the sun, Pour away the ocean and sweep up the wood; For nothing now can ever come to any good.'" He swallowed hard, opened his eyes, brushed away a tear, and held Klaus by the shoulders.

*"The demon is now gone?"*

Klaus joined the conversation. "I pray we will see no more of it. Sam's bravery and determination sent it back to hell. But we still face problems."

Guillaume looked at Klaus from under his eyebrows and smiled. "Opportunities, as the modern businessman says."

Klaus chuckled. "They always see problems as that, because they don't expose themselves to the problems. Just like generals, and their troops at the front line."

Guillaume smiled warmly.

*"What are these things?"* Isaac's reply, sounded a little peeved.

Klaus brought Isaac up to speed with events at the two houses.

*"So the main issues seem to be well in hand?"*

Guillaume and Klaus glanced at each other and nodded.

*"That means yes?"* Isaac asked, sounding a little more himself.

Guillaume walked a few yards away, clearly deep in thought.

"Guillaume?" Klaus called after him. "What is it?"

"I have been thinking a great deal about my 'journey.'"

Klaus frowned slightly at him and titled his head to one side. "And?"

"We have a select group who can travel back and forth through time. The Spirit Walkers."

"We know this?" Klaus sounded a little exasperated.

Guillaume nodded. "Have we considered everything they could do?"

"We know what they can do." Klaus shook his head and sat down.

"Hear me out. Without the two World Wars, how many souls would now need our help?"

Isaac remained uncharacteristically silent.

"Some, but clearly not as many," Klaus conceded.

"And consequently," Guillaume continued. "Papaver Rhoeas would not have been required?

"All this, I think the British say, is the bleeding obvious," Klaus replied, his exasperation growing.

Isaac understood his brother. *"What do you have in mind, Guillaume?"*

"What if Spirit Walkers took actions in the past which could have positive effects on the future?"

A silence smothered the air like a thick winter sea fog.

"Was würden sie tun? *(What would they do?)*"

"In erster Weltkrieg Hitler zu töten. *(To kill Hitler in World War One.)*"

"In erster Weltkrieg Hitler zu töten?" Klaus was concerned that after his 'journey', Guillaume was beginning to lose his grip on reality.

Guillaume sat down and shrugged. "Warum nicht? *(Why not?)*"

*"English, please."* Isaac reminded them.

"Tut mir leid Bruder. (I'm sorry brother.)" Guillaume bit his tongue. "English. Yes."

Klaus was still in shock. "You are proposing we send someone back to 1918, and kill the 'Austrian Corporal'?"

Guillaume nodded. "I have been researching this. On September 28, 1918, Private Henry Tandey, a British soldier serving near the French village of Marcoing, came across a wounded German soldier. He spared the soldier's life." Guillaume paused. "Tandey later told sources, that in the final moments of the battle, as the German troops were in retreat, a wounded German soldier entered his line of fire. He took aim, but couldn't shoot a wounded man, and he let him go. The soldier was twenty-nine-year-old Lance Corporal Adolf Hitler. What I propose, is a Spirit Walker goes back, takes over Private Tandey, and this time, kills Lance Corporal Hitler. Kills him before he develops his ideas for national socialism and writes 'Mein Kampf'." He shrugged and raised his hands to the ceiling. "What have we got to lose?"

"Have you never heard of the 'Butterfly Effect'?" Ralph said as he entered the gallery.

Klaus and Guillaume turned quickly, glanced at each other, and waved Ralph over to join them.

*"How are you Ralph?"* Isaac asked.

Ralph stared around the room, back at Klaus and Guillaume, frowned deeply, shook his head, scratched his ear, and smiled. "Isaac?"

*"Yes, old friend."*

Ralph answered as if Isaac was in the room with him. "It's good to hear from you again, my friend."

*"And you Ralph. You were about to tell us about this butterfly?"*

Ralph smiled. "In chaos theory, the butterfly effect is the sensitive dependence on initial conditions, in which a small change in one state of a deterministic nonlinear system, can result in large differences in a later state."

Klaus and Guillaume stared at each other, and back at Ralph, like a pair of bemused teenagers, who'd been played 'Are You Lonesome Tonight?' by Elvis Presley and the Jordanaires, and told that it had reached number one in the charts.

"Or to put it another way." Ralph chuckled at their expressions. "It refers to the idea that a butterfly's wings might create tiny changes in the atmosphere that may ultimately alter the path of a tornado, or delay, accelerate, or even prevent the occurrence of a tornado in another location." He raised his eyebrows to check their understanding, and decided another example was needed. "OK. Try this. If you make tiny changes in the past, they could have profound effects in the future. On the face of it, killing Hitler would seem to be an awesome idea, but why not go back a few more years, kill his parents, grandparents? Why not go back to Sarajevo on 28 June 1914, and prevent the assassination of Archduke Franz Ferdinand of Austria? Where do you start, and where do you stop? This line of action has profound, unknown, and potentially dangerous consequences for the world."

Guillaume looked crestfallen.

"I am simply pointing out the potential pitfalls of this type of intervention." Ralph said reassuringly.

This didn't help Guillaume's mood. "But it all seems so straightforward."

"My friend, have you ever known anything in this life, or any other, to be straightforward?" Ralph replied sympathetically. "But we shouldn't simply dismiss the idea. Admittedly there are major risks, but we should discuss this in detail, and only then determine if the benefits outweigh the risks. Einstein put it very well, 'I know not with what weapons World War III will be fought, but World War IV will be fought with sticks and stones'.

If we have a way to stop mankind reaching for sticks and stones, then we must investigate all options which may prevent it."

Guillaume brightened a little.

# Chapter Hundred-Twenty-One

Matt and Mark were stood open-mouthed, staring at Robert's extensive scientific library.

"Have you ever seen such a collection of volumes, dissertations, opuscules, codex... Mark, there's a copy of J. Wheeler and W. Quantum 'Theory and Measurement', 1983," Matt whispered. "Look at this, Marion & Thornton: Classical Dynamics of Particles and Systems, 2nd edition, 1970."

Mark was otherwise occupied. "Great heavens, you've got Andrzej Krasinski: 'Inhomogeneous Cosmological Models'." He was about to pick up the tome, when he spotted another treasure. "L. Lederman, D. Teresi: 'The God Particle: If the Universe Is the Answer, What Is the Question?' 2006." He turned and stared at Robert in total admiration, coated with some small degree of envy.

For twenty minutes they gasped and drooled until Robert finally suggested they sit down and discuss how they were going to move forward.

"But can't I just take a quick peak at this?" Matt held up Huw Price's 'Time's Arrow and Archimedes' Point'.

"Once we've made some preliminary decisions on what we do next, you can read to your heart's delight."

The brothers begrudgingly moved away from the book shelves, Matt carrying 'Time's Arrow', and Mark holding tightly onto Guckenheimer and Holmes' 'Nonlinear Oscillations, Dynamical Systems, and Bifurcations of Vector Fields'.

"So," Robert started, "how should we analyse this wonder?"

Matt looked at Mark who indicated he should be their spokesman. "We believe that we should consider the analytic solutions of massive (bi)gravity, which as I'm sure you know, can be written in a simple form using advanced Eddington-Finkelstein coordinates. We should then analyse the stability of these solutions against radial perturbations. Initially recover a previously obtained result on the instability of the bidiagonal bi-Schwarzschild solutions, and in the non-bidiagonal case, which contains, in particular, the Schwarzschild solution with Minkowski fiducial metric, we should be able show generically that there are physical spherically symmetric perturbations, but no unstable modes."

Robert stared at Matt in utter disbelief. "I, uh I … yes, of course, I … could you possibly put it in words that the others would understand?"

Matt took a very deep breath and spoke quietly to Mark for a few minutes. "No."

"No?" Robert was taken aback.

"No, we can't." He shrugged. "Is it important they understand this? Surely the entire point of us looking into this, is that we can use appropriate technical language."

Robert sat back in the chair and glanced from brother to brother. He felt as if he was sitting in the same room as Einstein and Newton. His first thought was for them to go to the university, but its distance from Takanun precluded any thought of this. "Let me call a few old colleagues from the university and get their views on this."

Mark stood up and walked to the window. "Are we determining if we can utilise its powers?" He paused for a few seconds, watching a blackbird heaving a resistant worm from the lawn "Or how we can shut it down?"

The statement was short, direct and to the point, and its implications far-reaching.

Matt joined his brother at the window and applauded as the blackbird finally won the life or death tug-of-war with the worm. "There is a quote which I think summarises our position better than I possibly could."

Robert raised his eyebrows. "And that is?"

"Thiruvallur said, 'Think wisely before you exercise an action. Having done so however, never look back and regret. That would be a shame.'"

Robert smiled. Whatever this Lazarus Pool was, it would be a monumental shame if they lost something which had the power to take the shapeless clay these two once were, and transform it into a pair of Michelangelo Davids.

"There is one thing I would like to raise," Mark said cautiously.

"Yes?" Robert sat back, anticipating he'd get an explanation for the two-loop hexagon Wilson loop, which, when he first saw it as a post graduate student in Cambridge, consisted of seventeen pages of Goncharov polylogarithms.

"Ralph suggested we should move in here with you. You have more free rooms, and we'd be living on the job so to speak."

"Yes." Robert was surprised by the request, but it made a lot of sense. "That's an excellent suggestion. I'll take you upstairs once we've completed business here and show you the rooms. All that's needed then, is for you to bring your things over."

Matt and Mark looked a little sheepishly at each other. "The truth is, that what we stand in is all we have. As Bertie Wooster said, 'There are moments, Jeeves, when one asks oneself, 'Do trousers matter?'"

"Well." Robert hid his surprise well. "We shall have to get you some things. Given that the effect of the Lazarus Pool appears to be inversely proportional to distance, we'd better use the internet. My daughter Marie's the expert on that. Once she comes up from the cellar, I'll get her onto it."

# Chapter Hundred Twenty-Two

"What should we do?" Marie was stood with her back to Charlie, closely examining the faceless images fixed to the melamine board. "We could do with Elizabeth being here."

Charlie stood alongside her. "Do you want me to ask her?"

"Please. Would you? See what she says, but for God's sake don't pressure her. She's got enough on her plate." She grinned at Charlie and winked. "But a few minutes of her time would be really helpful." She dragged out the word 'really'.

Charlie stared at the Lazarus Pool. "You going to be alright with that?" He nodded in its direction.

She followed his eyes. "God yes. Worst thing it could do, would be to turn me into a genius." She laughed at the thought. "Go on. I'll be fine."

He turned away and had one last glance at the Lazarus Pool. It hummed gently as blue stars erupted from its surface and flew around the room like demented blue bottles. As his foot stood on the first cellar step, a voice called from the door above him.

"Leaving just as we got here?"

Never before had Charlie been pleased to hear Ivor's voice. He looked up and smiled as Ivor and Gloria came down the steps, passed straight through him, and moved across the cellar floor to Marie.

"Keep an eye on her," Charlie called out as he trotted up the steps. Even with Ivor and Gloria here, he didn't want to be away for long.

"How are you two?" Marie asked.

"Never better," Gloria replied, linking arms with Ivor. "How things got so bad, is almost impossible to comprehend. But such is life, and thank God so's death. Don't you agree, darling?"

Ivor's attention was focused on the Lazarus Pool. "Sorry, love." He nodded his head in its direction. "I was thinking about that." He gently slipped his arm from Gloria's and walked cautiously towards it.

"Be careful," she called after him. "I know how nosey the policeman in you is." She pointed at him. "That's what made you such a good one." She frowned. "Well, at least at the start."

Ivor waved her away. "I'll be fine. I just want a closer look."

Gloria turned back to Marie and peered at the faceless images fixed on the wall. "These are all still missing?"

Marie nodded. "They're all from the Second World War. Plan is to put names to them and eventually all the blue spirits in the houses."

"OK DOWN THERE?" Patricia was stood in the cellar doorway. "COFFEE OR TEA?"

Marie looked at Gloria and raised her eyebrows. "Anything?"

She shook her head.

"IVOR?" Marie called across to him. "TEA OR COFFEE?"

He was standing close to the vortex, completely lost in himself. Marie's call made him jump, and step into the Lazarus Pool.

"IVOR!" Gloria screamed. "GET OUT OF IT!"

Inside the Lazarus Pool, Ivor had never felt such serenity and peace, and Gloria's screams were unheard as it filtered out her cries. He felt as if the spinning stars had entered his mind, probing, searching, discovering, stimulating, restoring, and filling sterile areas of his brain. Images of every conceivable aspect of planet Earth and the cosmos, words in hundreds of languages, sounds of nature, music, industry, smells, tastes, pages upon pages of text of fiction, poetry, science, philosophy, drama, and unfathomable calculations, all fought to occupy the unused neural spaces of his brain. His head began to feel like an overinflated balloon. His hands flew to the sides of his head, the pressure becoming unbearable, and he fell out of the vortex at Gloria's feet.

"IVOR?" Gloria was terrified of what may have happened to her rediscovered husband.

He sat up slowly, looked around, and smiled. "Never felt better."

"You stupid sod, what the hell were you thinking?" Her fear had been transformed into anger. "You, you've … you've always been too … oh … stop bloody smirking."

"Gloria, 'Where's the life we lost in living?' Once you and I spoke 'Of lovers whose bodies smell of each other Who think the same thoughts without need of speech.'"

"He's quoting TS Eliot."

Marie span around and Elizabeth was stood close behind her.

"He's always been one of my favourite poets."

Ivor stood up and smiled at Elizabeth. "You have excellent taste, my dear. 'If time and space, as sages say, Are things which cannot be, The sun which does not feel decay No greater is than we. So why, Love, should we ever pray To live a century? The butterfly that lives a day Has lived eternity.'" He took a deep breath and savoured the air. "Thomas Stearns Eliot, September 26, 1888 to January 4, 1965. Essayist, publisher, playwright, literary and social critic, and one of the twentieth century's major poets. A genius in the truest sense of the word."

Elizabeth, Marie, and Gloria, stood close together, shaking their heads, all utterly lost for words.

Ivor wasn't finished. He stared deep into Gloria's eyes. "'This form, this face, this life living to live in a world of time beyond me; let me resign my life for this life, my speech for that unspoken, the awakened, lips parted, the hope, the new ships.'" He opened his arms wide, smiled as broadly as a lottery winner, stepped towards Gloria, and walked straight through her.

"My God! He's alive," Elizabeth uttered incredulously.

Charlie appeared at the bottom of the steps, just in time to see Ivor pass through Gloria, who fell to the floor in a dead faint.

Ivor stopped dead in his tracks. "What the…" He thought twice about cursing, but couldn't help himself. "Fuck was that? A few minutes ago we were holding hands and now she's turned into thin air. How can…" He turned to Elizabeth. "What's happened to me?"

She raised her hands, as if in prayer, to her mouth, shook her head and shrugged.

"Life basically pissing sucks. Picks you up, and then kicks you in the balls. I should have known this wouldn't bloody last. Shit!" Ivor walked up to Elizabeth and held her arms. "I can feel you!" His mind was whirling widely like a typhoon in the Pacific. He turned and stabbed his finger at the Lazarus Pool. "Lived up to your fucking name, didn't you? Lazarus my arse." Suddenly his face began to change, until it was frozen in an expression of what could only be described as pure rapture. "'A man named Lazarus was sick. He lived in Bethany with his sisters, Mary and Martha.'" He dropped to his knees. "'Then Jesus shouted, 'Lazarus, come out!' And the dead man came out, his hands and feet bound in graveclothes, his face wrapped in a headcloth. Jesus told them, 'Unwrap him, and let him go!'" Ivor opened his mouth to speak again, but his eyes glazed over, and he collapsed into a crumpled heap on the floor.

Klaus and Guillaume were enjoying a cold beer, when Charlie, sucking in lungfuls of air, came charging into the lounge, knocking over a small mahogany side table, and smashing a crystal glass vase full of orange roses.

Klaus leapt to his feet, lifted Charlie off the floor, and sat him on the sofa. "In Gottes Namen! Was ist passiert? *(In the name of God! What happened?)*"

Charlie grimaced, as he tried to get air into his lungs, and understand what Klaus was asking him.

Guillaume remained calm and sat next to Charlie. "What's happened?"

"The Lazarus ... Pool's lived up ... to its ... name."

The two men stared at each other, frowned, and shrugged.

"You are not making any sense, Charlie." Guillaume maintained an air of calm.

Charlie sat up and looked wide-eyed at Guillaume. "Ivor walked, well actually, he tripped into the Lazarus Pool." He drew in a few more deep breaths.

"Und!" Klaus was less restrained.

Guillaume squeezed Klaus's arm and tapped his lips with his index finger.

"When he came out of the Lazarus Pool, he was different. Like Lazarus."

"Wie so?"

Guillaume glared at Klaus, who finally understood.

"He was quoting poetry and the Bible."

"Not so strange, Charlie," Guillaume said with a reassuring smile. "Our new friends the brothers, do exactly the same. But why do you say Lazarus?"

"Maybe not strange, but ..."

"What happened?"

"Well, he sort of... He walked through Gloria." Charlie tapped his chest. "You know, like I would. Like a live person would." He sat in silence, as it sank into Klaus and Guillaume.

Klaus prowled around the room, muttering unintelligible German to himself. He disappeared into the kitchen and came back with a large glass of water. After more prowling, he eventually stopped and sat down on the sofa. "I believe you say, a light has come on, when you begin to see things clearly?"

Charlie nodded. "Near enough."

"It is completely understandable what has happened to Ivor. We know these spirit-energies have the power to repair and heal."

Charlie and Guillaume, uh, huh'd.

"What is it they seek the most?"

"Release from purgatory?"

Klaus tilted his head to one side. "We have always assumed, that in the main, this is the case. But what if there are some, who do not wish to move over to the other side, and would prefer to start a new life? A life which was ripped from them by war. Wouldn't they look for a host?"

Guillaume's expression made it clear that he understood Klaus's logic. "A ghost. A spirit still with a 'physical' form, which when occupied by the spirit-energy, would become alive again."

"But if that's true, then why does Ivor still have control of his body?" Charlie needed more convincing.

"The spirit-energy doesn't know how to control Ivor?" Klaus frowned. "But I am sure that with time, it will grow to understand what to do, and drive Ivor out of his body."

Guillaume stood up. "We must warn all the other ghosts to keep away from it."

Klaus nodded. "Well away from it, or we could lose them all."

# Chapter Hundred-Twenty-Three

Morris was sat at his desk waiting for Charlie's call. Since the 'meeting' with his senior officer, he'd been somewhat muted as everything and everyone seemed to be conspiring against him. His so-called colleagues were constantly taking the piss, he was facing an internal inquiry into his actions during the interview with the drug dealer, he'd broken a crown on a molar, and couldn't see his dentist for three days, the damage to his relationship with his wife seemed irreparable, and to cap it all, his car had been stolen and torched.

*"Bollocks,"* he thought. *"Pointless sitting around here like a clay pigeon for these bastards to take pot shots at. I'll check out for myself the storage companies in Cardiff."* Twenty minutes later after a few internet searches and phone calls, he'd found the company, and that they had a unit which was now owned by a Mr S. Morbeck. "Gotcha you little beauty!"

"Shit. You haven't actually caught somebody, have you Minor? The stats office will be taking on extra staff. Probably ought to give the CPS a ring and warn them." A balding, overweight, red-faced, detective inspector quipped as he passed his desk. He stopped, turned around, and stood with his hands on his hips. "Jesus! It's not the Ripper of old London town?" He bent double with laughter, providing a WPC with an expansive glimpse of the cleavage of his behind.

"My God," she called out. "The things you see when you haven't got a harpoon."

The office fell into hysterics and the flustered detective inspector decided the toilets were his nearest escape route.

Despite his tormentor's embarrassment, Morris decided not to join in. He resisted the temptation to tell him to shove his comments up his arse, grabbed his car keys, and walked briskly out of the office to a series of cat calls, enquiries about his wife's sexual leanings, the results of his STI tests, and his inability to recognise a criminal even if he sat on one.

Half an hour later, after stopping off at McDonalds for a Chicken Select, fries, and a diet Coke, he arrived at Safestore. Nicola was as helpful as she'd been for Sam, and led Morris to the unit, opened it, and stayed with him as he examined the contents.

He turned and walked out of the storage unit. "But there's only cans of old films in there." He looked across at Nicola. "This is all of it? He didn't have any other units?"

"No, this is it."

"Contents are a bit odd, aren't they?"

"People keep all sorts of things in these units. We're just here to provide a service for them." She thought for a few moments. "The units were owned by Mr Morbeck's uncle and aunt. They were quite old and the films belonged to them. Maybe they were collectors?"

This seemed perfectly plausible to Morris, but his 'Morbeck's up to something' antenna, told him there had to be some shadowy motive for him wanting these films.

Nicola moved forward to lock the unit.

"I'd like to take a proper look at the contents. Have you got somebody who could empty this for me?"

Nicola looked at him as if he'd asked her to have sex with him in public.

"I'm conducting a murder enquiry," Morris emphasised.

The simple sentence sprung her into action.

After a long wait in reception, and three cups of probably the worst coffee he'd ever drank, Bernard the store-man waved at Morris to follow him. The unit was emptied, and the boxes stacked in a receiving area at the back of the main building. Morris nodded at Bernard, who looked him up and down, and muttered under his breath. "Bloody police, think they're pissing God almighty."

The unit was now as empty as a Scotsman's purse on Hogmanay. Morris sucked his teeth, chewed his bottom lip, walked outside, and stared dismally at the pile of boxes. *"What's the bloody point? If I do find anything, that bunch of wankers at the station won't lift a finger to help,"* he thought angrily.

"What do you want to do with them?" the warehouseman asked.

"Oh, put them back." Morris turned away and walked disconsolately back to reception.

The warehouseman stared at Morris's back, firing imaginary bullets into it. "Thanks for that. No really it was no problem. Piece of shit." He fired a few extra bullets, spat, breathed deeply, stared at the pile, and walked back into the warehouse to get a coffee. *"That can sodding wait,"* he thought.

Morris stopped in reception to thank Nicola for all her help, and drove to Morrisons for lunch. After an 'All-Day-Full-English-Breakfast', the world seemed a little rosier. Returning to the station definitely wasn't an option, so he bought a coffee and a double-chocolate muffin, and twenty minutes later, feeling almost himself, he drove home.

As he walked into the hall, his antennae twitched. Something wasn't right. The house seemed to have lost its pulse. Like a victim of Count Dracula, its life force had been drained. There was a penetrating coldness which made him shiver uncontrollably. A yawning emptiness, which seemed to make his words echo like the footsteps of a night sentry. There was no shouted hello from the kitchen. In fact, there was no sensation at all that anyone else was in the house. He felt completely isolated. Utterly alone.

"FRANKIE," he shouted up the stairs. "YOU UP THERE?"

Tumbleweed rolled down the stairs, driven on by a numbing wind.

*"Where the hell are you?"* he thought, as his fear of what he suspected to be true grew. He walked into the kitchen turned on the light, walked to the sink, filled the kettle, turned it on, took his favourite mug from the mug tree, and sat down at the breakfast bar waiting for the kettle to boil. He leaned his elbow on the table, and felt something under it. He glanced down. A white envelope glared back at him.

*"Alan."*

His fears twisted and tightened a double overhand noose knot in his stomach. He pushed the envelope around like a kitten with a ball of wool, picked it up, turned it over, sniffed it, held it up to the light, and finally tore it open.

*"I've tried to live with you and cope with what little life I have. But it's not enough. Whatever there was between us left a long time ago. There's no-one else. Maybe someday there will be. I've taken everything I need. Don't try to follow me. My solicitor will be in touch.*

*Frankie."*

Alan slowly and deliberately, rolled the letter into a ball and threw it at the wall. "Work your balls off, and what do you get?" He jumped up from the table and kicked the chair over. "Bloody shat on from a great height." He opened the fridge, took two bottles of Sol, and marched into the lounge. The TV offered him no comfort, and after suffering the first half an hour of 'Gravity', he decided bed was the only remaining option. He undressed on the landing, leaving his clothes in untidy piles. Spent a few minutes in bathroom cleaning his teeth, and washing his essential bits, slouched into the cold, hollow, darkened bedroom, stubbed his little toe on the bed, gritted his teeth, swore, and sat on the bed.

"Feeling better now?"

"JESUS CHRIST! WHAT THE …!" Morris's heart vaulted into his mouth. He stubbed his big toe on the bed, hopped, fell into the wardrobe, swore, crawled back to the bed, and leaned his elbows on the duvet.

"Enjoy that, dear?"

Morris's mind desperately tried to understand how he was hearing her voice. "Frankie? Is that you?"

"You remember my name. I see so little of you lately that I wasn't sure if you'd know who I was."

"But the note. It said …" He frowned. "Why would …" He was close to losing his easily raised temper, but chewed on his lower lip, and swallowed a big slice of pride from a well-cooked humble pie.

"I thought it was pretty clear what it said. Didn't you understand it?"

He stared at the dim silhouette in the darkness, and decided that silence would definitely be golden.

"Just in case you didn't understand my letter, it said I'd had enough." She switched the bedside light on, illuminating herself, sat up propped up by three pillows. Her expression gave nothing away.

"I thought you'd left. Gone for good," he continued, almost chewing through his bottom lip.

"Listen very closely, Alan, if you want me to be in this house in the morning, then the choice is pretty simple. Me or the police." She stared at him, waiting for a reply. "Nothing to say. Christ that speaks volumes to me." She began to swing her legs off the bed.

"You. I chose you." He stood up, sat close to her on the bed, and held her hand. "It's always been you. Bloody police and me have had it. If I have to interview another drug dealer, or those Stroudle morons, then I think I'll probably kill somebody. I, we, need a fresh start. Somewhere bloody miles away from here. Not sure what the hell I'll do for work, but I can't stick this shit anymore." He looked down at her hands and stroked them tenderly with his thumb. "I am so sorry. I've been a total bastard for ages. How in God's name you've put up with me 'til now is a miracle. I deserve everything you want to throw at me." He carried on stroking her fingers and softly kissing their tips. "But if you can," he said and looked longingly into her eyes, "give me another chance?"

"I wouldn't be doing *this* if I didn't want to try again." She smiled at the top of his head and pulled his face up in line with hers. "I love you, God only knows why." She stared deep into his eyes. "I'm not getting any younger, Alan. I want children."

It was the one constant topic of conversation between them, and it was clear from Frankie's expression, that it had to be concluded.

He breathed deeply, and thought about his reply before speaking. "But we had tests, and we know that you … well, we know, don't we?"

"I know. I've a womb that no baby's going to set up home in."

Alan looked startled. "You don't want me to … with another woman do you?"

She shook her head. "*No.*" She paused before replying. "There's adoption."

He stayed silent.

Her expression gave nothing away about the maelstrom of emotions churning inside her. "We've never considered it, but it is a viable option for us."

He moved towards her, kissed her tenderly on the lips, and ran his fingers through her hair. "If it's what you want."

For the first time in months, she threw her arms around him, kissed him full on the lips, and they made love like it was the first time.

# Chapter Hundred-Twenty-Four

Charlie trotted down the cellar steps with Klaus and Guillaume closely following.

"Where is he?" Guillaume asked, a deep frown spreading across his face.

Gloria pointed towards the photos on the wall. "He's taken a keen interest in those."

Ivor was standing with his nose pressed against the photos. He seemed to be particularly interested in a photo of a Sherman tank.

Klaus moved cautiously forward, reached out, touched Ivor on the shoulder, and even though his mind warned him what to expect, he jumped back when his hand came into contact with solid flesh. "Mein Gott! Es ist wahr! Er ist am Leben! *(My God! It's true! He is alive!)*" He turned around to the others, his face frozen in an expression of disbelief.

Ivor was totally unaware of Klaus. His attention was on the Sherman DD (Duplex Drive) tank, and its commander, a faceless first lieutenant. He reached up and touched the photo.

Gloria made a move towards him, but Elizabeth held her arm, and stopped her.

"Wait. Let's see what happens." Elizabeth was absorbed with Ivor's fixation on the photo.

As Ivor pressed his index finger against the photo, like a child pushing its finger into a marshmallow, it began to sink into it. As he maintained the pressure of his finger on the photo, his hand, wrist, arm, shoulder, and gradually all of him began to disappear into the scene of conflict. The past absorbing him into a frozen moment of its own reality.

Gloria screamed, ran to the wall, and tore the photo away from the melamine board. She lifted it close to her face, which congealed into an expression of absolute terror. Her hands flew to her face and the crumpled photo fell to the cellar floor.

Klaus raced forward, knelt down, picked up the photo, stared at it intently, shook his head vigorously, looked up at the others, shook his head again, stood up, flattened the creased photo on the palm of his hand, walked close to Guillaume, stared him directly in the eyes, and tapped the photo.

As Guillaume took the photo from Klaus, he was plainly shocked. "Comment? *(How?)*" He looked up at Klaus and massaged his temple with his free hand. "Nous n'avons jamais vu ça avant. *(We have never seen it before.)*" He handed the photo back to Klaus. "C'est sans précédent. *(This is unprecedented.)* Personne n'a jamais pénétré une photo comme ça. *(Nobody has ever entered a photo like this.)*"

Marie squeezed Charlie's arm so hard that he squealed in pain.

"That hurt."

But Marie's attention was fixed on Guillaume. "Que voulez - vous dire, quelqu'un est entré dans l'image? *(What do you mean, someone entered the picture?)*" she said loudly.

Guillaume's head turned, like a clockwork marionette, to face Marie, and Klaus held out the picture to her. "Voyez par vous-même. *(See for yourself.)*"

She carefully took the photo, and initially couldn't see anything out of the ordinary. She looked up, raised an eyebrow, and shrugged at Guillaume.

"Look closely." Klaus replied.

Marie held the photo close to her face and peered intently at it. Then she saw what had caused Klaus and Guillaume's dramatic reaction. Staring back at her from the turret of the tank, was the face of Ivor Lidsay.

Ivor rubbed his eyes, looked around, rubbed his eyes again, looked around again, pinched his hand, looked down at himself, and fell back against the metal rim of the turret.

"Lootenant!" The accent was thick New York Italian.

"What is it Innocenti?" Ivor's mind was in utter turmoil. Where the hell had that voice come from?

"We should take out dose houses on de right. Dat's where the bastards post snipers."

Ivor stayed silent, his mind as frozen as a King penguin's beak in a mid-winter blizzard.

"Lootenant?"

"Target the inn on the right, and the cafe on the left. Take them out. Masters?"

"Lootenant."

"And if you get a sniff of a Tiger. Scream. That son of bitch will end our war in the blink of an eye. And if you see any type of kraut. Spray 'em. They've been taking reprisals and shooting civilians in this town."

Alfredo had finished photographing the cans of film. "Fancy a coffee, Bill?"

Bill looked up from his laptop, "Black, two sugars." And he immediately returned to building the database.

Alfredo smiled. Bill was a genius, but communication wasn't one his greatest strengths. "Just be a couple of minutes."

As he waited for the kettle to boil, he heard what sounded like raised voices coming from the cellar. He walked to the open cellar door, peered down, and called out. "ANYONE DOWN THERE?"

Elizabeth called back. "COME DOWN, YOU'VE GOT TO SEE THIS!"

Alfredo's curiosity-switch was flicked to maximum. "I'LL BE THERE NOW." He jumped down the steps two at a time and ran across the cellar to where the group was gathered. "Cos'è? *(What is it?)*" His eagerness to know what had happened made him slip into his native tongue.

Marie handed him the photograph.

"Merda! Come ... come ha fatto questo? *(Shit! How ... how did this?)*" Alfredo stared closely at the photo, looked back at Marie, and then back at the photo. "This is Ivor?"

Marie nodded. "Si."

"È sicuramente Ivor? *(It's definitely Ivor?)*"

"Sì. Dev'essere Ivor. *(Yes. It has to be Ivor.)*"

The M4 Sherman turned the corner of a house into what once had been the busy main street of the town.

"TIGER! TWO O' CLOCK!" Innocenti shouted over the noise of the engine.

1st Lieutenant Charles Redvers's head snapped to his right. "IT'S A PANTHER NOT A TIGER! JESUS BIGHAM GET SOME SHOTS OFF, AND GET US THE HELL OUT OF HERE."

Sergeant John Bigham got off three shots at the front of the Panther, and all three bounced off like ping pong balls. The Sherman Continental R975 C1, air-cooled, radial, gasoline 400 hp engine roared, as Bigham slammed it into reverse and disappeared as rapidly as he could around the corner of the shell of what had once been the house of the mayor.

The Panther's high-velocity 75 mm gun spewed smoke and fire, and its shell, like a hot knife through butter, penetrated the two sides of the mayor's house and the sides of the Sherman. The hit was low on the side of the tank, and its interior was lit up by a fire-ball caused by the enormous friction of the penetration of the shell through the Sherman's inadequate armour. The appalling consequence of which was to turn its interior into a blast furnace which incinerated the crew. A second white-hot, eighteen-pound projectile, hammered into the empty ammunition rack under the tank's floor, but the steel walls of the compartment prevented the molten metal from striking the interior of the hull and ricocheting throughout the tank.

The tormented screams of the crew below him, and the stomach-churning stench of broiled flesh as they burned to death in the body of the tank, acid etched themselves into Ivor's psyche. Like a pyroclastic flow, the phosphorescent heat from the 'crematorium' below smashed into him, and Ivor lost consciousness.

Gloria had dropped to her knees and was smashing her fists into the cellar wall. "It had to end like this. There was no other way it could have happened. Life smiles, picks you up, and then kicks you in the teeth." She dropped onto her haunches and buried her face in her hands.

"Gloria!" Elizabeth said softly. "Over there! Behind you!"

Gloria, apart from her chest heaving from the seemingly bottomless sobs, didn't move.

Elizabeth walked close to her and squeezed her shoulder. "Gloria, look over here."

A puffy face with reddened eyes looked up at her. "Mmmm?"

Elizabeth lifted her to her feet, gently held her chin, and turned her face to look at the floor just to the left of the melamine board. "Look."

Gloria's eyes stared questioningly at a smoking pile of rags, which was rhythmically moving up and down. "Ivor?" She tried to shuffle forward, but Elizabeth gently held her back.

"It looks like Ivor, but let's be careful. We don't know if it's him."

"She's right, my dear." Klaus joined them and put his arm reassuringly around Gloria's shoulders. "These are things of which we have no knowledge. Let Alfredo check first."

Alfredo looked back at Klaus who nodded, and he moved his hand closer to a smoking shoulder. The heat was just about bearable, so Alfredo tentatively gripped the shoulder, and instantly a hand flew up and gripped his hand like Scrooge gripping his money. Alfredo tried to pull away, but the grip grew tighter. He turned to the others, and Charlie ran to his side.

"Alfredo, hold my hand," Charlie said as calmly as he could.

He nodded and gave him his left hand.

Immediately, the smoking rags stood up. Ivor dropped Alfredo's hand, and turned to face him.

Ivor's expression screamed 'Does not compute,' "Please tell me that didn't just happen." He shook his head rapidly from side to side, blew loudly down his nose and brushed himself down with his hands.

Gloria ran to Ivor and passed straight through him. "Oh bugger!" She stopped the other side of the cellar wall, turned, walked back into Takanun's cellar, half-smiled, and shook her head. "I'll be bloody glad when you're a ghost again."

"Any bright ideas on how I'm going to do that? Aside from throwing myself off a tall building?"

Klaus chewed his top lip. "I believe I know what has happened to you Ivor, but at present, I'm not sure how to reverse it." He straightened up, his expression full of positivity. "We will find an answer."

Ivor stabbed a finger at Charlie. "Have *you* got a clue?"

"How about walking away from the house?" He suggested.

"And when I get back?"

Charlie stared at his shoes and Klaus shrugged.

Ivor mimed banging his head against a wall. "Fine bloody pair you are."

"Ivor, it's not their fault. This is still new to everyone." Gloria blew him a kiss. "They'll find an answer."

Charlie turned towards Marie for moral support, but she was staring wide-eyed at Alfredo. Charlie stood in front of her, but she stepped to one side and continued to stare. Charlie turned and followed her gaze.

Alfredo, like a melting snowman, was sliding slowly down the cellar wall, his eyes closed, with tears streaming down his cheeks.

# Chapter Hundred-Twenty-Five

For the first time in many a year, Alan and Frankie woke in the same bed, and then, establishing another first, made love in daylight.

"What are you going to tell them?" Frankie was walking out of their en-suite, drying her hair with a towel.

Morris studied her as she rubbed her head with a pink towel. He'd forgotten what an amazing body she had. How could he have risked losing everything for the sake of a career? The greasy pole only had one certainty. Slipping down to the bottom when you least expected it.

"I'll go in today and speak to the boss. I'll have to work some time to ensure a smooth handover, but that shouldn't take long."

Frankie frowned slightly. "Will this affect your pension much?"

He shrugged. "Not sure, but I can get all those details over the next few days." He raised his palms to the ceiling. "If it does, it does. Nothing's going to make me change this decision."

When eventually they made it to the kitchen for breakfast, Morris grabbed a protein drink from the fridge, and unhooked his keys from a gift from Brittany their parents had bought them. "I won't be late," he said insistently, kissing the top of Frankie's head.

Chief Superintendent Stuart Wedgwood Peach, was leaning back in his black leather chair, looking over his steepled fingers at Morris. "You're sure about this, Alan? You've done your time in the trenches. I know all about recent 'events', but your future still looks pretty rosy to me. This is a major thing you're asking me to accept. Why don't you take a few days off, and think about it. Come back on Monday, and let's talk again."

Morris shook his head. "I can't go back on this. If I do, then I kiss goodbye to my marriage."

"Plenty more fish in the sea. Good looking man like you." Wedgwood Peach said, tapping the side of his nose. "There's plenty here to take your mind off any divorce proceedings."

Morris's hackles rose, but he controlled his temper and smiled. "Plenty more fish, but only one Frankie."

"Head against a brick wall?"

Morris nodded.

Wedgwood Peach stood up and offered him his hand. "I know what you're going to say, but nonetheless, go home, and I'll see you Monday morning."

Morris shook his hand and smiled knowingly. "I'll be back Monday, sir." As he left the station, heads turned, eyebrows raised questioningly, teeth were sucked, and sides of noses were tapped.

"Told you he was having problems."

"Knew he was up for a bloody good kicking."

"Always knew he didn't have the balls for the job."

"Wanker."

"I liked him."

"Piss-head."

"I'm having his desk."

"Parking slot's mine."

*"Jesus,"* thought Morris. *"And he thinks I need to take some time to consider my decision?"* He chuckled to himself as he walked out of the station, looked up at the faces at the windows, and slowly lifted the middle finger of his right hand.

"Everything OK?" Frankie knew his answer before he'd said a word and threw her arms around his neck. "We are going to be so happy." She kissed him tenderly on the cheek. "Coffee?"

"Please."

"There's a message on the phone for you."

"Who is it?"

Frankie shook her head. "No idea. Marie Stridham? Is it a case you're working on?"

"Stridham?" He frowned and pouted. *"Marie* Stridham?"

Frankie nodded as she stirred the coffee.

He walked to the phone and pressed the play button.

*"Hi. This is Marie Stridham. You won't know me. We're cousins, and I was hoping you'd like to meet. You can get me on 07736888967. Please call, I'd love to meet one of the few living relatives I know I have."*

Morris stood silently as the message came to an end.

"You OK?"

"Mmmm?"

"OK?"

"Mmmm. Yeah, I'm fine."

# Chapter Hundred-Twenty-Six

Robert had organised a telephone call with two senior lecturers he'd worked with at Cardiff University. It had taken quite a few phone calls before both ex-colleagues would accept he was no longer suffering from dementia, and that in the cellar of his house was an extraordinary 'natural' phenomenon he needed to discuss with them.

Robert, Mark, and Matt, were sat around the telephone in the lounge at Takanun, listening to Professor Dennis Counsell, bringing Robert up to speed with the latest gossip.

"…and so he left his wife, and now he's living with him in Worcester."

"Thank you Dennis. Shall we get started?" Robert interjected as tactfully as he could. Dennis had always been an 'old woman', but his knowledge of quantum mechanics had almost won him the Nobel Prize. "Ready to start, Charles?"

"As ready as I'm ever going to be at my age." The avuncular voice of Dr Charles Bartle always made Robert feel that all was well with the world. He'd decided to ask him to join their team because of his expertise in radio astronomy, and his treatise on black holes.

"Good. I have two colleagues with me. Matthew and Mark Stroudle. You won't have heard of them, but they will make an undisputed, positive contribution to our discussion."

There was the sound of a whispered conversation on the other end of the line, and then Charles spoke.

"Good to speak with you both. I hope we soon have the opportunity of meeting face to face."

"Thank you, Charles," Matt replied as if this type of thing occurred daily.

"Yes indeed, thank you, Charles for your kind words. I think that Helen Keller put it very well, when she said, 'Alone we can do so little; together we can do so much,'" Mark said calmly.

There were a few seconds of stunned silence, then Charles coughed slightly and replied. "Excellent sentiments ... Mark?"

"Indeed."

"Down to business then." Robert again tried to steer the conversation where he wanted it to go.

"Robert?"

"Dennis?"

"Getting together over the phone like this is a good start, but we need to see this ... what was it you called it?"

"Lazarus Pool."

"Yes. This Lazarus Pool. Let's agree on a mutually compatible date to come over to the house and take a close look at it. We can bring some instrumentation and start a controlled analysis. What do you think?"

Robert was used to Dennis taking things over, but in this instance he was absolutely right. There really was very little they could discuss over the phone, other than agreeing a future date for them to start a detailed scientific analysis of the anomaly.

"How are you both fixed for next Wednesday?"

There was a short silence as diaries were checked.

"OK by us. Any particular time?" Dennis replied.

"I'd say early to give us a full day. Nine?"

"Look forward to it. This is very exciting. No, it's astonishing, Robert. We'll be with you at nine. Make sure the coffee's on and the croissants are warm. Bye for now."

The line went dead.

"Sound like very nice men," Matt said quietly, as he stood up and stretched his back. "I look forward to working with them." He turned away and started to walk to the door. "Coming, Mark? We should start our analysis."

Mark jumped up and trotted after his brother.

Robert sat back on the sofa, scratched his head, and smiled at the brothers as they disappeared out of the door. A few days ago, he had been pretty much unaware of everything going on around him. And now, here he sat, physically energised, sharper than a samurai's sword, and about to analyse what he was certain, would become one of the greatest scientific discoveries of the age.

*"My God,"* he thought. *"I could be remembered like Newton, Einstein, or Crick and Watson."* He stood up and followed the brothers.

# Chapter Hundred-Twenty-Seven

Everyone had gathered in the kitchen at Takanun, trying to make some sense of the events in the cellar, and after a silence that seemed to last for minutes, Ivor was the first to speak.

"So this thing heals diseases, and apparently, can also take over lucky sods like me. But, you've got to stay near it for the effect to last?"

Klaus nodded. "Ja."

Ivor walked to an open cupboard, and picked up a bag of salted peanuts. He tossed four into his mouth. "But, what's the point of curing cancer, if by the time you get home you've got it again? Bit bloody pointless, isn't it?" He looked around the kitchen looking for support, but couldn't see any. "It's just my personal point of view." He carried on chewing peanuts for a minute, and then seemed to have his own personal epiphany. He turned slowly, and raised the index finger of his right hand like a parent about to chide their child. "So if I go for a stroll into Cardiff, I'll get rid of my passenger? I'll be a bloody ghost again."

"Don't know." Klaus replied. "But there is an easy way to find out."

Ivor smiled. "Next thing on my 'To Do' list."

Karsten had been quiet for some time, but had to speak. "Ivor."

He turned to face Karsten. "What?" He wasn't feeling particularly in the mood for a comforting talk from a German.

"I understand how this is difficult for you."

"You have no pissing idea."

"I think I do."

Ivor simply shrugged, and threw another handful of peanuts into his mouth.

"I also have come back from the 'dead'."

Ivor immediately stopped chewing the peanuts, stared wide-eyed at Karsten, and coughed as he choked on half-chewed peanuts. "You." Cough cough. "Did bloody." Cough. "What." Spit, cough, spit. "Bloody nuts." Cough, cough." Rose from the." Spit, cough, cough. "Dead?"

Karsten nodded, trying not to laugh at Ivor's discomfort. "I haven't experienced what you have. Yours is a particularly unique experience."

"You 'aint whistling dixie. My arse hasn't …"

"Ivor!" Gloria flashed him a look he knew well.

"Mmmm. OK."

"Karsten, you were saying?" Gloria continued in a gentle conciliatory tone.

Karsten was finding it increasingly difficult to maintain any sort of outward appearance of calm and control. "We find ourselves in an impossible situation. We have discovered, it is the wrong word, but it will have to do. We have discovered something which could change life as we know it."

Klaus leaned against the kitchen work surface and beamed at his son, who over the last few days had been assembling his thoughts into a well-structured argument.

"What do we have?" The question was rhetorical. "Something which may, or may not, be unique to this house. Either way, if it does what we believe it is capable of, then an enormous responsibility has been thrust upon us."

There were sounds of agreement from everyone in the room.

"It has already directly affected some of us, and some of us have had thoughts of saving loved ones." He glanced at Ivor, Charlie, and Marie. "But, is this a blessing, or a well-disguised curse?"

"Bloody curse if you ask me," Ivor said, finally recovered from his peanut 'encounter'. He was about to add some rather more colourful points, when out of the corner of his eye, he noticed Gloria staring at him through half-closed eyes. "However, in this instance, I have to agree with you?" He looked smug and nodded towards Gloria.

"With what I've seen, and so far know about this," Karsten said and glanced towards Charlie who'd just entered the kitchen, "Lazarus pool, I can only see risk and danger."

Klaus's expression darkened.

"Hardly." Robert was leaning against the door jam. "I am risen from the metaphorical dead."

"But you're a prisoner in your own home, Robert," Karsten said. "A life prisoner with no chance of payroll."

Robert shrugged. "I'd prefer this life, and all its uncertainties, to the living death of dementia."

"Are you sure of that?" Karsten's tone was a little too condescending.

*"Of course."* He stepped into the kitchen and scowled at him. "Until *you* have suffered the hell of losing your mind, of not knowing the ones who deeply loved you, and the loss of your dignity." His eyes were welling with tears. "Have you any idea what it's like not to be able to pee by yourself, and have someone wipe your behind after you've been to the toilet?"

Patricia held his hand and spoke softly to him. "He is only trying to help, Robert."

He squeezed her hand, looked across at Karsten, and half smiled. "I apologise. The last few days have been somewhat traumatic for us. And despite my anger, the points you make are well made."

Karsten shook his head. "It is for me to apologise. My comments were insensitive."

"No, my young friend. Your comments precisely address the problems this vortex presents us with. Shall we all move into the lounge?" He looked around the congested room, acknowledged the nods of agreement, and then slowly walked out of the kitchen.

As everyone began to settle themselves in the lounge, a loud knock from the front door reverberated down the hall.

Sam wandered across to the window and peered between the curtains. "Bollocks. It's that bloody policeman Morris. It looks like he's got a policewoman with him."

"That's probably his wife," Marie said sheepishly from the other side of the room. She'd forgotten to tell anyone she'd invited her erstwhile cousin to the house for a cup of coffee. "He's my cousin."

Heads span around and eyebrows were raised.

"I've only met him a few times when I was young." She shrugged and blushed. "Family argument, many years ago. I've invited him round for a cup of coffee."

Guillaume stood up quickly and started shepherding everyone out of the room. "I think we should leave." He gently held Marie's shoulder. "I'll leave this one to you, my dear. He doesn't need to know anything about anyone. Keep it to family business."

She nodded, waited for everyone other than Robert and Patricia to leave, walked down the hall, opened the front door, smiled warmly, and offered her hand.

"Alan? Alan Morris?"

Morris nodded, still unsure why out of the blue, this pretty young woman had contacted him.

An uncomfortable silence fell over them, until Frankie stepped forward and offered her hand to Marie. "I'm Frankie. I'm his," she said and nodded to Alan, "his better half. Can we come in?"

Marie shook her head as if she was coming out of a deep sleep. "I'm so sorry. Please, please come in. Follow me." She walked down the hall, and turned into the lounge where Robert and Patricia were sitting. "This is my mum and dad."

Robert stood up, walked across to meet Frankie and Alan, shook their hands, and then gestured for them to sit on the sofa.

Patricia linked arms with her daughter and smiled at their visitors. "So pleased to meet you. Would you like something to drink? Tea, coffee."

Frankie smiled. "Tea would be lovely. Mine's white, no sugar, and his," she said and nodded to Alan, who still seemed struck dumb, "is white, one sugar."

"Excellent." Patricia replied with genuine warmth in her voice. "I'll put the kettle on."

"We were intrigued by your invitation." She softly elbowed Alan in the ribs. "Weren't we, darling?"

"Mmmm?" Alan sat up and finally smiled. "Yes. Came like a bolt out of the blue."

Marie smiled and sat down opposite them on a pouffe. "Sorry about the 'out of the blue', but I didn't really know the best way to contact you." She smiled. "At least it worked."

Over the next hour, they discussed why the break had happened, drank tea, ate cake and biscuits, caught up on their recent pasts, and finally agreed they should keep in touch.

"How long have you been in the force, Alan?" Robert asked.

"Too long to remember. The police was the only job I ever wanted, but over the years it's done its best to break me and my marriage. That's why I'm resigning. We're going to move away, and start afresh."

"Good on you. It takes a hell of a lot to do what you're planning. I wish you the very best of luck."

"Thank you. The one thing today's shown me, is life's too short to be wasted."

"It can't possibly be that theory, it was disproved in 1978." Matt and Mark were again discussing quantum mechanics as they walked into the lounge.

A proverbial feather could have knocked Alan down if he'd been standing up. He pointed at the brothers, started to stand up, but was pulled back into his seat by Frankie. She stood up, and at the same time, pressed Alan back into the sofa. "Sorry, we haven't been introduced. I'm Frankie." She turned and glanced at Alan. "His better half."

"Matthew Stroudle. It's a great pleasure to meet you at last. Alan has spoken a lot about you at our 'meetings'." He gently lied. "This is my brother, Mark."

"Pleasure, Mrs Morris. We have had a long and fruitful working relationship with your husband." Mark replied as he leaned forward and kissed her hand.

"Why don't you join us?" Frankie said with a smile. "I'm sure you have a lot to talk about with Alan."

*"Fucking right they do!"* Morris thought in utter disbelief at what he was hearing. "Good to see you again," he said with a massive spoonful of sarcasm.

"I don't know what the problem is, but if you aren't pleasant to these two, then the deal's off." Frankie hissed in his ear. "Marie, this is a lovely house," she said as she looked around the room. "We're pretty short on space where we live. I'd give my eye teeth for a house like this. Can I take a look around?"

Marie got up from her chair. "Of course." She offered her arm to Frankie, and they walked out of the lounge, chatting like friends who'd known each other for years.

"Have fun," Frankie called over her shoulder.

Robert got up and gestured for Patricia to come with him. "Excuse us, won't you? Need to make the bed." They held hands and walked out of the lounge.

Morris jumped to his feet and walked quickly over to Matt and Mark. "I don't know what scam you two are pulling, but it's pissing got me beat."

Matt and Mark stared at each other in complete bafflement at Morris's comments. "A scam? You believe that we are, how do you put it, ah yes, trying to pull one over on these punters? Is that what you are suggesting?" Mark asked with incredulity in his voice.

"Jesus! Have you pair swallowed a bloody encyclopaedia and a dictionary?" He prodded Mark in the shoulder. "You haven't got enough brain cells between you to raise a slug's IQ." He turned to Matt. "Come on, we've known each other for long enough. What the hell's going on?"

"We are simply helping with the resolution of a complex scientific problem. Nothing more. Nothing less," Matt said matter-of-factly. "Would you like me to explain it to you?"

"Please do. I'm intrigued to hear what bullshit you're going to spout." Five minutes later, Morris couldn't find the words to express his utter disbelief at what he was being told. He waved his hands in the air. "OK. OK. You've got me as well. But for Christ's sake, tell me, how the hell have you remembered all that stuff?"

The brothers looked at each other and chuckled.

"Should we tell him?" Matt said quietly to Mark.

"We should check with Klaus first," Mark replied, glancing at Morris.

Matt nodded in agreement, "We need a minute to speak to someone," he said to Morris. Then, arm in arm with Mark, they turned, smiled at Morris, and walked out of the room.

# Chapter Hundred-Twenty-Eight

Charlie stayed to keep an eye on Alfredo. They were sat on the cellar steps, staring at the far wall.

"What happened to you?" Charlie finally broke the silence.

Alfredo kept his gaze fixed on the wall. "I heard a name."

"I didn't hear anything."

Alfredo tapped the side of his head. "In here. Someone called out. Shouted." He tapped the side of his head again and frowned. "It was in here."

Charlie's eyebrows did their best to meet in the middle. "Who was it?"

Alfredo shrugged. "I don't know. It sounded American. He was shouting. Ordering." He sat upright, his eyes still fixed on the wall. "There was a lot of shouting. Shouting and explosions."

A few weeks earlier, Charlie would have thought he was talking to a lunatic, but what he was hearing, sounded very much like Alfredo's links with the past had begun to strengthen.

"What name was it?" He pressed.

"Innocenti."

"Innocenti?" Charlie's eyebrows now tried to reach his hairline.

"Si. La mia famiglia. My family. I am certain it was a soldier. Un soldato nella seconda guerra. *(A soldier in the second war.")*

Charlie's eyebrows relaxed into a frown. "World War Two?"

Alfredo nodded. "I felt a terrible heat. Terrible. Like a furnace." He stood up, and like a zombie, walked towards the photos on the melamine board.

"Alfredo!" Charlie jumped up, ran after him, grabbed hold of his arm, and stopped him a couple of feet away from the photos. The despair in Alfredo's eyes made Charlie instantly release his grip on his arm.

He watched as Alfredo moved closer to the wall, and stretched out his right hand close to the photo of the tank, Klaus had replaced on the board. He moved even closer and whispered to the faceless commander.

"È il momento di venire casa. *(It's time to come home.)*"

# Chapter Hundred-Twenty-Nine

Marie was walking down the stairs with Frankie, having carefully omitted a tour of the loft.

"This place is wonderful," Frankie said, desperately trying not to show too many signs of envy. "My nephew would call it lush. Lush or sick. Never sure which means the best." She chuckled and smiled warmly at Marie.

"Shall we have a cup of coffee?" Marie suggested, adopting the same diversionary tactics she'd used upstairs, to avoid taking Frankie down into the cellar.

"What's in here?"

Marie was about to say it was full of building materials, and was a little dangerous, when Frankie decided she'd open the door herself, and take a look.

"The cellar!" She exclaimed. "I love cellars. Always full of things you've forgotten or tucked away because you didn't have room for them. Full of memories and surprises."

*"You have no idea how right you are,"* Marie thought. "Yes, but it's only full of rubbish. You know, all the stuff everybody says they really need or might use, and then ten years later, it's still there gathering dust."

"I know, that's what makes them so much fun." Frankie's expression was like a child pleading to be allowed to play a little longer in the park. "Can I take a look?"

Marie knew that refusing would cause more problems than showing her around the bits of the cellar she'd let her see. "OK, come on then. But please, be careful. Follow me, and I'll show you around."

Frankie lifted, peered, chuckled, sighed, knelt down, turned, pointed, checked CDs, read a few pages of some old magazines, and finally shook her head. "What an amazing place. I could spend days in here. Be alright if I came back?"

Marie smiled and edged towards the stairs. "Of course. Shall we go back upstairs?" It wasn't a question, but Frankie's attention had been taken by the far side of the cellar.

"What's over there?" She turned back to Marie. "We' haven't been over there, have we?"

Marie swallowed hard, shook her head, and linked arms with Frankie. "Come on, we can check that out next time."

Frankie resisted. "Can't we just take a quick peak?" She held up her hands in silent prayer. "Just for a few seconds?"

"For a few seconds, and then we go back upstairs." She looked at her with a single raised eyebrow and a slight scowl. "OK?"

Frankie kissed her on the cheek. "Thanks. I just feel like I need to take a look."

Marie led the way, and did her best to take Frankie away from the Lazarus Pool, which flickered at her in the dim light, like a sputtering blue candle.

"They're taking their time?" Morris said questioningly to Robert.

Robert pushed himself up on the arms of the chair. "Come on, let's find out what's so interesting."

They walked out into the hall and Robert saw the cellar door was open. "I'll just check if they're down there."

Morris nodded, and followed him.

"ANYONE THERE?" Robert called out.

Marie's attention was switched to her father's call, and Frankie took the opportunity to move closer to where she was being drawn.

"DOWN HERE, DAD." Marie called back. "WE'LL BE UP IN A…"

"Ooooh!"

Marie span around. Frankie was stood in the middle of the Lazarus Pool.

"Ooooh, this feels wonderful. Like a jacuzzi. What's here?"

Marie was a few yards away from her. "There's a draft from a duct which takes warm air up into the house." She offered her hand to Frankie. "Come on, let's go back and join your husband."

Frankie ran her fingers through her hair, and threw her head back. "It feels so good. Can't I stay for a little longer?"

*"In for a penny, in for a pound,"* Marie thought. "Yeah, that's fine."

Frankie's hands dropped to her sides, and then started massaging her abdomen. Unseen by her, the Lazarus Pool had wrapped itself around her, and a deep blue spinning star was slowly penetrating her abdomen. As it disappeared from view, Frankie shuddered, and like a deflating balloon, sank to the floor.

"Oh shit!" Marie ran forward, and cradled her in her arms.

"YOU OK DOWN THERE?" Robert called.

"YES, DAD. BE UP IN A COUPLE OF MINUTES. CAN YOU PUT THE KETTLE ON?"

"NO PROB. TEA OR COFFEE?"

"TWO TEAS PLEASE." She turned her attention back to Frankie. "Frankie, come on," She lightly patted her cheeks. "Come on." She squeezed the end of her nose, closing off her nostrils, and after a few seconds, Frankie was coughing and spluttering.

"What happened?"

"I think it must have been the heat. It can get very hot and airless down here." Marie gripped her arm, and helped her to her feet. "Come on. Let's get you upstairs. A hot, sweet tea is what you need."

As they made their way upstairs, cell division had already started in Frankie's fallopian tubes. An indisputable miracle of nature had started. Another spirit-energy had found a host.

# Chapter Hundred-Thirty

Karsten was still feeling a little unsettled after outlining his thoughts about the Lazarus Pool to the group. He wandered out of Takanun and waved to an old man resting on a Zimmer frame, who'd stopped outside the gate.

"Lovely weather," Karsten called out to him.

The old man looked up and smiled. "Beautiful. You live there?" He pointed at the High Wood.

"Just staying with friends."

He shook his head. "You should be careful. Bloody odd house that one."

Karsten walked closer to him. "Odd?" he said, tipping his head to one side.

"Damn odd. My dad told me things about that place that'd make your hair curl. When I was a boy, we used to give it a wide berth."

Karsten was intrigued. "Why was that?" He was now a few feet away from the old man. "You know, walk around it?"

The old man scanned around him, looking for some unseen 'enemy', shrugged, stepped away from his Zimmer, and leaned on the gate. "He told me." He had one last glance over his shoulder to check no-one was around. "That not long after the First World War, two men in the house, brothers they were, locked up their mother in a bedroom. Locked her up. Hard to credit, isn't it?"

Karsten nodded.

"Apparently," he said and leaned on the gate, "they said she was possessed by demons, or evil things like them. Mad woman, or something like that, that's what they called her. If it was me, I'd have had the place exercised. All day and night, she'd just sit up there," he said and looked over Karsten's shoulder, and pointed at the house, "in that …" Suddenly his jaw dropped and his eyes opened to the point where Karsten thought they would fall out of his head. The old man stepped back. "Don't you go in there. She's still there!" He grabbed his Zimmer and 'sped' off down the street. "DON'T GO IN THERE." He shouted over his shoulder to Karsten, as he disappeared around a corner.

Karsten stared in puzzlement at the back of the old man, shook his head, turned to back to the house, and smiled. Waving at him from an upstairs window, was Rebecca. He waved back, walked up the path to the house, made himself a ham sandwich, mug of coffee, and settled onto the sofa in the lounge.

"Sit down here, and I'll make us a hot drink," Charlie said comfortingly.

Karsten stirred on the sofa.

"Could I have a couple of those chocolate biscuits?" Alfredo replied.

Karsten slowly opened his eyes and peered blearily around the room.

Alfredo smiled wanly at him.

"Sorry. I must have fallen asleep." Karsten, rubbed his eyes, stretched, smiled at Alfredo, and immediately understood that something profound had affected him. "What's happened?"

"I'm not really sure. I was close to the photos, the one of the tank, and I heard a voice inside my head." He sat forward and scratched the side of his head. "A voice which spoke a name."

Karsten tilted his head to one side and looked questioningly at Alfredo. "What name?"

"Mine, I mean ours. My family name. Innocenti."

Charlie walked in with two cups of strong coffee and a packet of chocolate digestives under his arm. He lifted one of the cups to Karsten. "Coffee?"

He shook his head and patted the sofa. "I'm fine. Sit down and tell me everything that's been happening."

Ten minutes later, Karsten was staring intently at Charlie. "Alfredo should join us as a Spirit Walker."

Charlie nodded and turned to Alfredo. "You would need to properly understand what this would mean."

Momentarily, fear flashed across Alfredo's face, but it was soon replaced with genuine interest. "Dimmi tutto." He smiled. "Tell me everything."

"You must understand," Karsten said, "that there is real danger in what we do. *Real. Genuine. Risks.*" He emphasised the individual words.

Alfredo looked dumbstruck. He stared at the wall for a few minutes, but then stood and smiled. "I fully understand the risks, but after helping my family to move on, I want to join you." He gestured for Charlie to get to his feet. "We will be like the Tre Moschettieri. The Three Musketeers." He grabbed their hands and raised them in the air. "Tutti per uno e uno per tutti."

Karsten laughed. "All for one, and one for all!"

"I want to be Aramis," Charlie said as he mimed a thrust with a rapier.

"PORTHOS!" Karsten parried Charlie's thrust.

"ATHOS!" Alfredo bowed deeply.

"Can I be d'Artagnan? And the full quote is 'All for one and one for all, united we stand divided we fall.'"

The Three Musketeers stared wide-eyed at each other.

"There are two other quotes I particularly like," D'Artagnan continued. "'I do not cling to life sufficiently to fear death.' And, 'The merit of all things lies in their difficulty.'"

As one, they slowly turned around.

"Good day, everyone."

Charlie's jaw cracked on the floor.

D'Artagnan stepped forward and shook Karsten and Alfredo by the hand. "I don't believe we've been introduced. My name is Peter Wallins." He smiled broadly and patted Charlie on the shoulder. "You feeling OK?"

"But you …"

"Spit it out, Charlie."

"I saw you. Your spirit was with gran. You were going over to the other side together." He stared hard at Peter. "Gran said you were back together."

"Did you see us pass over together?"

Charlie shook his head. "Well, no. Only mum and gran." He massaged his temples and suddenly raised his eyebrows. "Are you alive?" He prodded Peter's chest with his index finger. "You are alive! You're not a spirit. How have you done that?"

"Still too many lost souls to help, and I like it here." He gripped Charlie's shoulder. "That's why I want to help you and become one of the team."

"But how are you alive?"

Peter tapped the side of his nose. "That's for me to know, and you to find out."

"But..."

"Could you tell us how you know Peter, Charlie?" Karsten asked with slight irritation in his voice. "Or rather *what* your friend is?"

Charlie rubbed the back of his head. "With anyone else this would be difficult, but with you, it will be a lot easier."

Half an hour later, Charlie and Peter's history had been fully explained to the open-mouthed Karsten and Alfredo.

Karsten crashed into amazement and bounced back into bewilderment. "*You* were with Charlie in Burma?" He shook his head. "During World War Two?"

Peter nodded.

"And you knew his gran?"

"Guilty as charged."

Alfredo patted Peter warmly on the back. "Benvenuto."

Karsten offered his hand. "Willkommen, Peter. I look forward to spending time discussing your experiences. We still have much to learn."

"I still don't know your names?" Peter said, tousling Charlie's hair.

Karsten and Alfredo looked at each other, back at Peter, shrugged, shook their heads, and smiled.

"Karsten Bauer." He bowed slightly from the waist.

"You're German," Peter said with a discernible frown.

"Yes. German and proud. However, I am of a generation which despises the monstrous actions of Hitler and supports the principle of a single European community." If Karsten had hackles, they would have been raised.

Peter smiled. "Please understand, I am from another time and generation which suffered terribly at the hands of Germany." He gestured at the room. "This century is new to me. But I'm learning." He offered his hand to Karsten, who looked down at it, frowned, but then looked up at Peter, smiled, and shook his hand warmly.

"Alfredo Innocenti. Welcome to the twenty-first century." He raised Peter's arm in the air. "'Tous pour un, un pour tous. All for one and one for all.'" He began to lower his arm, but paused. "United we stand, divided we fall."

Later, after a lengthy and detailed discussion with Klaus, Ralph, and Guillaume, it was agreed that Peter would join the Spirit Walker group, with the proviso that Alfredo's reaction to the photo of the tank had to be properly understood and resolved.

# Chapter Hundred-Thirty-One

"What do we have which can be reported to the Astrea?" Ralph, with Klaus and Guillaume, was walking up and down the rows of photos in the gallery at High Wood.

*"You have enough. More than enough."* The voice was clear and strident. *"You seem to have forgotten the principles of the organisation you have responsibility for."*

"Isaac!" The name was spoken in chorus, as the three men glanced back and forth between him and themselves, their expressions betraying their surprise.

*"You have all been diverted from your main purpose in life. Papaver Rhoeas has always been a secret organisation, and you have opened us up to charlatans, quacks, fakes, con artists. How did it come to this? Those of us who have passed on are unhappy. You will make a statement, which will make it very clear, that everything which has been said was false. All monies will be returned. You will return to our principles. Elizabeth will focus solely on her task in High Wood. Nothing else will distract her. The four 'Musketeers', a very apt name, our Spirit Walkers, must become active. I will come again, to confirm you have returned to our chosen path. Tell the others what has been decided."* And suddenly, he was gone.

For a full minute, they stood in an uncomfortable silence until Klaus spoke.

Ralph scowled. "Should we do as he demands?" he asked firmly.

Guillaume's expression said more than words ever could.

"Guillaume, we have to manage this situation. We're here today, in the present, not in heaven," Ralph continued, in his level mid-western accent. "We help souls to move on to the other side, but does that mean we have to take their advice?" He raised his eyebrows. "Does it?"

"Mein Bruder…" Guillaume started to speak, but Klaus jumped in.

"Ralph is right to raise this, Guillaume. It is a question we must ask"

Guillaume shook his head and stormed off down the stairs.

The two men looked after him and sighed.

"He will calm down," Klaus said none too convincingly. "The loss of Isaac is still very raw."

"Should we take Isaac's advice? Couldn't we come up with a compromise position, Klaus? Surely that's not beyond the wit of man?"

Klaus pursed his lips. "Let's find Guillaume and discuss this calmly."

Guillaume was in the garden, trying his best to be polite to Matt and Mark. "I'm sure Klaus will be down shortly."

Matt and Mark whispered to each other for a few seconds. "We'll wait."

Guillaume's curiosity button had been firmly pressed. He turned to the brothers. "What is it you want to ask him?"

"That policeman." Matt nodded towards the house. "He wants to know how we became like this. He seems to have a very clear memory of two individuals, who were, to say the least, somewhat anti-social in their behaviour. We however," he said and nodded at Mark, "have only an extremely vague recollection of these alleged earlier incarnations of ourselves."

"And what do you want to ask Klaus?"

"Can we show him the Lazarus Pool?"

"NEIN!" The voice was clarion clear and belonged to Klaus. "Why would you want to do such a thing? This man is no friend of ours."

Matt and Mark squeezed tightly up against each other and looked in shock and fear at Klaus.

"Klaus." Ralph was close behind him. "Calm down. They were only asking a question."

"Ja, but …"

"But me no buts," Ralph replied, putting his arm around Klaus's shoulders.

"'But me no buts' is circa 1820. Mrs Centlivre used the phrase in 1708, but actually it was Scott's employment of it in 'The Antiquary' in 1816 which made it fashionable," Mark said with a perfectly straight face.

Klaus, Ralph, and Guillaume stared open-mouthed at him, glanced at each other, and smiled.

"Let us talk to him first and decide what to do," Ralph suggested to Matt.

The brothers glanced quickly at each other and nodded in agreement.

"We'll be a couple of minutes," Ralph said, indicating that Matt and Mark should leave them alone.

"OK?" Ralph asked Guillaume.

Guillaume tried to put on a serious face, but the mood had been broken, and as Isaac had always said, life was too short to waste on petty disagreements. "I am OK, but we must talk about what Isaac said."

"Not here though," Ralph said quietly.

Guillaume nodded in agreement.

# Chapter Hundred-Thirty-Two

"You OK?" Morris jumped up from his chair in a panic, ran to Frankie's side, wrapped his arm around her waist, and helped her to the sofa.

"Don't fuss. Really, I'm fine. It was just a little stuffy in the cellar, and I got a little woozy." She gently pushed Morris away. "Just get me a glass of water will you. I still feel a little queasy."

He turned and jogged into the kitchen.

"He's very attentive," Marie said with a raised eyebrow.

"We're," she said and looked up to check that Morris wasn't coming back, "getting back together after some pretty bad years." She shrugged and screwed up her face. "Never marry a policeman. The force takes over their life. He's resigning, and we're going to make a fresh start."

Marie smiled and squeezed her hands. "You look good together. I hope everything works out for you."

Morris walked quickly back into the lounge with a tumbler of iced water. "Drink that." He sat down close to her. "How are you feeling?"

She smiled and nodded as she drank the water. "Much better thanks."

"What happened?" Morris asked with a concerned tone.

"Nothing really. It was pretty stuffy, and I stayed down there too long." She looked at Marie who smiled.

Morris stroked her cheek and kissed her tenderly. "We'd better leave you in peace," he said to Marie as he stood up.

"There's so much more I want to ask you. Can't you stay for a little longer?" Marie asked.

Frankie looked longingly at Morris, whose new persona couldn't refuse anything she wanted. "Thanks. Yes, we'd love to."

"I'm going down to take a look at the pool," Bill called from the hall. "Shouldn't be too long. I'll take a look at the tank while I'm down there."

Morris looked up at Marie, with a frown as deep as the Marianas Trench. "You've got a pool in your cellar?"

Marie's expression gave nothing away. "Pool table. Bill's American. He plays in a league in Boston and needs to keep his hand in."

Morris seemed to accept this, but then a little niggle needed an answer. "What's an American doing here?"

"Oh, Bill's over here working on … he's working with Dad on a project." She smiled. *"Shit, I hope he doesn't ask anything else,"* she thought.

Morris nodded and smiled. "Uh huh."

"Anyone fancy a glass of wine?" Marie wanted to change the subject.

Morris and Frankie looked at each other and said a few quiet words. "Thanks. White for me, and red for Frankie."

"No problem. Sauvignon Blanc OK?" Marie asked Alan who nodded. "Merlot Frankie?"

"Please."

As Marie knelt down to get the Merlot, Bill came trotting into the lounge.

"The pool's got bigger," he said loudly as he came to a sudden stop. "Oh, hi." He stepped close to Morris and offered his hand. "Name's Bill."

"Alan, and this is my wife Frankie."

"Cool. Good to meet you. You know Marie then?"

"Yes. We're related, and were catching up. She was telling us you like pool."

Bill chuckled to himself and raised an eyebrow. "Don't know where she got that idea from. Bowling's my game. Started with my dad when I was eight."

Marie stood up sharply behind Morris and Frankie, shaking her head and waving her arms at Bill. *"You. Love. Pool,"* she mouthed slowly at him.

Morris glanced back at her, and she quickly held up the bottle of Merlot. "I was asking Bill if he wanted a glass." She shook her head again at Bill, who smiled. "I'd prefer a glass of Sauvignon."

Marie sighed, and began to walk to the kitchen to get a bottle of Sauvignon Blanc from the fridge. She gestured at Bill to follow her, but he was already chatting with Morris and Frankie. *"Piss, shit, and balls,"* she thought. *"This is going to take some explaining."*

Klaus, Guillaume, and Ralph, came in from the relative calm of the garden to the nuclear potential of the kitchen.

"We may have a problem," Marie said as calmly as she could.

The four Musketeers came in from High Wood, and as they were walking down the hall, a call from the lounge stopped them dead in their tracks.

"Charlie?"

Charlie recognised the voice. "Detective Sergeant Morris." He walked nervously into the lounge, forced a smile, and stood close to the fireplace.

"Not detective sergeant for much longer, Charlie. I've decided to leave the force, and if you've got any sense, you'll do the same."

Charlie could hear the echo of his father's words, who'd done his best to dissuade him from going down the same destructive path as he'd chosen. "Why?" He couldn't disguise his surprise.

"Oh, mainly personal reasons." He turned to Frankie and smiled.

Charlie shrugged.

"Sorry, Charlie, you haven't met my wife." He put his arm around her shoulder. "This is my darling Frankie, who I'm glad to say I remembered before it was too late."

"Pleased to meet you." Charlie felt uncomfortable in this private moment.

Frankie picked up on Charlie's embarrassment and stood up. "I've heard a lot about you."

"All good, I hope?"

"Well, mostly." Frankie smiled warmly. "Joining us?"

"Got a few things to do in the cellar."

"Popular place the cellar," Morris said with a slight frown.

"You coming Aramis?" Alfredo called from the cellar door. "We need to take another look at that photo."

"If I was going to stay as a detective sergeant Charlie, you'd have tickled my antenna," Morris said to him with a knowing smile. "You'd better check out that photo."

"Thanks, I'd better go."

"Get out of the force while you can, Charlie. You'll regret it if you don't." Morris stood and took a firm grip on his hand and wrist. "Promise me you'll finish with the force." He looked deep into his eyes. "Do this for me and anyone you love."

Charlie looked across at Marie, who blew him a kiss, which Morris saw.

With tears in his eyes, he put his other hand on Charlie's shoulder. "Do it for her. Don't go down the same path I took. Promise me."

"I promise." Charlie was already close to making his decision about his future, and his way forward was now crystal clear.

Morris looked across at Bill. "Do you need to go with them?"

Bill nodded. "It'd probably be a good idea if I did."

He took Frankie's hand. "Come on, let's leave these good people. It looks like they've got a lot to do." He smiled at Marie. "Give me a ring, and we'll arrange to get together again."

She nodded. "I'd like that." She walked to Morris and kissed him on the cheek.

# Chapter Hundred-Thirty-Three

Charlie rejoined the Musketeers in the hall with Bill close in tow.

"Problem?" Karsten asked as he held open the cellar door.

"No." Charlie smiled. "Quite the opposite really." He walked through the open cellar door, grinned at Karsten, and trotted down the steps. "You coming?"

Bill nodded and followed them into the cellar.

"Shit! It is getting bigger." Charlie was leaning against the wall close to the Lazarus Pool. "Bigger and bluer." He turned to the others. "Do you think it's affecting us?"

"Probably, when we're this close," Alfredo said none too convincingly. "Maybe you have to go into it like the others?"

Peter was stood within inches of the spinning blue wonder. "So this is it." He brushed his hand through the surface. "Mmmm, warm. Warm, but also comforting." He took a few steps back. "A bit too comforting." He looked around at the others. "What do you think it is?"

"What do you think it is?" Karsten asked softly, stepping closer to Peter.

He slowly turned his head to face Karsten and smiled. "I would say that this whirlpool. This, what did you call it?" He looked across at Charlie.

"Lazarus Pool."

Peter stroked his chin. "Good name that." He looked back at Karsten. "I would say that this Lazarus Pool," he said, as he tossed something into it. Immediately they were showered in an explosion of cerulean stars. "Was magic."

"Scheiße! Was war zum Teufel das? *(Shit! What the hell was that?)*" Karsten's automatic reaction was to brush the stars off his sweater, but they were already settling back into the Lazarus Pool. He wasn't sure if he should be angry or scared. "What did you throw into it?"

"I've seen one of these before." Peter avoided Karsten's question.

"What did you say?" Charlie said with puzzlement.

"I've seen one of these before." He sat on the floor, and stared into the 'pool'.

"Wo? Wo hast du das gesehen? I am sorry. Where have you seen this before?" Karsten was stabbing his finger at the Lazarus Pool. "Wo? And what did you throw into it?"

Peter span around on his bottom, and looked up at Karsten and the other Musketeers. "I saw it below a crypt at Wewelsburg Castle, and I threw a Totenkopf into the pool. A Death's Head."

Charlie and Alfredo shrugged, shook their heads, glanced at Karsten, and raised their hands to the ceiling.

Karsten remained silent and still.

Peter stood up. "I believe Karsten has heard of Wewelsburg Castle, and a Death's Head." He looked across at him, and Karsten's eyes told him he knew very well what they were.

Karsten spoke quietly, and deliberately. "It was planned by the Nazis, that when they had established themselves as rulers of the world, Wewelsburg Castle would be the 'Grail Castle' of their regime. For Himmler, Wewelsburg Castle was not so much the location where the Grail was hidden, but where his Grail Order, the SS, the Schutzstaffel, and its sacred treasures, the most important of which was the Spear of Destiny, would be brought, and from which the magical power of the Nazi regime would radiate out."

"But that sounds like *Raiders of the Lost Ark* stuff," Charlie said with a frown which had turned his forehead into a corrugated roof. "You're not serious, are you?"

Karsten slowly nodded. "Deadly serious. The castle's history started several centuries before the National Socialists came to power in 1933."

He pulled an old camping chair out from under a pile of cushions, sat down, and after some heaving and swearing, the others were all sat on tattered camping chairs.

"Today, Wewelsburg Castle is part museum, part youth hostel, part bar-restaurant. When the estate was redesigned, it was shaped like a spear, which followed Himmler's belief, that the site would become the location where the Spear of Destiny would be kept. It is believed that Hitler had a vision of his future when he visited the museum in Vienna, where the Spear was on display, and he became convinced that whoever possessed it would control the fate of the world. Wewelsburg Castle was going to be the New Jerusalem and the centre of Germany. From 1941 onwards, the architects called the complex the 'Centre of the World. The work was done by slave labour, and about thirteen hundred died building it." He paused for a few seconds, his face not giving away his growing feelings of disquiet. "The Totenkopf, the Death's Head skull, was the universal cap badge of the SS." He stared at Peter, but said nothing.

Charlie frowned and turned to Peter. "And you've been in this castle?"

"I was bringing back the spirit of a British POW who was a slave labourer at Wewelsburg Castle. Beneath the crypt, behind a pillar, was a concealed secret room and in the room was something which looked remarkably like that." Peter jerked his thumb over his shoulder at the Lazarus Pool.

Charlie raised his hands to the ceiling, and shook his head. "Now there's a crypt and a secret room?"

Peter looked peeved. "It's there. It was a lot bigger than this one. And I know what it's made up of."

Karsten leaned forward, resting his elbows on his knees. "Which is?"

"The souls of tens of thousands murdered by the SS, and imprisoned below the crypt at Wewelsburg Castle. The Nazis believed it would provide a source of immense power, but fortunately, they never worked out how to harness it." He turned and stared at the Lazarus Pool. "The souls of the dead. That's what's in this." He turned around. "Isn't it?"

"That is what we believe," Karsten replied. "Why did you throw a Death's Head into it?"

"The crypt was littered with piles of Death's Head insignia. I picked up a couple, because they looked like they were important." He turned back again to the Lazarus Pool. "And its reaction, is exactly the same as the one in Wewelsburg. I don't know why, but souls don't react well to it."

"Do you need me for this?" A trembling American voice from somewhere in the shadows, reminded them that Bill was still there, and had been listening attentively to their conversation.

Karsten turned and smiled at Bill. "No. Not for this, Bill, but we still need your expertise to help us resolve how we identify the faces on the photos."

Bill breathed a deep sigh of relief. "Thank the Lord for that. I'll get back upstairs and get on to it."

Peter frowned deeply. "There is no known reason why the other pool of souls isn't still below the crypt at Wewelsburg Castle."

# Chapter Hundred-Thirty-Four

"Shut down the web site, all social media, Twitter, Facebook, and start to organise reimbursement of all donations."

There was a stunned silence on all the phones. The conference call had been hastily organised by Ralph.

"And how do you propose we explain this sudden retraction of the stated facts?" Renaat wasn't happy, despite understanding this had come from Isaac.

There was a chorus of agreement over the phones from the other members of the Astrea.

"We remain on our agreed course."

"I won't accept this."

"Ridiculous."

"Who runs Papaver Rhoeas?"

"Absolutely not!"

Renaat continued, "*We* run this organisation, not the dead." He regretted his insensitive words the instant they'd left his mouth. "Je présente mes excuses sans réserve. *(I offer my unqualified apologies.)* But what I say still remains true. It is *our* responsibility, the *living* members of Papaver Rhoeas, to determine what we do. Isaac was our Chef Charon, a great Chef Charon, but he is no longer with us." He turned to Guillaume. "You were appointed Chef Charon, and it is you who must lead, and not be led."

Guillaume, who initially looked like he would burst with anger, was now more relaxed. "Merci Renaat. Excuses acceptées. *(Thank you Renaat. Apology accepted.)* However, I am glad you have expressed your concerns so strongly. We cannot be led by our emotions. Our decisions must be based on pragmatism, and that *we*," he said and emphasised the word, "the Astrea, determine the best way forward for this organisation."

*"You take far too much upon yourself brother!"*

Guillaume ignored Isaac's ill-tempered utterance. "I had to put Isaac's demands to you, but I am persuaded by you, that our current strategy should remain."

*"I will not allow this!"*

*"I'm afraid you have no other option, brother."*

*"No true brother of mine would ignore my views!"*

*"I am your true brother, but I am also Chef Charon, and have responsibilities to lead, which I intend to do. With or without your support."*

An uncomfortable silence smothered the conversation.

"We all know the way forward will not be easy, but it has to be done. We will not lose sight of our raison d'être. We will continue, by whatever methods possible, to save the souls of the missing of World War One, and now, those of the second conflict."

"We are all agreed then on continuing with the current strategy?" Ralph's tone was one which didn't ask for replies.

There was unanimous agreement.

*"You will regret this decision."* Isaac's voice could now be heard by everyone. *"Do not expect any further support."*

Ralph shrugged. "Our decision to go public remains, and if some feathers have been ruffled, then so be it. However, this organisation will remain focused on its first principles."

"Uh huh. Full steam ahead?" Bill asked.

"What was it Bush said?"

Bill smiled. "Read my lips."

"Can we talk?" Bill said to the four Musketeers who were sat in the kitchen drinking coffee.

"Yeah ... of cou ... rse." Charlie mumbled through a mouthful of chocolate digestive biscuit. "Sorry. What is it?"

"I need to spend some time on the web site, and social media programmes."

"How long before you come back to us?" Alfredo asked.

"Maybe a day?"

Smiles broke out around the table. "OK. Meet you back here tomorrow when you've finished." Charlie looked at his watch. "Around three?"

"Works for me." Bill took his coffee and walked briskly out of the kitchen.

"We have a few hours to kill," Karsten remarked. "Why don't we discuss exactly what we are going to do?"

# Chapter Hundred-Thirty-Five

Robert, Matt, and Mark, were stood outside the front door waiting for Professor Dennis Counsell and Dr Charles Bartle.

Matt was a little annoyed. "They're late."

Robert glanced at his watch and raised an eyebrow at Matt. "Three minutes? Hardly what I'd call late, Matt."

"When a time is agreed, it should be held to." He shook his head, but then smiled and waved, as the two distinguished scientists pushed open the gate.

Robert walked down the path to meet them. "So good to see you both again. Come, let's show you what all the excitement is about."

"You're looking particularly well, Bob. We were all very concerned when you left the department," Charles said caringly.

"Needed a break." He jogged on the spot for a few seconds. "Cardiff half marathon next year." He raised an eyebrow and chuckled.

Charles and Dennis stared at the cellar wall and looked confused.

"You were going to show us this marvel?" Dennis said with a subtle hint of irritation. "This," he said and pointed at the wall, "invisible marvel."

"Ah? Of course. You're not able to see it, are you?" Charles and Dennis's 'status' in life, and 'sensitivity', finally struck Robert. He walked around for a few seconds. "But you will be able to feel it."

He took Charles and Dennis by the hand, and walked into the Lazarus Pool.

"The air here is warm." Dennis looked down. "It has substance. And it's moving. It feels like a warm current of water." His eyes were fixed on his feet. "But there is nothing here."

Charles was also transfixed by the warmth rippling through his fingers.

Robert turned and gestured for them to follow. "We need to show you its effect."

Matt stepped forward. "Do you have a knife about you?"

Charles was a little disturbed. "A small fruit knife, but be extremely careful, it's very sharp."

Matt took the knife from him, and drew the blade across his palm, drawing gasps from Dennis and Charles, as copious blood came from his hand. "Please don't worry. There is really no need for concern." He walked slowly forward into the unseen swirling blue vortex, ran his bleeding hand through the cerulean currents for just over a minute, made a fist, and walked back to Dennis and Charles. "Do not be unduly shocked by what I am about to show you."

Dennis and Charles quickly looked at each other, shrugged, and then gestured for Matt to continue.

Finger by finger, he slowly opened his hand, until the pristine palm of his hand was exposed to them. Despite their assurances, they gasped like female fans, who'd come face to face with George Clooney.

"But your cut was … it was bleeding." They moved forward, held Matt's hand, and examined it closely.

"But this is impossible. Quite impossible," Charles exclaimed, as he gently prodded the palm of Matt's hand.

Mark moved closer. "I believe Conan Doyle, put it very well. 'When you have eliminated all which is impossible, then whatever remains, however improbable, must be the truth.' This, gentlemen, is the truth, the whole truth, and nothing but the truth." He raised his right hand. "So help me God."

"This can only be described as miraculous. Do you have a chair? I think I need to sit down," Charles asked Mark, who pulled a camping chair forward for him.

He sat down, pulled at his upper lip, breathed out loudly, pulled at his ear lobe, steepled his fingers, stood up, sat down again, leaned forward, stared intently at the air where the Lazarus Pool was, sat back in the chair, and threw his hands up in a sign of surrender. "This is so far beyond the boundaries of anything I understand, or anything that can be explained by the known laws of science and nature. It contradicts everything …"

"Is it alien?" Dennis asked quietly.

Robert answered. "No. It is definitely of this Earth."

"What Robert is implying, is we believe that this Lazarus Pool, has been formed by the spirit-energies of the souls of missing, and unknown soldiers of the Second and First World Wars," Mark said in a firm matter-of-fact way.

Dennis scanned Robert, Matt, and Mark's faces. "You're serious, aren't you?"

"Deadly." Robert smiled at his unintended pun. "All the evidence we have points to this being an agglomeration of spirit-energies."

"Ghosts?"

Robert shook his head. "No, Charles. Ghosts still have their souls. The Lazarus Pool is a quintessence of the human soul. It is formed, from the purest, undiluted form of human life energy."

"Exposure to which, generates the effect we saw with the cut hand."

Robert nodded. "But none of that has been empirically confirmed. QED, the reason we are all here." He turned his hands over, raising his palms to the ceiling. "How do we prove what this is, quantify its effects, and determine if it can be replicated?"

# Chapter Hundred-Thirty-Six

"Anyone want to start?" Peter asked.

Karsten spoke first. "We have been given a God-given opportunity to change the past, and bring about a better future for the world. The horrors I witnessed in Auschwitz-Birkenau has made me certain, that whatever the cost we must stop this abomination from ever happening."

"But where do we start?" Alfredo said through pursed lips. "Kill everyone who was involved in the Holocaust?"

Karsten nodded. "Somewhat implausible, but the ends would justify the means."

Peter leaned forward and rested his elbows on the kitchen table. "Trotsky put it much better. 'The end may justify the means as long as there is something that justifies the end.'" He clasped his hands together. "Alfredo is right. Where do we start? If any period in history is available to us, then where do we start? How far back do we go?" He looked intensely at Karsten. "It's an impossible task. To rid the world of this evil, do you kill the snake in the Garden of Eden, and prevent original sin?"

"You're taking this to a ridiculous conclusion," Karsten, clearly frustrated, replied. "I am simply saying, that if Hitler hadn't survived the First World War, it is likely that the Holocaust would not have happened."

Charlie shook his head and glanced sideways at Karsten. "But how can you be sure of that? There would have been thousands of Germans who strongly objected to the reparations paid to the allies. It may not have been the Jews, but some other group which would have been made a scapegoat."

Karsten began to feel he was fighting an uphill battle, but also had to concede that his idea did have pretty big holes in it. He slowly and begrudgingly nodded his head. "Ja. Du hast Recht. You are right. But we must try to do something?"

"But what? Wouldn't our time be better spent working on the photos, and helping these lost souls?" Charlie said.

"When I found my uncles in Kefalonia, I never felt so Euforico e beato. Uh, elated and blessed. Is this not what we must do?" Alfredo said passionately.

Karsten stood up and prowled around, deep in thought.

"Is he OK?" Peter asked Charlie.

Charlie looked over his shoulder at Karsten. "He's pretty intense sometimes, but I have absolute trust in him."

Peter smiled. "Pretty intense. Mmmm, that was my feeling. Seems solid."

Charlie nodded. "As a granite rock."

Karsten walked briskly back to the others.

"You look like the proverbial cat who found the cream," Charlie chirped.

Karsten frowned and shrugged.

"Never mind. What have you thought up?"

Karsten sat down and leaned forward on his knees. "If we go back to the First World War, and ensure that the Austrian corporal …"

"Che? Who?" Alfredo said with a grimace.

"Adolph Hitler."

"Si."

Karsten showed a little frustration with Alfredo, but smiled and continued. "If we go back, and are able to kill Hitler, and when we return, we find history has changed for the worse, then surely if we go back, and ensure Hitler isn't killed, we can put history's jig-saw back in place." He raised his hands to the ceiling and looked around at everyone. "What do you think?"

Peter was chewing the inside of his cheek. "That's a lot of ifs."

Karsten nodded. "Alfredo?"

"What you say makes sense, but there is so much that could go wrong." He ran his fingers through his hair. "And even if this works, and we stop the Holocaust, what do we do next? For me it would be to stop the massacre in Kefalonia, and save my uncles."

Karsten smiled. "Eliminating Hitler may possibly achieve that."

Alfredo pursed his lips. "Possibly."

"What you're proposing is almost unimaginable. There are too many variables. And what about the butterfly effect?" Bill had returned to the cellar.

Peter frowned. "Enlighten me."

"Basically, if you mess around with the past, you mess around with the future."

Peter smiled.

"Has anyone ever tested this butterfly effect?" Karsten asked slowly and deliberately.

Bill smiled and raised an eyebrow. "Not that I'm aware of, given the lack of time machines."

"Then how do we know it is true?" Karsten smiled and raised both eyebrows.

"Well quantum mechanics postulates …" Bill decided that even he found this hard to argue against. "Well no-one has ever been in a position to test the theory." As the words spilled out of his mouth, Bill realised he was supporting Karsten's proposal.

Karsten stood up, and theatrically bowed. "Thank you. I think you British say, I rest my case."

Bill raised his index finger.

Karsten sighed. "Yes, Bill?"

"It could be worthwhile looking into a potential bootstrap paradox."

The others, looked at him as if he'd spoken in ancient Coptic.

"A what?" Charlie just about managed two words.

"A bootstrap paradox, is also called a causal loop. It's postulated that a later, future event is the cause of an earlier, past event, through some sort of time travel. The past event is then partly or entirely the cause of the future event, which is the past event's cause." Bill frowned and looked at the floor. "Admittedly, it is a bit difficult to understand."

Alfredo was listening intently. "I think I understand."

Karsten and Charlie span around and stared in amazement at him.

"Do explain." Charlie was still limited to two words.

Alfredo took a deep breath. "In the novel *'Somewhere in Time'*, an object from the future is brought to the past. In the past, it ages, until it is brought back to the past again, apparently unchanged from its previous journey. An object making such a circular passage through time, must be identical whenever it is brought back to the past, otherwise it would create an inconsistency."

"Any wiser?" Charlie asked Karsten, still functioning with two words.

Karsten seemed to have lost the power of speech and simply shook his head.

"It was just something I read," Alfredo said with crimson cheeks.

Through this 'discussion', Peter had remained silent. "Butterflies, bootstraps, and bollocks."

"Sounds like a country and western song." Bill chuckled.

"We need to go back and kill this bastard." Peter stretched his arms behind his back. "Not much else to say is there?"

# Chapter Hundred-Thirty-Seven

"You feeling OK?" Alan was standing outside the bathroom listening to Frankie throwing up. "Shall I come in?"

"Go away. I'm fine."

"You don't sound fine."

"Alan, just leave me alone. I'll be fine."

The vomiting seemed to have stopped.

"You OK?"

"Jesus! Will you just piss off? I'll be out in a minute."

"I'll go down and make us a cup of tea."

"Great."

"Want a biscuit or some toast?"

"PISS OFF!"

He finally took the hint, trotted downstairs, but despite Frankie's assurances, he was concerned about her. Since they'd come back from Takanun, she hadn't been herself, and now this vomiting had started. The policeman in him started to re-emerge from the mental shadows.

*"This all started after we spent time at that bloody house,"* he thought angrily. *"Sod resigning, I'm going to get to the bottom of what goes in there, and the house next door."*

"You were making a cup of tea?" Frankie was stood in the kitchen doorway, a little pale, but looking herself again.

"Mmmm?"

"Penny for them?"

Alan turned and half smiled. "Just putting the kettle on."

"I'll have a piece of toast," Frankie said as she sat at the breakfast bar. "I'll butter it hot. Could you pass me the butter and marmite?"

"Yes m'lady."

She leaned forward on her elbows. "What happened to all the concern?"

Alan looked at her sheepishly from under his eyebrows. "Sorry, love. Just worried about you. I hate it when you're not well."

She stood up, walked around the breakfast bar, and hugged him. "I'm fine. Probably something I ate. Anyway, whatever it was is gone now. Every last diced piece of carrot's flushed away."

Alan pulled a face. "Didn't need the details."

The colour in Frankie's face suddenly drained away, she ran to the sink, and whatever remained in her stomach, bounced off the stainless steel of the sink.

Alan ran across to her and stroked her back. "I'm taking you to the doctor. This isn't right."

"Well your blood pressure, lungs, temperature, and heart are excellent," Dr Hurl said with a comforting smile. "Still got pains in your stomach?"

Frankie shook her head. "Just the nausea and sickness."

"And this was this morning?"

Alan's eyes sprang wide open. "She's not pregnant." He looked quickly across at Frankie. "You can't be." He looked back at the GP. "It's in her notes. We can't have children. How could you even suggest it?"

Dr Hurl tapped Frankie's notes. "I know your wife's history, Mr Morris. I was simply trying to understand what happened."

Frankie dug him in the ribs, and threw him a look which could have curdled milk. "Shhh!"

He leaned back in the chair, looking duly admonished. "Sorry. I'm really concerned."

"I fully understand, Mr Morris." She turned her attention back to Frankie. "Nothing like this before?"

She shook her head.

Dr Hurl tapped the end of her nose with her right index finger. "Hop up on the couch, and let's have a feel of this stomach of yours."

Alan sat nervously behind the drawn curtain as Dr Hurl examined Frankie. After a few minutes, they both emerged, smiling broadly. "Everything OK?"

"Yes. I'd like your wife to have some blood tests."

"Why's that?"

"Usual routine checks. Nothing at all to worry about." She turned back to her computer. "Make an appointment to come back and see me in ten days, and the results should be back by then." She typed in a few notes, and turned back to Frankie and smiled. "See you in ten days then."

They stood up, thanked her, and walked down the corridor to a nurse who took the bloods.

Alan started reading the request for blood tests.

"What are you reading that for? You don't know what the hell any of it means." Frankie said.

"I know a bit."

"You know what they say about a little knowledge."

He tapped the form and looked up. "What's a Quantitative HCG?"

"How the hell should I know?"

"Mrs Morris?"

Frankie stood up, smiled at the nurse, and gestured for Alan to stay where he was. "You wait here."

Back home, Morris was soon googling quantitative HCG, he couldn't believe what he was reading.

*'After How Many Days Can Pregnancy Be Detected? There are two types of pregnancy tests that will determine whether you should start preparing for a new member of the family or not. There are two types of blood tests. Quantitative HCG and Qualitative HCG. The good thing about a blood test is that you can take the test within 7 to 12 days of having unprotected sex.'*

Simultaneously he felt elation, desperate concern, disbelief, distrust, love, fear, and utter confusion.

"What have you found?"

Morris jumped out of his skin and quickly shut the lid of the laptop. "Nothing."

"Didn't seem like nothing to me."

"Oh, just looking at some …"

"Brain dried up?"

"Just some places we could move to."

"Show me?"

"Let me narrow them down a bit first."

*"Show me."* This time it was an instruction. "Just open the lid, and let me see. We can decide together."

"But ..."

"Show. Me. Now."

Morris slowly opened the laptop.

Frankie scanned the text, and clenched her fists. "This can't be right. They've mixed up the tests. This can't be mine!" She turned and ran out of the room in floods of tears.

Morris followed her to where he knew she'd be. A bedroom at the back of the house, which they'd decided would be the nursery when they were first married. "Frankie?"

"I'm fine." Her back was towards him, and the dim light of the room didn't help him check how she was.

"We'll go to the doctors in the morning and see what's happened."

"They can't mess around with me like this! It's cruel."

"Let's see tomorrow. Come on, let's go downstairs and have a drink. Things will look better in the morning."

"This should be the happiest day of my life, Alan. Why can't I believe this?"

"Because you've had too many disappointments." He walked to her, sat on the floor, and held her close. "For now, why don't we believe it? Who knows, it could be true? You're having the right symptoms."

She turned in his arms, looked up at him, and smiled. "Yes. Let's enjoy it. Even if it's only for tonight. Let's drain as much joy out of it as we can."

# Chapter Hundred-Thirty-Eight

Karsten spent most of the night collecting his thoughts, and was now putting his case to the members of the Astrea.

"This goes against …" Klaus was not in favour of his son's proposal.

"It goes against nothing, vater. This is an experiment. A test of a theory. What is there to lose?"

Klaus shook his head, sighed deeply, but said nothing else.

"How do you propose to do this?" The voice on the phone was Patrice's.

"We do not need to hear this." Klaus had rediscovered his voice.

"I'm afraid we do, Klaus. How can we make a decision on this, if we do not fully understand what Karsten is proposing?" Patrice was obviously annoyed with Klaus's arrogance.

"As I stated, we do not …"

"Karsten, please carry on." Patrice cut across Klaus. "Karsten. Please."

Klaus shrugged, stood up, and walked out.

Karsten frowned, but carried on. "On September 28, 1918, Private Henry Tandey, a British soldier serving near the French village of Marcoing, reportedly encountered a wounded German soldier, but decided not to shoot him. Private Tandey spared the life of twenty-nine-year-old Lance Corporal Adolf Hitler." He paused, giving the significance of the event time to sink in. "My proposition, is that one of us takes over the body of Private Tandey, and shows no mercy to this wounded soldier, who would go on to cause the deaths of millions." He took a few steps back and sat on the arm of the sofa close to Charlie.

"Well done," Charlie whispered to him. "Stick with it."

"Carry on, Karsten," Guillaume said softly. "How would this happen?"

He smiled and nodded. "Thank you."

Marie wandered into the room.

Charlie looked across, stood up, and walked across to her. "Let's get a coffee."

She frowned at him. "Something you don't want me to hear?"

"No, no, just thought you'd like a coffee."

"You're not a good liar, Charlie. Excuse me." She squeezed past him and sat on the arm of Alfredo's chair.

Karsten glanced across at Charlie, who looked back, and nodded for him to continue.

"Given that Private Tandey was a British soldier, we felt that Charlie would be the best person to take on this task."

Marie's head snapped up. She stared at Charlie, raised her hands to the ceiling, shook her head, and mouthed, *"Why didn't you tell me?"*

He hung his head and hoped she'd understand.

"Are you OK with this, Charlie?" Ralph asked with concern. "It's asking a lot of you."

He quickly glanced at Marie, who was looking away from him, and nodded. "Burma taught me a lot. I'm sure I can do this."

"Didn't you consider Peter for this?" Ralph continued, turning to Karsten.

"Ja, but if this works, there will be other tasks, which Peter can undertake."

Ralph raised his eyebrows. "More difficult than this?"

"The actual task is very simple. Shoot someone. Others will need a longer period of involvement."

"Such as?" Ralph was clearly very interested in what was being proposed.

"I would rather determine first, if what we believe works."

Ralph nodded in understanding. "When would you propose to start this?"

"As soon as we have your approval."

"Does anyone else have any questions for Karsten?" Ralph was clearly drawing proceedings to a close. The silence was his answer. "In that case, if you will leave us, we will debate this, and give you our answer." He stood and shook Karsten's hand. "Thank you. It takes bravery like this to change the world."

Karsten smiled. "Some might call it stupidity."

"Such as me," Klaus said as he walked past his son and sat on the sofa.

Ralph frowned at Klaus, patted Karsten on the shoulder, and whispered, "You have my support." He followed him to the door and closed it. "Who wants to start?" Klaus moved to stand up, but Ralph waved him to sit down. "I think we know your position only too well Klaus. I propose that we each have five minutes to say our piece and make our vote. Guillaume, will you keep a record of the votes?"

Guillaume nodded and turned to Klaus. "I presume I can put you down as a no?"

Klaus was staring directly at Ralph, firing mental bullets into him. "Sie sind richtig. Ich stimme Nein. *(You are correct. I am voting no.)*"

Guillaume placed a tick in the no column. "Danke."

Half an hour later, the votes were tied.

"Guillaume, we need your casting vote," Ralph said.

*"Think very carefully brother. You have already seriously ignored our wishes."*

*"I will vote yes?"*

*"Spirit Walkers have always had the ability to move through time, and so far as we can tell, whenever they have done this, the currents and ripples of time were never disturbed."*

*"How will you vote?"*

*"We here in the afterlife vote yes. We must take this opportunity to discover if the future can be engineered for the better. As Karsten pointed out, we have the ability to correct this if it does not work."*

"Guillaume? Are you OK?" Ralph was sat close to him, gently massaging his shoulder.

"He's speaking with Isaac. I have seen this before," Klaus said with remorse in his voice. "I am sorry for my reaction, Ralph. It was uncalled for and unprofessional."

Ralph offered his hand, and Klaus shook it strongly and warmly.

"Apologies are never needed among good friends," Ralph said with a beaming smile, and then turned back to Guillaume.

"I change my vote to yes," Klaus exclaimed.

Ralph frowned and slowly turned. "You now vote yes?"

"Ja," Klaus said with a strong nod of the head. "We should take this chance to rid the world of this diabolical man. However slim and dangerous this chance may be."

"Isaac and the architects vote yes." Guillaume suddenly murmured. "This has the approval of my brother. They believe we should attempt to change history."

Ralph stood in the centre of the room. "Gentlemen, Papaver Rhoeas enters a new phase in its history. If we are successful in this enterprise, then the world as we know it, will change forever. Change as we see fit, and for the betterment of mankind." He turned to Klaus. "Will you tell your son of our decision?"

Klaus stood up, and walked out to the hall where the four Musketeers were waiting. He put his hands on Karsten's shoulders and smiled. "You and your friends can try to change the world."

Karsten beamed and hugged his father. "Danke Vater. Wir werden Sie nicht enttäuschen." *(Thank you father. We will not disappoint you.)*

Klaus clasped his hands together. "I pray that you don't. The consequences are too dire to imagine." He turned to Charlie. "Take absolutely no risks. If achieving your objective becomes impossible, you must leave immediately. All our prayers will go with you. Grasp this opportunity in both hands. Do what another young English Tommy couldn't, and rid the world of this devil."

Marie had finally, and grudgingly, accepted that Charlie's mind couldn't be changed. "You'd bloody well better come back to me." She slapped his cheek. "You get one sniff of trouble, and you get your arse out of wherever it is you are, like a greased rat up a drain pipe." She slapped his cheek again, only a little harder. "You hear me?"

Charlie nodded and held her tightly against his chest. "I love you," he whispered in her ear. "What we have will pull me back. Nothing's going to stop me marrying you."

Marie pushed him away and stared deep into his eyes. "You planning on asking me then?"

He dropped onto one knee and held her hand gently. "Will you …"

"Bloody right I will."

"… Marry me?"

A bond had been forged which even time itself would find impossible to fracture.

# Chapter Hundred-Thirty-Nine

The three remaining Musketeers were sat around Charlie's bed, staring at his motionless, comatose body.

Alfredo was very anxious. "Is this going to work?"

"Bit late to start worrying now." Peter was a little more relaxed.

Charlie became aware of an acerbic burning at the back of his throat. His eyes snapped open. It was night, and a full moon lit up a scene of utter desolation and destruction. He scanned the ground around him, and close to him on his right was a deep trench filled with a thick, syrupy, white mist. Suddenly, his eyes felt scorched, his breathing became increasingly laboured, suffocation and an intense pain tightened the invisible band around his chest. He peered out through streaming eyes, and could just make out soldiers, desperately trying to pull what looked like canvas bags over their heads. Others were collapsing onto the trench floor, writhing in agony, vomiting, frothing at the mouth, coughing, rubbing their streaming eyes, and screaming in agony. As they fell onto the sodden, muddy, duck boards, their torment was only increased, as the heavy chlorine gas had settled into a deep acrid layer on the bottom of the trench. It was like the 'Enchanted Ground', in the 'Pilgrim's Progress' which had air with the power to make pilgrims want to stop and sleep, and if they should fall asleep, they would never wake up.

The cause of Charlie's torment was generated from the opposing side of the front, where eight hundred and sixty-five Gaswurfminen, metal tubes filled with six hundred ml of 'White Star Mixture', chlorine and phosgene gas, had been electrically triggered to release their noxious contents into the still early morning air, and then slither across the fields of the valley floor into the British trenches.

The excruciating torture continued unabated in what had become an eerie silence, only broken by the harrowing moans of the gassed soldiers. A silence which every soldier expected at any moment to be broken. At six am, their thoughts were answered, as two thousand German artillery pieces opened fire. The incessant barrage continued unbroken until eight o' clock, when two enormous mines were exploded under the British lines and the German infantry attacked.

A hand grabbed Charlie's arm, and someone pulled him to his feet. A voice screamed at him. "THIS WAY! WE'VE GOT TO GET AWAY FROM HERE!"

Charlie scrabbled to his feet and followed close behind his unknown saviour. The trenches were being overrun by the German Infantry, helped by 08/15 Maxim light machine guns, hand grenades, and flame throwers. As he was pulled over the top of the trench, he suddenly felt himself being thrown to the floor under the weight of his saviour. The horrifying scream and stench of burning flesh which immediately followed, meant that the Kleinflammenwerfer, using pressurised air and carbon dioxide, had belched out a thirty foot, twelve hundred degree stream of burning oil, and his saviour had 'sacrificed' himself. The sound of masses of troops marching past them froze Charlie to the ground beneath his roasted saviour, who was slowly seeping hot, liquid fat onto him. He lay beneath this gruesome horror for what seemed like hours, until he could take no more, and with a great effort, he managed to roll out from under what was now just the blackened remains of a man. He knelt down and tenderly touched what remained of the scorched hand. "God be with you my friend."

"TANDEY!" a voice shouted from his right. "THIS WAY!"

Charlie picked up his Lee Enfield and ran in the direction of the British trenches. The fate of the Austrian corporal, and the future history of the world was held uncertainly in his young hands.